This book belongs to

....

....

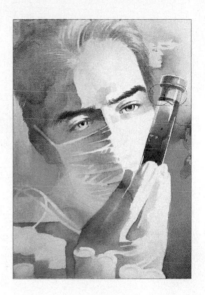

HIDDEN RICHES

Nora Roberts

Dora Conroy loves a bargain. An
enthusiastic dealer in unusual
antiques, she has just struck a
fantastic deal on a collection of
bric-a-brac at an auction. But Dora
is unnerved when her new assets
become a magnet for murder.
Before long, she and her new
neighbour, rugged ex-cop Jed
Skimmerhorn, find themselves
matching wits against an
international smuggler. And
discovering, too, that there is more
between them than they could ever
have bargained for.

A first-class mystery, laced with
humour and sparkling romance.

THE MAGIC BULLET

Harry Stein

The odds against finding a safe
and effective cure for cancer are
high. But that doesn't stop gifted
young medical researcher Dan
Logan in his new post at the
world-famous American Cancer
Foundation. Dan is thrilled to be
working with the best brains in the
business. However, when he and a
colleague, Sabrina Como, make a
dramatic breakthrough, they find
their progress blocked by rivals
every bit as deadly as the disease
they are fighting.

A chilling drama set in a high-
powered medical institution.

Ken Follett

A PLACE CALLED

FREEDOM

Illustrated by Kevin Tweddell

Jay Jamisson: spoilt younger son of one of Scotland's most powerful families, will stop at nothing to get what he thinks is his by right.

Malachi McAsh: a young man of courage and high ideals, determined to fight for his own freedom and that of his fellow workers.

Lizzie Hallim: rich, beautiful and unpredictable, destined to make a sensible match—until her wayward heart leads her to love elsewhere.

The destinies of these three very headstrong characters become irrevocably intertwined in this magnificent historical adventure from the best-selling Ken Follett.

I did a lot of gardening when I first moved into High Glen House and that's how I found the iron collar.

The house was falling down and the garden was overgrown. A crazy old lady had lived here for twenty years and never given it a lick of paint. She died and I bought it from her son, who owns the Toyota dealership in Kirkburn, the nearest town, fifty miles away.

You might wonder why a person would buy a dilapidated house fifty miles from nowhere. But I just love this valley. There are shy deer in the woods and an eagles' nest right at the top of the ridge. Out in the garden I would spend half the time leaning on my spade and staring at the blue-green mountainsides.

But I did some digging too. I decided to plant some shrubs around the outhouse. It's not a handsome building and I wanted to screen it with bushes. While I was digging the trench, I found a plain, unvarnished wooden box. I broke it open with my spade.

Inside was an oilcloth bag, and inside that a crudely made iron ring. At first I thought it might have been part of a cart or a plough. But why had someone wrapped it carefully in oilcloth to preserve it? There was a break in the ring and it had been bent. I began to think of it as a collar that some prisoner had been forced to wear. When the prisoner escaped the ring had been broken with a heavy blacksmith's tool, then bent to get it off.

I took it into the house and started to clean it up. It was slow work,

9

so I steeped it in RustAway overnight then tried again in the morning. As I polished it with a rag, an inscription became visible. It was engraved in old-fashioned script and it took me a while to figure it out, but this is what it said:

> This man is the property of Sir George Jamisson of Fife, AD 1767.

It's here on my desk, beside the computer. I use it as a paperweight. I often pick it up and turn it in my hands, rereading that inscription. If the iron collar could talk, I think to myself, what kind of story would it tell?

Part I: Scotland
Chapter 1

Snow crowned the ridges of High Glen and lay on the wooded slopes in pearly patches. In the valley bottom a hasty stream dodged between icy rocks. The bitter wind that howled inland from the North Sea brought flurries of sleet and hail.

Walking to church the McAsh twins, Malachi and Esther, followed a zigzag trail along the eastern slope of the glen. Malachi, known as Mack, wore a plaid cape and tweed breeches, but his legs were bare below the knee and his feet froze in his wooden clogs. However, he was young and hot-blooded and he hardly noticed the cold.

This was not the shortest way to church but High Glen always thrilled him. He had watched a pair of eagles raise three sets of nestlings here. Like the eagles, he had stolen the laird's salmon from the teeming stream. And, like the deer, he had hidden in the trees, silent and still, when the gamekeepers came.

The laird was Lady Hallim, a widow with a daughter. The land on the far side of the mountain belonged to Sir George Jamisson, and it was a different world. Engineers had torn great holes in the mountainside; man-made hills of slag disfigured the valley, and massive wagons loaded with coal ploughed the muddy road. There the twins lived, in a village called Heugh, a long row of low stone houses marching uphill like a staircase.

They were male and female versions of the same image. Both had fair hair and striking pale green eyes. Both were short and broad-backed. Both were opinionated and argumentative.

Arguments were a family tradition. Their father had been an all-round nonconformist, eager to disagree with the government or any

10

other authority. Their mother had worked for Lady Hallim before her marriage and she had always identified with the upper class. One bitter winter Father had died of the black spit, the cough that killed so many coalminers, and Mother got pneumonia and followed him within a few weeks. But the arguments went on, usually on Saturday nights in Mrs Wheighel's parlour, the nearest thing to a tavern in the village of Heugh.

The estate workers took Mother's view. They said the king was appointed by God, and people had to obey him. The coalminers had heard newer ideas, those of the radical philosophers like John Locke who said a government's authority could come only from the consent of the people. This theory appealed to Mack.

Few miners in Heugh could read, but Mack's mother could and he had pestered her to teach him. She had taught both her children, ignoring the gibes of her husband, who said she had ideas above her station. At Mrs Wheighel's Mack was called on to read aloud from *The Times*, the *Edinburgh Advertiser*, and political journals such as the radical *North Briton*. The papers were always weeks out of date, but the men and women of the village listened avidly to the accounts of strikes, protests and speeches.

It was after a Saturday-night argument at Mrs Wheighel's that Mack had written the letter to Caspar Gordonson, a London lawyer who wrote articles ridiculing the government.

The reply had come yesterday, and it was the most exciting thing that had ever happened to Mack. It would change his life, he thought: it might set him free. As a child he had envied Davy Patch, the one-eyed pedlar who roamed from village to village selling knives and string and ballads. Davy could get up at sunrise and go to sleep when he felt tired. Mack, from the age of seven, had been shaken awake by his mother a few minutes before two in the morning, and had worked down the mine for fifteen hours, finishing at five in the afternoon; then he had staggered home, often to fall asleep over his evening porridge. Mack no longer wanted to be a pedlar, but he still dreamed of a different life. And the letter meant his dreams might come true.

'I'm still not sure you should read it aloud in church,' Esther said as they tramped along. 'Ratchett will be furious.' Harry Ratchett was the viewer, the man who managed the mine for the owner. 'He might even tell Sir George, and then what will they do to you?'

'If I keep the letter to myself, it's pointless,' Mack said. He glanced at his twin. She looked troubled rather than combative. He felt a surge of affection for her. Whatever happened, she would be on his side.

'Don't give them reason to punish you,' she said worriedly.

He tried to reassure her. 'I'm just going to say what the law is— how can that be wrong?'

'It's incautious.'

'Aye, that it is,' he conceded. 'But I'm going to do it anyway.'

They crossed a ridge and dropped down the far side, into Coalpit Glen. A few moments later the small stone church came into view, beside a bridge over the river. A closed carriage stood at the church porch. Several ladies in hooped skirts and fur wraps were getting out, helped by the pastor.

Esther touched Mack's arm and pointed to the bridge. Riding across on a big chestnut hunter was the owner of the mine, the laird of the glen, Sir George Jamisson.

Jamisson had not been seen here for five years. He lived in London, which was a week's journey by ship, two weeks by stage-coach. He had once been a penny-pinching Edinburgh chandler, people said, selling candles and gin from a corner shop. Then a relative had died childless, and George had inherited the castle and the mines. On that foundation he had built a business empire that stretched as far as Barbados and Virginia. And he was now starchily respectable: a baronet, a magistrate and alderman of Wapping, responsible for law and order along London's waterfront.

'Well, that's that,' Esther said with relief. 'You won't be able to read out your letter now. Not in front of the laird himself!'

'On the contrary,' Mack said. 'This makes it all the better.'

LIZZIE HALLIM REFUSED to go to church in the carriage. She insisted on riding.

Such unladylike behaviour made her mother despair. 'How will you ever get a husband if you always act like a man?' Lady Hallim said.

'I can get a husband whenever I like,' Lizzie replied. It was true: men fell in love with her all the time. 'The problem is finding one I can put up with for more than half an hour.'

'The problem is finding one that doesn't scare easily,' her mother muttered.

Lizzie laughed. Last year Mother had taken her to London and 'launched' her into English society. It had been a disaster. Lizzie had talked too loud, laughed too much and openly mocked the elaborate manners of the dandified young men who tried to court her.

'It's because you grew up without a man in the house,' her mother added. 'It's made you too independent.' With that she got into the carriage.

Lizzie walked across the flinty front of Castle Jamisson, heading

12

for the stables. Her father had died when she was three, leaving them penniless. For years Mother had scraped by, mortgaging more and more of the Hallim estate, waiting for Lizzie to grow up and marry a wealthy man. Now Lizzie was twenty years old and it was time to fulfil her destiny.

That was undoubtedly why the Jamisson family were visiting their Scottish property again, and why their principal house guests were their neighbours, Lizzie and her mother. The pretext for the party was the twenty-first birthday of the younger son, Jay; but the real reason was that they wanted Lizzie to marry the older son, Robert, in order to add the Hallim estate to the Jamisson family's land.

She saw Robert standing in the stable yard, waiting for the horses to be saddled. He resembled the portrait of his mother that hung in the castle hall—a grave, plain woman with a determined look about the mouth. Lizzie was not in love with him, but she knew her duty.

She decided to banter with him a little. 'It really is most inconsiderate of you to live in London,' she said.

'Inconsiderate?' He frowned. 'Why?'

'You leave us without neighbours.' Still he looked puzzled. It seemed he did not have much of a sense of humour. She explained: 'With you away there isn't another soul between here and Edinburgh.'

A voice behind her said: 'Apart from a hundred families of coalminers and several villages of crofters.'

'You know what I mean,' she said, turning. 'Anyway, who are you?'

'Jay Jamisson,' he said with a bow. 'How could you forget?'

'Oh!' She had heard he had arrived late last night, but she had not recognised him from five years ago. He was taller and handsomer now.

Robert said: 'Hello, Jay. Welcome to Castle Jamisson.'

Jay looked suddenly sulky. 'Drop the proprietorial air, Robert. You may be the elder son but you haven't inherited the place yet.'

Lizzie intervened, saying: 'Congratulations on your birthday.'

'Thank you.'

Robert said impatiently: 'Are you going to church with us?'

Lizzie saw hatred in Jay's eyes but his voice was neutral. 'Yes. I've told them to saddle a horse for me.'

'We'd better get going.' Robert turned towards the stable. 'Hurry up in there!'

'All set, sir,' a groom called as three horses were led out: a sturdy black pony, a light bay mare and a grey gelding.

Lizzie mounted the black pony, riding sidesaddle, and trotted out

13

of the yard. The brothers followed, Jay on the gelding and Robert on the mare. Snow underfoot made the road treacherous, for it hid potholes that caused the horses to stumble. Lizzie said: 'Let's ride through the woods. The ground is not so uneven.' Without waiting for agreement she turned her horse off the road.

Underneath the tall pines the forest floor was clear. Lizzie urged her pony into a canter. After a moment the grey horse passed her. She glanced up and saw a challenging grin on Jay's face: he wanted to race. She gave a whoop and kicked the pony, who sprang forward eagerly. Jay's horse was bigger and would have been faster in a gallop, but the pony's short legs and light frame were better adapted to this terrain, and gradually Lizzie pulled ahead. When she could no longer hear Jay's horse she slowed down and brought the pony to a standstill.

Jay soon caught up, but there was no sight of Robert. She and Jay walked on, side by side, catching their breath. She studied him out of the corner of her eye. His mother, Alicia, Sir George's second wife, was a fair-haired coquette, and Jay had her blue eyes and winning smile. 'What do you do in London?' Lizzie asked him.

'I'm in the Third Regiment of Foot Guards.' A note of pride came into his voice and he added: 'I've just been made a captain.'

'Well, Captain Jamisson, what do you brave soldiers do?' she said mockingly. 'Is there a war in London at the moment?'

'There's plenty to do keeping the mob under control.'

Lizzie suddenly remembered Jay as a mean, bullying child and she wondered if he enjoyed his work.

'And how do you control them?' she asked.

'For example, by escorting criminals to the gallows, and making sure they don't get rescued by their cronies,' he said. 'One day I'd like to resign my commission and go abroad.'

'Oh—why?'

'My family has a sugar plantation in Barbados. I'm hoping my father will give it to me for my twenty-first birthday, as my portion.'

Lizzie felt deeply envious. 'Lucky you,' she said. 'There's nothing I'd like more than to go to a new country.' Now if Robert would take me to Barbados I'd marry him like a shot, she thought.

'And you'd have slaves to do all the work,' Jay added.

They emerged from the forest a few yards from the bridge. On the other side of the water, the miners were filing into church.

Lizzie was still thinking about Barbados. 'It must be very odd, to own slaves, and be able to do anything you like to them, as if they were beasts,' she said. 'Doesn't it make you feel strange?'

'Not in the least,' Jay said with a smile.

THE LITTLE CHURCH was full. The miners and crofters who formed the usual Sunday congregation left a space around the Jamisson family and their guests, as if afraid they might besmirch the fine clothes with coal dust and cow dung.

Mack had spoken defiantly to Esther, but now he was full of apprehension. Coal-owners had the right to flog miners, and on top of that Sir George was a magistrate, which meant he could order someone hanged. For a moment Mack considered backing out. Then the hymn began, and the miners filled the church with their thrilling voices. Behind him Mack heard the soaring tenor of Jimmy Lee, the finest singer in the village. The singing made him think of High Glen, and the dream of freedom, and he resolved to go through with his plan.

The pastor, Reverend John York, was a mild-mannered forty-year-old with thinning hair. His sermon was about truth. How would he react to Mack's letter? His instinct would be to take the side of the mine-owner. But he was a clergyman: wouldn't he be obliged to speak out for justice, regardless of what Sir George might say?

Mack studied the castle folk. He recognised most of the Jamisson family. When he was a boy they had spent much of their time here. And he recognised Lady Hallim and her daughter Lizzie. Mack's mother had once been a lady's maid at High Glen House, and after she married she had sometimes gone back to see her old friends and show off her twin babies. Mack and Esther had played with Lizzie on those visits. She had been a little minx: bossy, selfish and spoilt. Mack had kissed her once, and she had pulled his hair and made him cry. She looked as though she hadn't changed much. She had a small impish face, curly dark brown hair and very dark eyes that suggested mischief.

The sermon came to an end. In addition to the usual Presbyterian service there was to be a christening today: Mack's cousin Jen had given birth to her fourth child. She stood at the font, looking weary. She was only thirty but she had worked down the pit for twenty-three years.

The Reverend sprinkled water on her baby's head. Then her husband, Saul, repeated the words that made a slave of every Scottish miner's son. 'I pledge this child to work in Sir George Jamisson's mines, boy and man, for as long as he is able, or until he die.'

This was the moment Mack had decided on. He stood up.

At this point the viewer, Harry Ratchett, would normally step up to the font and hand over to Saul the 'arles', the traditional payment for pledging the child, a purse of ten pounds. However, to Mack's surprise, Sir George rose to perform this ritual personally.

As Sir George walked to the font Mack stepped into the central aisle and said loudly: 'The payment of arles is meaningless.'

There was a moment of shocked silence, and all heads turned to look at Mack.

'This ceremony has no force,' Mack declared. 'The boy may not be pledged to the mine. A child cannot be enslaved.'

Sir George said: 'Sit down, you young fool, and shut your mouth.'

'You sit down,' Mack said recklessly. He pointed a finger at Mr York. 'You spoke about truth in your sermon, Pastor—will you stand up for truth now?'

The clergyman looked at Mack with a worried air. 'Now, you know the law of Scotland,' he said in a reasonable tone. 'Coalminers are the property of the mine-owner. As soon as a man has worked a year and a day, he loses his freedom.'

'Aye,' Mack said. 'It's wicked, but it's the law. I'm saying the law does not enslave children, and I can prove it.'

The baby's father, Saul, spoke. 'We need the money, Mack!' he protested.

'Take the money,' Mack said. 'Your boy will work for Sir George until he's twenty-one, and that's worth ten pounds. But'— he raised his voice— 'but when he's of age, he will be free!'

Sir George flushed purple. 'I'll deal with you when the service is over,' he said angrily. He handed the purse to Saul, then turned to the pastor. 'Carry on, please, Mr York.'

The pastor said: 'Let us sing the final hymn.'

A voice behind Mack said: 'No, no—not yet.'

He looked round. It was Jimmy Lee, the young miner with the wonderful singing voice. He had run away once already, and as a punishment he wore round his neck an iron collar stamped with the words *This man is the property of Sir George Jamisson of Fife.*

'You can't stop now,' Jimmy said. 'I'm twenty-one next week. If I'm going to be free, I want to know about it.'

'You're not going to be free,' Sir George rasped.

Esther tugged at Mack's sleeve. 'The letter!' she hissed.

Mack had forgotten it in his excitement. 'The law says differently, Sir George,' he cried, waving the letter.

Reverend York said: 'What is that paper, McAsh?'

'It's a letter from a London lawyer that I've consulted. I'll read it. "The ceremony of arles has no foundation in English or Scottish law. The parents cannot sell what they do not own, namely the freedom of a grown man. They may compel their child to work in the mine until he reaches the age of twenty-one, but"'—Mack paused dramatically—' "but then he will be free to leave!" '

16

There was uproar as a hundred people tried to speak.

Mack held up a hand for quiet. 'Let me read one more line,' he said. '"Once the man is adult, the law applies to him as to everyone else in Scotland: when he has worked a year and a day *as an adult* he loses his freedom."'

There were grunts of anger and disappointment. Most of the men were no more free than they had ever been.

Sir George said: 'Who is this so-called lawyer?'

Mack said: 'His name is Caspar Gordonson.'

'Oh yes, I've heard of him. He's an associate of John Wilkes,' said Sir George scornfully. Everyone knew the name of Wilkes: he was the celebrated Liberal leader, living in exile in Paris but constantly threatening to return and undermine the government.

Robert Jamisson stood up, flushed with anger like his father. 'You're a coalminer,' he said. 'What have you to do with the law? As for writing to lawyers—' He snatched the letter out of Mack's hand. 'This is what I think of your lawyer.' He tore the paper in half.

The miners gasped. Their future was written on those pages.

Anger made Mack defiant. 'I see you're frightened enough to destroy that letter,' he said. 'But you can't tear up the law of the land. That's written on a paper that's not so easily ripped.'

Robert hesitated, not sure how to respond to such eloquence. After a moment he said angrily: 'Get out.'

Mack looked at the Reverend York. No layman had the right to order a member of the congregation to leave a church. 'Is this God's house, or Sir George Jamisson's?' Mack demanded.

It was a decisive moment, and York was not equal to it. He looked shamefaced and said: 'You'd better leave, McAsh.'

Mack could not resist a retort. 'Thank you for the sermon on truth, Pastor,' he said. 'I'll never forget it.'

He turned away. Esther stood up with him. As they started down the aisle, Jimmy Lee got up and followed. One or two others stood and suddenly the exodus became general: every miner in the place was following him out of the church.

The miners gathered around Mack in the churchyard. 'That was wrong, to tear up the letter,' Jimmy said angrily.

Several others agreed. 'We'll write again,' said one. 'The law is the law.'

'Aye, but the laird is the laird,' said a more cautious one.

As Mack calmed down he began to wonder realistically what he had achieved. The Jamissons had flatly refused to acknowledge the law. If they stuck to their guns what could the miners do?

A small figure in black fur shot out of the church porch. It was

Lizzie Hallim. She made straight for Mack, her black eyes flashing fire. 'How dare you talk to the laird and his son that way?'

'How dare they enslave us when the law says they may not?'

The miners murmured their agreement.

Lizzie looked around at them. 'You're fortunate to have paid work,' she said. 'You should all be grateful to Sir George for providing your families with the means to live.'

'If we're so fortunate, why do they need laws forbidding us to leave the village to seek other work?'

'Because you're too foolish to know when you're well off!'

Mack lowered his voice and adopted an enquiring tone. 'Miss Hallim, have you ever been down a coalmine?'

Lizzie said: 'Don't be ridiculous.'

'If you do, I guarantee you'll never again call us lucky.'

He felt an elbow dig painfully into his side: it was Esther, telling him to watch his step. She said: 'We'll think about what you've told us, Miss Hallim, and thank you for your advice.'

Lizzie nodded condescendingly. She turned to Mack. 'You should listen to your sister, she's got more sense than you.'

'That's the first true thing you've said to me today.'

Esther hissed: 'Mack—shut your gob.'

Lizzie grinned, and suddenly all her arrogance vanished. She seemed another person, friendly and gay. 'I haven't heard that phrase for a long time,' she laughed. Mack could not help laughing with her.

She turned away, still chuckling, and he watched her walk back to join the Jamissons at the church porch. 'My God,' he said, shaking his head. 'What a woman.'

As JAY LEFT THE CHURCH some of the crofters offered congratulations on his birthday, but not one of the miners spoke to him. They stood in a crowd to one side of the graveyard, arguing in low, angry voices. Jay hurried through the snow to where a groom held the horses. Robert was already there, but Lizzie was not. 'Where's Miss Elizabeth?' he said to the groom.

'Over by the porch, Mr Jay.'

Jay saw her talking animatedly to the pastor.

Robert tapped Jay on the chest with an aggressive finger. 'Listen here, Jay—you leave Elizabeth alone, do you understand?'

'What the devil are you talking about?' he said.

'You're not going to marry her, I am.'

'I don't want to marry her.'

'Then don't flirt with her.'

Jay knew that Lizzie had found him attractive, and he had enjoyed

18

bantering with her, but he had no thought of capturing her heart. Father's plan was for Robert to marry Lizzie, and neither Jay nor anyone else would oppose the wishes of Sir George. So Jay was surprised at this show of insecurity. Robert, like his father, was not often unsure of himself.

'Miss Hallim is a guest at our house,' Jay said reasonably. 'I can't ignore her, can I?'

Robert's mouth set in a stubborn line. 'Do you want me to speak to Father about it?'

Those were the magic words that had ended so many childhood disputes. Both brothers knew that their father would always rule in favour of Robert. 'All right, Robert,' Jay conceded. 'I'll try not to interfere with your courting.' He swung onto his horse and trotted away, leaving Robert to escort Lizzie back to the castle.

CASTLE JAMISSON WAS a dark grey stone fortress with turrets and a battlemented roof line. Although it was Jay's childhood home he did not like the place. The huge, draughty rooms on the ground floor— hall, dining room, drawing room—were impossible to heat. Big coal fires in every bedroom made little impression on the chill air.

Jay rode round to the stables and dismounted. He patted the gelding's neck. 'He's no steeplechaser, but he's well behaved,' he said to the groom. 'I'd be glad to have him in my regiment.'

The groom looked pleased. 'Thank you, sir,' he said.

Jay went into the great hall. It was a big gloomy chamber with dim shadowy corners into which the candlelight hardly penetrated. Over the fireplace was the portrait of his father's first wife, Robert's mother, Olive. Jay hated that painting. There she was, solemn and saintly, looking down her long nose at all who came after her. When she caught a fever and died suddenly at twenty-nine his father had remarried, but he never forgot his first love. He treated Jay's mother, Alicia, like a mistress, a plaything, and he made Jay feel almost like an illegitimate son.

Jay turned his back on the picture. A footman brought him a goblet of hot mulled wine and he sipped it gratefully. Perhaps it would settle the tension in his stomach. Today Father would announce what Jay's portion would be.

He knew he was not going to get half, or even a tenth, of his father's fortune. Robert would inherit this estate, with its rich mines, and the fleet of ships he already managed.

Jay's mother had counselled him not to argue about that: she knew Father was implacable. Robert was not merely the only son. He was Father all over again, clever, heartless and mean. Jay was different, easy-going and spendthrift. Father hated people who were careless with money, especially his money. Just a few months ago Jay had run up a huge gambling debt, nine hundred pounds. He had got his mother to ask Father to pay. It was a small fortune, enough to buy Castle Jamisson, but Sir George could easily afford it. All the same he had acted as if he was losing a leg.

Don't fight your father, Mother reasoned, but ask for something modest. Younger sons often went out to the colonies: there was a good chance his father would give him the sugar plantation in Barbados. Both he and his mother had spoken to his father about it, and he had high hopes.

His father came in a few minutes later and a footman helped him off with his cloak. 'Send a message to Ratchett,' Father said to the man. 'I want two men guarding the bridge twenty-four hours a day. If McAsh tries to leave the glen they should seize him.'

Jay said: 'What if McAsh goes over the mountain?'

'In this weather? He can try. As soon as we learn he's gone, we can send a party round by road and have the sheriff and a squad of troops waiting on the other side. But I doubt he'd ever make it.'

Lady Hallim arrived next. She was dark-haired and dark-eyed like her daughter, but she had none of Lizzie's spark and crackle. 'Let me take your coat,' Jay said, and helped her shrug off her heavy fur. 'Would you like some mulled wine?'

'What a nice boy you are, Jay,' she said. 'I'd love some.'

The other churchgoers came in, rubbing their hands for warmth. Robert was doggedly making small talk to Lizzie. Father began to discuss business with Henry Drome, a Glasgow merchant who was a relation of his first wife. The pastor had not come: perhaps he was sulking about the row in the church. There was a handful of other guests invited for dinner, mostly relatives, and one or two neighbours. Most of the conversations were about Malachi McAsh and his letter.

Lizzie's raised voice was heard over the buzz of conversation. 'But why not?' she was saying. 'I want to see for myself.'

Robert said gravely: 'A coalmine is no place for a lady.'

'What's this?' Sir George asked. 'Does Miss Hallim want to go down a pit?'

Robert said: 'Apart from any other considerations, female clothing would make it almost impossible.'

'Then I'll disguise myself as a man,' she shot back.

Sir George chuckled. 'There are some girls who could manage that,' he said. 'But you, my dear, are much too pretty to get away with it. Has everyone got a full cup?' He went on: 'Let us drink to my younger son James on his twenty-first birthday. To Jay!'

They drank the toast, then the women retired to prepare for dinner. The talk among the men turned to business.

Henry Drome said: 'I don't like the news from America. It could cost us a lot of money.'

Jay knew what he was talking about. The government had imposed taxes on various commodities imported into the American colonies—tea, paper, glass, lead—and the colonists were outraged.

'The Boston town meeting has announced a boycott of all British imports,' said Drome. 'They're giving up tea, and they've even agreed to save on black cloth by skimping on mourning clothes!'

Sir George said: 'The colonists are a damned gang of bandits, that's all they are—and the Boston rum distillers are the worst. The law obliges them to buy molasses from British plantations, but they smuggle in French molasses and drive the price down.'

'The Virginians are worse,' said Drome. 'The tobacco planters never pay their debts.'

'Don't I know it!' said Sir George. 'I've just had a planter default—leaving me with a bankrupt plantation. A place called Mockjack Hall.'

Robert said: 'Thank God there's no import duty on convicts.'

There was a general murmur of agreement. Every year the courts sentenced several hundred people to transportation to America, and the government paid five pounds per head to the shipper. Nine out of ten transportees crossed the Atlantic on a Jamisson vessel. But that was not the only way money was made. On the other side the convicts were obliged to do seven years' unpaid labour, which meant they could be sold as seven-year slaves. It was a lucrative trade.

'Aye,' said Father, turning to Robert. 'But even that would stop if the colonists had their way.' Adopting a jocular tone, he said: 'What about the Hallim girl, then, eh? A little jewel, if you ask me.'

'Elizabeth is very spirited,' Robert said dubiously. 'She may make a troublesome wife.'

'Nothing like a mettlesome mare,' Sir George said. 'You could do a lot worse.' He lowered his voice. 'Lady Hallim holds the estate in trust until Elizabeth marries. Since a woman's property belongs to her husband, the whole place will become yours. There must be a million tons of coal under High Glen—all the seams run in that direction. It'll be worth a fortune.'

'But I'm not sure how much she likes me,' Robert said dourly.

'I'll tell you a secret,' Sir George said. 'You know Lady Hallim has mortgaged the entire estate? I happen to know that her creditor is not willing to renew.'

'But surely she could raise the money from another lender, and pay him off.'

'Probably,' Sir George said. 'But she doesn't know that, and I've made sure her financial adviser won't tell her.' He chuckled. 'So you see young Elizabeth can't afford to turn you down.'

The ladies came back. Jay thought his mother wore a suppressed smile, as if she had an amusing secret. Before he could ask her what it was another guest arrived. The newcomer was a pockmarked young man, in clerical grey with spectacles and an old-fashioned curly wig. Alicia spoke to him, then took him to Sir George. 'This is Mr Cheshire,' she said. 'He's come in place of the pastor.'

Sir George gave a curt greeting, then turned away. He was not interested in obscure young clergymen.

They went in to dinner. The long table was laid with an elaborate spread: joints of venison, beef and ham, a whole roast salmon and several different pies. But Jay could hardly eat. Would Father give him the Barbados property? If not, what else? He could not guess, so he toyed with his food and waited.

Mr Cheshire proved mildly embarrassing. He belched loudly two or three times and spilt his claret, and Jay noticed him staring rather obviously into the cleavage of the woman sitting next to him.

They had sat down at three o'clock and, by the time the ladies withdrew, the winter afternoon was darkening into evening. A servant brought a bottle of port, a drum of tobacco and a box of clay pipes. The young clergyman filled a pipe, put a taper to it, inhaled, and began to cough. He had obviously never smoked before. The coughs shook him so hard that his wig and spectacles fell off— and Jay saw immediately that this was no clergyman.

He began to laugh. The others looked at him curiously.

Robert was the first to realise. 'Good God, it's Miss Hallim.'

There was a moment of startled silence, then Sir George began to laugh. The other men laughed too.

As Lizzie recovered, Jay admired her costume. The spectacles had hidden her flashing dark eyes, and the side curls of the wig had partly obscured her pretty profile. A white linen stock covered the smooth feminine skin of her throat. She had used charcoal to give her cheeks the pockmarked look. In the gloomy rooms of the castle, on a dull winter's afternoon, no one had been able to see through her disguise.

'Well, you've proved you can pass for a man,' said Sir George. 'But you still can't go down the pit. Go and fetch the other ladies, and we'll give Jay his birthday present.'

They met up with the women in the hall and Sir George led the whole party out through the main doors. It was dusk. 'Here,' he said to Jay. 'This is your birthday present.'

In front of the house a groom held the most beautiful horse Jay had ever seen. It was a white stallion about two years old, with the lean lines of an Arab. Jay was lost in admiration, but his mother's voice cut through his thoughts like a knife. 'Is that all?' she said.

'Now, Alicia, I hope you aren't going to be ungracious—'

'Is that all?' she repeated.

'Yes,' Sir George admitted.

It had not occurred to Jay that this present was instead of the Barbados property. He felt so bitter that he could not speak.

His mother spoke for him, her voice shrill with fury. 'This is your son,' she said. 'He is twenty-one years old—he's entitled to his portion in life . . . and you give him a horse? For God's sake give him the Barbados property.'

Robert protested: 'That's mine!'

At last Jay found his voice. 'The plantation has never been properly administered,' he said. 'I thought I would run it more like a regiment, get the slaves working harder, make it more remunerative.'

'Do you really think you could do that?' said his father.

Jay's heart leapt: perhaps Father would change his mind. 'I do!' he said eagerly.

'Well, I don't,' Father said harshly. 'I don't believe you have an inkling of how to run a plantation or any other enterprise. I think you're better off in the army where you're told what to do.'

Jay was stunned. He looked at the beautiful white stallion. 'I'll never ride that horse,' he said. 'Take it away.'

Alicia spoke to Sir George. 'Robert's getting the castle and the coalmines and the ships and everything else—does he have to have the plantation too?'

'Yes, for the sake of his mother,' Sir George said.

Alicia stared at her husband, and Jay realised then that she hated him. 'Damn you, then,' she said. 'Damn you to hell.' And she turned and went back into the house.

Chapter 2

The McAsh twins lived in a one-room house fifteen foot square, with a fireplace on one side and two curtained alcoves for beds on the other. The front door opened onto a muddy track that ran downhill from the pit to the bottom of the glen, where it met the road that led to the church, the castle and the outside world. The water supply was a mountain stream at the back of the row of houses.

All the way home Mack had been agonising over what had happened in the church, but he said nothing, and Esther tactfully asked him no questions. Earlier that morning they had put a piece of bacon on the fire to boil, and when they returned home the smell of it filled the house and made Mack's mouth water, lifting his spirits. Esther shredded a cabbage into the pot while Mack went across the road to Mrs Wheighel's for a jug of ale.

The two of them ate with gargantuan appetites. Then Esther belched and said, 'Well, what will you do?'

Mack knew there was only one answer. 'I've got to go away. I can't stay here, after all that. My pride won't let me.'

'That's what I thought.' Tears came to Esther's eyes. 'You're pitting yourself against the most powerful people in the land.'

'I'm right, though. If I don't do it now, I never will—and I'll spend the rest of my life regretting it.'

She nodded sadly. 'If they catch you they'll bring you back with an iron collar round your neck, like Jimmy Lee.'

Mack winced. To wear a collar like a dog was a humiliation the miners all feared. 'I'm cleverer than Jimmy,' he said. 'He tried to get work at a pit in Clackmannan, and the owner reported him.'

'That's the trouble. How will you earn your bread?'

Mack had thought about this. 'I'll go to Edinburgh,' he said. 'Then I'll get on a ship—I hear they always want strong men to work on the coalers. In three days I'll be out of Scotland.'

'A ship,' Esther said wonderingly. Neither of them had ever seen one. 'Where will you go?'

'London, I expect.' Most coal ships out of Edinburgh were destined for London. 'I'll go anywhere that's not Scotland—anywhere a man can be free. Think of it: to live where you like, to choose your work. To be your own man, and nobody's slave—won't that be grand?'

There were hot tears on Esther's cheeks. 'When will you go?'

'I'll stay another day or two, and hope the Jamissons relax their vigilance a bit. But Tuesday's my twenty-second birthday. If I'm at the pit on Wednesday I'll have worked my year-and-a-day, and I'll be a slave again. So I'll be away Tuesday night.'

In a small voice she said: 'I want to go with you.'

He was surprised. 'You've never said anything about it!'

'Why do you think I've never married? Because if I get wed and have a child I'll never get out of here.'

It was true. He saw the desperation in her eyes, and it hurt him to refuse her, but he had to. It would be much harder for two to escape than one. 'Stay a little while,' he said. 'As soon as I get work I'll save money and send for you.'

'Spit and swear!'

It was something they had done as children, to seal a promise. He spat on his palm, reached across the table and took her hand in his own. 'I swear I'll send for you.'

A DEER HUNT had been planned for the following morning, and Jay decided to go along. He felt like killing something.

He sat on the steps at the front of the castle and fitted a new wedge-shaped flint into the firing mechanism of his gun, fixing it firmly with a wad of soft leather. He cocked the flintlock and aimed at a tree across the lawn. Sighting along the barrel, he imagined he saw a big stag with spreading antlers. Jay pulled the trigger. The flint struck steel and gave a satisfactory shower of sparks, but there was no gunpowder in the pan and no ball in the barrel.

He heard his mother say: 'Hello, Jay.'

He stood up and kissed her good morning. He had not seen her since yesterday, when she had damned his father and stormed off. Now she looked weary and sad.

'You slept badly, didn't you?' he said.

She nodded. 'I've had better nights. I shouldn't have cursed your father like that.'

Hesitantly Jay said: 'You must have loved him . . . once.'

She sighed. 'I don't know. He was handsome and rich and a baronet, and I wanted to be his wife.'

'But now you hate him.'

'Ever since he began to favour your brother over you.'

Jay felt angry. 'You'd think Robert would see the unfairness of it!'

'I'm afraid Robert is a greedy young man. He wants it all. Come, let's take a turn up and down the drive.' She was wearing a fur-lined coat with a hood, and Jay had his plaid cloak. They walked across the lawn, their feet crunching the frosted grass.

'What made my father like this?' Jay said. 'Why does he hate me?'

She touched his cheek. 'He doesn't hate you,' she said, 'although you could be forgiven for thinking otherwise.'

'Then why does he treat me so badly?'

'Your father was a poor man when he married Olive Drome. He had nothing but a corner shop in a low-class district of Edinburgh. He feels he owes everything to Olive, and that it would be some kind of insult to her memory if he gave anything to you.'

Jay shook his head. 'There must be more to it than that.'

They reached the end of the drive and walked back in silence.

When they reached the castle she said: 'I've spent all night trying to think of a way to make things right for you, and so far I haven't succeeded. But I haven't given up. Good morning, Miss Hallim.'

Lizzie was coming down the steps dressed for hunting, looking like a pretty pixie in a black fur cap and little leather boots. She smiled and seemed happy to see Jay. 'Good morning!'

The sight of her cheered Jay up. 'Are you coming with us?'

'I wouldn't miss it for the world.'

'Splendid!' he said. 'You'll add a rare touch of refinement to what might otherwise be a coarsely masculine expedition.'

'Don't bet on it,' she said.

Alicia said: 'I'm going in. Good hunting, both of you.'

When she had gone Lizzie said: 'I'm so sorry your birthday was spoiled.' She squeezed his arm sympathetically. 'Perhaps you'll forget your troubles for an hour or so this morning.'

He could not help smiling back. 'I'll do my best.'

A gamekeeper walked round the corner of the castle with two dogs on a leash, and Lizzie went to pet them. The dogs were the long-legged, grey-haired breed sometimes called Highland deerhounds and sometimes Irish wolfhounds. Their role was to chase and bring down any deer wounded but not felled by the hunters' fire.

The rest of the party emerged from the castle: Robert, Sir George, and Henry Drome. Jay stared at his brother, but Robert avoided his eye. Father nodded curtly, almost as if he had forgotten the events of last night.

Highland ponies were brought round by stable hands. The party mounted them and rode out of the courtyard.

As they jogged down the glen Jay found himself brooding over his father's rejection again. He wished he were the only son. He wished Robert were dead. If there were an accident today, and Robert was killed, all Jay's troubles would be over. He touched the barrel of the gun slung across his shoulder. He could make it look like an accident. With everyone shooting at the same time, it might be hard to tell who had fired the fatal ball.

When they had ridden about three miles the gamekeepers saw a herd of twenty or thirty hinds half a mile further on, above the tree line on a south-facing slope. The party halted and Jay took out his spyglass. Hinds made perfectly good eating but it was more usual to shoot the big stags with their spectacular antlers. Jay examined the mountainside above the hinds. He saw what he had hoped for. 'Look—two stags . . . no, three . . . uphill from the females.'

'I see them, just over the first ridge,' Lizzie said. 'And another, you can just see the antlers of the fourth.'

Her face was flushed with excitement, making her even prettier. This was exactly the kind of thing she would like, of course: being out of doors, with horses and dogs and guns. Jay glanced at his brother. Robert looked ill-at-ease, out in the cold weather on a pony. He would rather be in a counting house, Jay thought. What a waste it would be for such a woman as Lizzie to marry Robert.

He turned away from them and studied the mountainside with his spyglass, searching for a route by which the stags could be approached. The stalkers had to be downwind so that the beasts could not pick up their scent. It was nearly impossible to shoot a deer from further away than about a hundred yards, and fifty yards was ideal; so the whole skill of deerstalking lay in creeping up on them and getting close enough for a good shot.

Lizzie had already devised an approach. 'There's a corrie a quarter of a mile back up the glen,' she said. A corrie was the depression formed by a stream, and it would hide the hunters as they climbed. 'We can follow that to the high ridge then work our way along.'

Sir George agreed. They returned to the corrie, then left the ponies and went up the mountainside on foot. Before long Henry and Robert were puffing and blowing, although the keepers and Lizzie showed no signs of strain. Sir George was red in the face and panting, and Jay found himself breathing hard.

They crossed the ridge. In its lee, hidden from the deer, they worked their way across the mountainside. The keepers took the lead, knowing the ground. When they thought they were coming close to the stags they edged downhill. Suddenly they dropped to their knees, and the others followed suit. Jay began to feel the thrill of the hunt and the prospect of a kill.

He decided to risk a look. Still crawling, he veered uphill and peered over an outcrop of rock. He saw the stags ranged across the mountainside in a straggling line. Up ahead someone yelped and cursed: it was Robert, slipping into a muddy puddle. 'Damn fool,' Jay said under his breath. One of the dogs let out a low growl. A keeper held up a warning hand and they all froze, listening for the sound of fleeing hoofs. But the deer did not run.

Sir George spoke in a low voice. 'There are four stags and five guns, so I shan't shoot this time, unless one of you misses,' he said. He could play the perfect host when he wanted to. 'Henry, you take the beast on the right here. Robert, take the next one along—it's the easiest shot. Jay, you take the next. Miss Hallim, yours is the furthest, but it has the best head—and I understand you're a pretty good shot. We'll let Miss Hallim shoot first, shall we?'

The hunters spread out, each looking for a lie from which to take aim. Jay worked his way uphill to a point where a stunted bush broke the skyline, giving him extra cover. Raising his head he looked down the mountain. He could see his stag about seventy yards away. He could also see the other hunters: Lizzie to his left, still crawling along; Henry to his far right; Sir George with the dogs—and Robert, below and to his right, twenty-five yards away—an easy target.

His heartbeat seemed to falter as he was struck again by the thought of killing his brother. He tried to push it out of his mind. He primed his gun, pouring a little powder into the flashpan, then closed the cover of the pan. Finally he cocked the firing mechanism.

He rolled over and looked across the slope. The deer grazed in peaceful ignorance. All the hunters were in position except Lizzie, who was still moving. Jay sighted on his stag. Then he slowly swung the barrel around until it pointed at Robert's back.

Lizzie's shot would be the signal for everyone to fire. But Lizzie was taking her time. Jay tried to breathe evenly but his heart was racing and his breath came in gasps. No, he thought. This can't be happening. I'm not going to kill my brother. By God I will, though. Hurry, Lizzie, please.

Out of the corner of his eye he saw something move near him. Before he could look up he heard the crack of Lizzie's gun. Holding his aim on Robert's spine, Jay squeezed his trigger. A bulky form loomed over him and he heard his father shout. Just as Jay's gun went off, a booted foot kicked the barrel. It jerked upwards and the ball went harmlessly up into the air. Fear and guilt possessed Jay's heart and he looked up into the enraged face of Sir George.

'You murdering little bastard,' his father said.

THE DAY IN THE OPEN air made Lizzie sleepy, and soon after supper she announced that she was going to bed. Robert happened to be out of the room so Jay politely sprang up to light her way upstairs with a candle. As they mounted the staircase he said quietly: 'I'll take you down the mine, if you like.'

Lizzie's sleepiness vanished. 'When can we go?' she said eagerly.

'Tonight. The hewers start work at midnight, the bearers an hour or two later.'

'Really?' Lizzie was mystified. 'Why do they work at night?'

'They work all day as well. The bearers finish at the end of the afternoon.'

She felt foolish. 'I had no idea they worked such long hours.'

'Be ready at midnight,' Jay said. 'You'll have to dress as a man again. Meet me in the stable yard. I'll saddle a couple of horses.' He handed her the candle. 'Until midnight,' he whispered.

She went into her bedroom. Jay was happy again, she noted. Earlier today he had had a row with his father, up on the mountain. No one had seen exactly what happened, but Jay had missed his stag and Sir George had been white with rage. Lizzie had killed her stag cleanly. Both Robert and Henry had wounded theirs. Robert finished his off with another shot, but Henry's got away and the dogs went after it and brought it down after a chase.

She took off her dress, her petticoats and her shoes, then she wrapped herself in a blanket and sat in front of the blazing fire. There was a tap at the door and her mother came in. Lizzie suffered a guilty pang. I hope Mother doesn't want a long chat, she thought anxiously. But it was not yet eleven: there was plenty of time.

Mother unpinned Lizzie's hair and began to brush it. Lizzie closed her eyes and relaxed. This always took her back to her childhood. 'You must promise me not to dress as a man again,' Mother said. Lizzie was startled. It was almost as if Mother had overheard her talking to Jay. 'You're much too old for such games now,' she added.

'Sir George was highly amused!' Lizzie protested.

'Perhaps, but it's no way to get a husband.'

'Robert seems to want me.'

'Yes—but you must give him a chance to pay court! Going to church yesterday you rode off with Jay and left Robert behind. Then again, tonight you chose to retire when Robert was out of the room, so that he lost the chance of escorting you upstairs.'

Lizzie loved her mother and would have liked to please her. But she could not be the daughter her mother wanted. 'I'm sorry, Mother,' she said. 'I just don't think of these things.'

'Do you . . . like Robert?'

'I'd take him if I were desperate.'

Lady Hallim put down the hairbrush and sat opposite Lizzie. 'My dear, we *are* desperate. And I've managed by borrowing, and mortgaging our land. But there's a limit to how much one can borrow. They're threatening to take away Hallim House and the estate.'

'Who are "they"?'

Mother looked vague. 'Well, your father's lawyer arranged the loans, but I don't exactly know who put up the money.'

'Mother . . . are you saying we're going to lose our home?'

'No, dear—not if you marry Robert.' Mother stood up and kissed her. 'Good night, dear. Sleep well.'

'Good night, Mother.'

Lizzie looked thoughtfully into the fire. She had known for years that it was her destiny to rescue their fortunes by marrying a wealthy man, but suddenly the prospect of marrying Robert appalled her.

She felt a kind of physical disgust, as if she had swallowed something putrid. But what could she do? She could not let her mother's creditors throw them out of their home!

She pinned up her hair, then dressed in the disguise she had worn yesterday, with a topcoat and a man's three-cornered hat but without the curly wig. For warmth she added fur gloves, and a plaid blanket that made her shoulders seem broader.

When she heard midnight strike she took a candle and went downstairs. Jay was waiting in the stable yard holding two ponies. She felt a glow of pleasure when he smiled at her in the moonlight. Without speaking, he handed her the reins of the smaller horse, then led the way out of the yard by a back path.

When they reached the road Jay unshrouded a lantern. They mounted their ponies and rode up the glen towards the coalpits. 'Did you have another row with your father?' Lizzie asked.

'Yes.'

'What about?' she said.

She sensed that he disliked her questioning. However, he answered mildly enough. 'The same old thing, I'm afraid—my brother, Robert.'

'I think you've been very badly treated, if that's any consolation.'

'It is—thank you.' He seemed to relax a bit.

As they approached the pits Lizzie began to feel apprehensive. But whatever happens, she thought, I'll know what it's like—and McAsh will no longer be able to taunt me with my ignorance.

The pithead itself was marked by a horse trotting in a circle, turning a drum. As they got closer Lizzie saw that the drum wound a rope that pulled buckets of water out of the pit. 'There's always water in a mine,' Jay explained. 'It seeps from the earth.'

They tied up their horses and went to the edge of the pit. It was a shaft about six foot square with a steep wooden staircase descending its sides in a zigzag. There was no handrail. Lizzie suffered a moment of panic. 'How deep is it?' she asked in a shaky voice.

'If I remember rightly, this pit is two hundred and ten feet.'

Lizzie swallowed hard. Gritting her teeth, she said: 'What are we waiting for?'

Jay went ahead, lighting the steps for her. As they descended, the wooden buckets of water waltzed up the well in the middle of the shaft, frequently splashing icy water on Lizzie. She had a scary vision of herself slipping off the stairs and tumbling crazily down the shaft, crashing into the buckets before she hit the bottom and died.

After a while Jay stopped to let her rest. Wanting to show she wasn't tired, she made conversation. 'You know a lot about the

mines—where the water comes from, how deep the pit is and so on.'
'I spent one summer with Harry Ratchett, the viewer. Mother decided she wanted me to learn all about the business, in the hope that one day Father would want me to run it. Foolish aspiration.'
Lizzie felt sorry for him.
They went on. A few minutes later the stairs ended in a deck that gave access to two tunnels. Jay stepped off the deck into one of them, turned and gave his hand to Lizzie. As he began to lead her on he kept hold of her hand. She was not sure what to make of this but she had no time to think about it. She had to concentrate on keeping her footing. She ploughed through thick coal dust and she could taste it in the air. The roof was low in places and she had to stoop much of the time.
On either side candlelight flickered in the gaps between broad columns. Jay said: 'Each miner works a twelve-foot section of the coalface, called a "room". Between one room and another they leave a pillar of coal to support the roof.'
Lizzie suddenly realised that above her head were two hundred and ten feet of earth and rock that could collapse if the miners had not done their work carefully, and she fought to suppress a feeling of panic. She gave Jay's hand a squeeze, and he squeezed back.
Jay stopped beside a room where a man was digging. To Lizzie's surprise the miner was not standing up: he lay on his side, attacking the coalface at floor level. A candle in a wooden holder threw its light on his work. Despite his awkward position he swung his pick powerfully, digging the point into the coal and prising out lumps. Lizzie was shocked to realise that he was lying in running water, which seeped out of the coalface and drained into a ditch that ran along the tunnel. Lizzie dipped her fingers into the ditch. The water was freezing cold. She shivered.
The tunnel was not level, but rose and fell with the seam of coal. Now it began to go up more steeply. Jay pointed ahead to where a miner was raising a candle slowly towards the roof. 'He's testing for firedamp,' Jay said.
Lizzie let go of his hand and sat on a rock, to relieve her back from stooping. 'What's firedamp?'
'An inflammable gas. It's lighter than air, so it concentrates at roof level. It's what causes most explosions in coalmines.'
This sounded mad. 'If it's explosive, why is he using a candle?'
'It's the only way to detect the gas—you can't see it or smell it. A small amount will give a blue tinge to the flame.'
'And what will a large amount do?'
'Blow us all to kingdom come.'

Lizzie felt this was the last straw. She was filthy and exhausted and now she was in danger of being blown up. 'And if he finds firedamp—how do you get rid of it?'

'Set fire to it. One of the miners is designated fireman. In this pit I believe it's McAsh, the young troublemaker. The job is generally handed down from father to son. The fireman is the pit's expert on gas. He knows what to do.'

In order to get away from this insanely dangerous test, Lizzie pointed to a side tunnel and said: 'What's down there?'

Jay took her hand again. 'Let's go and see.'

There was a strange hush throughout the mine, Lizzie thought as they walked along. Nobody spoke much and the clang of picks hitting the face was muffled by the thick dust underfoot. They found themselves in a deserted section. Jay stopped. 'This part seems to be worked-out,' he said, swinging his lantern in an arc. Lizzie noticed that his face was smeared black, like the miners', and she smiled.

'Your face is black!' she said.

He grinned. 'And what do you think yours is like?'

'Oh, no!' she said with a laugh.

'You're still beautiful, though,' he said, and he kissed her.

She was surprised, but she did not flinch: she liked it. When he drew back she said, 'Is that what you brought me down here for?'

'Are you offended?'

She ought to be offended, she knew. 'Perhaps we should retrace our steps.'

'May I keep holding your hand?'

'Yes.'

He seemed satisfied with that, and he led her back.

At this point the bearers began to arrive, carrying their candles and wooden shovels, and Lizzie suffered her most horrifying shock yet. They were nearly all women and girls.

'Why do women do this?' she asked Jay incredulously.

'A miner is paid by the weight of coal he delivers to the pithead,' he replied. 'If he has to pay a bearer, the money goes out of the family. So he gets his wife and children to do it.'

The bearers got to work shovelling the coal into big baskets. Lizzie watched as two women picked one up between them and heaved it onto the bent back of a third. She grunted as she took the weight, then she headed slowly down the tunnel, bent double. Lizzie wondered how she could possibly carry it up two hundred feet of steps. 'Is the basket as heavy as it looks?' she said.

One of the miners overheard her. 'We call it a corf,' he said. 'It holds a hundred and fifty pounds of coal. Would you like to feel the weight, young sir? Or perhaps a half-corf, such as this wee one is carrying.'

Approaching them was a girl of ten or eleven. She was barefoot, and carried on her back a corf half full of coal.

'Yes,' said Lizzie. 'Let me feel the weight.'

The miner stopped the girl and one of his women lifted the corf and swung it onto Lizzie's back.

Although she was braced for it, the weight was much more than she had anticipated. Her legs buckled under her and she collapsed. The miner, seemingly expecting this, caught her, and she felt the weight lifted from her back.

The miner who had caught Lizzie easily supported her on his strong forearm. A calloused hand, hard as a horse's hoof, squashed her breast through the linen shirt and she heard the man grunt with surprise. He held her by her shoulders and astonished eyes stared at her out of his coal-blackened face.

'Miss Hallim!' he whispered. She realised the miner was Malachi McAsh.

They looked at one another for a spellbound moment. Then a voice said: 'Mack—look at this!'

A woman was holding a candle up to the roof. McAsh released his hold on Lizzie. He looked at the candle flame and said: 'You're right, Esther.' He turned back and addressed the others. 'There's a little firedamp. It's not enough to sound the alarm, not yet anyway. We'll check in different places and see how far it extends.'

Jay took Lizzie's arm. 'I think we've seen enough, don't you?'

Lizzie did not argue. Her curiosity had been satisfied long ago. They hurried along the tunnel towards the shaft. The mine was busy now and there were bearers in front of them and behind. The women moved slowly under their enormous burdens.

They reached the shaft and started up the stairs. After a while Lizzie had to rest, but the bearers never stopped, and she felt humiliated as she watched little girls pass her with their loads, some of them crying from pain and exhaustion. All the emotions of the night came together and turned into anger. 'I swear,' she said vehemently, 'I'll never allow coal to be mined on my land, as long as I live.'

Before Jay could make any reply, a bell began to ring.

'The alarm,' Jay said. 'They must have found more firedamp.'

Lizzie groaned and got to her feet.

'I'll carry you,' Jay said, and without more ado he slung her over his shoulder and began to climb the stairs.

33

THE FIREDAMP SPREAD with terrifying speed and Mack had to stop testing for fear of setting fire to it before the pit was evacuated.

His first priority was to get everyone out as fast as possible. He rang the handbell vigorously while he counted to twelve. By the time he stopped, miners and bearers were hurrying towards the shaft.

His two bearers stayed—his sister Esther and his cousin Annie. Using their coal shovels the two women began frantically to dig a shallow trench, the length and breadth of Mack, in the floor of the tunnel. Meanwhile Mack snatched an oilcloth bundle hanging from the roof of his room and ran for the mouth of the tunnel.

The last stragglers were heading up the stairs. Now Mack had to get rid of the gas. It was evilly bad luck that this should happen today. It was his birthday: he was leaving. He felt sick at heart that in his final hours as a coalminer he had to risk his life to save the pit. But if the firedamp were not burned off, the pit would close. And a pit closure in a mining village was like a failed harvest in a farming community: people starved.

He stepped out onto the deck and tore the waterproof wrappings off his bundle. Inside was a big torch made of dry sticks and rags, a ball of string and a large version of the wooden candleholder the miners used. Mack stuck the torch firmly in the holder, tied the string to the base and lit the torch with his candle. Here it would burn safely, for the lighter-than-air gas could not gather at the bottom of the shaft. But his next task was to get the burning torch into the tunnel.

He took a moment to soak himself in the drainage pool at the bottom of the shaft, to give a little extra protection from burns. Then he hurried back along the tunnel unwinding the ball of string. When he reached Esther and Annie, he saw that all was ready. The trench was dug. Esther was dipping a blanket into the drainage ditch, and now she quickly wrapped it round Mack. Shivering, he lay down in the trench, still holding the end of the string. Annie knelt beside him and, somewhat to his surprise, kissed him full on the lips. Then she covered the trench with a heavy board, closing him in.

He counted to one hundred, to give them time to get out of the tunnel. Then, with his heart full of dread, he started to pull on the string, drawing the blazing torch towards where he lay, in a tunnel half full of explosive gas.

JAY CARRIED LIZZIE to the top of the stairs and set her down at the pithead. Daybreak was still hours away, and it had started to snow. As the last of the miners and bearers came out of the shaft, Lizzie noticed the young woman whose baby had been christened on

Sunday—Jen, her name was—darting among the crowd of mine workers calling: 'Wullie! Wullie!' It seemed she was searching for a child. She found her husband Saul and had a rapid conversation with him. Then she screamed 'No!', ran to the pithead and started back down the stairs.

The husband went to the edge of the shaft then came back, visibly distressed. Lizzie said to him: 'What's the matter?'

He replied in a shaky voice. 'We can't find our laddie, and she thinks he's still down the pit.'

MACK HAD DONE THIS on three previous occasions, but this time he was dealing with a far greater concentration of firedamp. He shivered in his sodden blanket. As he steadily wound in the string, pulling the blazing torch closer to himself and to the gas, he tried to calm his fear by thinking about Annie. They had grown up together and had always been fond of one another. Annie had never kissed him in public before, but she had often done it secretly. They had explored one another's bodies, only stopping short of what Annie called 'making bairns'. And they had almost done that . . .

It was no use: he still felt terrified. If I survive this night, he vowed, I will leave the glen today, so help me God.

The string which had gathered in his hands told him the torch was now about halfway to him. Surely the gas must blow.

Then he heard a voice.

Mack's heart stopped. It was a voice of a terrified child, crying and saying: 'Where is everyone?'

He knew what had happened. As a small boy working in the mine he had often fallen asleep during his fifteen-hour day. This child had done the same, and had slept through the alarm. He pushed the board aside and sprang out of his trench. The scene was illuminated by the torch and he could see the boy coming out of a side tunnel. It was Wullie, the son of his cousin Jen.

Mack ran for the boy, unwrapping the sodden blanket from around himself as he went. He wrapped the boy in the blanket, saying: 'There's firedamp, Wullie, we've got to get out!' He picked him up and ran on. As he approached the burning torch he heard himself shouting: 'Not yet! Not yet!' Then they were past it.

The boy was light, but it was hard to run stooping, and the uneven floor made it more difficult. As Mack rounded the curve in the tunnel, the light from the torch dimmed to nothing. He was forced to go on more slowly, feeling the tunnel wall with his free hand. Then, mercifully, a candle flame appeared at the entrance of the tunnel and Mack heard Jen's voice calling: 'Wullie! Wullie!'

'I've got him here, Jen!' Mack shouted, breaking into a run. 'Get yourself up the stairs!'

She ignored his instruction and came towards him.

He crashed into her and swept her up in his free arm.

Then the gas blew. A force like a massive fist struck Mack's back and he was lifted off his feet, losing his grip on Wullie and Jen. He felt a wave of scorching heat, then he splashed headfirst into the drainage pool at the bottom of the mine shaft.

He broke the surface and dashed water from his eyes. The wooden decking and staircase were burning in places, and the flames illuminated the scene fitfully. Mack located Jen, splashing about and choking. He grabbed her and heaved her out of the water.

Choking, she screamed: 'Where's Wullie?'

Mack pushed himself from one side of the pool to the other, bumping into the bucket chain which had ceased to operate. At last he found a floating object that turned out to be Wullie. He shoved the boy onto the deck beside his mother and clambered out himself.

'Thank God,' Jen sobbed. 'He's alive.'

'Away up the stairs with us,' Mack said. 'There might be a secondary blast.' He pulled Jen and Wullie to their feet and pushed them up ahead of him.

When he reached the top he was surrounded by a crowd who shook his hand and congratulated him. The crowd parted for Jay Jamisson and his companion. 'Well done, McAsh,' said Jay. 'My family appreciates your courage.'

You smug bastard, Mack thought.

Lizzie said: 'Is there no other way to deal with firedamp?'

'No,' said Jay.

'Of course there is,' Mack gasped. 'You sink ventilation shafts that let the gas escape before ever it can accumulate. The Jamissons have been told time and time again.'

One or two of the miners shouted: 'Aye! That's right!'

'Now, McAsh,' Jay remonstrated. 'Don't spoil everything by getting above your station again. You'll get into real trouble.'

'I'm in no trouble,' Mack said. 'Today is my twenty-second birthday. I haven't worked here the full year-and-a-day, not quite—and I'm not going to.' The crowd was suddenly quiet. 'I'm leaving, Mr Jamisson,' he said. 'I quit. Goodbye.' He turned his back on Jay and, in total silence, walked away.

BY THE TIME Jay and Lizzie got back to the castle, servants were about, lighting fires and sweeping floors. Lizzie, black with coal dust and almost helpless with fatigue, thanked Jay in a whisper and

staggered upstairs. Jay ordered a tub and hot water to be brought to his room, then took a bath, scrubbing the coal dust off his skin.

As he lay there he thought about Lizzie. Her impish face appeared before him in the steam from his bath, smiling mischievously, mocking him, daring him. He wondered if she was thinking about him.

He did not feel sleepy. He wanted to talk to someone about the night's adventure. He shaved and put on fresh clothes, then he went along to his mother's room. As he expected, she was up, sitting at her dressing table while her maid did her hair. He kissed her and dropped into a chair.

She dismissed her maid. 'Why are you up so early?' she asked.

'I haven't been to bed. I went down the pit.'

'With Lizzie Hallim?'

She was so clever, he thought fondly. 'How did you guess?'

'It wasn't difficult. She was itching to go.'

'We chose a bad day to go down. There was an explosion.'

'Dear God, are you all right?'

'Yes. I was out of the pit by the time it blew. So was Lizzie.'

Mother calmed down. 'What did Lizzie think of it?'

'She swore she would never allow mining on the Hallim estate.'

Alicia laughed. 'When Robert is her husband he will have the power to go against her wishes . . . in theory. We shall see. But how do you think the courtship is progressing?'

'Flirting isn't Robert's strong point,' Jay said scornfully.

'Perhaps she won't marry him after all.'

'I think she will have to. Lady Hallim is having trouble renewing her mortgages—Father has made sure of it.' He sighed. 'She's a wonderful girl. She'll be wasted on Robert.'

Mother put a hand on his knee. 'She's not Robert's yet. She might marry you. You're in love with her, I can tell.'

'Love? Is that what this is?'

'Of course—your eyes light up at the mention of her name, and when she's in the room you can't see anyone else.'

She had described Jay's feelings exactly. 'But marry her?'

'If you're in love with her, ask her! You'd be the laird of High Glen. You'd clear land for grazing, sell more venison. You could produce a decent income from it, even without mining for coal.'

'What about the mortgages?'

'You're a much more attractive borrower than Lady Hallim—you're young and vigorous and come from a wealthy family. You would find it easy enough to renew the loans. And then, in time . . .'

'What?'

'Well, Lizzie is an impulsive girl. Today she vows she will never allow mining on the Hallim estate. Tomorrow, who knows?'

Jay grimaced. He wanted to be a Barbadian sugar grower, not a Scottish coal-owner. But he wanted Lizzie, too.

'HOW COULD YOU DO such a thing?' Lady Hallim wailed as she scrubbed Lizzie's back with a pumice stone.

'I had to see for myself,' Lizzie replied. 'Mack McAsh riled me when he said I didn't know what I was talking about.'

'And why should you?' said her mother. 'What business has a young lady to know about coalmining, may I ask?'

'I hate it when people dismiss me by saying that women don't understand about politics, or farming, or mining, or trade—it lets them get away with all kinds of nonsense.'

Lady Hallim groaned. 'I hope Robert doesn't mind you being so masculine.'

'He'll have to take me as I am, or not at all.'

Her mother gave an exasperated sigh. 'My dear, this won't do. You must give him more encouragement. Now promise me you'll be nice to him today.'

'Mother, what do you think of Jay?'

Mother smiled. 'A charming boy, of course, but a little vain and self-absorbed, I think—' She stopped suddenly and stared hard at Lizzie. 'Why do you ask?'

'He kissed me in the coalmine.'

'No!' Lady Hallim stood upright and hurled the pumice stone across the room. 'No, Elizabeth, I will not have this!' Lizzie was taken aback by her mother's fury. 'I have not lived twenty years in penury to see you grow up and marry a handsome pauper!'

'He's not a pauper—'

'Yes, he is, you saw that awful scene with his father—his patrimony is a horse. Lizzie, you cannot do this!' She seized her daughter's hand. 'Promise me you won't marry him, Lizzie. Promise me!'

Lizzie pulled her hand away. She felt disloyal, but she had to tell the truth. 'I can't,' she said. 'I love him.'

WHEN JAY LEFT his mother's room he felt suddenly hungry. He went down to the dining room. His father and Robert were there, eating grilled ham and talking to Harry Ratchett. Ratchett, as manager of the pits, had come to report the firedamp blast. Father looked sternly at Jay and said: 'I hear you went down Heugh pit last night. Who was your companion?'

'Lizzie Hallim,' he confessed.

Robert coloured. 'Damn you,' he said. 'You know that Father

did not wish her to be taken down the pit.'

Father wagged a finger. 'I warn you not to disregard my orders.'

'You should be worrying about McAsh, not me,' Jay said, trying to turn away his father's wrath. 'He told everyone he was leaving today.'

Robert said: 'Insubordinate tyke.'

Harry Ratchett coughed. 'You might just let McAsh go, Sir George,' he said. 'He's a troublemaker and we'd be well rid of him.'

'I can't do that,' Father replied. 'If McAsh gets away with it, every young miner will think he can leave too.'

There was a thoughtful silence.

'He could be flogged,' Robert suggested.

Ratchett looked uneasy. 'It's many years since that right was exercised by a coal-owner. And who would wield the lash?'

Robert said impatiently: 'Well, what do we do with troublemakers?'

Sir George smiled. 'We make them go the round,' he said.

Chapter 3

Mack would have liked to start walking to Edinburgh right away, but he knew that would be foolish. He went home, took off his wet clothes, lit the fire and got into bed. The night's adventures had made him dirtier than usual, but his blankets were so black that a little more made no difference. Like most of the men, he bathed once a week, on Saturday night.

The other miners had gone back to work after the explosion. Esther had stayed at the pit, with Annie, to bring the coal Mack had hewed up to the surface: she would not let hard work go to waste.

When Mack woke up he knew it was a momentous day but he could not remember why. Then it came back to him: he was leaving the glen. The first thing he had to do was get clean. He built up the fire then made several trips to the stream with the water barrel. He heated the water on the fire and brought in the tin tub that hung outside the back door. He filled the bath, then got in with a piece of soap and a stiff brush and scrubbed himself.

While he was in the bath, Annie came in.

She hesitated, looking troubled.

Mack offered her the brush and said: 'Would you do my back?'

She took it from him and began to scrub. 'They say a miner shouldn't wash his back. It's supposed to be weakening.'

'I'm not a miner any more.'

She stopped. 'Don't go, Mack,' she pleaded. 'Don't leave me.'

He had been afraid of this: that kiss down the mine had been a forewarning. He was fond of his cousin, but he did not want to spend his life with her, especially if it meant staying in Heugh. Could he explain that without crucifying her? 'I must go away,' he said. 'I'll miss you, Annie, but I have to go.'

She knelt beside the tub and put her hand on his knee above the water. 'Don't you love me, Mack?'

To his shame he began to feel aroused. 'You're dear to me, Annie, but I never said "I love you," no more than you did.'

'Stay here and let's get married,' Annie said, caressing him.

'If I get married I'm stuck here for life,' Mack said, but he felt his resistance weakening.

Annie stood up and pulled off her dress. She wore nothing else: underwear was reserved for Sundays. Her body was lean and hard, with small flat breasts. To Mack's astonishment she climbed into the tub with him, kneeling astride his legs. 'Say you'll stay,' she pleaded. 'Let's do it. I want to feel you inside me.'

He knew that if he gave in his fate was sealed. 'No,' he said, but his voice was a whisper.

She came closer, pulling his face to hers. 'Say yes,' she said.

He groaned and gave up the struggle. 'Yes,' he said. 'Quickly.'

There was a terrific crash and the door flew open. Four men burst in: Robert Jamisson, Harry Ratchett and two of the Jamissons' keepers. Robert wore a sword and a pair of pistols, and one of the keepers carried a musket. Traditionally the keepers looked after the deer and tried to catch poachers, but nowadays many of them enforced discipline at the pits.

Annie got off Mack and stepped out of the bath. Dazed and frightened, Mack stood up shakily.

The keeper with the musket looked at Annie. 'Cosy cousins,' he said with a leer. Mack knew the man: his name was McAlistair. He recognised the other one, a big bully called Tanner.

Robert laughed harshly. 'Is that what she is—his cousin?'

Mack suppressed his anger. 'I'm a free man and I've broken no laws,' he said. 'What are you doing in my house?'

McAlistair was still staring at Annie's body. 'What a pretty sight,' he said thickly.

Mack turned to him. In a low, even voice he said: 'If you touch her I'll tear the head off your neck with my hands.'

McAlistair paled and took a step back. But Tanner was bigger and more reckless, and he reached out and grasped Annie's breast.

A second later Mack was out of the bath and seizing Tanner by the wrist. Before anyone else could move he had thrust Tanner's hand into the fire. 'Run, Annie!' he yelled.

Tanner screamed and writhed. 'Let me go!' he screeched.

Annie snatched up her dress and flew out of the back door.

The butt of a musket cracked into the back of Mack's head, and for a moment he swayed, stunned. Then Ratchett grabbed him from behind, pinning his arms, and the point of Robert's sword was at his throat. Robert said: 'Tie him up.'

They threw him across the back of a horse and covered his nakedness with a blanket, then they took him to Castle Jamisson and put him in the larder, still naked and tied hand and foot.

He lay on the stone floor, shivering, surrounded by the dripping carcasses of deer, cattle and pigs. His head hurt from the musket blow, but what pained him most was how easily the Jamissons had taken him. What a fool he was to have delayed his departure, allowing them time to plan his downfall.

It did not help to speculate on what they had in store for him. If he did not freeze to death here in the larder they would probably send him to Edinburgh and have him tried for assaulting the gamekeeper. Like most crimes, that was a hanging matter.

THE LIGHT COMING through the cracks around the door gradually faded as night fell. Jamisson's men came for him just as the stableyard clock struck eleven.

Davy Taggart, the blacksmith, fitted an iron collar like Jimmy Lee's round Mack's neck. It was the ultimate humiliation: a sign telling all the world he was another man's property.

They untied his bonds and threw some clothes at him: a pair of breeches, a threadbare flannel shirt and a ripped waistcoat. He put them on hastily, then the keepers tied his hands again and put him on a pony. They rode to the pit.

The Wednesday shift would begin in a few minutes' time, at midnight. The ostler was putting a fresh horse in harness to drive the bucket chain. Mack realised they were going to make him go the round. He roared: 'You've no right to do this! No right!' The keepers laughed at him.

They stood him in the muddy circular track around which the pithead horses trotted day and night. Then they tied him to the harness, facing the horse, so that he could not get out of its way. The ostler whipped the horse into a trot.

Mack began to run backwards. He stumbled almost immediately, and the horse drew up. The ostler whipped it again, and Mack scrambled to his feet just in time. He began to get the knack of running backwards. Then he became overconfident and slipped on icy mud. The horse trod on his stomach and kicked his thigh, then stopped.

They made Mack stand up, then they lashed the horse again. The blow to the stomach had winded Mack, and his left leg felt weak, but he was forced into a limping backwards run. His mind dulled with pain, he thought of nothing but staying on his feet and avoiding those deadly hoofs.

He was aware of the hewers arriving at midnight to begin their shift. They came up the hill together, talking and shouting as usual; then they fell silent as they approached the pithead and saw Mack. The keepers hefted their muskets menacingly whenever a miner seemed disposed to stop.

Gradually Mack lost all sense of time. The bearers arrived, women and children chattering on their way up the hill, then falling silent, as the men had. He heard Annie cry: 'Oh dear God, they've made Mack go the round!' Esther appeared, and before the keepers could prevent her she stopped the horse. She held a flagon of hot sweetened milk to Mack's lips. He gulped it frantically before they pulled her away.

The night wore on as slow as a year. There came a moment when he realised that it was daylight once more. Now it could be only an hour or two until the hewers stopped work, but an hour would last for ever.

A pony came up the hill. Out of the corner of his eye Mack saw the rider get off and stand staring at him, and he recognised Lizzie Hallim. Was she here to mock him? he wondered. He felt humiliated and wished she would go away. But when he looked again at her elfin face he saw no mockery there. Instead there was compassion, anger, and something else that he could not read.

Another horse came up the hill and Robert got off. He spoke to Lizzie in an irate undertone. Lizzie's reply was clearly audible: 'This is barbaric!' While they were arguing, the men began to come up from the pit. They stood around the horse-gin, watching without speaking. The women also began to join the silent crowd.

Robert ordered the ostler to stop the horse.

Mack at last stopped running. He tried to stand proud, but his legs would not support him and he fell to his knees.

Robert spoke loud enough for everyone to hear. 'Well, McAsh, you said yesterday that you were one day short of servitude. Now you have worked that extra day. You're my father's property now.' He turned round to address the crowd.

But before he could speak again, Jimmy Lee started to sing. The notes of a familiar hymn soared out across the glen:

43

Behold a man in anguish bending,
Marked by pain and loss,
Yonder stony hill ascending,
Carrying a cross.

The others joined in, some singing the harmonies, and a hundred voices swelled the melody.

Robert turned away, helpless. He stamped across the mud to his horse and rode off down the hill with the thrilling voices of the miners shaking the mountain air like a thunderstorm.

Look no more with eyes of pity,
See our victory.
When we build that heavenly city,
All men shall be free!

JAY WOKE UP knowing he was going to propose marriage to Lizzie. It was only yesterday that his mother had put it into his mind, but now it seemed natural, even inevitable.

To his disappointment he found she had gone out early. Too tense to wait around the house, he went out to the stables and looked at the white stallion his father had given him for his birthday. The horse's name was Blizzard. Jay had vowed never to ride him, but he could not resist the temptation. He took Blizzard up to High Glen and galloped him along the springy turf. He felt as if he were on the back of an eagle, soaring through the air, borne up by the wind.

Riding home, he reached the stable yard at the same time as his brother. Robert was in a bad mood. He threw his reins to a groom and stomped indoors. While Jay was stabling Blizzard, Lizzie rode up. She, too, was upset, but the flush of anger on her cheeks made her look even prettier. She jumped off her horse and before he could speak she said: 'I know that people who misbehave must be punished, but I don't believe in torture, do you?'

Jay saw nothing wrong in torturing criminals but he was not going to tell her that. 'Of course I don't,' he said. 'Have you come from the pithead?'

'It was awful. I told Robert to let the man go but he refused.'

So she had quarrelled with Robert. Jay concealed his delight. My chances are improving by the minute, he thought exultantly.

A groom took her horse and they walked across the yard into the castle. Robert was talking to Sir George in the hall. 'It was a piece of brazen defiance,' he was saying. 'We must make sure McAsh doesn't get away with this.'

Lizzie made an exasperated noise and Jay saw a chance to score points with her. Recalling Harry Ratchett's argument, he said to his father, 'I think we should consider letting McAsh go. We'd be better off without him.'

'He has defied us openly,' Robert protested. 'He can't be allowed to get away with it.'

'He hasn't got away with it!' Lizzie declared. 'He's suffered the most savage punishment!'

Sir George said: 'It's not savage, Elizabeth—you have to understand that they don't feel pain as we do.' Before she could expostulate he turned to Robert. 'But it's true that he hasn't got away with it. The miners now know they can't leave at the age of twenty-one. McAsh could be dangerous, he's already halfway to becoming a hero from what you've just told me. I wonder if we shouldn't discreetly let him vanish.'

Robert was not satisfied. 'I still think it looks bad,' he said.

'Then make it look better,' Father said. 'Leave the guard on the bridge. McAsh will go over the mountain, probably: we just won't chase him. I don't mind them thinking he's escaped—so long as they know he did not have the right to leave.'

'Very well,' said Robert. He disappeared towards the back of the house, still looking grumpy. Father went into his study.

When they were alone Lizzie threw her arms round Jay's neck. 'You did it!' she said. 'You set him free!' She gave him an exuberant kiss.

It was scandalously bold, and he was shocked, but he soon recovered. He put his arms round her waist and held her close. He leaned down and they kissed again. With a thrill of anxiety he realised that this was the moment to ask her to marry him, but he didn't know how to bring the subject up.

'Lizzie . . . you can't marry Robert, now.'

Lizzie leaned her head on his chest. 'Of course I can't, not now. Because I'm going to marry you—am I not?' she said with a grin.

He could hardly believe she had said that. 'Well . . . yes!'

'There you are, then. Now you can kiss me again.'

Feeling a little dazed, he bent his head to hers. As soon as their lips met she opened her mouth and he was shocked and delighted to feel her tongue teasing its way through. He did not hear the door into the hall open. Suddenly Robert was shouting: 'What the devil is this?'

The lovers broke apart. 'It's all right, brother,' said Jay. 'You see, we're engaged to be married.'

'YOU BLOODY FOOL, you'll have nothing to live on,' Sir George said.

The families had separated to discuss the shocking news privately. Lady Hallim and Lizzie had gone upstairs. Sir George, Jay and

Alicia were in the study. Robert had stomped off somewhere alone.

Jay bit back a hurt retort. Remembering what his mother had suggested, he said: 'I'm sure I can manage High Glen. It should produce an income large enough for us to live on.'

His mother cut in: 'Jay can raise new mortgages.'

Father looked taken aback. 'Are you on the boy's side, then?'

'You refused to give him anything. You want him to fight for everything, as you did. Well, he's fighting. You can hardly complain.'

Sir George's tone became resigned. 'Oh, well. They're both over twenty-one, so I don't suppose we can stop them.' A crafty look came over his face. 'At any rate the coal in High Glen will come into our family.'

'Oh no it won't,' said Alicia. 'Jay may lease the mining rights to someone else. After the way you insulted him on his birthday, what does he owe you?'

'I'm his father, damn it!'

'Then start acting like his father. Congratulate him on his engagement. Plan a lavish wedding celebration.'

He stared at her for a moment. 'Is that what you want?'

'It's not all.'

'I might have guessed. What else are you after, Alicia?'

'Barbados.'

Jay almost jumped out of his chair. How crafty Mother was!

His father said: 'Barbados is promised to Robert.'

Mother went to the door and Jay followed her. 'If you don't give Jay the plantation,' she said, 'you won't have the coal. It's a simple choice, and you have plenty of time to think about it.' She went out.

Jay went with her. In the hall he whispered: 'You were marvellous! But Lizzie won't allow mining in High Glen.'

'I know, I know,' Mother said impatiently. 'We'll cross that bridge when we come to it.'

LIZZIE CAME DOWN the stairs wearing a fur cloak so big it went round her twice and brushed the floor. With the house full of tension she had to get outside for a while. She stepped out of the castle door and pulled her furs more tightly around her. The clouds had partly cleared and there was a moon: she could see well enough to pick her way across the drive and down the sloping lawn towards the river.

She felt no remorse about letting Robert down. He had never loved her. Instead of being distraught about losing her, he was furious that his brother had got the better of him. She put him out of her mind. She had got what she wanted: Jay instead of Robert. Now she was eager to plan the wedding and set up house.

46

Mother was upset. Her dream was for Lizzie to marry a rich man and end the years of poverty. But she had to accept that Lizzie had her own dreams. Lady Hallim had also said that Jay was vain and self-absorbed, but Lizzie had never met a man who wasn't. At first she too had thought he was weak, for not standing up more to his brother and his father; but now she thought she must have been wrong about that, for in proposing to her he had defied them both.

She reached the bank of the river. This was no mountain stream, trickling down the glen. Thirty yards wide, it was a deep, fast-moving torrent. The moonlight gleamed off the troubled surface in patches of silver, like smashed mosaic.

As she looked over the river she saw movement on the far bank some way upstream. At first she thought it must be a deer: its head was too large for a man. Then she saw that it was a man with a bundle tied to his head. He stepped to the river bank and slipped into the water.

The bundle must be his clothes. But who would swim the river at this time of night in the middle of winter? Lizzie shivered inside her fur cloak when she thought how bitterly cold the water must be.

She stood motionless, watching his head move across the torrent at a steady speed. The strong current forced him into a diagonal course, but his pace did not falter. He would reach the near bank twenty or thirty yards upstream from where Lizzie stood.

But halfway across he suffered a stroke of bad luck. Lizzie saw the dark shape of a fallen tree rushing towards him. A heavy branch struck his head, and his arms became entangled in the foliage. Lizzie gasped as he went under. She stared at the branches, looking for the man, but he did not reappear. 'Please don't drown,' she whispered. The tree passed her and still there was no sign of him. As she stood there in an agony of suspense he surfaced, a yard behind the floating tree.

Lizzie went down to the river's edge. 'Over here!' she called. 'I'll pull you out!' He seemed not to hear but appeared to look about him to get his bearings. Lizzie called to him again. 'Over here! Let me help you!' He struck out towards her, thrashing and spluttering but moving in the right direction.

She knelt down and reached out to him. As his hands flailed the air, she grabbed a wrist and pulled it to her. Grasping his arm with both hands, she heaved. He hit the side and collapsed, half on the bank and half in the water. She changed her grip, holding him under the arms, and heaved again. He pushed with his hands and feet and, at last, flopped out of the water and lay on the bank, naked and sodden. The man whose life she had saved was Malachi McAsh.

He lay gasping and shivering uncontrollably. She untied the sodden bundle on his head, then she put her hand on his shoulder. He felt as cold as the grave. 'Stand up!' she said urgently. 'Get up or you'll die!' He did not move. She grabbed him with both hands but could not shift him at all. 'Mack, please don't die,' she said, and there was a sob in her voice.

Slowly he got on all fours, then he reached up and took her hand. With a heave from her he struggled to his feet. 'Thank God,' she murmured. He clung to her and she felt a powerful sense of intimacy with him, almost as if they were lovers.

Somehow she had to dry him. She needed a rag, anything she could use as a towel. She was wearing several linen petticoats: she could spare him one. 'Can you stand up alone now?' she said. He managed to nod between coughs. She let go of him and swiftly removed one petticoat. Then she began to rub him with it.

She wiped his face and rubbed his hair, then went behind him and dried his broad back. She realised that if he put on wet clothes now he would probably die of pneumonia. But he could not stay naked. 'Let me get you some clothes,' she said.

He shook his head. 'I'll not delay here. As soon as I start walking I'll get warmer.' He started to squeeze water out of a plaid blanket.

On impulse she took off her long fur cloak. She refused to think about how she would explain its disappearance to her mother. 'Wear this, then, and carry your clothes until you get a chance to dry them.' Without waiting for his assent she put the fur over his shoulders. He hesitated, then drew it around him gratefully.

She picked up his bundle and took out his boots. He handed her the wet blanket and she stuffed it into the bag. As she did so she felt the iron collar. She took it out. The iron ring had been broken and the collar bent to get it off. 'How did you do this?' she said.

He pulled on his boots. 'Broke into the pithead smithy and used Taggart's tools.'

'Why are you taking it with you?'

His eyes blazed with anger. 'Never to forget,' he said bitterly. 'Never.' He took the bag from her. He was ready to go.

'The keepers won't come after you,' she said.

He looked hard at her. 'How do you know?'

'Sir George decided you're such a troublemaker he'll be glad to be rid of you. He left the guard on the bridge because he doesn't want the miners to know he's letting you go; but he's expecting you to sneak past.'

A look of relief came over his face. 'So I needn't worry about the sheriff's men,' he said. 'Thank God.' He held out his hand. She was about to shake it when to her surprise he raised her fingers to his white lips and kissed them. Then he walked away.

MACK'S BOOTS crunched the ice on the puddles as he strode down the glen in the moonlight, but his body warmed quickly under Lizzie Hallim's fur cloak. As he got further from the castle he began to see the funny side of their encounter. There was she, in an embroidered dress and silk shoes, and he had come swimming across the river as naked as the day he was born. She must have had a shock!

Last Sunday at church she had acted like a typical arrogant Scottish aristocrat. But she'd had the guts to take up his challenge and go down the pit. And tonight she had saved his life. He was sorry to think he might never see her again.

Happily he did not have far to go tonight. He would walk to Craigie, a pit village six miles down the glen. There he would take refuge in the home of his mother's brother, Uncle Eb, and in the morning he would set out for Edinburgh. Once there he would leave on the first ship that would hire him.

As he strode along he began to feel solemn about his journey. He was leaving the only home he had ever known. He was leaving Esther, his friend and ally, although he hoped to rescue her before too long. He was leaving Annie, the cousin who had taught him how to kiss. But he had always known this would happen. As long as he could remember he had dreamed of escape. Now he was filled with elation. He had got away.

PART II: London
Chapter 4

Mack loved London. He felt a thrill every morning when he woke up and remembered where he was. The city was full of sights and surprises, strange people and new experiences. He stared at the gorgeous colours of the clothes worn by men and women, he heard the bellowing herds of cattle being driven through the narrow streets to the city's slaughterhouses, and he dodged the swarms of nearly naked children, begging and stealing. He went to bull fights and theatres, he tasted bananas and ginger and red wine. Everything was exciting. Best of all, he was free to go where he would and do as he liked.

Of course he had to earn his living. It was not easy. London swarmed with starving families who had fled from country districts where there had been two years of bad harvests. There were also thousands of handloom silk weavers, put out of work by the new northern factories, so Dermot said. Dermot Riley was a weaver himself. He had a wife and five children living in two rooms in Spitalfields. In order to get by they had to sublet Dermot's workroom, and Mack slept there, on the floor, beside the big silent loom.

Mack and Dermot looked for work together. Today they had got portering work, carrying huge baskets of fish in the waterfront market at Billingsgate. At the end of the day Mack had been reluctant to waste his money on a theatre ticket, but Dermot swore he would not regret it. Dermot had been right: it was worth twice the price to stand in the pit and see the Irish actor Charles Macklin play Shylock.

Walking east from the theatre, heading for Spitalfields, they passed through Covent Garden, where whores—young and old—accosted them from doorways. None of them tempted Mack, although he thought wistfully of his lusty cousin Annie. In the Strand was the Bear, a rambling tavern with several bars around a courtyard. The heat of the theatre had made them thirsty, and they went inside for a quart of ale. Dermot said: 'Let's take a look out the back.'

Mack had been here before, and he knew that bear-baiting, dogfights and all kinds of entertainments were held in the back yard. Tonight a prize-fighting ring had been set up, lit by numerous oil lamps. A dwarf in a silk suit was haranguing the crowd. 'A pound for anyone who can knock down the Bermondsey Bruiser!'

Dermot said to Mack: 'You could knock him down, I'd say.'

The Bermondsey Bruiser's face bore the marks of many fights. He was tall and heavy, but he looked stupid and slow. 'I suppose I could,' Mack said.

Dermot was enthusiastic. He grabbed the dwarf by the arm. 'Here's a customer for you.'

'A contender!' the dwarf bellowed, and the crowd cheered.

A pound was a lot of money, a week's wages for many people. Mack was tempted. 'All right,' he said, taking off his coat.

'Be ready for him to jump you as soon as you get in the ring,' Dermot said.

The ring was a waist-high circle of rope. As Mack lifted his foot to step into it, the Bermondsey Bruiser rushed him.

Mack was ready for it, and he stepped back, catching a glancing blow to his forehead from the Bruiser's massive fist. The crowd gasped. Mack stepped quickly up to the ring and kicked the Bruiser's shin under the rope, causing him to stumble. A cheer went up, and Mack heard Dermot's voice yelling: 'Kill him, Mack!'

Before the man could regain his balance, Mack hit him on each side of the head, left then right, then on the chin with an uppercut that had all his force behind it. The Bruiser's legs wobbled, his eyes rolled up, then he staggered and fell flat on his back.

The fight was over. The crowd roared their enthusiasm.

Scowling, the dwarf handed Mack a gold sovereign.

A rough-faced man in expensive clothes appeared at Mack's side. 'That was well done,' he said. 'I'm putting on a prize fight at the Pelican in Shadwell next Saturday. If you want the chance of earning twenty pounds, I'll put you up against Rees Preece, the Welsh Mountain.'

Mack looked at the Bruiser, lying in a useless heap, damaged and good for nothing. 'No,' he said.

The promoter shrugged. 'If you don't need the money. . .'

Mack thought of his twin, Esther, still carrying coal up the ladders of Heugh pit fifteen hours a day. Twenty pounds would pay her passage to London. 'On second thoughts, yes,' he said.

LIZZIE HALLIM AND HER MOTHER rattled northwards through the city of London in a hackney carriage. Lizzie was excited and happy: they were going to meet Jay and look at a house.

'Sir George has certainly changed his attitude,' said Lady Hallim. 'Bringing us to London, planning a lavish wedding, and now offering to pay the rent on a London house for the two of you to live in. I wonder what his motive might be? There isn't anything he wants from you, is there?'

Lizzie laughed. 'Perhaps he just wants me to make his son happy.'

'Which I'm sure you will. Here we are.'

The carriage stopped in Chapel Street, a quietly elegant row of houses in Holborn. Lizzie got down and looked at number twelve. She liked it right away. There were four storeys and a basement, and the windows were tall and graceful. However, two of the windows were broken and the number '45' was crudely daubed on the front door. Lizzie was about to comment when another carriage drew up and Jay jumped out.

He kissed Lizzie, then handed his mother down from the carriage and knocked on the door of the house.

An elderly caretaker opened the door. 'Who broke the windows?' Jay said immediately.

'The hatters, it was,' the man said as they stepped inside.

Lizzie had read that the people who made hats were on strike, as were the tailors and grinders. She said: 'Why are they on strike?'

'They want better wages, miss, and who can blame them, with the price of a fourpenny loaf gone up to eightpence-farthing?'

Lizzie went through the building excitedly throwing back curtains and opening windows. The furniture was new and expensive, and the drawing room was a wide, light room with three big windows at each end. The place needed only a thorough airing and a lick of paint to make it delightfully habitable.

She and Jay ran ahead of the two mothers, and when they reached the attic floor they were alone. 'What's the significance of the number forty-five?'

'It's all to do with that traitor John Wilkes,' Jay replied. 'He used to edit a journal called the *North Briton*, and the government charged him with seditious libel over issue number forty-five, in which he as good as called the king a liar. He ran away to Paris, but now he's come back to stir up more trouble among ignorant common people.'

'Is it true they can't afford bread?'

'There's a shortage of grain all over Europe, so it's inevitable that the price of bread should go up. And the unemployment is caused by the American embargo on British goods.'

'I don't suppose that's much consolation to the hatters and tailors.'

Lady Hallim and Lady Jamisson came into the room. Alicia said: 'Well, Lizzie, do you like the house?'

'I adore it!'

'Then you shall have it.'

Lizzie beamed and Jay squeezed her arm.

Lizzie's mother said: 'Sir George is so kind, I don't know how to thank him.'

'Thank my mother,' Jay said. 'She's the one who's made him behave decently.'

Alicia gave him a reproving look, but Lizzie could tell she did not really mind. She and Jay were obviously very fond of one another.

As they left the room, Lizzie remembered something. 'Oh, I must show you this!' she said to Jay. She had picked up a handbill in the street and saved it for him. She took it from her pocket and gave it to him to read. It said:

> *At the sign of the Pelican near Shadwell*
> *A Fist Fight—for Twenty Pounds!*
> *Rees Preece, the Welsh Mountain*
> *versus Mack McAsh, the Killer Collier*
> *Saturday next at Three o' Clock*

'So that's what's become of him,' said Jay. 'He's a prize fighter.'

'I've never seen a prize fight,' Lizzie said wistfully.

Jay laughed. 'I should think not! It's no place for a lady.'

'Nor is a coalmine, but you took me there.' Lizzie was disappointed. Jay's daring seemed to have deserted him momentarily. However, if he would not take her she would go alone.

LIZZIE ADJUSTED her wig and hat and looked in the mirror. A young man looked back at her. A heavy waistcoat flattened her bosom, the tail of her coat concealed the rounded curves of her womanly bottom, and knee boots covered her calves.

She opened her bedroom door. She and her mother were staying in a small house in the grounds of Sir George's mansion in Grosvenor Square. Mother was taking an afternoon nap. Lizzie ran down the stairs and slipped out of the door into the street. She waved down a sedan chair and said in a deep croak: 'Take me to the Pelican tavern, and look sharp about it.'

The chairmen carried her further east than she had ever been in London. They deposited her outside a big waterfront tavern with a crude painting of a pelican on its wooden sign. The courtyard was full of noisy, excited people: working men in boots and neckerchiefs, waistcoated gentlemen and low-class women in shawls and clogs.

She went into the tavern, banged on the counter with a fist and said to the barman: 'A pint of strong ale, Jack.' It was wonderful to address the world in such arrogant tones. What would these people do if they realised she was an upper-class lady dressed as a man?

She went outside, carrying her beer. She saw McAsh right away. He stood close to the ring talking to another man.

His opponent, Rees Preece, deserved his nickname of 'the Welsh Mountain'. He was the biggest man Lizzie had ever seen, at least a foot taller than Mack, with a vicious look about the face. Lizzie felt frightened for McAsh. He could be killed, she realised. She was tempted to leave, but she could not drag herself away.

Then, suddenly, the fight was on. Lizzie saw no signal. The two men were at one another like cats, punching and kicking and butting in a frenzy. The crowd roared and Lizzie realised she was screaming. She covered her mouth with her hand.

The initial flurry lasted only seconds: it was too energetic to keep up. The men separated and began to circle one another. Preece rushed Mack again, but Mack jumped back, dodging, then suddenly stepped in and hit Preece once, very hard, on the side of the head. The spectators cheered wildly. Preece seemed to hesitate and Lizzie guessed he was surprised by Mack's strength. Perhaps Mack could defeat this huge man after all.

Mack danced back out of reach. Preece shook himself like a dog, then lowered his head and charged, punching wildly. Mack ducked and sidestepped, but somehow Preece managed to land several mighty punches. Then Mack hit him hard on the side of the head again, and once more Preece was stopped in his tracks.

The same dance was repeated, and Lizzie heard Mack's second's yell: 'In for the kill, Mack!' She realised that after delivering a punch Mack always backed off and let the other man recover. Preece, by contrast, always followed one punch with another until Mack fought him off.

Soon Preece had one eye closed, but Mack was bleeding from his mouth and from a cut over one eye. How long could they stand there pounding one another into dead meat? Lizzie wondered. Even she could see that in a crude trial of strength Preece would win, simply because he was bigger and more hardened to punishment.

There was a flurry of activity in the ring. Mack hit Preece once, twice, and a third time, making him stagger. Lizzie was seized by the hope that Preece would collapse. But then Mack backed off, waiting for his opponent to fall. The crowd urged him to finish Preece off, but he took no notice.

To Lizzie's dismay Preece recovered yet again, and hit Mack with a low punch in the belly. Mack bent forward and gasped—and then, unexpectedly, Preece butted him, putting all the force of his broad back into it. Mack's legs gave way and he fell to the ground. Preece kicked him in the head as he lay prone. Mack did not move. Lizzie heard herself screaming: 'Leave him alone!' Preece kicked Mack again and again, until the seconds from both sides jumped into the ring and pulled him away.

Lizzie was afraid Mack might be dead. She pushed through the crowd and stepped into the ring. Mack's second knelt beside his prone body. His eyes were closed, but Lizzie saw that he was breathing. 'Thank God he's alive,' she said.

His second stared at her and said in an Irish accent: 'Who are you, the boy soprano?' She realised she had forgotten to put on a man's voice.

'A friend,' she replied. 'Let's carry him inside.'

After hesitating the man said: 'All right.' He grasped Mack under the arms. Two spectators took his legs and they lifted him.

Lizzie led the way into the tavern. In her most arrogant male voice she shouted: 'Landlord—show me your best room.'

A woman came from behind the bar. 'Who's paying?'

Lizzie gave her a sovereign.

'This way,' said the woman.

She led them up the stairs to a bedroom overlooking the court-yard. The men laid Mack on the bed, then the helpers left. Lizzie said to the woman: 'Light the fire then bring us some French brandy. Do you know of a physician who could dress this man's wounds?'

'I'll send for Dr Samuels.'

Mack's face was swollen and bloody. Lizzie undid his shirt and saw that his chest was covered with bruises and abrasions.

The Irishman said: 'I'm Dermot Riley—Mack lodges in my house.'

'My name is Elizabeth Hallim,' she replied. 'I've known him since we were children.' She decided not to explain why she was dressed as a man: Riley could think what he liked. 'We should bathe his wounds. Ask for some hot water, will you?'

He went out, leaving her alone with Mack.

Hesitantly, she put her hand on Mack's chest. The skin was warm and the flesh beneath it was hard. She felt the thump of his heartbeat, regular and strong. He opened his eyes and looked at her blankly. 'Where am I? Who are you?'

'You were in a prize fight,' she said. 'You lost.'

He stared at her for several seconds, then at last he grinned. 'Lizzie Hallim, dressed as a man again.'

'Thank God you're all right!'

He gave her a peculiar look. 'It's very . . . kind of you to care.'

'I can't think why I do,' she said. 'You're only a coalminer who doesn't know his place.' Then to her horror she felt tears running down her face. 'It's very hard to watch a friend being beaten to a pulp,' she said.

He watched her cry. 'Lizzie Hallim,' he said wonderingly, 'will I ever understand you?'

BRANDY EASED THE PAIN of Mack's wounds that evening, but on the following morning, back at Dermot's lodgings, he woke up in agony. He hurt in every part of his body. The face he saw in the mirror was all cuts and bruises, and too tender to be touched, let alone shaved.

All the same his spirits were high. Lizzie Hallim never failed to stimulate him. When he had recognised her, sitting on the edge of the bed, he had felt a barely controllable urge to take her in his arms. He had resisted the temptation by reminding himself that such a move would mean the end of their peculiar friendship. And when she had told him she was going to marry Jay Jamisson, he had bitten his tongue instead of telling her she was a damn fool. It was none of his business and he did not want to offend her.

Dermot's wife, Bridget, made a breakfast of salt porridge and afterwards Mack and Dermot went out to look for work.

It was not a lucky day. They toured the food markets of London, offering themselves as porters, but there were too many men and not enough work. By the end of the afternoon they were as weary as if they had worked all day, but they had nothing to show for it.

As they walked along the Strand a small figure shot out of an alley and crashed into Dermot. It was a girl of about thirteen, ragged and thin and scared. After her came a brawny young man in expensive but dishevelled clothes. He came within an inch of grabbing her as she bounced off Dermot, but she dodged and ran on. Then she slipped and fell, and he was on her.

She screamed in terror. The man was mad with rage. He picked up the slight body and punched the side of her head, knocking her down again, then he kicked her puny chest with his booted foot.

The last thing Mack wanted was another fight, but he could not stand still and watch this. As the man was about to kick her again Mack grabbed him by the collar and the seat of the breeches and lifted him bodily off the ground. The man roared with anger and began to writhe violently, but Mack held him.

'Get your filthy hands off me,' the man shouted.

Mack set him on the ground. 'Just leave the child alone.'

Dermot helped the girl stand up and held her gently but firmly.

'She's a damned thief!' said the man aggressively.

'Is that all?' Mack said. 'By the way you were kicking her I thought she'd murdered the king. Whatever she's done you've punished her enough.'

The man looked at him. 'You're obviously just off the boat,' he said. 'You won't last long in London if you put your trust in the likes of her.' With that he walked off.

The girl said: 'Thanks, Jock—you saved my life.' People knew Mack was Scottish as soon as he spoke.

He looked at the girl. She had dark hair roughly cropped, and a pretty face that was bruised from the beating. Her body was that of a child but there was a knowing, adult look in her eyes. He said: 'Are you all right?'

'I hurt,' she said, holding her side. 'I wish you'd killed him!'

'What did you do to him?'

'I tried to rob him while he was having Cora.'

Mack had heard that prostitutes sometimes had accomplices who robbed their clients. 'Would you like a drink?'

'I'd kiss the Pope's arse for a glass of gin.'

Mack didn't know whether to be shocked or amused.

They crossed the road to a tavern and Mack bought three mugs of beer. The girl tossed most of hers down in a few gulps and said: 'You're a good man, Jock.'

'My name is Mack,' he said. 'This is Dermot.'

'I'm Peggy. They call me Quick Peg.'

'On account of the way you drink, I suppose.'

She grinned. 'In this city, if you don't drink quick someone will steal your liquor.'

A voice said breathlessly: 'Peg, are you all right?'

Mack looked up to see a young woman wearing an orange dress.

Peg said: 'Hello, Cora. I was rescued by a handsome prince. Meet Scotch Jock McKnock.'

Cora smiled at Mack and said: 'Thank you for helping Peg. I hope you didn't get those bruises in the process.'

Mack shook his head. 'That was another brute.'

Cora sat beside Mack. She was about twenty years old, with an angelic face and a mass of flaming red hair. It was shocking to think that someone so young and pretty was a whore.

'What are you doing in London, Jock?'

'Looking for work.'

'Find any?'

'Not much.'

She shook her head. 'It's been a bitch of a winter and the price of bread is shocking. There's too many men like you.'

Peg put in: 'That was what made my father turn to thieving, only he didn't have the knack. He danced with the sheriff's collar on.'

Dermot explained. 'It means he was hanged.'

Mack said: 'Oh dear, I'm sorry.'

'Don't feel sorry for me. It makes me sick.'

'All right, all right, I won't,' Mack said mildly.

Cora said: 'If you want work, I know someone who's looking for coal heavers, to unload the coal ships.'

'I'll do anything,' Mack said, thinking of Esther.

'The coal-heaving gangs are all run by tavern-keepers down in Wapping. I know one of them, Sidney Lennox at the Sun. He's a lying, cheating, evil-smelling drunken pig, but they're all the same.'

'Will you take us to the Sun?'

'Be it on your own head,' said Cora.

A WARM FOG of sweat and coal dust filled the airless hold of the wooden ship. Mack stood on a mountain of coal, wielding a broad-bladed shovel. The work was brutally hard but he felt good. He was earning good money, and he was no one's slave.

It was Saturday afternoon, and the sixteen-strong gang had almost emptied this ship, the *Black Swan* from Newcastle. This was the second ship they had unloaded this week, and the gang got a penny per man for every score, or twenty sacks of coal. Mack reckoned each man had earned six pounds gross.

However, there were deductions. Sidney Lennox, the middleman or 'undertaker', sent vast quantities of beer and gin on board for the men. They had to drink a lot to replace the fluid they lost by sweating, but Lennox gave them more than was necessary and the liquor had to be paid for. So Mack was not sure how much he would receive when he lined up for his wages tonight. However, he should be able to send for Esther in a few weeks. His heart leapt at the prospect.

The last of the coal was shovelled into sacks and stacked in a barge to be rowed ashore. Mack stretched his aching back and shouldered his shovel. Up on deck the cold air hit him, and he put on the fur cloak Lizzie Hallim had given him. The coal heavers rowed to shore and walked to the Sun to get their wages.

Mack and Dermot were the first to arrive. They found Peg in the bar smoking a clay pipe. She lived at the Sun, sleeping on the floor in a corner of the bar. Sidney Lennox was a receiver as well as an undertaker, and Peg sold him the things she stole. When she saw Mack she said cheerfully: 'What-ho, Jock—rescued any more maidens?'

'Not today,' he grinned. He sat beside Peg. 'How's business?'

She took his question seriously. 'Me and Cora tumbled a rich old gent this afternoon so we're having the evening off.'

Mack found it odd to be friends with a thief. He knew what drove her to it: she had no alternative but starvation.

He had no money to pay for his supper, but Lennox gave all the coal heavers credit against their earnings. Mack ordered soup with oysters floating in it, a slab of bread and a tankard of dark beer, and when it arrived he fell on the food like a wolf.

The other coal heavers drifted in. There was no sign of Lennox and Mack guessed he was keeping the men waiting so that they would spend more in drinking.

Cora came in after an hour or so. She looked as striking as ever, in a mustard-coloured outfit. All the men greeted her, but to Mack's surprise she came and sat with him. 'I hear you had a profitable afternoon,' he said.

'Easy money,' she said. 'A man old enough to know better.'

The coal heavers' wives began to appear, many of them with babies in their arms and children clinging to their skirts. Mack guessed they were hoping to get hold of some of the wages before all the money was drunk, gambled or stolen. Bridget Riley came in with her five children and sat with Dermot and Mack.

Lennox finally showed up at midnight. He carried a leather sack

full of coins and a pair of pistols, presumably to protect him from
robbery. He was a surly man of about thirty with a cruel twist to
his mouth. He pulled a table into a corner and put the sack down
and the pistols next to it. The men and women crowded round,
pushing and shoving. Mack hung back: it was beneath his dignity to
scramble for the wages he had earned.

He heard Lennox's voice raised over the hubbub. 'Each man has
earned a pound and elevenpence this week, after bar bills.'

Mack was not sure he had heard right. They had unloaded two
ships, some fifteen hundred score, giving each man a gross income of
about six pounds. How could it have been reduced to little more than
a pound each? He said: 'Just a minute. How do you work that out?'

Lennox looked up with a scowl. 'You've unloaded one thousand
four hundred and forty-five score which gives each man six pounds
and fivepence gross. Deduct fifteen shillings a day for drink—'

'What?' Mack interrupted. 'Fifteen shillings a day?' That was
three-quarters of their earnings!

'You're new here and you don't know the rules, McAsh,' Lennox
grated. 'Why don't you shut your mouth, or no one will get paid.'

Mack was outraged, but the system was obviously well established,
and the men must have accepted it. However, his protest had struck
a chord among the others, and Dermot Riley now raised his voice. 'I
didn't drink fifteen shillings' worth of liquor a day,' he said.

'Nor did I,' said another man.

Lennox replied angrily: 'That's how much I sent on board for
you—do you think I can keep a tally of what every man drinks?'

Mack said, 'If not, you're the only innkeeper in London who
can't!' The men laughed.

Lennox was infuriated by Mack's mockery. 'The system is, you pay
for fifteen shillings' worth of liquor, whether you drink it or not.'

Mack stepped up to the table. 'Well, I have a system too,' he said.
'I don't pay for liquor that I haven't asked for and haven't drunk. You
may not have kept count but I can tell you exactly what I owe you.'

'So can I,' said another man. He was Charlie Smith, an English-
born Negro with a Newcastle accent.

Lennox said: 'You're lucky to be paid at all, you black villain, you
ought to be a slave in chains.'

Mack said to Lennox: 'You'll not leave that table until you've paid
me what you owe.'

Lennox's eyes fell to his pistols.

With a swift movement Mack swept the guns to the floor. 'You'll
not escape by shooting me either, you damn thief,' he said angrily.

Lennox looked like a cornered mastiff. He had made the coal

heavers drunk and they would kill him unless he paid them.

He gave Mack a look of pure hatred and said: 'You'll suffer for this, McAsh, I swear by God you will.'

Mack said mildly: 'Come on, Lennox, the men are only asking you to pay them what they're due.'

Scowling darkly, Lennox began to count out money. He paid Charlie Smith first, then Dermot Riley, then Mack, taking their word for the amount of liquor they had consumed.

Mack was elated. He had three pounds and nine shillings in his hand: if he put half of it aside for Esther he would still be flush.

As the last man was being paid, Mack picked up Lennox's guns from the floor. He blew the flintlocks clear of powder, so that they would not fire, then placed them on the table.

Lennox took his disarmed pistols and the nearly empty money bag and stood up. The room went quiet. 'Go home, all of you,' he said malevolently. 'And don't come back on Monday. There'll be no work for you. You're all dismissed.'

MACK GOT UP EARLY on Sunday morning and went into the other room. Dermot and his wife lay on a mattress and the five children slept together in the opposite corner. Mack shook Dermot awake. 'We've got to find some work for our gang before tomorrow morning,' Mack said.

Dermot got up. Bridget mumbled from the bed: 'Wear something respectable, now, if you want to impress an undertaker.' Dermot put on an old red waistcoat, and he lent Mack a blue silk neckcloth. They called for Charlie Smith on the way. Charlie had been a coal heaver for five years and he knew everyone. He put on his best blue coat and they went together to Wapping.

The waterfront neighbourhood was almost deserted. The three men went first to the Frying Pan, a few yards from the Sun. They found the landlord boiling a ham in the yard. The smell made Mack's mouth water.

'What-ho, Harry,' Charlie addressed him cheerfully.

He gave them a sour look. 'What do you boys want?'

'Work,' Charlie replied. 'Have you got a ship to uncoal tomorrow?'

'Yes, and a gang to do it, thanks all the same.'

They left. Dermot said: 'What was the matter with him? He looked at us like lepers.'

'We'll try Buck Delaney at the Swan,' Charlie said. 'He runs two or three gangs at a time.'

The Swan was a busy tavern with stables, a coffee room and a number of bars. They found the landlord in his private room overlooking the courtyard. 'Let me give you a tip, boys,' he said. 'Every undertaker in London has heard what happened last night. There's not one will employ you, Sidney Lennox has made sure of that.'

Mack's heart sank. He said: 'What's to stop us going to the captains ourselves and undertaking to unload ships?'

'Everything,' said Delaney. 'There's too many people making too much money out of the present arrangement.' He shook his head. 'If I were you I'd take ship and get out of town for a year or two. When you come back it will all be forgotten.'

Feeling defeated the three men went downstairs, sat in one of the bars and ordered beer and bread for their breakfast. Mack thought of Caspar Gordonson, the radical lawyer who had started all this by telling Mack his legal rights. If I could get hold of Gordonson, he thought, I'd let him know what legal rights are worth.

The law was only useful to those who had the power to enforce it, it seemed. Coalminers and coal heavers had no advocate at court. Mack picked up his tankard then froze with it halfway to his mouth. Caspar Gordonson lived in London, of course. Mack *could* get hold of him. He could let him know what legal rights were worth—but perhaps he could do better than that. Perhaps Gordonson would be the coal heavers' advocate. It was worth a try.

CASPAR GORDONSON lived in a three-storey brick terrace house in Fleet Street. A manservant let them in, showing no surprise when they asked for Mr Gordonson.

Gordonson's home was more like a printer's shop than a lawyer's home. Pamphlets and journals were stacked in the hall, and the sound of machinery from below stairs suggested that a press was being operated in the basement.

The servant stepped into a room off the hall. 'McAsh?' came a shrill voice from within. 'Never heard of him.'

A moment later a balding man appeared in the doorway and peered at the three coal heavers through spectacles. 'I don't think I know any of you,' he said. 'Who are you, anyway?'

'Malachi McAsh, known as Mack. I was a coalminer at Heugh, near Edinburgh, until you wrote and told me I was a free man.'

Understanding lit up Gordonson's expression. 'You're the liberty-loving miner! Shake hands, man.'

Mack introduced Dermot and Charlie.

'Come in, all of you.' They followed him into an untidy room furnished with a writing table and lined with bookcases. More publications were piled on the floor, and printer's proofs were scattered across the table. 'Now, McAsh, what do you want with me?'

Mack told him the story of how he had left Heugh. Gordonson lit a pipe as he listened, shaking his head in disgust from time to time. 'I know the Jamissons of old—they're greedy, heartless people,' he said when Mack had finished. 'What did you do when you got to London?'

'I became a coal heaver.' Mack related what had happened in the Sun tavern last night.

Gordonson said: 'The liquor payments to coal heavers are a long-standing scandal. Parliament actually passed a law against the practice ten years ago, but it has never been enforced. The government is afraid of disrupting the supply of coal. London runs on coal: without it no bread is made, no beer brewed, no iron smelted—'

'I understand,' Mack interrupted impatiently. 'I ought not to be surprised that the law does nothing for men such as us.'

'Now you're wrong there,' Gordonson said. 'The law has no will of its own. It's like a weapon, or a tool: it works for those who pick it up and use it.'

'The rich.'

'Usually,' Gordonson conceded. 'But it might work for you. Suppose you devised an alternative ganging system for unloading coal ships. It wouldn't be difficult,' he said. 'The men could choose one of their number to be undertaker and deal with the captains. The money would be shared out as soon as it's received.'

Charlie Smith said lugubriously: 'It's been tried before. The undertakers just bribe the ships' captains not to use the new gangs.'

Gordonson put in: 'I remember the last coal heavers' dispute. They were defeated because they had no champion.'

'Why should it be different this time?' said Mack.

'Because of John Wilkes.'

Wilkes was the defender of liberty, but he was in exile. 'He can't do much for us in Paris.'

'He's not in Paris. He's back. He's going to stand for Parliament.'

That was a surprise. 'But I still don't see how it helps us.'

'Wilkes will take the coal heavers' part, and the government will side with the undertakers. Such a dispute, with working men having the law on their side, would do Wilkes nothing but good.'

'How do you know what Wilkes will do?'

Gordonson smiled. 'I'm his electoral agent. I love my country and I hate the greedy brutes who would destroy its people and ruin its prosperity. So I spend my life fighting for justice.' He smiled and put his pipe back in his mouth. 'I hope that doesn't sound too pompous.'

'Not at all,' said Mack. 'I'm glad you're on our side.'

Chapter 5

Jay Jamisson's wedding day was cold and damp. From his bedroom in Grosvenor Square he could see Hyde Park, where his regiment was bivouacked. A low mist covered the ground, and the soldiers' tents looked like ships' sails on a swirling grey sea.

He turned from the window. Chip Marlborough, his brideman, was holding Jay's new coat. Jay shrugged into it with a grunt of thanks. Chip was a captain in the 3rd Foot Guards, like Jay. His father was Lord Arebury, who had business dealings with Jay's father. Jay was flattered that such an aristocratic scion had agreed to stand beside him on his wedding day.

'Have you seen to the horses?' Jay asked anxiously.

'Of course,' said Chip.

Although theirs was an infantry regiment, officers always went mounted, and the horses were Jay's responsibility. He was good with horses, he understood them. He had only two days' leave for his wedding but he still worried that the beasts were being looked after properly.

His leave was so short because the regiment was on active service. There was no war, but the people of London were so restless and turbulent that the troops were standing by to suppress riots.

'I hope the regiment isn't called out while I'm on leave,' Jay said. 'It would be just my luck to miss the action.'

'Stop worrying!' Chip poured brandy from a decanter into two glasses. 'To love!' he said.

'To love,' Jay repeated.

The door opened and a footman said: 'Will you see a Mr Sidney Lennox, sir?'

Jay's heart sank. He owed Lennox money: gambling losses. 'You'd better show him in,' Jay said. 'I'm sorry about this,' he said to Chip.

'I know Lennox,' Chip said. 'I've lost money to him myself.'

Lennox walked in and Jay noticed the distinctive sweet-sour smell of the man, like something fermenting. Lennox wore a yellow suit and silk stockings with buckled shoes, but he still looked like a jackal. However, Jay could not quite bring himself to break with Lennox. He was a very useful acquaintance, willing to give credit to young officers who ran out of cash but wanted to continue gambling. Jay owed Lennox a hundred and fifty pounds. It would be embarrassing if Lennox insisted on collecting the debt now.

'You know I'm getting married today, Lennox,' Jay said.

'Yes, I know that,' Lennox said. 'I came to drink your health.'

'By all means. Chip, a tot for our friend.'

Chip poured three generous measures of brandy.

Lennox said: 'To you and your bride.'

'Thank you,' said Jay, and the three men drank.

Lennox addressed Chip. 'There'll be a big faro game tomorrow night, at Lord Archer's coffee-house, Captain Marlborough. I'll hope to see you there. No doubt you'll be too busy, Captain Jamisson.'

'I expect so,' Jay replied. Anyway, I can't afford it, he thought.

Lennox put down his glass. 'I wish you a good day and hope the fog lifts,' he said, and went out.

Jay concealed his relief. Nothing had been said about the money. Lennox knew that Jay's father had paid the last debt, and perhaps he felt confident that Sir George would do the same again. Jay heard the sound of carriages drawing up in front of the house. 'Let's go downstairs,' he said.

Jay's mother, father and brother were waiting in the drawing room, a grand space, with expensive Chippendale furniture. It smelt of wax polish. Alicia kissed her son. Sir George and Robert greeted him awkwardly.

A footman was pouring coffee. Jay and Chip each took a cup. Before they could sip it the door flew open and Lizzie came in like a hurricane. 'How dare you?' she stormed, her eyes flashing. She was wearing her bridal outfit and looked ravishing.

'What have I done?' Jay asked plaintively.

'The wedding is off!' she replied.

Lady Hallim hurried in after her, looking distraught. 'Lizzie, please stop this,' she said.

Jay's mother took charge. 'Lizzie dear, what is the trouble?'

'This!' she said, and she fluttered a sheaf of papers.

Lady Hallim was wringing her hands. 'It's a letter from my head keeper.'

Lizzie said: 'It says that surveyors employed by the Jamissons have been sinking boreholes on the Hallim estate.'

'Oh, no!' Jay protested. He understood what had happened. His father was so eager to get at Lizzie's coal that he had not been able to wait until the wedding. 'You damn fool!' he said recklessly. 'Look what you've done!'

It was a shocking thing for a son to say. Sir George went red in the face and his eyes bulged. 'Call off the damned wedding, then!' he roared. 'What do I care?'

Alicia intervened. 'Calm down. There has obviously been a mistake. No doubt Sir George's surveyors misunderstood some instructions.

Lady Hallim, please take Lizzie back to the guesthouse while we sort this out.'

Chip Marlborough coughed. 'If you'll excuse me . . .' he said, 'I'll wait upstairs,' and he went out of the door.

Alicia ushered Lizzie and Lady Hallim out behind him. 'Just give me a few minutes and everything will be all right.'

As Lizzie went out she was looking more doubtful than angry, and Jay hoped she realised he hadn't known about the boreholes. His mother closed the door and turned to Sir George. 'If there's no wedding you won't get your coal,' she said.

There was a pause while that threat sank in. Jay was afraid his father would explode. But Mother was a good judge of how far he could be pushed and in the end he said: 'What do you want, Alicia?'

'First of all, Jay must speak to Lizzie and convince her that he didn't know about the surveyors. If he can do that, they can get married as planned.'

'Then what?'

'Then be patient. In time, Jay and I can talk Lizzie round.'

Sir George shook his head. 'It's not good enough—I can't wait.'

He looked at Robert, who shrugged. 'I suppose I might as well tell you. I've got debts of my own. You know we have always run on borrowed money—most of it from Lord Arebury. In the past we've made profits for ourselves and for him. But our trade with America has fallen very low since the trouble started in the colonies. Now our biggest debtor has gone bust, leaving me with a tobacco plantation in Virginia that I can't sell.'

Jay was stunned. He began to see why his father had been so enraged at having to pay his gambling debts.

Father went on: 'Lord Arebury wants his money. So I have to have the Hallim estate. Otherwise I could lose my entire business.'

There was silence. Eventually Alicia said: 'Then there is only one solution. High Glen will have to be mined without Lizzie's knowledge.'

Jay frowned anxiously. But he decided not to say anything just yet.

'How could it be done?' said Sir George.

'Send her and Jay to another country.'

Jay was startled. What a clever idea! 'But Lady Hallim would know,' he said. 'And she'd be sure to tell Lizzie.'

Alicia shook her head. 'No, she won't. She'll do anything to make this marriage happen. She'll keep quiet if we tell her to.'

Jay said: 'But where would we go? What country?'

'Barbados,' said his mother.

'No!' Robert interjected. 'The sugar plantation belongs to me.'

Alicia looked enquiringly at Sir George. 'Is that true?'

65

Sir George nodded. 'I made it over to him three years ago.'

That was another shock. Jay felt wounded. 'That's why you wouldn't give it to me for my birthday,' he said sadly.

Alicia did not give up. 'What's this Virginia property, George?'

'Mockjack Hall—it's a tobacco plantation, about a thousand acres and fifty slaves . . . What are you thinking?'

'You could give that to Jay.'

Jay's heart leapt. It would be the fresh start he had longed for, a place of his own to manage. And Lizzie would jump at the chance.

Sir George's eyes narrowed. 'I couldn't give him any money. He'd have to borrow what he needed to get the place going.'

Jay said quickly: 'I don't care about that.'

'But you'd have to pay the interest on Lady Hallim's mortgages,' Alicia put in. 'Otherwise she could lose High Glen.'

'I can do that out of the income from the coal,' Father went on. 'They'll have to leave for Virginia straight away, within a few weeks. I need that coal immediately.'

'That's all right. Lizzie won't want to make the journey back to Scotland—she'll be too busy preparing for her new life.'

Sir George said: 'It could work. All right—we'll do it.'

Alicia put her arms round Jay and kissed him. 'Bless you, my dear son,' she said. 'Now go to her and tell her that you and your family are desperately sorry about this mistake, and that your father has given you Mockjack Hall as a wedding present.'

Jay hugged her and whispered: 'Well done, Mother—thank you.'

As he walked across the garden he felt jubilant and apprehensive at the same time. He had got what he had always wanted. He wished it could have been done without deceiving Lizzie. But if he had refused he would have lost the property and he might have lost her as well.

AT NOON ON THE THIRD DAY, the hold of the *Durham Primrose* was empty of coal. Mack looked around, hardly able to believe it. They had done it all without an undertaker. They had picked out a ship that arrived in the middle of the day, when the other gangs were already working. While the men waited on the river bank, Mack and Charlie rowed out to the ship and offered their services. The captain knew that if he held out for a regular gang he would have to wait until the following day, and time was money to ships' captains, so he hired them. The men seemed to work faster knowing they would be paid in full, and they uncoaled the ship in forty-eight hours.

Mack conferred with the first mate. They had both kept count of the number of round trips, and they agreed the total. Then he went to the captain's cabin.

'Finished?' the captain said. 'You're quicker than the usual gangs. What's the tally?'

'Six hundred score, all but ninety-three,' the first mate said, and Mack nodded. Each man was paid a penny a score.

The captain unlocked a chest that stood in the corner. Mack stared as he took out a smaller box, put it on the table and opened it. 'If we call the odd seven sacks a half-score, I owe you thirty-nine pounds fourteen shillings exactly.' He counted out the money and gave Mack a linen bag to carry it in.

Mack felt a tremendous sense of triumph. Each man had earned almost two pounds and ten shillings—more in two days than they got for two weeks with Lennox. But, more importantly, they had proved they could stand up for their rights and win justice.

When the men had been paid and they had all rowed to shore, he and Dermot walked to Spitalfields. Mack had a tune on his lips and a spring in his step. When he entered his room a pleasant surprise was waiting for him. Sitting on a three-legged stool, swinging a shapely leg, was Peg's red-haired friend Cora, in a chestnut-coloured coat and a jaunty hat.

She had picked up his fur cloak, which lay on the straw mattress that was his bed. 'Where did you get this?' she said.

'It was a gift from a fine lady,' he said with a grin. 'What are you doing here?'

'I came to see you,' she said. 'If you wash your face you can walk out with me—if you don't have to go to tea with any fine ladies.'

He went down to the standpipe in the yard, stripped to the waist and washed the coal dust from his skin. He borrowed a clean shirt from Dermot, put on his coat and hat and took Cora's arm.

They walked west, through the heart of the city into Mayfair. Mack enjoyed having Cora on his arm. Because of her striking colouring and her dashing clothes she attracted a lot of attention, and Mack got envious looks from other men.

Outside one of the very grandest homes, carriages were drawing up and depositing guests as if for a party. The house was a blaze of light, although it was midafternoon, and the entrance was decorated with flowers. 'It must be a wedding,' Cora said.

As they watched, another carriage drew up and Jay Jamisson stepped out. He handed his bride down from the carriage, and a small crowd of bystanders cheered and clapped.

Lizzie smiled and looked round, acknowledging the applause. Her eyes met Mack's, and for a moment she froze. He smiled and waved.

She averted her eyes quickly and hurried inside.

'She's pretty,' Cora said. 'Do you know her?'

'She's the one who gave me the fur,' Mack said. 'She's throwing herself away on Jay Jamisson.'

'I suppose you think she'd be better off marrying you,' Cora said sarcastically.

'She would, too,' Mack said seriously. 'Shall we go to the theatre?'

JAY AND LIZZIE moved into the Chapel Street house on the day after the wedding. For the first time they ate supper alone, with no one present but the servants. For the first time they went upstairs hand in hand, undressed together and got into their own bed. For the first time they woke up together in their own house.

Jay had one more day's leave. The weather was cold but sunny. Lizzie got up and went naked to the window. The church bells were ringing muffled because it was a hanging day: one or more criminals would be executed this morning. Half the city's working people would take an unofficial holiday and people would flock to Tyburn Cross, where the gallows stood, to see the spectacle.

She turned to face Jay and said: 'Take me to the hanging.'

He looked disapproving. 'A gruesome request.'

'Don't tell me it's no place for a lady.'

He smiled. 'I wouldn't dare. But why do you want to go?'

That was a good question. She had mixed feelings about it. It was shameful to make entertainment of death but her curiosity was overwhelming. 'I want to know what it's like,' she said.

Jay said: 'Perhaps we could hire a room overlooking the gallows— that's what a lot of people do.'

'Oh, no—I want to be in the crowd!' she protested.

'Women of our class don't do that.'

'Then I'll dress as a man.'

He looked doubtful.

She grinned at him and jumped onto the bed. 'Don't be an old curmudgeon. Let's go to the hanging.'

He could not help laughing. 'All right,' he said.

She performed her daily chores rapidly. She told the cook what to buy for dinner; decided which rooms the housemaids would clean; told the groom she would not be riding today; and took delivery of twelve brassbound trunks for the voyage to Virginia.

Then she put on her disguise.

THE STREET KNOWN as Tyburn Street or Oxford Street was thronged with people. The gallows stood at the end of the street, outside Hyde Park. People stood shoulder to shoulder on the stone wall of the park. Hawkers moved through the crowds selling hot sausages and tots of gin and printed copies of what they said were the dying speeches of the condemned.

Mack held Cora's hand and pushed through the crowd. Nowadays Mack wanted to spend all his free time with Cora. He liked just looking at her; he liked her devil-may-care attitude. He had no desire to watch people getting killed but she insisted on going. A friend of hers was going to be hanged. Her name was Dolly Macaroni, and she was a brothel-keeper, but her crime was forgery.

'What did she forge, anyway?' Mack said as they approached the gallows.

'A bank draft. She changed the amount from eleven pounds to eighty pounds.'

'Where did she get a draft for eleven pounds?'

'From Lord Massey. She says he owed her more.'

The gallows was just three posts with crossbeams. Five ropes hung from the beams, their ends tied in nooses ready for the condemned. A chaplain stood nearby, with a handful of law officers. Soldiers with muskets kept the crowd at a distance.

They became aware of a roaring sound from further down Tyburn Street. 'They're coming,' said Cora.

First there was a squad of peace officers on horseback, led by the city marshal. Next were the constables, on foot and armed with clubs. Then came the tumbril, a high four-wheeled cart drawn by two horses. A company of javelin men brought up the rear.

In the cart, their hands and arms bound with ropes, were five people: three men, a boy of about fifteen and a woman. 'That's Dolly,' Cora said and she began to cry.

Mack stared in horrid fascination at the five who were to die. One of the men was drunk. The other two looked defiant. Dolly was praying aloud and the boy was crying.

The cart was driven under the scaffold. The two sober men were greeted by a group at the front of the crowd. After a moment Mack distinguished their accents as Irish. One of the condemned men shouted: 'Don't let the surgeons have me, boys!' There was a roar of assent from his friends.

'He must be a murderer,' said Cora. 'The bodies of murderers belong to the Company of Surgeons. They cut them up to see what's inside.'

Mack shuddered.

The hangman climbed on the cart. One by one he placed the nooses round their necks. The priest got up on the cart and spoke to each of them in turn. When he had finished, the hangman blindfolded the five people then got down, leaving only the condemned on the cart. The drunk man could not keep his balance: he stumbled and fell, and the noose began to strangle him.

The hangman whipped the horses.

LIZZIE HEARD HERSELF scream: 'No!'

The hangman lashed the horses again and the cart was drawn from under the condemned people. One by one, they fell.

Lizzie stared at the five bodies and was filled with loathing for herself and the crowd around her.

The sheriff stepped up to cut the bodies down and that was when the trouble started. The Irish group surged forward, trying to get past the guards to the scaffold. The constables fought back, and the javelin men joined in. Blood began to flow.

'I was afraid of this,' Jay said. 'Let's get clear as fast as we can.'

Many around them had the same idea, but those at the back were trying to get closer and see what was happening. As some surged one way and some the other, fist fights broke out. Jay tried to force a way through. Lizzie stuck close to him. The scaffold was now swarming with Irish, some of whom were beating off the guards while others tried to cut down the bodies of their friends.

For no apparent reason the crush around Lizzie and Jay eased suddenly. 'Jay, come on!' Lizzie shouted, and darted through a gap. As she turned to make sure Jay was behind her the gap closed. 'Jay!' she screamed. 'Jay!' He shouted back but the crowd forced them further apart. A moment later he was lost from sight.

She was on her own. She gritted her teeth and turned her back on the scaffold. She faced a solid pack of people. She tried to push herself between a small man and a big-bosomed matron. 'Keep your hands to yourself, young man,' the woman said. Lizzie persisted and managed to squeeze through. Then she saw a familiar face and recognised Mack McAsh. He was with the red-haired woman who had been at his side in Grosvenor Square. 'Mack!' she yelled gratefully. He saw her and recognised her. Then a tall man's elbow jabbed her eye and when she could see again Mack and the woman had vanished.

Grimly she pressed on and eventually came up against the front of a house. She worked her way along to the corner and stepped into an alley to catch her breath. She hoped Jay was all right. She turned round to look for him and was startled to see two men staring at her.

One was middle-aged and unshaven with a fat belly; the other a youth of about eighteen. Something about their stares frightened her, but before she could move away they pounced and threw her to the ground. They went through her pockets, taking her purse, her pocket watch and a handkerchief.

71

The older man said: 'That's a good coat—nearly new.'

They both bent over her again and began to pull off her coat and waistcoat. She struggled, but all she achieved was to rip her shirt. Hastily she covered her breasts but she was too late. 'Hey, it's a girl!' cried the younger man.

The fat one stared at her. 'And a pretty girl, too, by God,' he said.

Fear flooded Lizzie and she screamed, but there was so much noise in the street she doubted whether anyone would hear.

Then, suddenly, Mack McAsh appeared. She glimpsed his face and a raised fist, then he struck the older man, who rocked sideways and staggered. Mack hit him again, and the man slumped to the ground.

The boy tried to run away but she grabbed his ankle and tripped him. Mack threw him against the house wall, then punched him on the chin. The boy fell unconscious on top of his partner.

Lizzie got to her feet. 'Thank God you were here!' she said fervently. She threw her arms round him and said: 'You saved me—thank you, thank you!'

He hugged her closely. 'You saved me, once—when you pulled me out of the river,' he said with a wry smile.

As soon as she felt safe again she began to worry about Jay. She detached herself from Mack's embrace. 'I have to look for my husband,' she said as he helped her put her coat on. 'Will you help me?'

'Of course.' He handed her her things.

'What about your red-haired friend?' she asked.

'Cora? I made sure she was safe before I came after you.'

'Did you?' Lizzie felt unreasonably irritated. Then, despite herself, she laughed. 'Thank you for rescuing me.' She kissed him briefly on the lips then turned towards the street.

Jay stood there watching, a thunderous look on his face.

'Oh, Jay!' she said. 'Thank heaven you're all right!'

'What happened here?' he said, taking her by the arm.

'Those two men robbed me. McAsh knocked them down and rescued me,' she said.

'That's no reason to kiss him,' said her husband.

Chapter 6

Jay's regiment was on duty in Palace Yard on the day of John Wilkes's trial. The Liberal hero had been convicted of criminal libel years ago, and had fled to Paris. On his return, he was accused of being an outlaw. But while the legal action dragged on he won the Middlesex by-election handsomely. However, he had not yet taken his seat in Parliament, and the government hoped to prevent him doing so by having him convicted in court.

Jay steadied his horse and looked nervously over the crowd of Wilkes supporters milling around outside Westminster Hall, where the trial was taking place. If violence broke out, Jay's regiment was supposed to keep order. There was a small detachment of guards, just forty men and a few officers under Colonel Cranbrough, Jay's commanding officer. They formed a thin red and white line between the court building and the mob.

Cranbrough took orders from the Westminster magistrates, represented by Sir John Fielding. Fielding was a famous reforming justice, although Tories like Jay and his father thought him too soft.

It was a long day, and the captains took turns to break off and drink a glass of wine. Towards the end of the afternoon, while Jay was giving his horse an apple, he was approached by Sidney Lennox.

His heart sank but he put on a show of bravado. 'What are you doing here, Lennox? I didn't know you were a Wilkesite.'

'John Wilkes can go to the devil,' Lennox replied. 'I've come about the hundred and fifty pounds you owe me.'

Jay blanched at the reminder. The thought that his father might find out made his legs feel weak. He would do anything to avoid that. 'I may have to ask you to wait a little longer,' he said feebly.

Lennox did not reply directly. 'I believe you know a man called Mack McAsh.'

'Unfortunately I do.'

'He's started his own coal-heaving gang, with the help of Caspar Gordonson. The two of them are causing a lot of trouble.'

'It doesn't surprise me,' Jay said. 'He was a damned nuisance in my father's coalmine.'

'The problem is not just McAsh. His two cronies, Dermot Riley and Charlie Smith, have gangs of their own now, and there'll be more by the end of the week. It will ruin the trade unless it's stopped.'

'All the same, it's not my problem.'

'But you could help with it. It would be worth money to me.'

'How much?' Jay said warily.

'A hundred and fifty pounds.'

Jay's heart leapt at the prospect of wiping out his debt. 'What would I have to do?' he said suspiciously.

'I want the shipowners to refuse to hire McAsh's gangs. The biggest owner in London is your father. If he gave a lead, the others would follow.'

Jay frowned. He had no influence with his father.

A roar from the crowd signalled that Wilkes was coming out. Jay mounted his horse hastily. 'I'll see what I can do,' he called to Lennox as he trotted away.

Jay found Chip Marlborough who told him: 'Wilkes has been refused bail and committed to the King's Bench Prison. Pass the word—no one is to fire unless Sir John Fielding gives the order.'

Jay suppressed an anxious protest. How were soldiers to control the mob if their hands were tied? But he rode around and relayed the instruction.

A carriage emerged from the gateway. The crowd gave a blood-curdling roar, and Jay felt a stab of fear. Wilkes's supporters ran across Westminster Bridge, and Jay realised that the carriage would have to cross the river into Surrey to get to the prison. Surrey was a separate district, and the Surrey magistrates had not asked for army support. Jay watched, helpless, as the carriage crossed the River Thames. Before it reached the Surrey side the crowd stopped it and detached the horses. A dozen strong men got between the traces and began to pull it back towards Westminster.

Once across the bridge the mob turned the carriage east. Cranbrough shouted to his men: 'Follow at a distance—don't take action!'

The carriage was drawn along the Strand and into the heart of the city. The mob shouted 'Wilkes and liberty!' and 'Number forty-five!' They did not stop until they reached Spitalfields. There, Wilkes got out and went into the Three Tuns tavern. He was followed by Sir John Fielding who had been following the carriage with the crowd.

Wilkes's supporters milled about in the street for a while, and then Wilkes appeared at an upstairs window to appeal for order.

During the speech one of Fielding's clerks came out and spoke to Colonel Cranbrough. Cranbrough whispered the news to his captains. A deal had been done: Wilkes would slip out of the back door and surrender himself at the King's Bench Prison tonight.

Wilkes finished his speech, waved and bowed, and vanished. The crowd began to drift away. Sir John came and shook Cranbrough's hand. 'A splendid job, Colonel. Bloodshed was avoided and the law was satisfied.' He was putting a brave face on it, Jay thought, but the truth was that the law had been laughed at by the mob.

WHEN HE HAD DISMISSED his men and checked that the horses were taken care of, Jay remembered Lennox's proposition. He decided to call in at Grosvenor Square on his way home.

It was late. The family had eaten supper and Sir George was in his study. Jay knocked on the door and went in.

Sir George was drinking wine and yawning over a list of molasses prices. Jay sat down and said: 'Wilkes was refused bail.'

'So I heard. What brings you here so late?'

'Malachi McAsh has surfaced in London. He's stirring up trouble among the coal heavers.'

'That doesn't take much doing—they're a quarrelsome lot.'

'I've been asked to approach you on behalf of the undertakers. McAsh and his friends have started independent gangs. The undertakers are asking shipowners to be loyal to them. They feel that if you give a lead the other shippers will follow.'

'I'm not sure I should interfere. It's not our battle.'

Jay was disappointed. He pretended indifference. 'It's nothing to me, but you're always saying we've got to take a firm line with seditious labouring men.'

At that moment there was a terrific hammering at the front door. Sir George frowned and Jay stepped into the hall to have a look. A footman hurried past and opened the door to a burly working man. 'Light up!' he ordered the footman. 'Illuminate for Wilkes!'

Sir George emerged from the study and Jay told him: 'They do this—make people put candles in all their windows in support of Wilkes.'

Sir George said: 'What's that on the door?'

They walked forward. The number 45 was chalked on the door. Outside a small mob was going from house to house.

'Will you light up for Wilkes?' the man said.

Sir George reddened. 'Go to the devil!' he said, and he slammed the door in the man's face.

He went back to the study and Jay followed him. As they sat down they heard the sound of breaking glass. They both jumped up again and rushed into the dining room at the front of the house. There was a broken windowpane and a stone on the polished wood floor. As they stood staring, another stone crashed through the other window.

Sir George stepped into the hall and spoke to the footman. 'Tell everyone to move to the back of the house, out of harm's way.'

Throwing caution to the wind, Jay said: 'You know, Father, we really have to deal more decisively with these troublemakers.'

'What the devil are you talking about?'

'I was thinking of McAsh and the coal heavers. If they're allowed to defy authority once, they'll do it again. Better to nip these things in the bud. Teach them their place.'

Sir George hesitated, scowled and said: 'You're absolutely right. We'll do it tomorrow.'

As Mack walked down Wapping High Street he felt he knew what it must be like to be king. From every tavern doorway, from windows and rooftops, men waved and called out his name. But the men's appreciation was nothing compared with that of their wives. The men were not only bringing home three or four times as much money, they were also ending the day more sober.

He reached the waterfront and looked over the broad grey river. The tide was high and there were several new ships at anchor. He hired a boatman to row him out to the *Prince of Denmark* and climbed aboard. The skipper was in his cabin, writing in the ship's log. 'Good day to you, Captain,' Mack said. 'I'm Mack McAsh.'

'What is it?' the man said gruffly.

'Would you like your ship uncoaled?' Mack said pleasantly.

'No.'

'Who's going to do it for you, then?'

'None of your damn business.'

'It certainly is my business; but if you don't want to tell me, no matter—someone else will.'

'Good day to you, then.'

Mack couldn't think of anything else to say, so he left. Another new ship, *Whitehaven Jack*, was anchored next to the *Prince*. Mack got his boatman to take him there.

He found the captain on the poop deck with a young gentleman in sword and wig. 'Captain, sir, good day to you both.'

This captain was polite. 'Good day to you. This is Mr Tallow, the owner's son. What's your business?'

'Would you like your ship uncoaled by a fast and sober gang?'

'Yes,' said the captain.

'No,' said Tallow. 'You're McAsh, aren't you?' he added. 'We don't want you.'

This second rejection riled Mack. 'Why not?' he asked challengingly.

'We've done business with Harry Nipper at the Frying Pan for years and never had any trouble.'

The captain interjected: 'I wouldn't say we've had no trouble.'

Tallow glared at him.

A suspicion crossed Mack's mind. 'Has someone told you not to hire my gang?' The look on Tallow's face told him he was right.

'You'll find that nobody on the river will hire your gang, or Riley's or Charlie Smith's,' Tallow said petulantly. 'The word has gone out that you're a troublemaker.'

Mack realised this was very serious. He had known that Lennox and the undertakers would move against him sooner or later, but he had not expected them to be supported by the shipowners.

'I'm sorry you've made that decision,' he said to Tallow. 'It's bad for the men and bad for the owners. I bid you good day.'

Mack had himself rowed ashore. He felt dashed. What had made him think he could defeat a group of men as wealthy and ruthless as the undertakers? He should have foreseen this.

He made his way to St Luke's coffee-house, which had become his unofficial headquarters. Cora was there, ready for work, dressed in the orange gown she had worn the first time they met. Mack sat down with her. Straight away she said: 'What's the matter?'

He told her. As he was finishing his story, Dermot and Charlie came in. Their expressions told him that they'd had no better luck than he. Charlie's black face was a picture of despondency, and Dermot said: 'The owners have conspired against us. We're finished, Mack.'

His readiness to give up angered Mack. 'Finished?' he said scornfully. 'Are you a man or what?'

'But what can we do?' said Dermot.

'We could organise a strike. All the coal heavers want to change to our system. We could persuade them to stop working for the old undertakers. Then the shippers would have to hire the new gangs.'

Dermot was sceptical. 'Suppose they still refuse to hire us? We couldn't hold out for ever.'

'Nor can the shippers—London must have coal!'

Dermot frowned, then his face cleared. 'I'd hate to go back to the old ways. I'll give it a try.'

'Good!' said Mack, relieved.

'It's the men that will have to be persuaded.'

'That's right,' Mack said decisively. 'We'll call a meeting. The gangs that are working today will finish as soon as it gets dark. You two go round all the taverns and spread the word.'

Charlie said: 'We can't meet here—it's too small.'

'The Jolly Sailor's got a big courtyard,' said Dermot. 'And the landlord's not an undertaker.'

'Right,' Mack agreed. 'Tell them to be there an hour after nightfall.'

Dermot and Charlie went out.

Mack looked at Cora. 'Are you taking an evening off?' he said.

She shook her head. 'Just waiting for my accomplice.'

It troubled Mack that Peg was a thief and Cora was responsible. 'I wish we could find a way for that child to make a living without stealing,' he said.

'Why? And how would *I* make a living without her?'

'You could do anything, you're shrewd and beautiful—'

'I don't want to do anything, Mack, I just want to do this. I like dressing up and drinking gin and flirting. It's exciting and it's easy and I make ten times as much as I'd get serving in a coffee-house.'

He was shocked. He had thought she would say she stole because she had to. 'I really don't know you,' he said, completely flummoxed.

Peg arrived. She was pale and thin and tired, as always. Mack said: 'Have you eaten anything today?'

'No,' she said, sitting down. 'I'd love a glass of gin.'

Mack waved at a waiter. 'A bowl of porridge with cream, please.'

Peg made a face, but when the food came she ate with relish.

While she was eating, Caspar Gordonson came in. Mack was glad to see him and swiftly ran over the day's events.

Gordonson looked worried. 'You have to understand that our rulers are frightened,' he said. 'What they really want is an excuse to call out the troops and shoot people. I got you into this, and if you get killed it will be on my conscience.'

His fear began to infect Mack. Just as Gordonson felt responsible for him, he was responsible for the coal heavers. 'What do you think we should do?' he asked.

'If the men agree to strike, your job will be to keep them under control. You'll have to stop them setting fire to ships, murdering strikebreakers and laying siege to undertakers' taverns.'

'I think I might be able to do that,' Mack said. 'They listen to me. They seem to respect me.'

'They worship you,' Gordonson said. 'And that puts you in even greater danger. You're the ringleader, and the government may break the strike by hanging you.'

'What should I do?' Mack was beginning to wish he had never mentioned the word 'strike'.

'Leave the place where you're lodging and move somewhere else. Keep your address secret from all but a few trusted people.'

Cora said: 'Come and live with me.'

Mack managed a smile. 'That part would not be difficult.'

Gordonson went on: 'Don't show yourself on the streets in daylight. Appear at meetings then vanish. Become a ghost.'

Cora got up to leave. To Mack's surprise, Peg put her arms round his waist and hugged him. 'Be careful, Jock,' she said.

Mack was touched by how much they all cared for him.

Cora kissed him and then sauntered out. Peg followed.

A few moments later Mack and Gordonson left for the Jolly Sailor. Mack was surprised to see the tavern's courtyard packed with men. There were about eight hundred coal heavers in London, and at least half of them were here. The news of his arrival spread quickly and the men started to cheer. By the time he reached the hastily erected platform they were roaring. He stepped up and gazed at them. Hundreds of coal-smeared faces looked back at him in the torchlight. He fought back tears of gratitude for their trust in him. He held up his hands for quiet, but it did no good. Some cried his name, others yelled 'Wilkes and liberty!' and other slogans. Gradually one chant came to dominate the rest, until they were all bellowing the same: 'Strike! Strike! Strike!'

JAY JAMISSON received a curt note from his father at breakfast time: *Meet me at my place of business at noon. G.J.*

His first guilty thought was that Father had found out about his deal with Lennox. It had gone off perfectly. The shippers had boycotted the new coal-heaving gangs, and Lennox had returned Jay's IOUs, as agreed. But now the coal heavers were on strike and no coal had been landed in London for a week. Had Father discovered that all that might not have happened but for Jay's gambling debts?

The church bells were striking twelve as he entered the Jamissons' riverside warehouse. The dusty air was laden with spicy smells—coffee and cinnamon, rum and port, pepper and oranges. He climbed a rickety wooden staircase to the counting house. Passing through a lobby occupied by clerks he went into his father's office.

'Good morning, Father,' he said. 'Where's Robert?' His brother was almost always at Father's side.

'He had to go to Rochester. But this concerns you more than him. Sir Sidney Armstrong wants to see me.'

Armstrong was the right-hand man of Secretary of State Viscount Weymouth. 'What does he want?'

'He wants this coal strike brought to an end and he knows we started it. He'll be here any moment now.'

'Why is he coming here?' Such an important personage would normally summon people to his office in Whitehall.

'Secrecy, I imagine.'

Before Jay could ask any more questions the door opened and a middle-aged man came in. Both Jay and Sir George stood up. Armstrong walked with his nose a little high, as if to show that he did not usually descend into the mire of commercial activity. Sir George shook hands and asked him to sit down.

Armstrong refused a glass of wine. 'This strike has to end,' he said. 'The coal heavers have closed down half of London's industry.'

Sir George said: 'But why have you come to me, Sir Sidney?'

'Because I understand you were influential in starting the shippers' embargo which provoked the coal heavers. May I ask why?'

Sir George looked at Jay, who swallowed and said: 'I was

approached by the undertakers who organise the gangs. My father and I did not want the established order on the waterfront to be disturbed.'

'Quite right,' Armstrong said. 'Who are the ringleaders?'

'The most important is a man called Malachi McAsh. As it happens, he used to be a coal heaver in my father's mines.'

'I'd like to see this McAsh arrested and charged with a capital offence under the Riot Act. But it would have to be plausible: there would have to be a real riot with firearms used against officers of the Crown, and numerous people killed and injured.'

Jay was confused. Was Armstrong telling the Jamissons to organise such a riot?

His father showed no sign of puzzlement. 'You make yourself very clear, Sir Sidney.' He looked at Jay. 'Do you know where McAsh can be found?'

'No,' he said. Then, seeing the expression of scorn on his father's face, he added hastily: 'But I can find out.'

AT DAYBREAK Mack woke Cora and made love to her. She had come to bed in the small hours, and he had kissed her and gone back to sleep. Now he was wide-awake and she was the sleepy one. Her body was warm and relaxed. She wrapped her arms round him and moaned quietly, and at the end she gave a small cry of delight. Then she went back to sleep.

He sighed and got up. Cora's home was the upstairs floor of a tumbledown building in a coal yard. There were two rooms, a big bed in one and a table and chairs in the other. The bedroom was full of what Cora spent all her money on: clothes. She had eight or ten different outfits, all in striking colours, with shoes to match each one.

He washed his face, dressed quickly and left. A few minutes later he was at Dermot's house. The family were eating their breakfast.

'You've got a letter,' Dermot said, and handed Mack a sealed note.

The letter was from Esther. Mack felt a stab of guilt. He was supposed to be saving money for her, but he was on strike and penniless.

'Where's it to be today?' Dermot said. Every day Mack met his lieutenants at a different location.

'The back bar of the Queen's Head tavern,' Mack replied.

'I'll spread the word.' Dermot put his hat on and went out.

Mack opened his letter: it was full of news. The Jamissons were sinking a new coalpit in High Glen, on the Hallim estate. That was surprising: Mack had heard Lizzie say she would never allow coalmining in High Glen. Reverend York's wife had taken a fever and died. And Esther was still determined to leave Heugh as soon as Mack had saved the money.

He pocketed the letter and went along to the Queen's Head. He would win the strike, then he would be able to save.

His men were already arriving, and he got down to business.

One-Eye Wilson, a coal heaver who had been sent to check on new ships anchoring in the river, reported that two coal carriers had arrived on the morning tide.

Mack turned to Charlie Smith. 'Go and talk to the captains. Explain why we're on strike and ask them to wait. Say we hope the shippers will soon give in and allow the new gangs to uncoal the ships.'

Caspar Gordonson arrived with a note in his hand. 'There's a barge train bringing coal to London along the River Lea. It should arrive at Enfield Lock this afternoon.'

'Enfield,' Mack said. 'How far away is that?'

'Twelve miles. We can get there by midday, even if we walk.'

'Good. We must get control of the lock and prevent the barges passing. I'll go myself. I'll take twelve steady men.'

'HE'S GONE TO GROUND,' said Sidney Lennox. 'He's left his lodgings and no one knows where he went.'

Jay felt awful. He had told his father, in front of Sir Sidney Armstrong, that he could locate McAsh. If he failed, his father's scorn would be blistering. 'Someone must know where he lays his head,' he said plaintively. 'Does McAsh have a woman?'

'Yes—Cora. But she's as tough as a boot. She won't tell.'

'There must be someone else.'

'There's the kid, Quick Peg,' Lennox said thoughtfully. 'She goes robbing with Cora. I wonder . . .'

AT MIDNIGHT Lord Archer's coffee-house in Covent Garden was packed with officers, gentlemen and whores. The air was full of tobacco smoke and the smell of spilt wine, and the fiddler could hardly be heard over the roar of a hundred shouted conversations. There were several card games in progress, but Jay and Chip Marlborough were not playing. Jay was hoping to meet Cora. Numerous girls had approached him during the evening, but none fitted her description. On the far side of the room a watchful Sidney Lennox smoked a pipe and played faro.

Jay was beginning to think they would be unlucky tonight. He might have to repeat this performance tomorrow, and even the day after. Just as he was thinking wistfully of climbing into a warm bed and finding Lizzie there, eager and waiting, Cora came in. Jay was sure it was she. She was easily the prettiest girl in the room, and her hair was the colour of the flames in the fireplace. As she scanned the room with a professional gaze, Jay saw Lennox look over at him and nod slowly twice.

Thank God, he thought. He caught Cora's eye and smiled. She smiled back and came over.

'I thought I knew every beautiful woman in London, but I was wrong,' Jay said gallantly. 'I'm Captain James and this is Captain Chip.'

'I'm Cora,' she said, giving them a once-over look. 'What a handsome pair. I can't decide which captain I like best.'

Chip said: 'My family is nobler than Jay's.'

'But mine's richer,' said Jay.

'If you're so rich, buy me a measure of brandy,' she said.

Jay waved at a waiter and offered Cora a seat. She squeezed in between him and Chip on the bench. Giving Jay a quizzical look she said: 'Do I know you?'

He felt a stab of anxiety. Surely they had never met? 'I don't think so,' he said. 'Now's our chance to get to know one another.' He put his arm over the back of the seat and stroked her neck. She closed her eyes as if enjoying it, and Jay began to relax. He began to wish he had not drunk so much. He might need his wits about him.

Her brandy came and she drank it in a gulp. 'Come on, Captain,' she said. 'We'd better get some air before you drink any more.' She stood up and headed for the door, and Jay followed.

She led him along the colonnaded sidewalk of the Covent Garden piazza and turned into an alley. They embraced and kissed, and he forgot all about Lennox and the plot. Cora was warm and willing and he wanted her. Her hands were all over him.

From behind him there came a childish scream. Cora gave a start and pushed Jay away. She turned as if to run, but Chip Marlborough appeared and grabbed her before she took the first step.

Jay turned round and saw Lennox struggling to keep hold of a wriggling child. As they struggled the child dropped several objects. In the starlight Jay recognised his own wallet and pocket watch, silk handkerchief and silver seal. She had been picking his pockets while he was kissing Cora, and he had felt nothing.

The child stopped struggling and Lennox said: 'We're taking you two before a magistrate. Picking pockets is a hanging offence.'

MOST WEALTHY and powerful men were magistrates and Sir George Jamisson was no exception. Although he never held open court, he had the right to try cases at home. He was expecting Jay, so he had not gone to bed, but he was irritable at having been kept up so late. 'I expected you around ten o'clock,' he said grumpily when they all trooped into the drawing room of the Grosvenor Square house.

Cora said: 'So this was all planned—you evil pigs.'

Sir George said: 'Shut your mouth or I'll have you flogged before we begin.' He drew paper towards him and dipped a pen in an inkwell. 'Jay Jamisson, Esquire, is the prosecutor. He complains that his pocket was picked by . . . what is your name, child?'

'Peggy Knapp, sir.'

'And the woman's name?'

'Cora Higgins,' said Cora.

'Pocket picked by Peggy Knapp, accomplice Cora Higgins. The crime witnessed by . . .'

'Sidney Lennox, keeper of the Sun tavern in Wapping.'

'Now, have the accused anything to say?'

Cora said: 'I'm not her accomplice—I've never seen her before in my life. I went for a walk with a handsome young man, that's all. I never knew she was picking his pockets.'

Lennox said: 'The two are known associates, Sir George.'

'I've heard enough,' Sir George said. 'You are both committed to Newgate Prison on charges of pickpocketing.'

Cora was white with fear. 'Why are you all doing this?' she said.

Sir George ignored her. 'Captain Marlborough, oblige me by taking the woman outside and guarding her.' Chip led Cora out and closed the door. Then Sir George turned to Peg. 'Now, child, what is the punishment for picking pockets—do you know?'

'The sheriff's collar,' she whispered.

'If you mean hanging, you're right. But did you know that some people who have influential friends to plead for them are not hanged, but sent to America instead?'

The child nodded.

'Well, now, what if I tell you that I will be your influential friend and intercede for you?'

She looked up at him and hope gleamed in her little face.

'But you have to do something for me. I will save you from hanging if you tell us where Mack McAsh is living.'

The room was silent for a long time.

'In the attic over the coal yard in Wapping High Street,' she said.

MACK WAS SURPRISED to wake up alone. Cora had never before stayed out until daybreak. He had been living with her for only two weeks and he didn't know all her habits, but he was worried.

He spent the morning at St Luke's coffee-house, sending messages and receiving reports. He asked everyone if they had seen or heard of Cora, but no one had.

In the afternoon he walked to Covent Garden and went round the taverns and coffee-houses. Several people had seen Cora last night. A waiter at Lord Archer's had noticed her leaving with a rich young drunk. After that there was no trace.

Mack walked home in the dark, hoping that when he arrived at Cora's lodgings she would be waiting for him. But the place was cold and dark and empty.

He lit a candle and sat brooding. Outside on Wapping High Street the taverns were filling up. He ate some bread and cheese and read a book, but he could not concentrate. Late in the evening there was a commotion in the street outside. Fearing that the coal heavers might start some kind of fracas he went to the window. Ten or twelve horse-drawn carts were lumbering down the road in the moonlight, evidently headed for the coal yard. A crowd of men followed the carts, jeering and shouting, and more spilled out of the taverns and joined them. The scene had all the makings of a riot.

Mack cursed and rushed down the stairs. If he could persuade the men with the carts not to unload, he might avert violence.

When he reached the street the first cart was turning into the coal yard. As he ran forward the men jumped off the carts and, without warning, began to throw lumps of coal at the crowd.

'Stop!' he yelled. He ran between the coal heavers and the carts with his hands held up. The men recognised him and for a moment there was quiet. He was grateful to see Charlie Smith in the crowd. 'Try to keep order here, Charlie,' he said. 'I'll talk to these people.'

'Everybody stay calm,' Charlie called out. 'Leave it to Mack.'

Mack approached the lead cart. 'Who's in charge here?' he said.

A figure stepped forward in the moonlight. 'I am.'

Mack recognised Sidney Lennox. He was shocked and puzzled. Why was Lennox trying to deliver coal to a yard?

He spotted the owner of the yard, Jack Cooper. 'Jack, close up the gates,' he pleaded. 'There'll be murder done if you let this go on.'

Cooper looked sulky. 'I've got to make a living.'

Mack gave him a hard look. 'Who asked you to do this, Jack?'

'I'm my own man—no one tells me what to do.'

Mack began to see what was happening. He turned to Lennox. 'You've paid him off. But why?'

They were interrupted by the sound of a handbell being rung loudly. Standing at the upstairs window of the nearby Frying Pan tavern was a man wearing the wig and sword that marked him as someone of importance. 'I am Roland MacPherson, a justice of the peace in Wapping,' he announced, 'and I hereby declare a riot.' He went on to read the key section of the Riot Act.

Once a riot had been declared, the law stated that everyone had to disperse within an hour. Defiance was punishable by death.

The magistrate had got here quickly, Mack thought. Clearly he had been expecting this. The whole episode had been carefully planned. It seemed they wanted to provoke a riot that would discredit the coal heavers and give them a pretext to hang the ringleaders. And that meant him. On top of that, the whole thing was taking place right outside Mack's window. Who had betrayed him?

He turned to the angry crowd of coal heavers. 'Listen to me,' he began. 'This is a plot to provoke us into a riot. If we all go home peacefully we will outwit our enemies. If we fight, we're lost.'

There was a rumble of discontent.

'He's right,' Charlie piped up. 'Look who's here—Sidney Lennox. He's up to no good, we can be sure of that.'

Some of the coal heavers were nodding now, and Mack began to think he might persuade them. Then Lennox yelled: 'Get him!'

Several men came at Mack at once. He turned to run, but one tackled him and he crashed to the ground. He was kicked and punched but he hardly felt the blows as he struggled to get up. Then his attackers were thrown aside by coal heavers and he knew that what he had dreaded was about to begin: a pitched battle.

He looked round and saw fierce hand-to-hand fighting on all sides. He grabbed Charlie. 'We'll try to get inside the coal yard and close the gates on them,' he said. 'Tell the men!'

Charlie ran from man to man, shouting: 'Inside the yard and close the gates! Keep them out of the yard!' Then, to his horror, Mack heard the bang of a musket. He saw a blunderbuss, a musket with a shortened barrel, pointed directly at him. Before he could move, Charlie snatched the gun, turned it on the man who held it and shot him dead. Mack cursed. Charlie could hang for that.

The first shots were followed by a ragged tattoo of gunfire. Mack cried out in protest as several coal heavers fell dead or wounded; their wives and widows would blame him, and they would be right: he had started something he could not control.

Most of the coal heavers got into the yard where they fought frenziedly to keep the coal drivers out. Mack saw that if he could get the high wooden gates closed the entire battle might peter out. He got behind one of the gates and started to push. Some of the coal heavers joined in. The big gate swept several scuffling men out of the way, and Mack thought they would get it shut; then it was blocked by a cart. A dozen coal heavers began to drag it out of the yard while others pushed the gates. 'Keep pushing, don't stop!' Mack yelled. The cart inched out and the gates closed with maddening slowness.

Then Mack heard a noise that wiped out all his hopes at a stroke: the sound of marching feet.

THE GUARDS MARCHED down Wapping High Street, their white and red uniforms gleaming in the moonlight. Jay rode at the head of the column. He was about to get what he had always wanted: action.

He could hear the roar of the battle Lennox had started: men shouting, horses neighing, muskets banging. He told himself that a rabble of coal heavers would be terrified of a trained troop of Guards, but he found it hard to be confident.

Seeing the soldiers, many of the rioters fled; but some threw coal, and a rain of lumps came down on Jay and his men. Without flinching they marched up to the gates and took up their firing positions.

Jay raised his sword. The coal heavers were trapped in the yard. It was like shooting chickens in a coop.

Suddenly McAsh appeared on top of the wall, his face lit by the moon. 'Stop!' he yelled. 'Don't shoot!'

Go to hell, Jay thought. He swept his sword down and shouted: 'Fire!'

The muskets cracked like thunder. Ten or twelve coal heavers fell, some shouting in pain, others deathly silent. McAsh jumped down from the wall and knelt by the motionless body of Charlie. He looked up and met Jay's eye, and the rage in his face chilled Jay's blood.

Jay shouted: 'Charge!' The coal heavers engaged the Guards aggressively, surprising Jay. He had expected them to flee, but they dodged swords and muskets to grapple hand to hand, fighting with sticks and lumps of coal and fists and feet. He was dismayed to see several uniforms fall.

Then, suddenly, McAsh was in front of him. Jay lifted his sword, and McAsh ducked around to Jay's left side. Jay struck awkwardly and missed. McAsh jumped up, grabbed Jay's sleeve and pulled. With dreadful inevitability Jay slid sideways in his saddle. McAsh gave a mighty heave and pulled him off his horse.

Jay managed to land on his feet. McAsh's hands were round his throat in an instant. Jay swung his sword wildly. It connected with something and he thought he had wounded McAsh, but the grip on his throat did not slacken. His vision returned and he looked into McAsh's eyes and saw murder there. Suddenly he feared for his life.

One of his men saw him in trouble and he swung the butt of a

musket. The blow hit McAsh on the ear, connecting with a loud crack. For a split second McAsh's stranglehold increased, then his eyes rolled up in his head, his hands slipped from Jay's neck and he slumped to the ground unconscious.

Jay drew breath raggedly and leaned on his sword. His face hurt like fire: his nose must be broken. But as he looked at the man crumpled at his feet he felt nothing but satisfaction.

JAY CAME HOME in the early hours with blood and dirt all over him and a bandage on his nose. Lizzie was so pleased to see him alive that she threw her arms round him and hugged him, ruining her white silk robe. She woke the servants and ordered hot water, and he told her the story of the riot as she helped him out of his filthy uniform and washed his bruised body.

Later, when they were lying side by side in the big four-poster bed, she said tentatively: 'Do you think McAsh will be hanged?'

'I certainly hope so,' Jay said. 'We have witnesses to say he incited the crowd to riot and personally attacked officers.'

She frowned. 'I never thought of him as a violent man.'

Jay looked smug. 'You may be right. But things were arranged so that he had no choice.'

'What do you mean?'

'Sir Sidney Armstrong told us he wanted McAsh arrested for rioting. So Lennox and I arranged a riot.'

Lizzie was shocked. 'And is Sir Sidney pleased now?'

'He is. And Colonel Cranbrough was impressed by the way that I handled the riot. I can resign my commission and leave the army now with an unimpeachable reputation.'

Jay made love to her then, but she was too troubled to enjoy his caresses. A few moments later he was asleep. Lizzie lay awake. It was the second time she had been shocked by her husband's attitude to justice—and both occasions involved Lennox. She was glad they were leaving England in a month's time and would never see Lennox again. Still she could not sleep. There was a cold, leaden feeling in the pit of her stomach. Mack McAsh was going to be hanged. She had been revolted to watch the hanging of total strangers at Tyburn Cross. The thought of the same thing happening to her childhood friend was unbearable.

When the light of dawn began to show round the edges of the curtains she got up. She decided to begin packing for the voyage, and when the servants appeared she told them to start filling the waterproof trunks she had bought with her wedding presents: table linen, cutlery, china and glassware, cooking pots and kitchen knives.

Jay woke up aching and bad-tempered. He drank a shot of brandy for breakfast and went off to his regiment. Lizzie had returned to her packing when a footman knocked and said that Caspar Gordonson was downstairs.

She asked the man to repeat the visitor's name, because she could hardly believe Gordonson would dare to call on any member of the Jamisson family. He supported the strike that was damaging her father-in-law's business. She should have refused to see him, she knew. But curiosity got the better of her, and she told the footman to show him into the drawing room.

However, she had no intention of making him welcome. 'You've caused a great deal of trouble,' she said as she walked in.

To her surprise he was not the aggressive know-it-all she had expected, but an untidy, shortsighted man with the manner of an absent-minded schoolteacher. 'I'm sure I didn't mean to,' he said. 'That is . . . I did, of course . . . but not to you personally.'

'Why have you come here? If my husband were at home, he would throw you out on your ear.'

'Mack McAsh has been charged under the Riot Act and committed to Newgate Prison. He will be tried at the Old Bailey in three weeks' time. It's a hanging offence.'

The reminder struck Lizzie like a blow, but she hid her feelings. 'I know. Such a tragedy—a man with his life in front of him.'

'You must feel guilty,' Gordonson said.

'You insolent fool!' she blazed. 'Who encouraged McAsh to think he had rights? You! You're the one who should feel guilty!'

'I do,' he said quietly.

His humility calmed her. Tears came to her eyes but she fought them back. 'Do you think there is hope?'

'It depends who is willing to speak for him. Influential friends are everything in our legal system. I will plead for his life, but my words won't count for much. However, if you would plead for him—'

'I can't do that!' she protested. 'My husband will be a prosecution witness. It would be dreadfully disloyal of me.'

'You could save his life. Think about it—'

'I won't! I'll do something else. I'll . . .' She cast about for ideas. 'I'll write to Mr York, the pastor of the church in Heugh. I'll ask him to come to London and plead for Mack's life at the trial.'

Gordonson said: 'A country parson from Scotland? I don't think he'll have much influence.' He went to the door. 'You can change your mind at any time. Just come to the Old Bailey three weeks from tomorrow. Remember that his life may depend on it.'

He went out, and Lizzie let herself cry.

Chapter 7

Mack woke to find himself in one of the common wards of Newgate Prison. It was cold and the place smelt foul. At least thirty people were crammed into a room about the size of Cora's lodgings—men, women and children, plus a dog and a pig.

There was constant coming and going. Some of the women left early in the morning, and Mack learned they were prisoners' wives who bribed the jailers and spent nights here. The warders brought in food, beer, gin and newspapers for those who could pay their grossly inflated prices. People went to see friends in other wards. Anything was permitted, it seemed, but everything had to be paid for.

Mack hurt all over, but his head was the worst. There was a lump at the back that was crusted with blood. He felt hopelessly gloomy. He had failed in every way. He had fought for the coal heavers' rights and had got some of them killed. He would be put on trial for treason, or riot, or murder. And he would probably die on the gallows. Poor Esther would never get out of the village now.

He was at a low point when a warder opened the door and Cora walked in. Her face was dirty and her red dress was torn but she still looked ravishing. Mack sprang to his feet and embraced her, to cheers from the other prisoners. 'What happened to you?' he asked.

'I was done for picking pockets—but it was on account of you. It was a trap. He looked like any other rich young drunk, but he was Jay Jamisson. They took us in front of his father. It's a hanging offence, picking pockets. But they offered Peg a pardon—if she would tell them where you lived.'

Mack suffered a moment of anger with Peg; but she was just a child, she could not be blamed. 'So that was how they found out.'

He told her the story of the riot. When he had done she said: 'By God, McAsh, you're an unlucky man to know.'

It was true, he thought. Everyone he met got into trouble.

'You must talk to Peg,' she said. 'She thinks you must hate her.' She banged on the door and a warder opened it. She gave him a coin, jerked a thumb at Mack and said: 'He's with me.' The warder nodded and let them out.

She led him along a corridor to a room very like the one they had left. Peg was sitting on the floor in a corner. When she saw Mack she stood up, looking scared. 'I'm sorry,' she said. Her eyes filled with tears. 'I let you down,' she whispered.

'Don't be silly.' He took her in his arms, and her tiny frame shook as she sobbed and sobbed.

ON THE DAY of the trial the prisoners were woken at five in the morning. With Cora and Peg and fifteen or twenty others Mack was tied up and marched out of the prison, along Newgate Street, down a side street called Old Bailey and up an alley to the Sessions House.

Caspar Gordonson met them there and explained who was who. The yard in front of the building was already full of people: witnesses, jurors, lawyers, friends and relatives.

Peg said: 'Will you be at the trial, Mr Gordonson?'

'Yes—but the judge may not let me speak.'

'For God's sake, why not?' Mack said indignantly.

'The theory is that if you're innocent you don't need legal expertise to prove it. But sometimes judges make exceptions.'

'I hope we get a friendly judge,' Mack said anxiously.

The prisoners were led across the yard and through a gate to the bail dock. From there Mack could see the imposing Sessions House. Stone steps led up to its ground floor, which was open on one side except for a row of columns. Inside was the judges' bench on a high platform. On either side were railed-off spaces for jurors, and balconies for court officers and privileged spectators.

He watched with grim fascination as the court began its long day of trials. The first cases were dealt with rapidly, few taking more than half an hour. Cora and Peg were tried together at about midafternoon. Jay Jamisson testified that Cora had just met him in the street and got him talking while Peg picked his pockets. He called Sidney Lennox as the witness who had seen what was happening. Neither Cora nor Peg challenged this version of events. Their reward was the appearance of Sir George, who testified that they had been helpful in the apprehension of another criminal and asked the judge to sentence them to transportation rather than hanging.

The judge nodded sympathetically, but the sentence would not be pronounced until the end of the day.

Mack's case was called a few minutes later. The prosecutor was a lawyer, Augustus Pym.

Gordonson approached the bench and addressed the judge. 'My lord, as the prosecution is to be done by a professional lawyer, will you allow me to speak for Mr McAsh?'

'Certainly not,' said the judge. 'If McAsh cannot convince the jury unless he has outside help, he can't have much of a case.'

Mack's throat was dry and he could hear his heartbeat. He was going to have to fight for his life alone.

Pym began. 'On the night in question a delivery of coal was being made to the yard of Mr John Cooper in Wapping High Street. The delivery men were attacked by a group of striking coal heavers, and the magistrates were alerted. Mr Roland MacPherson, Justice of the Peace, arrived and declared a riot. The coal heavers refused to disperse.'

'We were attacked!' Mack said.

They ignored him. 'Mr MacPherson then summoned the troops, as was his right and duty. A detachment of the Third Foot Guards arrived under the command of Captain Jamisson. The prisoner was among those arrested. The Crown's first witness is John Cooper.'

Cooper testified that he went to Rochester to buy coal that had been unloaded there. He had it driven to London in carts.

Mack asked: 'Who did the ship belong to?'

'I don't know—I dealt with the captain.'

'Could it have belonged to Sir George Jamisson?'

'I don't know.'

'Who suggested that you might be able to buy coal in Rochester?'

'Sidney Lennox.'

'A friend of the Jamissons.'

'I don't know about that.'

Pym's next witness was Roland MacPherson, who swore that he had been summoned to the scene to read the Riot Act at a quarter past eleven in the evening, and the crowd had refused to disperse.

Mack said: 'You arrived very quickly. Who summoned you?'

'Harold Nipper, the landlord of the Frying Pan.'

'Where were you when he summoned you?'

'In the back parlour of his tavern.'

'That was handy! Was it planned?'

'I knew there was going to be a coal delivery and I feared there might be trouble.'

'Who forewarned you?'

'Sidney Lennox.'

One of the jurors said: 'Ho!'

Mack looked at him. He was a youngish man with a sceptical expression, and Mack marked him down as a potential ally.

Finally Pym called Jay Jamisson, who said he had been in command of a detachment of Guards at the Tower of London.

The sceptical juror interrupted: 'Is that your usual barracks?'

'No.'

'Where then?'

'Hyde Park, at the moment.'

'On the other side of London. How did you come to be at the Tower that night?'

'I assume my commanding officers feared trouble.'

'Sidney Lennox warned them, I suppose,' the juror said, and there was a ripple of laughter.

Jay said that when he and his men arrived at the coal yard there was a riot in full progress. He told how Mack had attacked him and had been knocked out by another soldier.

Mack asked him: 'Do you think the riot will turn folk against the coal heavers?'

'I'm sure of it.'

'So the riot makes it more likely that the authorities will take drastic action to end the strike?'

'I certainly hope so.'

Beside Mack, Caspar Gordonson was muttering: 'Brilliant, brilliant, he fell right into your trap.'

'And when the strike is over, the Jamisson family's coal ships will be unloaded and you will be able to sell your coal again.'

Jay began to see where he was being led, but it was too late. 'Yes.'

'So an end to the strike is worth a lot of money to you. Is that why you cooperated with Sidney Lennox in provoking the riot?' Mack turned away.

'I did no such thing!' said Jay, but he was speaking to the back of Mack's head.

Pym had no more witnesses. Now it was up to Mack to defend himself.

'I didn't riot,' he began. 'I simply refused to let undertakers steal my wages. That's my crime, gentlemen of the jury.'

The judge said irritably: 'Can you prove that you did not riot?'

Mack was not put off by the interruption. 'Gentlemen,' he continued, 'ask yourselves some questions.' He turned and looked straight at Jay. 'Who ordered that wagons of coal should be brought down Wapping High Street at an hour when the taverns are full of coal heavers? Who sent them to the very coal yard where I live? Who gave them muskets and ammunition? Who made sure the troops were standing by in the neighbourhood? Who orchestrated the entire riot?' He swung round and looked at the jury. 'You know the answer, don't you?' He held their gaze a moment longer, then turned away. He had done his best, and now his life was in their hands.

Gordonson got to his feet. 'We were expecting a character witness to appear on McAsh's behalf—the Reverend Mr York, pastor of the church in the village of his birth—but he has not yet arrived.'

The judge said: 'If he arrives he may speak before sentencing.' Gordonson raised his eyebrows. 'That is, unless the jury finds the defendant not guilty. Gentlemen, consider your verdict.'

Mack studied the jurors as they conferred. He thought, to his dismay, that they looked unsympathetic. He could see the sceptical one making a point forcefully, wagging his finger. Were the others listening attentively, or ranged against him? The sceptical one shrugged and half turned away, and Mack feared he had lost the argument. The foreman approached the bench.

The judge said: 'Have you reached a verdict?'

'We have.'

'And how do you find the prisoner?'

'We find him guilty as charged.'

LIZZIE COULD THINK of nothing but the trial. She had dinner at three o'clock and, as Jay was at the court all day, her mother, who was still living in the Jamissons' house, came to dine and keep her company.

'You're looking quite plump, my dear,' Lady Hallim said. 'Have you been eating a lot?'

'On the contrary,' Lizzie said. 'Sometimes food makes me feel ill. It's all the excitement of going to Virginia, I suppose. And now this dreadful trial.'

'It's not your concern,' Lady Hallim said briskly. 'Dozens of people are hanged every year for much less dreadful crimes. McAsh can't be reprieved just because you knew him as a child.'

There was a knock at the dining-room door and a footman came in. 'The Reverend Mr York, madam,' he said.

'What's he doing here?' Lizzie said anxiously. 'He's supposed to be at the Old Bailey. Show him in, quickly.'

The pastor came in, but before Lizzie could speak he said something that momentarily took her mind off Mack. 'Lady Hallim, Mrs Jamisson, I arrived in London a few hours ago, and I've called on you at the earliest possible moment to offer you my sympathies—'

Lizzie's mother said: 'No—' then clamped her lips tight.

Lizzie shot a puzzled look at her mother and said: 'What are you talking about, Mr York?'

'The pit disaster, of course.'

'I know nothing about it—although I see my mother does—'

'There was a roof collapse at your pit and twenty people killed.'

Lizzie gasped. 'How absolutely dreadful.' In her mind she saw twenty new graves in the little churchyard by the bridge. 'But what do you mean by "your" pit?'

'High Glen, of course, the one that was begun when you married Mr Jamisson.'

Lizzie went cold. She rounded on her mother. 'You knew?'

Lady Hallim had the grace to look ashamed. 'My dear, it was the only thing to do. We thought you'd never know, you're going to America—' Her mother began to cry.

Her tears did nothing to blunt Lizzie's outrage. 'You thought I'd never know? I can hardly believe my ears!' An awful thought struck her. She turned to the pastor. 'Mack's twin sister . . .'

'I'm afraid Esther McAsh was among the dead,' he said.

'Oh, no.' Esther was dead and her twin brother Mack was about to be condemned to death. 'The trial is today!'

York said: 'Oh my goodness, I didn't know it was so soon—am I too late?'

'Perhaps not, if you go now. I'm coming with you.'

Mother said: 'No, please—'

Lizzie made her voice harsh. 'Don't try to stop me, Mother. I'm going to plead for Mack's life myself.'

'I'm coming with you,' said Lady Hallim.

THE SESSIONS YARD was crammed with people. Lizzie pushed through the crowd and at last saw Mack and Caspar Gordonson through the railings that enclosed an inner yard. When she called, Gordonson came out through a gate. At the same time Sir George and Jay appeared.

She ignored them and spoke to Gordonson: 'This is the Reverend Mr York, from our village in Scotland. He's come to plead for Mack's life. And I'm going to plead for him, too.'

'Thank you,' Gordonson said fervently. 'It's the best thing you could possibly do.'

Lady Hallim said: 'I tried to stop her, Sir George.'

Jay grabbed Lizzie by the arm, squeezing hard. 'You can't go against your own husband,' he stormed. 'It's disloyal!'

'Disloyal?' she repeated scornfully. 'Who the hell are you to talk to me about loyalty? You swore to me that you would not mine coal on my land—then went ahead and did exactly that.'

They all went quiet. 'You know about the accident, then,' said Jay.

She took a deep breath. 'I might as well say now that Jay and I will be leading separate lives from today. We'll be married in name only. I shall return to my house in Scotland, and none of the Jamisson family will be welcome there.'

Sir George was too stupefied to say anything.

Caspar Gordonson addressed Jay. 'May I make a suggestion? Mrs Jamisson might be persuaded not to testify—on condition that you plead for Mack's life.'

'Absolutely not,' said Jay.

Gordonson went on: 'It would save the embarrassment of a wife going against her husband in open court. You could say that Mack was a miner in the Jamisson pits and for that reason the family wishes to be merciful.'

Lizzie could see hesitation flicker across Jay's face. Then he said sulkily: 'I suppose I have to accept this.'

Sir George looked at her. 'There's one condition, which I know Jay will insist upon. You must forget all this nonsense about separate lives. You are to be a proper wife to Jay.'

'No!' she cried. 'He has betrayed me—how can I trust him?'

Her mother said: 'You have to. You're going to have his baby.'

Lizzie stared at her. 'How would you know?'

'Your bosom has got bigger and food makes you feel sick. You've been married for two months: it's not exactly unexpected.'

'Oh, my God.' Lizzie was dumbfounded. A baby! Could it be? She looked at her husband. On his face she saw anger mixed with a pleading look. 'Why did you lie to me?' she said.

'I didn't want to, but I had to,' he said.

She felt bitter. Her love for him would never be quite the same, she knew. But he was still her husband.

'All right,' she said. 'I accept.'

'OH YES! OH YES!' shouted the court crier. 'My Lords, the King's Justices, command silence while the sentence of death is passing on the prisoners at the bar.'

The judge put on his black cap and stood up.

Mack suffered a wave of terror. Nineteen cases had been tried and twelve people had been found guilty. Lizzie had forced Jay to plead for mercy, but what if the judge decided to discount Jay's plea?

The judge looked at each of the twelve prisoners. 'The law is that thou shalt return to the place whence thou camest, and from thence to the Place of Execution, where thou shalt hang by the neck, till the body be dead! dead! dead! and the Lord have mercy on thy souls.'

There was an awful pause. Cora held Mack's arm, and he felt her fingers digging into his flesh.

'Peg Knapp is reprieved and recommended for transportation,' the judge intoned. 'Cora Higgins is reprieved and recommended for transportation. Malachi McAsh is reprieved and recommended for transportation. The rest are left to hang.'

Mack put his arms round Cora and Peg, and the three of them stood in a mutual embrace. Their lives had been spared.

Caspar Gordonson took Mack's arm and said solemnly: 'I have to give you some dreadful news. There has been a roof collapse in one of the Jamisson pits. Twenty people were killed.'

'Esther . . .?'

'I'm sorry, Mack. Your sister was among the dead.'

Mack put his hands over his face and wept.

THE DAY OF DEPARTURE came quickly. One morning, without warning, all the prisoners who had been sentenced to transportation were told to pick up their possessions and then herded into the courtyard. There, a blacksmith shackled them in pairs with heavy leg-irons. Mack was paired with a filthy old drunk called Mad Barney. Cora made eyes at the blacksmith and got herself paired with Peg.

Mack looked up and down the line of convicts. There were more than a hundred, he reckoned; around a quarter of them female, with a sprinkling of children. Among the men was Sidney Lennox.

Lennox's fall had caused much glee. Although the coal heavers' strike had been broken, no one would work for him at any price. He had tried to coerce a woman into stealing for him, but she and two friends had informed against him for receiving stolen property, and he had duly been convicted. The Jamissons had saved him from the gallows, but they could not prevent his being transported.

The great wooden doors of the prison swung wide. Escorted by a squad of guards the prisoners moved out into the busy city street. The irons slowed them down, and it took more than an hour to shuffle to the waterfront. A boat was waiting to take them out to their ship, anchored midstream. Mack read its name: 'The *Rosebud*.'

'Is it a Jamisson ship?' said Cora.

'I think most of the convict ships are.'

As he stepped into the boat, Mack realised this would be the last time he stood on British soil for many years, perhaps for ever. He had mixed feelings: fear and apprehension mixed with a certain reckless excitement at the prospect of a new country and a new life.

The ship was about forty foot long by fifteen wide. Mack had an impression of coiled ropes and furled sails, the smell of varnish; then they were shoved over the lip of a hatch and down a ladder.

There seemed to be three lower decks. On the first, four sailors were eating their midday meal, sitting crosslegged on the floor. On the third, all the way down at the foot of the ladder, two men were stacking barrels. At the middle level, which was obviously for the convicts, a sailor roughly pulled Mack and Barney off the ladder and shoved them through a doorway.

Mack peered at his surroundings in the gloom. The ceiling was an inch or two above his head: a tall man would have to stoop. It was pierced by two gratings which admitted a little light and air from the deck above. Along both sides of the deck were rows of wooden racks, six foot wide, one at waist height and one a few inches off the floor. With horror Mack realised they were for the convicts to lie on.

They shuffled along the narrow walkway between the rows. The first few berths were already occupied by convicts lying flat, still chained in pairs. A sailor directed Peg and Cora to lie next to Mack and Barney, like knives in a drawer. Peg was able to sit upright but the grown-ups were not, for there was not enough headroom. At the end of each row was a large, cone-shaped earthenware jar about two foot high. Mack realised they were the toilets.

'How long will it take to get to Virginia?' said Peg.

'Seven weeks,' he said. 'If we're lucky.'

LIZZIE WATCHED as her trunk was carried into the large cabin at the rear of the *Rosebud*. She and Jay had the owner's quarters, a bedroom and a day room, and more space than she had expected. Everyone talked of the horrors of the transatlantic voyage, but she was determined to try to enjoy the novel experience.

Making the best of things was now her philosophy of life. Only a few weeks ago she would have been thrilled by this trip. Going to America was her great ambition. But the dream had lost some of its glow when she learned of Jay's betrayal. She tried to pretend that he was as dear to her as ever, but her body told the truth. When he touched her at night she did not respond as she once had.

Her pregnancy made her disappointments seem less important. She would love the baby without reservation. And he, or she, would grow up a Virginian.

As she was taking off her hat there was a tap at the cabin door. A wiry man in a blue coat and a three-cornered hat stepped inside and bowed. 'Silas Bone, first mate, at your service.'

'Good day to you, Bone,' Jay said stiffly, assuming the dignity of the owner's son.

'Captain's compliments to you both,' Bone said. 'We'll get under way at the turn of the tide.'

Jay said: 'Are my horses on board?'

'Yes, sir.'

'Let's have a look at their accommodation.'

They stepped out of the cabin and walked along the deck to an open hatch. The mate scampered down a ladder, agile as a monkey. Jay went after him and Lizzie followed. They went to the second of the lower decks. Jay's favourite horses, the two greys, and the birthday present, Blizzard, stood in narrow stalls. Each had a sling under its belly, attached to a beam overhead, so that if it lost its footing in heavy seas it could not fall. They were nervous and Jay petted them for a while, speaking to them soothingly.

Lizzie became impatient and wandered along the deck to where a heavy door stood open. Bone followed her. 'That's the convict hold ahead,' he said. 'It's no place for a lady.'

He had said the magic words that guaranteed she would persist. She turned round and fixed him with a look. 'Mr Bone, this ship belongs to my father-in-law and I will go where I like. Is that clear?' 'Aye, aye, Mrs Jamisson.'

She was keen to see the convict hold because McAsh might be there: this was the first convict ship to leave London since his trial. She went forward a couple of paces, ducked under a beam, pushed open a door and found herself in a big space filled with what looked like storage racks. Something moved on the shelf beside her, with a clank like a chain, and she jumped. Then she saw to her horror that there was someone lying on the shelf; no, two people, fettered together at their ankles. As her eyes adjusted to the gloom she realised there were dozens packed together on these racks.

'Lizzie Jamisson!' said a voice.

She recognised the Scots accent: it was Mack. She took a few paces along the narrow walkway, saying: 'Mack—where are you?' An arm was stretched out to her, ghostly grey in the twilight. She squeezed Mack's hand. 'This is dreadful,' she said. 'What can I do?'

'Nothing, now,' he said.

She saw Cora lying beside him, and the child, Peg, next to her. At least they were all together. 'Perhaps I can make sure you get enough food and water,' she said.

'That would be kind.'

She retraced her steps with an indignant protest on her lips, but when she caught the eye of Silas Bone she saw such a look of scorn on his face that she bit back her words. The ship was about to set sail, and nothing she could say would change matters now.

'The horses are comfortable,' Jay said with an air of satisfaction when he caught sight of her.

Lizzie could not resist a retort. 'They're better off than the human beings!'

'Ah, that reminds me,' said Jay. 'Bone, there's a convict called Lennox. Have his irons struck and put him in a cabin, please.'

'Aye, aye, sir.'

'Why is Lennox with us?' Lizzie said, aghast.

'He was convicted of receiving stolen goods. But the family has made use of him in the past and we can't abandon him.'

Lizzie turned away. What bad luck that he too had been transported. Would Jay never escape from his malign influence?

A few minutes later Lizzie and Jay stood in the bows as the ship began to move downriver on the tide. As the dome of St Paul's slipped below the skyline of warehouses she said: 'I wonder if we'll ever see London again?'

PART III: Virginia
Chapter 8

An excited cry from *Rosebud*'s deck penetrated the convicts' hold: 'Land ho!'

A cheer went up from the crew. Despite his weakness Mack longed to go on deck. This is America, he thought. I've crossed the world to the far side and I'm still alive!

He had often felt he would not make it. Twenty-five of the prisoners had died at sea. They had not starved: Lizzie had kept her promise and ensured they had enough to eat and drink. But the drinking water was foul and the diet of salt meat and bread unhealthily monotonous, and all the convicts had been violently ill with what was called jail fever. Mad Barney had been the first to die of it. Peg had always been thin but now she looked as if she was made of sticks. Cora's once voluptuous body was scraggy and disfigured with sores.

That night the *Rosebud* anchored in calm waters. The seaman who brought the prisoners' rations was one of the friendlier crew members: Ezekiel Bell, known as Beau Bell. He told them they were off Cape Henry, near the town of Hampton in Virginia.

'Mack, what happens when we get to Virginia?' Peg asked.

'We'll be sold, and have to work for whoever buys us.'

'Will we be sold together?'

He knew there was little chance of it. 'We might be,' he said. 'Let's hope for the best. And anyway it's only for seven years. Then we'll be free.'

'Seven years,' she said dismally. 'I'll be grown-up!'

'And I'll be almost thirty,' Mack said. It seemed middle-aged.

They weighed anchor the following morning, and Mack could feel the ship bowling along in a strong favourable wind. In the evening he learned they were almost at the mouth of the Rappahannock River. He went up on deck for one of the exercise periods, and as the ship tacked upriver he got his first sight of America.

Thick woods and cultivated fields lined both banks. At intervals there would be a jetty and a lawn rising up to a grand house. Here and there around the jetties he saw the huge barrels known as hogsheads, used for transporting tobacco. Most of the people in the fields were black, he noted.

That brief survey was all he saw for the next four days. When at last they anchored he learned they were at Fredericksburg, their

A Place Called Freedom

destination. The voyage had taken eight weeks.

That night the convicts got cooked food. Next morning they were brought up on deck in groups of ten, and they saw Fredericksburg. The town, which was built around a bluff, looked as though a couple of hundred people might live there: it was not much bigger than Heugh, but it seemed a cheerful, prosperous place, with houses of wood painted white and green. On the opposite bank, a little upstream, was a town called Falmouth.

The prisoners were given soap and made to wash, and a barber came on board to shave the men and cut their hair. Those whose clothes were too indecent were given replacement garments, but their gratitude was diminished when they recognised them as having been taken from those who had died on the voyage.

That afternoon two men were brought down to the hold to inspect them. Beau Bell whispered to Mack that they were 'soul drivers': they would buy up groups of slaves, convicts and indentured servants and herd them upcountry like sheep, to sell to remote farmers. Mack did not like the look of them. They went away without making a purchase. Tomorrow was race day, Bell said: the gentry came into town from all around for the horse races. Most of the convicts would be sold by the end of the day. Then the soul drivers would offer a knockdown price for all those who remained.

That night there was another good meal, and in the morning they got a breakfast of porridge and molasses and a ration of rum and water. Consequently, despite the uncertain future that faced them, it was a cheerful group that hobbled, still chained, on deck.

A fat-bellied man in a straw hat came on board accompanied by a tall, grey-haired Negro. The two of them looked over the convicts, picking out the youngest and strongest men. Inevitably Mack was among those chosen. No women or children were picked.

When the selection was finished the captain said: 'Right, you lot, go with these men.'

Peg began to cry. 'Take me with you!' she wailed.

Mack embraced her. He had guessed this was going to happen, and it broke his heart. He hugged her hard, then detached himself from her. 'Try and stay with Cora, if you can,' he said.

Cora kissed him with desperate passion. Hot tears ran down her face. 'Try and find us, Mack, for God's sake,' she pleaded.

'I'll do my best—'

'Come on, lover-boy,' the fat-bellied man said. Mack looked back over his shoulder as he was pushed down the gangway onto the wharf. Cora and Peg stood watching with their arms round one another, crying. Then they were lost from sight.

101

It felt strange to put his feet on solid ground, after weeks at sea. As he hobbled down the unpaved main street he stared about him. The town centre had a church, a market house, a pillory and a gallows. Brick and wood houses stood widely spaced along either side of the street. The town was thronged with people, horses, carts and carriages, most of which must have come from the countryside all around. The women had new bonnets and ribbons, and the men wore polished boots and clean gloves. He overheard talk of races and betting odds. Virginians seemed keen on gambling.

The town petered out after half a mile. They waded across the river at a ford, then set off along a rough track through wooded countryside. Mack put himself next to the middle-aged Negro. 'My name is Malachi McAsh,' he said. 'They call me Mack.'

The man kept his eyes straight ahead, but spoke in a friendly way. 'I'm Kobe,' he said, pronouncing it to rhyme with Toby.

'The fat man in the straw hat—does he own us now?'

'No. Bill Sowerby's just the overseer. Him and me was told to go aboard the *Rosebud* and pick out the best field hands.'

'Who has bought us?'

'You ain't exactly been bought. Mr Jay Jamisson decided to keep you for hisself, to work at Mockjack Hall.'

'Jamisson!'

'S' right.'

So Mack was once again owned by the Jamisson family. The thought made him angry. I'll run away again, he vowed. 'There were two people on the ship with me, a woman and a girl,' he said. 'Will I be able to find out who bought them?'

Kobe gave a humourless laugh. 'Everybody's trying to find someone they were sold apart from. People ask around all the time.'

'The child's name is Peg,' Mack persisted. 'She's only thirteen. She doesn't have a mother or father.'

'When you've been bought, nobody has a mother or father.'

Kobe had given up, Mack realised; he'd abandoned all hope of freedom. I swear I'll never do that, Mack thought.

They walked about ten miles. It was slow, because the convicts were fettered. Some were still chained in pairs. The overseer, Sowerby, was on horseback, but he seemed in no hurry, and as he rode he sipped some kind of liquor from a flask.

The road followed the rocky river, which wound through a lush forest. Mack felt bitter about being the property of a Jamisson again, but Lizzie's presence would be some consolation. Her sense of justice had saved his life in the past and might do so again.

It was noon when they arrived at the Jamisson plantation. A path led through an orchard to a muddy compound with a dozen or so cabins. Two elderly black women were cooking over open fires, and four or five naked children played in the dirt. The cabins were crudely built and their shuttered windows had no glass.

Sowerby exchanged a few words with Kobe and disappeared.

Kobe said to the convicts: 'These are your quarters. White and black live in separate cabins, and each cabin takes six people. Before we rest we have one more chore. Follow me.'

They walked along a footpath between fields of green wheat, tall Indian corn and the fragrant tobacco plant. Men and women were at work in every field, weeding between the rows.

They emerged onto a wide lawn and went up a rise towards a sprawling, dilapidated clapboard house: Mockjack Hall, presumably. Skirting the house, they came to a group of outbuildings, one of which was a smithy. Working there was a Negro whom Kobe addressed as Cass. He began to strike the fetters from the convicts' legs.

When Mack felt the irons fall from his legs he had to make an effort not to run away. While he was still fighting the impulse, Kobe began to speak. 'Now you've lost your chains, some of you are already figuring how far you can get by sundown.' He paused for effect, then went on: 'People who run away are generally caught, and they get punished. First they're flogged, but that's the easy part. Then they have to wear the iron collar, which some find shameful. But the worst is, your time is made longer. We got people here run away so many times they won't be free until they're a hundred years old.' He caught Mack's eye. 'If you're willing to chance that much, all I can say is, I wish you luck.'

IN THE MORNING the old women cooked a boiled corn dish called hominy which the convicts and slaves ate with their fingers out of wooden bowls. There were about forty field hands altogether, mostly black slaves. There were four indentured servants, people who had sold four years' labour in advance to pay for their transatlantic ticket, and three regular waged employees: two free blacks and a white woman, all past fifty years old.

The hands were given their orders by Bill Sowerby and Kobe. They were marched a mile or two across broad fields to where the tobacco was ready to harvest. There they were divided into three groups. The first was set to cutting down the ripe plants. The next group went into a field that had been cut the previous day. Newcomers were shown how to split the stacks of the cut plants and spear them on long wooden spikes. Mack was in the third group, which had the job of carrying the loaded spikes across the fields to the tobacco house, where they were hung from the high ceiling to cure.

It was a long, hot summer day. Mack had been weakened by disease, malnutrition and inactivity on the *Rosebud*, and he found himself constantly overtaken by women and children. Bill Sowerby carried a whip but Mack did not see him use it.

At noon they got a meal of coarse cornbread that the slaves called pone. While they were eating Mack was dismayed to see the familiar figure of Sidney Lennox, dressed in new clothes, being shown around the plantation by Sowerby. No doubt Jay felt that Lennox could be useful to him.

At sundown, feeling exhausted, they left the fields; but instead of returning to their cabins they were marched to the tobacco house, now lit up by dozens of candles. After a hasty meal they worked on, stripping the leaves from cured plants and pressing them into bundles. It was past midnight when at last the hands were allowed to return to their cabins. Mack fell asleep immediately.

It seemed only seconds later that he was being shaken awake to go back to work. Wearily he staggered outside. Leaning against the cabin wall he ate his bowl of hominy. No sooner had he stuffed the last handful into his mouth than they were marched off again.

As they entered the field in the dawn light, he saw Lizzie. She was on a white horse and wore a loose linen dress and a big hat. She looked well; rested, comfortable, the lady of the manor riding about her estate. She had put on some weight, Mack noticed. Then, looking at her rounded body, he realised she was pregnant.

Lizzie caught his eye. She stared at first, unsure who he was; then she seemed to recognise him with a jolt. Perhaps she was shocked by the change in his appearance caused by the voyage.

He held her eye for a long time, hoping she would come over to him; but then she turned away without speaking, kicked her horse into a trot, and disappeared into the woods.

MOCKJACK HALL was a big, long-fronted house with a pillared portico facing down a sloping lawn to the muddy Rappahannock River. It had been painted white with green shutters, many years ago, but now the paint was peeling and the colours had faded to a uniform drab. The house had grand reception rooms—drawing room, dining room, and even a ballroom—and spacious bedrooms upstairs, but the interior needed redecoration and the whole place had an air of lost grandeur.

Nevertheless Jay felt good as he surveyed his estate from the portico. It was a thousand acres of cultivated fields, wooded hillsides, bright streams and broad ponds, and it all belonged to him. At last he was a gentleman in his own right.

He planned to cut a dash in Virginia society. He didn't know just how colonial government worked, but he understood that the assembly in Williamsburg was composed of burgesses, the equivalent of Members of Parliament. Given his status, he thought he might stand for election to the House of Burgesses. He wanted everyone to know that Jay Jamisson was a man of importance.

Lizzie came across the lawn riding Blizzard. She was riding him well, Jay thought, almost like a man—and then he realised, to his irritation, that she was riding astride. When she reined in he said: 'You shouldn't ride like that.'

Her face fell, but her rejoinder was defiant, as always: 'I'll ride sidesaddle when we're with company, but not on my own.'

'Anyway, quite soon you'll have to stop riding altogether, for the sake of the baby,' he said sulkily.

'But not just yet,' she said. She was five months pregnant: she planned to stop riding at six. She changed the subject. 'I've been looking around. The land is in better condition than the house. Sowerby is a drunk, but he has kept the place going. We probably should be grateful, considering he hasn't been paid for a year.'

'He may have to wait a little longer—cash is short.'

'Your father said there were fifty hands, but in fact there are only twenty-five. It's a good thing we have the fifteen convicts from the *Rosebud*. I presume we didn't pay for the new men.'

'Certainly not—why should I pay for something that belongs to my family? I gave the captain a receipt for the men. He will hand that to Father and Father will probably send me a bill, which I will pay—when I can.'

'How will your father take it?'

Jay grinned. 'He'll be furious, but what can he do?'

'I suppose it's all right,' Lizzie said dubiously.

He did not like her questioning his judgment. 'These things are best left to me.'

That annoyed her. She went on the attack. 'I'm sorry to see Lennox here—I can't understand your attachment to that man.'

Jay had mixed feelings about Lennox. Once he had been rescued from the hold of the *Rosebud*, the man had assumed he would be living on the Jamisson plantation, and Jay had never summoned the nerve to discuss the matter. 'Sowerby needs an assistant,' he said.

'Lennox knows nothing about tobacco.'

'He can learn.' Jay did not want to discuss Lennox. 'I may go into public life here, get elected to the House of Burgesses,' he said.

'I wonder how soon it could be arranged.'

'You'd better meet our neighbours and talk to them about it.'

He nodded. 'In a month or so we'll give a big party and invite everyone of importance from round about Fredericksburg.'

'A party,' Lizzie said dubiously. 'Can we afford it?'

Once again she was questioning his judgment. 'Leave the finances to me,' he snapped. 'I'm sure we can get supplies on credit—my name must be worth quite a lot.'

THE BALLROOM WAS SMALL, but it had a good floor and a little balcony for the musicians. Twenty or thirty couples were dancing, in bright satin clothes. Dozens of candles lit up the floral decorations. In the other rooms, guests played cards, drank and flirted.

Jay and Lizzie moved from the ballroom to the dining room, smiling and nodding at their guests. Jay had drunk plenty of wine and was feeling good. The party had cost a small fortune, but it was a success: everyone who was anyone had come.

In the dining room the Jamissons' nearest neighbours were standing at the fire, eating cake and talking politics. They were Colonel and Mrs Thumson, Bill and Suzy Delahaye, and Roderick Armstead, a bachelor. The Thumsons were very elevated: the colonel was a burgess, a member of the General Assembly, grave and self-important. He explained to Jay: 'The governor of Virginia died last March, and we're waiting for his replacement.'

Jay assumed the air of an insider in the London court. 'The king has appointed Norborne Berkeley, the Baron de Botetourt. I believe he was hoping to leave London soon after I did.'

Thumson said: 'The President of the Council is acting as his deputy in the interim.'

Jay was keen to show a knowledge of local affairs. He said: 'I assume that's why the burgesses were so unwise as to support the Massachusetts Letter.' The letter, a protest against customs duties, had been sent to King George by the Massachusetts legislature. The Virginia legislature had passed a resolution approving of it. Jay and most London Tories considered both actions to be disloyal.

Thumson said stiffly: 'I trust the burgesses were not unwise.'

'His Majesty certainly thought so,' Jay rejoined. 'I'm quite sure the new governor will demand that the resolution be withdrawn.' He had learned this before leaving London.

Bill Delahaye, younger than Thumson, said hotly: 'The burgesses will refuse.' His pretty wife, Suzy, put a restraining hand on his arm.

Jay said: 'If the burgesses refuse, the governor will have to dissolve the assembly.'

106

Roderick Armstead said: 'It's curious how little difference that makes, nowadays. Colonial parliaments are constantly being dissolved for one reason or another. They simply reassemble informally, in a tavern or a private house, and carry on their business.'

'Then they have no legal status!' Jay protested.

Colonel Thumson answered him. 'Still, they have the consent of the people they govern, and that seems to be enough.'

To Jay, the idea that governments got their authority from the people was dangerous nonsense. 'In London a man could be jailed for talking that way, Colonel.'

'Quite,' said Thumson enigmatically.

Lizzie intervened. 'Have you tried the syllabub, Mrs Thumson?'

The colonel's wife responded with exaggerated enthusiasm. 'Yes, it's very good, quite delicious.'

'Ah, I see Dr Finch—I must have a word with him,' Thumson said, and smoothly moved, with his wife, to another group.

Bill Delahaye said: 'You've only just arrived, Jamisson. You may find that living here gives you a different perspective.'

His tone was not unkind, but Jay was offended. 'I trust, sir, that my loyalty to my sovereign will be unshaken, no matter where I live.'

Delahaye's face darkened. 'No doubt,' he said, and he too moved away, taking his wife with him.

Roderick Armstead said: 'I must try this syllabub,' and turned to the table.

JAY CAME DOWN to breakfast at midday. He had a headache. He found Lizzie eating grilled ham while the house slaves cleaned up after the ball.

There was a letter for him. He sat down and opened it, but before he could read it Lizzie glared at him and said: 'Why on earth did you start that quarrel last night?'

'What quarrel?'

'With Thumson and Delahaye, of course. You offended them. You practically called Colonel Thumson a traitor!'

'It seems to me he probably is a traitor.'

'He's a landowner, a member of the House of Burgesses and a retired British army officer—how can he be a traitor?'

'Well, you heard him talk.'

'After spending all that money to get to know our neighbours you succeeded only in making them dislike you.' She resumed eating.

Jay looked at his letter. It was dated August 29, 1768 and was from a lawyer in Williamsburg.

*I am commanded to write to you, dear Mr Jamisson, by your father,
Sir George. I welcome you to Virginia and hope that we shall soon
have the pleasure of seeing you here in the colonial capital.*

Jay was surprised. This was uncharacteristically thoughtful of his
father. Would he start to be kind, now that Jay was half a world away?

*Until then, please let me know if I may be of any assistance. I know
that you have taken over a plantation in difficulties. Allow me to offer
my services should you require a mortgage. I am sure a lender could be
found without difficulty. I remain, Sir, your most humble and obedient
servant—Matthew Murchman.*

Jay smiled. This was just what he needed. The repair and redecoration of the house, and the lavish party, had already put him up to
his neck in debt with local merchants; and Sowerby kept asking for
supplies: seed, new tools, the list was endless. 'Well, you needn't
worry about money any longer,' he said to Lizzie.
   She looked sceptical.
   'I'm going to Williamsburg,' he said.

WHILE JAY WAS IN Williamsburg Lizzie got a letter from her mother.
The first thing that struck her was the return address: The Manse, St
John's Church, Aberdeen. What was Mother doing in a vicarage in
Aberdeen?

*I have so much to tell you, my dear daughter! Soon after I
returned to High Glen your brother-in-law Robert took over the
management of the estate. Sir George is now paying the interest
on my mortgages so I am in no position to argue. Robert asked
me to leave the big house and live in the old hunting lodge, for the
sake of economy. I confess I was not best pleased with the
arrangement but he insisted . . .*

A surge of impotent anger possessed Lizzie. How dare Robert
evict her mother from her home? Gritting her teeth, she read on.

*Then Mr York announced that he was leaving us. He has been
pastor at Heugh for fifteen years and he is my oldest friend. I
understood that after the tragic early death of his wife he felt the
need to go and live in a new place. But then the most astonishing
thing happened. My dear, I blush to tell you that he asked me to
marry him!! And I accepted!!!*
   So you see we are wed, and have moved to Aberdeen, from

*where I write. I know many will say I have married beneath
myself, but I know how worthless a title is. Indeed I am happier
now than I ever have been . . .*

'Good God!' Lizzie said aloud. She had never thought of her
mother remarrying. There was no reason why not, of course:
Mother was only forty. What shocked Lizzie was a sense of being
cast adrift. She had always been the centre of her mother's life. But
now her mother was a minister's wife living in Aberdeen. It meant
Lizzie had no home but this plantation, no family but Jay.

She put her letter in a drawer, got her coat and went outside. The
air was cool. It was now mid-October: they had been here two
months. She headed across the lawn and down towards the river. She
went on foot: she was past six months now, and she was afraid she
might harm the baby if she rode.

She walked round the estate almost every day. She was usually
accompanied by Roy and Rex, two deerhounds Jay had bought. She
kept a close eye on the work of the plantation, for Jay took no interest at all. Today was Sunday, the hands' day of rest, and it gave her
an opportunity to poke around while Sowerby and Lennox were
elsewhere. Roy followed her, but Rex lazily remained on the porch.

The tobacco harvest was in. There was still a lot of work to do
processing the crop, but the hands should have some reward, she
thought, for all their effort. It occurred to her that she might give
them a party. Jay might be against it, but he would not be home for
a couple of weeks—Williamsburg was three days away—so it could
be over by the time he returned.

She walked along the bank of the Rappahannock River, turning
the idea over in her mind. The river was shallow and rocky here,
upstream from Fredericksburg. She skirted a clump of half-sub-
merged bushes and stopped suddenly. A man was standing waist-
deep in the water, washing, his broad back to her. It was McAsh.

Roy bristled, then recognised Mack.

Lizzie had seen him naked in a river once before, almost a year
ago. She remembered drying his skin with her petticoat. Now, as she
watched the water roll off Mack's skin, she thought that, despite all
he had been through, he still had the powerful grace of a young animal. As he pulled on his breeches Roy loped up to him. Mack looked
up, saw Lizzie and froze, startled. Then he said: 'You might turn
your back.'

'You might turn yours!' she replied.

'I was here first.'

'I own the place!' she snapped.

110

Mack seemed amused now as he tied the string that held up his breeches. 'You own me, too,' he said.

She was looking at his chest. He was getting his muscles back. 'And I've seen you naked before.'

Suddenly the tension was gone and they were laughing.

'I'm going to give a party for the field hands,' she said. 'What kind of party would they like?'

He looked thoughtful. 'You could have a bonfire in the back yard. What the hands would like most of all would be a good meal, with plenty of meat. They never get enough to eat.'

'What do they like to drink?'

'Rum. But if I were you I'd give them apple cider, or beer. How about some music? The Negroes love to dance and sing.'

Lizzie was enjoying herself. It was fun planning a party with Mack. 'All right—but who would play?'

'There's a free black called Pepper Jones who performs in the taverns in Fredericksburg. You could hire him. He plays the banjo.'

'How do you know about this man? When have you been to Fredericksburg?'

A shadow crossed his face. 'I went once on a Sunday to look for Cora.'

'Did you find her?'

'No.' He turned away, looking sad.

'I'm sorry.' She wanted to put her arms round him and comfort him, but she restrained herself. To hide her feelings she changed the subject. 'I'd better talk to Bill Sowerby about this party.'

'You haven't heard? Bill Sowerby has left.'

'Left? What do you mean?'

'He disappeared two nights ago.'

Lizzie realised she had not seen Sowerby for a couple of days. 'Did he say when he was coming back?'

'I don't know that he talked to anyone directly, but I'd say he isn't coming back at all.'

'Why?'

'He owes a lot of money to Sidney Lennox and he can't pay.'

Lizzie felt indignant. 'And I suppose Lennox has been acting as overseer ever since.'

'It's only been one day . . . but yes, he has.'

'I don't want that brute taking over the plantation!' she said hotly.

'Amen to that,' Mack said. 'None of the hands wants it either.'

Lizzie frowned suspiciously. Sowerby was owed a lot in wages. Jay had told him he would be paid when the first tobacco crop was sold. Why had he not simply waited? He must have been frightened. 'I

111

believe Lennox has forced Sowerby out,' she said.

Mack nodded. 'That's my guess too.'

'I'm going to speak to him right away,' Lizzie said. Lennox had a small house down by the tobacco sheds. 'I hope he's at home.'

'He's not there now. At this time on a Sunday he'll be at the Ferry House—that's a tavern three or four miles upriver.'

Lizzie could not bear to postpone the confrontation. 'Will you come with me?' she said. 'I'd feel safer if you were there.'

'Of course.'

'You can drive the pony trap.'

They walked up from the river to the house. The stableboy, Jimmy, was watering the horses. Mack and he got the trap out and put a pony in the traces while Lizzie went into the house to put on a hat.

They drove out of the estate and followed the road upstream to the ferry crossing. The Ferry House was a wood-frame building not much bigger than the two-room houses lived in by Sowerby and Lennox. It was gloomy and smoky inside. Ten or twelve people sat drinking and playing dice. There were no women and no blacks.

Mack followed Lizzie into the room but stood back, by the door, his face in shadow.

A man came in from a back room, wiping his hands on a towel, and said: 'What can I bring you, sir—oh! A lady!'

'Nothing, thank you,' Lizzie said in a clear voice, and the room went quiet. She looked round at the upturned faces. Lennox was in the corner, bent over a shaker and a pair of dice. On the little table in front of him he had several piles of small coins.

He carefully scooped up his coins before he stood up slowly and took off his hat. 'What are you doing here, Mrs Jamisson?'

'I didn't come to play dice, obviously,' she said crisply. 'Where is Mr Sowerby?'

She heard one or two approving murmurs, as if others in the place would like to know what had happened to Sowerby; and she saw a grey-haired man turn in his chair and look at her.

'He's run off, it seems,' Lennox answered.

'Why did he leave?'

'How should I know?'

The grey-haired man piped up: 'He owed Lennox money.'

She turned back to Lennox. 'Why did he borrow money from you?'

'He didn't, exactly. He lost it to me.'

'Gambling?'

'Yes.'

'And did you threaten him?'

'I asked for my money,' Lennox said coolly.

'I believe he was frightened of you.'

A nasty smile crossed Lennox's face. 'Many people are,' he said, and the threat in his voice was hardly veiled.

Lizzie felt scared as well as angry. 'Let's get something clear,' she said. There was a tremor in her voice and she swallowed to get it under control. 'I am the mistress of the plantation and I shall take charge of the place until my husband returns. Then he will decide how to replace Mr Sowerby.'

Lennox shook his head. 'Oh, no,' he said. 'I'm Sowerby's deputy. Mr Jamisson has told me that I'm in charge if Sowerby should fall ill or anything, and I take my orders from him.'

Lizzie could have screamed with frustration. 'I'm warning you, Lennox, you'd better obey me!'

'And if I don't?' He took a step towards her, grinning. 'What will you do, Mrs Jamisson? Knock me down?' As he said this he lifted his hand over his head, in a gesture that might have been an illustration of what he was saying, but could just as easily have been a threat.

Lizzie gave a cry of fear and jumped back. Suddenly Mack was there, standing between Lennox and her. 'You've raised your hand to a woman, Lennox,' he said. 'Now let's see you raise it to a man.'

'You!' Lennox said. 'I didn't know it was you in the corner.'

'And now that you know, what are you going to do?'

'I didn't come here to argue. I came to play dice.' Lennox turned and went back to his table.

Lizzie felt as angry and frustrated as she had when she arrived. 'Let's go,' she said to Mack, and went out.

SHE HAD TO KNOW more about tobacco growing, she decided, when she calmed down. The only way she could defeat Lennox was by persuading Jay that she would do a better job.

Next day she got out the pony and trap and went over to Colonel Thumson's place. As she drove through his plantation she was struck by how prosperous it looked. There were rows of hogsheads on the jetty; the slaves looked active and fit; the sheds were painted and the fields were neat. She saw the colonel across a meadow, talking to a small group of hands. Jay never spent any time in the fields.

Mrs Thumson was a fat and kindly woman past fifty. She poured tea and chatted to Lizzie about the pregnancy until the colonel came in for tea. Colonel Thumson was in his fifties, tall and white-haired, and vigorous for his age. Remembering the party, he shook her hand stiffly but she softened him with a smile and a compliment. 'Why does your plantation look so much more impressive than anyone else's?'

'Well, it's kind of you to say so,' he replied. 'I'd say the main factor is that I'm here. Bill Delahaye is always going away to horse races and Roderick Armstead spends every afternoon at the Ferry House.'

'Why do your slaves look so energetic?'

'Now, that depends on what you feed them.' He was obviously enjoying sharing his expertise with this attractive young woman. 'They can live on hominy and corn pone, but they'll work better if you give them salt fish every day and meat once a week.'

'Why have so many plantations gone bankrupt recently?'

'You have to understand the tobacco plant. It exhausts the soil. After four or five years the quality deteriorates. You have to switch the field to wheat or Indian corn and find new land for your tobacco.'

'Why, you must be constantly clearing ground.'

'Indeed. Every winter I clear woodland for cultivation. There's woodland aplenty on your place. Why not start with Pond Copse? It's close to your curing sheds and the soil is right. Which reminds me.' He glanced at the clock. 'I have to visit my sheds before it gets dark.'

Lizzie stood up. 'I must get back and speak to my overseer.'

Mrs Thumson said: 'Don't do too much now, Mrs Jamisson—remember your baby.'

Lizzie smiled. 'I'm going to take plenty of rest too, I promise.'

NEXT MORNING she sent Jimmy, the stableboy, to summon Lennox to her drawing room. She waited for him in a great carved chair that must have been brought from England a century before.

'We're going to clear Pond Copse ready for tobacco planting next spring,' she said, when he arrived. 'I want you to begin today.'

For once he was taken by surprise. 'Why?' he said.

'Tobacco farmers must clear new land every winter. It's the only way to maintain high yields.'

'There's nothing wrong with the old fields.'

'Tobacco cultivation exhausts the land.'

'Ah, yes,' he said. 'But we manure heavily.'

Thumson had not mentioned manuring. 'I don't know . . .'

Her hesitation was fatal. 'These things are best left to men,' he said. 'If you want to change you'll have to speak to Mr Jamisson.'

She hated to let Lennox win, even temporarily, but she would have to wait until Jay returned. She said: 'You can go now.'

He gave a little smile of victory and went out.

Lizzie forced herself to rest for the remainder of the day, but on the following morning she made her usual tour of the plantation. Some of the hands were sowing winter wheat in Stream Quarter.

Lizzie spotted Mack there, working alongside a young black woman. They crossed the ploughed field in a line, distributing the seed from heavy baskets. Lennox followed, hurrying the slower workers with a kick or a touch of the whip.

Lizzie turned away, but before she was out of earshot she heard a cry and turned back. The hand working next to Mack had collapsed. It was Bess, a girl about fifteen years old, tall and thin.

Lizzie hurried towards the prone figure, but Mack was nearer. He put down his basket and knelt beside Bess. He touched her forehead and her hands. 'I think she's just fainted,' he said.

Lennox came up and kicked the girl in the ribs with a heavily booted foot. Her body jerked but her eyes did not open.

Lizzie cried out: 'Stop it, don't kick her!'

'Lazy black bitch, I'll teach her a lesson,' Lennox said, and he brought the whip down on the back of the unconscious girl.

'Stop!' Lizzie cried.

As Lennox lifted the whip again Mack sprang to his feet. 'Your mistress told you to stop,' he said.

Lennox changed his grip and slashed Mack across the face.

Mack staggered and his hand flew to his face. A purplish weal appeared on his cheek and blood trickled between his lips.

Lennox raised his whip again, but the blow never fell. In a moment he was flat on the ground and Mack had the whip. He snapped it over his knee, then contemptuously threw it at Lennox.

Lizzie felt a surge of triumph. The bully was broken. 'Get on with your work, everyone!' she said. 'Can you carry Bess to the house?' she asked Mack.

'Of course.' He picked her up in his arms.

They walked back to the house and took the girl into the kitchen. By the time Mack put her down in a chair she had recovered consciousness. Lizzie sent Sarah, the cook, to fetch some of Jay's brandy. After a sip Bess declared she felt all right except for bruised ribs. Lizzie told her to have something to eat and rest until tomorrow.

Leaving the kitchen, Mack said: 'I shouldn't have humiliated Lennox. He's a vengeful man.'

'How can he take revenge on you?'

'Easily. He's the overseer.'

She frowned, thinking, then she was struck by an idea. 'I know what to do—you can work in the house.'

He smiled. 'I'd love to. I might not be much of a butler, though.'

'No, no—not as a servant. You could be in charge of repairs. I have to have the nursery painted and fixed up.'

He looked suspicious. 'Do you really mean it?'

'Of course! I'll feel safer with you close by, anyway.'

'It would be . . . just wonderful to get away from Lennox.'

'That's settled,' she said decisively. 'You can start straight away.'

THE HOUSE SLAVES were a little grumpy about the party at first. They looked down on the field hands. Sarah resented having to cook for 'trash that eats hominy and corn pone'. But Lizzie jollied them along, and in the end they entered into the spirit of it.

At sundown on Saturday the kitchen staff were cooking up a banquet and Pepper Jones had arrived with his banjo.

When darkness fell all was ready. Lizzie paced up and down impatiently, waiting for the slaves to come in from the fields. She hoped they would sing. She had sometimes heard them from a distance, singing plaintive laments or rhythmic work songs, but they always stopped when one of the masters came near.

As the moon rose, the old women came up from their quarters with the babies on their hips and the toddlers trailing behind. They did not know where the field hands were. Lizzie supposed they must have been working at the furthermost reaches of the plantation, and so were taking a long time to return.

When it had been dark for an hour she admitted to herself that something had gone wrong. With anger mounting in her breast she summoned Mack and said: 'Get Lennox up here.'

It took almost an hour, but eventually Mack returned with Lennox, who had obviously been drinking. 'Where are the field hands?' Lizzie demanded. 'They should be here!'

'Ah, yes,' Lennox said. 'That was not possible today. They've been cutting wood for barrels at Stafford Park.' Stafford Park was ten miles upriver. 'There's a few days' work to be done so we made camp. The hands will stay there, with Kobe, until we finish.'

He had done it to defy her. It was enough to make her scream. But until Jay came home there was nothing she could do. 'Get out of here, and stay out of my sight until my husband comes home.'

She felt tears spring to her eyes. Not wanting the staff to see her cry, she turned and ran into the house. As soon as she was alone in the drawing room she began to sob with frustration. After a minute she heard the door open. Mack's voice said: 'I'm sorry.'

His sympathy made her cry fresh tears. A moment later she felt his arms around her. It was deeply comforting. She laid her head on his shoulder and cried and cried. He stroked her hair and kissed her tears. Slowly her sobs became quieter and her grief eased.

Then she realised what she was doing. She was a married woman, six months pregnant, and she had let a servant kiss her! She pulled away in horror. 'What am I thinking about?' she said.

'You're not thinking,' he said.

'I am now,' she said. 'Go away!'

Looking sad, he turned and left the room.

THE NEXT DAY was Sunday, and Mack went into Fredericksburg wearing his new clothes. Pepper Jones, who had stayed in the slave quarters overnight, went with him, carrying his banjo.

Pepper was a thin, energetic man about fifty years old. Mack asked him: 'How did you come to be free?'

'Born free,' he replied. 'My ma was white, though it don't show. My daddy was a runaway, recaptured before I was born—I never saw him.'

'Is it right what Kobe says, that all runaways get caught?'

Pepper laughed. 'Hell, no. Most get caught, but most are stupid.'

'So, if you're not stupid . . .?'

He shrugged. 'It ain't easy. As soon as you run away, the master puts an advertisement in the newspaper, giving your description.'

'But you could keep out of sight.'

'Got to eat, though. That means you need a job, if you stay inside the colonies, and any man that's going to employ you has probably read about you in the newspaper.'

'What do you mean when you say "if you stay inside the colonies"?'

'West of here is the mountains, and on the other side of the mountains, the wilderness. No newspapers there. No sheriffs either.'

'Then surely a man could disappear over the mountains and never be found!'

'That's the truth. Also, he could be scalped by Indians and killed by mountain lions. More likely he could starve to death.'

'But some succeed?'

'Must do. Otherwise there wouldn't be no such place as America.'

'West of here, you said,' Mack mused. 'How far are the mountains?'

'About a hundred miles, they say.'

'So close!'

'It's further than you think.'

THE TOWN WAS BUSY: Sunday was the day the field hands from the plantations came in to go to church or get drunk or both. Mack and Pepper went to Whitey Jones's tavern. Whitey was so called because of his colouring, a mixture of black and white. Mack had no money, but Pepper had been paid and he bought Mack a quart of ale.

While they were drinking, Pepper said: 'Hey, Whitey, have you ever run into anyone who crossed the mountains?'

'Sure have,' Whitey said. 'There was a trapper in here one time, said there was the best hunting he ever saw over there.'

Mack said: 'Did he tell you what route he took?'

'Seems to me he said there was a pass called the Cumberland Gap.'

'Cumberland Gap,' Mack repeated.

Whitey said: 'Say, weren't you asking after a girl called Cora?'

Mack's heart leapt. 'Yes—have you heard tell of her?'

'Seen her—so I know why you're crazy for her.' He rolled his eyes. 'Down by the river. She was wearing a green coat and carrying a basket, and she was getting the ferry over to Falmouth.'

Mack smiled. The coat, and the fact that she was taking the ferry instead of wading across the ford, indicated that she had landed on her feet again. 'How did you know who she was?'

'The ferryman called her by name.'

Mack swallowed the rest of his beer. 'She must be living on the Falmouth side of the river. And I'm going to find her. Pepper, thanks for the beer.'

'Good luck!'

Fredericksburg had been built just below the fall line of the Rappahannock River, at the limit of navigation. Mack walked to the point where the water was shallow enough to wade across. He was full of excitement. Who had bought Cora? How was she living? And did she know what had become of Peg? If only he could locate the two of them, and fulfil his promise, he could make serious plans to escape. For the last three months he had been suppressing his yearning for freedom, but Pepper's talk of the wilderness beyond the mountains had brought it all back, and he longed to run away.

Falmouth was a smaller version of Fredericksburg: it had the same wharves, warehouses, taverns and painted wood-frame homes. He went into the first tavern he came across and spoke to the proprietor. 'I'm looking for a young woman called Cora Higgins.'

'Cora? She lives in the white house on the next corner.' The man took a watch from his waistcoat pocket and glanced at it. 'But she won't be there now, she'll be in church.'

'I've seen the church. I'll go there.'

Cora had never been a churchgoer, but perhaps her owner forced her to go, Mack thought as he walked towards the little wooden church.

The service had ended and the congregation were coming out, all in their Sunday best. Mack saw Cora right away.

He smiled broadly. The starved, filthy woman he had left on the *Rosebud* might have been a different person. Cora was her old self: clear skin, glossy hair, rounded figure. She was as well dressed as ever, in a dark brown coat and a wool skirt, and she wore good boots. She was talking animatedly to an old woman. She broke off her conversation as he approached her. 'Mack!' she said delightedly. 'This is a miracle!'

He opened his arms to embrace her but she held out a hand to shake. He took it and said: 'You look wonderful.'

'What happened to you?' she said, withdrawing her hand.

'I'm on the Jamisson plantation—Lennox is the overseer.'

'Did he hit your face?'

Mack touched the sore place where Lennox had slashed him. 'Yes, but I broke his whip. Have you any news of Peg?'

'She was taken off by the soul drivers, Bates and Makepiece.'

Mack's heart sank. 'Damn. It's going to be hard to find her. And who bought you? Somebody kind, by the look of you!'

As he spoke a plump, richly dressed man in his fifties came up. Cora said, 'Here he is, Alexander Rowley, the tobacco broker.'

Rowley shook hands with the old woman and said a word to her, then turned to Mack. Cora said, 'This is Malachi McAsh, an old friend of mine from London. Mack, this is Mr Rowley—my husband.'

Mack stared, speechless. Rowley put a proprietorial arm round Cora's shoulders and shook Mack's hand. 'How do you do, McAsh?' he said, and without another word he swept Cora away.

Why not? Mack thought as he trudged along the road back to the Jamisson plantation. Cora had obviously been bought by Rowley and had made him fall in love with her. Good for her. All the same he was disappointed. She had made him promise to search for her; but she had forgotten him as soon as she got the chance of an easy life.

Chapter 9

Jay went to Williamsburg with high hopes that in the colonial capital he would find men loyal to the king who would welcome a valuable political ally.

Williamsburg was small but grand. The main street, Duke of Gloucester Street, was a mile long and a hundred feet broad. The Capitol was at one end and the College of William and Mary at the other—two stately brick buildings built in the English style. There was a theatre and several shops, and plenty of inns with rooms to let.

Jay moved into the Raleigh Tavern, a low white clapboard building with bedrooms in the attic.

He left his card at the palace, but he had to wait three days for an appointment with the new governor, Lord de Botetourt. When finally he got his invitation it was a reception with fifty other guests. Clearly the governor had yet to realise that Jay was an important ally.

Unfortunately Botetourt was the very opposite of what Jay had hoped for. Virginia needed a tough governor who would strike fear into the hearts of mutinous colonists, but Botetourt turned out to be a fat, friendly man with the air of a prosperous wine merchant.

Jay watched him greeting his guests in the long ballroom. Bill Delahaye was there, and shook hands with Jay. 'What do you think of our new governor?'

'I'm not sure he realises what he's taken on,' Jay said.

Delahaye said, 'He may be cleverer than he looks.'

'I hope so.'

'There's a big card game tomorrow night, Jamisson—would you like me to introduce you?'

Jay had not spent an evening gambling since he left London. 'Certainly.'

He did not get Botetourt to himself until the end of the party, when the guests were leaving. He took the governor's sleeve and said in a low voice: 'I want you to know that I'm completely loyal to you and the Crown. Whenever you're ready to stamp out treachery and crush disloyal opposition, I'm on your side.'

Botetourt looked hard at him and Jay perceived that there was a shrewd politician behind the affable exterior. 'How kind—but let's hope that not too much stamping and crushing will be required. I find that persuasion and negotiation are so much better—the effects last longer. Major Wilkinson—goodbye! Mrs Wilkinson—so good of you to come.'

Persuasion and negotiation, Jay thought as he passed out into the garden. Botetourt had fallen into a nest of vipers and he wanted to negotiate with them. Jay said to Delahaye: 'I wonder how long it will take him to grasp the realities out here.'

'I think he understands already,' Delahaye said. 'He just doesn't believe in baring his teeth before he's ready to bite.'

Sure enough, next day the amiable new governor dissolved the General Assembly.

MATTHEW MURCHMAN was a small, nervous grey squirrel of a man. He lived and did business in a green-painted clapboard house on Duke of Gloucester Street.

Jay signed the papers mortgaging the plantation. He was disappointed at the amount of the loan: only four hundred pounds.

'I was lucky to get so much,' Murchman twittered, 'what with tobacco doing so badly.'

'Who is the lender?' asked Jay.

'A syndicate, Captain Jamisson. That's how these things work nowadays. Are there any liabilities you would like me to settle?'

Jay had brought bills for all the debts he had run up in Virginia. Murchman glanced through them and said: 'About a hundred pounds here. I'll give you notes for all these before you leave town. And let me know if you buy anything while you're here.'

'I probably will,' Jay said. 'A Mr Smythe is selling a carriage with a beautiful pair of grey horses. And I need two or three slaves.'

'I'll let it be known that you're in funds with me.'

'And let me have a hundred pounds in gold,' Jay said. 'There's a card game at the Raleigh tonight.'

'Certainly, Captain Jamisson. It's your money!'

THERE WAS NOT MUCH left of the four hundred pounds when Jay arrived back at the plantation. He had lost at cards, he had bought four slave girls, and he had failed to beat down Mr Smythe's price for the carriage and horses. However, his first tobacco crop would soon be ready for sale, and he would pay his future bills from the proceeds.

He was apprehensive of what Lizzie might say about the carriage, but she hardly mentioned it. She obviously had something else on her mind that she was bursting to tell him. As soon as he had kissed her she said: 'Bill Sowerby has left.'

'Really? Good thing we've got Lennox to take over.'

'I think Lennox drove him away. Apparently Sowerby had lost a lot of money to him at cards.'

That made sense. 'Lennox is a good card player.'

They were standing on the front portico, and at that moment Lennox came round the side of the house. 'There's a consignment of salt cod in barrels just arrived,' he said.

'It's for the field hands,' Lizzie said. 'Colonel Thumson says they work better when they're well fed. He gives his slaves salt fish every day and meat once a week.'

'Thumson is richer than I am. Send it back, Lennox.'

'They're going to have to work hard this winter,' Lizzie protested. 'We have to clear all the woodland in Pond Copse ready for planting with tobacco next spring.'

Lennox said quickly: 'That isn't necessary. There's plenty of life left in the fields, with good manuring.'

Lizzie snapped: 'Leave us, please, Mr Lennox—immediately.'

Lennox looked angry but he went away.

'You must get rid of him, Jay,' she said.

'I don't see why—'

'It's not just that he's brutal. He doesn't know anything about tobacco—and the worst of it is he's not interested in learning.'

'But who would take over?'

'We could do it together.'

'I don't want to be a farmer!'

'Then let me do it.'

Jay nodded. 'All this is just so that you can be in charge, isn't it?'

He was afraid she would explode, but instead she went quiet. 'If that's what you think of me, that I just want to order people around, why did you marry me?'

'In those days you used to be pretty,' he said.

Her eyes flashed fire, but she did not speak. Instead she turned round and walked into the house.

After a moment he followed her. He was surprised to see McAsh in the hall, dressed in a waistcoat and indoor shoes, putting a new pane of glass in a window. He found Lizzie in the drawing room. 'I just saw McAsh in the hall,' he said.

'I've put him in charge of maintenance.'

'I don't want that man in my house.'

Her reaction took him by surprise. 'Then you'll just have to suffer it!' she blazed. 'If McAsh goes, I go too! I will not be alone here while Lennox is on the estate.' She stormed out of the room.

'All right!' he said to the door as it slammed. He was not going to fight a war over one damned convict.

IN THE OLD NURSERY wing Mack found a map.

He had redecorated two of the three rooms and he was clearing out the schoolroom. There was a chest full of mouldy books and the map was there, carefully folded in a leather case. It was a map of Virginia.

He pored over it, fascinated and thrilled: this was his passport to freedom. He discovered that the Rappahannock was one of several rivers running across Virginia from the mountains in the west to the Bay of Chesapeake in the east. He found Fredericksburg on the south bank of the Rappahannock. There was no way to tell distances, but Pepper Jones had said it was a hundred miles to the mountains. If the map was right, it was the same distance again to the other side of the range. Far to the south was what looked like a pass, where the Cumberland River rose. He remembered Whitey

122

A Place Called Freedom

talking about the Cumberland Gap. That was it: that was the way
out. On the far side of those mountains a man could be free.
He folded the map carefully and restored it to its case. If only he
could find Peg, he thought as he swept the room. He had to know
whether she was all right before he ran away.
When it became too dark to work he left the nursery and went
downstairs. He took his old fur cloak off a hook by the back door
and wrapped it around him: it was cold outside. As he went out a
knot of excited slaves came towards him. In the middle of the group
was Kobe, and he was carrying Bess, the slave girl who had fainted a
few weeks ago. Her eyes were closed and there was blood on her
smock.
Mack held the door open, then followed Kobe inside.
'Put her in the drawing room and I'll fetch Mrs Jamisson,' he said.
'The drawing room?' Kobe asked dubiously.
It was the only room where the fire was lit, apart from the dining
room. 'Trust me—it's what Mrs Jamisson would prefer.'
Kobe nodded.
Mack knocked on the dining-room door and entered. Lizzie and
Jay were eating at a small round table in front of a blazing fire. Mack
addressed Lizzie. 'Bess has had an accident—Kobe's put her in the
drawing room.'
'I'll come at once,' Lizzie said, pushing back her chair.
Jay said: 'Don't let her bleed on that yellow silk upholstery!'
Mack held the door and followed Lizzie out.
Lizzie bent over the injured girl. Bess's dark skin had gone paler
and her breathing seemed shallow. 'What happened?' asked Lizzie.
'She cut herself,' Kobe answered. 'She was hacking at a rope with
a machete. The blade slipped off the rope and sliced her belly.'
Lizzie enlarged the tear in Bess's smock and gazed at the wound
beneath. It looked bad. There was a lot of blood and the cut seemed
deep. 'Go to the kitchen, one of you, and get me some clean rags and
a bowl of warm water.'
Mack admired her decisiveness. 'I'll do it,' he said.
A few moments later he was back. Lizzie dipped a rag in the water
and washed the skin. As the wound became more clearly visible it
looked worse. 'I can't deal with this,' Lizzie said. 'She needs a doctor.'
Jay came into the room, took one look and paled.
Lizzie said to him: 'I'll have to send for Dr Finch.'
'As you wish,' he said. 'I'm going to the Ferry House.'
Lizzie looked at Kobe and Mack. 'One of you has to ride into
Fredericksburg in the dark.'
Kobe said: 'Mack ain't much of a horseman. I'll go.'

123

FREDERICKSBURG WAS ten miles away, but Kobe knew the road and he was back two hours later.

When he walked into the drawing room his face was like thunder. 'Dr Finch won't come out at this time of night for no nigger girl,' he said in a shaky voice.

'Curse the damn fool,' Lizzie said furiously.

They all looked at Bess. Her skin was beaded with perspiration and her breathing had become ragged. She was obviously dying.

'If the doctor won't come, we'll just have to take her to him,' Lizzie said. 'Kobe, take the mattress from my bed and put it in the back of the buggy for her to lie on. And some blankets.'

Mack hurried to the stables and put Stripe, the pony, in the traces. He got a taper from the kitchen fire and lit the carriage lamps on the buggy. When he pulled round to the front Kobe was waiting.

While Kobe arranged the bedding Mack went into the house. Lizzie was putting her coat on. 'Do you think you should, in your condition?' Mack asked.

'I'm afraid that doctor will refuse to treat her if I don't.'

Mack picked Bess up gently and carried her outside. He laid her on the mattress and Kobe covered her with the blankets. Lizzie climbed up and settled herself beside Bess, cradling the girl's head in her arms. Mack got up in front and picked up the reins.

The trail was rocky and rutted, and the buggy bounced along. Mack was worried about jolting Bess, but Lizzie kept saying: 'Go faster! Go faster!'

They reached Fredericksburg and drew up outside Dr Finch's home. Lizzie went to the door while Mack wrapped Bess in the blankets and carefully lifted her up. She was unconscious.

The door was opened by Mrs Finch, a mousy woman in her forties. She showed Lizzie into the parlour and Mack followed with Bess. The doctor, a thickset man with a bullying manner, looked distinctly guilty when he realised he had forced a pregnant woman to drive through the night to bring him a patient. When he had looked at Bess's wound he asked Lizzie to make herself comfortable in the other room. Mack went with her and Mrs Finch stayed to help her husband.

Lizzie eased herself very gingerly into a chair. 'What's the matter?' Mack said.

'That ride has given me the most awful backache. Do you think Bess will be all right?'

'I don't know. She's not very robust.'

At last Dr Finch came in, drying his hands. 'It's a nasty wound but she's young and she will heal,' he said.

124

'Thank goodness,' Lizzie said.

The doctor nodded. 'She shouldn't travel far tonight. She can sleep here in my maid's quarters, and you can send for her tomorrow or the day after. When the wound closes I'll take out the stitches. She should do no heavy work until then.'

'Of course.'

A few minutes later she and Mack were on their way. This time he drove slowly, glancing behind him from time to time to where Lizzie lay sleeping on the mattress. She was restless, shifting her position and muttering in her sleep.

They were driving along a deserted stretch when the stillness of the night was shattered by a scream.

It was Lizzie. Mack frantically hauled on the reins. Before the pony had stopped he was clambering into the back. He put his arm round her shoulders and raised her a little.

'Oh, Mack, it hurts!' she cried. 'I think the baby is coming.'

'But it's not due . . .'

'Another two months.'

Mack knew little about such things but he guessed that the birth had been brought on by the bumpy ride to Fredericksburg.

'How long have we got?'

She groaned long and loud, then answered him. 'Not long. My waters broke, I think.'

When the pain passed she shivered. Mack covered her with his fur. 'You can have your cloak back,' he said, and she smiled briefly before the next spasm took her.

When she could speak again she said: 'You must take the baby when it comes out.'

'All right,' he said, but he was not sure what she meant. He knelt at her feet and pushed up her skirts. Lizzie lifted her legs and put her feet up against his shoulders to brace herself.

The baby came very quickly. Lizzie gave a mighty groan and Mack felt a warm, slippery object pushing its way out. A moment later the baby's head was in his hands. Lizzie seemed to rest for a few moments, then start again. He held the head with one hand and put the other under the tiny shoulders as they came into the world. A moment later the rest of the baby slid out.

He held it and stared at it: the closed eyes, the dark hair of its head, the miniature limbs. 'It's a girl,' he said.

'She must cry!' Lizzie said urgently.

Mack had heard of smacking a newborn baby to make it breathe. It was hard to do, but he turned her over in his hand and gave her bottom a sharp slap. Nothing happened.

As he held the tiny chest in his big hand he realised there was something dreadfully wrong. He could not feel a heartbeat.

Lizzie struggled to sit upright. 'Give her to me!' she said. She put her lips to the baby's and blew into her mouth. Mack willed the child to gasp air into her lungs, but nothing happened.

'She's dead,' Lizzie said. She held the baby to her bosom and drew her cloak round the naked body. 'My baby's dead.' She began to weep.

Mack put his arms round them both and held them while Lizzie cried her heart out.

AFTER HER BABY girl was born dead, Lizzie lived in a world of grey colours, silent people, rain and mist. She let the household staff do as they pleased, realising vaguely that Mack had taken charge of them. She left the tobacco fields to Lennox. Sometimes she visited Mrs Thumson or Suzy Delahaye, for they were willing to talk about the baby as long as she liked.

She was quite sure it was all her fault. She had not rested as much as she should; and she had ridden ten miles in the buggy, urging Mack to go faster and faster, on the night the baby was stillborn.

She could not talk to Jay about it. At first he had been angry. He had railed at Lizzie, vowed to shoot Dr Finch and threatened to have Mack flogged; but his rage had evaporated when he learned the baby had been a girl, and now he acted as if she had never been pregnant.

One day, three months after the birth, she went to the nursery wing, still gleaming with fresh paint, and sat alone. She imagined a little girl there in a cradle, gurgling happily or crying to be fed. The vision was so intense that tears rolled down her face.

Mack came in while she was like that. 'This will not do you any good,' he said in a hard voice.

'I expected more sympathy from you,' she said miserably.

'Don't be so damned pathetic, Lizzie—it's not your nature.'

She was shocked. No one had spoken unkindly to her since the stillbirth. 'You have no right to talk to me like that.'

He surprised her then by grabbing her by both arms and pulling her up out of her chair. 'Don't tell me about my rights,' he said.

She was afraid he would do violence to her, but he put her down. 'What am I supposed to do?' she said.

'Anything you like. Get a ship back home and go and live with your mother in Aberdeen. Run away to the frontier with some ne'er-do-well.' He paused and looked hard at her. 'Or make up your mind to be a wife to Jay, and have another baby.'

That surprised her. 'I thought . . .'

'What did you think?'

'Nothing.' She had known for some time that he was at least half in love with her. After the failed party for the field hands he had touched her tenderly, in a way that could only be loving. And there was more in her response than the need for sympathy. But all those feelings had faded since the baby. She had no passions, just regrets.

She felt ashamed and embarrassed to have had such desires. Jay was her husband. He was weak and foolish, and he had lied to her, but she had married him and she had to be faithful to him.

Mack was still staring at her. She wondered what was going through his mind. She thought he was referring to himself when he said *Run away to the frontier with some ne'er-do-well.*

He reached out tentatively and stroked her cheek. There was yearning in his green eyes. Lizzie hardened her heart. A sudden impulse seized her and she slapped his face as hard as she could.

It was like slapping a rock. He did not move. But his expression changed. He looked so shocked and dismayed that she had to resist an urge to apologise and embrace him. In a shaky voice she said: 'Don't you dare touch me!'

She could not look at his hurt expression any longer, so she stood up and walked out of the room.

HE HAD SAID *Make up your mind to be a wife to Jay, and have another baby.* The idea of having Jay in her bed had become unpleasant to her, but it was her duty. That evening after the meal was over she said: 'It's been three months since the baby. I'm all right now.'

'What do you mean?'

'My body is back to normal. I mean, I've healed.'

He still did not understand. 'Why are you telling me this?'

Trying to keep the exasperation out of her voice, she said: 'We can make love again, that's what I'm saying. Will you come to my room tonight?'

He looked annoyed. 'It's the man who's supposed to make these suggestions,' he said irritably.

Feeling hurt, she went up to her room. Her maid Mildred came to help her undress. As she took off her petticoats Lizzie said, in a voice as casual as she could manage: 'Has Mr Jamisson gone to bed?'

'No, I think he went out.'

Lizzie looked at the maid's face. There was something puzzling in her expression. 'Mildred, are you hiding something from me?'

Mildred was young—about eighteen—and she had no talent for deceit. She averted her eyes. 'No, Mrs Jamisson.'

Lizzie was sure she was lying. But why? Did her husband have another woman?

A week later he still had not come to her room.

She became obsessed with the idea that he was having an affair. The only person she could think of was Suzy Delahaye, she was young and pretty, and her husband was always away from home, at the races. On the seventh night she looked out of her bedroom window and saw the flicker of a candle lamp moving across the dark lawn. She decided to follow. She drew a shawl around her shoulders and ran down the stairs.

She slipped out of the house and ran across the grass. Soon the light disappeared into the woods, but by then she was close enough to discern that Jay, if it was he, had taken the path that led to the overseer's quarters.

There were two cottages. Lennox occupied one. The other had been Sowerby's and was now vacant. But there was someone in it now. The windows were shuttered but light shone through the cracks. Lizzie tried the door. It was not locked. She opened it and went inside.

The house had two rooms. The kitchen, at the front, was empty, but she could hear a low voice coming from the bedroom at the back. She tiptoed to the door, took a deep breath and flung it open.

Jay lay on the bed in his shirt and breeches. At the end of the bed stood the slave called Felia. She was one of the four Jay had bought in Williamsburg. She was slim and very beautiful, with soft brown eyes, and she was completely naked. As Lizzie stared, the girl threw her a haughty, triumphant look. You may be the mistress of the house, it said, but he comes to my bed every night, not yours.

Jay spoke as if from a great distance: 'Lizzie, oh my God!'

She turned her face to him and saw him flinch at her look. 'Go to hell, Jay,' she said quietly, then she turned and left the room.

SHE WENT TO HER ROOM, got her keys from the drawer, then went down to the gun room. In the rack with Jay's guns were a pair of pocket pistols in a leather case. Checking the case, she found a full powder horn, plenty of linen wadding, some spare flints and a box of lead shot. Then she went to her bedroom and locked the door. When she had loaded both pistols and placed them on her bedside table she went to bed.

AT FIRST MACK HATED Lizzie for that slap. Every time he thought of it he felt enraged. But on reflection he realised that she was at the mercy of conflicting emotions. She was attracted to him, but she was married to someone else. She had a well-developed sense of duty, and in desperation she had tried to put an end to the dilemma by quarrelling with him.

128

He had longed to tell her that her loyalty to Jay was misplaced. All the slaves had known for months that Jay was spending his nights in a cottage with Felia, a beautiful and willing girl from Senegal. But he had felt sure Lizzie would soon find out for herself, and sure enough she had, two nights ago. How would it all end?

Mack was lying restlessly in his bed before daybreak, turning these things over in his mind, when he heard a horse whinny softly outside. Frowning, he slipped off his bunk and went to the cabin door in his breeches and shirt. Dawn was breaking and he could see two women entering the compound, one leading a pony.

A moment later he recognised the taller woman as Cora. Then he recognised the other one. 'Peg!' he cried delightedly.

She saw him and came running to him. She had grown up, he thought as she threw herself into his arms. 'Mack!' she said. 'Oh, Mack, I've been so frightened!'

'I thought I'd never see you again,' he said. 'What happened?'

Cora answered his question. 'She's in trouble. She was bought by a hill farmer called Burgo Marler. He tried to rape her and she stabbed him to death with a kitchen knife. Now every sheriff in the colony is looking for her.'

Mack was aghast. If Peg were caught she would certainly be hanged. 'How did you get to Fredericksburg?' he asked her.

'Walked,' she said. 'I travelled in the dark and got directions from people who are out at night—slaves, runaways, army deserters.'

Cora said: 'I hid her in my house for a few days—my husband's in Williamsburg on business. But then I heard that the local sheriff was about to raid everyone who was on the *Rosebud.*'

'But that means he'll come here!' Mack said.

'Yes—he's not far behind me, with a search party.'

'So why did you bring her here?'

Cora's face hardened. 'Because she's your problem. I've got a rich husband and a nice house and my own pew in the church, and I don't want the sheriff to find a murderer in my damn stable loft!'

Mack stared at her in dismay. 'By God, you're hardhearted,' he said angrily.

'I saved her, didn't I?' Cora said. 'Now I've got to save myself!'

Peg said: 'Thank you for everything, Cora. You did save me.'

Kobe had come out and was watching the proceedings silently. Now Mack turned to him. 'Where could she hide? They'll search every inch of the quarters, the stables, the tobacco sheds . . .'

Cora said: 'Would Lizzie Jamisson hide Peg—for your sake?'

He was not sure. 'She might do it out of kindness,' he said.

They heard dogs barking. It sounded like the deerhounds on the porch of the big house. What had disquieted them? Then there was an answering bark from down by the river.

'Strange dogs in the neighbourhood,' Kobe said. 'Could it be the search party already?'

Cora turned away and mounted her pony. 'I'm getting out of here before I'm seen.' She walked the pony out of the compound. 'Good luck,' she called softly. Then she disappeared into the woods.

Mack turned to Peg. 'Come with me to the house. It's our best chance.'

They hurried through the cold fields and across the damp lawns in the grey light. He led her in through the back entrance. They crept up the stairs. Mack looked out of the landing window and saw five or six men and some dogs coming up from the direction of the river. The party split: two men headed for the house and the rest turned towards the slave quarters with the dogs.

Mack went to Lizzie's bedroom and tapped gently, fearful of waking Jay in the next room.

Nothing happened. He tapped harder.

He heard soft footsteps, then Lizzie's voice: 'Who's there?'

'Hush! It's Mack!' he whispered. 'Open the door!'

He heard a key turn, and the door opened. In the pale light he saw her, wearing a dressing gown, looking deliciously tousled. 'Explain yourself, fast,' she said. Then she saw Peg. 'You're not alone.'

'Peg Knapp,' he said.

'I remember,' Lizzie said. 'How are you, Peggy?'

'I'm in trouble again,' Peg said.

Mack explained. 'She killed a man who tried to rape her.'

'Oh, dear God,' Lizzie said. She put her arms round Peg, drawing her inside the room. 'You poor child.'

'The sheriff is looking for her. He's outside now, searching the slave quarters.'

Lizzie said: 'You just leave the sheriff to me. I'll explain that Peg was defending herself against rape.'

Mack shook his head impatiently. 'That's no good, Lizzie. The sheriff will say that the court has to decide whether she's guilty, not you, and no Virginian court is going to acquit a convict who kills her owner. They're all terrified of being attacked by their slaves.'

Lizzie bit her lip. 'What do you think we should do?'

One of the dogs growled outside, and Mack heard the voice of a man calming it. 'I want you to hide Peg in here while they search the place. Will you do it?' If you say no, he thought, I'm in love with the wrong woman.

'Of course I'll do it,' she said. 'What do you think I am?'

130

He smiled happily, flooded with relief. Then he heard a sound from Jay's bedroom. 'I must get out of here,' he said. 'Good luck!'

He stepped across the landing and ran downstairs. When he reached the hall he pasted a smile on his face and opened the door.

Two men were on the porch. They wore the dress of prosperous Virginians: riding boots, long waistcoats and three-cornered hats. Both carried pistols with shoulder straps.

Mack stood squarely in the doorway to discourage them from entering. 'Good morning, gentlemen,' he said. 'This looks like a search party.'

The taller of the two said: 'I'm the sheriff of Spotsylvania County, and I'm looking for a girl by the name of Peggy Knapp. Is your master at home?'

'Yes.'

'Take us to him.'

Mack stood aside and let them into the hall. 'I believe I heard Mr Jamisson moving around,' he said. 'Shall I ask him to come down?'

'No—I don't want to put him to the trouble of getting dressed.'

Mack cursed under his breath. He said: 'This way, please,' and led them up the stairs.

He knocked on Jay's door. Jay opened it, wearing a wrap over his nightshirt. 'What the devil is all this?' he said irritably.

'I'm Sheriff Abraham Barton, Mr Jamisson. I apologise for disturbing you, but we're searching for the murderer of Burgo Marler. Does the name Peggy Knapp mean anything to you?'

'It certainly does. The girl was always a thief and I'm not surprised she's turned into a killer. Have you asked McAsh here if he knows where she is?'

Barton looked at Mack in surprise. 'So you're McAsh! When did you last see Peggy Knapp?'

'When I disembarked from the *Rosebud* half a year ago.'

The sheriff turned back to Jay. 'The niggers may be concealing her. We've brought dogs.'

Jay waved a generous hand. 'Do whatever you need to.'

'We should search the house, too.'

Jay hesitated, and Mack hoped he would tell the sheriff to go to hell. But after a moment he shrugged and said: 'Of course. Search everywhere, by all means. I'll leave you to it.' He closed his door.

Barton said to Mack: 'Which is Mrs Jamisson's room?'

Mack swallowed. 'Next door.' He stepped along the landing and knocked gently. 'Mrs Jamisson? Are you awake?'

There was a pause, then Lizzie opened the door. Feigning sleepiness, she said: 'What on earth do you want at this hour?'

'The sheriff is looking for a fugitive.'

Lizzie opened the door wide. 'Well, I haven't got one in here.'

Barton said: 'May we step inside for a moment?'

There was an almost imperceptible flash of fear in Lizzie's eyes. But she shrugged with a semblance of apathy and said: 'Feel free.'

The two men stepped inside. The sheriff looked under the bed while his assistant opened the wardrobe. Lizzie sat on the bed. With a hasty gesture she picked up a corner of the bedspread and tugged it. Mack glimpsed a small, dirty foot before it was covered up.

Peg was in the bed. She was so thin that she hardly made a bulge in the piled-up covers.

The sheriff opened a blanket chest and the other man looked behind a screen. Would they pull the covers off the bed?

The same thought must have gone through Lizzie's mind, for she got into bed saying: 'Now, if you're done, I'm going back to sleep.'

Barton looked hard at Lizzie and the bed. Did he have the nerve to demand that she get out again? After a moment's hesitation he said, 'Thank you, Mrs Jamisson. We're sorry to have disturbed your rest. We'll carry on and search the slave quarters.'

'Good luck,' Lizzie said. 'And, Sheriff—when you've finished your work, bring your men back here and have some breakfast!'

LIZZIE STAYED in her room while the men and dogs searched the plantation. At the usual time Sarah, the cook, came in with Lizzie's breakfast on a tray. Peg hid under the bedclothes, but the woman said to Lizzie: 'I know all about Peggy, so don't you worry.'

Peg came out again and Lizzie said bemusedly: 'Who doesn't know?'

'Mr Jamisson and Mr Lennox.'

Lizzie shared her breakfast with Peg. The child shovelled down grilled ham and scrambled eggs as if she had not eaten for a month.

The search party left as she was finishing. Lizzie and Peg went to the window and watched the men cross the lawn and make their way down to the river. They watched the men out of sight, then Lizzie sighed and said: 'You're safe.'

They hugged happily. Peg was painfully bony, and Lizzie felt a surge of maternal feeling for the poor child. 'You'll have to stay in this room until we're sure Jay and Lennox are out of the way.'

'Aren't you worried that Mr Jamisson will come in?' Peg asked.

'No, he never comes in here.'

Peg looked puzzled but she did not ask any more questions. Instead she said: 'When I'm older I'm going to marry Mack.'

Lizzie had the strangest feeling that she was being warned off.

132

MACK SAT in the old nursery going through his survival kit. He had a stolen ball of twine and six hooks, so he could catch fish. There was a tinderbox to light fires and an iron pan to cook his food. He had an axe and a heavy knife, purloined while the slaves were felling trees and making barrels.

Peg's return had removed the last obstacle preventing him from running away. She had moved into the female slave quarters. The girls would all keep her secret. As soon as they chose, he and Peg could simply walk away from the plantation at the end of the day's work. By dawn they could be thirty miles away.

But Peg had been back a week, and he was still at Mockjack Hall.

He stared at his map and his fish-hooks and his tinderbox. He was a step away from freedom, but he could not take that step. He had fallen in love with Lizzie, and he could not bear to leave her.

LIZZIE STOOD naked in front of the cheval glass in her bedroom, looking at her body. She had told Jay she was back to normal after the pregnancy, but the truth was that she would never be quite the same. Her breasts had gone back to their previous size, but they seemed to hang a little lower on her chest. Her tummy would never return to normal, she now realised: the slight bulge was with her for ever. She wondered if anyone would ever find this body attractive again. She took a deep breath, pulling in her stomach and sticking out her chest. There, that was almost how she had looked before.

The door opened.

Mack stood there, speechless. He had come to repair a broken tile in the fireplace. He had said to Mildred: 'Is Mrs Jamisson up yet?' Mildred had replied: 'Just gone over to the stables.' She must have thought he said Mr Jamisson. He knew he should mutter an apology and get out fast, but his feet seemed clamped to the floor.

She turned to him. Her face was troubled, and he wondered why. At last he found his voice. 'Oh, but you're beautiful,' he whispered.

Her face changed, as if a question had been answered.

'Close the door,' she said.

He pushed the door behind him and a moment later she was in his arms. He crushed her naked body to him, feeling her soft breasts against his chest. He kissed her lips and her mouth opened to him and he gloried in the hunger of her kiss.

At last he broke away and looked at her. How dark her eyes were, almost black. 'Do you love me?' he said.

'Oh, Mack, how could you ask?' Tears came to her eyes. 'Of course I do. I love you, I love you.'

Chapter 10

When the first of the tobacco crop was ready for sale, Lennox took four hogsheads into Fredericksburg on a flatboat. He would take the tobacco to a public warehouse where the official inspector would issue a certificate saying it was 'merchantable'. Such certificates, known as tobacco notes, were used as money throughout Virginia.

Jay would use the note to pay his most pressing debts. Fortunately Lizzie had not noticed that they were broke. After the baby was born dead she had lived in a daze for three months. Then, when she caught him with Felia, she had become furiously silent.

Today she looked happier and seemed almost friendly. 'What's the news?' she asked him at dinner.

'Trouble in Massachusetts,' he replied. 'There's a group of hotheads called the Sons of Liberty—they've even had the nerve to send money to that damned fellow John Wilkes in London. Meanwhile, the Customs Commissioners are afraid to set foot in Boston. They've taken refuge aboard HMS *Romney*.'

'It sounds as if the colonists are ready to rebel.'

Jay shook his head. 'They just need a dose of the medicine we gave the coal heavers—a taste of rifle fire and a few good hangings.'

Lizzie shuddered and asked no more questions. They finished the meal in silence. While Jay was lighting his pipe, Lennox came in. Jay could see that he had been drinking, as well as doing business, in Fredericksburg. 'Is all well, Lennox?'

'Not exactly,' Lennox said in his habitual insolent tone.

Lizzie said impatiently: 'What's happened?'

'Our tobacco has been burned, that's what's happened.'

'Burned!' said Jay. 'How?'

'By the inspector. Burned as trash. Not merchantable.'

Jay had a sickening feeling in the pit of his stomach. He swallowed and said: 'I didn't know they could do that.'

Lizzie said: 'What was wrong with it?'

Lennox looked uncharacteristically flustered. 'They say it's cowpen,' he said at last.

'What do you mean, "cowpen"?' Jay asked. 'What's that?'

Lizzie said coldly: 'It means cattle have been penned on the land where the crop was grown. When land is overmanured the tobacco acquires a strong, unpleasant flavour.'

A terrible thought struck Jay. 'How much of our crop was grown this way?'

Lennox said nothing, but Lizzie answered. 'All of it.'

Then Jay understood that he was ruined. The plantation was mort-gaged, he was in debt up to his ears, and the entire crop was value-less. 'God help me,' he said, and he buried his face in his hands.

THAT NIGHT HE KNOCKED on Lizzie's door. She was sitting by the fire in her nightdress, thinking about Mack, trying to be practical. She was ecstatically happy. She loved him and he loved her. But what were they going to do?

The knock startled her. She jumped out of her chair and stared at the locked door. The handle rattled and Jay's voice came: 'Lizzie, open this door!'

She said nothing.

'I'm going to Williamsburg early in the morning to try to borrow more money,' he said. 'I want to see you before I go.'

Still she said nothing.

There was a thud as if he had thrown his shoulder against the door. A moment later she heard his footsteps recede, but she guessed he had not yet given up, and she was right. A few minutes later he came back and said: 'If you don't open the door I'm going to break it down.'

There was a bang as an axe crashed into the door. Another crash split the woodwork and she saw the blade come through.

Lizzie began to feel scared. She went to her bedside table and picked up her pistols.

As Jay continued to attack the door, Lizzie checked the loading of the pistols, pouring a little gunpowder into the priming pan of each. She released the safety catches and cocked them both.

The door flew open and Jay burst in, red-faced and panting.

She stretched out her left arm and fired a shot over his head.

In the confined space the bang was like a cannon. Jay stopped and held up his hands in a defensive gesture, looking scared.

'I've only got one shot left,' she said to him, 'so the next will go into your heart.'

'You cold bitch,' he said.

It was a clever barb. Coldness was what she accused herself of. Slowly she lowered the pistol. 'What do you want?'

He dropped the axe. 'To bed you one time before I leave.'

She felt sick. The image of Mack came into her mind. No one but he could make love to her now.

Jay grasped the pistols by the barrels and she let him take them away. She stared at him in horror. She could not believe this was going to happen. He came close and punched her in the stomach.

'Never point a gun at me again!' he yelled.

She let out a cry of shock and pain, and doubled up.

As she fell to the floor he kicked her head and she passed out.

ALL THE NEXT MORNING Lizzie lay in bed with a headache so severe she could barely speak. Sarah came in with breakfast, looking frightened. Lizzie sipped some tea then closed her eyes again.

When the cook came to take the tray away Lizzie said: 'Is Mr Jamisson gone to Williamsburg?'

'Yes, madam. Mr Lennox has gone with him.'

A few minutes later Mack burst into the room. He stood and stared at her, shaking with rage. He reached out and felt her face with trembling fingers. She took his hand and kissed his palm. They sat together for a long time, not speaking. Lizzie's pain began to ease. After a while she fell asleep.

In the afternoon Mack came in with Dr Finch.

'I didn't send for you,' Lizzie said.

'I was told you had a headache.'

'I'm not ill,' she replied. What the hell, she thought, why not tell the truth? 'My head hurts because my husband kicked it.'

Finch looked embarrassed. 'Is your vision blurred?'

'No.'

He put his hands on her temples and probed gently with his fingers. 'Is that where the blow landed?'

'Yes, damn it.'

'You're lucky to have so much curly hair. It cushioned the impact. I'll give you a drug to ease the pain. Send for me again if you have any trouble with your eyesight.'

When he had gone Mack sat on the edge of the bed and held her hand. After a while he said: 'You should leave him.'

'I wouldn't know where to go,' she said.

'I would. I'm going to run away.'

Her heart missed a beat. She could not bear to lose him.

'Peg will go with me,' he added. 'Come with us.'

There—it was out. He had hinted at it before—*Run away with some ne'er-do-well*, he had said—but now he was not hinting. 'Where will you go?' she said.

'About a hundred miles west of here is a long mountain range. It's high, too. But people say there's a pass called the Cumberland Gap. Beyond the mountains is wilderness.'

She began to feel excited. 'How would you get there?'

'Peg and I would walk. We'd head west from here to the foothills. If you come with us we can take a wagon and supplies. I won't be a runaway then, I'll be a servant, travelling with his mistress and her maid. In that case I'd go south to Richmond then west to Staunton. It's longer, but Pepper Jones says the roads are better.'

'And once you reach the mountains?'

He smiled. 'We'll look for a valley with fish in the stream and deer in the woods, and perhaps a pair of eagles nesting in the highest trees. And there we'll build a house.'

AS LIZZIE PACKED, her feelings seesawed from elation to terror. She was deliriously happy at the thought of running away with Mack. Then she thought of the hazards. The Indians might be hostile. What if they got snowed in? They could starve to death!

Glancing out of her bedroom window she saw the buggy from MacLaine's tavern in Fredericksburg. There was luggage on the back and a single figure in the passenger seat. The driver had obviously come to the wrong plantation. She went down to redirect him.

But when she stepped out onto the porch she recognised the passenger. It was Jay's mother, Alicia. She was wearing black.

'Lady Jamisson!' Lizzie said in horror.

'Hello, Lizzie,' said her mother-in-law. 'Sir George is dead.'

'Heart failure,' she explained a few minutes later, sitting in the drawing room with a cup of tea. There was no hint of tears as she spoke of the death of her husband.

Lizzie remembered the young Alicia as pretty, rather than beautiful, and now there was little remaining of her youthful allure. She was just a middle-aged woman who had come to the end of a disappointing marriage.

'Where's Jay?' Alicia asked.

'He's gone to Williamsburg to try to borrow money.'

'The plantation hasn't prospered, then.'

'Our tobacco crop was condemned.'

A shadow of sadness crossed Alicia's face. Lizzie realised that Jay was a disappointment to his mother, just as he was to his wife. 'I suppose you're wondering what's in Sir George's will,' Alicia said.

The will had not crossed Lizzie's mind. 'Did he have much to bequeath? I thought the business was in trouble.'

'It was saved by the coal from High Glen. He died a rich man.'

'Did he provide for you?'

'Oh, yes—my portion was settled before we married.'

'And Robert has inherited everything else?'

'That's what we all expected. But my husband left a quarter of his wealth to be divided among any legitimate grandchildren alive within a year of his death. So your little baby is rich. When am I

137

going to see him, or her? Which did you have?'

'A little girl,' Lizzie said. 'She was born dead.'

Alicia offered no sympathy. 'Hell,' she swore. 'You must be sure to have another, quickly.'

MACK HAD LOADED the wagon with seed, tools, rope, nails, cornmeal and salt. Also a ploughshare: when they reached their destination he would convert the wagon into a plough. He had opened the gun-room and taken all the rifles and ammunition. He would put four mares in the traces, he decided, and take two stallions so that they could breed. Jay Jamisson would be furious at the theft of his precious horses: he would mind that more than the loss of Lizzie, Mack felt sure.

While he was roping down the supplies Lizzie came out. She told him about Alicia's arrival. 'Sir George is dead.'

'Praise be. The world is well rid of him.'

'Can we still leave?'

'I don't see why not. Alicia can't stop us.'

'What if she goes to the sheriff and says we've run away and stolen all this?' She indicated the pile of supplies on the wagon.

'Remember our story. You're going to visit a cousin who has just started to farm in North Carolina. You're taking gifts.'

Lizzie nodded. 'I'll make sure Colonel Thumson and Suzy Delahaye hear of my plans.'

'Tell them that your mother-in-law disapproves and she may try to make trouble for you.'

'Good idea.' Hesitantly, she said: 'When shall we leave?'

He smiled. 'Before first light. I'll have the wagon taken down to the quarters tonight, so that we won't make much noise as we go. By the time Alicia wakes up we'll be gone.'

WHEN MACK CAME for her she was sitting at the window in her coat and three-cornered hat. He smiled to see her in her favourite clothes. They held hands and tiptoed down the stairs and out of the house.

The wagon was waiting down by the road, out of sight. Peg was already sitting on the seat, wrapped in a blanket. All the slaves were there to say goodbye. Bess, the field hand who had been injured on the night Lizzie lost her baby, threw her arms round Lizzie and sobbed. They all stood and watched as Mack and Lizzie climbed onto the wagon.

Mack cracked the reins and said: 'Hup! Walk on!'

The horses took the strain and they moved off. Lizzie looked ahead. In the distance, dawn was breaking.

Chapter 11

Matthew Murchman was out of town when Jay and Lennox reached Williamsburg. He might be back tomorrow, his servant said. Jay scribbled a note saying he needed to borrow more money and he would like to see the lawyer at his earliest convenience.

Next day, forced to kill time, he went along to the Capitol building. Dissolved by the governor last year, the assembly had reconvened after an election. In the House of Burgesses they were discussing taxation: griping as usual about paying taxes while having no voice in the Westminster Parliament. 'No taxation without representation' was their parrot cry. This time, however, they went further than usual, and affirmed their right to cooperate with other colonial assemblies in opposition to royal demands.

Jay felt sure the governor could not let that pass and he was right. Just before dinnertime the serjeant at arms handed a sheet of paper to the clerk, who read it and said: 'Mr Speaker, the governor commands the immediate attendance of your House in the council chamber.'

Jay followed the burgesses as they trooped up the stairs to the council chamber. Governor Botetourt spoke very briefly. 'I have heard of your resolves,' he said. 'You have made it my duty to dissolve you. You are dissolved accordingly.'

Jay concealed his glee as the burgesses slowly filed back out of the chamber. They collected their papers downstairs and drifted out into the courtyard.

He made his way to the Raleigh tavern and ordered his midday meal. As he waited he was surprised to see many of the burgesses go past, heading for one of the larger rooms in the rear. When he had eaten he went to investigate.

As he had guessed, the burgesses were holding a debate. They made no attempt to hide their sedition. They were blindly convinced of the rightness of their cause, and that gave them a kind of mad self-confidence. No one protested when Jay took a seat at the back of the room, although many there knew he was loyal to the Crown.

One of the hotheads was speaking, and Jay recognised George Washington, a former army officer who had made a lot of money in land speculation. He was not much of an orator, but there was a steely determination about him that struck Jay forcibly.

Washington had a plan. In the northern colonies, he said, leading men had formed associations whose members agreed not to import

British goods. If Virginians really wanted to put pressure on London they should do the same.

Not everyone agreed. Some burgesses pointed out that the northern colonies had more industry and could make many essentials for themselves, whereas the south depended on imports.

Washington said there might be exceptions, and suggested a small committee to thrash out the technicalities. The proposal was passed and the committee members were chosen.

Jay left the room in disgust. As he passed through the hall Lennox approached him with a message. It was from Murchman. He was back in town and would be honoured to receive Mr Jamisson at nine o'clock in the morning.

JAY GOT TO Murchman's house early. This was his only chance. If he could not borrow more money his creditors would foreclose the mortgage and he would be homeless as well as penniless.

Murchman seemed nervous. 'I've arranged for your creditor to come and meet you,' he said.

'Creditor? You told me it was a syndicate.'

'Ah, yes—a minor deception, I'm sorry. The individual wanted to remain anonymous.'

'So why has he decided to reveal himself now?'

'I . . . I couldn't say. I think I'll let him introduce himself.'

The door opened and in walked Jay's brother, Robert.

'You!' Jay said, astonished. 'When did you get here?'

'A few days ago,' Robert said.

Jay held out his hand and Robert shook it briefly. 'So it was you who lent me the money?' Jay said.

'It was Father,' Robert said.

'Thank God! I was afraid I might not be able to borrow more from a stranger.'

'But Father's not your creditor any more. He's dead.'

'Dead?' Jay sat down abruptly. Father was not yet sixty. 'How . . .?'

'Heart failure.'

Jay looked again at his brother. There was an expression of vindictive triumph on Robert's face. Why was he pleased?

'I'm your creditor now,' Robert said.

Jay saw what was coming. 'You swine,' he whispered.

Robert nodded. 'I'm foreclosing on your mortgage. The tobacco plantation is mine. I've done the same with High Glen: bought up the mortgages and foreclosed. That belongs to me now.'

Jay could hardly speak. 'You planned this,' he said with a struggle. 'You and Father . . .'

140

'Yes.'

'I've been ruined by my own family.'

'You've ruined yourself. You're lazy and foolish and weak.'

Jay ignored the insults. All he could think of was that his own father had plotted his downfall. He remembered how Murchman's letter offering a mortgage had come just after his arrival in Virginia. Father must have anticipated that the plantation would get into difficulties and he had planned to take it back from Jay. His father was dead, but had sent this message of rejection from beyond the grave.

JAY WAS DRUNK by dinnertime. That evening he passed out in the bar of the Raleigh. Lennox must have put him to bed, for he woke up in his room the following morning.

He was drinking brandy again at eleven o'clock in the morning when his mother walked into the bar.

He stood up and stared at her, frightened. She said: 'No, I'm not a ghost.' She kissed him and sat down.

When he recovered he said: 'How did you find me?'

'I went to Fredericksburg and they told me you were here. Prepare yourself for a shock. Your father's dead.'

'I know.'

That surprised her. 'How?'

'Robert is here.' Jay told her the story and explained that Robert was now the owner of both the plantation and High Glen. 'I'm ruined,' he said. 'I was thinking of killing myself.'

Her eyes widened. 'Then Robert didn't tell you what was in your father's will. A quarter of the estate goes to any legitimate grandchildren of your father born within a year of his death. If there are none after a year Robert gets everything.'

'A quarter? That's a fortune!'

'All you have to do is make Lizzie pregnant again.'

Jay managed a grin. 'Well, I know how to do that, anyway.'

'Don't be so sure. She's run away with that coalminer.'

'Good God! She's left me? And gone off with a convict?' It was deeply humiliating. Jay looked away. 'I'll never live this down.'

'They took a wagonload of supplies and six of your horses.'

'Damned thieves! Couldn't you stop them?'

'I tried—but Lizzie gave out a story that she was taking gifts to a cousin in North Carolina. The neighbours told the sheriff I was just a cantankerous mother-in-law trying to stir up trouble.'

'And we've no idea where they've gone.'

'I do. I followed them.'

He shook his head in admiration. 'How did you do that?'

'I kept asking people if they'd seen a four-horse wagon with a man, a woman and a child. There's not so much traffic that people forget.'

'Where did they go?'

'They came south to Richmond. There they took a road called Three Notch Trail and headed west. I turned east and came here. If you leave now you'll be only three days behind them.'

'What if Lizzie won't come back?'

His mother's face set in grim lines of determination. 'There is one other possibility, of course,' she said. 'You could make another woman pregnant, marry her, and still inherit—if Lizzie suddenly died.'

He stared at his mother for a long moment.

She went on: 'They're headed for the wilderness, beyond the law. Sudden death is normal and no one questions it.'

Jay swallowed drily and reached for his drink. His mother put her hand on the glass to prevent him. 'You have to get started,' she said. 'Take Lennox with you. If you can't persuade or force Lizzie to come back with you—he will know how to manage it.'

Jay nodded. 'Very well,' he said. 'I'll do it.'

THE ANCIENT BUFFALO-HUNTING TRACK known as Three Notch Trail went due west across the rolling Virginia landscape. It ran parallel to the James River, as Lizzie could see from Mack's map. At first they passed many large estates like the ones around Fredericksburg, but as they went further west the houses and fields became smaller and the tracts of undeveloped woodland larger.

They pushed the horses hard, for they feared they might be followed. Alicia would not sit quietly in Fredericksburg waiting for Jay to come home. She would have sent a message to Williamsburg, or gone there herself, to warn him of what had happened. He would almost certainly chase after Lizzie: he needed her to provide the necessary grandchild. And he would travel faster, for he had no need of a wagonload of supplies.

On the third day the countryside became more hilly and a blue mountain range appeared in the distant haze. As the miles went by the horses became overtired, stumbling on the rough road and stubbornly slowing down. On uphill stretches their heads drooped and they became unresponsive to the whip.

'What's the matter with them?' Mack asked anxiously.

'We have to give them better food,' Lizzie replied. 'They're existing on what they can graze at night. For work like this, horses need oats.'

'I should have brought some,' he said regretfully.

That afternoon they reached Charlottesville, a new settlement growing up where Three Notch Trail crossed the north–south Seminole Trail. Lizzie noticed a tavern identified by a crude painting of a swan. 'We could get oats here,' she said.

'Let's not stop,' Mack said. 'I don't want people to remember us.'

Lizzie understood. The crossroads would present Jay with a problem. He would have to find out whether the runaways had turned south or continued west. Stopping at the tavern for supplies would call attention to themselves.

A few miles beyond Charlottesville they stopped where the road was crossed by a barely visible track. Mack built a fire and Peg cooked hominy. Lizzie found the glutinous texture disgusting, but she forced herself to eat a few spoonfuls. She felt ashamed that her field hands had eaten this every day.

While Mack washed their bowls in a stream Lizzie hobbled the horses so that they could graze at night but not run away. Then the three of them wrapped themselves in blankets and went to sleep under the wagon.

NEXT DAY they crossed a mountain range by a pass then dropped down into the plain beyond. Lizzie and Peg rode the wagon downhill while Mack ranged ahead on one of the spare horses. Lizzie could tell that Peg had something on her mind.

'What's troubling you?' she asked her.

'Why did you decide to run away with us?'

It was hard to find a simple answer to that question. Lizzie thought about it and eventually replied: 'Mainly because my husband doesn't love me any more, I suppose.'

Peg looked sulky, and Lizzie guessed there was more to come.

'You're in love with Mack, aren't you?'

'Of course!'

'But you've only just got rid of your husband—isn't it a bit soon?'

Lizzie winced. She herself felt this was true, but it was galling to hear the criticism from a child. 'My husband hasn't touched me for six months—how long do you think I should wait?'

'Mack loves me.'

'He loves us both, I think,' Lizzie said, 'but in different ways. He's been like a father to you. And I'll try to be like a mother, if you'll let me.'

'No!' Peg said angrily. 'That's not how it's going to be!'

Lizzie was at a loss to know what to say to her. Looking ahead she saw a shallow river with a low wooden building beside it, obviously a tavern used by travellers fording the river. Mack was tying up his horse outside the building.

She pulled up the wagon. A big, roughly dressed man came out. 'We need to buy oats for our horses,' Mack said.

The man replied with a question. 'You folks going to rest your team and step inside and take a drink?'

Lizzie felt a tankard of beer was the most desirable thing on earth. 'Yes,' she said decisively, and swung down from the wagon.

'I'm Barney Tobold—they call me Baz,' said the tavern-keeper. He led the way inside the gloomy, earth-floored room and poured beer from a cask into wooden mugs. Mack came in with his map in his hand and said: 'What river is this?'

'We call it South River.'

'Once you cross over, where does the road lead to?'

'A town called Staunton, about twenty miles away. Where are you people headed, anyway?'

Lizzie answered: 'I'm on my way to visit a cousin.'

'In Staunton?'

Lizzie was flustered by the question. 'Uh . . . near there.'

'Is that so? What name?'

She said the first name that came to her. 'Angus . . . Angus James.'

Baz frowned. 'That's funny. I thought I knew everyone in Staunton.'

The sound of hoofbeats came from outside. Could Jay have caught up with them so soon? The sound made Mack uneasy too and he said: 'If we want to make Staunton by nightfall . . .'

'We don't have time to linger,' Lizzie finished. She emptied her tankard and took out her purse. 'Let me pay you.'

Two men walked in, blinking in the dim light. Out of the corner of her eye Lizzie saw Peg give a start, then turn her back on the newcomers, as if she did not want them to see her face.

One of them spoke cheerily. 'Hello, strangers!' He was an ugly man with a broken nose and one closed eye. 'I'm Chris Dobbs, known as Deadeye Dobbo. A pleasure to meet you. Let me buy you a drink.'

'We're leaving,' Lizzie said. 'Thanks all the same.'

Mack went out and Lizzie and Peg moved to the door. Dobbs looked at Peg and registered surprise. 'I know you,' he said. 'I've seen you with Burgo Marler, God rest his soul.'

'Never heard of him,' Peg said boldly, and walked past.

'Hey, you must be the little bitch that killed him!'

'Wait a minute,' Lizzie said. 'Jenny has been a maid in my family since she was ten and she's never met anyone called Burgo Marler, let alone killed him.'

He was not to be put off so easily. 'Her name isn't Jenny; it's Betty, or Milly, or Peggy. That's it—she's Peggy Knapp.'

Lizzie felt sick with fear.

Dobbs turned to his companion. 'Ain't it her, now?'

The other man shrugged. 'I never saw Burgo's convict more than a time or two,' he said dubiously.

Baz said: 'She fits the description in the *Virginia Gazette*, though.' He reached under the counter and came up with a musket. 'Maybe you should all stay around while we get a message to the sheriff in Staunton. I know he'll want to check your story.'

Lizzie's fear turned to anger. 'I'm walking out of here with this child, and if you shoot the wife of a wealthy Virginian gentleman, no excuse on earth is going to keep you from the gallows.' She stepped between Peg and the gun and pushed her forward.

Baz cocked the flintlock with a deafening click.

Peg twitched under Lizzie's hands, and Lizzie tightened her grip, sensing the girl wanted to break into a run. It was three yards to the door but they seemed to take an hour to get there.

No shot rang out. Lizzie felt sunshine on her face. She could contain herself no longer. Shoving Peg forward she broke into a run.

Peg jumped up on the seat of the wagon and Lizzie followed. Mack was already in the saddle. 'What happened?' he said.

'Let's get out of here!' Lizzie said, snapping the reins. 'That one-eyed fellow recognised Peg.' She turned the wagon to the east. If they headed for Staunton they would be riding into the sheriff's arms. They had to go back the way they had come.

Looking over her shoulder she saw the three men in the doorway, Baz still holding the musket. She whipped the horses into a trot.

When they were out of range, Lizzie slowed the horses to a walk and Mack brought his horse alongside. 'We forgot to buy oats,' he said.

THEY STOPPED where they had made camp the night before. They drove the wagon off the main road and concealed it in the woods: they were now fugitives from justice.

In the morning Mack decided they would have to go back to Charlottesville and take the Seminole Trail south. They could turn west again after a day or two without coming within fifty miles of Staunton. However, it occurred to him that Dobbs might be heading for Charlottesville. He could have passed by their hidden campsite after dark. Mack proposed riding into Charlottesville alone to check that the coast was clear. Lizzie agreed.

He rode hard and reached the town before sunrise. The door of the Swan was open and smoke came from its chimney. Mack tied his horse to a bush, then cautiously approached the tavern.

There was no one in the bar. A mouth-watering smell was coming from somewhere. He went round to the back and saw a middle-aged woman frying bacon. 'I need to buy oats,' he said.

Without looking up she said: 'You'll find a store just opposite the courthouse.'

'Thanks. Have you seen Deadeye Dobbs?'

'Who the hell is he?'

'Never mind.' Leaving his horse, he went up the hill to the wooden courthouse. Across the square was a smaller building with a sign saying *Seed Merchant*. It was locked up, but in an outhouse at the back he found a half-dressed man shaving. 'I need to buy oats,' he said again.

The man wiped his face and led Mack into the store.

'Any strangers in town?' Mack asked him.

'You,' he replied.

It seemed Dobbs had not come here last night.

Mack paid with money Lizzie had given him and took the two big sacks on his back. When he went outside he heard hoofs, and looked up to see two horsemen riding in from the east. He hurried down the hill. The riders pulled up at the Swan. Mack slowed his pace as he approached and tipped his hat down over his eyes. As they dismounted he studied their faces.

One of them was Jay Jamisson. He had almost caught up, thanks to yesterday's trouble at South River.

Now Mack had to reach his horse and get away without being seen. Suddenly he realised that 'his' horse had been stolen from Jay, and it was roped to a bush not three yards away from where Jay now stood: one glance and he would recognise it as his own.

Lennox was with Jay; he tied up his mount next to Mack's, partly masking the stolen horse from Jay's view. Jay tied up next to Lennox. A drop of sweat rolled down Mack's forehead and into his eye, and he blinked it away. When his vision cleared the two were walking into the Swan.

He walked quickly across the road to the tavern and transferred the two sacks of oats to the horse. He mounted and rode off. A minute later he had left the town behind.

He was anxious to get back to Lizzie and Peg, but he was forced to go more slowly because of the weight of the oats, and the sun was warm by the time he reached the crossing. He turned down the side trail to the hidden campsite. 'Jay is in Charlottesville,' he said as soon as he saw Lizzie.

She paled. 'So close!'

'He'll probably follow Three Notch Trail across the mountains later today. But as soon as he reaches the South River ford he'll find out that we turned back. That will put him only a day and a half behind us. We'll have to abandon the wagon.'

'And all our supplies!'

'Most of them. We'll take whatever the horses will carry.' Mack looked along the narrow trail leading south from the camp. 'Instead of going back to Charlottesville we could try taking this track south. It probably cuts a corner and meets up with the Seminole Trail a few miles out of town.'

Lizzie was not the type to whine. Her mouth set in a determined line. 'All right,' she said grimly. 'Let's start unloading.'

They had to abandon the ploughshare, and some of the cornmeal, but they managed to keep the guns, the tools and the seed.

By midmorning they had mounted up and were on their way.

FOR THREE DAYS they followed the Seminole Trail southwest, through a majestic series of valleys that wound between lush forested mountains. They rode three abreast, with three packhorses following in a line.

On the morning of the fourth day they breasted a rise and saw, in the valley below, a wide river with a cluster of wooden buildings on the far bank. A flat-bottomed ferry-boat was tied up at a jetty.

Mack reined in. 'My guess is that this is the James River, and that that settlement is a place called Lynch's Ferry.'

Lizzie guessed what he was thinking: 'You want to turn west again.'

He nodded. 'We've seen almost nobody for three days—Jay will have trouble picking up our scent. But if we cross that ferry we'll meet the ferryman, and it might be hard to avoid the local busybodies.'

They turned off the trail at an angle and went down through sloping woodland to reach the river half a mile or so upstream from the settlement. A flat track ran west along the bank for several miles. Then it turned away from the river, skirting a range of hills. They ended the day beside a fast-running mountain stream. Lizzie shot a small deer and Mack butchered it, then made a spit to roast a haunch. Leaving Peg to watch the fire, he went to wash his bloodstained hands.

He made his way downstream to where a small waterfall dropped into a deep pool. He knelt on a ledge and rinsed his hands in the falling water. Then he decided to bathe, and took off all his clothes. He stepped out of his breeches and looked up to see Lizzie.

'Every time I take off my clothes and jump in a river—'

'You find me watching!'

They both laughed. 'Come and bathe with me,' he said.

His heart beat faster as she stripped. He gazed lovingly at her body. She stood naked in front of him with a what-the-hell expression on her face. They embraced and kissed.

Out of the corner of his eye he saw something move on the bank. He turned his head and glimpsed a flash of colour, then it was gone. Someone had been watching. Had Peg stumbled on them accidentally, or was it a stranger?

When they returned to the campsite Peg was gone.

'I think she's run off,' Lizzie said.

Mack narrowed his eyes. 'What makes you so sure?'

'She's jealous of me because you love me. She told me she was going to marry you. Of course it's just a girlish fantasy, but she doesn't know that. I think she saw us kissing and ran away.'

Mack had a dreadful feeling this was true. He imagined how Peg felt and the thought was agonising. Now that poor child was wandering alone in the mountains at night. 'At least she can't have gone far. She hasn't taken a horse. We'll search together. Let's make torches. She's probably gone back the way we came.'

They backtracked for hours, shining their lights into the woods on either side of the winding trail. There was no sign of her.

At dawn they loaded up the horses and went on. It was possible she had gone west, and Mack hoped they would stumble on her on the track, but all that morning they walked without finding her.

At midday they came upon another trail. It was just a dirt road, but it was wider than a wagon and there were hoof marks in the mud. It ran from northeast to southwest, and in the distance beyond it they could see a range of majestic mountains rising into the blue sky.

This was the road they had been searching for, the way to the Cumberland Gap. With heavy hearts, they turned southwest and rode on.

THE NEXT MORNING, Jay Jamisson walked his horse down the hill to the James River and looked across the water to Lynch's Ferry.

Jay was exhausted, aching and dispirited. He was weary of bad food, filthy clothes, long days in the saddle and short nights on the hard ground. He had been excited on reaching the South River ford to learn that Lizzie and her partners had been forced to turn back. Now he was puzzled about how they had passed him on the road.

'They turned off the trail somewhere,' Deadeye Dobbs had said confidently as they sat in the tavern beside the river. Dobbs had seen the three fugitives the previous day and had recognised Peg Knapp as the missing convict who had killed Burgo Marler.

'But did they go north or south?' Jay said worriedly.

'If you're running from the law, south is the direction you head— away from sheriffs and courthouses and magistrates.'

Jay supposed he must be right. He told Dobbs, as he told everyone he met on the trail, that he would pay a reward of fifty English pounds to anyone who arrested the fugitives. The money—enough to buy a small farm out here—had come from his mother. When they parted, Dobbs crossed the ford and went west, towards Staunton. Jay returned to Charlottesville, expecting to find that Lizzie had passed through there and turned south. However, the wagon had not been seen again. Jay could only guess they had found another route to the southbound Seminole Trail. Gambling on that assumption, he and Lennox had taken the trail. But the countryside was becoming lonelier, and they met no one who recalled seeing the fugitives on the road.

However, Jay had high hopes of getting some information here at Lynch's Ferry. He questioned the ferryman as they crossed the river. 'We're looking for a group of three people: a young Englishwoman, a Scotsman of about the same age, and a young girl of fourteen. Have they been through here?'

The man shook his head.

Jay's heart sank. 'Could someone have passed through here without you seeing them?'

The man took his time replying. Eventually he said: 'He'd have to be a heck of a good swimmer.'

Jay cursed under his breath. She had not been seen for six days. She had outwitted him and cheated him of his inheritance. If ever I see her again, by God I'll shoot her in the head, he thought.

The ferry reached the other side. As they disembarked, the ferry- man said casually: 'There's somebody waiting for you all in the tavern. Mean-looking fellow with one closed eye.'

Dobbs! How had he got here ahead of them? And why?

Jay was eager to solve the riddle. 'You deal with the horses,' he told Lennox. 'I'll go and see Dobbs.'

The tavern was a two-storey building alongside the ferry dock. Dobbs was sitting at a table eating stew from a bowl. He raised his good eye and spoke with his mouth full. 'I come to claim that reward, Captain Jamisson. Look over there.' He nodded towards the corner.

There, tied to a chair, was Peg Knapp.

Jay stared at her. 'Where the hell did she come from?'

'I found her on the road south of Staunton, heading towards the town. I asked her how she got there, but she won't talk.'

Jay looked again at the girl and saw bruises on her face. Dobbs had not been gentle with her.

'I'll tell you what I think,' Dobbs said. 'They came almost this far but they never crossed the river. Instead they turned west. They must have abandoned their wagon somewhere. They went on horseback up the river valley to the Staunton road.'

'But how did you get here ahead of us?'

He grinned. 'I came down the river on a raft.'

'There must have been a quarrel,' Jay said. 'This murdering little bitch left the others and turned north. So they must have gone south.' He frowned. 'Where do they imagine they're going?'

'The road leads to Fort Chiswell. Beyond that there's not much in the way of settled land. Further south there's a place called Wolf Hills, and after that it's Cherokee country. I'd guess they'll turn west at Wolf Hills and head up into the mountains. Hunters talk about a pass called the Cumberland Gap.'

'What's on the other side?'

'Wilderness, they say. They call it the bluegrass country.'

Jay saw it now. Lizzie was planning to start a new life in undiscovered country. But she would fail, he thought excitedly. He would catch her and bring her back—dead or alive.

'The child is not worth much on her own,' he said to Dobbs. 'You have to help us catch the other two, if you want your fifty pounds.'

TEN DAYS AFTER PEG ran off, Mack and Lizzie rode across a wide, flat plain and reached the mighty Holston River. Mack was elated. 'This is it,' he said to Lizzie. 'This is the edge of civilisation.'

For several days they had felt almost alone in the world. Yesterday they had seen one white man—a trapper—and three Indians on a distant hill; today, no white men and several groups of Indians. The Indians were neither friendly nor hostile. They kept a distance.

As the farms became fewer, the game had increased: bison, deer, rabbits and millions of edible birds—turkeys, duck, woodcock and quail. Lizzie shot more than the two of them could eat.

They watered the horses in the river and sat down to rest on the rocky shore. The trail had petered out as they crossed the plain, and beyond the river there was no sign of a track. To the north a high ridge rose forbiddingly into the sky.

Mack said: 'There must be a pass.'

'I don't see it,' said Lizzie. 'If it isn't there . . .'

'We'll look for another one.' He spoke confidently but at heart he was fearful. They were going into unmapped country. They might be

A Place Called Freedom

attacked by mountain lions or wild bears. The Indians could turn hostile. At present there was plenty of food for anyone with a rifle, but what would happen in the winter?

He took out his map. 'The river valleys slant from northeast to southwest, and we have to go northwest, at right angles to the rivers, across a series of high ridges. When we come up against a ridge that looks impassable, we turn west and follow the valley, all the time looking out for our next chance to turn north. The passes are in there somewhere.'

'Well, there's nothing to do now but try,' she said. Her face became solemn again. 'I just wish Peg was here.'

Mack felt the same way. They had done all they could to look for her, but that was small consolation. Sighing, he got to his feet. 'I'll be happier when we're out of sight of this river,' he said. 'Jay might guess our route thus far—but this is where we shake him off.'

Reflexively he looked back the way they had come. There was no one in sight. Then he became conscious that they were being watched. Tensing, he slowly turned his head.

Two Indians were standing a few yards away. They were boys of about seventeen years old. They had the straight black hair and reddish-tan skin characteristic of the original Americans, and wore the deerskin tunics and trousers that the new immigrants had copied.

The taller one held out a large fish. 'I want a knife,' he said.

'You want to trade?' Mack asked.

The boy smiled. 'I want a knife.'

Lizzie said: 'We don't need a fish, but we could use a guide. I'll bet he knows where the pass is.'

Mack said eagerly: 'Will you guide us?'

The boy smiled, but it was obvious he did not understand.

Lizzie said: 'Let me try.'

She went to one of the packhorses, opened a leather satchel and took out a long-bladed knife. It had been made at the forge on the plantation, and the letter 'J', for Jamisson, was burned into the handle. She showed it to the boy.

He smiled broadly. 'I'll buy that,' he said, and reached for it.

Lizzie withdrew it. 'Look,' she said. She bent over a large stone with a flat surface. Using the point of the knife she drew a jagged line. She pointed at the mountains, then at the line. 'This is the ridge.'

Mack could not tell whether the boy understood or not.

Below the ridge she drew two stick figures, then pointed at herself and Mack. 'This is us,' she said. 'Now—' She drew a second ridge, then a deep V shape joining the two. 'This is the pass,' she said. Then she pointed at the boy. 'You take us to the pass—and you get the knife.'

He drew a V shape in the air. 'Pass,' he said.

Mack said: 'Do you think he got the message?'

'I don't know.' She took her horse's bridle and began to walk on. 'Shall we go?' she said to the boy.

He started to walk beside her. The other Indian came too. They struck out along the bank of a stream. The terrain rose remorselessly, but the ground seemed less rough and the horses went a little faster. Mack realised the boys were following a trail only they could see. They went all the way to the foot of the mountain and suddenly turned east; then, to Mack's enormous relief, they saw the pass. 'Well done, Fish Boy!' he said joyfully.

They forded a river and curved round the mountain to emerge on the far side of the ridge. As the sun went down they found themselves in a narrow valley with a fast-flowing stream. Ahead of them was another ridge. 'Let's make camp,' Mack said. 'In the morning we'll go up the valley and look for another pass.'

Lizzie gave Fish Boy the knife. 'Thank you,' she said.

Mack hoped the Indians would stay with them. But they turned back the way they had come, the taller of them still carrying his fish.

JAY WAS CONVINCED they would catch Lizzie today. He kept up a fast pace, driving the horses hard.

However, there was still no sign of the fugitives when he reached the Holston River at dusk. They hobbled the horses and tied Peg to a tree while Lennox prepared hominy for supper.

They were all blistered and exhausted and Dobbs was losing heart. 'I should give up and go back,' he said. 'It ain't worth fifty pounds to get lost in the mountains and die.'

Jay did not want him to go: he was the only one with any local knowledge. 'Give it one more day. Everyone says the way across the mountains is north of here. We may catch her tomorrow.'

'And we may waste our damn time.'

Lennox spooned the lumpy porridge into bowls. Dobbs untied Peg's hands long enough for her to eat, then tied her up again and threw a blanket over her. No one cared much for her well-being but Dobbs wanted to take her to the Staunton sheriff: he seemed to think he would be rewarded for capturing her.

They wrapped themselves in their blankets and made desultory conversation while they passed round a bottle of rum. The hours went by and the moon rose. Jay dozed fitfully. At some point he opened his eyes and saw a strange face, young but alien, at the edge of the circle of firelight. He realised that it belonged to an Indian.

The face was focused on Peg. She was making faces at the Indian, and Jay figured that she was trying to get him to untie her.

There were two Indians, he saw. They were young boys.

One of them stepped silently into the circle. He was carrying a big fish. He put it down, then drew a knife and bent over Peg.

Lennox was as quick as a snake. There was a blur of movement and he had the boy in an armlock. The knife fell to the ground. The second Indian vanished.

Jay stood up. 'What have we here?'

Dobbs rubbed his eyes and stared. 'Just an Indian boy, trying to rob us. We should hang him as a lesson to the others.'

'Not yet,' said Lennox. 'Hold him for me, Dobbo.' Dobbs took over and Lennox picked up the knife. 'Look at this. It's one of ours—it has the letter "J" burned into the handle.'

Jay looked. It was true. The knife had been made at his plantation! 'Why, then he must have met Lizzie!'

Lennox said: 'Exactly.' He held the knife in front of the Indian's eyes and said: 'Which way did they go, boy?'

'No trade today,' he said in a terrified voice.

Lennox took the boy's left hand. He hooked the point of the knife under the nail of the index finger. 'Which way?' he said, and he pulled out the nail.

The boy and Peg screamed at the same time. 'Stop it!' Peg yelled. 'Leave him alone!'

Lennox took the other hand and pulled out another fingernail. 'Which way to the pass?' he said.

'Pass,' the boy said, and with a bleeding hand he pointed north.

Jay gave a sigh of satisfaction. 'You can take us there,' he said.

Chapter 12

Mack dreamed he was wading across a river to a place called Freedom. He kept striding forward but the bank never got any closer, and the river became deeper with every stride. Eventually it closed over his head. Gasping, he woke up.

He heard one of the horses whinny.

'Something's disturbed them,' he said. There was no reply. He turned over and saw that Lizzie was not beside him. He rolled quickly out of his blanket and stood up.

Someone was coming. 'Lizzie!' he called.

Then Jay stepped from behind a tree with a rifle pointed at Mack's heart.

A moment later Lennox appeared with a pistol in each hand.

Mack stood there helpless. Despair engulfed him like the river in his dream. Where was Lizzie?

Deadeye Dobbs rode up with Peg on another horse beside him, her feet tied together under the horse's belly. Fish Boy was walking alongside Dobbs's horse, tied by a long rope to Dobbs's saddle. He must have led them here. His hands were covered with blood and Mack realised with disgust that he had been tortured.

Jay was staring at the blankets on the ground. It was obvious that Mack and Lizzie had been sleeping together. 'You filthy pig,' he said. He reversed his rifle and swung the butt at Mack's head, hitting him a bone-crunching blow. Mack staggered and fell. 'Where is she, where's my wife?'

Mack tasted blood. 'I don't know.'

'If you don't know I might as well have the satisfaction of shooting you through the head!'

Peg screamed: 'No—don't shoot—please!'

Jay pointed the rifle at Mack's head. His voice rose to a hysterical pitch. 'This is for all the times you've defied me!' he screamed.

LIZZIE LAY BELLY-DOWN behind a rock, with her rifle in her hand, waiting. She had picked her spot the night before, after inspecting the river bank and seeing the footprints and droppings of deer. As the light strengthened she waited for the animals to come to drink.

There was a movement in the trees. A moment later a young deer came out of the woods, stepped daintily to the water's edge and began to drink. Lizzie cocked the flintlock of her rifle. As always, she suffered a moment of regret for the beautiful animal she was about to destroy. Then she pulled the trigger.

THE SHOT CAME from further up the valley, two or three hundred yards away. Jay froze, his gun still pointed at Mack.

Dobbs drawled: 'If you shoot now, Jamisson, you'll warn her and she could get away.'

Jay hesitated, then slowly lowered his gun. 'I'll go after her. The rest of you stay here.' He left the clearing, gun held ready.

Mack realised that to warn Lizzie he had to make one of them fire. Before his resolve could weaken he broke into a run.

There was a moment of stunned silence. Then Peg screamed.

Mack ran for the trees, expecting a bullet to slam into his back.

There was a bang, followed by another.

He felt nothing. The shots had missed him. He stopped and raised his hands, then turned slowly, keeping his hands up. It's up to you now, Lizzie, he thought. Good luck, my love.

154

JAY STOPPED WHEN HE HEARD shooting. It had come from behind him. He guessed that Lennox or Dobbs had shot McAsh.

Whatever the truth, the all-important task was to capture Lizzie. Unfortunately, the shooting had warned her.

He knew his wife. Patience and caution were foreign to her. By now she would be running this way. She would be almost back in the clearing before she thought to slow down and make a plan.

He found a spot where he could see clearly along the bank of the stream and hid himself in the bushes. Then he cocked the flintlock of his rifle. He tried to pretend he was hunting deer. He would aim for the heart, just below the shoulder, for a clean kill.

She came into view, half walking and half running along the river bank. She carried two rifles under her arm.

He aimed at her heart, but he saw her naked on the bed in the Chapel Street house when they were first married: and he could not shoot.

When she was ten yards away he stepped out of the undergrowth.

She stopped and gave a cry of horror.

'Hello, darling,' he said.

She gave him a look of hatred. 'Why couldn't you just let me go?' she said. 'You don't love me.'

'No, but I need a grandchild,' he said.

She looked scornful. 'I'd rather die.'

'That's the alternative,' he said.

THERE WAS A MOMENT of chaos after Lennox fired his pistols at Mack.

The horses were frightened by the close-range shooting. Peg's mount ran away. She stayed on, tied as she was, and they disappeared into the trees. Dobbs's horse was bucking and he fought to bring it under control. Lennox began hastily to reload his weapons.

That was when Fish Boy made his move. He ran at Dobbs's horse, jumped on behind him and wrestled Dobbs out of the saddle.

Lennox dropped his pistols and ran to the rescue.

Mack stuck out a foot and tripped Lennox.

Dobbs fell off his horse, but one ankle got tangled in the rope by which Fish Boy was tied to the saddle. The horse, now terrified, bolted. Fish Boy clung to its neck for dear life. It ran into the woods, dragging Dobbs along the ground after it.

Only Mack and Lennox were left in the clearing. At last it had come to a fist fight between them. I'll kill him, Mack thought.

Lennox rolled over and came up with a knife in his hand. He lunged at Mack. Mack dodged, then kicked Lennox's kneecap and danced out of range.

Limping, Lennox came at him. This time he feinted with the knife, let Mack dodge the wrong way, then struck again. Mack felt a sharp pain in his left side. He swung with his right fist and hit Lennox a mighty blow to the side of the head. Lennox dropped the knife.

He backed away, fear in his eyes, but Mack was after him fast. He punched Lennox in the belly, then hit him on each side of the head. Dazed and terrified, Lennox staggered. Mack was about to hit him again when he heard Jay's voice say: 'Stop or I'll kill her.'

Lizzie walked into the clearing and Jay followed, holding his rifle to the back of her head.

Mack stared, paralysed. He could see that Jay's rifle was cocked. If Jay even stumbled, the gun would blow her head off. Mack turned away from Lennox and moved towards Jay. 'You've only got one shot,' he snarled. 'If you shoot Lizzie, I'll kill you.'

'Then perhaps I should shoot you,' Jay said.

'Yes,' Mack said madly, moving towards him. 'Shoot me.'

Jay swung the rifle.

Mack felt a wild jubilation: the gun was no longer pointed at Lizzie. He walked steadily towards Jay.

Jay took careful aim at Mack.

There was a strange noise, and suddenly an arrow was sticking out of Jay's cheek. He screamed in pain and dropped the rifle. It went off with a bang and the ball flew past Mack's head. The noise came again, and a second arrow pierced Jay's neck. He fell to the ground.

Into the clearing came Fish Boy, his friend and Peg, followed by five or six Indian men, all carrying bows. Mack guessed that when Jay captured Fish Boy the other Indian had gone for help. The rescue party must have met up with the runaway horses. He didn't know what had happened to Dobbs, but one of the Indians was wearing Dobbs's boots.

Lizzie stood over Jay, staring at him, her hand covering her mouth. Mack went and put his arms round her and they stood looking down at the man on the ground. Blood was pouring from his mouth.

'He's dying,' Lizzie said shakily. Mack nodded.

The other Indians seized Lennox, threw him flat and held him down. There was some conversation between Fish Boy and the oldest Indian. Fish Boy kept showing his fingers. They looked to Mack as if the nails had been pulled out.

The older Indian drew a hatchet from his belt. With a swift, powerful motion he cut off Lennox's right hand at the wrist. Blood gushed from the stump and Lennox fainted.

The man picked up the severed hand and, with a formal air,

presented it to Fish Boy who took it solemnly. Then he turned round
and hurled it into the woods.

'God forgive them,' said Lizzie.

But they hadn't finished. They tied a rope to Lennox's ankle,
looped it over a bough of the tree and raised him until he was hanging upside-down. Blood pumped from his severed wrist and pooled
on the ground beneath him. The Indians stood around, looking at
the grisly sight, watching Lennox die.

Peg came up to them and said: 'We ought to do something about
the boy's fingers.'

Lizzie nodded. 'I'll see to it.'

'No,' Peg said firmly. 'Let me do it.'

Lizzie found a jar of ointment and a silk handkerchief and Peg
detached Fish Boy from the group around the tree. She led him down
to the stream and began to bathe his wounds.

'Mack,' said Lizzie. 'Jay is dead.' She was crying.

Mack looked down at him. The bleeding had stopped and he was
white and motionless. Mack felt for a heartbeat. There was none.

'I loved him once,' Lizzie said. 'I want to bury him.'

Mack got a spade from their kit and dug a shallow grave. He and
Lizzie lifted Jay's body and placed it in the hole. Lizzie bent down
and gingerly withdrew the arrows from the corpse. Mack shovelled
soil over the body and Lizzie began to cover the grave with stones.

Suddenly Mack wanted to get away from this place of blood. He
rounded up the horses and began to load the supplies.

The Indians stirred. Lennox seemed to be dead. They left the tree
and came over to Mack. The oldest man spoke. Mack didn't
understand a word, but from the man's formal tone he guessed he
was saying that justice had been done.

Fish Boy and Peg came up from the waterside together. Mack
looked at the boy's hand: Peg had made a nice job of the bandage.

Fish Boy said something, and there followed an exchange in the
Indian language which sounded quite angry. At last all the Indians
but Fish Boy walked away. They soon disappeared into the woods.

Mack got on his horse. Fish Boy unroped a spare horse from the
line and mounted it. He went ahead. Peg rode beside him. 'Is Fish
Boy going to guide us?' Mack said to Lizzie.

'It looks like it.'

'But he hasn't asked a price. I wonder what he wants?'

Lizzie looked at the two young people riding side by side. 'Can't
you guess?' she said.

'Oh!' said Mack. 'You think he's in love with her?'

'I think he wants to spend a little more time with her.'

'Well, well.' Mack became thoughtful.

As they headed west, along the river valley, the sun came up behind them, throwing their shadows on the land ahead.

IT WAS A BROAD VALLEY, beyond the highest range but still in the mountains. There was a fast-moving stream of pure cold water bubbling along the valley floor, teeming with fish. The hillsides were densely forested and alive with game. On the highest range, a pair of golden eagles came and went, bringing food to their young.

'It reminds me of home,' said Lizzie.

'Then we'll call it High Glen,' Mack replied.

They unloaded the horses in the flattest part of the valley bottom, where they would build a house and clear a field. They camped on a patch of dry turf beneath a wide-spreading tree.

Peg and Fish Boy were rummaging through a sack, looking for a saw, when Peg found the broken iron collar. She pulled it out and stared quizzically at it. 'Why did you bring this?' she said.

Mack exchanged glances with Lizzie. They were both recalling the scene by the river in the old High Glen, back in Scotland, when Lizzie had asked Mack the same question.

Now he gave Peg the same answer, but this time there was no bitterness in his voice, only hope. 'Never to forget,' he said with a smile. 'Never.'

KEN FOLLETT

The idea that Scottish coalmines were worked by slave labour as recently as the eighteenth century seems particularly shocking from today's perspective. 'But it's absolutely true,' says author Ken Follett. 'It wasn't until the Emancipation Act of 1799 that slave labour was actually abolished.' This kind of historical research is one of the elements that make this best-selling author's novels so compelling. Inspiration for the plots is also drawn from history books. 'I just read out of idle curiosity and every now and then something strikes me as being tremendously dramatic and interesting. I work on the theory that I have to be fascinated by the background of the novel in order to make the readers fascinated by it.' In the course of researching *A Place Called Freedom*, Follett  visited a working mine at Longannet in Scotland. Luckily he doesn't suffer from claustrophobia, but says that for anyone going underground for the first time 'there is a moment when something or other reminds you of just exactly how much earth and rock there is over your head. Just how many millions of tons—and that's quite a chilling thought.'

The ever-popular Follett, who started his career as a reporter, built his reputation as a novelist with a string of impressive thrillers including *Eye of the Needle*, *Storm Island* and *Lie Down with Lions*. Then his work took a new direction with historical novels such as *Night Over Water* and the recent best seller *A Dangerous Fortune*. But Follett is anything but predictable and reveals that his next book will be a contemporary story about the psychology of twins.

The author lives in Chelsea with his wife Barbara in a 200-year-old house overlooking the Thames. He relaxes by playing bass guitar with friends in a blues band. 'We just play to enjoy ourselves,' says the multi-talented Follett.

DEAN KOONTZ
Icebound

ILLUSTRATED BY GEOFF HUNT

In the depths of an Arctic winter, in subzero temperatures and semi-darkness, eight scientists are working on a project to save the world from drought. Suddenly, a fierce storm leaves them stranded on an iceberg, adrift in a hostile sea. Explosives laid during the early stages of their work have been carefully set to detonate at midnight—and there is no way to defuse them. Dr Harry Carpenter and his team are trapped. . .

BEFORE . . .

From *The New York Times*:

POLAR ICE: PUREST WATER IN THE WORLD

Moscow, Feb 10—According to Russian scientists, the water consti-
tuting the Arctic ice cap has a far lower bacteria count than any
water we now drink, a discovery that might make this vast frozen
reservoir a valuable resource of the future. Because tapping the polar
ice cap might be cheaper than any desalinisation process, some
Russian researchers speculate that millions of acres of farmland
might be irrigated with melted icebergs in the next decade.

ICEBERGS COULD PROVIDE FRESH WATER

Boston, Mass., Sept 5—Speaking before the annual convention of
the American Society of Environmental Engineers, Dr Harold
Carpenter said today that chronic shortages of water in California
and other regions could be alleviated by a controlled melting of icebergs towed south from the Arctic Circle. Dr Carpenter's wife and
research partner, Dr Rita Carpenter, said the investment necessary
for research would be 'repaid a hundredfold within ten years'.

According to the Carpenters, a large iceberg would be 'blown
loose' from the edge of the ice field and allowed to drift south in natural currents. Later, steel cables would be affixed to tow the ice to a
shore-based conversion facility near thirsty farmland.

THOUSANDS STARVING IN DROUGHTS

United Nations, Oct 18—The director of the United Nations
Disaster Relief Office announced that poor harvests owing to water

shortages in the United States, Canada and Europe have made it impossible for drought-stricken Africans and Asians to purchase grain from the usually food-rich Western nations. Already, more than 200,000 people have died . . .

UN FUND TO SEND SCIENTISTS TO POLAR ICE CAP

United Nations, Jan 6—Eleven members of the United Nations today contributed to a fund which will pay for a series of experiments on the polar ice cap. The primary intent of the project will be to study the feasibility of towing huge icebergs south, where they can be tapped for the irrigation of crops.

RESEARCH STATION ON ARCTIC ICE FIELD

Thule, Greenland, Sept 28—This morning, a team of UN scientists under the direction of Drs Harold and Rita Carpenter, landed on the Arctic ice cap between Greenland and Spitsbergen, Norway. They began construction of a research station two miles from the edge of the ice field, where they will conduct United Nations-funded studies for at least nine months . . .

EXPEDITION TO BLOW LOOSE PIECE OF ICE CAP

Thule, Greenland, Jan 14—At midnight tomorrow, scientists at the United Nations-funded Edgeway Station will detonate a series of explosive devices to separate a half-mile-square iceberg from the edge of the winter ice cap, just 350 miles off the northeast coast of Greenland. Two United Nations trawlers, equipped with electronic tracking gear, are waiting 230 miles to the south, where they will monitor the progress of the 'bugged' iceberg . . .

JANUARY 15, NOON . . .

With a crystal-shattering shriek, the bit of the power drill bored deep into the Arctic ice. Grey-white slush churned out of the hole, sluiced across the crusted snow, and refroze in seconds.

Watching the drill, Harry Carpenter had a curious premonition of imminent disaster. A faint flicker of alarm. Inside his heavily insulated clothing, he shivered.

As a scientist, Harry respected the tools of logic, method and reason, but he had learned never to discount a hunch—especially on the ice, where strange things could happen. He was unable to identify the source of his sudden uneasiness, though occasional dark forebodings were to be expected on a job involving high explosives.

Peter Johnson, the electronics engineer who doubled as the team's demolitions expert, switched off the drill and stepped back. In his white storm suit, fur-lined parka and fur-lined hood, Peter resembled a polar bear—except for his dark-brown face.

Claude Jobert shut down the portable generator that supplied power to the drill. The resultant hush had an eerie quality so intense that Harry glanced behind him and then up into the sky, half convinced that something was rushing or falling towards him.

As the bleak afternoon began, the three men were preparing to lower the last explosive charge deep into the ice. It was the sixtieth demolitions package that they had handled since the previous morning, and they were all uneasily conscious of standing upon enough high-yield plastic explosives to destroy them in an apocalyptic flash.

The ice cap was a perfect graveyard, utterly lifeless, and it encouraged thoughts of mortality. Ghostly bluish-white plains led off in all directions, sombre and moody during that long season of nearly constant darkness. The only points of elevation were the jagged pressure ridges and slabs of ice—some only as large as a man, others bigger than houses—that had been forced up from the plateau and that stood on end like giant tombstones.

'The shaft's twenty-eight yards deep. One more extension for the bit, and the job's done,' Pete Johnson told Harry and Claude.

'Thank God!' Claude Jobert shivered as if his thermal suit provided no protection whatsoever. 'We'll make it back to base camp tonight. Think of that! I haven't been warm one minute since we left.'

Ordinarily, Claude didn't complain. He was a jovial, energetic little man, lean, wiry and hard. He had a mane of white hair now tucked under his hood, a face weathered and made leathery by a lifetime in extreme climates, and bright blue eyes as clear as those of a child.

Since they had left the comfort of Edgeway Station, however, Claude had been neither jovial nor energetic, and he had complained frequently about the cold. At fifty-nine, he was the oldest member of the expedition, and, although he was a fine Arctic geologist, the current expedition would be his last trip to either pole. Henceforth, his research would be done in laboratories.

Harry wondered if Jobert, who was eighteen years his senior, was bothered less by the bitter cold than by the knowledge that the work he loved had grown too demanding for him. One day Harry would have to face the same truth, and he wasn't sure that he would be able to exit with grace.

'It's snowing.'

Even as Pete Johnson spoke, Harry saw the lazily spiralling flakes descending.

Claude Jobert frowned. 'We weren't due for this storm until later.'

The trip out from Edgeway Station—which lay six miles northeast of their temporary camp—had not been difficult. Nevertheless, a bad storm might make the return journey impossible. Visibility could quickly deteriorate to zero, and they could easily get lost because of compass distortion. If their snowmobiles ran out of fuel, they would freeze to death, for even thermal suits would be insufficient protection against prolonged exposure to the murderous cold of a blizzard.

Studying the sky, Harry said, 'Maybe it's a local squall.'

'Yes, that's just what Online Weather said *last* week,' Claude reminded him. 'We were to have only local squalls on the periphery of the main event. Then we had so much snow and ice it would've kept Père Noël home on Christmas Eve.'

'So we'd better finish this job quickly.'

As if to confirm the need for haste, a wind sprang up from the west, and the snowflakes began to descend at an angle, no longer spiralling prettily like flakes in a crystal bibelot.

Pete freed the drill from the shank of the buried bit and lifted it out of its supportive frame, handling it as if it weighed a tenth of its actual eighty-five pounds.

A decade ago he had been a football star at Penn State University, turning down offers from several National Football League teams. He hadn't wanted to play out the role that society dictated for every six-foot-four-inch, 200-pound black football hero. Instead, he had won scholarships, earned two more degrees, and taken a well-paid position with a computer-industry think tank.

Now he was vital to Harry's expedition. He maintained the electronic data-gathering equipment at Edgeway, and, having designed the explosive devices, he was the only one among them who could deal with them in full confidence if something went wrong. Furthermore, his tremendous strength was an asset out there on the inhospitable top of the world.

As Pete swung the drill out of the way, Harry and Claude lifted a three-foot bit extension from one of the cargo trailers that were coupled to the snowmobiles. They screwed it onto the threaded shank, which was still buried in the ice, and Claude started the generator.

Peter clamped the drill firmly in place, and finished boring the

166

twenty-nine-yard-deep shaft, at the bottom of which they would plant a tubular charge of explosives.

While the machine roared, Harry gazed at the heavens. Within the past few minutes, the weather had deteriorated alarmingly. Above them was only a deep, whirling whiteness. The wind had escalated to perhaps twenty miles an hour, and its song was a mournful drone. Harry still sensed an oncoming disaster. The feeling was formless, vague, but unshakable.

As a boy, growing up on an Indiana farm, Harry had yearned for adventure. He had never realised that adventure was hard work, although he *had* understood that it was dangerous. To a kid, danger was part of the appeal. In the process of growing up, however, as he'd lost both parents and learned the violent ways of the world, he had ceased to see anything romantic about death.

Claude Jobert leaned close and shouted above the noise from the wind and the grinding auger. 'Don't worry, Harry. We'll be back at Edgeway soon. Good brandy, a game of chess, all the comforts.'

Harry Carpenter nodded. He continued to study the sky.

12:20pm

In the telecommunications shack at Edgeway Station, Gunvald Larsson stood at the single small window, chewing nervously on the stem of his unlit pipe and peering out at the escalating storm.

From Gunvald's slightly elevated viewpoint, Edgeway Station contrasted so boldly with the environment in which it stood that it might have been humanity's only outpost on an alien planet. The six canary-yellow Nissen huts had been airlifted onto the ice cap in pre-fabricated sections at tremendous expense. Each one-storey structure measured twenty by fifteen feet. The walls were riveted to hooped girders, and the floor of each hut was countersunk into the ice. A hundred yards north of the camp, a smaller structure stood by itself. It housed the fuel tanks that fed the generators.

The son of a Swedish father and a Danish mother, Gunvald had been on the Swedish ski teams at two winter Olympics, had earned one silver medal, and was proud of his heritage; he cultivated the image of an imperturbable Scandinavian and possessed an inner calm that matched his cool exterior. During the past hours, however, he had lost a large measure of his characteristic composure. Chewing on the pipe stem, he turned away from the window and scowled at the computers that lined three walls of the shack.

Early the previous afternoon, when Harry and the others had gone south towards the edge of the ice, Gunvald had stayed behind to monitor incoming calls on the radio and to keep a watch over the station. After weeks of living in a tiny community with eight too-close neighbours, he had been eager for his session of solitude, but by four o'clock, when Edgeway's seismographs registered the first quake, Gunvald had begun to wish that the other eight members of the team had not ventured so near to the edge of the ice, where the polar cap met the sea. At 4:14, the jolt was confirmed by radio reports from Reykjavik and from Hammerfest, Norway. Severe slippage had occurred in the seabed sixty miles northeast of Raufarhöfn in Iceland, and the tremor registered a solid 6.5 on the Richter scale.

From the outset they had intended to study, among other things, ocean-bed temblors—or tremors—in the Greenland Sea to learn more about local suboceanic fault lines in this geologically active part of the earth. If ships were to be towing colossal icebergs in those waters, they would need to know how often the sea was disturbed by major submarine quakes and by resultant high waves. Gunvald should have been pleased with the opportunity to observe, at such close quarters, the characteristics and patterns of major temblors on the Greenland Sea fault network. But he wasn't pleased at all.

Edgeway Station itself was in no imminent danger. If major seabed slippage occurred nearby, a tsunami (or tidal wave) might roll beneath the ice cap and precipitate the formation of new chasms and pressure ridges. But most of the polar terrain would be unchanged, and the likelihood that the base camp would be damaged was slim.

The other expedition members, however, couldn't be as certain of their safety. In addition to creating pressure ridges and chasms, a hot tsunami—or tidal wave—was likely to snap off sections of the ice at the edge of the winter field. Harry and the others might find the cap falling out from under them.

At nine o'clock last night, five hours after the first tremor, the second quake—5.8 on the Richter scale—had hit the fault chain. The epicentre had been thirty-five miles nearer Edgeway than that of the initial shaker. Gunvald took no comfort from the fact that the second quake had been less powerful than the first. The diminution in force was not absolute proof that the more recent temblor had been an aftershock to the first. Both might have been foreshocks, with the main event still to come.

At nine thirty, when the radio had confirmed the location and force of the second shock, Gunvald had put through a call to the temporary camp six miles to the southwest. He told Harry about the quakes and explained the risks that they were taking by remaining on the perimeter of the polar ice.

'We've got a job to do,' Harry had said. 'Forty-six packages are in place, armed and ticking. If we don't place the other fourteen tomorrow, we likely won't break off the size berg we need. In effect, we'll be aborting the mission, which is out of the question.'

'I think we should consider it.'

'No, no. The project's too damned expensive to chuck it all just because there *might* be a seismic risk.'

'I suppose you're right,' Gunvald said, 'but I don't like it.'

The open frequency crackled with static as Harry said, 'Can't say I'm doing cartwheels, either. At any rate, the ice is seven hundred feet thick where we are. It won't just splinter apart like the first coat on a winter pond.'

'Nevertheless, I suggest you wrap things up quickly tomorrow.'

'No need to worry about that. Living out here in these damned inflatable igloos makes any shack at Edgeway seem like a suite at the Ritz-Carlton.'

After that conversation, Gunvald Larsson had gone to bed. He hadn't slept well. In his nightmares, the world crumbled apart, dropped away from him in enormous chunks, and he fell into a cold, bottomless void.

At seven thirty in the morning, while Gunvald had been shaving, the seismograph had recorded a third tremor: Richter 5.2.

The fourth tremor had hit at eleven fifty. The epicentre was approximately one hundred and ten miles due south. Much closer than any previous tremor, essentially on their doorstep: 4.2 on the Richter scale.

He'd called the temporary camp, and Rita Carpenter had assured him that the expedition would leave the edge of the ice cap by two o'clock.

'The weather will be a problem,' Gunvald worried. 'The storm is shifting course and picking up speed. We'll have heavy snow this afternoon.'

'We'll be back at Edgeway by four,' she'd said. 'Maybe sooner.'

At twelve minutes past noon another slippage had occurred in the subsea crust, 100 miles south: 4.5 on the Richter scale.

12:30pm

The temporary camp stood on a flat section of ice in the lee of a pressure ridge. Three inflatable, quilted, rubberised nylon igloos, equipped with space heaters, were arranged in a semicircle approximately five yards from the fifty-foot-high bank of ice. The accommodation wasn't spacious or cosy, but it was temporary, to be used only while the team planted the sixty packages of explosives.

A hundred yards to the south, on a plateau that was five or six feet above the camp, a six-foot steel pipe rose from the ice. Fixed to it were a thermometer, a barometer and an anemometer.

With one gloved hand, Rita Carpenter brushed snow from the faces of the three instruments and read the temperature, the atmospheric pressure and the wind velocity. She didn't like what she saw. The storm had not been expected to reach them until at least six o'clock that night, but it was liable to be on them in full force before they had completed the return journey to Edgeway Station.

Negotiating the forty-five-degree slope between the plateau and the lower plain, Rita started back towards the temporary camp. Movement was awkward because she was wearing full survival gear: knitted thermal underwear, two pairs of socks, felt boots, fleece-lined outer boots, a quilted thermal suit, a fur-lined coat, a knitted mask that covered her face from chin to goggles, a fur-lined hood and gloves.

Though Rita was warm enough, the bitter-cold wind and the barren landscape chilled her emotionally. By choice, both she and Harry had spent a large portion of their professional lives in the Arctic and Antarctic; however, she did not share Harry's love of the vast open spaces. In fact, she'd driven herself to return repeatedly to the polar regions primarily because she was afraid of them.

Now, as she approached the igloo at the west end of the camp, she suddenly suffered a phobic reaction so intense that it nearly brought her to her knees. Cryophobia: the fear of ice. Frigophobia: the fear of cold. Chionophobia: the fear of snow. Rita knew those terms because she suffered from mild forms of all three phobias. Frequent confrontation with the sources of her anxieties had ensured that she usually suffered only minor uneasiness, seldom flat-out terror. Sometimes, however, she was overwhelmed by memories against which no number of inoculations was sufficient protection. Like now. The tumultuous white sky seemed to descend at the speed of a falling rock, to press relentlessly upon her as though the sheeting snow had magically metamorphosed into a massive slab of marble that would crush her into the frozen plain.

Outside the igloo entrance, she halted and held her ground, refusing to run from that which terrified her. She forced herself to endure the isolation of that bleak and gloom-shrouded realm. That isolation, in fact, was the aspect of the Arctic that most troubled Rita. In her mind, since she'd been six years old, winter was inextricably associated with the grey and distorted faces of corpses, with the frost-glazed stares of sightless eyes, with suffocating despair.

She was trembling so violently that the beam of her flashlight jittered across the snow at her feet. She breathed deeply through her knitted mask. To help quell her irrational fear of the ice cap, she told herself that she had a greater problem waiting in the igloo beside her: Franz Fischer.

She had met Fischer shortly after earning her doctorate and taking her first research position with International Telephone and Telegraph. Franz, who had also worked for ITT, was attractive and not without charm when he chose to reveal it, and they'd been together for nearly two years. They'd separated nine years ago, as the publication of her first book approached, when it became clear that Franz would never be entirely comfortable with a woman who was his professional and intellectual equal. He expected to dominate, and she would not be dominated. She had walked out on him, met Harry, got married a year later and never looked back.

Harry felt, in his unfailingly sweet and reasonable way, that Rita and Franz's history was none of his concern. He was secure in his marriage and sure of himself, and therefore had no qualms about recruiting Franz to be the chief meteorologist at Edgeway Station. The German was the best man for the job.

In this one instance, unreasonable jealousy would have served Harry—and all of them—better than rationality. Nine years after their separation, Franz still insisted on playing the lover scorned. In the confines of a polar outpost this was as disruptive, in its way, as shouted insults would have been.

The wind groaned, the snow churned round her and the ice stretched out of sight as it had since time immemorial—but gradually her racing heartbeat subsided to a normal rate. She stopped shaking. The terror passed. She'd won again.

When at last Rita entered the igloo, Franz was packing instruments into a carton. He glanced up at her, nodded, and continued packing.

With his thick blond hair and deep-set dark eyes he possessed a certain animal magnetism, and Rita could see why she had been drawn to him when she was younger. At forty-five he was as muscular and trim as a boy.

'Wind is up to twenty-four miles,' she said, removing her goggles. 'Air temp's down to ten degrees Fahrenheit and falling.'

'With the wind-chill factor, it'll be minus twenty or worse by the time we break camp.' He didn't look up.

'We'll make it back all right.'

'In zero visibility?'

'It won't get that bad so fast.'

'Take another look outside, Rita. This front's pushing in a lot faster than predicted. We could find ourselves in a total whiteout.'

'Honestly, Franz, your gloomy Teutonic nature—'

A thunderlike sound rolled beneath them, and a tremor passed through the ice cap. The rumble was augmented by a high-pitched squeal as dozens of ice strata moved against one another.

Rita stumbled but kept her balance, as though lurching down the aisle of a moving train.

The rumble quickly faded away, and blessed stillness returned.

Franz cleared his throat. 'Larsson's much-heralded big quake?'

'No. Too small. Major movement on this fault chain would be much larger than that, much bigger all down the line. That little shake would hardly have registered on the Richter scale.'

'When can we expect the main event?'

She shrugged. 'Maybe never. Maybe a minute from now.'

Grimacing, he continued packing instruments into the waterproof carton. 'And you were talking about *my* gloomy nature . . .'

12:45pm

Pinned by cones of light from two snowmobiles, Roger Breskin and George Lin finished anchoring the radio transmitter to the ice with four two-foot-long belaying pins, and then ran a systems check on the equipment.

Even the murky glow of the winter twilight had now been frozen out of the sky. Without the snowmobile headlamps, visibility would drop to ten yards. As the wind had gathered speed, it had become an increasingly deadly enemy. Already the fine snow was being driven so hard that it appeared to be sheeting past them on a course parallel to the ice cap. Every few minutes they were forced to scrape their goggles and break the crust of snow off the knitted masks that covered the lower half of their faces.

Standing behind the amber headlights, Brian Dougherty wondered why he had come to that godforsaken terminus. He had never before seen a place so barren; every aspect of the landscape was a blunt reminder that all of life was nothing but a prelude to inevitable and eternal death. Of course, that was precisely why he had come to the ice cap: adventure, danger, the possibility of death. He knew at least that much about himself, though he had only a shadowy notion of *why* he was obsessed with taking extreme risks. He had compelling reasons for staying alive, after all. He was young. He was not wildly handsome, but he wasn't the Hunchback of Notre Dame, either, and he was in love with life. Not least of all, his family was enormously wealthy, and in fourteen months, when he turned twenty-five, he would gain control of a $30 million trust fund.

His family's fame and the sympathy accorded to the whole Dougherty clan would open any door that couldn't be battered down with money. Brian's uncle, once President of the United States, had been assassinated by a sniper. And his father, a United States Senator from California, had been shot and crippled during a primary campaign nine years ago. The tragedies of the Doughertys were the stuff of endless magazine covers, a national obsession that sometimes seemed destined to evolve into a formidable political mythology, in which the Doughertys were not merely ordinary men or women but demigods, embodiments of virtue, goodwill and sacrifice.

In time, Brian could have a political career of his own if he wished. But he was still too young to face the responsibilities of his family tradition and, in fact, he was fleeing those responsibilities. Four years ago, he'd dropped out of Harvard after only eighteen months of law studies. Since then he had travelled the world, and his escapist adventures had put him on the front pages of newspapers on every continent. He had confronted a bull in one of Madrid's rings. He'd broken an arm on an African safari when a rhinoceros attacked his Jeep, and while shooting rapids on the Colorado River he had nearly drowned. Now he was passing the long, merciless winter on the polar ice.

His name and the quality of several magazine articles that he had written were not sufficient credentials to obtain a position as the official chronicler of the expedition. But the Dougherty Family Foundation had made an $850,000 grant to the Edgeway Project, which had guaranteed Brian a place on the team. Brian was genuinely interested in the project, and his sincerity won friends.

He supposed his interest arose from the fact that he was unable to imagine himself making a commitment to any lifelong work that was even half as arduous as theirs. Although a political career was part of his legacy, Brian loathed that vile game: politics was lies, deception, self-interest and self-aggrandisement. Unfortunately, it had infected him with a cynicism that made him question the value of *any* achievement, either inside or outside the political arena.

He *did* take pleasure in the act of writing, and he intended to produce three or four articles about life in the far, far north. Already, in fact, he had enough material for a book, which he felt increasingly compelled to write. Yet such an ambitious undertaking daunted him.

His family thought that he had been attracted to the Edgeway Project because of its humanitarian potential, that he was getting serious about his future. He hadn't wanted to disillusion them, but they were wrong. Initially he'd been drawn to the expedition merely because it was another adventure. It was a way to avoid, for a while longer, thinking about the past and the future.

Lin and Breskin got to their feet and wiped snow from their goggles.

Brian approached them, shouting over the wind, 'Are you done?'

'At last!' Breskin said.

The two-foot-square transmitter would be sheathed in snow and ice within hours, but that wouldn't affect the strong signal that it would put out ten times every minute for eight to twelve days. When that segment of ice was blasted loose from the winter field, the transmitter would drift with it into those channels known as Iceberg Alley and from there into the North Atlantic. Two trawlers, part of the United Nations Geophysical Year (UNGY) fleet, were standing at the ready 230 miles to the south to monitor the radio signal. With the aid of geosynchronous polar satellites, they would home in on the berg until it could be identified visually by the red dye that had been spread across wide areas of its surface.

The purpose of the experiment was to gain an understanding of how winter sea currents affected drift ice. Before any plans could be made to tow ice south to drought-stricken coastal areas, scientists must learn how the sea would work against the ships and how it might be made to work for them.

'Could I get a few pictures?' Brian asked.

'No time for that,' George Lin said shortly. 'Storm could cut us off. By morning we'd be part of the landscape, frozen solid.'

'We can spare a minute,' Roger Breskin said.

Brian smiled thankfully.

'You crazy?' Lin asked. 'See this snow? If we delay—'

'George, you've already wasted a minute carping.' Breskin's tone was not accusatory, merely that of a scientist stating a fact.

Although Roger Breskin had emigrated to Canada from the United States only eight years ago, he was every bit as quiet and calm as the stereotypical Canadian.

Behind his goggles, Lin's eyes narrowed. 'Take your pictures. I guess Roger wants to see himself in all the fancy magazines. But hurry.'

Brian had no choice but to be quick. Weather conditions allowed no time for setting up shots and focusing to perfection.

'This OK?' Roger Breskin asked, standing to the right of the transmitter.

'Great.'

Roger dominated the frame in the viewfinder. He was five foot eleven, shorter and lighter than Pete Johnson but no less muscular than the former football star. He had been a weightlifter for twenty

174

of his thirty-six years, and his biceps were enormous. In Arctic gear, he was an impressively bearish figure, who seemed to belong in these vast frozen wastes as none of the others did.

Standing to the left of the transmitter, George Lin was shorter and slimmer than Roger, but the differences were not merely physical. While Roger stood as silent and still as a pinnacle of ice, Lin swayed from side to side as if he might explode with nervous energy. Unlike Breskin, he didn't belong in these frozen wastes, and he knew it.

George Lin had been born Lin Shen-yang in Canton in 1946, one year before Mao Tse-tung's revolution had ousted the Kuomintang government and established a totalitarian state. His family had not managed to flee to Taiwan until George was seven. In those early years, something monstrous had happened that had forever traumatised and shaped him. Occasionally he alluded to it, but he refused ever to speak of it directly.

'Just hurry,' Lin urged.

Brian focused and pressed the shutter release.

The electronic flash was reflected by the snowscape. Then the deep darkness swarmed back to crouch at the edges of the headlamps.

Brian said, 'One more for—'

The ice cap rose abruptly, precipitously, like the motorised floor in a carnival fun house. It tilted left, right, then dropped out from under him.

He fell, slammed so hard into the ice that even the heavy padding of his clothing did not adequately cushion him from the painful impact. The ice heaved up again, shuddered and bucked, as though striving mightily to fling him off the top of the earth and out into space.

One of the snowmobiles crashed onto its side, inches from his head, and sharp shards of ice exploded in his face, glittery needles, stinging his skin, barely sparing his eyes.

Dizzy, shocked, Brian cautiously raised his head and saw Breskin and Lin sprawled in the snow nearby. Brian started to get up—but he fell again as the wasteland leaped more violently than it had the first time. Gunvald's suboceanic earthquake had come at last.

Brian tried to brace himself within a shallow depression in the ice, wedging between the natural contours to avoid being thrown into the snowmobiles or the transmitter. Evidently a massive tsunami was passing directly under them, hundreds of millions of cubic yards of water rising with all the fury and force of an angry god awakening.

The overturned snowmobile revolved on its side. The headlights swept across Brian twice, harrying shadows like wind-whipped leaves, and then stopped as they illuminated the other men.

Behind Roger Breskin and George Lin, the ice suddenly cracked open with a deafening *boom!* and gaped like a ragged, demonic mouth. Brian shouted a warning.

Roger grasped one of the large steel anchor pins that fixed the transmitter in place, and held on with both hands.

The ice heaved a fourth time. The white field tilted towards the new, yawning crevasse. Although he tried desperately to brace himself, Brian slid out across the ice towards the chasm. He grabbed the transmitter as he sailed past it, crashed hard against Roger Breskin, and held on with fierce determination.

Roger shouted something about George Lin, but the wailing of the wind and the rumble of fracturing ice masked his words.

Squinting through snow-filmed goggles, unwilling to risk his precarious hold to wipe them clean, Brian looked over his shoulder.

Screaming, George Lin slid towards the brink of the new crevasse. He flailed at the slick ice. As the last surge of the tsunami passed beneath them and as the winter cap settled down, Lin fell out of sight into the chasm.

THE SIXTIETH PACKAGE of explosives was no different from the fifty-nine that had been placed in the ice before it: a tube two and a half inches in diameter, sixty inches long, with smooth, rounded ends. A sophisticated timing device and detonator occupied the bottom of the cylinder, synchronised to the timers in the other fifty-nine packages. The upper end of the cylinder terminated in a steel loop, and a gated carabiner hook connected a tempered-steel chain to the loop.

Harry Carpenter wound the chain off the drum of a small hand winch, lowering the package into the narrow hole, working carefully because the charge was equivalent to 3,000 pounds of TNT. When he felt the cylinder touch bottom in the eighty-seven-foot shaft, he connected another carabiner to the free end of the chain, and secured the carabiner to a peg that was embedded in the ice.

Pete Johnson was kneeling beside Harry. He looked over his shoulder at the Frenchman and called out above the keening wind: 'Ready here, Claude.'

A barrel, which they had filled with snow, stood on electric heating coils in one of the cargo trailers. It brimmed with boiling water. Claude Jobert fixed a metal-ring hose to a valve on the barrel. He opened the valve and handed the nozzle to Carpenter.

Loosening the petcock, Harry let hot water pour out of the hose into the deep shaft. In three minutes the hole was sealed: the bomb was suspended in new ice. If he left the shaft open, the explosion would vent upwards to no purpose. The charge had been shaped to blow downwards and expend its energy to all sides, and the hole must be tightly sealed to achieve the desired effect.

Pete Johnson rapped his gloved knuckles against the newly formed plug. 'Now we can get back to Edge—'

The ice cap jolted up, lurched forwards, tilted sharply in front of them, squealed like a great monster and then groaned, before collapsing back into its original plane.

Harry was thrown on his face. His goggles jammed hard against his cheeks and eyebrows. Pain swelled across his cheekbones, and the taste of blood was in his mouth.

Pete and Claude had fallen and were holding each other. Harry caught a brief glimpse of them, grotesquely locked in each other's embrace as though they were a pair of wrestlers.

The ice shook again.

Harry's first thought had been that the plastic explosives had blown up in his face and that he was dead or dying. But, as the ice swelled once more, he realised that tidal waves must be surging beneath the polar cap, no doubt spawned by a seabed quake.

As the fourth wave struck, the white world round Harry cracked and canted, and he found himself suspended at the top of an ice ramp. In the distance, the sound of shattering, grinding ice pierced the night and the wind: the ominous protests of a brittle world cracking asunder. The roar grew nearer by the second, and Harry steeled himself for the worst.

Then, as suddenly as the terror had begun—no more than a minute ago—it ended. The ice plain dropped, became a level floor, and was still.

AT THE FIRST TREMOR, Rita had shouted a warning to Franz, then sprinted far enough to be safely out of any icefall from the looming pressure ridge. When she stopped running and spun round to look back at the temporary camp she saw she was alone. Franz had not emerged from the igloo.

A truck-size piece of the ridge wall cracked off and fell with eerie grace, smashing into the uninhabited igloo at the east end of the crescent-shaped encampment. The inflatable dome popped as if it were a child's balloon.

'Franz!'

A much larger section of the ridge collapsed. Sheets, spires, boulders, slabs of ice crashed into the camp, flattening the centre igloo, overturning a snowmobile, ripping open the igloo at the west end of the camp, from which Franz had still not escaped, casting up thousands of splinters of ice that glinted like showers of sparks.

Then she watched as Franz crawled out of the ruined nylon dome and scrambled towards her. Mortar shells of ice exploded to the left and right of him, but he had the grace of a broken-field runner and the speed born of terror. He raced beyond the avalanche to safety.

As the ridge stabilised and ice stopped falling, Rita was shaken by a vivid vision of Harry crushed beneath a shining white monolith, elsewhere in the cruel polar night. She staggered, ceased trying to keep her balance, sat on the ice and began to shake uncontrollably.

ONLY THE SNOWFLAKES moved, cascading out of the darkness. Harry held on to the snowmobile and pulled himself erect. His heart thudded so hard that it seemed to knock against his ribs. When he regained his breath, he wiped his goggles and looked round.

Pete Johnson was helping Claude to his feet. The Frenchman was rubber-legged but evidently uninjured. Pete didn't even have weak knees; perhaps he was every bit as indestructible as he appeared to be.

High on adrenalin, Harry briefly felt like a boy again, pumped up by the danger, exhilarated by the very fact of having survived.

Then he thought of Rita, and his blood ran cold. The temporary camp was shadowed by a high wall of ice. Ordinarily, that was the best place for it. But, with all the shaking that they had just been through, the ridge might have broken apart . . .

Get moving, he thought, awash with fear far greater than that which he had felt only moments ago. Get packed, get moving, get to her.

He hurried to the other men. 'Anyone hurt?'

'Just rattled,' Claude said. He was not only a man who refused to surrender to adversity but one who was actually buoyed by it. With a brighter smile than he'd managed all day, he said, 'Quite a ride!'

Pete glanced at Harry. 'What about you?'

'Fine.'

'You're bleeding.'

When Harry touched his upper lip, bright chips of frozen blood like fragments of rubies adhered to his glove. 'Nosebleed. It's already stopped. They may be in serious trouble at camp,' he said.

'My thoughts exactly,' Pete said.

As Harry strapped down the last of the instruments in the second snowmobile's cargo trailer, Pete called to him. He wiped his goggles and went to the other machine. Even in the uncertain light, Harry could see the worry in Pete's eyes. 'What is it?'

'During that shaking . . . did the snowmobiles do a lot of moving round?'

'Hell, yes, they bounced up and down as if the ice was a damn trampoline.'

'Just up and down? I mean, is it possible they slid round, sort of swivelled round?'

Harry leaned closer to Pete. 'I was holding tight to one of them. It didn't turn. But what's that have to do with anything?'

'Bear with me. What direction were the snowmobiles facing before the tsunami?'

'East. Towards the temporary camp.'

Pete bit his lower lip. 'Then am I losing my mind or what?'

'Why?'

'Well, for one thing . . .' He tapped the snowmobile's compass.

Harry read the compass. According to the needle, the snowmobile was facing due south, a ninety-degree change from where it had stood before the ice was shaken by the seismic waves.

'That's not all,' Pete said. 'When we parked here, I know damned well the wind was hitting this snowmobile from behind. Now it's blowing across the flank, from my right side. Blizzard winds are steady. They don't change ninety degrees in a few minutes.'

'But if the wind didn't change and the snowmobiles didn't move, that means the ice we're on . . .' Harry's voice trailed away into silence.

At last Pete finished the thought: '. . . so the ice must have revolved one full quarter of the compass.'

'But how's that possible?'

'I have one good idea.'

Harry nodded reluctantly. 'Yeah, so do I.'

'We're in deep trouble, Harry.'

They hurried to the second vehicle, and the fresh snow crunched and squeaked under their boots.

Pete tapped the face of the compass. 'This one's facing south too.'

Harry said nothing. Their situation was so dire that he didn't want to have to put it into words.

Pete surveyed the inhospitable wasteland that surrounded them. 'If the temperature keeps dropping . . . and it *will* keep dropping . . . then how long could we survive out here?'

'With our current supplies, not even one day.'

'The nearest help . . .'

'Would be those UNGY trawlers. Two hundred miles away.'

'And they're not going to head north into a major storm, not with so many ice floes to negotiate.'

Neither of them spoke. The banshee shriek of the wind filled the silence. Harry shook his head. 'Only one thing's certain. We won't be driving back to Edgeway Station this afternoon.'

Claude Jobert joined them in time to hear that last exchange. Even though the lower part of his face was covered by a snow mask, his alarm was unmistakable. He put one hand on Harry's arm. 'What's wrong?'

Harry glanced at Pete.

To Claude, Pete said, 'Those waves . . . they broke up the edge of the ice field. We're adrift on an iceberg.'

'That can't be,' Claude said, tightening his grip on Harry's arm.

'Outrageous, but it's true,' Harry said. 'We're moving further away from Edgeway Station with every passing minute.'

Claude looked from Harry to Pete, then round at the forbidding landscape, as if he expected to see something that would refute what they had told him. 'You can't be sure.'

'All but certain,' Pete disagreed.

Claude was a reluctant convert to the truth. 'But under us . . . those bombs . . .'

'Exactly,' Harry said. 'Those bombs.'

1:00pm

One of the snowmobiles was on its side; the other was canted against a low hummock of ice. The four headlamps parted the curtains of snow, illuminating nothing, pointing away from the precipice over which George Lin had disappeared. Although Brian Dougherty was convinced that any search for him was a waste of time, he scrambled to the edge of the new crevasse and sprawled face down on the ice at the jagged brink. Roger Breskin joined him, and they lay side by side, peering into a terrible darkness.

Queasiness coiled and slithered in Brian's gut. He tried to dig the metal toes of his boots into the iron-hard ice, and he clutched at the flat surface. If another tsunami set the world adance, he might be tipped into the abyss.

Roger directed his flashlight outwards, towards the distant wall of the crevasse. Except for falling snow, nothing was revealed within the reach of the yellow beam. The light dwindled away into blackness.

'It isn't a crevasse,' Brian said. 'It's a damned canyon!'

The beam moved slowly back and forth: nothing lay out there. Nothing whatsoever. Brian was baffled. 'I don't understand.'

'We've broken off from the main ice field,' Roger explained, with characteristic yet nonetheless remarkable equanimity.

Brian needed a moment to absorb that news and grasp the full horror of it. 'Broken off . . . You mean we're adrift?'

'A ship of ice.'

The wind gusted so violently that for half a minute Brian could not have been heard above it even if he'd shouted at the top of his

180

voice. When the gust died out at last, he leaned towards Roger Breskin. 'What about the others?'

'Could be on this berg too. But let's hope they're still on safe ice.'

'Dear God.'

Roger directed the flashlight away from the darkness where they had expected to find the far wall of a crevasse. The pale light angled to the left and right, then touched upon the choppy, black, unfrozen sea that raged eighty or ninety feet below them. Irregular chunks of ice bobbled and swirled in the deep troughs of frigid dark water, crashed together on the crests of the waves; touched by the light, they glittered as if they were diamonds spread on black velvet.

Mesmerised by the chaos that the flashlight revealed, swallowing hard, Brian said, 'George fell into the sea. He's gone.'

'Maybe not.' Pushing with his elbows against the ice, Roger inched forwards until he was able to peer over the brink and straight down the face of the precipice. The flashlight beam found the place where their ice island met the sea. The cliff did not plunge cleanly into the water. At its base, it was shattered into three ragged shelves, each six or eight feet below the one above it. The shelves were as fissured and sharp-edged and jumbled as the base of any rocky bluff on dry land. Storm waves crashed across the shelves and broke against the glistening palisades, exploding into fat gouts of foam and icy spray. Lin would have been dashed to pieces in that maelstrom.

The light moved slowly backwards and upwards, revealing more of the cliff. Just twenty feet below them, another shelf crossed the face of the berg. This one was only a few feet wide. Roger Breskin used the flashlight to explore it.

Eight feet to the right of them, twenty feet down, previously cloaked in darkness, lay George Lin. He was on his left side, facing out towards the open sea. His left arm was wedged under him, and his right arm was across his chest. He had assumed the foetal position, with his knees drawn up and his head tucked down.

Roger cupped his free hand to his mouth and shouted: 'George! You hear me? George!'

Lin didn't move or respond.

'You think he's alive?' Brian asked.

'Must be. Didn't fall far. Clothes are quilted, insulated—absorbed some impact.'

Brian cupped both hands round his mouth and shouted at Lin.

The only answer came from the steadily increasing wind, and it was easy to believe that its shriek was full of gleeful malevolence, that this wind was somehow alive and daring them to remain at the brink just a moment longer.

'Have to go down and get him,' Roger said.

Brian studied the slick, vertical wall of ice that dropped twenty feet to the ledge. 'How?'

'We've got rope, tools. We'll improvise.'

'Improvise?' Brian said in astonishment. 'You done any climbing?'

'No.'

'This is nuts.'

Brian stared down at the crumpled figure on the ledge. In a Spanish bullring, on the African veld, on the Colorado River . . . in so many ways he had tempted death without much fear. He wondered why he was hesitating now. Virtually every risk he'd ever taken had been pointless, a childish game. This time he had a good reason for risking everything: a human life was at stake. Was that the problem? Was it that he didn't want to be a hero? Too damned many heroes in the Dougherty family.

'Let's get working,' Brian said at last. 'George'll freeze if he lies there much longer.'

1:05pm

Harry Carpenter leaned into the handlebars and squinted through the curve of Plexiglas at the white landscape. Hard sprays of snow and sleet slanted through the headlights. The windshield wiper thumped monotonously, crusted with ice but still doing its job. Visibility had decreased to ten or twelve yards.

The only vehicles in use by the Edgeway expedition were custom-stretched snowmobiles with rotary-combustion engines and specially engineered suspension. Each machine could carry two adults in bulky thermal clothing on a thirty-six-inch padded bench. The driver and passenger rode in tandem, one behind the other.

Of course, the machines had been adapted further for operations in the rugged polar winter, where conditions were dramatically more severe than those encountered by snowmobile enthusiasts back in the States. Aside from a pair of special heavy-duty Arctic batteries, the major modification on each vehicle was the addition of a cabin that extended from the hood to the end of the stretched passenger bench. That enclosure was fabricated of riveted aluminium sheets and thick Plexiglas. An efficient little heater had been mounted over the engine, and two small fans conducted the warm air to the driver and passenger. Without the cabin, the continuous pounding of the wind would chill any driver to the bone and might kill him on a trip longer than four or five miles.

A few of the sleds had been further modified in unique ways.

Harry's was one of those, for he was transporting the power drill. The drill was too important to be exposed to the shocks that rattled the bed of a cargo trailer; therefore, the last half of the bench was fitted with locking braces, and the drill was now dogged down tightly behind Harry, occupying the space where a passenger ordinarily would have been. With those few modifications, the sled was well suited for work on the Greenland ice.

Although the vehicle had a top speed of forty-five miles per hour, at the moment, Harry was holding the snowmobile to a crawl. If the brink of the iceberg abruptly loomed out of the storm, and he were going at all fast, he would not be able to stop the machine in time, and he would pitch down into the sea. Haunted by that mental image, he kept the engine throttled back to just five miles per hour.

They had struck out due south from the sixtieth blasting shaft, maintaining that heading as well as they could, on the assumption that what had been east prior to the tsunami was now south.

Harry glanced in the side-mounted mirror. The headlamps of the second sled—carrying Pete and Claude—sparkled in the darkness behind him.

Although distracted for only a second, he quickly returned to his scrutiny of the ice ahead, hoping to see a glimmer of light from the temporary camp. Rita and Franz would realise that without a marker the camp would be difficult if not impossible to find in such weather. They would switch on the snowmobile lights and focus on the ridge of ice behind the camp: the glow, reflected and intensified, would be an unmistakable beacon.

But he was unable to see even a vague, shimmering luminescence ahead. The darkness worried him, for he took it to mean that the camp was gone, buried under tons of ice.

He squinted through the falling snow: nothing.

If he found Rita alive, he would thank God every minute of the rest of his life—which might total precious few. For she had brought him more joy than he had ever expected to know.

Just thirty feet ahead, in the headlights, a narrow black line appeared on the snow-swept plain: a crack in the ice, barely visible from his perspective. Harry hit the brakes hard. The machine slid round thirty degrees on its axis, skis clattering loudly. He turned the handlebars into the slide until he felt the track gripping again, and then he steered back to the right.

Still moving, gliding like a hockey puck, twenty feet from the looming pit and *still* sliding . . .

The black line grew clearer. Ice was visible beyond it. So it must be a crevasse. Not the ultimate brink, with only night on the far side and only the cold sea at the base of it. Just a crevasse.

Sliding, sliding . . .

The skis rattled. Something knocked against the undercarriage. The snow cover was thin. Ice offered poor traction. Snow billowed from the skis, from the churning polyurethane track, like clouds of smoke.

Fifteen feet . . . ten feet . . .

The sled stopped smoothly, so near the crevasse that Harry was not able to see the edge of the ice over the sloped front of the machine. The tips of the skis must have been protruding beyond the brink. He slipped the machine into reverse and backed up two or three feet, until he could see the precipice.

Shivering, but not because of the cold, he pulled his goggles from his forehead, fitted them over his eyes, opened the cabin door and got out. The headlights revealed that the crevasse was only about four yards wide at the centre and narrowed drastically towards both ends. Gazing down into the blackness, he suspected that the depth of the chasm could be measured in hundreds of feet.

He shuddered and turned his back to it. Twenty feet behind his sled, the second snowmobile was stopped with its engine running, lights blazing. Pete Johnson squeezed out through the cabin door.

Harry waved and started towards him. The ice rumbled and moved. Surprised, Harry halted.

For an instant he thought that another seismic wave was passing beneath them. But they were adrift now and wouldn't be affected by a tsunami in the same way as they had been when on the fixed ice cap. No, the disturbance was entirely local—in fact, it was directly under his feet. Suddenly the ice opened in front of him, a zigzagging crack about an inch wide, wider, wider, now as wide as his hand, then even wider. He was standing with his back to the brink, and the badly fractured wall of the newly formed crevasse was disintegrating beneath him.

He staggered, flung himself forwards, jumped across the jagged fissure, aware that it was widening under him even as he was in mid-leap. He fell on the far side and rolled away from that treacherous patch of ice. Behind him, the wall of the crevasse calved off thick slabs that crashed into the depths, and thunder rose from below. The plain shivered.

Harry pushed up onto his knees, not sure if he was safe. Hell, no. The edge of the chasm continued to disintegrate into the pit, the crevasse widened towards him, and he scrambled frantically away from it.

Gasping, he glanced back in time to see his snowmobile slide into the chasm. It slammed against the far wall and was pinned there for an instant by a truck-size slab of ice. The fuel in the main and auxiliary tanks exploded. Flames gushed high but quickly subsided as the burning wreckage sought the depths. Around and under him, red-orange phantoms shimmered briefly in the milky ice; then the fire puffed out, and darkness took command.

1:07pm

Cryophobia. The fear of ice. Circumstances made it far harder than usual for Rita Carpenter to repress that persistent, debilitating terror.

Portions of the pressure ridge had partially collapsed, while other sections had been radically recontoured by the tsunami. Now a shallow cave—approximately forty feet deep and thirty feet wide—pocked the white ramparts.

She hesitated in the entrance to that cold haven, reluctant to follow Franz Fischer inside, plagued by the irrational feeling that she would be moving not merely forwards a few feet but simultaneously backwards in time to that winter day when she was six, to the living death of the white tomb . . .

Clenching her teeth, struggling to repress a sense of almost paralysing dread, she went inside. The storm raged behind her, but she found comparative quiet within those white walls, as well as relief from the biting wind and snow.

With her flashlight, Rita studied the ceiling and the walls, searching for indications that the structure was in imminent danger of collapsing. The cave appeared to be stable enough at the moment.

'Risky,' she said, unable to prevent her voice from breaking.

Franz agreed. 'But we don't have any choice.'

All three inflatable shelters had been destroyed. To remain in the increasingly fierce wind for an extended period of time would be courting hypothermia.

They went outside again and carried the short-wave radio—which appeared to have survived the destruction of the camp—into the ice cave and set it on the floor against the rear wall. Franz ran wires in from the back-up battery of the undamaged snowmobile, and they hooked up the transceiver. Rita switched it on, and the selection band glowed sea-green.

'It works,' she said, relieved.

Franz had no sooner stepped outside to see what else he could salvage than an urgent transmission came through from Gunvald at Edgeway Station.

'What a relief to hear your voice,' Gunvald said. 'Is everyone all right?'

'The camp was destroyed, but Franz and I are OK. We've taken shelter in an ice cave.'

'Harry and the others?'

'We don't know what's happened to them,' she said, and her chest tightened with anxiety. 'They're out on work details. We'll give them fifteen minutes to show up before we go looking.' She hesitated and cleared her throat. 'The thing is . . . we're adrift.'

For a moment, Gunvald was too stunned to speak. Then: 'Are you certain?'

'A change in wind direction alerted us. Then the compasses.'

'Give me a moment,' Larsson said, with audible distress. 'Let me think.'

In spite of the storm and the strong magnetic disturbances that accompany bad weather in those latitudes, Larsson's voice was clear a few moments later as he said, 'What's the size of this iceberg of yours? Do you have any idea?'

'None at all. We haven't had an opportunity to reconnoitre. Right now, we're just searching for whatever's salvageable in the wreckage of the camp.'

'If the iceberg isn't very large . . . Harry and the others might not be adrift with you.'

Rita closed her eyes. 'I hope that's true.'

'Whether they are or aren't, the situation is far from hopeless. I'll get a message by satellite relay to the USAF base at Thule. Once I've alerted them, they can contact those trawlers standing south of you.'

'But what then? No sensible captain would bring a trawler into a storm. He'd lose his ship and his crew trying to save us.'

'They've got the most modern rescue aircraft at Thule, helicopters capable of manoeuvring in almost any conditions.'

'There isn't a plane yet invented that can fly safely in this kind of storm—let alone set down on an iceberg in gale-force winds.'

The radio produced only crackling static and warbling electronic squeals, but she sensed that Gunvald was still there.

Yeah, she thought. It leaves me speechless too.

Finally the Swede said, 'OK, you're right about the aircraft. But we can't give up hope of rescue. Take turns getting warm in the snowmobiles. Do you have a good supply of fuel?'

'Enough to get back to Edgeway—if that were possible. Not a hell of a lot more than that. Enough to run the engines for a few hours, not a few days.'

'Well then . . .'

Silence. Static.

He came back after several seconds. '. . . I'll put through that call to Thule all the same. They might see an answer that we've overlooked.'

She said, 'Edgeway came through unscathed?'

'Fine here. I'll live. And so will you, Rita.'

'I'll try,' she said. 'I'll sure as hell try.'

1:10pm

Brian Dougherty siphoned gasoline from the tank of the upright snowmobile and poured it onto a two-foot section of ice at the brink of the cliff.

Roger Breskin twisted open a chemical match and tossed it into the gasoline. Flames erupted, flapped like bright tattered flags in the wind, but burned out within seconds.

Kneeling where the fire had been, Brian examined the edge of the precipice. The ice had been jagged; now it was smooth and slick. A climber's rope would slide over it without fraying.

'Good enough?' Roger asked.

Brian nodded.

Roger stooped and snatched up the free end of a thirty-five-foot nylon rope that he had tied to the frame of the snowmobile and had also anchored to a long threaded-piton identical to those used to secure the radio transmitter. He quickly looped it round Brian's chest and shoulders, fashioning a harness of sorts. He tied three sturdy knots at the centre of the younger man's chest and said, 'It'll hold. Just remember to grip the rope above your head with both hands so you'll keep some of the pressure off your shoulders.'

Because he did not trust himself to speak without a nervous stammer, Brian nodded.

Roger returned to the snowmobile, which was facing towards the precipice and which he had disconnected from its cargo trailer. He climbed into the cabin, closed the door, then held the brakes and revved the engine.

Trembling, Brian stretched out on his stomach, flat on the ice. He took a deep breath through his knitted ski mask, hesitated only briefly, and pushed himself feet first over the edge of the cliff. Although he didn't drop far, his stomach lurched, and a thrill of terror like an electrical current sizzled through him. The rope pulled tight, checking his descent when the crown of his head was only inches below the top of the iceberg.

As yet, too little of the line hung past the brink to enable him to reach overhead and get a firm grip on it. He was forced to take the strain entirely with his shoulders.

'Come on, come on, Roger,' he muttered. 'Be quick.'

Because Roger was highly experienced with the snowmobile, it had seemed logical and reasonable to Brian that he should be the one to go down to retrieve George Lin. Now he wished that he had been the snowmobile expert. What the hell was taking so long?

His impatience evaporated when he suddenly dropped as if the rope had been cut. He landed on the ledge with such force that pain shot up his legs to the top of his spine. His knees crumpled as though they were sodden cardboard. He fell against the face of the cliff, bounced off, and toppled off the narrow ledge, out into the wind-shattered night.

He was too terrified to scream.

Roger had hit the brakes immediately after he released them, but, because the ice had been swept free of snow and polished by the incessant wind, it provided little traction. The snowmobile had lurched forwards too fast. As smoothly as a shuffleboard puck gliding along polished pine, it slid another ten feet, headlights spearing out into an eternal blackness, before it finally stopped less than ten feet from the edge of the cliff.

The harness jerked tight across Brian's chest and under his arms. Compared to the throbbing pain in his legs and the ache in his back, however, the new agony was endurable. He was surprised that he was still alive. Unclipping his flashlight from the tool belt that encircled his waist, he cut open the perfect blackness round him with a blade of light, and torrents of snowflakes gushed over him.

Trying not to think about the icy sea below, he peered up at the ledge that he had overshot. It was four feet above his head. A yard to his left, the gloved fingers of George Lin's inert right hand trailed over the shelf.

A flashlight beam stabbed down from above.

Brian raised his eyes and saw Roger Breskin peering at him from the top of the cliff. 'You all right?' Roger shouted. His voice sounded as if it came from the far end of a five-mile-long railroad tunnel.

Brian nodded as best he could: Yes, I'm all right. There was no way to convey, with only a nod, the degree of his fear and the worry that was caused by the lingering pain in his legs.

Breskin shouted, but only a few of his words reached Brian: 'Going . . . snowmobile . . . draw you . . . up.'

Again, Brian nodded.

Roger disappeared, hurrying back to the snowmobile.

Leaving his flashlight on, Brian clipped it to his tool belt, with the beam shining down on his right foot. He reached overhead and gripped the taut line with both hands, hoisting himself slightly to take a measure of the strain off his upper arms.

The snowmobile drew up some of the line. The movement was smooth compared to the style of his descent, and he was not thrown against the cliff. From the knees down, his legs were still below the ledge. He swung them up and over, planted both feet on the narrow shelf of ice, crouching there. He let go of the rope and stood up. His ankles ached, his knees felt as if they were made of jelly, and pain laced his thighs. But his legs held him.

He took a large piton—a five-inch shaft tapered to a sharp point, topped by a one-inch-diameter eye loop—from a zippered pocket of his coat. He freed a small hammer from his tool belt and pounded the pin into a tight crack in the face of the cliff.

Again, Roger's flashlight shone down from the top.

When the anchoring pin was secure, Brian unhooked an eight-foot coil of nylon rope from his belt. Before descending, he had knotted one end of it to a carabiner; now he linked the carabiner to the piton and screwed shut its safety gate. He tied the other end of the line round his waist. The resultant tether would bring him up short of death if he slipped and fell off the ledge, yet he was free enough to attend to George Lin. Thus belayed, he untied the harness that ran across his chest and coiled the rope round his neck.

He got on his hands and knees and crawled to Lin. He took his flashlight from his belt and placed it on the ledge, against the cliff face, with the beam shining on the unconscious man.

Unconscious—or dead?

Before he could answer that question, he had to get a look at Lin's face. Turning the man onto his back was not an easy chore, because Brian had to be careful that the scientist did not roll off into the abyss. By the time Lin was on his back, he'd regained consciousness. His amber skin—at least on those few square inches of his face that were exposed—was shockingly pale.

'How do you feel?' Brian shouted above the shrill wind.

Lin stared at him uncomprehendingly and tried to sit up.

Brian pressed him down. 'Be careful! You don't want to fall.'

Lin turned his head and stared into the darkness. When he looked at Brian again, his pallor had deepened.

'Are you badly hurt?' Brian asked.

'Some chest pain,' Lin said, barely loud enough to be heard.

'Heart?'

'No. When I went over the edge . . . the ice was still rocking . . . from the wave . . . the cliff face was slanted. I *slid* down . . . and landed here hard on my side. That's all I remember.'

'Broken ribs?'

Lin took a deep breath and winced. 'No. Probably not. Only bruised, I think. Damn sore. But nothing's fractured.'

Brian removed the coil of rope from round his neck. 'I'll have to make a harness under your arms. You'll have to sit up.'

Groaning, Lin eased cautiously into a sitting position, with his back towards the cliff and his legs dangling in the void.

Brian quickly fashioned a harness, tied a tight double knot over Lin's breastbone, and got to his feet. He reached down and helped the injured man to stand.

'Ready?' Roger called from twenty feet above.

'Yeah. But take it easy!'

Lin clapped his hands rapidly, loudly. 'Feel numb . . . all over. I can move my fingers . . . but hardly feel them.'

'You'll be OK.'

'Can't feel . . . toes at all. Sleepy. Not good.'

He was right about that. When the body became so cold that it encouraged sleep to maintain heat, death might not be far away.

'As soon as you're topside, get into the sled,' Brian said. 'Fifteen minutes, you'll be as warm as toast.'

'You risked your life. Why?'

'Well, wouldn't you have done the same?'

The taut line was pulled smoothly upwards, taking George Lin with it. At the top of the precipice, however, Lin got stuck, with his shoulders past the brink and the rest of him dangling in the wind. He was too weak to pull himself to safety.

Roger Breskin's years of training as a weightlifter served him well. He left the snowmobile and easily manhandled George Lin the last few feet onto the top of the iceberg. He untied the harness from the man's shoulders and threw the main line down to Brian.

'Check with you . . . soon as . . . George settled!' he shouted. Even though his voice was wind-tattered, the anxiety in it was evident.

Only an hour ago, Brian couldn't have conceived that Roger—rock solid as he was, with his bull's neck, massive biceps and air of self-reliance—might ever be afraid of anything whatsoever. Now that the other man's fear was evident, Brian was less ashamed of the terror that knotted his own guts.

He picked up the main line and harnessed himself to it. Then he untied the safety tether at his waist, loosened the other end from the piton, coiled it and hooked it to his tool belt. He plucked the flashlight from the ledge and also fastened it to the belt. He would have salvaged the piton too, if he'd had the strength to prise it out of the ice. Their supplies, the fuel and the tools were priceless. No one could predict what scrap, now insignificant, might eventually be essential to their survival. A flashlight beam found him in the darkness.

'Are you ready to go?' Roger Breskin shouted.

'Whenever you are.'

Roger returned to the snowmobile.

No sooner had Brian braced himself than the rope was drawn up, putting a new and more terrible strain on his aching shoulders. Battered by the wind, half-dazed by pain, unable to stop thinking about the immense watery grave that lapped far below him, he slid along the face of the cliff as smoothly as George Lin had done five minutes ago. When he came to the brink, he was able to push and kick over the top without Roger's help.

He got up and took a few uncertain steps towards the snow-mobile's headlamps. His legs were sore, but he had come through virtually unscathed. 'Incredible,' he said, untying the knots that held the harness together.

'What are you talking about?' Roger asked as he joined him.

'Didn't expect to make it.'

'You didn't trust me?'

'It wasn't that. I thought the rope would snap or something.'

'You're going to die eventually,' Roger said, his voice almost theatrical in its effect. 'But this wasn't your place. It wasn't the right time.'

Brian was as amazed to hear Roger Breskin waxing philosophical as he had been to learn that the man knew fear.

'If you're not hurt, we'd better get moving.'

Working his throbbing shoulders, Brian said, 'What now?'

Roger wiped his goggles. 'Find the temporary camp. Join up with the others.'

'What if the camp isn't on this iceberg with us?'

Roger had already turned away towards the toppled snowmobile.

THE CABIN of the remaining snowmobile would seat only two men; therefore, Harry elected to ride behind in the open cargo trailer. Claude was willing to surrender his place, and Pete Johnson insisted on giving up his seat behind the handlebars, as though riding in the trailer was desirable, when in fact the exposure might prove deadly. Harry cut them short and pulled rank in order to obtain that worst of all positions for himself.

Three or four inches of snow had accumulated in the trailer bed. Harry brushed it out with his hands. He turned his back squarely to the wind and pulled on the drawstring at his chin, loosening his hood. He reached inside the neck of his coat and got hold of the thick woollen snow mask that had been folded against his throat. He tugged it over his mouth and nose; now not even a fraction of his face was exposed. What the mask did not cover, the hood and the goggles concealed. He drew the hood tight once more and knotted the drawstring.

The snowmobile began to move.

Conditions in the trailer were even worse than Harry had expected. The suspension system was primitive at best, and every irregularity of the ice cap was instantly transmitted through the skis to the trailer bed. Even his heavy clothing could not fully cushion him from the cruellest shocks. The wind roared at him from every direction; blasts of frigid air searched relentlessly for a chink in his Arctic armour.

Aware that dwelling on his condition would only make it seem much worse, he guided his thoughts into other channels. He closed his eyes and conjured a vivid picture of Rita. But in order not to think of her as she might be—cold, frightened, injured or even dead—he cast his mind back in time, back to the day they had first met. The second Friday of May. Nearly nine years ago. In Paris . . .

HE HAD BEEN ATTENDING a conference of scientists who had participated in the previous United Nations Geophysical Year. From all over the world, 300 men and women of different disciplines had met in Paris for seminars, lectures and intense discussions.

At three o'clock on Friday afternoon, in a small room off the hotel mezzanine, Harry addressed a handful of geophysicists and meteorologists who were interested in his Arctic studies. When he had made his final point, he put away his notes and suggested they switch to a question-and-answer format.

He was surprised and enchanted by a beautiful young woman who asked more intelligent, incisive questions than the twenty eminent grey heads in the room. She looked as though she might be half-Irish and half-Italian. Her amber-olive skin seemed to radiate heat. Wide mouth, ripe lips: very Italian. But there was something Irish in her curious, lopsided smile which gave her an elfin quality. Her eyes were Irish, too, green, clear—but almond-shaped. Long, lustrous auburn hair. In a group that opted for tweeds, sensible spring suits and plain dresses, she stood out in tan corduroy jeans and a dark-blue sweater that accentuated her exciting figure. But it was her mind—quick, inquisitive, well informed, well trained—that most engaged Harry.

When the meeting broke up, he reached her before she left the room. 'I wanted to thank you for making this a more interesting session than it might otherwise have been, but I don't even know your name.'

She smiled crookedly. 'Rita Marzano.'

'Marzano. I thought you looked half-Italian, half-Irish.'

'Half-English, actually.' Her smile developed into a full, lopsided grin. 'My father was Italian, but I was raised in London.'

'Marzano . . . that's familiar. You've written a book, haven't you?'

'*Changing Tomorrow*.'

Changing Tomorrow was popularised science, a study of mankind's future projected from current discoveries in genetics, biochemistry and physics. It was on the best-seller lists.

'Have you read it?' she asked.

'No,' he admitted.

'My British publisher shipped four hundred copies to the convention. They're on sale in the news corner off the lobby.' She glanced at her watch. 'I'm scheduled for an autograph session now. If you'd like a signed copy, I won't make you wait in line.'

That night he was unable to put the book down until he turned the last page at three o'clock in the morning. He was fascinated by her way of ordering facts and her unconventional but logical approaches to problems, because they were startlingly like his own thought processes. He felt almost as though he was reading his own book.

He slept through the Saturday morning lectures and spent most of the afternoon looking for Rita. When he wasn't looking for her, he was thinking about her. As he showered and dressed for the evening's gala affair, he realised he couldn't recall a word spoken in the one lecture to which he had gone.

For the first time in his life, Harry Carpenter wondered what life was like for a settled man sharing a future with one woman. He was what many women would call 'a good catch': five foot eleven pleasant-looking if not handsome, with grey eyes and aristocratic features. But he had never wanted to be anyone's catch. He'd always wanted a woman who was his equal, a woman with whom he could share his work and hopes and ideas, from whom he could get feedback. He thought perhaps he had found her, but he didn't know what to do about it. At thirty-three, he had spent far too many hours in academic pursuits and too few learning the rituals of courtship.

The programme for the evening included a film study of the major UNGY projects, a banquet and a floor show, followed by dancing to a twelve-piece band. Ordinarily, he would have gone only to the film, if that. But there was a good chance that he'd see Rita Marzano at one of the social functions.

She was last in line at the hotel's exhibition hall, where the film was to be shown. She was alone, and she smiled when she saw him.

With a candour that he could not control and a blush that he hoped she didn't notice, he said, 'I've been looking for you all day.'

'And just why were you looking for me all day?'

'Well, the book. I'd like to talk about it if you have a minute.'

'Minute?'

'Or an hour.'

'Or an evening?'

Damn if he wasn't blushing again. He felt like an Indiana farm boy. 'Well . . .'

She looked along the exhibition-hall line, turned to Harry again, and grinned. 'If we skip out on this, we'll have all evening to talk.'

'Aren't you interested in the film?'

'No. Besides, dinner will be awful.'

'How about Laperouse for dinner then?'

She frowned. 'That's pretty expensive. You needn't take me first class. I'm as happy with beer as with champagne.'

'This is a special occasion. For me if not for you.'

Dinner was perfect. Paris offered no more romantic atmosphere than that in the upstairs room at Laperouse. From their table they had a view of the night-clad city, and below them lay the light-stained, oily river like a storybook giant's discarded black silk scarf. Throughout the meal, they unravelled an endless skein of conversation, immediately as comfortable as friends who have been dining together for a decade. When he finished his cognac, Harry was reluctant to let the night end so soon.

She shared his reluctance and said, 'Shall we go? We haven't talked about my book, and that's really what you wanted to do. Tell you what. We'll walk to the Hotel George V, have some champagne in my room and talk.'

He was somewhat confused. 'You're not staying at the convention hotel? I know it's dull, but the George V is terribly expensive.'

'I've made a tidy sum from *Changing Tomorrow*. I'm splurging, for once. I have a small suite overlooking the gardens.'

In her room a bottle of champagne stood beside her bed in a silver bucket full of crushed ice.

She pointed to the bottle. 'Moët. Open it, please.'

He took it out of the bucket—and saw her wince.

'The sound of the ice,' she said.

'What about it?'

She hesitated. 'Puts my teeth on edge. Like fingernails screeching against a blackboard.'

By then he was so attuned to her that he knew she wasn't telling him the truth, that she had winced because the rattle of the ice had reminded her of something unpleasant. For a moment her eyes were far away, deep in a memory that furrowed her brow.

'The ice is hardly melted,' he said. 'When did you order this?'

Shedding the troubling memory, she focused on him and grinned again. 'When I went to the ladies' room at Laperouse.'

Incredulous, he said, '*You're* seducing *me.*'

'Are you offended? It's very late in the twentieth century, you know.'

'Good heavens, no.'

'Actually, I've never done anything like this before. I mean, going to bed on a first date.'

'Neither have I.'

'But it feels right, doesn't it?'

He eased the bottle into the ice and pulled her into his arms. Her lips were the texture of a dream, and her body against his felt like destiny.

They skipped the rest of the convention and stayed in bed. They talked, made love and slept as if they were drugged.

SOMEONE WAS SHOUTING his name.

Stiff with cold, crusted with snow, Harry raised himself from the bed of the cargo trailer and from the delicious memories.

Claude Jobert was staring at him through the rear window of the snowmobile cabin. 'Harry! Hey, Harry!' He was barely audible above the wind and the engine noise. 'Lights! Ahead! Look!'

At first he didn't understand what Claude meant. He was stiff, chilled, and still half in that Paris hotel room. Then he lifted his gaze and saw that they were driving towards a hazy yellow light that shimmered languidly across the ice.

Pete Johnson drove the snowmobile along the familiar ice plateau and down into the basin where the igloos had been. The domes were deflated, crushed by enormous slabs of ice. But one snowmobile was running, headlights ablaze, and two people in Arctic gear stood beside it, waving.

One of them was Rita.

Harry launched himself out of the trailer while the snowmobile was still in motion, and ran to her.

'Harry!'

He grabbed her, nearly lifted her above his head, then put her down and lowered his snow mask. He tried to speak, couldn't, and hugged her instead.

Eventually, voice quivering, she said, 'Are you hurt?'

'Nosebleed, that's all. And you?'

'Just frightened.'

He knew that she struggled against her fear of snow, ice and cold, and he never ceased to admire her determination to confront her phobias. 'You've good reason this time,' he said. 'Listen, you know what we'll do if we get off this damned berg?'

She shook her head and shoved up her misted goggles, so he could see her lovely green eyes, which were wide with curiosity.

'We'll go to Paris,' he told her.

Grinning, she said, 'To the Hotel George V.'

'A room overlooking the gardens.'

He pulled up his own goggles, and she kissed him.

Clapping one hand on Harry's shoulder, Pete Johnson said, 'Have some consideration for those whose wives don't like frostbite. And didn't you hear what I said? The gang's all here.' He pointed to a pair of snowmobiles racing towards them through the snow.

'Roger, Brian and George,' Rita said with obvious relief.

'The gang's all here,' Harry agreed. 'But where in the name of God does it go next?'

1:32pm

On the fourteenth day of a 100-day espionage mission, the Russian nuclear submarine *Ilya Pogodin* reached its first monitoring station on schedule. The captain, Nikita Gorov, ordered the manoeuvring room to hold the boat steady in the moderate southeasterly currents north of Jan Mayen Island, forty miles from the coast of Greenland and 100 feet beneath the stormy surface of the North Atlantic.

The *Ilya Pogodin* had been named after an official Hero of the Soviet People, in the days before the corrupt bureaucracy had failed and the totalitarian state had crumbled under the weight of its own inefficiency and venality. The boat's name had not been changed: in part because the navy was tradition-bound, and in part because Russia was now so fearfully poor that the country could spare no funds for the repainting of boat names.

Gorov was unable to obtain even adequate maintenance for his vessel. In these trying days after the fall of empire, he was too worried about the integrity of the pressure hull, the nuclear power plant and the engines to spare any concern for the fact that the *Ilya Pogodin* was named after a despicable thief and murderer who had been nothing more noble than a dutiful defender of the late, unlamented regime.

Although the *Pogodin* was an ageing fleet submarine, it was nonetheless a substantial boat, measuring 360 feet from bow to stern. The southeasterly currents had a negligible influence on it and it would not drift more than 100 yards from where Gorov had ordered it to be held steady.

Peter Timoshenko, the communications officer, was in the control centre at Gorov's side. Around them, the electronic equipment pulsed and glowed and blinked in the half light. When the manoeuvring room acknowledged Gorov's order to hold the boat steady, Timoshenko said, 'Request permission to run up the aerial, Captain.'

'That's what we're here for.'

After giving Timoshenko a while to deploy the aerial and scan a wide spectrum of frequencies, Captain Gorov stepped into the doorway of the communications shack. He nodded at the communications officer and said, 'Anything of interest?'

'Not much as yet. There's a group of American Marines winter-testing some equipment near the coast.'

Although they were living in the long shadow of the Cold War's passage, in a world where old enemies were supposed to have become neutral towards one another or were even said to have become fine friends, the greater part of the former Soviet intelligence apparatus remained intact. The Russian navy continued to conduct extensive information-gathering along the coastline of every major Western nation, as well as at most points of strategic military importance in the Third World. If enemies could become friends virtually overnight, they could become *enemies* again with equal alacrity.

'Keep me informed,' Gorov said, then went to lunch.

CROUCHED AT THE SHORT-WAVE radio, in contact with Edgeway Station, Harry said, 'Have you got through to Thule?'

Although Gunvald Larsson's voice was filtered through a sieve of static, it was intelligible. 'I've been in continuous contact with them and with Norwegian officials at a meteorological station on Spitsbergen for the past twenty-five minutes.'

'Can either of them reach us?'

'The Norwegians are pretty much locked in by ice. The Americans have several rescue helicopters at Thule, but conditions at ground level aren't really good enough to allow them to lift off. Terrific winds. And by the time they got to you—if they *could* get to you—the weather would have deteriorated so much they probably wouldn't be able to put down on your iceberg. Do you think you can ride it out?'

Harry said, 'We haven't taken an inventory of our remaining supplies, but I'm sure we don't have enough fuel to keep us warm any longer than twenty-four hours.'

198

Gunvald hesitated. Then: 'According to the latest forecasts, this is bigger than any other major weather pattern we've had all winter. We're in for a week of bitter storms. One atop the other. Not even a brief respite between them.'

A week. Harry closed his eyes. Even in thermal clothing, even sheltered from the wind, they could not survive for a week with no heat. They were virtually without food; hunger would weaken their resistance to the subzero temperatures. 'It doesn't look good, does it? What about the UNGY trawlers?'

'The Americans have relayed the news to them. Both the *Melville* and the *Liberty* are making for you at their best possible speed. But, according to Thule, seas are extremely rough. And those trawlers are two hundred and thirty miles away.'

They had to know precisely where they stood, no matter how tenuous their position might be. Harry said, 'Can a ship that size push a hundred miles or more into a storm as bad as this one without being torn to pieces?'

'I think those two captains are courageous—but not suicidal,' Gunvald said flatly. 'I would guess they'll be forced to turn back.'

Harry sighed. 'OK, Gunvald, I'll call you again in fifteen minutes. We've got to have a conference here. There's a chance we'll think of something.'

'I'll be waiting.'

Harry put the microphone on top of the radio. He stood and regarded the others. 'You heard.'

Everyone in the ice cave was staring either at Harry or at the now silent radio. Eventually Rita said what they were all thinking. 'Even if the trawlers can reach us, they won't be here until tomorrow at the earliest. They can't possibly make it in time to take us aboard before midnight. And at midnight all sixty bombs go off.'

'We don't know the size or the shape of the iceberg,' Franz Fischer said. 'Most of the charges may be in the ice shafts that are still part of the main winter field.'

Pete Johnson disagreed. 'Claude, Harry and I were at the end of the bomb line when the first tsunami passed under us. I think we followed a fairly direct course back to camp, the same route we took going out. So we must have driven right by or across all sixty charges. And I'd bet my right arm this berg isn't anywhere near large enough to withstand all those concussions.'

After a short silence Brian cleared his throat. 'You mean the iceberg's going to be blown into a thousand pieces?'

No one responded.

'Isn't there anything we can do to save ourselves?' Brian asked, as his gaze travelled from one member of the team to another. 'Surely there's *something* we could do.'

Throughout the conversation, George Lin had stood motionless and quiet as a statue, but suddenly he turned and took three quick steps towards Dougherty. 'Are you scared, boy? You *should* be scared. Your almighty family can't bail you out of this one!'

Startled, Brian backed away from the angry man.

Lin's hands were fisted at his sides. 'How do you like being helpless?' He was shouting. 'How do you like it? Your big, rich, powerful family doesn't mean a goddamned thing out here. Now you have to scramble to save yourself. Just exactly like the rest of us.'

'That's enough,' Harry said.

Lin turned on him. His face had been transformed by hatred. 'His family sits back with all its money and privileges, isolated from reality but so damned sure of its moral superiority, yammering about how the rest of us should live, about how we should sacrifice for this or that noble cause. It was people like them who started the trouble in China, brought in Mao, lost us our homeland, tens of millions of people butchered. You let them get a foot in the door, and the communists come right after them. The—'

'Brian didn't put us on this berg,' Harry said sharply. 'And neither did his family. For God's sake, George, he saved your life less than an hour ago.'

When Lin realised that he'd been ranting, the flush of anger drained from his cheeks. He seemed confused, then embarrassed. He shook his head as if to clear it. 'I . . . I'm sorry.'

'Don't tell me,' Harry said. 'Tell Brian.'

Lin turned to Dougherty, but didn't look him in the face. 'I'm sorry. I really am. I don't know what came over me. You did save my life. Harry's right.'

'Forget it, George. It's all right,' Brian reassured him.

After a brief hesitation, Lin nodded and went to the far end of the cave. He walked back and forth, exercising his bruised muscles, staring at the ice over which he trod.

Harry wondered what experiences in the man's past had prepared him to regard Brian Dougherty as an antagonist.

'Is there anything at all we can do to save ourselves?' Brian asked again, graciously dismissing the incident with Lin.

'Maybe,' Harry said. 'First we've got to get some of those bombs out of the ice and defuse them.'

Fischer was amazed. 'Impossible! How could they be retrieved?'

Claude rose to his feet. 'We've got an auxiliary drill, ice axes and the power saw. If we had a lot of time, we might be able to angle down towards each bomb, more or less dig steps in the ice. But, Harry, we would need at least a week to retrieve them, maybe two.'

'We only have ten hours,' Fischer reminded them unnecessarily.

Stepping to the middle of the room, Pete Johnson said, 'Wait a minute. You folks didn't listen to the man. Harry said we had to defuse *some* of the bombs, not all of them.' He looked at Harry. 'You want to explain yourself?'

'The nearest package of explosive is three hundred yards from our position. Nine hundred feet. If we can retrieve and disarm it, then we'll be nine hundred and forty-five feet from the *next* nearest bomb. Each charge is forty-five feet from the one in front of it. So, if we take up ten of them, we'll be over a quarter of a mile from the nearest explosion. The other fifty will detonate at midnight—but none of them will be directly under us. Our end of the iceberg might survive the shock. With luck, it might be large enough to sustain us.'

'Might,' Fischer said sourly.

'It's our best chance.'

'If we can't *dig* up the explosives, then how do we get to them?'

'With the auxiliary drill. Reopen the shafts.'

Fischer frowned. 'What if we drill into a bomb casing?'

'It won't explode,' Harry assured him. 'The plastic charge responds only to a certain voltage of electric current. Neither shock nor heat will do the job.'

'And when we've opened the shaft?' the German asked with obvious scepticism. 'Just reel in the bomb by its chain?'

'Something like that. We'll snap the upper end of the chain to a snowmobile and try to pop it and the cylinder out of the shaft.'

'Won't work,' Fischer said dismissively.

Brian said, 'We can't just lie down and wait for the end, Franz. That doesn't make a whole hell of a lot of sense.' He turned to Harry. 'But if your plan works, if we can get the bombs out of the ice, will it be possible to uncover ten of them in ten hours?'

'We won't know till we try,' Harry said, resolutely refusing either to play up to Fischer's stubborn pessimism or to raise false hopes.

Pete Johnson said, 'If we can't get ten, maybe eight. If not eight, surely six. Every one we get buys us more security.'

'Even so,' Fischer said, 'what will we have gained? We'll still be adrift on an iceberg, for God's sake. We'll still freeze to death.'

Getting to her feet, Rita said, 'Franz, goddammit, stop playing the devil's advocate, or whatever it is you're doing. You're a good man. You can help us survive. Or, for the lack of your help, we may all die. We need you on our side, pulling with us.'

'My sentiments exactly,' Harry said. He pulled his hood over his head and laced it tightly beneath his chin. 'And if we can buy some time by retrieving a few of the bombs, even just three or four—well, there's always the chance we'll be rescued sooner than seems possible right now. And if that happens I want to be around to say hello. What about the rest of you?'

No one disagreed with him.

'All right, we'll need every man on the bomb-recovery project,' Harry said, fitting the tinted goggles over his eyes. 'Rita, will you stay here and watch over the radio?'

'Sure.'

'Let's get moving then. I can hear those sixty clocks ticking. I don't want to be too near them when the alarms go off.'

2:30pm

Within a minute or two of lying down, Nikita Gorov knew that he was not going to be able to get any rest. From out of the past, one small ghost materialised to haunt him and ensure that he would not find the peace of sleep. When he closed his eyes, he could see little Nikolai, his Nikki, running towards him through a soft yellow haze. The child's arms were open wide, and he was giggling. But, regardless of how fast Nikki ran or how desperately Gorov reached out, the unbreachable veil between life and death separated them.

Suddenly charged with nervous energy, Gorov got up from his bunk and sat at the desk. He picked up a silver-framed photograph of Nikolai and himself on a cruise ship and spoke softly to the golden-haired boy in the picture. 'I am not responsible for your death, Nikki.'

Gorov knew that was true. Yet oceans of guilt washed through him in endless, corrosive tides. 'I know you never blamed me, Nikki. But I wish I could hear you tell me so.'

IN MID-JUNE, seven months ago, the *Ilya Pogodin* had been sixty days into an ultrasecret, ninety-day surveillance mission on the Mediterranean route. The boat had been submerged nine miles off the Egyptian coast. The multicommunications aerial was up, and thousands of bytes of data, important and otherwise, were being filed in her computer banks every minute.

At two o'clock in the morning on June 15, a message came in from the Naval Intelligence Office at Sevastopol, relayed from the Naval Ministry in Moscow, shattering the radio silence that was an absolute necessity during a clandestine mission.

The message began with latitude and longitude coordinates, followed by orders to rendezvous in twenty-two hours with the *Petr*

Vavilov, a Vostok-class research ship that was currently in the same part of the Mediterranean. That much of it pleasantly piqued Gorov's curiosity: a midnight meeting in the middle of the sea was a more traditional and intriguing piece of cloak-and-dagger work than that to which he was accustomed in an age of electronic spying. But the rest of it brought him straight to his feet, trembling.

> YOUR SON IN SERIOUS CONDITION KREMLIN HOSPITAL STOP YOUR PRESENCE REQUIRED MOSCOW SOONEST STOP ALL TRANSPORTATION HAS BEEN ARRANGED STOP FIRST OFFICER ZHUKOV TO ASSUME COMMAND YOUR SHIP STOP CONFIRM RECEIPT

At midnight Gorov passed control of his submarine to his first officer, Zhukov, and transferred to the *Petr Vavilov*. From the main deck of the research ship, a helicopter took him to Damascus, Syria, where he boarded a Russian diplomatic jet for a flight to Moscow. He arrived at Sheremetyevo Airport at three o'clock in the afternoon.

Boris Okudzhava, a functionary from the Naval Ministry, met him at the terminal. Okudzhava had eyes as dirty grey as laundry water. 'A car is waiting, Captain Gorov.'

'What's wrong with Nikki? What's wrong with my son?'

'I think we'd better not waste time here. I'll explain in the car.'

The Ministry car was immediately in front of the terminal, parked illegally, with the engine running. The moment Gorov and Okudzhava got in the back seat and closed the doors, the driver—a young man in a navy uniform—sped away from the kerb.

'What's wrong with Nikki?' Gorov demanded once again.

'He entered the hospital thirty-one days ago with what was first thought to be a glandular fever or influenza. He was dizzy, sweating and nauseous. You weren't notified,' said Okudzhava, 'because you were on a highly classified mission. Besides, the situation didn't seem all that critical. Then there was a brief remission of the symptoms. He seemed in the best of health for four days. When the symptoms returned, new diagnostic tests were begun. And then . . . eight days ago, they discovered he has a cancerous brain tumour.'

'Cancer,' Gorov said thickly.

'The tumour is too large to be operable, far too advanced for radiation treatments. When it became clear that Nikolai's condition was rapidly deteriorating, we broke radio silence and called you back.'

A cold sweat had sprung up along the back of Gorov's neck, as if Death had lightly touched him with icy fingers. 'He's only eight years old,' he said, more to himself than to either of the men with whom he shared the car.

Neither replied.

Since he had read that decoded message in his quarters aboard the *Ilya Pogodin* thirty-seven hours ago, Gorov had known that Nikki must be dying. The Admiralty was not cruel, but on the other hand it would not have interrupted an important espionage mission on the Mediterranean route unless the situation was quite hopeless. He had prepared himself for this news.

At the hospital, the elevators were out of order. Boris Okudzhava led Gorov to the service stairs and they climbed to the seventh floor.

Nikki was in an eight-patient ward with four other dying children, in a small bed under stained and tattered sheets. No ECG monitor or other equipment surrounded him. Deemed incurable, he had been brought to a terminal ward to suffer through the last of his time in this world.

The boy was fearfully pale. Waxy skin. A grey tint to his lips. Eyes closed. His golden hair was lank, damp with sweat.

Trembling, finding it increasingly difficult to maintain a submariner's traditional calm, Gorov stood beside the bed, gazing down at his son, his only child.

'Nikki,' he said, and his voice was unsteady, weak.

The boy didn't answer or even open his eyes.

Gorov sat on the edge of the bed. He put one hand over his son's hand. 'Nikki, I'm here.'

Someone touched Gorov's shoulder, and he looked up. A white-coated physician stood beside the bed. He indicated a woman at the end of the room. 'She's the one who needs you now.'

It was Anya. Gorov had been so focused on Nikki that he hadn't noticed her standing at the window, pretending to watch the people down on the old Kalinin Prospekt.

Gradually Gorov became aware of the defeat in the slope of his wife's shoulders and the hint of grief in the tilt of her head, and he began to apprehend the full meaning of the doctor's words. Nikki was already dead. Too late to say 'I love you' one last time. Too late for one last kiss. Too late to look into his child's eyes and say 'I was always so proud of you.'

Although Anya needed him, he couldn't bear to get up from the edge of the bed—as though to do so would ensure that Nikki's death was permanent, while sheer stubborn denial might eventually cause a miraculous resurrection. He spoke her name, and, though it was only a whisper, she turned to him. Her eyes shimmered with tears. She was biting her lip to keep from sobbing. At last he found the strength to leave the bed. He went to his wife and held her. She wept against his shoulder. He held her and stroked her golden hair.

DURING THE REMAINDER of that summer, they tried to find things to smile about. They went to the Taganka Theatre, the ballet, the music hall and the circus. Once a week they ate dinner at Aragvi, the best restaurant in the city, where they both drank too much vodka with their caviar, too much wine with their *sulguni* cheese and bread. They made urgent love every night, as though their passion was a refutation of suffering, cancer and death.

Although no longer as light-hearted as she had always been, Anya appeared to recover from the loss more quickly and more completely than did Nikita. For one thing, she was thirty-four, ten years younger than he. Her spirit was more resilient. Furthermore, she was not burdened with the guilt that he bore like a leaden yoke. He knew that Nikki had asked for him repeatedly during the last weeks of life and especially during the final few hours. Although aware that he was being foolish and irrational, Gorov felt as if he had failed his only son. He only feigned recovery.

Nothing is more terrible for a parent to endure than to outlive his child. The natural order seems demolished.

On January 2, he took the *Ilya Pogodin* to sea on a 100-day espionage mission. He looked forward to the fourteen weeks beneath the North Atlantic, because that seemed like a good time and place to absolve himself of his remaining grief and of his unshakable guilt. But at night Nikki continued to visit him, came down through the fathoms, through the dark sea and into the deeper darkness of Gorov's troubled mind, asking the familiar and unanswerable questions: *Why did you abandon me, Father? Why didn't you come to me when I needed you, when I was afraid and calling for you? Why didn't you help me?*

SOMEONE RAPPED discreetly on the cabin door. Like a faint note reverberating in the bronze hollow of a bell, the knock echoed softly in the small room. Gorov returned from the past and looked up from the silver-framed photograph. 'Yes?'

'Timoshenko, sir.'

The captain put down the picture and turned away from the desk. 'Come in, Lieutenant.'

The door opened, and Timoshenko peered in at him. 'We've been intercepting a series of messages you ought to read.'

'About what?'

'That United Nations study group. They call their base Edgeway Station. Remember it?'

'Of course.'

'Well, they're in trouble.'

3:05pm

Harry Carpenter fixed the steel chain to a carabiner and the carabiner to the frame-mounted tow ring on the back of the snowmobile. 'Now we just need a little luck.'

'It'll hold,' Claude said, patting the chain. He was kneeling on the ice beside Harry with his back to the wind.

The snowmobile was parked virtually on top of the reopened blasting shaft. Inside it, Roger Breskin was at the controls, watching the rearview mirror for the go-ahead sign from Harry.

Once he had pulled his snow mask over his mouth and nose, Harry got wearily to his feet and signalled Breskin to begin. Then he turned into the wind and stared at the small, perfectly round hole in the ice.

Pete Johnson knelt to one side of the shaft, waiting to monitor the progress of the bomb when it began to move.

After he revved the engine several times, Roger slipped the sled into gear. The machine moved less than a yard before the chain held it. The engine noise changed pitch, and gradually its shriek became louder than the wailing wind.

But the bomb did not move. Not an inch.

The chain appeared to vibrate. Breskin accelerated until the sled was at peak power, screaming.

With a crack like a rifle shot, the links of the chain broke out of the side of the shaft and the cylinder tore free of its icy bed. The snowmobile surged forwards, the chain remained taut, and the bomb scraped and clattered upwards.

Pete Johnson got to his feet and straddled the hole as Harry joined him. Directing a flashlight into the narrow black well, he peered down for a moment and then signalled Breskin to stop. Grasping the chain with both hands, he hoisted the tubular pack of explosives halfway out of the shaft and, with Harry's help, extracted it completely. They laid it on the ice.

One down. Nine to go.

THE COMMUNICATIONS CENTRE of the *Ilya Pogodin* was full of light and motion as seven radiant video-display terminals flickered with intercepted messages. Two technicians worked at one end of the cramped chamber, and Timoshenko stood near the entrance with Nikita Gorov.

Among the hundreds of communications being continuously sorted and stored by the *Ilya Pogodin*'s computers, a steady stream of data pertained to the Edgeway crisis. The computer had been instructed to create a special file for any intercepted messages that contained one or more of five key words: Carpenter, Larsson, Edgeway, *Melville*, *Liberty*.

'Is this complete?' Gorov asked when he finished reading the Edgeway material.

Timoshenko nodded. 'The computer produces an updated print-out every fifteen minutes. This one is only ten minutes old.'

'The captain of the trawler *Melville* is turning back. If the weather on the surface is half as bad as they're saying, the *Liberty* will turn back too.'

Gorov stared at the print-out, no longer reading it, not even seeing it. Behind his night-black eyes was the image of a fresh-faced little boy with arms open wide. The son he had been unable to save.

At last he said, 'I'll be in the control room until further notice. Let me know at once if there's any important news about this.'

'Yes, sir.'

Because the *Pogodin* was not actually under way but was hanging motionless in the sea, the control-room watch consisted of only five men in addition to First Officer Zhukov, who was perched on a metal stool in the centre of the chamber, reading a novel.

Emil Zhukov was the sole potential opposition with which Gorov would have to contend if he were to carry out the plan that he had begun to formulate. Zhukov was the only man aboard the submarine with the authority to relieve the captain of his command if, in Zhukov's opinion, Gorov had lost his senses or had disobeyed a direct order of the Naval Ministry.

Emil Zhukov, at forty-two, was not a great deal younger than his captain, but their relationship had a subtle child-and-mentor quality, primarily because Zhukov placed such a high value on discipline that his respect for authority bordered on an unhealthy reverence. Tall, lean, with a long, narrow face, intense hazel eyes, and thick dark hair, the first officer reminded Gorov of a wolf; he had a lupine grace when he moved, and his direct stare sometimes seemed predatory. In fact, he was not as dangerous as he appeared to be; he was merely a good man and a reliable, though not brilliant, officer. Ordinarily, deference to his captain would ensure his cooperation—but under extreme circumstances, his obedience could not be taken for granted. Emil Zhukov would never lose sight of the fact that there were many men of higher authority to whom he owed greater respect and allegiance than he owed his captain.

At the chart table, Gorov put the Edgeway material on top of the novel that Zhukov was reading. 'You'd better take a look at this.'

When he reached the last page of the document, the first officer said, 'Quite a trap these Carpenters have got themselves into.'

'It isn't the Carpenters who caught my eye. Another name.'

Quickly scanning the print-out, Zhukov said, 'You must mean Dougherty. Brian Dougherty.'

Gorov sat on the other stool at the lighted chart table. 'Yes.'

'Is he related to the assassinated American President?'

'Nephew.'

'I much admired his uncle,' said Zhukov. 'But I suppose you think I'm naive in that regard.'

Gorov's disdain for politics and politicians was well known to his first officer, who quietly disapproved of his attitude. Shrugging, he said, 'Politics is strictly about power. I admire achievement. A scientist who discovers a cure for disease—that's a great man or woman. But politicians . . .'

Zhukov frowned. 'You think he wasn't a great man?'

'No matter what I think of the late President, I'll admit the Dougherty family handled their tragedy with grace and fortitude. Very dignified,' said Gorov.

Zhukov nodded solemnly. 'An admirable family. Very sad.'

Gorov felt as if his first officer were a sophisticated musical instrument that he had just finished tuning. Now he was about to attempt a complicated melody with him. 'The boy's father is a Senator, isn't he?'

'Yes, and highly regarded,' Zhukov said.

'He was also shot, wasn't he?'

'Another assassination attempt.'

'After all the American system has done to that family, why do you suppose the Doughertys remain such ardent supporters of it?'

'They're great patriots,' Zhukov said.

Pulling thoughtfully at his well-trimmed beard, Gorov said, 'How difficult it must be for a family to remain patriotic to a nation that kills its best sons.'

'Oh, but it wasn't the country that killed them, sir. Blame a handful of reactionaries. But not the American people.'

Gorov pretended to think about it for a minute. Then he said, 'I suppose you're right. From what I read, Americans seem to have considerable respect and sympathy for the Doughertys.'

'Of course. Patriotism in adversity is the only kind that earns respect. It's easy to be patriotic in times of plenty.'

The melody that Gorov had hoped to play with his first officer was progressing without a sour note, and the captain almost smiled. Instead, he said, 'What an opportunity for Russia.'

As the captain had expected, Zhukov did not immediately follow the change of thought. 'Opportunity?'

'For goodwill.'

'Oh?'

'And in a time when Mother Russia desperately needs goodwill more than at any other moment in her history. Goodwill leads to lots of foreign aid, preferential trade treatment, even military cooperation.'

'I don't see the opportunity.'

'We're only five hours from their position. And if we were to go to the aid of those miserable people stranded on the iceberg, we'd be heroes. Worldwide heroes. You see? And Russia would be heroic by association.'

Blinking in surprise, Zhukov said, 'Rescue them?'

'After all, we'd be saving the lives of eight valued scientists from half a dozen countries, including the nephew of the assassinated President. Such an opportunity for propaganda and goodwill comes no more than once a decade.'

'But we'd need permission from Moscow.'

'Of course.'

'To get a quick answer, you'll have to send your request by satellite relay. And to use that equipment, we'll have to surface.'

'I'm aware of that.'

Emil Zhukov's face was lined with anxiety, because he realised that he was going to have to choose to disobey one authority or another—either the captain himself or the captain's superiors in Moscow. 'If we surface, sir, we'd compromise the entire mission.'

'This far north, in the middle of a raging winter storm, we should be able to go up, send and receive in total anonymity.'

'Yes, but we're under orders to maintain strict radio silence.'

Gorov nodded solemnly, as if to show that he was conscious of his awesome responsibility. 'When my son was dying, Moscow broke our radio silence.'

'That was a matter of life and death.'

'People are dying here too. Certainly, we're under orders to maintain radio silence. I know how serious a matter it is to set aside such orders. On the other hand, in an emergency, a captain is permitted to disobey the Ministry at his discretion.'

Frowning even more deeply, Zhukov said, 'I'm not so sure this is the type of emergency they had in mind when they wrote the rules.'

'Well, that's what I'm calling it,' Gorov said, issuing a quiet but not particularly subtle challenge.

'You'll have to answer to the Naval Board of Inquiry when it's all over,' Zhukov said. 'And this is an intelligence mission, so the intelligence services will have some questions.'

'I'm prepared,' Gorov said.

'You know what they're like.'

'I can be tough. Mother Russia and the navy have taught me endurance.' He knew they were approaching the last bars of the tune.

'My head will be on the block too,' Zhukov said morosely.

'No one's head will be on the block. They aren't all fools at the Ministry.'

The first officer was not convinced. His frown deepened.

'When they weigh the alternatives,' Gorov said confidently, 'they'll give the permission I want. I'm absolutely positive of it. Clearly, Russia has more to gain by sending us on this rescue mission than she does by insisting upon the continuation of what is, after all, nothing more than another routine surveillance run.' Getting up from the stool, Gorov said, 'Lieutenant, I want the crew at battle stations in five minutes.'

'Is that necessary?'

'If we're going to break a Ministry rule at our own discretion, we can at least take all precautions,' Gorov said.

For a long moment they stared at each other, each trying to read the other's mind, trying to see the future.

Finally Zhukov stood up without breaking eye contact. He hesitated . . . then saluted. 'Yes, sir. It will be done.'

'We'll surface as soon as the multicommunications aerial has been wound down and secured.'

'Yes, sir.'

Gorov felt as if hundreds of painful knots were coming untied inside him. He had won. 'Go to it, then.'

Zhukov left the control room.

Walking to the circular, railed command pad at the end of the control room, Gorov thought about little Nikki and knew that he was doing the right thing. In the name of his dead son, in honour of his lost boy, not for the advantage of Russia, he would save the lives of those stranded people. This time he had the power to thwart death, and he was determined not to fail.

4:00pm

Bang! Sparks shot out of the vents in the steel-alloy casing of the auxiliary drill. It chugged, sputtered and cut out.

Roger Breskin had been operating the drill at the third sealed shaft. 'What the hell?' He thumbed the power switch.

When the drill wouldn't start, Pete Johnson stepped in and dropped to his knees to have a look at it.

Everyone crowded round, expecting the worst. They were, Harry

210

thought, like people gathered at an automobile accident—except that the corpses in this wreckage might be their own.

'What's wrong with it?' George Lin asked.

'You'll have to take apart the casing to find the trouble,' Fischer told Pete.

'Yeah, but I don't have to take it apart to know I can't repair it.' Pointing to the snow and frozen slush round the partially reopened third shaft, Pete said, 'See those black specks?'

Harry crouched and studied the bits of metal scattered on the ice. 'Gear teeth. And we don't have a spare set.'

Everyone was silent.

'What now?' Brian asked eventually.

With Teutonic pessimism, Fischer said, 'Back to the cave and wait for midnight.'

'That's giving up,' Brian said, shaking his head.

Getting to his feet, Harry said, 'But I'm afraid that's all we can do at the moment, Brian. We lost the other drill when my sled went into that crevasse.'

Dougherty shook his head, refusing to accept that they were powerless. 'Earlier, Claude said we could use the ice axe and the power saw to cut some steps in the ice, angled down to each package.'

The Frenchman interrupted him. 'That would only work if we had a week. We'd need six more hours, perhaps longer, to retrieve this one bomb by that method.'

'OK. Let's go, let's pack up,' said Harry. 'No point standing here, losing body heat. We can talk about it back at the cave, out of this wind. We might think of something yet.'

AT 4:02 THE COMMUNICATIONS centre reported that a message was coming in from the Naval Ministry. Five minutes later the decoding sheet was passed up to the bridge, where Nikita Gorov began to read it with some trepidation.

YOUR REQUEST UNDER STUDY BY ADMIRALTY STOP IMMEDIATE DECISION CANNOT BE MADE STOP SUBMERGE AND CONTINUE SCHEDULED MISSION FOR ONE HOUR STOP A CONTINUATION OR NEW ORDERS WILL BE TRANSMITTED TO YOU AT 1700 HOURS YOUR TIME STOP

Gorov was disappointed. The Ministry's indecision had cranked up the level of his tension. The next hour would be even more difficult for him. He turned to the other two men. 'Clear the bridge and prepare to dive.'

HARRY HAD NOT YET finished telling Rita how the auxiliary drill had broken down, when she interrupted him. 'Hey, where's Brian?'

He turned to the men who had entered the ice cave behind him. Brian Dougherty was not among them.

Harry frowned. 'Where's Brian? Why isn't he here?'

'He must be around. I'll take a look outside,' Roger Breskin said. Pete Johnson left with him.

'He probably just had to go to the john,' Fischer said.

'No,' Harry disagreed. 'He would have told someone.'

Out on the ice cap, no one could afford to be modest about bladder and bowel habits. When going to the latrine, they all accepted that it was necessary to inform at least one other person as to exactly where to start looking if they didn't make a timely return.

Roger and Pete reappeared in less than two minutes, pulling up their goggles, tugging down their ice-veined snow masks.

'He's not at the sleds,' Roger said. 'Or anywhere else we can see.' His grey eyes, usually expressionless, were troubled.

'Who rode back here with him?' Harry asked.

They looked at one another. 'Claude?'

The Frenchman shook his head. 'Not me. I thought he rode with Franz.'

'I rode with Franz,' George Lin said.

Rita was exasperated. 'For God's sake, you mean he was left behind in the confusion?'

'He might have been hurt,' Pete said. 'A fall.'

Claude Jobert said, 'Fell, hit his head, unable to cry out, and we were so eager to get back here, we didn't notice.'

'It's impossible,' Pete insisted.

Dubious, Harry said, 'Maybe. All right, we'll go back and look. You and me, Pete. Two snowmobiles.'

Roger stepped forwards. 'I'm going with you.'

'Two can handle it,' Harry said, fixing his goggles in place.

'I insist,' Breskin said. 'Look, Brian handled himself damn well out there on the ice today. He didn't hesitate when he had to go over that cliff to get a line round George. And if it was me in trouble now, he'd do whatever he could. So you can count me in on this.'

As far as Harry could remember, that was the longest speech that Roger Breskin had made in months. He was impressed. 'OK then. You'll come along. You're too damn big to argue with.'

AFTER RETURNING to the third blasting shaft, Pete and Roger parked the two snowmobiles and left their engines running and headlights blazing. They set out in different directions, and Harry set out in a third to search for Brian in the drifts, waist-high pressure ridges and low ice hummocks round the site.

Cautious, aware that he could be swallowed by the storm as quickly and completely as Brian had been, Harry probed the black and white landscape before he committed himself to it, sweeping his flashlight from side to side. Every ten steps, he looked over his shoulder to see if he was straying too far from the snowmobiles. He was already well out of the section of the ice field that was illuminated by the head-lights, but he knew that he must not lose sight of the sleds. If he got lost, no one would hear his cries for help above the screeching wind.

Even as he searched assiduously behind every drift and canted slab of ice, he nurtured only a slim hope that he would ever locate Dougherty. The snow was mounting at the rate of two inches an hour or faster. If Brian had lain on the ice, unconscious or unable to move, for the past fifteen minutes, maybe longer . . . Well, by this time the kid would be covered over, a smooth white lump like any hummock or drift, frozen fast to the winter field.

It's hopeless, Harry thought.

Then, not forty feet from the blasting shaft, he stepped round a monolith of ice as large as a truck and found Brian on the other side. He was on his back, laid out flat, still wearing his goggles and snow mask. Because the upturned slab of ice acted as a windbreak, the snow had not drifted over him and he'd been spared the worst of the bitter cold. Nevertheless, he didn't move.

Harry knelt beside the body and pulled the snow mask from the face. Thin, irregularly spaced puffs of vapour rose from between the parted lips. Alive. But for how long? Brian's skin was no less white than the snow round him. After lying motionless on the ice for at least a quarter of an hour, he would already be suffering from exposure.

He was deciding how best to get Brian out of there when he saw someone approaching through the turbulent gloom. A shaft of light appeared in the darkness, hazy at first, getting sharper and brighter as it drew nearer. Roger Breskin staggered through a thick curtain of snow, holding his flashlight before him as a blind man holds a cane. Pulling down his snow mask, he asked, 'Is he alive?'

'Not by much.'

'What happened?'

'I don't know. Let's get him into one of the snowmobile cabins and let the warm air work on him.'

AT 4:50 THE AMERICANS at Thule radioed Gunvald Larsson with bad news. Like the *Melville* before her, the trawler *Liberty* had found the storm to be an irresistible force against which only big warships and fools tried to stand. She had turned back five minutes ago when a seaman discovered minor buckling of the starboard bow plates. The radioman repeatedly assured Gunvald that everyone stationed at Thule was praying for those poor bastards on the iceberg.

No number of prayers would make Gunvald feel better. The cold, hard fact was that the captain of the *Liberty*, although certainly with great remorse, had made a decision that virtually sentenced eight people to death.

Gunvald couldn't bring himself to pass on the news to Rita. Not right away. He had to have time to think about how he would tell them. Although he was not a man who usually sought to relieve tension with liquor, he poured himself a shot of vodka from the communications-hut pantry. When he had finished the vodka, he was still unable to call Rita.

ALTHOUGH THE SNOWMOBILES were stationary, the five small engines rumbled steadily. On the ice cap, the machines must never be switched off, because the batteries would go dead and the lubricants in the engines would freeze up within two or three minutes.

Harry came out of the ice cave and hurried to the nearest snowmobile. When he was settled in the warm cabin, he screwed off the top of the Thermos flask that he'd brought with him. He took several quick sips of the thick, fragrant vegetable soup, brewed from freeze-dried mix and brought to boiling point on the hot plate that they had used earlier to melt snow at the open blasting shafts. For the first time all day, he was able to relax temporarily.

In the three snowmobiles to his left, George Lin, Claude and Roger were eating dinner in equal privacy. He could barely see them: dim shapes inside the unlighted cabins. Franz Fischer and Pete Johnson were in the ice cave, waiting for their turn at warm cabins and Thermos flasks full of hot soup.

Rita knocked and opened the cabin door, startling Harry.

Swallowing a mouthful of soup, he said, 'What's wrong?'

She leaned inside. 'Brian wants to talk to you.'

'Is he still improving?'

'Oh, yes. Nicely.'

'Does he remember what happened?'

'Let him tell you,' she said.

In the fifth snowmobile, the one parked furthest from the cave, Brian was slowly recuperating. Rita had been in the cabin with him for the past twenty minutes, massaging his chilled fingers, feeding him soup and making sure that he didn't lapse into a dangerous sleep. He had regained consciousness during the ride back from the third demolition shaft, but he had been in too much agony to talk.

Harry capped his Thermos flask, and went to visit Dougherty.

The snowmobile cabin was uncomfortably cramped. Harry sat backwards on the narrow passenger bench, facing the rear of the machine, where Brian Dougherty was facing forwards.

Harry said, 'How do you feel?'

'Like hell.'

'You will for a while yet.'

'My hands and feet sting. It's like someone's jabbing lots of long needles into them.' His voice was shaded with pain.

'Frostbite?'

'We haven't looked at my feet yet. But they feel about the same as my hands. And there doesn't seem to be any frostbite on my hands. I think I'm safe. But—' He gasped in pain, and his face contorted. 'Oh, God, that's bad.'

Opening his Thermos, Harry said, 'Soup?'

'No, thanks. Rita pumped a quart of it into me.' He rubbed his hands together, apparently to ease another especially sharp prickle of pain. 'By the way, I'm head over heels in love with your wife.'

'Who isn't?'

'And I want to thank you for coming after me. You saved my life.'

'Another day, another act of heroism,' Harry said. He took a mouthful of soup. 'What happened to you out there?'

Brian hesitated. His eyes glittered in the shadows. At last he said, 'Someone clubbed me on the back of the head.'

Harry almost choked on his soup. 'Knocked you out?'

'I've got the lumps to prove it.'

'Let me see.'

Brian leaned forwards, lowered his head.

Harry stripped off his gloves and felt the boy's head. The two lumps were easy to find, both on the back of the skull. 'Concussion?'

'None of the symptoms.'

'Headache?'

'Oh, yeah. A real bastard of a headache.'

'Double vision?'

'No.'

'You're certain you didn't faint?'

'Positive,' Brian said, sitting up straight again. 'I distinctly remember being struck from behind. Twice. The first time he didn't put enough force into it. My hood cushioned the blow. I stumbled, kept my balance, started to turn round—and he hit me a lot harder the next time. The lights went out but good.'

'And he dragged you out of sight? That doesn't sound likely.'

'The wind was gusting. The snow was so thick I couldn't see more than two yards. He had excellent cover.'

'You're saying someone tried to murder you.'

'That's right.'

Harry didn't want to believe it. He had too much on his mind as it was.

'It happened as we were getting ready to leave the third site.' Brian hissed in pain. 'I was loading some equipment into the last of the trailers. Everyone was busy. The wind was gusting hard, the snow was falling so heavily I'd lost sight of the rest of you, then he hit me.'

'But who?'

'I didn't see him.'

'Did he speak to you?'

'No.'

'If he wanted you dead, why wouldn't he wait for midnight? The way it looks now, you'll die then with the rest of us. Why would he feel he had to hurry you along?'

'Well, maybe . . . This sounds crazy . . . but, well, I *am* a Dougherty.'

Harry understood at once. 'To a certain breed of maniac, yes, that would make you an appealing victim. Killing a Dougherty, any Dougherty—there's a sense of history involved. I suppose I can see a psychopath getting a real thrill out of that.'

They were silent. Then Brian said, 'But who among us is psychotic?'

'Like to take a guess?' Harry said.

'Guess who it was? No.'

'I expected you to say George Lin.'

'For whatever reasons, George doesn't care for me or my family. I still can't believe he's a killer.'

'You can't be sure. You don't know what's going on inside his head any more than I do. There're few people in this life we can ever really know. With me . . . Rita's the only person I'd ever vouch for and have no doubts.'

'Yes, but I saved his life today.'

'If he's psychotic, why would that matter to him? In fact, through his twisted logic, that might even be why he wants to kill you.'

For the first time all day, Harry was on the verge of despair. He was exhausted both physically and mentally. 'If he's nuts, obsessed with you and your family, then he's not going to give up easily. What does he have to lose? He's going to die at midnight anyway.'

Rubbing his hands together, massaging his still-cold fingers, Brian said, 'Are you going to tell the others?'

'No. We'll say you don't remember what happened, that you must have fallen and hit your head on an outcropping of ice. Better that your would-be killer thinks we don't know about him. If he thinks we don't know about him, he might get careless the next time he tries for you.'

'If he's a lunatic, then I must be nuts too. Here I am worrying about being murdered even though midnight's only seven hours away.'

'No. You've got a strong survival instinct, that's all. It's a sign of sanity.'

'Unless the survival instinct is so strong that it keeps me from recognising a hopeless situation. Then maybe it's a sign of lunacy.'

'It isn't hopeless,' Harry said. 'We've got seven hours. Anything could happen in seven hours.'

THE TURBULENT SEA smashed against the rounded bows of the *Ilya Pogodin* and geysered into the darkness, an endless series of waves that sounded like window-rattling peals of thunder. Because the boat rode so low in the water, it shuddered only slightly from the impact, but it could not withstand that punishment indefinitely.

Captain Gorov was on the bridge with two other men. They were all wearing fleece-lined pea jackets, hooded black rain slickers and gloves. The two young lookouts stood back to back, one facing port and the other starboard. All three men had night-service field glasses and were surveying the horizon.

The satellite tracking gear rose from the sail behind the bridge and opened like spring's first blossom. The five petal-form radar plates, which quickly joined together to become a dish, were already beginning to search the sky.

At three minutes past the hour, a note from Timoshenko was sent up to the bridge. The communications officer wished to inform the captain that a coded message had begun to come in from the Ministry in Moscow. The moment of truth had arrived.

Gorov kept his eyes to the night glasses. He scanned ninety degrees of the storm-swept horizon, but it was not waves and clouds and snow that he saw. Instead, two visions plagued him, each more vivid than reality. In the first, he was sitting at a table in a conference room listening to the state's testimony at his own court-martial, and he was forbidden to speak in his own defence. In the second vision, he stared down at a young boy who lay dead in a hospital bed. The night glasses seemed to be a conduit to both the past and the future.

At 5:07 the decoded message was passed through the conning-tower hatch and into the captain's hands. Gorov's eyes went straight to the body of the communiqué.

YOUR REQUEST GRANTED STOP MAKE ALL SPEED TO RESCUE
MEMBERS EDGEWAY EXPEDITION STOP WHEN FOREIGN NATION-
ALS ABOARD TAKE ALL PRECAUTIONS AGAINST COMPROMISE OF
CLASSIFIED MATERIAL STOP EMBASSY OFFICIALS IN WASHINGTON
HAVE INFORMED AMERICAN GOVERNMENT OF INTENT TO
RESCUE EDGEWAY GROUP STOP

At the bottom of the decoding sheet, Timoshenko had written two words in pencil: *Receipt acknowledged.* There was nothing to do now but act upon their new orders.

Although he was not at all sure that sufficient time remained in which to get those people off the iceberg, Gorov was happier than he had been in a long time. At least he was *doing* something. At least he had a chance of reaching the Edgeway scientists before they were all dead. He stuffed the decoded message into a coat pocket and sounded two brief blasts on the electric diving horns.

5:30pm

Brian had been in the snowmobile nearly an hour and was suffering from claustrophobia. 'I'd like to go out and walk.'

'Don't rush yourself.' Rita switched on a flashlight, and the sudden brightness made her eyes water. She studied his hands. 'Numb? Tingling?'

'Not any more. And my feet feel a lot better.' He saw that Rita still had her doubts. 'My legs are cramped. I really need to exercise them. Besides, it's too warm in here.'

She hesitated. 'Your face *does* have some colour now. Well . . . all right. But when you've stretched your muscles, if you still feel any tingling, any numbness, you've got to come back here right away.'

'Good enough.'

Rita patted her lap. 'Put your feet up here, one at a time.' She worked the outer boot onto his somewhat swollen foot. While Rita threaded the laces through the eyelets and drew them tight, she said, 'Well, if nothing else, you've a wealth of material for those magazine pieces.'

He was surprised to hear himself say, 'I've decided not to write them. I'm going to do a book instead.' Until that moment his obsession had been a private matter. Now that he had revealed it to someone he respected, he had forced himself to regard it less as an obsession and more as a commitment.

'A book? You'd better think twice about that. Writing a book is an ordeal. I've done three, you know, and I know how it is. Writing the

218

first third is pure pleasure. But you lose that feeling. Believe me, you do. In the second third, you're just trying to prove something to yourself. When you get to the last third, it's simply a matter of survival.'

'But I've figured out how to make everything hang together in the narrative. I've got my theme.'

Rita winced and shook her head sadly. 'So you're too far gone to respond to reason.' She helped him get his right foot into the sealskin boot. 'What *is* your theme?'

'Heroism.'

'Heroism?' She grimaced. 'What in the name of God does heroism have to do with the Edgeway Project?'

'I think maybe it has everything to do with it.'

'You're daft. I never noticed any heroes here.'

Brian was surprised by her apparently genuine astonishment. 'Have you looked in a mirror?'

'Me? A hero? Dear boy, I'm scared sick half the time.'

'Heroes can be scared and still be heroes. That's what makes them heroes—acting in spite of fear. This is heroic work, this project.'

'It's work, that's all. Dangerous, yes. Foolish, perhaps. But heroic? You're romanticising it.'

He was silent as she finished lacing his boots. 'Well, it's not like politics. You're not in it for power, privilege or money. You're not out here because you want to control people.'

Rita raised her head and met his gaze. Her eyes were beautiful—and as deep as the clear Arctic sea. He knew that she understood him, in that moment, better than anyone ever had. 'The world thinks your family is full of heroes.'

'Well, I know them better.'

'They've made sacrifices, Brian. Your uncle was killed. Your father took a bullet of his own.'

'This will sound mean-spirited, but it wouldn't if you knew them. Getting shot isn't an act of bravery—any more than it is for some poor bastard who gets gunned down while he's withdrawing money from an automatic teller machine. He's a victim, not a hero.'

'Some people get into politics to make a better world.'

'Not anyone I've known, Rita. It's all about envy and power. But out here, everything's so clean. The work is hard, the environment is hostile—but *clean*.'

He couldn't recall anyone ever having met his gaze as unwaveringly as she did. After a thoughtful silence, she said, 'So you're not just a troubled rich boy out for thrills, the way the media would have it.'

He broke eye contact first, taking his foot off the bench and contorting himself in the small space in order to slip his arms into the sleeves of his coat. 'Of course, maybe I'm deluding myself. Maybe that's just what I am, everything they write in the papers.'

'There's precious little truth in the papers,' she said. 'In fact you'll only find it one place.'

'Where's that?'

'You know.'

He nodded. 'In myself.'

She smiled. Putting on her coat, she said, 'You'll be fine.'

'When?'

'Oh, in twenty years maybe.'

He laughed. 'I hope I'm not going to be screwed up that long.'

'Maybe longer. Hey, that's what life's all about: little by little, day by day, each of us learning how to be less screwed up.'

When he followed Rita out of the snowmobile, Brian was surprised by the bitter power of the storm wind. It took his breath away and almost drove him to his knees.

The wind was a reminder that his unknown assailant was not the only threat to his survival. For a few minutes he'd forgotten that they were adrift, had forgotten about the time bombs ticking towards midnight. The fear came back to him. Now that he had committed himself to writing the book, he wanted *very* much to live.

THE HEADLAMPS on one of the snowmobiles shone through the mouth of the cave. The eight distorted shadows of the expedition members rippled and slid across the walls of the white chamber, swelled and shrank, mysterious but perhaps no more so than the people who cast them—one of whom was a potential murderer.

Harry watched Roger Breskin, Franz Fischer, George Lin, Claude and Pete as they argued about how they should spend the six hours and twenty minutes remaining before midnight. He ought to have been leading the discussion, but he couldn't keep his mind on what the others were saying. He couldn't prevent himself from studying them intensely, as though psychotic tendencies ought to be evident in the way a man walked, talked and gestured. His train of thought was interrupted by a call from Edgeway Station. Larsson's voice, shot through with static, rattled off the ice walls.

When Harry went to the radio and responded to the call, Gunvald said, 'Harry, the trawlers have turned back. The *Melville* and the *Liberty*. Some time ago. I've known, but I couldn't bring myself to tell you.' He was unaccountably buoyant. 'But now it doesn't matter. It doesn't matter, Harry!'

Pete, Claude and the others had crowded round the radio, baffled by the Swede's excitement.

Harry said, 'Gunvald, what in the hell are you talking about? What do you mean, it doesn't matter?'

Static shredded the airwaves, but then the frequency cleared as Larsson said, 'Just got word from Thule. Relayed from Washington. There's a submarine in your neighbourhood, Harry. Do you read me? A Russian submarine.'

8:20pm

Gorov, Zhukov and Seaman Semichastny clambered onto the bridge and faced the port side. The sea was neither calm nor as tumultuous as it had been when they had surfaced earlier to receive the message from the Naval Ministry. The iceberg lay off to port, sheltering them from some of the power of the storm waves and the wind.

They couldn't see the berg, even though the radar and sonar images had indicated that it was massive both above and below the waterline. They were only fifty or sixty yards from the target, but the darkness was impenetrable. Instinct alone told Gorov that something enormous loomed over them, and the awareness of being in the shadow of an invisible colossus was one of the eeriest and most disconcerting feelings that he had ever known.

Above and behind them on the sail, the 100-watt bridge lamp illuminated the immediate steelwork and allowed the three men to see one another. Clotted with scattered small chunks of ice, choppy waves broke against the curved hull, reflecting just enough of that red light to give the impression that the *Pogodin* was sailing not on water but on an ocean of wine-dark blood.

Tapping the bridge anemometer, the first officer said, 'We've got wind velocity of thirty miles an hour, even leeward of the iceberg.'

With the wind factored in, Gorov suspected that the temperature atop the iceberg had to be at least –60 or –70. Rescuing the Edgeway scientists under those hideous conditions was a greater challenge than any he had ever faced in his entire naval career. It might even be impossible. And he began to worry that, once again, he had arrived too late.

'Let's have some light,' Gorov ordered.

Semichastny immediately swung the floodlight to port and closed the switch. The piercing beam blazed against a towering palisade of ice, so enormous that the sight of it made all three men gasp.

Semichastny moved the floodlight slowly to the right, then back to the left. The cliff was so long and high that Gorov could not get an idea of the overall appearance of it. Each brilliantly lit circle of ice, although visible in considerable detail from their front-row seat, seemed disassociated from the one that had come before it.

'Lieutenant Zhukov, put up a flare.'

'Yes, sir.'

Zhukov was carrying the signal gun. He raised the pistol, held it at arm's length and fired up into the port-side gloom.

The rocket climbed swiftly. It was visible for a moment, but then it vanished into the blizzard as though it had passed through a veil into another dimension.

Three hundred feet . . . 400 feet . . . 500 . . . High above, the rocket burst into a brilliant incandescent moon.

Beneath the flare, 300 yards in every direction, the ocean was painted with cold light that revealed its green-grey hue. The iceberg loomed: a daunting presence, at least 100 feet high, a huge rampart more formidable than the fortifications of any castle in the world. During their radar- and sonar-guided approach to the site, they had discovered that the berg was four-fifths of a mile long. Rising dramatically from the mottled green-grey-black sea, it was curiously like a man-made monolith with mysterious religious significance. It soared, glass-smooth, gleaming, marred by neither major outcroppings nor indentations.

Gorov had hoped to find a ragged cliff, one that shelved into the water in easy steps. The sea was not discouragingly rough there in the leeward shadow, and a few men might be able to get across to the ice. Among the submarine's equipment stores were three inflatable motorised rubber rafts and a large selection of the highest-quality climbing gear. But they had to find a place to land. A small shelf. A tiny cove. A niche above the waterline. *Something.*

As if reading the captain's mind, Zhukov said, 'Even if we could land men there, it would be one hell of a climb. It's as straight and smooth as a hundred-foot sheet of window glass.'

'We could chop footholds out of the ice,' Gorov said. 'We have the climbing picks. Axes. Ropes and pitons. We've got the climbing boots and the grappling hooks. Everything we need.'

'But these men are submariners, sir. Not mountain climbers.'

'The right men could make it,' Gorov insisted.

'Yes, sir,' Zhukov said. 'I know they could. But we don't have a single man aboard who could make that climb in even half the time it would take a trained mountaineer. We'd need hours to get to the top and rig a system for bringing the Edgeway scientists down to the rafts. And by the time—'

'—by the time we've worked out a way to land them on the ice, they'll be lucky to have even an hour left,' Gorov said, finishing the first officer's argument for him.

Midnight was fast approaching.

'Let's have a look at the windward flank,' Gorov said. 'Maybe it'll have something better to offer.'

IN THE CAVE, waiting for more news from Gunvald, they were exhilarated by the prospect of rescue—but sobered by the thought that the submarine might not arrive quickly enough. At times, they were all silent; at other times, they all seemed to be talking at once.

After waiting until the chamber was filled with excited chatter and the others were particularly distracted, Harry quietly excused himself to go to the latrine. Passing Pete Johnson, he whispered, 'I want to talk to you alone.'

Pete blinked in surprise.

Not even breaking stride as he spoke, barely glancing at the engineer, Harry put his goggles in place, pulled up his snow mask and walked out of the cave, past the rumbling snowmobiles.

He doubted that much fuel remained in their tanks. The engines would conk out soon. No more light. No more heat.

Past the snowmobiles, the area that they had used for the temporary camp lavatory lay on the far side of a U-shaped, ten-foot-high ridge of broken ice and drifted snow. Harry actually had no need to relieve himself, but the call of nature provided the least suspicious excuse for getting out of the cave and away from the others. He reached the opening in the crescent ridge that formed the windbreak and stood with his back to the ridge wall.

He supposed he might be making a mistake with Pete Johnson. Even a friend or loved one, known and trusted, might harbour some unspeakable dark urge. Everyone was a mystery within a mystery. Nevertheless, he had decided to risk confronting Pete Johnson alone.

During the past few months, he had come to like and respect this big, broad-faced man. Beneath Pete Johnson's fierce-looking competence, there was a kid with a love for science and technology and adventure. Harry recognised himself in Pete.

In a minute, the engineer joined him at the back wall of the U-shaped, roofless shelter. Pulling his snow mask down, he said, 'Are we here to gossip about someone? Or have you suddenly taken a romantic interest in me?'

'This is serious, Pete.'

'Damn right it is. If Rita finds out, she'll beat the hell out of me.'

'Let's get right to the point. I want to know . . . why did you try to kill Brian Dougherty?'

'I don't like the way he parts his hair.'

'Pete, I'm not joking.'

Above their heads, at the crest of the sheltering ridge, the wind whistled through the natural crenellations in the slabs of ice.

Pete's grin faded. 'Man, you *are* serious. What's going on here?' The bafflement on the big man's broad, black face seemed as genuine as any lamb's sweet look of innocence. 'Are you saying somebody actually *did* try to kill him? Back at the third blasting site, when he got left behind? But he fell, you said. *He* said. He told us that he fell and hit his head. Didn't he?'

Harry sighed. 'Damn. If you *are* the one, you're good. I believe you really don't know.'

'Hey, I *know* I really don't know.'

'Brian didn't fall and knock himself unconscious. Someone struck him on the back of the head. Twice.'

Pete was speechless.

As quickly as he could, Harry recounted the conversation that he'd had with Brian in the snowmobile cabin a few hours ago.

'If I'd been this psycho,' Pete said, 'and if I'd decided to kill you here and now, you wouldn't have had much chance.'

'Yeah, but I didn't have any choice. I needed an ally, and you were

the best prospect. Thanks for not tearing my head off, anyway.'

'I've changed my mind about you, Harry. I thought you had a hero complex, but this is just perfectly natural for you, this kind of courage. You're built this way. This is how you came into the world.'

'I only did what I had to do,' Harry said impatiently. 'I figured our would-be killer might make another attempt on the boy's life. And I need someone besides Rita and me to help stop him when the time comes.'

'And I've been nominated.'

'Congratulations.'

A whirl of wind swooped down on them. They lowered their heads while a column of spinning snow passed over them and then whistled out of the open end of the crescent ridge.

Pete said, 'So far as you're concerned, is there any one of them we should watch more closely than the others?'

'I ought to have asked you that question. I already know what Rita, Brian and I think. I need a fresh perspective.'

Pete didn't have to ponder the question to come up with an answer. 'George Lin,' he said at once.

'That was my own first choice. But don't you think he's too obvious?'

'Maybe. But that doesn't rule him out. What's wrong with him, anyway? I mean, the way he acts with Brian, the anger—what's that all about?'

'I'm not sure,' Harry said. 'Something happened to him in China when he was a child, something traumatic. He seems to connect Brian to that, because of his family's politics.'

'And the pressure we've been under these past nine hours might have snapped him.'

'I suppose it's possible.'

'But it doesn't feel right.'

'Not quite.'

After a minute or so, Pete said, 'What about Franz Fischer?'

'What about him?'

'He's cool towards you. And towards Rita. Not cool towards *her* exactly . . . but there's sure something odd in the way he looks at her.'

'You're observant.'

'Maybe it's professional jealousy because of all these science awards the two of you have piled up the last few years.'

'He's not that petty.'

'What then?' When Harry hesitated, Pete said, 'None of my business?'

'They were lovers before we were married.'

'So he *is* jealous. You ever think maybe that should have been a reason not to bring Franz onto this team?'

'If Rita and I could put the past behind us, why couldn't he?'

'Because he's not you and Rita, man. He's a self-involved science nerd, for one thing. Probably accepted the invitation to join the expedition just so Rita would have a chance to compare him and you. He probably thought you'd stumble round like a dweeb here on the ice, while he'd be Nanook of the North, a macho man by comparison. From day one he must have realised it wasn't going to work out that way, which explains why he's been so bitchy.'

'Franz might hate me and perhaps even Rita, but how do his feelings towards *us* translate into an attack on Brian?' Harry shook his head. 'It might be Franz. But not because he's jealous of me.'

'Breskin?'

'He's a cipher.'

'He strikes me as *too* self-contained.'

'We always tend to suspect the loner,' Harry said, 'the quiet man who keeps to himself. But that's no more logical than suspecting Franz merely because he had a relationship with Rita years ago.

Besides, Roger had a chance to kill the kid early this afternoon. When Brian was dangling over the cliff, trying to reach George, Roger could have cut the rope. Who would have been the wiser?'

'But then George would have been a witness.'

'What psychopath has that degree of self-control? Besides, I'm not sure that George was in any condition to be a witness, little more than half-conscious at that point.'

'But, like you said, Roger's a cipher.'

'We're going in circles.'

As they breathed, the vapour they expelled crystallised between them. The cloud had become so thick that they could not see each other clearly, though they were no more than two feet apart.

Waving the fog out of their way, Pete said, 'We're left with Claude.'

'He seems the least likely of the lot. I've known him fifteen years, and I've been on the ice with him several times before. He's a wonderful man.'

'He often talks about his late wife, Collette. He still gets teary about it, shaky. When did she die?'

'Three years ago this month. Claude was on the ice, his first expedition in two and a half years, when she was murdered.'

'*Murdered?*'

'She'd flown from Paris to London on a short holiday. The IRA had planted a bomb in a restaurant where she went for lunch. She was one of the eight killed in the blast.'

'Good God!'

'They caught one of the men involved. He's still in prison.'

Pete said, 'And Claude took it very hard.'

'Oh, yes. Collette was great. You'd have liked her.'

For a moment neither of them spoke. At the top of the ridge, the wind moaned like a revenant trapped between this world and the next.

'His wife was killed by Irishmen,' said Pete.

'So?'

'Dougherty is Irish.'

'That's a stretch, Pete. Irish–American, actually. Third generation.'

'I guess it is. But you know . . . some people say Brian's family sympathised with the IRA to the extent that for years they secretly funnelled donations to them.'

'I've heard it all too. But it was never proved. Political slander, as far as we know. The actual fact is . . . we have four suspects, and none of them looks like a sure bet.'

'Correction. Six suspects.'

'Franz, George, Roger, Claude . . .'

'And me.'

'I've ruled you out, Pete. After the conversation we've just had—'

'Is there a law that says a killer can't be a good actor?'

Harry stared at him, trying to read his expression. 'I know you told me the truth, you're not the guy,' he said finally. 'But what you're saying is that I mustn't trust anyone, not even for a moment.'

'Precisely. And it goes for both of us. That's why the sixth name on the list of suspects is yours.'

'What? *Me?*'

'You were at the third blasting shaft with the rest of us.'

'But I'm the one who found him when we went back.'

'And you were the one who assigned search areas. You could have given yourself the right one, so you'd make sure he was dead before you "found" him. Then Breskin stumbled on you before you had a chance to deal Brian the *coup de grâce*.'

Harry gaped at him.

'You don't really think I'm capable of murder?'

'It's a chance in a million. But I've seen people win on longer odds.'

Although he knew that Pete was just giving him a taste of his own medicine, Harry felt a tension ache return to his neck and shoulders. 'You know what's wrong with you Californians?'

'Yeah. We make you Bostonians feel inferior, because we're so self-aware and mellow, but you're so repressed and uptight.'

'Actually, I'd been thinking that all the earthquakes and fires and riots and serial killers out there have made you paranoid.'

They smiled at each other.

Harry said, 'We'd better be getting back.'

THE WINDWARD FLANK of the iceberg had not been as forbidding as the featureless leeward wall. Three rugged shelves stepped back and up from the waterline. Beyond the shelves, the cliff rose at an angle for fifty feet or more. Rafts could have landed on the shelves in fair weather, but the huge waves that crashed now across the steps at the base of the iceberg would tear one of the *Pogodin*'s motorised rubber rafts to pieces, and so Gorov had given orders to return to leeward. He had no choice but to shoot a line across and rig a breeches buoy.

In his quarters Gorov changed into a dry uniform. Then he sat at the corner desk and picked up the photograph of his dead son. The boy's smile was genuine, not assumed for the camera. He was gripping his father's hand. In his other hand, he held a large cone of vanilla ice cream that was dripping onto his fingers. Even on the flat, two-dimensional surface of the photo, one could sense the aura of delight, love and pleasure that the child had always radiated in life.

'I swear I came as quickly as I could,' Gorov murmured to the photograph.

The boy stared, smiling.

'I'm going to get those people off the iceberg before midnight.' Gorov hardly recognised his own voice. 'I know I can do it. I'm not going to let them die. That's a promise.'

LIEUTENANT TIMOSHENKO had been off duty for the past four hours. He had eaten dinner and napped. Now, at 8:45, fifteen minutes ahead of schedule, he had returned to the communications centre once more, preparing to take the last watch of the day. One of his subordinates manned the equipment while Timoshenko sat at a corner work desk, reading a magazine and drinking a mug of hot tea.

Gorov stepped in from the companionway. 'Lieutenant, I believe it's time to make direct radio contact with those people on the iceberg.'

Timoshenko put down his tea and got up. 'Do you want to talk to them, sir?'

'I'll leave that to you,' Gorov said.

'And what should I tell them?'

Gorov quickly explained what they had found on their trip round the huge island of ice—the hopelessly stormy seas on the windward side, the sheer wall on the leeward side—and outlined his plans for the breeches buoy. 'And tell them that from here on out, we'll keep them informed of our progress every step of the way.'

'Yes, sir.'

Gorov turned to go.

'Sir? They're certain to ask—do you think we've a good chance of saving them?'

'Not good, no. Only fair. But tell them that if it's at all humanly possible, we'll do it, one way or the other. I'm more determined about this than I've been about anything else in my life. Tell them that, Lieutenant. Make sure you tell them that.'

8:57pm

Harry was surprised to hear his mother tongue spoken so fluently by a Russian radio operator. The man sounded as though he had taken a degree at a good middle-level university in Britain. Gradually, however, as Timoshenko explained why the leeward flank was the only approach to the iceberg worth investigating, Harry became accustomed to the man's decidedly English accent.

'A breeches buoy,' Harry said doubtfully. 'It can't be easy to rig one of those between two moving points, and in this weather.'

'We can match speeds with the ice pretty much dead on, which makes it almost like rigging between two stationary points. Besides, a breeches buoy is only one of our options. If we're unable to make it work, we'll get to you some other way. You needn't worry about that.'

'Wouldn't it be simpler to send divers across to the ice? You must have scuba equipment aboard.'

'And we've a number of well-trained frogmen,' Timoshenko said. 'But even the leeward sea is much too rough for them.'

'We certainly don't want anyone put at too great a risk on our behalf. From what you said, your captain sounds confident. So I guess we're better off leaving all the worrying to you. Have you anything else to tell me?'

'That's all for the moment,' Timoshenko said. 'Stay by your radio. We'll keep you informed of developments.'

EVERYONE EXCEPT HARRY and George had something to say about the call from the *Ilya Pogodin*'s communications officer—suggestions about preparations to be made for the rescue party, ideas about how they might be able to help the Russians scale the leeward wall—and everyone seemed determined to say it first, now, instantly.

When George Lin saw that their excitement had begun to abate and that they were growing quieter, he joined the group and faced Harry. He had been waiting until he was certain he would be heard. 'What is a Russian submarine doing in this part of the world? It doesn't belong here.'

'But these are international waters.'

'They're a long way from Russia.'

'Not all that far, actually.'

Lin's face was distorted by anger, and his voice was strained. 'But how did they learn about us?'

'From monitoring radio reports, I suppose.'

'Precisely,' Lin said, as if he had proved a point. He looked at Fischer and then at Claude, searching for a supporter. 'Radio reports. *Monitoring.*' He turned to Roger Breskin. 'And why would the Russians be monitoring communications in this part of the world?' When Breskin shrugged, Lin said, 'I'll tell you why. The *Pogodin* is on a surveillance mission. It's a goddamned spy ship, that's what it is.'

'Most likely,' Claude agreed, 'but that's hardly a startling revelation, George. We may not like it, but we all know how the world works.'

'Of course it's a spy ship,' Fischer said. 'If it had been a nuclear sub, they wouldn't even let us know they were in the area. We're *lucky* it's a spy ship, actually, something they're willing to compromise.'

230

Lin was determined to make them see the situation with the same degree of alarm that he himself obviously felt. 'Listen to me, think about this: it isn't *just* a spy ship. It's carrying motorised rafts, for God's sake, and the equipment to rig a breeches buoy to a point on land. That means it puts spies ashore in other countries, saboteurs and maybe even assassins.'

'Assassins and saboteurs may be stretching it,' Fischer said.

'Not stretching it at all!' Lin responded ardently. His face was flushed, and his sense of urgency grew visibly by the moment. 'These communist bastards—'

'They aren't communists any more,' Roger noted.

'Their new government's riddled with the same old criminals, and, when the moment's right, they'll be back. You'd better believe it. And they're barbarians, they're capable of anything. *Anything.*' He slammed his left fist into the open palm of his right hand.

Brian winced at the gesture and glanced at Harry.

Gently putting one hand on Lin's shoulder, Rita said, 'George, calm down. You aren't making a great deal of sense.'

Whipping round to face her as though she had threatened him, Lin said, 'Don't you realise why these Russians want to rescue us? They aren't really concerned about whether we live or die. It's strictly the propaganda value of the situation that interests them. They're going to use us to generate pro-Russian sentiment in the world press.'

'That's certainly true,' Harry said. 'But we're in no position to reject them.'

'Unless we stay here and die,' Roger Breskin said. His deep voice gave his simple statement the quality of an ominous prophecy.

Pete's patience with Lin had been exhausted. 'Is that what you want, George? Do you want to stay here and die?'

Lin was flustered. He shook his head: no. 'But you've got to see—'

Pete pressed his point. 'Do you want to stay here and die? That's the only question that matters. That's the bottom line.'

Lin fidgeted, searched their faces for a sign of support, and then looked down at the floor. 'No. Of course not. Nobody wants to die. I'm just . . . just . . . Sorry. Excuse me.' He walked to the far end of the cave and began to pace.

Roger Breskin took his watch from a zippered pocket in his parka. 'Five after nine.'

'Less than three hours,' Claude said.

'Can they get to us and take us off the ice in just three hours?' Brian wondered aloud.

'If they can't,' Harry said, trying to lighten the moment, 'I'm going to be really pissed off.'

9:10pm

Emil Zhukov climbed onto the bridge with a Thermos of hot tea and three aluminium mugs. 'Have they assembled the gun?'

'A few minutes yet,' Gorov said. He held one of the mugs while the first officer poured the tea.

Suddenly the night smelt of herbs and lemons and honey, and Nikita Gorov's mouth watered. He sipped the brew and smiled. Already the tea was growing cool, but sufficient heat remained to put an end to the chills that had been racing along his spine.

Below the bridge, on the forward section of the main deck, framed by four emergency lights, three crewmen were busy assembling the special gun that would be used to shoot a messenger line to the iceberg. The gun looked so wicked that an uninformed observer might have expected it to fire nuclear mortar rounds. Nearly as tall as any of the men assembling it, weighing 350 pounds, it consisted of just three primary components. The square base contained the motor that operated the pulleys for the breeches buoy, and it was fastened to four small steel rings recessed in the deck. The blocklike middle component of the gun fitted into a swivel mount on the base and contained the firing mechanism and a large drum of messenger line. The final piece was a four-foot-long barrel with a five-inch-diameter bore, which the three-man team had just inserted in its socket.

The tallest of the three crewmen stepped away from the gun, glanced up at the bridge and signalled to the captain that they were ready.

Gorov threw out the last of his tea. He gave the mug to Zhukov. 'Alert the control room.'

If his risky plan to use the breeches buoy was to have any chance of success, the submarine had to match speeds perfectly with the iceberg. If the boat outpaced the ice, or if the ice surged ahead by even a fraction of a knot, the messenger line might pull taut, stretch and snap faster than they could reel out new slack.

Gorov glanced at his watch. A quarter past nine. The minutes were slipping away too quickly.

One of the men on the forward deck uncapped the muzzle of the gun. Another man loaded a shell into the breech at the bottom.

The projectile, which would tow the messenger line, looked rather like a firework rocket: two feet long, nearly five inches in diameter. Trailing the nylon-and-wire line, it would strike the face of the cliff, explode on impact, and fire a four-inch bolt into the ice.

That bolt, to which the messenger line was joined, could slam eight to twelve inches into a solid-rock face, essentially fusing with the natural material round it, extruding reverse-hooked pins to prevent extraction. Welded to granite or limestone, the bolt was a reliable anchor. Unfortunately, Gorov thought, they were not dealing with granite or limestone. A large unknown element had been introduced. The anchor might not penetrate the ice properly or fuse with it as it did with most varieties of stone.

One of the crewmen took hold of the handgrips, in one of which the trigger was seated. With the help of the other two men, he got a range fix and a wind reading.

Zhukov put up two flares.

Gorov lifted his night glasses. He focused on the circle of light on the face of the cliff, thirty feet above the waterline.

A heavy *whump!* was audible above the wind.

Even before the sound of the shot faded, the rocket exploded against the iceberg fifty yards away.

'Direct hit!' Zhukov said.

With cannonlike volleys of sound, the cliff fractured. Cracks zigzagged outwards in every direction from the tow rocket's point of impact. The ice shifted, rippled like jelly at first, then shattered as completely as a plate-glass window. A prodigious wall of ice—200 yards long, seventy or eighty feet high and several feet thick—slid away from the side of the berg, collapsed violently into the sea and sent shimmering fountains of dark water more than fifty feet into the air. The messenger line went down with the ice.

A twenty-foot-high tidal wave of displaced water surged across the fifty yards of open sea towards the port flank of the submarine, and there was no time to take evasive action. One of the three crewmen on the deck cried out as the small tsunami crashed across the main deck with enough power to rock the *Pogodin* to starboard. With the messenger-line gun, all three vanished under that black tide. If they hadn't been tethered, they would have been washed overboard.

As the crewmen struggled to their feet, Gorov turned his field glasses on the iceberg again. 'It's still too damned sheer.'

The tremendous icefall had done little to change the vertical topography of the leeward flank of the berg. A 200-yard-long indentation marked the collapse, but even that new feature was uncannily smooth, unmarked by ledges or projections or wide fissures that might have been of use to a climber, nor any shelves or sheltering niches where a motorised raft could put in and tie up.

Gorov lowered his night glasses. Turning again towards the three men on the forward main deck, he signalled them to dismantle the gun and get below.

Dispirited, Zhukov said, 'What now?'

Gorov wiped his goggles with the back of one ice-crusted glove. He studied the cliff through binoculars. At last he said, 'Tell Timoshenko to put through a call to the Edgeway group. Find out where their cave is located. If it's near the leeward side, they ought to move out of there altogether, right now.'

'Move?' Zhukov said.

'I'm going to see if I can create a landing shelf if I torpedo the base of the cliff.'

'THE REST OF YOU go ahead,' Harry insisted. 'I've got to let Gunvald know what's happening here. As soon as I've talked to him, I'll bring out the radio.'

'You've only got a few minutes,' Rita said worriedly and reached for his hand, as if she might pull him out of the cave with her. But then she seemed to sense that he had another and better reason for calling Gunvald, a reason that he preferred to conceal from the others. Their eyes met, and understanding passed between them. She said, 'A few minutes. You remember that. Don't you start chatting with him about old girlfriends.'

Harry smiled. 'I never had any.'

'Just young ones, right?'

Claude said, 'Harry, I really think it's foolish to—'

'Don't worry. I promise I'll be out of here long before the shooting starts. Now the rest of you get moving. Go, go.'

The ice cave was neither along the leeward flank of the berg nor near the midpoint of its length, where the Russian radioman had said the torpedo would strike. Nevertheless, they had unanimously decided to retreat to the snowmobiles in case the concussion from the torpedo dislodged the hundreds of interlocking slabs of ice that formed the ceiling of the cave.

As soon as he was alone, Harry knelt in front of the radio and called Larsson.

'I read you, Harry.' Gunvald's voice was overlaid with static.

'Have you been listening in to my conversations with the Russians?' Harry said.

'What I could hear of them. This storm is beginning to generate a hell of a lot of interference.'

'At least you've got a general idea of the situation here,' Harry said. 'I haven't time to chat about that. I'm calling to ask you to do something important for me. Something you may find morally repugnant.'

As succinctly as he could, Harry told Gunvald Larsson about the attempt to kill Brian Dougherty and then quickly explained what he wanted done. Although shocked, the Swede appreciated the need for haste and didn't waste time asking for more details. 'What you want me to do isn't especially pleasant,' he agreed. 'But under the circumstances it seems necessary. I'll do it.'

'Good. But hurry.'

As Harry put down the microphone, Pete Johnson entered the cave. 'Man, are you suicidal? Maybe I was wrong about you being a natural-born hero. Maybe you're just a natural-born masochist. Let's get the hell out of here before the roof falls in.'

Harry unplugged the microphone and picked up the radio by the thick, crisscrossing leather straps atop the case. Stepping out of the cave into the wildly howling night, he discovered that the snow had at last given way entirely to an ice storm. The tiny spicules were needle-sharp, coming along like great clouds of diamond dust, on a course nearly horizontal to the ground. They stung the exposed sections of Harry's face and began immediately to plate his storm suit with transparent armour.

THE SUPPLY SHED at Edgeway Station was a pair of adjoining Nissen huts, in which the expedition stored tools, spare parts, any equipment that wasn't in use and other provisions. Just inside the door, Gunvald stripped out of his heavy coat and hung it on a wooden rack near one of the electric heaters.

Reaching overhead in the blackness, he located the light chain and tugged it. A naked 100-watt bulb blinked on, shedding cold white light.

Along the back wall, nine metal lockers stood like narrow, upright caskets. A name was stencilled on the grey door of each, white letters above the narrow ventilation slits: H. CARPENTER, R. CARPENTER, JOHNSON, JOBERT, and so forth.

Gunvald went to the tool rack and took down a heavy hammer and an iron crowbar. He was going to have to force open those lockers, one after the other, as quickly as possible, before he had any second thoughts. If a member of the Edgeway expedition was a psychopathic killer and if evidence existed to identify that man, then the lockers were the logical place to look.

Gunvald used the hammer to smash the combination dials from five of the lockers, one after the other. Wedging the hook of the crowbar into the round hole where the dial had been, Gunvald pulled backwards with all his might and tore the lock from the first locker. The metal squealed and bent, and the door popped open. He didn't pause to look inside but quickly proceeded to wrench open the other four: *bang, bang, bang, bang!* Done.

235

After he had taken a minute to catch his breath, he picked up a wooden crate, put it down in front of the first locker and sat on it.

All right then. Where should he start?

Roger Breskin, Franz Fischer, George Lin, Claude Jobert, Pete Johnson. Those were the five suspects. All were good men, as far as Gunvald was aware, although some were friendlier and easier to get to know than others. They were smarter and more well balanced than the average person on the street; they *had* to be so, in order to have successful research careers in the Arctic, where the arduousness of the job and the unusual pressures quickly eliminated those who weren't self-reliant and exceptionally stable.

He decided to begin with Roger Breskin, because Roger's locker was the first in line. All the shelves were bare except the top one, on which was a cardboard box. Gunvald lifted the box out and put it between his feet.

As he had expected, the Canadian travelled light. The box contained only four items. A laminated eight-by-ten colour photograph of Roger's mother: a strong-jawed woman with a winning smile and curly grey hair. One silver brush-and-comb set: tarnished. A rosary. And a scrapbook filled with newspaper clippings of Breskin's career as an amateur weightlifter.

Gunvald left everything on the floor and moved the wooden crate two feet to the left. He sat in front of Fischer's locker.

THE SUBMARINE was submerged again, holding steady just below the surface, at its highest periscope depth. It was lying in wait along the iceberg's projected course.

On the conning-tower platform in the control room, Nikita Gorov stood at the periscope. Even though the top of the scope was eight or nine feet above sea level, the storm waves exploded against it and washed over it, obscuring his view from time to time.

The iceberg had already begun to cross their bow, 300 yards north of their position. That gleaming white mountain was starkly silhouetted against the black night and sea.

Zhukov stood next to the captain. He was wearing headphones and listening on an open line that connected him to the petty officer in the forward torpedo room. He said, 'Number one tube ready.'

The *Ilya Pogodin* was not primarily a warship, but an information gatherer. It didn't carry nuclear missiles. However, the Russian Naval Ministry had planned that every submarine should be prepared to bring the battle to the enemy in the event of a non-nuclear war. Therefore, the boat was carrying twelve electric torpedoes, each weighing over a ton and a half.

236

'Number one tube ready,' Zhukov said again as the officer in the torpedo room repeated that announcement over the headset.

After a protracted and almost reverent silence, Nikita Gorov said, 'Match bearings . . . and . . . *shoot!*'

'Fire one!' Zhukov said.

Gorov squinted through the eyepiece of the periscope, tense and expectant. The torpedo had been programmed to strike the cliff fifteen feet below the waterline. With luck, the configuration of the ice after the explosion would be more amenable than it was now to the landing of a couple of rafts.

The torpedo hit its mark. The black ocean swelled and leaped at the base of the cliff, and for an instant the water was full of fiery yellow light, as if sea serpents with radiant eyes were surfacing.

Gorov felt the echoes of the concussion vibrate through the submarine's outer hull.

The bottom of the white cliff began to dissolve. A house-size chunk of it tumbled into the water and was followed by an avalanche of broken ice.

Lifting the headset from one ear, Zhukov said, 'How's it look out there, sir?'

Keeping his eye to the periscope, Gorov said, 'Not much better than it did.'

'No landing shelf?'

'Not really. But the ice is still falling.'

Zhukov paused, listening to the petty officer at the other end of the line. 'Muzzle door shut.'

'Green and check.'

Gorov wasn't listening closely to the series of safety checks, because his full attention was riveted on the iceberg. Something was wrong. The floating mountain had begun to act strangely. Or was it his imagination? He squinted, trying to get a better view of the behemoth between the high waves. The target seemed not to be advancing eastwards any longer. Indeed, he thought the 'bow' of it was even beginning to swing round slightly to the south. No. Absurd. Couldn't happen. He closed his eyes and told himself that he was seeing things. But, when he looked again, he was even more certain that—

The radar technician said, 'Target's changing course!'

'It can't be,' Zhukov said, startled. 'Not all that quickly.'

'Nevertheless, it's changing,' Gorov said.

'Not because of the torpedo. Just one torpedo couldn't have such a profound effect on an object that large.'

'No. Something else is at work here,' Gorov said worriedly. The captain turned away from the periscope. From the ceiling, he pulled down a microphone on a steel-spring neck and spoke to both the control room round him and to the sonar room, which was the next compartment forward in the boat. 'I want an all-systems analysis of the lower fathoms to a depth of seven hundred feet.'

Through the use of limited-range sonar, thermal-analysis sensors, sophisticated listening devices and other marine-survey equipment, the *Ilya Pogodin*'s technicians were able to plot the movements of both warm- and cold-blooded forms of sea life beneath and to all sides of the boat, thereby identifying the direction of a major current strong enough to affect an object as large as the iceberg.

Two minutes after Gorov had ordered the scan, the squawk box crackled again. 'Strong current detected, travelling due south, beginning at a depth of three hundred and forty feet.'

Gorov looked away from the scope and pulled down the overhead microphone again. 'How fast is it moving?'

'Approximately nine knots, sir.'

Gorov blanched. 'Impossible!'

He released the microphone, which sprang up out of the way, and, with a new sense of urgency, returned to the periscope. They were in the path of a juggernaut. The massive island of ice had been swinging slowly, ponderously into the new current, but now the full force of the fast-moving water was squarely behind it.

'Target closing,' the radar operator said. 'Five hundred yards!'

Before Gorov could reply, the boat was suddenly shaken as if a giant hand had taken hold of it. Zhukov fell. Papers slid off the chart table. 'What the hell?' Zhukov asked, scrambling to his feet.

'Collision.'

'With what?'

The berg was still 500 yards away.

'Probably a small floe of ice,' Gorov said.

He ordered damage reports from every part of the boat. He knew that they hadn't collided with a large object, for if they had done so they would already be sinking. The submarine's hull wasn't tempered, because it required a degree of flexibility to descend and ascend rapidly through realms of varying temperatures and pressures. Consequently, even a single ton of ice, if moving with sufficient velocity, would cave in the hull as if crashing into a cardboard vessel. Whatever they had encountered was clearly of limited size; nevertheless, it must have caused at least minor damage.

The sonar operator called out the position of the iceberg: 'Four hundred and fifty yards and closing!'

Gorov was in a bind. If he didn't take the boat down, they would collide with that mountain of ice. But, if he dived before he knew what damage had been sustained, they might never be able to surface again. There simply wasn't enough time to bring the big boat round and flee either to the east or to the west; because the iceberg was rushing at them sideways, it stretched nearly two-fifths of a mile both to port and starboard.

He snapped up the horizontal bar on the periscope and sent it into its hydraulic sleeve.

'Four hundred and twenty yards and closing!' called the sonar operator.

'Dive!' Gorov said. '*Dive!*'

The diving klaxons blasted throughout the boat. Simultaneously the collision alarm wailed.

'We're going under the ice before it hits us,' Gorov said.

Zhukov paled. 'It must be six hundred feet below the waterline!'

Heart racing, Nikita Gorov said, 'I know. I'm not certain we'll make it.'

The damage reports disclosed that no bulkheads had buckled; no water was entering the boat. The shock had been worse in the forward quarters than anywhere else, and it had been especially unsettling to the men in the torpedo room, two decks below the control room. The boat had apparently sustained some exterior hull damage immediately aft and starboard of the bow.

If the outer skin had only been scraped, or if it had suffered only a minor dent, the boat would survive. However, if the hull had sustained even moderate compaction at any point—and, worst of all, distortion that lay across welded seams—they might not live through a deep dive. The pressure on the submarine would not be uniformly resisted by the damaged areas, and the boat might implode and sink straight to the ocean floor.

The young diving officer's voice was loud but, in spite of the circumstances, not shaky. 'Two hundred feet and descending.'

The sonar operator reported: 'The profile of the target is narrowing. She's continuing to come bow-around in the current.'

'Two hundred and fifty feet,' said the diving officer.

They had to get down at least 600 feet. To be safe, Gorov preferred to descend to 700 feet, though the speed of the target's approach reduced their chances of attaining even 600 in time to avoid it.

The sonar operator called: 'Three hundred and eighty yards and closing.'

'If I wasn't an atheist,' Zhukov said, 'I'd start praying.'

No one laughed. At that moment none of them was an atheist. Even though everyone appeared cool and confident, Gorov could smell the fear in the control room, the tang of an unusually acrid sweat. The place was redolent of fear.

'Three hundred and twenty feet,' the diving officer announced.

They were in a crash dive. Going down fast. A lot of strain on the hull. Even as each man monitored the equipment at his station, he found time to glance repeatedly at the diving stand, which had suddenly become the very centre of the room. The needle on the depth gauge was falling rapidly.

Four hundred feet.

Four hundred and twenty feet.

Everyone aboard knew that the boat had been designed for sudden and radical manoeuvres, but the *Pogodin* was not in the best shape of its life, and might be running with a stress crack serious enough to spell doom at any moment.

'Four hundred and sixty feet,' said the diving officer.

'Target at three hundred yards.'

'Depth at four hundred and eighty feet.'

With both hands, Gorov gripped the command-pad railing tightly and resisted the pull of the inclined deck until his arms ached.

'Target at *two* hundred yards!'

Zhukov said, 'It's picking up speed like it's going downhill.'

'Five hundred and twenty feet.'

Their descent was accelerating, but not fast enough to please Gorov. They would need to get down at least another hundred and eighty feet until they were without a doubt safely under the iceberg.

'Five hundred and forty feet.'

'Target at one hundred and sixty yards. Closing fast!' called the sonar operator.

'Five hundred and sixty feet,' the diving officer said, although he must have known that everyone was watching the depth gauge.

'Target at one hundred and twenty yards and closing.'

The diving officer's voice had softened almost to a whisper, yet it carried clearly through the control room. 'Six hundred feet and descending.'

Emil Zhukov's face was as gaunt as a death mask.

Still bracing himself against the railing, Gorov said, 'We've got to risk another eighty feet or a hundred, anyway. We've got to be well under the ice.'

Zhukov nodded.

'Six hundred and twenty feet.'

The sonar operator struggled to control his voice. Nevertheless, a faint note of distress coloured his next report: 'Target at sixty yards and closing. Dead ahead of the bow. It's going to hit us!'

240

'None of that!' Gorov said sharply. 'We'll make it.'

'Depth six hundred and seventy feet.'

'Twenty yards.'

'Six hundred and ninety.'

'Target lost,' the sonar operator said, his voice rising half an octave on the last word.

They froze, waiting for the grinding impact that would smash the hull.

I've been a fool to jeopardise my own and seventy-nine other lives just to save one-tenth that number, Gorov thought.

The technician who was monitoring the surface fathometer cried, 'Ice overhead!'

They were under the berg.

'What's our clearance?' Gorov asked.

'Fifty feet.'

No one cheered. They were still too tense for that. But they indulged in a modest, collective sigh of relief.

'We're under it,' Zhukov said, amazed. 'We're safe.'

'Stabilise at seven hundred and forty,' Gorov said. He pulled on his neatly trimmed beard and found it wet with perspiration. 'No. Not entirely safe. Not yet. No iceberg will have a flat bottom. There'll be scattered protrusions below six hundred feet, and we might even encounter one that drops all the way down to our running depth. Not safe until we're completely out from under.'

GUNVALD FOUND NOTHING incriminating in the lockers. Five suspects. No sinister discoveries. No clues.

He got up from the wooden crate and went to the far end of the room. At that distance from the violated lockers—although distance itself didn't make him any less guilty—he felt that he could fill and light his pipe. He needed the pipe to calm him and to help him think. Soon the air was filled with the rich aroma of tobacco.

He closed his eyes and leaned against the wall and thought about the items that he had taken from the lockers. If one of those men was mentally unbalanced, a potential killer, then he was damned clever. He had hidden his madness so well that no sign of it could be found even in his most personal possessions.

Frustrated, Gunvald emptied his pipe into a sand-filled waste can, put the pipe in his vest pocket and returned to the lockers. The floor was littered with the precious detritus of five lives. As he gathered up the articles and put them back where he had found them, his guilt gave way to shame at the violation of privacy that he had committed.

And then he saw the envelope. Ten by twelve inches. About one inch thick. At the very bottom of the locker, taped against the back wall. In his haste, he had overlooked it, because it was in the lowest part of the locker, at foot level, tucked at the rear of the twelve-inch-high space under the lowest shelf.

It was firmly taped to the locker wall. He tore it free and opened it. The envelope contained only a spiralbound notebook with what appeared to be newspaper and magazine clippings hidden among the pages. Gunvald began to page through the notebook. The contents hit him with tremendous force, shocked him as he had never imagined that he could be shocked. Hideous stuff. Page after page of it. He knew at once that the man who had compiled this collection, if not a raving maniac, was seriously disturbed.

He closed the book and hurriedly pulled on his coat and outer boots. Kicking through snowdrifts, head tucked down to protect his face from a savage wind, he ran back to the telecommunications hut, frantic to let Harry know what he had found.

'ICE OVERHEAD. One hundred feet.'

Gorov left the command pad and stood behind the technician who was reading the surface fathometer.

'Ice overhead. One hundred and twenty feet.'

'How can it be receding?' Gorov frowned, reluctant to believe the proof provided by the very technology that he had always before trusted. 'By now the iceberg's turned its narrow profile to us, so we can't have passed under even half its length. There's still a huge, long mountain hanging over us.'

The technician frowned too. 'I don't understand it, sir. But now it's up to a hundred and forty feet and still rising.'

'A hundred and forty feet of clear water between us and the bottom of the iceberg?'

'Yes, sir.'

The surface fathometer broadcast high-frequency sound waves upwards in a tightly controlled spread, bounced an echo off the underside of the ice—if any lay overhead—and determined the distance between the top of the sail and the frozen ceiling of the sea.

'One hundred and sixty feet, sir.'

The stylus on the surface fathometer wiggled back and forth on a continuous drum of graph paper. The black band that it drew was steadily growing wider.

'Ice overhead. One hundred and eighty feet.'

The ice continued to recede above them. It made no sense.

The squawk box above the command pad hissed and crackled. The torpedo officer reported news that Gorov had hoped never to hear at *any* depth, let alone at 740 feet: 'Captain, our forward bulkhead is sweating.'

Everyone in the control room stiffened. Their attention had been riveted on the sonar readings, because the greatest danger had seemed to be that they would ram into a long stalactite of ice hanging from the bottom of the berg. The torpedo officer's warning was an unnerving reminder that they had had a collision before initiating a crash dive and that they were more than seven hundred feet beneath the surface, where every square inch of the hull was under brutal pressure. Millions upon millions of tons of seawater lay between them and the world of sky and sun and open air that was their true home.

Pulling down an overhead microphone, Gorov said, 'Captain to torpedo room. There's dry insulation behind that bulkhead.'

The squawk box was now the centre of interest. 'Yes, sir. But it's sweating just the same. The insulation behind it must be wet now.'

Evidently they had sustained a dangerous amount of damage when they had collided with that floe ice. 'Is there much water?'

'Just a film, sir. Along the weld between number four tube and number five tube.'

'Any buckling?'

'No, sir.'

'Watch it closely,' Gorov said.

'I've got eyes for nothing else, sir.'

The operator seated at the surface fathometer announced, 'Ice overhead. Two hundred and fifty feet.'

The mystery of the receding ice again. They were not descending. And Gorov knew damned well that the iceberg above them was not magically levitating out of the sea. So why was the distance between them steadily widening?

'Should we take her up, sir?' Zhukov suggested. 'A little closer to the ice. If we ascend even to just six hundred feet, that torpedo-room bulkhead might stop sweating. The pressure would be considerably less.'

'We can't go up,' Gorov said curtly. 'There's still all that ice above us. I don't know what's happening here, how the ice can be receding like this, but we'll be cautious until I understand the situation.'

'Ice overhead. Two hundred and eighty feet.'

Gorov looked again at the surface-fathometer graph. Abruptly the stylus stopped jiggling. It produced a straight, thin, black line down the centre of the drum.

'Clear water!' the technician said, with obvious astonishment. '*No* ice overhead.'

'We're out from under?' Zhukov asked.

Gorov said, 'Impossible. That berg's at least four-fifths of a mile long. No more than half of it has passed over us. We can't—'

'Ice overhead again!' the surface-fathometer operator called out. 'Three hundred feet. Ice at three hundred feet and *falling* now.'

Gorov watched the stylus closely. The channel of open water between the top of the *Pogodin*'s sail and the bottom of the iceberg narrowed rapidly, until it steadied at fifty feet for a few seconds and then began to fluctuate wildly in utterly unpredictable peaks and troughs. Then it reached fifty feet of clearance once more, and at last the stylus began to wiggle less erratically.

'Could the fathometer have been malfunctioning back there?' Gorov asked.

The technician shook his head. 'I don't think so, sir. It seems fine now.'

'Then do I understand what just happened? Did we pass under a *hole* in the middle of the iceberg?'

Keeping a close watch on the graph drum, the technician said, 'Yes. I think so. From every indication, a hole. Approximately in the middle.'

'A funnel-shaped hole.'

'Yes, sir. It began to register as an inverted dish. But when we were directly under, the upper two-thirds of the cavity narrowed drastically.'

With growing excitement, Gorov said, 'And it went all the way to the top of the iceberg?'

'I don't know about that, sir. But it went up at least to sea level.'

The surface fathometer, of course, couldn't take readings further up than the surface of the sea.

'A hole,' Gorov said thoughtfully. He had a seed of an idea, the germ of an outrageously daring plan to rescue the Edgeway scientists. If the hole was—

'Clear water,' the technician announced. 'No ice overhead.'

Zhukov pressed a few keys on the command-pad console. He looked at the computer screen to his right. 'It checks. This time the berg's really gone.'

Gorov glanced at his watch: 10:02pm. Less than two hours remained until the sixty explosive charges would shatter the iceberg. The scheme that he had in mind might seem to some to border on outright lunacy, but it had the advantage of being a plan that could work within the limited time they had left.

Pulling down the steel-spring microphone, Gorov said, 'Captain to torpedo room. How's it look there?'

244

From the overhead speaker: 'Still sweating, sir. It's not any better, but it's not any worse, either.'

'Keep watching.' Gorov released the microphone and returned to the command pad. 'Engines at half speed. Left full rudder.'

Astonishment made Emil Zhukov's long face appear even longer. He swallowed hard. 'You mean we aren't going up?'

'Not this minute,' Gorov said. 'We've got to make another run under that behemoth. I want to have another look at that hole in the middle of it.'

THE VOLUME on the short-wave radio was at its maximum setting, so the Russian communications officer aboard the *Pogodin* could be heard over the roar of the storm beast that prowled at the entrance to the cave.

The others had joined Harry and Pete in the ice cave to hear the astounding news first-hand.

When Lieutenant Timoshenko had described the hole and the large area of dramatically scalloped ice on the bottom of their floating prison, Harry had explained the probable cause of it. The iceberg had been broken off the cap by a tsunami, and the tsunami had been generated by a seabed earthquake almost directly beneath them. If ocean-floor volcanic activity had been associated with the recent event, enormous quantities of lava could have been discharged into the sea, flung upwards with tremendous force. Spouts of white-hot lava could have bored that hole, and the millions of gallons of boiling water that it produced could easily have sculpted the troughs and peaks that marked the bottom of the iceberg just past the hole.

'As Captain Gorov sees it, there are three possibilities. First, the hole in the bottom of your berg might end in solid ice above the waterline. Or, second, it might lead into a shallow crevasse. Or, third, it might even continue above sea level and open at the top of the iceberg. Does that analysis seem sound to you, Dr Carpenter?' Timoshenko asked.

'Yes,' Harry said, impressed by the captain's reasoning. 'And I know which of the three it is.' He told Timoshenko about the crevasse that had opened midway in the iceberg's length when the gigantic seismic waves had passed under the edge of the winter field. 'I nearly drove my snowmobile straight into it.'

'Then if the hole is at the bottom of the crevasse—I suppose we should call it a shaft or tunnel, rather than a hole—would you be willing to try to reach it by climbing down *into* the crevasse?' Timoshenko enquired.

The question seemed bizarre to Harry. He could not see the point of going down into that chasm where his snowmobile had vanished. 'I don't understand where you're going with this,' he said.

'That's how we're going to try to take you off the ice. Through that tunnel and out from underneath the berg.'

In the cave behind Harry, the seven others responded to that suggestion with noisy disbelief.

He gestured at them to be quiet. To the Russian radioman, he said, 'Down this tunnel, and somehow into the submarine? But how?'

Timoshenko said, 'In diving gear.'

'We haven't any.'

'Yes, but *we* have.' Timoshenko explained how the gear would get to them.

Harry was more impressed than ever with the Russians' ingenuity but still doubtful. 'A man can't dive that deep unless he's trained and has special equipment.'

'We've got the special equipment,' Timoshenko said. 'I'm afraid you'll have to do without the special training.' He spent the next five minutes outlining Captain Gorov's plan in some detail.

The scheme was brilliant, imaginative, daring and well thought out. Harry wanted to meet this Captain Nikita Gorov, to see what kind of man could come up with such a stunningly clever idea. 'It might work, but it's risky. And there's no guarantee that the tunnel from your end actually opens into the bottom of the crevasse at our end. Maybe we won't be able to find it.'

'Perhaps,' Timoshenko agreed. 'But it's your best chance. In fact, it's your only chance. There's just an hour and a half until those explosives detonate. We can't get rafts across to the iceberg, climb up there and bring you down as we'd planned. Not in ninety minutes.'

Harry knew that was true. 'Lieutenant Timoshenko, I need to discuss this with my colleagues. Give me a minute, please.' Still hunkering before the radio, he turned to face the others and said, 'Well?'

Rita would have to control her phobia as never before, because she would have to go down *inside* the ice, be entirely surrounded by it. Yet she was the first to speak in favour of the plan: 'Of course we'll do it. We can't just sit here and wait to die.'

Claude Jobert nodded. 'We haven't much choice.'

'We've got one chance in ten thousand of getting through alive,' Franz estimated. 'But it's not altogether hopeless.'

'Teutonic gloom,' Rita said, grinning.

In spite of himself, Fischer managed a smile. 'That's what you said when I was worried that a snowstorm might strike before we got back to base camp.'

'Count me in,' Brian said.

Roger Breskin nodded. 'And me.'

Pete Johnson said, 'I joined up for the adventure. Now I'm sure as hell getting more of it than I bargained for.'

Turning to Lin, Harry said, 'Well, George?'

With his goggles up and his snow mask pulled down, Lin revealed his distress in every line and aspect of his face.

'George? Are you with us or not?' Harry persisted.

Finally Lin nodded.

Harry picked up the microphone again. 'Lieutenant Timoshenko?'

'I read you, Dr Carpenter.'

'We've decided that your captain's plan makes sense, if only because it's a necessity. We'll do it—if it can be done.'

'It can be done, Doctor. We're convinced of it.'

'We'll have to move quickly,' Harry said. 'There isn't any hope in hell of our reaching the crevasse much before eleven o'clock. That leaves just one hour for the rest of it.'

Timoshenko said, 'If we all keep in mind a vivid image of what's going to happen at midnight, we should be able to hustle through in the time we have. Good luck to all of you.'

EVEN THE MOST SOPHISTICATED telecommunications equipment was unable to cope with the interference that accompanied a storm in polar latitudes in the bitter heart of winter. Gunvald could no longer pick up the powerful transmissions emanating from the US base at Thule. He tried every frequency band, but across all of them the storm reigned. The speakers were choked with static: a wailing, screeching, crackling concert of chaos unaccompanied by even a single human voice.

He returned to the frequency where Harry was supposed to be awaiting his call. 'Harry, can you read me?'

Static.

For perhaps the fiftieth time, he read off their call numbers, raising his voice as if trying to shout above the interference.

No response. It wasn't a matter of hearing them or being heard through the static. They simply weren't receiving him at all. He ought to give up.

He glanced at the spiralbound notebook that lay open on the table beside him. Although he had looked at the same page a dozen times already, he shuddered. He *couldn't* give up. They had to know the nature of the beast in their midst.

He called them again.

Static.

10:56pm

When they were in the vicinity of the chasm, Harry brought his snowmobile to a stop and, with a measure of reluctance, climbed out. The other snowmobiles pulled up behind him. The last vehicle was only thirty yards away, but he could see nothing more than vague yellow aureoles where the headlights should have been.

He hurried forwards with his flashlight, scouting the ice, until he ascertained that the next 100 feet were safe. The air was bone-freezing, so cold that breathing it even through his snow mask hurt his throat and made his lungs ache. He scrambled back to the comparative warmth of his snowmobile and cautiously drove the 100 feet he knew to be safe before getting out to conduct further reconnaissance.

Again he had found the crevasse, although this time he had avoided nearly driving over the brink. The chasm was ten or twelve feet wide, narrowing towards the bottom, filled with more darkness than his flashlight could dispel. As far as he could see through his frosted goggles, the wall along which he would have to descend was pretty much a flat, unchallenging surface. Less than a hundred feet down was a wide ledge, which he thought he could reach without killing himself.

Harry turned his sled round and gingerly backed it to the edge of the chasm, a move that might reasonably have been judged suicidal; however, considering that barely sixty precious minutes remained to them, a certain degree of recklessness seemed essential.

By the time the others parked their snowmobiles, got out and joined him near the brink of the crevasse, Harry had fixed two 1,000-pound-test, ninety-strand nylon lines to the tow hitch of his sled. The first rope was an eighty-foot safety line that would bring him up short of the crevasse floor if he fell. He knotted it round his waist. The second line, the one that he would use to attempt a measured descent, was 100 feet long, and he tossed the free end into the ravine.

Pete Johnson arrived at the brink and gave Harry his flashlight.

Harry had already snapped his own flashlight to the tool belt at his waist and it hung at his right hip. Now he clipped Pete's torch at his left hip. Twin beams of yellow light shone down his legs.

Neither he nor Pete attempted to speak. The wind was shrieking like something that had crawled out of the bowels of Hell on Judgment Day. They couldn't have heard each other even if they had screamed at the top of their lungs.

Harry stretched out on the ice, flat on his stomach, and took the climbing line in both hands.

Pete patted him reassuringly on the shoulder. Then he slowly pushed Harry backwards, over the ledge, into the crevasse.

Harry thought he had a firm grip on the line and was certain that he could control his descent, but he was mistaken. As though greased, the line slipped through his hands, and he plunged unchecked into the abyss. A wall of ice flashed past him, two or three inches from his face, flickering with the reflections of the two flashlight beams that preceded him. He clenched the rope as tightly as he could and also tried to pin it between his knees, but he was in what amounted to freefall.

The rope burned through the surface slickness of his gloves, and abruptly he was able to stop himself, perhaps seventy feet below the brink of the crevasse. His heart was pounding, and every muscle in his body was knotted tighter than the safety line round his waist. Gasping for breath, he swung back and forth on the line, banging painfully—and then more gently—against the chasm wall.

After easing down the rope another fifteen or twenty feet, he reached the bottom of the crevasse. He unclipped one of the flashlights from his tool belt and began to search for the entrance to the tunnel that Lieutenant Timoshenko had described.

At the moment he did not have a view of the entire floor of the crevasse. When part of one wall had collapsed under his snowmobile earlier in the day, it had tumbled to the bottom; now it constituted a ten-foot-high divider that partitioned the chasm into two areas of roughly equal size. The badly charred wreckage of the sled was strewn over the top of that partition.

The section into which Harry had descended was a dead end. It contained no side passages, no deeper fissures large enough to allow him to descend further and no sign of a tunnel or open water.

Slipping, sliding, he climbed to the top of that sloped mound, and over the smashed and burnt ruins of the snowmobile to the far side.

There he found a way out, into deeper and more mysterious realms of ice. The right-hand wall offered no caves or fissures, but the left-hand wall didn't reach all the way to the floor. It ended four feet above the bottom of the crevasse.

Harry dropped flat on his stomach and poked his flashlight into that low opening. The passageway was about thirty feet wide and no higher than four feet. It appeared to run straight and level for six or seven yards under the crevasse wall, before it curved sharply downwards and out of sight.

He looked at his watch: 11:02. Detonation in fifty-eight minutes.

Holding the light in front of him, Harry quickly wriggled into the passage. He wasn't claustrophobic, but he had a healthy fear of being confined in an extremely cramped place ninety feet beneath the Arctic ice, while surrounded by fifty-eight packages of live explosive.

Nevertheless, he twisted and pulled himself forwards with his elbows and his knees. When he'd gone twenty-five or thirty feet, he discovered that the passageway led into the bottom of what seemed to be a large open space, a hollow in the heart of the ice. He moved the flashlight to the left and right, but, from his position, he was unable to get a clear idea of the cavern's true size. He slid out of the crawl-space, stood up and unclipped the second flashlight from his belt.

He was in a circular chamber 100 feet in diameter, with dozens of fissures and cul-de-sacs and passageways leading from it. Apparently the ceiling, a nearly perfect dome had been formed by a great upwards rush of hot water and steam. The floor descended towards the centre of the room in seven progressive steps, two or three feet at a time, so the overall effect was of an amphitheatre. At the nadir of the cavern, where the stage would have been, was a forty-foot-diameter pool of thrashing sea water. The tunnel.

Hundreds of feet below, that wide tunnel opened into the hollow in the bottom of the iceberg, to the lightless world of the deep Arctic Ocean, where the *Ilya Pogodin* would be waiting for them.

Harry was suddenly energised by hope.

Nature had been set firmly against them for the past twelve hours. Perhaps now she was ready to show them a little mercy.

Harry clipped one of the flashlights to his belt. Holding the other light in front of him, he wriggled back through the crawlspace between the domed cavern and the bottom of the open crevasse, eager to signal the others to descend and begin their tortuous escape from that prison of ice.

11:06pm

At the command pad, Nikita Gorov monitored a series of five video-display terminals which provided data regarding the boat's and the iceberg's positions, relative attitudes and speeds.

'Clear water,' said the technician who was operating the surface fathometer. 'No ice overhead.'

Gorov had jockeyed the *Ilya Pogodin* under the quarter-mile-long concavity in the bottom of the iceberg. The sail of the submarine was directly below the tunnel in the centre of that concavity, and there they would remain for the duration of the operation.

'Speed matched to target,' Zhukov said, repeating the report that had come over his headset from the manoeuvring room.

The captain hesitated, reluctant to act until he was absolutely certain that they were properly positioned. He studied the five screens for another half-minute. When he was satisfied that the speed of the boat was as closely coordinated with the iceberg's progress as was humanly possible, he pulled down a microphone and said, 'Captain to communications centre. Release the aerial at will, Lieutenant.'

Timoshenko's voice grated from the overhead speaker. 'Aerial deployed.'

Topside, eight watertight aluminium boxes nestled among the masts and periscopes on the *Pogodin*'s sail. They were held in place by multiple lengths of nylon cord, some of which had no doubt snapped, as expected, during the submarine's second descent to 700 feet.

When Timoshenko released the aerial, a helium balloon had been ejected in a swarm of bubbles from a pressurised tube on top of the sail. If it was functioning properly, the balloon would be rising rapidly in the dark sea, trailing the multicommunications wire behind it. As an intelligence-gathering boat, the *Ilya Pogodin* had deployed that aerial in the same fashion on thousands of occasions over the years.

The eight watertight boxes fastened atop the sail, however, were not a standard feature. They were secured to the communications wire with a fine-link, titanium-alloy chain and spring locks. When the rising helium balloon was twenty feet above the sail, it should jerk the chain tight and draw the boxes upwards, pulling hard enough against the remaining nylon restraining lines to cause them to slip their knots. Because the aluminium boxes were buoyant, they would then rise instantly from the sail into the entrance to the long tunnel and continue to rise effortlessly, higher, higher.

Bending over the graph of the surface fathometer, the operator said, 'I'm registering a fragmented obstruction in the tunnel.'

'The boxes?' Gorov asked.

'Yes, sir.'

'It's working,' Zhukov said.

'Seems to be,' the captain agreed.

'Now if the Edgeway people have located the other end of the tunnel—'

'We can get on with the hard part,' Gorov finished for him.

11:10pm

The helium balloon broke through at the upper end of the tunnel and bobbed merrily on the swell. One by one, as Timoshenko reeled out additional wire at the far end, the eight watertight aluminium boxes burst through the surface. They bumped against one another with dull, almost inaudible thumps.

Harry was no longer alone in the dome-ceilinged cavern. Rita, Brian, Franz, Claude and Roger had joined him. George Lin and Pete Johnson were following on behind.

Picking up the grappling hook that they had jerry-rigged from lengths of copper pipe and heavy-gauge wire, Harry said, 'Come on. Let's get that stuff out of the water.'

With Franz's and Roger's assistance, he managed to snare the chain and drag the boxes out of the pool. All three men got wet to the knees in the process, and within seconds the storm suits had frozen solid round their calves. Cold, shuddering, they hurriedly popped open the aluminium cargo boxes and extracted the gear that had been sent up from the *Ilya Pogodin*.

Each box held underwater breathing apparatus. But this was not ordinary scuba gear. It had been designed for use in especially deep and extremely cold water. Each suit came with a battery pack that was attached to a belt and worn at the waist. When this was plugged into both the skintight pants and jacket, the lining provided heat in much the same fashion as an electric blanket.

A compressed-air tank came with each suit. The tank contained an oxygen-helium mixture with several special additives to allow the user to reach great depths. The diving mask was large enough to cover most of the face from chin to forehead, eliminating the need for a separate mouthpiece; air was fed directly into the mask, so the diver could breathe through his nose.

George Lin had entered the cavern while they were unpacking the boxes. He studied the equipment with unconcealed suspicion. 'Harry, there must be some other way. There's got to be—'

'No,' Harry said. 'This is it. This or nothing. There's no time for discussion, George. Just shut up and suit up.'

Lin looked glum.

Harry glanced at the others, who were busy unpacking their own boxes of gear. *None* of them looked like a killer, yet one of them had clubbed Brian and might give them a lot of trouble when they were under water and moving down through the long tunnel of ice.

Bringing up the rear, Pete Johnson squirmed laboriously out of the crawlspace from the crevasse into the cavern, cursing the ice round him. His broad shoulders had made it difficult for him to squeeze through the narrowest part of that passageway.

'Let's get dressed,' Harry said. 'No time to waste.'

They changed from the Arctic gear into the scuba suits with haste born of acute discomfort and desperation. Harry, Franz and Roger were already paying for their knee-deep immersion in the pool: their flesh from calves to toes prickled, ached, *burned*. The others had been spared that additional suffering, but they cursed and complained bitterly during their brief nakedness. No wind circulated through the cavern, but the air temperature was perhaps twenty or more degrees below zero.

Modesty was potentially as deadly as sloth. When Harry looked up after tucking himself into his insulation-lined scuba pants, he saw Rita struggling into her scuba jacket. Her flesh was blue-white and textured with enormous goose pimples. She zipped up her jacket, caught Harry's eye and winked.

He marvelled at that wink. He could guess at the agonising fear that must be afflicting her. She wasn't just *on* the ice any more. She was now *in* the ice. Entombed. Her terror must already be acute.

Pete was having trouble squeezing into his gear. He said, 'Are all these Russians pygmies?'

Everyone laughed. The joke hadn't been *that* funny. Such easy laughter was an indication of how tense they were. Harry sensed that panic was near the surface in all of them.

11:15pm

The overhead speaker brought the bad news that everyone in the control room had been expecting: 'That bulkhead is sweating again, Captain.'

Gorov turned away from the video displays and pulled down a microphone. 'Captain to torpedo room. Is it still just a thin film?'

'Yes, sir. About the same.'

'Keep an eye on it.'

Zhukov said, 'Now that we know the lie of the ice above us, we could take her up to six hundred feet, into the bowl of the funnel.'

Gorov shook his head. 'Right now we have only one thing to worry about—the sweat on that torpedo-room bulkhead. If we ascend to six hundred feet, we might still have that problem, and we'd also have to worry that the iceberg might suddenly enter a new current.' He knew that if the berg began to move faster or slower than it was travelling at the moment they might not realise what was happening until it was too late. They would collide with the deeper ice lying beyond their bow or with that to their stern.

'Steady as she goes,' Gorov said.

THE NOTEBOOK HAD AN EVIL POWER that Gunvald found horribly compelling. The contents shocked, disgusted and sickened him, yet he couldn't resist looking at one more page, then another.

In a sense, the notebook was a diary of dementia, a week-by-week chronicle of a mind travelling from the borderlands of sanity into the nations of madness. Newspaper and magazine clippings had been arranged according to their dates of publication. In the margin alongside each clipping, the compiler had written his comments.

The earliest entries seemed to have been snipped from various amateurishly produced political magazines of limited circulation, published in the US by extreme left- and right-wing groups. They were wildly overwritten scare stories of the most mindless sort: the President was a dedicated hard-line communist—yet, in another clipping, he was a dedicated hard-line fascist; the Pope was alternately a despicable right-wing zealot *and* a left-wing maniac intent on funding the destruction of democracy and confiscating all the wealth of the world for the benefit of the Jesuits. One clipping claimed that in China girls were raised from infancy on government-funded 'prostitute farms' and given at the age of ten to politicians in the West in return for national-security secrets.

With the newspaper clipping on page twenty-four, the notebook became uglier and more disturbing. It was a photograph of the late President Dougherty. Above the photograph was a headline: DOUGHERTY ASSASSINATION—TEN YEARS AGO TODAY. From that point forwards, more and more space in the notebook was devoted to the Dougherty family. By page 100, a third of the way through the book, they had become his sole obsession. Every clipping in the subsequent 200 pages dealt with them: a report of a campaign speech that Brian's father had made two years ago, a piece about a surprise birthday party given for the late President's widow, a United Press International dispatch concerning Brian's adventures in one of Madrid's bullrings . . .

On page 210 was a family portrait taken at the wedding of Brian's sister and reprinted in *People* magazine. Beneath it was a two-word, handwritten notice in red: *The enemy*.

The pages that followed were hair-raising.

Gunvald tried calling Harry once more. No response. He could communicate with no one. The storm was his only companion.

What in the name of God was happening on that iceberg?

BRIAN DOUGHERTY and Roger Breskin were the only members of the group who had extensive diving experience. Because Brian was not an official member of the expedition, merely an observer, Harry didn't think the kid should have to assume the front position in the descent through the tunnel. Therefore, Roger Breskin would lead. Harry would follow Roger, then Brian, Rita, George, Claude, Franz and Pete. A lot of thought had gone into that arrangement. Brian would be between Harry and Rita, the only two people that he could fully trust. George Lin was behind Rita and might be a threat to her and Brian. Because of his age and convivial temperament, Claude Jobert seemed the least likely of all suspects other than Pete, so he would be behind Lin, where he would notice and attempt to prevent any foul play. If Franz was the guilty party, his freedom to strike out at Brian would be severely limited by the fact that Pete would be keeping a watch on him from behind. And, in the unlikely event that Pete Johnson was the would-be murderer, he wouldn't find it easy to get past Franz, Claude, Lin and Rita to reach Brian.

Each of the heated wet suits came with a waterproof watch that featured a large, luminescent digital read-out. Harry looked at his when he had finished suiting up. Eighteen minutes past eleven. Detonation in forty-two minutes.

He said, 'Ready to go?'

Everyone was suited up, masks in place. Even George Lin.

Harry said, 'Good luck, my friends.' He slipped up his own mask, reached over his left shoulder to activate the air feed on his tank and took a few deep breaths to be sure that the equipment was working properly. He turned to Roger Breskin and gave him the thumbs-up sign.

Roger picked up one of the three halogen lamps that they had found in the aluminium boxes, hesitated for only a second—and jumped feet first into the forty-foot-wide mouth of the tunnel.

Harry followed. The water was murky. Millions of particles of dirt, clouds of tiny diatoms in sufficient quantity to feed a pack of whales, and beads of ice drifted in the diffused, yellowish beam of the waterproof lamp. Behind the halogen glow, Roger was a half-seen shape, perfectly black and mysterious in his rubber suit.

As instructed, Brian plunged into the water without delay, to thwart a possible attempt on his life after Harry and Roger had departed the cavern.

Roger had already begun to pull himself downwards on the multi-communications wire that led back to the *Ilya Pogodin*.

Harry followed him down into the unknown.

11:22pm

In the control room, the technician seated at the surface fathometer said, 'I'm picking up a partial blockage of the hole again.'

'Divers?'

The technician studied the graph for a moment. 'Yes. That could be the interpretation. I've got downward movement on all the blips.'

The good news affected everyone. The men were no less tense than they had been a minute ago. For the first time in several hours, however, their tension was qualified by guarded optimism.

'Torpedo room to Captain.'

Gorov surreptitiously blotted his damp hands on his trousers and pulled down the microphone once more. 'Go ahead.'

The voice was controlled, though an underlying note of distress was apparent. 'The sweat on the bulkhead between number four tube and number five tube is getting worse, Captain. Water's trickling down to the deck now.'

'Any buckling?'

'Nothing visible.'

'Any sounds of metal fatigue?'

'We've been going over it with a stethoscope, sir. No alarming noise, no fatigue signatures, just the usual.'

'Then why do you sound so concerned?' Gorov demanded.

The torpedo officer didn't respond immediately, but finally he said, 'Well, sir, when you lay your hand against the steel . . . there's a strange vibration. Something I've never felt before. I think . . .'

'What do you think?' Gorov demanded. 'Spit it out. What do you think you feel when you put your hand to the steel?'

'Pressure.'

Gorov was aware that the control-room crew had already lost its optimism. To the torpedo officer, he said, 'Pressure? You cannot feel pressure through the steel. I suggest you control your imagination. There's no reason to panic. Just keep a close watch on it.'

Morosely, the torpedo officer said, 'Yes, sir.'

Zhukov's lupine face was distorted by fear and doubt. He spoke so softly that Gorov had to strain to hear: 'One pinhole, one hairline crack in the pressure hull, and the boat will be smashed flat.'

True enough. And it could all happen in a fraction of a second. At least death would be mercifully swift.

'We'll be all right,' Gorov insisted.

He saw the confusion of loyalties in the first officer's eyes, and he wondered if he was wrong. He wondered if he should take the *Pogodin* up a few hundred feet to lessen the crushing pressure on it, and abandon the Edgeway scientists.

He was a stern enough judge of himself to face the possibility that saving the Edgeway expedition might have become an obsession with him, an act of personal atonement, which was not in the best interests of his crew. If that was the case, he was no longer fit to command.

Are we all going to die because of me? he wondered.

11:27pm

The descent along the communications wire proved to be far more difficult and exhausting than Harry Carpenter had anticipated. He had failed to take into account that a diver ordinarily spent the larger part of his time swimming more or less parallel to the ocean floor; their headfirst descent on that 700-foot line was perpendicular to the seabed, which he found to be inexplicably tiring. His arms ached and blood pounded at his temples. He soon realised that he would have to pause periodically and get his head up to regain equilibrium; otherwise, although his weariness and growing disorientation were no doubt psychological, he would black out.

In the lead, Roger Breskin appeared to progress effortlessly. He slid his left hand along the communications wire as he descended, held the lamp in his other hand, and relied entirely on his legs to propel him, kicking smoothly. His technique wasn't substantially different from Harry's, but he had the advantage of many hours of underwater experience and muscles built through regular, diligent workouts with heavy weights.

Harry glanced over his shoulder to see if Brian and Rita were all right. The kid was trailing him by about twelve feet, features barely visible in the full-face diving mask. In spite of all that he'd endured in the past few hours, he seemed to be having no trouble keeping up.

Behind Brian, Rita was barely visible, only fitfully backlit by the halogen lamp that George Lin carried in her wake. The yellowish beams were defeated by the murky water; against that eerily luminous but pale haze, she was but a rippling shadow. Harry couldn't get a glimpse of her face, but he knew that her psychological suffering, at least, must be great.

CRYOPHOBIA: FEAR OF ICE. The frigid water in the tunnel was as dark as if it had been tainted with clouds of squid. Rita wasn't able to see the ice that lay only twenty feet from her in every direction, but she remained acutely aware of it. At times her fear was so overwhelming that her throat tightened and she was unable to breathe. Each time, however, on the shuddering edge of blind panic, she finally exhaled explosively, inhaled the metallic-tasting mixture of gases from the scuba tank, and staved off hysteria.

Down, ever down. Embraced by a coldness that she couldn't feel. Surrounded by ice that she couldn't see. Curved white walls out of sight to the left of her, to the right, above and below. Prison of ice. Silent but for the susurrant rush of her breathing and the thud-thud-thudding of her heart. Inescapable. Deeper than a grave.

As she swam down into depths unknown, Rita was repeatedly flashing back to the winter when she had been only six years old.

Happy. Excited. On her way to her first skiing holiday with her mother and father, who are experienced on the slopes and eager to teach her. The car is an Audi. Her mother and father sit up front, and she sits alone in the back. Ascending into increasingly white and fantastic realms. A winding road in the French Alps. An alabaster wonderland all round them; below, great vistas of evergreen forest shrouded with snow. Her mother sees the avalanche first, to the right of the roadway and high above, and she cries out in alarm. Rita looks through the side window, sees the wall of white further up the mountain, growing as rapidly as a storm wave sweeping across the ocean towards shore, so white and silent and beautiful that she can hardly believe it can hurt them. Her father says, 'We can outrun it,' as he jams his foot on the accelerator; her mother says, 'Hurry, for God's sake, hurry,' and it comes onwards, silent and white and huge and dazzling, and bigger by the second . . . then a barely audible rumble like distant thunder . . .

Rita heard strange sounds. Hollow, faraway voices. Shouting or lamenting. Then she realised that it was only a single voice. Her own.

She squinted past Brian and desperately concentrated on the shadowy shape further along the line: Harry. He was dimly visible in the murk, kicking down into the black void, so near and yet so far away. As long as she thought about Harry and kept in mind the good times that they would have together when this ordeal ended, she was able to stop screaming into her face mask and continue swimming. Paris. The Hotel George V. A bottle of fine champagne. His kiss. His touch. They would share it all again if she just didn't let her fears overwhelm her.

WHEN THEY WERE PERHAPS a hundred and fifty feet down the dark tunnel, Harry saw Roger Breskin pause for a rest. He performed a somersault as though engaged in a water ballet and turned round on the line until he faced Harry in a more natural position: head up and feet down.

Five yards behind Roger, Harry also paused and was about to do a somersault of his own when Roger's halogen lamp winked out. He was enveloped in darkness.

An instant later Breskin collided with him. Harry couldn't hold on to the communications wire. They tumbled away into the blackness towards the tunnel wall, and for an instant Harry didn't understand what was happening. Then he felt a hand clawing at his throat, and he knew that he was in trouble. He flailed at Breskin, putting all his strength into the blows, but the water absorbed the energy of his punches and transformed them into playful pats.

Breskin's hand closed tightly round Harry's throat. Harry tried to wrench his head away; the weightlifter had an iron grip.

Breskin drove a knee into Harry's stomach, but the water worked against him, slowing and cushioning the blow. Then Harry's back thumped against the tunnel wall, and pain coruscated along his spine. The bigger man pinned him against the ice.

The two remaining halogen lamps—one held by George and one by Pete—were far above and about twenty feet closer towards the centre of the tunnel, vaguely luminous ghost lights haunting the cloudy water. Harry was essentially blind. Even at close range, he could not see his assailant.

The hand at his throat slipped higher, pawed at his chin. His face mask was torn off. With that strategic stroke, Harry was denied his breath and what little vision he'd had, and he was exposed to the killing cold of the water. Helpless, disoriented, he was no longer a threat to Breskin, and the big man let him go.

The cold was like a fistful of nails rammed hard into his face, and his body heat seemed to pour out as though it were hot liquid.

Terrified, on the verge of panic but aware that panic might be the death of him, Harry rolled away into the darkness, grappling behind himself for the precious mask that floated at the end of his air hose.

A SECOND AFTER THE LAMP went out at the head of the procession, Rita realised what was wrong: Breskin was the would-be killer of Brian Dougherty. And a second after *that*, she knew what she had to do.

Although she couldn't see Harry or Breskin in the gloom below, she was certain that the two men were struggling for their lives. As tough as he was, Harry wouldn't stand much of a chance against an experienced diver. She started to go to his aid, but that was a foolish idea, and she rejected it at once. If Harry was no match for Roger Breskin, then neither was she. The best she could do was trust in Harry to survive, one way or another, and meanwhile fade into the darkness away from the communications wire, wait for her chance and be prepared to come in behind Breskin when he went after Brian.

She let go of the line and swam out of the amber light from George Lin's lamp, which was silhouetting her for Breskin. Praying that George wouldn't follow her and blow her cover, she soon came up against the wall of the tunnel, the smooth curve of . . . ice.

The rumble swells into a roar, and again her father says, 'We'll

outrun it,' but his words are now more of a prayer than a promise. The
great white wall comes down down down, and her mother screams...

Rita strove to repress her fear. Swinging round, putting her back
to the wall, she looked out towards the commotion along the communications wire. In the centre of the tunnel, Roger Breskin soared
out of the black depths and into the dim light from George Lin's
lamp. He went straight for Brian.

As Brian saw Roger Breskin soar like a shark from the lightless
depths, he recalled Breskin's words earlier in the day, just after they'd
rescued George from the ledge. Brian had been hoisted back to the
top of the cliff, shaking, weak with relief. *It wasn't that. I thought the*
rope would snap or something.

You're going to die eventually. But this wasn't your place. It wasn't
the right time.

Brian had thought that Roger was being uncharacteristically
philosophical. Now he realised that it had been a blunt threat, a
heartfelt promise of violence. Maybe Breskin hadn't wanted George
to be a witness, or maybe he hadn't struck earlier for other inexplicable and insane reasons of his own. This time, he had more than
one witness, but he seemed not to care.

Even as that conversation replayed in Brian's memory, he tried to
turn from Breskin and kick towards the tunnel wall, but they
collided and tumbled away together into the darkness. Breskin's
powerful legs encircled Brian, clamping like a crab pincer. Then a
hand at his throat. At his face mask. *No!*

THE AIR HOSE trailed along the side of Harry's head, and the diving
mask was attached to the end of it, floating above him. He pulled
the mask down and clamped it to his face. It was full of water, and
he dared not breathe immediately, even though his lungs felt as
though they were on fire. When he peeled up one corner of the
rubber rim, the influx of oxygen–helium mixture forced the water
out from behind the Plexiglas faceplate, and, when all the water had
been purged, he pressed that corner down tight again and sucked
in a deep breath, another, another, spluttering and choking and
gasping with relief. The slightly odd smell and taste of the gas was
more delicious than anything that he had ever eaten or drunk before
in his entire life.

His chest was sore, his eyes burned, and his headache was so fierce
that his skull seemed to be splitting apart. He wanted only to hang
where he was, recuperating, suspended in the tenebrous sea. But he
thought of Rita, and he swam up towards the two remaining lights
and a turmoil of shadows.

BRIAN GRIPPED Breskin's left wrist with both hands and tried to wrench the big man's steely hand from his face, but he wasn't able to resist. The diving mask was torn loose.

When the cold water gushed across his face, the shock was nearly as painful as having a blazing torch shoved against his skin. Nevertheless, Brian reacted so calmly that he surprised himself. He squeezed his eyelids shut before the water could flash-freeze the surface tissues of his eyeballs, clenched his teeth and managed not to breathe either through his mouth or nose.

He couldn't hold out long. A minute. A minute and a half. Then he would breathe involuntarily, spasmodically—

Breskin clamped his legs tighter round Brian's waist, pushed his rubber-sheathed fingers between Brian's compressed lips and tried to force his mouth open.

Rita swam in behind Roger Breskin and wrapped her long legs round his waist as he had wrapped his legs round Brian. With reflexes sharpened by maniacal frenzy, Breskin let go of Brian and seized Rita by the ankles. She felt as though she were riding a wild horse. He twisted and bucked, a powerful beast, but she gripped him with her thighs and grabbed for his mask.

Sensing her intent, Breskin released her ankles and seized her wrists just as her hands touched the rim of his faceplate. He bent forwards, kicked his flippers, did a somersault. Rolling through the water, he tore her hands from his face and, using the dynamics of the sea to achieve a leverage that she couldn't hope to match, he pitched her away from him.

When she oriented herself again, she saw that Pete and Franz had descended on Breskin. Franz struggled to maintain a wrist lock while Pete tried to pin at least one of the madman's arms.

Breskin was a trained diver, however, and they were not. They were slow, clumsy, confused by the physics of the gravity-free realm in which they battled, while Breskin writhed as if he were an eel, supple and quick and fearfully strong. He broke their hold on him, rammed an elbow into Pete's face, ripped Pete's mask over his head and shoved him into Franz.

Brian was at the wire with Claude. The Frenchman held Pete's lamp in one hand and was using his free hand to steady Brian while the kid got the water out of his mask.

Kicking away from Pete and Franz as they tumbled in disarray, Breskin streaked towards Brian again.

Rita glimpsed movement out of the corner of her eye, turned her head, and saw Harry shoot up from the darkness below.

Harry knew that Breskin didn't see him coming. Certain that he had temporarily disabled all opposition, the big man went directly for his prey. He was no doubt sure that he could deal swiftly with a man of Claude's age and then finish Brian before he was able to clear his fouled mask and draw a restorative breath.

Rising under Breskin, Harry could have collided with him and hoped to deflect him from Brian. Instead, he shot past the madman and grabbed the air hose that connected his face mask to the pressurised tank on his back. Harry jerked the hose both out of the clamp that held it to the feed valve at the top of the tank and from the diving mask.

Breskin fumbled for the hose, but he realised that it had been ripped away not merely from the mask but from the tank on his back. It was gone and couldn't be reconnected.

Alarmed, he scissored his legs and went up towards the mouth of the tunnel as fast as he could. His only hope was to reach the surface.

Then he remembered that the pool in the domed ice cavern was more than a hundred and fifty feet above him, too far to reach with the weight belt pulling him down, so he fumbled at his waist, trying to free himself of the burdensome lead. The release wasn't where it ought to be, because the damn belt was made by the Russians, and he had never before used Russian equipment.

Roger stopped kicking, so he could concentrate on the search for the belt release. At once he began to sink slowly back into the tunnel. He wrenched at the belt, but he *still* could not find the release. Finally he knew that he had wasted too much time, didn't dare waste another second, would have to get to the surface even with the hampering belt. Arms straight down at his sides, creating as little resistance to the water as possible, kicking smoothly, rhythmically, he struggled up, up.

His chest ached, and his heart was hammering as if it would burst, and he couldn't any longer resist the urge to breathe. He opened his mouth, exhaled explosively, desperately inhaled, but there was nothing to breathe except the meagre breath that he had just expelled. His lungs were *ablaze*. He ripped off his mask and inhaled water so bitterly cold that pain shot through his teeth. He closed his mouth, choking violently, but at once he tried to breathe again. There was only more water, water, nothing but water. He clawed at the water with both hands, as if it were a thin curtain that he could tear apart to get to the blessed air just beyond it. Then he realised that he wasn't kicking any longer, was just drifting down and down, gasping, and it felt as though he had more lead weights inside his chest than round his waist . . .

He saw that Death was a woman. A pale woman, not without

262

beauty. Her eyes were a lovely, translucent grey. Roger studied her face as it rose out of the water before him, and he realised that she was his mother, in whose arms he had first heard that the world was a hostile place and that people of exceptional evil secretly conspired to rule ordinary men and women, with no intention but to crush the free spirit of everyone who defied them. And, now, although Roger had made himself strong to resist those conspirators, they had crushed him, too. They had won, just as his mother had told him they would. But losing wasn't so terrible. There was a peace in losing. Grey-haired, grey-eyed Death smiled at him and took him into her motherly embrace.

11:37pm

The tension had sharpened Nikita Gorov's mind and had forced him to confront an unpleasant but undeniable truth. Fools and heroes, he saw now, were separated by a line so thin that it was the next thing to invisible. He had been so intent on being a hero. And for what? For whom? For a dead son? It was inexcusable to have risked the crew of the *Ilya Pogodin* merely because, in some strange way, he wanted to fulfil an obligation to his dead son. He'd been playing hero, but he'd been only a fool.

Regardless of what he *should* have done, the submarine was committed to the rescue mission now. They couldn't abandon it this close to success. Not unless those two sweating bulkheads began to show signs of structural deterioration. He had got his men into this, and it was up to him to get them out.

'Sir, the divers are stationary.'

The captain stared at the ceiling, as if he could see through the double hull. What were they doing up there?

'Don't they realise there's no time left?' Zhukov said. 'When those explosives split the iceberg at midnight, we've got to be out from under. We've *got* to be.'

Gorov looked at the clock. He pulled on his beard and said, 'If they don't start moving down again in five minutes, we'll have to get out of here. One minute later than that, and they can't make it aboard before midnight, anyway.'

RITA SWAM up to Claude and hugged him. He returned her embrace. Her eyes glistened with tears. They pressed the faceplates of their diving masks flat against each other. When she spoke, he could hear her as if she were in another room. The Plexiglas conducted their voices well enough.

'Brian didn't fall earlier today. He was clubbed, left to die. We didn't know who did it. Until now.'

Claude said, 'I wondered what the hell—? Is Pete all right?'

'Yes. Just a bloody nose when the mask was pulled up over his head. He'll make it.'

'Something's wrong with George.'

'Shock, I think. Harry's explaining to him about Roger.'

'You've got tears on your cheeks,' Claude said.

'I know.'

'What's wrong?'

'Nothing,' she said. 'Harry's alive.'

BRIAN SWAM DOWN along the wire. He wasn't worried much about the ticking bombs overhead. He was increasingly convinced that he and the others would reach the submarine and survive the explosions. He was worried instead about the book that he intended to write.

The theme would definitely be heroism. He had come to see that there were two basic forms of it: heroism that was sought, as when a man climbed a mountain or challenged an angry bull in one of Madrid's rings. Because a man had to know his limits, heroism sought was important. It was far less valuable, however, than heroism *unsought*. Harry, Rita and the others had put their lives on the line in their jobs because they believed that what they were doing would contribute to the betterment of the human condition, not because they wanted to test themselves. Yet, although they would deny it, they were heroes every day of the week. They were heroes in the way that cops and firemen were heroes, in the way that millions of mothers and fathers were quiet heroes for taking on the responsibilities of supporting families and raising children to be good citizens. Brian understood now that it was this selfless, unsought heroism that was the truest courage and the deepest virtue. When he had finished writing the book, when he had worked out all his thoughts on the subject, he would be ready to begin his adult life at last. And he was determined that quiet heroism would be the theme.

THE TECHNICIAN LOOKED UP from the surface-fathometer graph. 'They're moving again.'

'Coming down?' Gorov asked.

'Yes, sir.'

The squawk box brought them the voice of the petty officer in the forward torpedo room. It contained a new note of urgency.

264

Taking the neck of the overhead microphone as gingerly as if he were handling a snake, Gorov said, 'Go ahead.'

'We've got a litre or two of water on the deck now, Captain. The forward bulkhead is sweating from overhead to deck.'

'Distortion of the rivet line?'

'No, sir.'

'Hear anything unusual with the stethoscope?'

'No, sir.'

'We'll be on our way in ten minutes,' Gorov said.

IN PLACES, the tunnel narrowed just enough for the halogen light to reflect off the ice, and then the fact of their imprisonment could not be as easily put out of mind as when darkness lay to all sides.

Rita was pulled continually between the past and the present, between death and life, courage and cowardice. Minute by minute, she expected her inner turmoil to subside, but it grew worse.

When the white tide hits the trees, they snap as though they're bread-sticks. Her mother screams, her father cries out, and Rita can't look away from the onrushing wave of snow, 100 feet high. The juggernaut hits the Audi, tumbles the car, shoves it across the roadway, casts it across the guard rail and into a ravine. The car turns over, over again, then sleds sideways, down, down, rebounds from a tree, turns into the slide, races down once more in a great river of snow, with another impact, yet another. The windshield implodes, followed by a sudden stillness and a silence deeper than the silence in a deserted church.

Rita wrenched herself from the memory, making meaningless, pathetic sounds of terror.

George Lin was urging her on from behind. She had stopped swimming. Cursing herself, she kicked her feet and started down again.

FOLLOWING THE WIRE further into the shaft, George Lin told himself that the Russians weren't communists any more. At least the communists weren't in charge. Maybe, one day in the future, they would be back in power; evil never really died. But he tried to convince himself that the men in the submarine were risking their lives, and they had no sinister motives.

Canton, autumn 1949. Three weeks before Chiang Kai-shek was driven from the mainland. George's father had been away, making arrangements to spirit the family and its dwindling assets to the island nation of Taiwan. There were four other people in the house: his grandmother; his grandfather; his mother; his eleven-year-old sister, Yun-ti. At dawn, a contingent of heavily armed Maoist guerrillas, seeking his father, invaded the house. His mother managed to hide him inside a fireplace. Yun-ti was hidden elsewhere, but the men found her. As George watched from within the fireplace, his grandparents were beaten to their knees and then shot in the head. In that same room, his mother and sister were raped repeatedly. Every degradation, every humiliation was perpetrated upon them. When they finally left, they slit Yun-ti's throat. Then his mother's throat. His father had come home twelve hours later—and found George still hiding in the fireplace, unable to speak. He remained silent for more than three years after they escaped to Taiwan.

Nevertheless, the men in the submarine below were Russians, not Chinese, and they weren't communists any more. The men below would not be like those who had violated his mother and sister and then killed them. These were different people in a different time. They could be trusted. He *must* trust them.

HARRY HAD A SENSE of vastly greater space round him. The tunnel had widened out. The water was clearer than it had been above, probably because there were fewer particles of ice in it. Within seconds, he saw coloured lights below, first green and then red. Then his handheld light revealed a great grey shape hovering in the abyss below him.

Even when he arrived at the sail of the *Ilya Pogodin* and rested against the radar mast, Harry was not sanguine about their chances of surviving the tremendous pressure. He was half convinced that his lungs would explode with the force of grenades and that his blood vessels would pop like balloons. Furthermore, Harry didn't like the look of the submarine. Waiting for the others to catch up with him, he had nearly a minute to study the boat. All the running lights were aglow: red on the port side, green on the starboard side, white on the sail, a yellow overtaking light . . . the *Pogodin* seemed too gaudy to be substantial. The boat resembled a damned slot machine or a Christmas tree. It seemed fragile, a construction of dark cellophane.

11:49pm

Rita expected her fear to abate when she reached the bottom of the tunnel and the ice was no longer to every side of her. But the island of ice was still overhead, as high as a seventy-storey building and four-fifths of a mile long. She was terrified by the thought of it hanging over her, and she dared not look up.

It's cold in the Audi, because the engine is dead. Snow and shattered tree limbs have poured into the front seat, through the shattered windshield, burying her parents to the waist. They sit silently in the snow,

both dead, and, as time passes, Rita draws her coat tightly round her and waits for help to come. After a while she begins to have trouble staying awake, and she drifts out of the cold car into colder places within her own mind. After what seems a long time, she hears the crack-crack-crackle of ice . . . and is that a voice whispering her name? And a cold hand reaching under the coat, envious of her warmth . . .

Someone touched Rita, and she cried out in horror, but at least the scream drove the Audi and avalanche back into the past.

Pete was on one side of her, Franz on the other. Evidently, she had stopped moving, and they were holding her by her arms and bringing her down the final few fathoms between them. The submarine was directly ahead. She saw Harry holding on to the radar mast above the sail.

A WARNING SIREN shrieked. The green numerals and dimensional diagrams disappeared from the central video display directly above the command pad. Red letters replaced them: EMERGENCY.

Gorov punched a console key labelled DISPLAY. The screen cleared immediately, and the siren shut off. A new message appeared in the usual green letters: MUZZLE DOOR COLLAPSED ON FORWARD TORPEDO TUBE NUMBER FIVE. TUBE FILLED WITH WATER TO BREACH DOOR.

'It's happening,' Zhukov said.

Number five tube must have torqued when they had collided with the ice floe earlier in the night. Now the muzzle door at the outer hull had given way.

Gorov said quickly, 'Only the outer door collapsed. Just the *muzzle* door. Not the breach door. There's no water in the boat. Not yet—and there won't be.'

A seaman monitoring one of the safety boards said, 'Captain, our visitors have opened the topside hatch to the air lock.'

'We're going to make it,' Gorov told the control-room crew. 'We're damned well going to make it.'

HARRY GAZED DOWN into a tiny, brightly lit, water-filled compartment. They had been warned that it was large enough to accommodate only four divers at a time—and, even at that size, it was twice as large as the escape trunks on many submarines.

One by one, Brian, Claude, Rita and George went down into the room and sat on the floor with their backs pressed to the walls.

From outside, as he had been instructed over the radio, Harry closed the hatch, which was faster than waiting for someone inside to use a lanyard to pull it down and then spin the sealing wheel.

He looked at his luminous watch: 11:54.

In the air lock, Rita held on to wall grips as powerful pumps extracted the water from the chamber in thirty seconds. She didn't remove her mask, but continued to breathe the mixture of gases in her scuba tank, as they had been instructed to do.

A hatch opened in the centre of the floor. A young Russian seaman appeared, smiled almost shyly, and beckoned with one finger.

They moved quickly from the air lock, down a ladder into the escape-chamber control room. The seaman pulled the inner hatch shut and water flooded into the upper chamber again.

Acutely aware that a huge island of ice, mined with explosives, loomed directly above the boat, Rita went with the others into an adjoining decompression chamber.

HARRY TRIED THE HATCH again, and it swung open.

He waited until Franz and Pete had entered, and then he followed them. They sat with their backs to the walls.

He didn't even have to look at his watch. An internal crisis clock told him that they were about four minutes from detonation.

The drains dilated, and the pumps drained the escape trunk.

GOROV PULLED DOWN an overhead microphone, called the manoeuvring room and ordered the boat into immediate full reverse. A moment later the ship shuddered in response to the abrupt change of engine thrust. Gorov was thrown against the command-pad railing, and Zhukov almost fell.

From the overhead speaker: 'Manoeuvring room to Captain. Engines full reverse.'

The iceberg was moving southwards at nine knots. The submarine was reversing *northwards* at ten ... twelve ... now fifteen knots against a nine-knot current, resulting in a separation speed of fifteen knots.

Gorov didn't know if that was sufficient speed to save them, but it was the best that they could do at the moment, because to build to greater speed, they needed more time than remained until detonation.

'Ice overhead,' the surface-fathometer operator announced. They were out from under the funnel-shaped concavity in the centre of the berg. 'Sixty feet. Ice overhead at sixty feet.'

HARRY ENTERED the decompression chamber and sat beside Rita. They held hands and stared at his watch: 11:58.

THE CENTRE OF ATTENTION in the control room was the six-figure digital clock aft of the command pad. Gorov imagined that he could detect a twitch in his crewmen with the passage of each second: 11:59.

The technician at the fathometer said, 'Clear water. No ice overhead.'

'We're out from under,' someone said.

'But we're not yet out of the way,' Gorov cautioned, aware that they were well within the fallout pattern of blast-hurled ice.

For the second time in ten minutes, a warning siren sounded, and EMERGENCY flashed in red on one of the overhead screens.

Gorov keyed up a display and found that another torpedo tube in the damaged area of the hull had partially succumbed: MUZZLE DOOR COLLAPSED ON FORWARD TORPEDO TUBE NUMBER FOUR. TUBE FILLED WITH WATER TO BREACH DOOR.

Pulling down a microphone, Gorov shouted, 'Captain to torpedo room! Abandon your position and seal all watertight doors.'

'Oh, dear God,' said Emil Zhukov, the atheist.

'The breach doors will hold,' Gorov said with conviction, and he prayed that he was right.

Eleven fifty-nine and fifty-nine seconds.

'Brace yourselves!'

'Clear water.'

'Where is it?'

The concussion hit them. Transmitted through the shattering iceberg to the water and through the water to the hull, it was a surprisingly mild and distant rumble. Gorov waited for the power of the shock waves to escalate, but it never did.

The sonar operator reported massive fragmentation of the iceberg.

By 12:02, however, when sonar had not located a substantial fragment of ice anywhere near the *Ilya Pogodin*, Gorov knew they were safe. 'Take her up.'

The control-room crew let out a cheer.

AFTER . . .

JANUARY 18, DUNDEE, SCOTLAND

Shortly before noon, two and a half days after escaping from their prison of ice, the survivors arrived in Scotland.

More than one hundred newsmen from all over the world had flown to Dundee to report on the conclusion of the Edgeway story. Among themselves, reporters apparently had got more conversational mileage from the bone-chilling weather than from the news event that they were there to cover.

Even after disembarking from the *Pogodin* and standing in the brisk breeze for nearly an hour, George Lin still enjoyed the feel of the wind on his face. It smelled clean and so much better than the canned air of the submarine. And it was neither so cold nor so fierce that he needed to fear frostbite, which was a vast improvement over the weather with which he had lived for the past few months.

Pacing energetically back and forth at the edge of the wharf, followed by a covey of reporters, he said, 'This boat—isn't she a beautiful sight?'

Anchored in a deep-water berth behind him, the submarine was flying an enormous Russian flag and, for courtesy, a Scottish flag of somewhat smaller dimensions. Sixty-eight of the crewmen were in two facing lines on the main deck, all in dress blues and navy pea coats, standing at attention for a ceremonial inspection. Nikita Gorov, Emil Zhukov and the other officers looked splendid in their uniforms and grey winter parade coats with brass buttons. A number of dignitaries were also on the bridge and on the railed gangplank that connected the submarine to the dock: a representative of Her Majesty's government, the Russian ambassador to Britain and the mayor of Dundee.

One of the photographers asked George to pose beside a weathered concrete piling with the *Ilya Pogodin* as a backdrop. Smiling broadly, he obliged.

A reporter asked him what it felt like to be a hero.

'I'm no hero,' George said at once. He turned to point at the officers and crew of the boat behind him. '*They* are the heroes here.'

JANUARY 25, E-MAIL MESSAGE TRANSMITTED FROM MONTEGO BAY, JAMAICA, TO PARIS, FRANCE

Claude, Franz and I got here January 23. Within an hour of arrival, both the taxi driver who brought us from the airport and the hotel clerk referred to us as 'an unlikely group'. Man, they don't know the half of it.

Can't get enough sun. I'm even acquiring a tan.

We're talking about maybe changing careers and opening a bar in some tropical resort. Maybe you and Rita want to think about going into business with us. We could sit round all day, swilling down rum drinks with funny little paper umbrellas in them. It sure beats frostbite, high explosives and underwater battles with psychopaths. The most serious problem we face here is humidity.

As ever, Pete.

In their suite at the Hotel George V, a bottle of Dom Pérignon stood in an ice bucket beside the bed.

They were in each other's arms, as close as two people could get without actually melting together and becoming a single entity, generating enough heat to keep an entire Arctic outpost warm for a long winter, when they were startled by a clatter beside the bed. They had been rescued by the *Pogodin* more than a week ago, but their nerves were still wound too tight. He sat up, and she fell off him, and they both turned towards the sound, but they were alone in the room.

'Ice,' she said.

'*Ice?*'

'Yes, ice. Shifting in the champagne bucket.'

He glanced at the bucket on its silver-plated stand, and the ice shifted again. He looked at her. She smiled. He grinned. She giggled as if she were a schoolgirl, and he roared with laughter.

DEAN KOONTZ

A large, luxurious home overlooking California's coast is just one of the rewards Dean Koontz has earned from his phenomenal twenty-eight-year writing career. His name regularly appears on best-seller  lists, five of his sixty novels have been filmed and he is estimated to sell some sixteen million books every year. These achievements seem all the more remarkable in view of his origins.

Born in Pennsylvania, Koontz grew up in a household dominated by his alcoholic father's violent rages. Ray Koontz, who also gambled and was unfaithful to his wife, was eventually diagnosed as a borderline schizophrenic. 'When I was a kid, living in these terrible circumstances,' the author recalls, 'books were a way to live other lives. They revealed to me that there *were* other lives. That was immensely valuable.'

He financed his own way through college and at twenty-one married his high school sweetheart, Gerda. A year later, Koontz had sold his first science fiction novel, *Star Quest*, and others followed while Gerda worked to support her husband's full-time writing career. Within four years Koontz was established, and by the end of the 1970s had turned from science fiction to the chilling novels of psychological suspense that he is most famous for today.

Koontz's father eventually became so ill that he arranged for him to be cared for in a nearby nursing home. His behaviour deteriorated, however, and he twice tried to kill his son. With Gerda's continuing support, Koontz has learned to deal with his painful past: 'Happiness is a choice,' he says. 'Terrible things happen to everybody, but that doesn't mean we can't deal with those things. It's dwelling on the bad things that ruins your life.'

When memories do come to haunt him, the fifty-year-old author retreats to his book-lined office and escapes once again into his imagination. He often works ten-hour days creating the chillingly vivid stories that are his speciality. 'I like a reader to be immersed in a scene—to see it, taste it, smell it: to have all their senses impacted by it,' he explains. The result is suspense that few writers can match.

HIDDEN RICHES

by **NORA ROBERTS**

Illustrated by Rick Johnson

*F*ed and Dora are worlds apart, so it is no surprise that they clash almost as soon as Jed moves into the flat opposite Dora's.

He is an ex-cop hiding from his troubled past and all he wants is to be left alone.

But warm-hearted, sociable Dora is intrigued by her handsome new neighbour—and, when she finds her antiques business and her flat under threat, it is to him that she turns. . .

PROLOGUE

He didn't want to be there. No, he hated being trapped in the elegant old house, prodded and pinched by restless ghosts. It was no longer enough to shroud the furniture in dust covers, lock the doors and walk away. He had to empty it and, by emptying it, purge himself of some of the nightmares.

'Captain Skimmerhorn?'

Jed tensed at the title. As of last week he was no longer captain. He'd resigned from the force, turned in his shield, but he was already weary of explaining it. He shifted aside as the movers carried a rosewood armoire down the staircase, through the grand foyer and out into the chilly morning.

'Yes?'

'You might want to check upstairs, make sure we got everything you wanted put in storage. Otherwise, looks like we're done here.'

'Fine.'

But he didn't want to go up those stairs, walk through those rooms. Even empty they would hold too much. Responsibility, he mused as he reluctantly started up. His life had been too crowded with responsibility to ignore it now.

Something nudged him along the hallway towards his old room, where he had grown up. But he stopped in the doorway. Hands jammed into his pockets, he waited for memories to assault him.

He'd cried in that room—in secret and in shame. And when the tears had dried, he'd plotted in that room. Useless, childish revenges that had always boomeranged on him. He'd learned to hate in that room.

Yet it was only a room. It was only a house. He'd convinced himself of that years before, when he had come back to live there as a man. And hadn't he been content? he asked himself now. Hadn't it been simple? Until Elaine.

'Jedidiah.'

He flinched. He'd nearly brought his right hand out of his pocket to touch a weapon that was no longer there.

He relaxed and glanced at his grandmother. Honoria Skimmerhorn Rodgers was wrapped in mink, discreet daytime diamonds at her ears. Her eyes, as vivid a blue as his own, were filled with concern.

'I hoped I'd convinced you to wait,' she said quietly.

'There was no reason to wait.'

'But there's a reason for this?' She gestured towards the empty room. 'A reason to move out of the family home?'

'Family? We were never a family here, or anywhere.'

Her eyes hardened. 'Pretending the past doesn't exist is as bad as living in it. What are you doing here, Jedidiah? Tossing away everything you've earned, everything you've made of yourself? Perhaps I was less than enthusiastic about your choice of profession, but it was your choice and you succeeded. You made more of the Skimmerhorn name when you were promoted to captain than all your ancestors did with their money and social power.'

'I didn't become a cop to promote my name.'

'No,' Honoria said quietly. 'You did it for yourself against tremendous family pressure—including my own. I saw you turn your life around, and it awed me.' She studied him, this son of her son. He had inherited the bold good looks of the Skimmerhorns. Bronzed hair, tousled by the wind; a lean, rawboned face taut with stress; the tall, broad-shouldered build; the defiant blue eyes.

'I might have had reservations when you moved back in here alone after your parents died, but it seemed you'd made the right choice again. This time your solution to your sister's tragedy is to sell your home and throw away your career. You disappoint me.'

'I'd rather disappoint you than be responsible for the life of a single cop. I'm in no shape to command.' He looked down at his hands, flexed them. 'I may never be. And as for the house, it should have been sold years ago. After the accident. It would have been sold if Elaine had agreed to it. Now she's gone, too, and it's my decision.'

'Yes, it's yours,' she agreed. 'But it's the wrong one.'

Rage sizzled in his blood. He wanted to hit something, someone. It was a feeling that came over him all too often. And because of it, he was no longer Captain J.T. Skimmerhorn of the Philadelphia Police Department, but a civilian. 'Can't you understand? I can't live here. I need to get out. I'm being smothered here.'

'Then come home with me. At least for the holidays. Give yourself a little more time before you do something irreversible.' Her voice was gentle again as she took his rigid hands in hers. 'Jedidiah, it's been months since Elaine—since Elaine was killed.'

'I know.' Yes, he knew the exact moment of his sister's death. After all, he'd killed her. 'I appreciate the invitation, but I've got plans. I'm looking at an apartment today. On South Street.'

'An apartment.' Honoria's sigh was ripe with annoyance. 'Don't bury yourself in some miserable room, Jedidiah.'

'The ad said it was quiet, attractive and well located. That doesn't sound miserable Grandmother.' He squeezed her hands before she could argue. 'Let it be.'

She sighed, tasting defeat. 'I only want what's best for you.'

'You always did.' He suppressed a shudder, feeling the walls closing in on him. 'Let's get out of here.'

I

Isadora Conroy absorbed the magic of the empty theatre as she stood in the wings of the Liberty Theater, watching a dress rehearsal for *A Christmas Carol*. As always, she enjoyed Dickens, but also the drama of edgy nerves, of creative lighting, of the well-delivered line. After all, the theatre was in her blood.

Her large brown eyes glinted with excitement and seemed to dominate the face framed by golden-brown hair. That excitement brought a flush to her ivory skin, a smile to her wide mouth. The energy inside her small, compact body shimmered out. She was a woman interested in everything around her, who believed in illusions. Watching her father rattling Marley's chains at the fear-struck Scrooge, she believed he was no longer her father, but the doomed miser wrapped for eternity in the heavy chains of his own greed.

Then Marley became Quentin Conroy again, veteran actor, director and theatre buff, calling for a minute change in the blocking.

'Dora.' Hurrying up from behind, Dora's sister Ophelia said, 'We're already twenty minutes behind schedule.'

'We don't have a schedule,' Dora murmured, nodding because the blocking change was perfect. 'I never have a schedule on a buying trip. Lea, isn't he wonderful?'

Lea glanced out onstage and studied their father. 'Yes.'

Dora beamed. Leaving the stage hadn't diminished her love of it, or her admiration for the man who had taught her how to milk a line. She'd watched him become hundreds of men onstage—Macbeth, Willie Loman, Nathan Detroit. She'd seen him triumph and seen him fail. But he always entertained.

'Remember Mom and Dad as Titania and Oberon?'

'Who could forget? Mom stayed in character for weeks. It wasn't easy living with the queen of the fairies. And if we don't get out of here soon, the queen's going to come out and tell us what might happen to two women travelling alone to Virginia.'

'Relax, honey,' Dora said to her sister. 'He's about to take five.'

Which he did, on cue. When the actors scattered, Dora stepped out to centre stage. 'Dad, you were great.'

'Thank you, my sweet.' He lifted an arm so that his tattered shroud floated 'I think the make-up is an improvement over last year.'

'Absolutely.' In fact, the greasepaint and charcoal were alarmingly realistic; his handsome face appeared just short of decay. She kissed him lightly. 'Sorry we'll miss opening night.'

'Can't be helped.' He did pout a little. Although he had a son to carry on the Conroy tradition, he'd lost his two daughters—one to marriage, one to free enterprise. 'So my two little girls are off on their adventure.' He kissed Lea in turn.

'Oh, Lea!' Trixie Conroy, resplendent in her costume, complete with bustle and feathered hat, rushed out onstage. 'John's on the phone, dear. He couldn't remember if Missy had a Scout meeting tonight at five or a piano lesson at six.'

'I left a list,' Lea muttered. 'How's he going to manage the kids for three days if he can't read a list?'

'Such a sweet man,' Trixie commented when Lea dashed off. 'The perfect son-in-law. Now, Dora, you will drive carefully?'

'Yes, Mom.'

'It's an awfully long way to Virginia. And it might snow.'

'I have snow tyres.' Dora gave her mother a kiss. 'And a phone in the van. I'll check in every time we cross a state line.'

'Won't that be fun?' The idea cheered Trixie enormously. 'Oh, and Quentin, darling, we're sold out for the week.'

'Naturally. A Conroy expects no less than standing room only.'

'Break a leg.' Dora kissed her mother again. 'You, too, Dad,' she said. 'And don't forget you're showing the apartment later today.'

'I never forget an engagement. Places!' he called out, then winked at his daughter. '*Bon voyage*, my sweet.'

Dora could hear his chains clanging when she reached the wings.

TO DORA'S WAY OF THINKING, an auction house was very like a theatre. You had the stage, the props, the characters. As she had explained to her baffled parents years before, she wasn't really retiring from the stage. She was merely exploring another medium.

She'd already taken the time to study the arena for today's performance. The building where Sherman Porter held his auctions had originally been a draughty slaughterhouse. Merchandise was displayed on an icy concrete floor, where people who were huddled in coats and mufflers wandered through, poking at glassware and debating over paintings, china cabinets and carved headboards.

Isadora Conroy loved a bargain. She'd always loved to buy and all too often had exchanged money for objects she had no use for. But it was that love of a bargain that had led Dora into opening her own shop, and the discovery that selling was as pleasurable as buying.

'Lea, look at this.' Dora offered a gilded cream dispenser shaped like a woman's evening slipper. 'Isn't it fabulous?'

Ophelia Conroy Bradshaw lifted a single honey-brown eyebrow. 'I think you mean frivolous, right?'

'Come on, there's a place for the ridiculous in the world.'

'I know. Your shop.'

Dora chuckled. Though she replaced the creamer, she'd already decided to bid on that lot. She noted the number. 'I'm really glad you came along on this trip, Lea. You keep me centred.'

'Somebody has to. Still, I feel guilty being away from home this close to Christmas and leaving John with the kids.'

'You were dying to get away,' Dora reminded her. Tossing one end of her red muffler over her shoulder, Dora crouched down to check a lady's cherrywood dressing table. 'Honey, it's only been three days. You'll be home tonight, and you can smother the kids with attention, seduce John, and everybody'll be happy.'

Lea rolled her eyes and smiled weakly.

Dora straightened, shook her hair from her face and nodded. 'I've seen enough for now. We'd better get some seats before—Oh, wait!' Her brown eyes brightened. 'Look.' She scurried across the floor.

It was the painting that had caught her attention. It wasn't large, perhaps eighteen by twenty-four inches, with a simple, streamlined ebony frame. The canvas was a wash of colour—streaks of crimson and sapphire, a dollop of citrine, a bold dash of emerald.

Dora smiled at the boy who was propping the painting against the wall. 'You've got it upside-down.'

'Huh?' The stock boy turned. 'Ah, no, ma'am.' He turned the canvas round to show Dora the hook at the back.

'Mmm.' When she owned it—and she would—she'd fix that.

'This shipment just came in.'

'I see.' She stepped closer and picked up a china basset hound curled up in a resting pose. No craftsman's mark or date, but the workmanship was excellent.

'Frivolous enough for you?' Lea asked.

'Just. Make a terrific doorstop.' After setting it down, Dora reached for a tall figurine of a man and woman in Victorian dress, caught in the swirl of a waltz. Her hand closed over thick, gnarled fingers. 'Sorry.' She glanced up at an elderly bespectacled man.

'Pretty, isn't it?' he asked her, grinning. 'My wife had one just like it. Got busted when the kids were wrestling in the parlour.'

Dora smiled back. 'Do you collect?'

'In a manner of speaking.' He set the figurine down and his old, shrewd eyes swept the display—pricing, cataloguing, dismissing. 'I'm Tom Ashworth. Got a shop here in Front Royal. Accumulated so much stuff over the years it was open a shop or buy a bigger house.'

'I know what you mean. I'm Dora Conroy.' She held out a hand. 'I have a shop in Philadelphia.'

'Thought you were a pro.' Pleased, he winked. 'Don't believe I've seen you at one of Porter's auctions before.'

'No. I've never been able to make it. Actually, this trip was an impulse. I dragged my sister along. Lea, Tom Ashworth.'

'Nice to meet you.'

'My pleasure.'

'Have you been in business long, Mr Ashworth?' Lea asked.

'Nigh on forty years. The wife got us started, crocheting doilies and scarves and selling them. Worked side by side in the shop till she passed on in the spring of eighty-six. Now I got me a grandson working with me. Got a lot of fancy ideas, but he's a good boy.'

'Family businesses are the best,' Dora said. 'Lea's just started working part-time at the shop.'

'Lord knows why. I don't know anything about antiques.'

'You just have to figure out what people want,' Ashworth told her. 'And how much they'll pay for it.'

'Exactly.' Delighted with him, Dora hooked a hand through his arm. 'It looks like we're getting started. Why don't we find seats?'

Ashworth offered Lea his other arm and, feeling like the cock of the walk, escorted the women to chairs near the front row, as Dora prepared to play her favourite role.

The bidding was low but energetic. Dora bought the cherrywood dressing table, snapped up the lot that included the creamer/slipper and competed briskly with Ashworth for a set of crystal saltcellars.

'Got me,' he said when Dora topped his bid yet again.

282

'I've got a customer who collects,' she told him.

'That so?' Ashworth leaned closer as the bidding began on the next lot. 'I've got a set of six at the shop. Cobalt and silver. You got time, you drop on by after this and take a look.'

'I might just do that. Now, here we go.' Spotting the abstract painting, Dora rubbed her hands together. 'Mine,' she said softly.

BY THREE O'CLOCK Dora was in front of Mr Ashworth's shop, adding half a dozen cobalt saltcellars to the treasures in her van.

'It was great meeting you, Mr Ashworth.' She offered her hand. 'If you get up to Philadelphia, I'll expect you to drop by.'

'You can count on it. Take care of yourselves. Drive safely.'

'We will. Merry Christmas.' Dora climbed into the van.

With a last wave she started the van and pulled away. She smiled as she saw Ashworth standing with his hand lifted in a salute.

'What a sweetheart. I'm glad he got that figurine.'

Lea shivered and waited impatiently for the van to heat up. 'I still can't believe you bought that hideous painting, Dory. You'll never be able to sell it. At least you only paid fifty dollars for it.'

Dora shrugged. 'Fifty-two seventy-five.'

With a sigh Lea settled back. 'This time tomorrow I'll be baking cookies and rolling out pie dough.'

'You asked for it. You had to get married, have kids, buy a house. Where else is the family going to have Christmas dinner?'

'I wouldn't mind if Mom didn't insist on helping me cook it.'

'Maybe Will can distract her. Is he coming alone or with one of his sweeties?' Dora asked, referring to their brother's list of glamorous dates.

'Alone, last I heard. Dora, watch that truck, will you?'

Dora raced the engine to pass a sixteen-wheeler. 'So when's Will getting in?'

'He's taking a late train out of New York on Christmas Eve.'

'Late enough to make a grand entrance,' Dora predicted. 'Oh, I just remembered. That new tenant Dad signed up is moving in across the hall today. I hope Dad remembers to be there with the keys. You know how absent-minded he is when he's in the middle of a production.'

'I know, which is why I can't understand how you could let him interview a tenant for your building. Just don't be surprised if you end up across the hall from a psychopath.'

Dora smiled. 'I specifically told Dad no psychopaths.' She swung towards the slip road, imagining unpacking her new possessions. The very first thing she would do, she promised herself, was find the perfect spot for the painting.

HIGH IN THE GLITTERY tower of a silver building overlooking the cramped streets of LA, Edmund Finley enjoyed his weekly manicure. The wall directly across from his rosewood desk flickered with a dozen television screens showing CNN headline news and one of the home-shopping networks. Other screens were tuned in to offices in his organisation so that he could observe his employees.

But unless he chose to listen in, the only sounds in the vast sweep of his office were the strains of a Mozart opera.

Finley liked to watch. His top-floor office gave him a feeling of power, and he would often stand at the wide window behind his desk and study the comings and goings of strangers far below. In his home, far up in the hills above the city, there were television screens and monitors in every room, and windows where he could look down on the lights of the LA basin. Every evening he would stand on the balcony outside his bedroom and imagine owning everything, everyone, for as far as his eye could see.

Edmund Finley—a tall, spare, distinguished-looking man in his early fifties who looked much younger—acquired. And once he acquired, he hoarded. His office reflected his taste for the exclusive. Sculptures by Rodin and Denécheau filled niches in the white walls. A Renoir hung above a Louis Quatorze commode. Two high glass cabinets held a stunning and esoteric display of *objets d'art*: carved snuff bottles of lapis and aquamarine, ivory netsukes, Dresden figurines, Limoges ring boxes, African masks.

His import-export business was enormously successful. His smuggling sideline more so. After all, smuggling was more of a challenge. It required a certain finesse and a ruthless ingenuity.

'You're all done, Mr Finley.' The manicurist placed Finley's hand gently on the spotless blotter on his desk. He smiled down at his buffed nails.

'Excellent work.' Taking a gold money clip from his pocket, Finley peeled off a fifty-dollar bill. 'Merry Christmas, dear.'

'Oh, thank you, Mr Finley. Merry Christmas to you, too.'

Still smiling, he dismissed her with a wave. Before the door had closed behind her, he had swivelled in his chair and, through the stream of sunlight, studied his view of Los Angeles.

Christmas, he thought. What a lovely time of year. One of good-will towards men, ringing bells and coloured lights. Of course, it was also the time of desperate loneliness, despair and suicide. But those small human tragedies didn't touch or concern him. Money had catapulted him above those fragile needs for companionship and family. He could buy companionship.

The knock on his door made him turn as he called out, 'Enter.'

'Sir.' Abel Winesap, a small man with the heavy title of executive assistant, cleared his throat. 'Mr Finley.'

'Do you know the true meaning of Christmas, Abel?' Finley's voice was warm. 'Acquisition. A lovely word, don't you agree?'

'Yes, sir.' Winesap shivered. What he had come to report was difficult enough. Finley's happy mood made the difficult more dangerous. 'I'm afraid we have a problem, Mr Finley.'

'Oh?' Finley's smile remained, but his eyes frosted.

Winesap gulped in fear. He knew that Finley's frigid anger was lethal. It was Winesap who had been chosen to witness Finley's termination of an employee who had been embezzling. And he remembered how calmly Finley had slit the man's throat with a sixteenth-century jewelled dagger. Betrayal, Finley believed, deserved quick punishment, and some ceremony.

Nervously Winesap continued with his story. 'The shipment from New York, sir. The merchandise you were expecting . . .'

'Has there been a delay?'

'No. That is, the shipment arrived today as expected, but the merchandise . . .' He moistened his thin, nervous lips. 'It isn't what you ordered, sir. Apparently there was a mix-up somewhere.'

Finley placed his pampered hands on the edge of the desk. 'Where is it?' His voice was a chilly hiss.

'In Receiving, sir. I thought—'

'Bring it up. Immediately.'

'Right away, sir.' Winesap escaped, grateful for the reprieve.

Finley had paid a great deal of money for the merchandise, and even more to have that merchandise concealed and smuggled; having each piece stolen, disguised, then transported from various locations to his factory in New York. Why, the bribes alone had run close to six figures. To calm himself, he poured generously from a decanter of guava juice. If there had been a mistake, he thought, more steadily, it would be rectified. Whoever had erred would be punished.

There was a knock on his door. 'Come,' he snapped out, and waited as one of his receiving clerks wheeled in a crate. 'Leave it there. And go. Abel, remain. The door,' he said.

Winesap scurried to shut it behind the departing clerk and walked back to the crate. 'I opened it as you instructed, Mr Finley.' Gingerly he dipped his hand into a sea of shredded paper. His fingers trembled as he pulled out a china teapot.

Finley took the teapot, turning it over in his hands. It was English, a lovely piece, worth perhaps $200 on the open market. But it was mass-produced, and to him it was worthless. He smashed it against the edge of the crate and sent shards flying.

'What else?'

Quaking, Winesap drew out a swirling glass vase.

Italian, Finley deduced as he inspected it. Handmade. A value of perhaps one hundred and fifty dollars. He hurled it against the wall.

'Where is my merchandise?' he demanded.

'Sir, I can't— I believe there's been . . . an error.'

'An error.' Finley's eyes were like jade as he clenched his fists at his sides. DiCarlo, he thought, conjuring up an image of his man in New York. Young, bright, ambitious. But not stupid, not enough to attempt a double-cross. Still, he would pay dearly for this.

'Get DiCarlo on the phone.'

'Yes, sir.' Winesap darted to the desk to place the call.

Systematically Finley destroyed the rest of the crate's contents.

2

Jed Skimmerhorn wanted a drink. But he wasn't going to get one until he'd finished carting boxes up these rickety back steps and into his new apartment.

Not that he had a lot of possessions. His old partner, Brent Chapman, had given him a hand with the heavier pieces of furniture. All that remained were a few cardboard boxes filled with books and assorted junk. He wasn't sure why he'd kept that much. Then again, he wasn't even sure why he'd found it so necessary to move across town into an apartment. It was something about fresh starts. But you couldn't start fresh until you'd ended.

Turning in his resignation had been the first step—perhaps the hardest. The police commissioner had refused to accept the resignation and put Jed on extended leave. It didn't matter what it was called, Jed mused. He wasn't a cop any more. Couldn't be a cop any more. He'd given fourteen years of his life to the force. It had to be enough.

Jed elbowed open the door to the apartment. He slid the boxes across the wooden floor before heading back down the narrow hall-way towards the rear entrance.

He hadn't heard a peep from his neighbour across the hall. The eccentric old man who had let the place had said that the second apartment was occupied but that the tenant was as quiet as a mouse. It certainly seemed that way.

Jed started down the outside steps, noting with annoyance that the banister wouldn't hold the weight of a three-year-old. The steps themselves were slick with the sleet that continued to spit out of the colourless sky. Though the apartment fronted onto Philadelphia's busy South Street, Jed didn't think he'd mind the noise and bohemian atmosphere, the tourists or the shops. In any case, it would be a dramatic change from the manicured lawns of Chestnut Hill, where the Skimmerhorn home had stood for years.

Through the gloom he could see the glow of coloured lights strung on the windows of neighbouring buildings. It reminded him that Brent had invited him to Christmas dinner. A big, noisy family event that Jed might have enjoyed in the past. There had never been big, noisy family events in his life—or none that were fun.

And now there was no family. No family at all.

He pressed his fingertips to the ache at his temples and willed himself not to think of Elaine. But memories knotted his stomach.

He hauled out the last of the boxes and slammed the boot with a force that rattled the reconditioned Thunderbird down to its tyres. He wasn't going to think of Elaine or Donny Speck or regrets. He was going to go upstairs, pour a drink and think of nothing at all.

Once inside, Jed dumped the last box onto the oak table in the dining area. The apartment was echoingly empty, which only served to satisfy him that he was alone. One of the reasons he'd chosen it was because he'd have only one neighbour to ignore. The other reason was just as simple: it was fabulous.

He imagined the old building had been converted into shop and apartments some time in the thirties. It had retained its lofty ceilings and spacious rooms, the working fireplace and slim, tall windows. The skirting board was walnut and uncarved, the walls a creamy ivory.

He unearthed a bottle of Jameson's, three-quarters full. He set it on the table. He was shoving packing paper aside in search of a glass when he heard noises. His hands froze. He turned, trying to locate the source of the sound. He thought he'd heard bells. And now laughter, a smoky drift of it, seductive and female.

His eyes turned to the brass openwork floor vent near the fireplace. The sounds floated up through it. There was some sort of antique shop beneath the apartment. It had been closed for the last couple of days, but it was apparently open for business now.

Jed went back to search for a glass and tuned out the sounds.

'I REALLY DO APPRECIATE your meeting us here, John,' Dora said.

'No problem.' Lea's husband puffed a bit as he carted another crate into the overflowing storeroom. He was a tall man with a skinny frame and an honest face that might have been homely but for the pale eyes that peered out behind thick lenses. He smiled at Dora. 'How did you manage to buy so much in such a short time?'

'Experience.' She had to rise on her toes to kiss John's cheek; then she bent and scooped up her younger nephew, Michael. 'Hey, frog-face, did you miss me?'

He grinned and wrapped his pudgy arms round her neck.

Lea turned to keep an eagle eye on her two other children. 'Richie, hands in your pockets. Missy, no pirouetting in the shop.' Lea sighed, smiled. 'I'm home.' She held out her arms for Michael. 'Dora, do you need any more help?'

'No. I can handle it from here. Thanks again.'

Dora herded her family outside, then locked up and engaged the security alarm.

Alone, she turned and took a deep breath. There was the scent of apple and pine from the potpourri set all around the shop. It was good to be home, she thought. She lifted the box containing the new acquisitions that she'd decided to take to her apartment upstairs.

She unlocked the door that led from the storeroom to the inside stairway while juggling the box, her handbag, her overnight bag and her coat. She was halfway down the hall when she saw the light spilling out of the neighbouring apartment. The new tenant. She walked to the open door and peered in.

She saw him standing by an old table, a bottle in one hand, a glass in the other. The room itself was sparsely furnished with a sofa, an overstuffed chair and some weightlifting equipment. But she was more interested in the man. He was tall, with a tough, athletic build. He wore a navy sweatshirt and Levi's. His hair was a bit unkempt, falling carelessly over his collar in a rich shade of ripening wheat. In contrast, the watch at his wrist was either an amazingly good fake or a genuine Rolex. His face seemed grim.

Before she had made a sound, she saw his body tense. His head whipped round and he pinned her with eyes that were hard, expressionless and shockingly blue.

'Your door was open,' she said apologetically.

'Yeah.' He set the bottle down, carrying the glass with him as he crossed to her. Jed took his own survey. A pretty, oval face, slightly pointed at the chin, with an old-fashioned roses-and-cream complexion; a wide, smiling mouth; big brown eyes that were filled with friendly curiosity; a swing of sable-coloured hair.

'I'm Dora, from across the hall,' she said. 'Need any help?'

'No.' Jed closed the door in her face.

Her mouth fell open. 'Well, welcome to the neighbourhood,' she muttered. She unlocked her own door and slammed it behind her.

Dora dumped her things on a settee. Marching to her phone, she decided to call her father and give him an earful.

Before she'd dialled the number, she spotted a sheet of paper with a big heart-shaped happy face drawn at the bottom. Dora hung up the phone and began to read. *Izzy, my darling daughter.*

Dora winced. Her father was the only one who called her that.

The deed is done. Well done, if I say so myself. Your tenant is a strapping young man who should be able to help with any menial work. His name, as you see on the lease, is Jed Skimmerhorn. I found him fascinatingly taciturn. I couldn't think of anything nicer to give my adored daughter than an intriguing neighbour.

Your devoted father

Dora couldn't help smiling. The move was so obvious.

'Sorry, Dad,' she murmured. 'You're in for a disappointment.'

Setting the note aside, she skimmed a finger down the lease until she came to Jed's signature and dashed her own name on both copies. Lifting one, she strode across the hall and knocked.

When the door opened, Dora thrust the lease out, crushing the corner against Jed's chest. 'You'll need this for your records.'

He took it. Her eyes weren't friendly now, but cool. Which suited him. 'Why'd the old man leave this with you?'

Her chin tilted up. 'The old man,' she said in mild tones, 'is my father. I own the building, which makes me your landlord.' She turned on her heel and was across the hall in two strides. With her hand on the knob she paused, turned. 'The rent's due on the twenty-first of each month. You can slip the cheque under my door and save yourself a stamp, as well as any contact with other humans.'

She slipped inside and closed the door with a satisfied click.

JED SPENT a gruelling ninety minutes at the gym around the corner the next morning, lifting weights and burning away most of his morning-after headache in the steam room. Now, feeling almost human, he craved a pot of black coffee. He pulled his key out of the pocket of his jogging pants and let himself into the hallway. He heard music, the rich-throated wail of Aretha Franklin. At least his landlord's taste in music wouldn't irritate him, he mused.

He noted her open door. An even trade, Jed figured, and wandered over. He knew he'd been deliberately rude the night before, and he thought it wise to make peace with the woman who owned his building. He nudged the door open a bit wider and stared.

Like his, her apartment was spacious, high-ceilinged and full of light from the front windows. That was where the similarity ended. He'd never seen so much stuff crammed into one single space. Glass shelves covered one wall and were loaded with knick-knacks. There were a number of tables, each topped by glassware and china. A floral couch was loaded with coloured pillows which picked up the faded tones of a large rug. To complement the season, there was a Christmas tree by the window, laden with coloured balls and lights.

It should have been messy, Jed thought. Instead, he had the impression of having opened some magic treasure chest.

In the midst of it was his landlord. She wore a scarlet suit with a fitted jacket over her slim body. Jed leaned against the doorjamb as she propped the painting she'd been holding on the sofa and turned. To her credit she managed to muffle her squeal when she spotted him.

'Your door was open,' he told her.

'Yeah.' She shrugged. 'I've been recirculating some things this morning—from up here to downstairs.' She crossed the room and stood beside a pedestal dining-room table, pouring what smelt gloriously like strong coffee from a china pot into a matching cup. Dora set the pot back down and lifted a brow. Her unsmiling lips were as boldly red as her suit. 'Is there something you need?'

He nodded towards the pot. 'Some of that wouldn't hurt.'

Saying nothing, Dora set down her cup, went to a curved glass cabinet and took out another cup and saucer. 'Cream? Sugar?'

'No.'

When he didn't come any further into the room, she took the coffee to him. His eyes were hard and inscrutable.

'Thanks.' He downed the contents of the fragile cup in two swallows. He looked back at the painting, studied it for a moment. Bold, he thought, like her colour scheme, like the punch-in-the-gut scent she wore. 'You know, that's upside-down.'

Her smile came quickly, brilliantly. She had indeed set it on the sofa the way it had been displayed at auction. 'I think so, too.' She went over and flipped it.

Jed narrowed his eyes. 'It's still ugly, but it's right side up.'

'The appreciation of art is as individual as art itself.'

'If you say so. Thanks for the coffee.' He handed his cup back.

'You're welcome. Oh, Skimmerhorn?'

He stopped, glanced back over his shoulder.

'If you're thinking of sprucing up your new place, come on down to the shop. Dora's Parlor has something for everybody.'

'I don't need anything.'

Dora was still smiling when she heard his door close. 'Wrong, Skimmerhorn,' she murmured. 'Everybody needs something.'

COOLING HIS HEELS in a dusty office of Premium Shipping wasn't how Anthony DiCarlo had pictured spending this morning. He wanted answers, and he wanted them now.

290

More to the point, Finley wanted answers yesterday. The phone call from LA the day before had been crystal clear. Find the merchandise within twenty-four hours or pay the consequences.

DiCarlo had no intention of discovering what those consequences were. He looked at the big clock—less than fifteen hours.

Through the glass panel stencilled with an overweight Santa, he could see a dozen shipping clerks busily stamping and hauling. DiCarlo sneered as the fat shipping supervisor approached the door.

'Mr DiCarlo, so sorry to keep you waiting. As you can imagine, we're pretty frantic around here these days.' Bill Tarkington waddled round his desk to his coffee machine. 'Some coffee?'

'No. There's been an error, Mr Tarkington,' DiCarlo said, his fury clear. 'An error that must be corrected immediately.'

'Well, can you give me the specifics?'

'The merchandise I directed to Abel Winesap in Los Angeles was not the merchandise that arrived there.' DiCarlo took the shipping invoice from his inside breast pocket.

'That's an odd one.' Tarkington rattled the keys on his computer. 'That was to ship out on December seventeenth. Yep, yep, there she is.' He sipped some coffee. 'Oh, wait, I remember. We provided the crate and the packing, and you supervised. So how in the world did the merchandise get switched?'

'That is my question,' DiCarlo hissed, slamming the desk.

Tarkington hit a few more keys. 'That shipment went out of section three. Let's see who was on the belt that day. Ah, Opal.'

'I want to speak to her.'

Tarkington leaned forward and flicked a switch on his desk. 'Opal Johnson, please report to Mr Tarkington's office.'

THE NIGHTMARE that had plagued Opal for a week was coming true.

'I'm sorry, Mr Tarkington,' she forced herself to say. 'It's hard to recall any one shipment. All I remember about last week is working three double shifts and going home to soak my feet every night.'

She was lying, DiCarlo decided. He could see it in her eyes. 'Things have been pretty harried for you the past few weeks, I imagine.'

'I guess so. The Christmas rush.'

'But I also figure you know exactly what happened to my shipment.'

Opal's stomach did a quick jig. 'Look, mister, I already told you I don't know what happened. I do the best job I can.'

'You want to protect your job, don't you, Opal? You don't want to get fired, do you?'

'I got kids,' she sobbed. 'I got kids.'

'Then help me out, and I'll do the same for you.'

Opal fumbled for a cigarette. 'I'm really sorry. I was late and . . . and I was so rushed I mixed up the invoices. I'm sorry,' she sobbed.

'You're going to be a lot sorrier if you don't find out what happened to my shipment,' DiCarlo said.

'I went through all the paperwork yesterday. There was only one other oversized crate that came through that morning.' She reached in her handbag and fished out an address. DiCarlo snatched it.

'Sherman Porter, Front Royal, Virginia.'

'Please, Mr DiCarlo, I got kids. I know I made a mistake . . . I can't afford to get fired.'

He put the paper into his pocket. 'I'll check this out, then we'll see.'

3

At the main counter in her shop, Dora put the finishing touch of a big red bow on a brightly wrapped box. 'She'll love them, Mr O'Malley.' Dora patted the box containing the cobalt saltcellars.

'Well, I appreciate your calling me, Miss Conroy. I don't know what Hester sees in these things, but she sure sets store by them.'

'You're going to be her hero. Happy Christmas, Mr O'Malley.'

'Same to you and yours.' He walked out, a satisfied customer.

There were another half a dozen customers in the shop, two being helped by Dora's assistant, Terri Starr, who was also a member of the Conroys' acting troupe. Dora skirted the counter.

'Oh, miss?'

Dora turned, smiling. There was something vaguely familiar about the stout matron with lacquered black hair.

'Yes, ma'am. May I help you?'

She gestured towards a display table. 'Are these doorstops?'

'Yes, they are. Of course, they can be used for whatever you like.' Automatically Dora glanced over as the bells jingled on her door. She merely lifted a brow when Jed walked in. 'Several of these are from the Victorian period,' she went on. She lifted one in the shape of a basket of fruit. 'This one was probably used for a drawing room.'

'My niece, Sharon, and her husband just moved into their first house,' the woman said. 'I'd like to get them a housewarming present.'

'Was there a reason you had a doorstop in mind?'

'Yes, actually. My niece does a lot of sewing. It's an old house, you see, and the door to her sewing room won't stay open. Since they have a baby on the way, I know she'd want to be able to keep an ear out.' Still, she hesitated. 'I bought Sharon a chamber pot here a few months ago for her birthday. She loved it.'

That clicked. 'The Sunderland, with the frog painted inside.'

The woman's eyes brightened. 'Why, yes. You remembered.'

'I was very fond of that piece, Mrs . . . '

'Lyle. Alice Lyle.'

'Mrs Lyle, yes. I'm glad it found a good home.' Dora tapped a finger to her lips. 'If she liked that, maybe she'd appreciate something along these lines.' She chose a brass figure of an elephant. 'It's Jumbo,' she explained. 'P.T. Barnum's?'

'Yes.' The woman chuckled as Dora passed Jumbo to her. 'He's perfect.' She took a quick, discreet glance at the tag dangling from Jumbo's front foot. 'Yes, definitely.'

'Would you like him gift-wrapped?'

'Yes, thank you.' She picked up the sleeping hound Dora had purchased at auction only the day before. 'I think I'll take him along, too—a nice, cosy watchdog for the nursery. You do take Visa?'

'Of course. This will just take a few minutes. Why don't you help yourself to some coffee while you wait.' Dora gestured to a table that was always set with tea and coffeepots and trays of pretty cookies. She carried the doorstops back to the counter. 'Christmas shopping, Skimmerhorn?' she asked as she passed him.

'I need a gift for a hostess.'

'Browse around. I'll be right with you.'

Jed wasn't completely sure what he was browsing around in. The packed apartment was only a small taste of the amazing array of merchandise offered in Dora's Parlor. Bottles of varying sizes and colours caught the glitter of sunlight and begged to be handled. Tin soldiers arranged in battle lines fought beside old war posters.

He wandered into the next room and found it equally packed. Teddy bears and teapots. Cuckoo clocks and corkscrews. A junk shop, he mused. Idly he picked up a small enamelled box decorated with painted roses. Mary Pat would like this, he decided.

'Well, Skimmerhorn, you surprise me.' Dora smiled and gestured towards the box he held. 'You show excellent taste. That was made *circa* 1770.' There was a laugh in her eyes. 'It goes for $2,500.'

'This?' It didn't fill the cup of his palm.

'Well, it is a George III.'

'Yeah, right.' He put it back on the table with the same care he would have used with an explosive device. The fact that he could afford it didn't make it any less intimidating. He scanned the room, afraid to touch anything now. 'Maybe I should just pick up some flowers.'

'That's nice, too. Of course, they don't last.' Dora was enjoying his look of pure discomfort. 'Tell me a little about your hostess so that I can help you select something. Is she the athletic, outdoors

type or a quiet homebody who bakes her own bread?'

'She's my partner—ex-partner's wife. She's a trauma nurse. She's got three kids and likes to read books.'

'All right. We have a busy, dedicated woman. The gift shouldn't be too personal. Something for the house.' She walked to a corner resembling an old-fashioned pantry. 'This would do nicely.' Dora took down a footed wooden jar trimmed in brass.

Jed frowned over it. 'What's it for—cookies?'

Dora beamed at him. 'How clever of you. Yes, it's a biscuit jar. This one's oak, from about 1870. A practical and ornamental gift, and at forty dollars it won't cost you more than a dozen long-stem roses.'

'OK. I guess she'd get a kick out of it.'

'See? That wasn't so painful. Can I help you with anything else?'

'No, that's it.' He followed her back into the main room. The place smelt cosy, he decided. Like apples. There was music playing softly. He recognised *The Nutcracker* and was surprised that he suddenly felt relaxed. 'You actually make a living out of all this?' he asked her.

Amused, she unfolded a box. 'People collect, Skimmerhorn. Didn't you ever have comic books as a boy, or baseball cards?'

'Sure.' He'd had to hide them, but he'd had them.

She lined the box with tissue, working quickly, competently. She glanced up to find him staring down at her hands.

His gaze lifted, locked on hers. He'd felt something watching her work that had gone straight to the gut, like a hot arrow. 'Just like you played with dolls,' he said.

'Actually, I never liked them much. I preferred imaginary play-mates because you could change them into any character you wanted.' With more care than necessary she fitted the lid on, with its gold-embossed DORA'S PARLOR. 'What I was getting at is that most children collect and trade. Some people never grow out of it. Shall I gift-wrap this for you? There's no extra charge.'

'Yeah, go ahead.'

He moved down the counter to give himself some breathing room. The sexual tug he'd felt wasn't new, but it was the first time he'd experienced it because a woman had pretty hands. And huge brown eyes, he added. Then there was that smile, he thought.

Dora set the gaily wrapped package in front of him. 'I hope your friend likes her gift.' She watched as Jed left the shop.

An unusual man, she mused. The unusual was her stock in trade.

DiCARLO RACED along the Van Wyck Expressway towards LaGuardia Airport, dialling his car phone. 'DiCarlo,' he stated, flipping the phone to speaker. 'Get me Mr Finley.' With his nerves bubbling, he checked his watch. He'd make it, he assured himself.

Finley's voice filled the car. 'Mr DiCarlo.'

'I tracked it all down, Mr Finley.' DiCarlo forced his words into a calm tone. 'Some idiot clerk at Premium sent our shipment to Front Royal, Virginia. I'll straighten it out in no time.'

'I see. And what is your definition of "no time"?'

'I'm on my way to the airport right now. I've got a flight booked to Dulles and a car waiting. I'll be in Front Royal before five.' His voice weakened. 'I'm handling all of this at my own expense, Mr Finley.'

'That's wise of you, Mr DiCarlo. You do know how important that merchandise is to me, don't you? You will use any means necessary to recover it. Any means at all.'

'Understood.' DiCarlo was more than ready to do just that.

'THIS IS QUITE a mix-up, isn't it?' While he asked this rhetorical—and to DiCarlo unamusing—question, Sherman Porter rummaged through his dented filing cabinet. 'Guess we'd have caught it here, but we had ourselves an auction going on,' Porter continued. 'Moved a lot of stuff.' He opened another file drawer.

DiCarlo looked at his watch. Six fifteen. Time was running out.

'Here now, this looks promising.' Porter unearthed a short stack of neatly typed invoices and handed them over.

DiCarlo took out his own list and compared. It was all there, he noted, torn between relief and despair. All sold. The china hound, the porcelain figurine, the abstract painting, the bronze eagle and the stuffed parrot. The enormous and ugly plaster replica of the Statue of Liberty was gone as well.

Inside his pocket DiCarlo had another list. On it were descriptions of what had been carefully and expensively hidden in each piece of merchandise. An engraved Gallé vase valued at nearly one hundred thousand dollars. An antique sapphire brooch, reputed to have been worn by Mary, Queen of Scots. The list went on.

Despite the chill of the room, his skin grew clammy. Not one item remained in Porter's possession. 'Nothing left,' DiCarlo said weakly.

'We had a good turnout,' Porter said, pleased with the memory. 'That shipment came in just before we started the auction, and there wasn't time to do an inventory. Best I can say is, go through a mailing list of our customers, match up the addresses with the names there next to the stuff we sold. You can get in touch, explain things.'

It would take days to round up Finley's stock, DiCarlo thought, sickened. Weeks.

Porter shuffled through a drawer and came up with the mailing list. 'Go ahead, take your time. I'm not in any hurry.'

TWENTY MINUTES LATER DiCarlo left, with one bright pinpoint of hope. The porcelain figurine was still in Front Royal, the property of a Thomas Ashworth, antiques dealer. Regaining possession of one piece quickly might placate Finley and buy time.

As he drove through light traffic to Ashworth's shop, DiCarlo worked out his strategy. Since Ashworth had paid only forty-five dollars for the figurine, DiCarlo was prepared to buy it back and include a reasonable profit for the dealer. Once he had the figurine, he would tell Finley everything was under control. With any luck Finley would have Winesap contact the rest of the list and DiCarlo would be back in New York to enjoy Christmas.

The scenario brightened his mood. It wasn't until he had parked in front of Ashworth's shop that his smile faded. Closed.

DiCarlo got out of the car and rattled the knob, pounding on the glass-fronted door. He raced to the display window, cupping his hands beside his face. He could see nothing but his own misery.

Finley would accept no excuses, he knew—nothing so vague as simple bad luck. Then DiCarlo saw the porcelain figurine of a man and woman in ballroom dress. He clenched his gloved hands into fists.

He moved the car two blocks away. From his glove compartment he took a flashlight, a screwdriver, his revolver. He slipped them all into the pockets of his cashmere coat.

This time he headed up a side street towards the rear entrance of Ashworth's shop. As he walked, his eyes darted from side to side, watchful, wary. It was a small town, and on a cold, blustery night most citizens were home. DiCarlo passed no one.

Nor did he spot any evidence of a security system. Moving quickly, he used the screwdriver to jemmy the door. The sound of splintering wood made him smile. DiCarlo slipped inside, shut the door behind him. He flicked on his flashlight, shielding the beam with his hand as he swung it right and left. To make the break-in appear to be a random burglary, DiCarlo smashed a lamp and a Capo di Monte vase at random. On impulse, for the thrill of stealing, he dropped a few cloisonné boxes into his pockets.

He was grinning when he snatched up the figurine. 'Gotcha, baby,' he murmured, then froze as light flooded into the shop from a stairway to his right. Swearing, DiCarlo squeezed himself between a rosewood armoire and a brass standard lamp.

'I've called the police.' An elderly man wearing a grey flannel robe and carrying a nine iron inched down the steps.

For a moment DiCarlo was baffled as he smelt roast chicken. The old man had an apartment upstairs, DiCarlo realised, and cursed himself for crashing through the shop. But there wasn't time for regrets. Tucking the figurine under his arm like a football, he hurtled towards Ashworth.

The old man grunted on impact, teetered on the steps, his bathrobe flapping over legs as thin as pencils. Wheezing, Ashworth swung the golf club. DiCarlo grabbed it and Ashworth pitched forward. His head hit a cast-iron coal scuttle with an ominous crack.

Disgusted, DiCarlo shoved Ashworth over. In the spill of the upstairs light he could see the flow of blood, the open, staring eyes. Fury had him kicking the body twice before he pulled himself back.

He was half a block away when he heard the sound of sirens.

'You have news for me?' Finley said.

'Yes. Yes, sir. I have the porcelain figurine with me, Mr Finley, as well as a list locating all the other merchandise.' DiCarlo spoke from his car phone as he drove back towards Dulles International.

Finley waited a beat. 'Explain.'

DiCarlo began with Sherman Porter, pausing every few seconds. 'There was a bit of a problem in recovering the figurine, sir. An antiques dealer in Front Royal had purchased it. His shop was closed when I arrived, and knowing that you wanted results quickly I broke in to retrieve it. Mr Finley, the dealer's dead.'

'I see. So I assume you took care of this Porter.'

'Took care of?'

'He can link you to the . . . accident, correct? And a link to you, Mr DiCarlo, is a link to me. I suggest you snap the link quickly. After you've finished tidying up in Virginia, I'll expect you here, with the figurine. We'll discuss the next steps.'

'You want me in California? Mr Finley—'

'By noon, Mr DiCarlo. We'll be closing early tomorrow. The holidays, you know. Contact Winesap with your flight information.'

'Yes, sir.' DiCarlo broke the connection. He hoped Porter was still in his shop so he could put a bullet in the man's brain.

'Really, Andrew, *really*, there's no need for you to walk me up.'

Andrew Dawd, an accountant who considered tax havens the height of intrigue, gave a hearty laugh and pinched Dora's cheek. 'Now, Dora, my mother taught me to always see the girl to her door.'

'Well, Mamma's not here.' She inched up the steps. 'And it's late.'

'It's not even eleven. You're going to send me off without a cup of coffee? You know you make the best coffee in Philadelphia.'

'It's a gift.' She was searching for some polite way to refuse when the outside door slammed open, slammed shut.

Jed strode down the hall. His scarred leather bomber jacket was left unzipped over a sweatshirt and jeans. His hair was wind-blown, his face unshaven—which suited the surly look in his eye.

Dora had to wonder why, at that moment, she preferred Jed's dangerous look to the three-piece-suited, buffed and polished accountant beside her. 'Skimmerhorn,' she said.

Jed summed up Dora's date with one glance as he fitted the key into his lock. 'Conroy,' he said, and slipped inside and closed the door.

Andrew's well-groomed eyebrows rose. 'Your new tenant?'

'Yes.' Dora sighed. She unlocked the door and let Andrew in.

Frowning, he folded his overcoat neatly over the back of a chair. Too frustrated for tidiness, Dora tossed her mink, *circa* 1925, towards the couch on her way to the kitchen. While she ground coffee beans in the hand-cranked grinder, she glanced at Andrew.

'Why don't you put on some music, Andrew?'

'Music?' His blandly handsome face cleared. 'Of course.'

Moments later she heard the quiet strains of an old Johnny Mathis recording. She thought, Uh-oh, then shrugged. If she couldn't handle an accountant who wore Brooks Brothers suits and Halston cologne, she deserved to pay the price. 'The coffee'll be a few minutes,' she said as she walked back into the living room.

Andrew was admiring Dora in the short dress covered with fiery bugle beads. She sat on the arm of the chair and crossed her legs without giving a thought to the way the movement urged her skirt higher.

Andrew gave it considerable thought.

Catching the predatory look in his eye, Dora leapt off the chair like a spring. 'I'll go check the coffee.'

But he caught her hand and swung her into his arms in what she imagined he considered a stylish move. 'We should take advantage of the music,' he told her as he glided over the rug.

Dora forced herself to relax. She smiled, and let the music and the movement take her. He wasn't such a bad guy, she mused.

Suddenly he clamped her against him, shattering the mellow mood, and his hands streaked under the hem of her dress.

'Hey!' Furious, she reared back, freeing herself.

'Oh, Dora, Dora, you're so beautiful, so irresistible.'

He pressed her against the side of a chair. Dora felt her balance going. 'Well, resist, or I'll have to hurt you,' she said.

He only continued to mumble seductive phrases as he tumbled with her to the floor, sending several of her treasures crashing down. Enough was enough. Dora brought her knee up between Andrew's thighs. Even as he grunted she popped him hard in the eye.

'Off!' she shouted, shoving at him. Groaning, he rolled, curling up like a boiled shrimp. Dora scrambled to her feet.

He heaved himself up. 'You're crazy,' he managed.

'You're right. Absolutely.' She picked up his coat and held it out, impatience snapping around her. 'Go away, Andrew.'

He snatched the coat from her. 'I took you out to dinner.'

'Consider it a bad investment. I'm sure you can find a way to deduct it.' She yanked open her door just as Jed opened his across the hall. 'Out! And you're fired.' Andrew scurried off, and Dora stood catching her breath. The quiet sound of Jed clearing his throat had her spinning back. He was grinning.

'See something funny, Skimmerhorn?' she said.

He thought about it. 'Yeah.' He leaned against the doorjamb and continued to grin. 'Interesting date, Conroy?'

'Fascinating.' Dora let out a long breath. 'Want a drink?'

'Sure.'

She went into her apartment and tossed her shoes aside.

He glanced at the broken china on the floor. That must have been the crash he'd heard. He'd had a bad moment deciding whether to intervene. Even when he'd carried a badge, he'd worried more about answering a domestic dispute than collaring a pro.

He looked over at Dora while she poured brandy into glasses. Her face was still flushed, her eyes narrowed.

'So, who was the jerk?' he asked.

'My former accountant.' Dora handed Jed a glass. 'He spends the evening boring me into a coma talking about capital gains, then figures he can rip my clothes off.' Pouting, she crouched over the china and held up a broken cup. 'This was Derby, 1815.'

'It's trash now. Get a broom or something.'

She rose and went out to the kitchen. She came back waving a dustpan and broom. 'I bet the guy was an Eagle Scout.'

'Probably had a change of underwear in his overcoat pocket,' Jed said. Gently he took the broom from her.

Dora winced as Jed dumped a load of broken glass into a wastepaper bin. 'Were you?' Resigned, she sat on the arm of the chair. The theatrics, it seemed, were over.

'Was I what?'

'An Eagle Scout.'

He dumped the last load, then sent her a long look. 'No. I was a delinquent. Watch your feet here. I might have missed some.'

'Thanks. So what do you do now?'

'You ought to know. I filled out an application.'

'I didn't have a chance to read it.'

He smiled. 'I'm independently wealthy.'

'Oh. So what do you do with yourself all day?'

'Nothing much.'

'I could keep you busy. That is, if you're any good with your hands. What I mean is, I need some new shelves in the storeroom.'

'Your outside banister's a joke,' he said.

'Oh.' Her lips moved into a pout. 'Can you fix it?'

'Probably. I'll think about it.' He was thinking about something else at the moment—about how badly he wanted to touch her. Just a brush of his thumb along the curve of her throat. He couldn't say why, but he wanted to do that, only that. Annoyed with himself, Jed set aside his glass and picked up the bin. 'I'll take this to the kitchen.'

'Thanks.' She had to swallow. There was something about the way the man looked at her that sent weird jangles through her system. Stupid, she told herself. It had simply been an exhausting day. She started towards the kitchen. 'Really, thanks,' she said again. 'If you hadn't come in, I'd be kicking things.'

'That's all right. I liked watching you kick him out.'

She smiled. 'Why?'

'I didn't like his suit.' He stopped in the doorway.

With the smile still curving her lips, she glanced up. Jed followed her gaze and studied the sprig of mistletoe over his head.

'Cute,' he said, and because he was a man who'd decided to stop taking chances, he started to move past her.

'Hey.' Amused by the situation and his reaction, Dora caught his arm. 'Bad luck,' she told him. Standing up on her toes, she brushed her mouth lightly over his. 'I don't like to risk bad luck.'

He reacted instinctively and brought his mouth down on hers in a kiss that had the blood draining out of her head. Her lips parted helplessly under his. It was quick—seconds only—but when he released her, she rocked back down on her heels, eyes wide.

He stared down at her for a moment, cursing himself and fighting a vicious urge to do exactly what the idiot accountant had tried.

'Lock your door, Conroy,' he said softly. He walked out.

'What are you so cranky about?' Lea demanded. She'd popped back into the storeroom to announce a $500 sale and had been greeted, for the third time that morning, by a short snarl.

'I'm not cranky,' Dora snapped. 'I'm busy.' She was boxing up a place setting of dinnerware.

'I know something's wrong.' Lea crossed her arms. 'Spill it.'

There was no way Dora was going to admit that she'd let one kiss tie her up into knots. She wrapped the last cup in newspaper. 'Where's that stupid packing tape?' She turned, then stumbled back against the desk when she spotted Jed at the base of the stairs.

'I came to see if you still wanted me to fix that banister,' he said.

'Banister? Oh . . . oh, well. You have to get wood or something?' He looked over when Lea firmly cleared her throat.

'Oh, Lea, Jed Skimmerhorn, the new tenant. Jed, my sister, Lea.'

'Nice to meet you.' Lea extended a hand. 'Settling in all right?'

'Not much to settle. Do you want the banister fixed or not?'

'Sure, go ahead.' Dora occupied herself by sealing the carton. 'You can slip the bill under my door if I'm not around.'

He couldn't resist. 'Another hot date?'

She smiled sweetly and yanked open the door. With that, he sauntered out.

'*That*'s the new tenant?' Lea whispered. She hurried to the door to peek through. 'Who is he? Tell,' she demanded. 'Tell all.'

'There's nothing to tell. I went out with Andrew last night and he made a pass at me. Jed met him when I was kicking him out.'

'What does he do? Jed, I mean. He must lift weights or something to have shoulders like that.'

'I never knew you had such a shoulder fixation.'

'I do when they're attached to a body like that one. Let's see, he's a construction worker.'

'You lose the trip for two to Maui. Would you like to try for the matching luggage set?'

'Just tell me.'

Dora had dug up Jed's application. His last place of employment had been the Philadelphia Police Department. 'He's an ex-cop.'

'Ex?' Lea's eyes went wide. 'He was fired from the force?'

'He resigned,' Dora said. 'A few months back. According to the notes Dad took when he called the commissioner of police, Jed's got a potful of commendations, and they're keeping his service revolver warm for him in the hope that he'll come back.'

'Well then, why did he quit?'

'That didn't seem to be anyone's business,' Dora said primly, but she was just as curious. She held up her hand to ward off more questions. 'We'd better get back to helping Terri.'

'All right, but I feel good knowing you've got a cop right across the hall. That should keep you out of trouble.'

UNDER ANY OTHER circumstances DiCarlo would have felt foolish sitting in an elegant reception area holding a cheap porcelain statue in his lap. In this particular reception area, decorated with muted

Impressionist prints and Erté sculptures, he didn't feel foolish at all. He felt scared, bone-scared.

He hadn't really minded putting a small-calibre bullet between Porter's eyes. But, considering his string of bad luck, he wondered whether he had the wrong statue in his lap. It certainly looked like the one he'd seen packed into the crate at Premium Shipping.

'Mr DiCarlo?' the receptionist said. 'Mr Finley can see you.'

'Right. Sure.' DiCarlo rose, hooking the statue under his arm.

Finley didn't rise from his desk. He enjoyed watching DiCarlo nervously cross the ocean of white carpet. He smiled coldly.

'Mr DiCarlo, you have tidied up in the great state of Virginia?'

'Everything there is taken care of.'

'Excellent.' Finley gestured to his desk, so that DiCarlo set the statue down. 'And this is all you've brought me?'

'I have a list of the other merchandise. And all the locations.' DiCarlo dived into his pocket. 'There were only three other buyers, and two of them are also dealers. I think it should be simple enough to go into those shops and buy back that merchandise.'

'You think?' Finley said softly. 'If you could think, Mr DiCarlo, my merchandise would be in my possession. However, I'm willing to let you redeem yourself.' He rose and ran a fingertip over the female face of the statue. 'A hideous piece, don't you agree?'

'Yes, sir.'

Finley picked up an unused marble ashtray from his desk and decapitated the woman. 'An ugly cocoon,' he murmured, 'to protect sheer beauty.' From inside the figurine he pulled a small object wrapped in bubble plastic. Delicately he unwrapped it, and DiCarlo saw what looked like a gold cigarette lighter, heavily ornate.

'Do you know what this is, Mr DiCarlo?'

'Uh, no, sir.'

'It is an étui.' Finley laughed then, caressing the gold. 'This small ornamental case was used to hold manicure sets or sewing implements, perhaps a buttonhook or a snuff spoon. This one is gold, and these stones, Mr DiCarlo, are rubies. There are initials etched into the base.' Smiling dreamily, he turned it over. 'It was a gift from Napoleon to his Josephine. And now it belongs to me.'

'That's great, Mr Finley.' DiCarlo was relieved that he'd brought his employer the right figurine.

'You think so?' Finley's emerald eyes glittered. 'Oh, I'm pleased to have it, but it reminds me that my shipment is incomplete. A shipment, I might add, that has taken me nearly a year to accumulate.' Finley caressed the étui in intimate little circles. 'Tomorrow is Christmas Eve. You have plans, I imagine.'

'Well, actually, yes. My family, you see . . .'

Finley's face lit up with a smile. 'There is nothing like family around the holidays, Mr DiCarlo. I'll give you until the first of the year—No, no, make it the second.' His smile spread and widened. 'I trust you won't disappoint me.'

'No, sir.'

JED COULDN'T SAY why he was doing it. He'd had no business going down to the shop that morning in the first place. He was perfectly content to spend his days working out, lifting weights, catching up on his reading. Lord knew what crazy impulse had had him wandering downstairs and somehow volunteering to fix the banister.

Now he was standing out in the cold, working on it. He was forced to work outside because Dora didn't have ten feet of unoccupied space inside. At least there was no one to bother him in the rear of the building, and he enjoyed working with his hands, liked the feel of wood under them. Once, he'd considered adding a small workshop onto the back of the house in Chestnut Hill. But that had been before Donny Speck. Before the investigation that had become an obsession.

And, of course, it had been before Elaine had paid the price.

Before Jed could switch off his mind, he saw it again. The silver Mercedes saloon sitting under the carport. He saw her blue eyes look with annoyance in his direction. He saw himself racing across the manicured lawn, between the rosebushes. Then the explosion had ripped through the air and sent him flying back. He hoped she'd felt nothing after her fingers had twisted the key in the ignition and triggered the bomb.

Swearing, Jed attacked the new banister with the power sander. It was over. Elaine was dead and couldn't be brought back. Donny Speck was dead. And however much Jed might have wished it, he couldn't kill the man again.

And he was exactly where he wanted to be. Alone.

DICARLO WAS FEELING FINE. His luck was back; the rented Porsche was tearing up Route 95. Boxed on the seat beside him were a bronze eagle and a Statue of Liberty, both from a novelty shop outside Washington DC, as well as the stuffed parrot from Virginia. After a quick detour to Philadelphia to pick up the last two items on his list, he would make it to New York in time for holiday celebrations.

The day after Christmas he would take up his schedule again. At this pace, he figured he would have all Mr Finley's merchandise in hand well before deadline. He might even earn a bonus.

He dialled Finley's private number on the car phone.

'Mr Finley. DiCarlo. I've recovered three more items—two from DC and the other one from Virginia. I'm on my way to Philadelphia now. The last two items are in a shop there.'

'Then I'll wish you Merry Christmas now, Mr DiCarlo. If you have something to report, you'll leave a message with Winesap.'

'I'll keep in touch, Mr Finley. Enjoy your holiday.'

DiCarlo walked into Dora's Parlor fifteen minutes before closing. He noticed a statuesque redhead wearing a green elf's cap.

Terri Starr beamed at DiCarlo. 'Merry Christmas,' she said. 'You've just caught us. We're closing early today.'

DiCarlo tried a smile. 'I bet you hate us eleventh-hour shoppers.'

'Are you kidding? I love them.' She'd already spotted the Porsche at the kerb and was calculating ending the business day with a whopping sale. 'Are you looking for anything in particular?'

'Actually, yes.' DiCarlo took a look around, hoping to spot either the painting or the china hound quickly. 'I'm on my way home, and I have an aunt who collects animal statues. Dogs in particular.'

'I might be able to help you.' Terri led him to a curved glass cabinet and took out an apple-green, carved Fo dog, one of their most expensive jade pieces. 'Gorgeous, isn't he?'

'I'm afraid my aunt's tastes aren't quite so sophisticated.'

'Let's see, then.' With some regret Terri replaced the jade. 'We've got a couple of nice cocker spaniels in plaster.'

'I'll take a look. Would it be all right if I just browsed around?'

'You go right ahead. Take your time.'

DiCarlo saw the plaster cockers. He saw cloisonné poodles, blown-glass retrievers, but not the china hound. He kept his eye peeled for the painting as well. There were dozens of framed prints, advertising posters. There was no abstract in an ebony frame.

'I think I've found the perfect thing.' Terri came up to him. 'It's Staffordshire pottery, a mamma English sheepdog and her puppy.'

DiCarlo kept a pleasant smile in place even after he'd spotted the four-figure price tag. 'I had something a little different in my mind, but this is Aunt Maria all over.' He pulled out a credit card. 'She used to have this mutt, you see,' he continued as he followed Terri to the counter. 'A brown and white spotted dog who slept curled up on the rug. I was hoping to find something that looked like him.'

'Too bad you weren't in a few days ago.' Terri nestled the Staffordshire in tissue paper. 'We had a piece very much like that. In china, a Basset hound. It was only here a day before we sold it.'

'Sold it?' DiCarlo said between smiling teeth. 'That's too bad.'

'It wasn't nearly as fine a piece as the one you've just bought,

Mr ... DiCarlo,' she added after a glance at his credit card.

'I'm sure you're right. I notice you also carry art.'

'Some. Mostly posters and family portraits from estate sales.'

'Nothing modern, then? I'm doing some redecorating.'

'Afraid not. I haven't noticed any paintings in the storeroom.'

While she wrote out his bill, DiCarlo drummed his fingers on the counter. If it hadn't been broad daylight, he might have stuck his gun under the salesgirl's pretty chin and forced her to look up who had bought the dog. Of course, then he'd have to kill her.

'Just sign here.' Terri passed him the sales slip and his card. 'I hope you and your aunt have a terrific Christmas, Mr DiCarlo.'

He'd go somewhere for a late lunch. When it was dark, when the shop was empty, he'd be back.

DORA GAVE JED'S DOOR her best businesslike rap. She knew he would growl at her when he opened it. He didn't disappoint her.

His short-sleeved sweatshirt was damp with sweat. His forearms glistened with it. Scowling, he gripped the ends of a towel he'd hooked round his neck. 'What do you want?'

'I see you're your usual bright and cheerful self.' She spotted his weight equipment scattered over the living area. 'My phone's out of order. I need to make a call.'

'There's a booth on the corner.'

'You're such a sweet guy, Skimmerhorn. Why hasn't some lucky woman snapped you up?'

'I beat them off with a stick.'

'Oh, I bet you do. Be a pal. It's a local call.'

For a minute she thought he was going to shut the door in her face. Again. But he swung the door wider and stepped back. 'Make it fast,' he told her, and stalked away.

Dora jiggled the phone, then swore softly. 'Yours is out, too.'

He looked at her, intrigued now rather than annoyed. 'You always dress like that to talk on the phone?'

She was wearing a slithery jumpsuit in silver, with strappy spiked heels. 'I have a couple of parties to drop in on. How about you? Are you spending Christmas Eve lifting weights?'

'I don't like parties. Why don't you run along?' He tossed the towel aside and picked up a dumbbell.

She sat on the arm of the couch, frowning, as she watched Jed lift his weights. She shouldn't feel sorry for him, she mused. He was the last person on earth to inspire sympathy. And yet she hated to imagine him spending the evening alone, with barbells. 'Why don't you come with me?'

306

The long, silent look he sent her had her hurrying on.

'It's not a proposition, Skimmerhorn. Just a couple of parties. It's Christmas Eve. A time of fellowship. You might have heard of it.'

'Take off, Conroy.'

She sighed, rose. 'Enjoy your sweat, Skimmerhorn.' She stopped. 'What's that noise?' Her eyes narrowed in concentration.

He lowered the dumbbell and listened. 'Someone down in the shop. The sound carries up through the vent.'

She froze. 'We closed hours ago. Terri left by three thirty.' Dora's heels clicked smartly on the floor as she crossed to the door.

'Where are you going?'

'Downstairs, of course. Somebody must have cut the alarm and broken in. They're in for a surprise.'

He took her arm and pushed her into a chair. 'Stay there.' He strode into the bedroom, then returned carrying a .38.

Her eyes rounded. 'What's that?'

'It's a parasol. Stay in here. Lock the door.' Jed closed the door behind him. It was probably Dora's assistant, he thought as he moved silently down the hall. But there was too much cop in him to take chances. And to dismiss the fact that the phones were out.

He reached the door that led down to the storeroom, eased it open. He heard a sound—a drawer closing.

A movement behind him had him braced and pivoting. And swearing under his breath. Dora was three steps back, a dumbbell hefted in one hand. Jed jerked a thumb. She shook her head.

He started down, halting when the third step groaned under his foot. There was a rapid series of pops, and the wall inches away from his face spat plaster.

Jed crouched, sprinted down the rest of the steps, rolling when he hit bottom and coming up, weapon drawn, in time to see the rear door slam shut. He hit the door at a run, went through low. The cold air bit into his lungs, like slivers of ice. He raced after the sound of running footsteps. After about two blocks, he heard the roar of an engine, the squeal of tyres, and he knew he'd lost his quarry. When he returned, he found Dora standing in the small gravel driveway, shivering.

Her fear had already turned to anger. 'Your face is bleeding.'

'Yeah?' He brushed at his cheek and his fingers came away wet. 'The plaster must have nipped it.' He looked down at the dumbbell she still carried. 'And what were you going to do with that?'

'When he wrestled you to the ground, I was going to hit him with it. Weren't you supposed to call for back-up or something?'

'I'm not a cop any more.'

Yes, you are, she thought. In your eyes, in your moves. Saying nothing, she followed him towards the rear entrance of the shop.

'Ever heard of security systems?' he asked.

'I have one. It's supposed to clang if anyone tries to get in.'

'Mickey Mouse,' Jed said in disgust after one look at the mechanism. 'All you have to do is cut a couple of wires.' He held out the frayed ends. 'This guy took out the phone for good measure. He'd have seen by the lights that there was somebody upstairs.'

Her teeth were chattering. 'Then he was stupid, wasn't he?'

'Maybe he was in a hurry. Don't you have a coat?'

'Silly of me not to have thought to grab my wrap. What was that popping noise right before you took your heroic flight downstairs?'

'Silencer.' Jed checked his pocket for loose change.

'Silencer?' The word came out in a squeak as she grabbed his arm. 'Like in gangster movies? He was shooting at you?'

'I don't think it was personal. We'd better call this in.'

Her hand slid away from his arm. 'He could have shot you.'

'Got a quarter on you?'

'I have a phone in my van.'

He strode over to her van, shaking his head when he found it unlocked. He punched in Brent's number and waited for two rings.

'Merry Christmas!'

'Hi, Mary Pat.' He could hear children yelling in the background over a forceful recording of 'Jingle Bells'.

'Jed, you're not calling with a lame excuse about tomorrow?'

'No, I'll be there. M.P., is Brent around?'

'Right here, making his famous sausage stuffing. Hang on.'

There was a clatter. 'Hey, Captain. Merry Christmas.'

'Sorry to bust in on your cooking, but we had a little problem over here. Break-in. The shop below the apartment.'

'They get anything?'

'I have to have her check.' He watched Dora shiver. 'Took a couple of pops at me. Used a silencer.'

'Jeez. You hit?'

'No.' The bleeding on his cheek had nearly stopped. 'He had a car close. From the sound of the engine, it wasn't an economy.'

'Sit tight, Kemo Sabe. I'll call it in and be on my way.'

'Thanks.' Jed hung up and looked at Dora. 'Come on.' He took her frozen hands, warming them as they walked back to the shop. 'You can take a look around, see if anything is missing.'

He took a brief glance at the jemmied lock, then closed out the cold. After he'd switched on the lights, he simply stood and absorbed. The storeroom was crammed with boxes. Shelves held uncrated merchandise in no sort of order he could discern. There was a desk, which seemed to be an island of sanity. It held a phone, a lamp, a porcelain pitcher stuffed with pencils and pens, and a bust of Beethoven that served as a paperweight.

'Nothing's gone,' Dora said.

'How can you tell?'

'I know my stock. You must have scared him off.'

'What about cash?'

'We deposit everything but about a hundred in small bills and change every night.' She walked over to the desk, opened the top drawer and took out an envelope. 'Here it is.' She turned to check the files. 'Look at this. These drawers are a mess.'

He came to peer over her shoulder. 'So he was after something in your files.'

'It's just business stuff.' Baffled, she ran a hand through her hair. 'There's no reason for anyone to break in here for paperwork. A crazed IRS agent? A psychopathic accountant?' As soon as she'd said it, Dora bit her tongue.

'What was that jerk's name the other night?'

'Don't be ridiculous. Andrew would never do anything like this.'

'Andrew what?'

She blew out a long breath. 'I'll give you his name and address. Then you can go do cop things like harass him for an alibi.'

'I'm not a cop.'

'If it looks like a cop, sounds like a cop . . .' She dropped her gaze, then lifted it slowly. 'You're tough, authoritative, a little mean.'

'I can be meaner.' He edged closer to her.

'Did I tell you I've always had this problem with authority?'

'Well, you're lousy at taking orders. I told you to stay put.'

She lifted her hand, rubbed her thumb over the cut on his cheek. 'You scared me. Were you scared?'

'No. I love having people shoot at me.'

'Then this is probably just a reaction we're having.' She slid her arms round his neck and liked the fit. 'You know, from the shock.'

Her lips were curved when his mouth came down. He knew it was a mistake. Even as he kissed her deeply, he knew. Somehow she'd already dug a hook into his mind he'd been unable to shake loose. Now she was trembling against him. He drew back, wanting to clear his head, but she pulled him towards her.

He was still sane enough at that moment to hear the spit of gravel under tyres outside and the rattle at the door upstairs.

'The troops are here.' He took Dora by the shoulders and set her firmly aside. She saw in his eyes what he would continue to deny. He was a cop again. 'Why don't you go put on some coffee, Conroy?

It doesn't look like you'll make your parties after all.'

She started up the stairs, her back to him. 'And that's it?'

'Yeah. That's it.'

DORA HAD BRANDY. Jed drank coffee. Wanting to ignore him as completely as he was ignoring her, she curled herself onto the couch and studied the cheerful lights of her Christmas tree.

She liked Jed's pal, though, Lieutenant Brent Chapman, with his wrinkled slacks and easy grin. He'd come in smelling of sausage and cinnamon, his heavy hornrims magnifying mild brown eyes. His questions were slow and thoughtful, his manner reassuring.

No, there was nothing missing as far as she could tell.

No, there was nothing in the files of any monetary value.

Yes, the shop had been crowded the past couple of weeks, but no, she couldn't remember anyone acting suspicious.

Enemies? This brought on a quick laugh. No.

'Tell him about the bean-counter,' Jed ordered her.

'For heaven's sake. Andrew wouldn't—'

'Dawd,' Jed interrupted. 'Andrew Dawd, accountant. He put some moves on her, so she gave him his walking papers.'

'I see.' Brent scribbled the name in his dogeared notepad. He would have liked to smile, but the gleam in Dora's eye warned him to keep a sober countenance. 'It wouldn't hurt to talk with him,' Brent pointed out gently. He picked up one of the cookies she'd spread on a pretty fluted dish. 'Great cookies.'

'Thanks. Why not take some home? You've got kids, don't you?'

'Three.' Brent reached for his wallet to show off pictures. While Jed rolled his eyes and paced away, Dora rose to admire the snapshots. There were two girls and a boy, all spit and polish for school pictures.

'That's Carly. She's ten,' Brent said. 'Fifth grade at Bester Elementary.'

'My niece Missy's in fifth at Bester, too.' They beamed at each other. 'I bet they know each other.'

'That wouldn't be Missy Bradshaw, would it?' Brent asked.

'Yes, that's right.'

'She's been to the house a dozen times. They live a block over. Missy's parents and my wife and I are in the same car pool.'

'Would you two like to be alone?' Jed asked.

'Tell me, Brent, is he always so crabby?' Dora said.

'Pretty much.' He tucked his wallet away and rose. 'But he was the best cop I ever worked with, so you can feel safe with him.'

'Thanks. I'll get those cookies.' She walked to the kitchen.

'Some landlord,' Brent commented, and wiggled his eyebrows.

'Get a grip. How soon will you have anything on the slugs?'

'It's Christmas, Jed. Give the lab boys a few days.'

Dora walked back in, carrying a paper plate covered with foil.

'Thanks, Miss Conroy.'

'Dora. You will let me know if you find out anything?'

'Count on it. You just relax. Merry Christmas.'

'I'll walk you out.' Jed nodded to Dora. 'I'll be back.'

As they walked down the hall, Brent said, 'You've been here what, about a week? How'd you get her mad already?'

'It's a gift. Look, why do you figure a pro would break into a junk shop and rifle a bunch of paperwork?'

'That's the sixty-four-thousand-dollar question.' Brent walked through the rear door, sucking in his breath at the slap of wind.

'And what would anyone look for in the files of a junk shop?'

Brent opened his car door. 'You can take the boy off the force, but you can't take the force out of the boy.'

'I take a personal interest when somebody shoots at me.'

'Can't blame you for that. We miss you downtown, Captain.'

'Save it.' He wasn't in the mood for a lecture or a pep talk or a guilt trip. 'Let me know what comes through.'

'You'll be the first.' Brent climbed into the car.

Jed headed back inside. He wanted to make certain Dora was locked up for the night before he went back downstairs for another look. Just as an interested civilian, he told himself.

'They've cleared out,' he told her when he breezed through her open door. 'You can count on Brent. He's a good detail man.'

'Terrific. Listen, I've got to ask. I know what you'll say—not to worry, it was just one of those freak things that happen. But I have to ask anyway. Do you think whoever was here before will be back?'

Jed studied her face. There was a strain in her eyes she'd done a good job of hiding up until now. 'I don't know,' he said flatly.

'Great.' Dora closed her eyes, drew a deep breath. 'I should have known better than to ask. If you can't figure out what the guy was doing here, how can you tell if he'll be back or not?'

He could have lied, Jed told himself, uneasy that her cheeks had gone pale. 'Look.' He rose, and surprised them both by reaching out to tuck her hair behind her ear. 'I don't think you've got anything to worry about tonight. You need to go to bed. Let the cops do their job.'

'Yeah. I'll be out most of tomorrow—at my sister's. I'll leave you the number just in case.'

'Fine. Lock up behind me. OK?' He stepped into the hall.

'You bet. You, too. Lock up, I mean.'

'Sure.' He waited until she'd closed and bolted the door. Then he went down to take another look at the storeroom.

IN A PRETTY Federal town house shaded by stately oaks, a well-to-do matron was enjoying a glass of sherry and a showing of Bing Crosby's *White Christmas* on her big-screen TV.

At the sound of a quiet footstep behind her, Mrs Lyle smiled. 'Come watch, Muriel,' she invited, addressing her housekeeper.

She didn't cry out when the blow came. The crystal wineglass shattered against the edge of the coffee table, splattering the Aubusson rug with blood-red sherry. Somewhere through the haze of pain that left her paralysed, Mrs Lyle heard the crashing of glass and a furious male voice demanding over and over, 'Where is the dog?'

Then she heard nothing at all.

IT WAS MIDNIGHT when DiCarlo rode the elevator up to his Manhattan apartment. His arms were laden with boxes. He'd been lucky to find the receipt for the stupid dog, he told himself, and wondered idly if the bullets he'd sprayed up the stairs of the antique shop had hit anything. Or anyone.

Not to worry, he thought. The gun was untraceable. And he was making progress. He had the bronze eagle, the plaster Statue of Liberty, the parrot, the china dog.

And a partridge in a pear tree, he thought, and chuckled.

5

So . . .' Dora snacked on a raw carrot while Lea checked the Christmas goose. 'Jed races out after the guy, waving a gun, while I stand there like a Hollywood heroine, clutching my hands.'

'Thank goodness you weren't hurt.' Harassed by the number of pots simmering on the stove, the sound of her children wreaking havoc in the family room and the very real fear that her mother would invade the kitchen at any moment, Lea shuddered.

'The cops came and did all this cop stuff—Dad would have loved the staging—and asked all these questions.' Dora purposely left out the part about the bullets. 'It turns out Jed's ex-partner is your neighbour. Carly Chapman's father. She goes to school with Missy.'

Lea lifted a lid and sniffed. 'Oh, yeah. Brent and Mary Pat.'

'Here's the good part. They're going to question Andrew.'

'You're kidding. Andrew?'

'Jilted accountant seeks revenge by destroying woman's tax files.' Dora ate a broccoli spear and shrugged. 'When's dinner?'

'Twenty minutes. If we can keep Mom busy for—' She broke off, swore under her breath as Trixie Conroy made her entrance.

Trixie always made an entrance, whether it was onto a stage or into a market. She'd dressed for the simple family dinner in a flowing caftan of bleeding colours that billowed round her willowy form. Her hair, cropped gamine-short, was a bold red. Her milk-pale face was striking. The blue eyes were lavishly lashed.

'Darlings!' Trixie's voice was as dramatic as the rest of her. 'It's so lovely to see my two girls together. Oh, and those glorious aromas. I do hope you're not overheating my meatballs, Ophelia.'

'Ah . . . ' Lea sent Dora a desperate look. 'No, of course not.' Lea hadn't heated them at all but had stuck them under the sink with hopes of palming them off on the dog later. 'Mom, did you know someone broke into Dora's shop last night?'

'Oh my baby. Oh my lamb.' Trixie rushed across the kitchen to clasp Dora's face between her heavily ringed hands. 'Are you hurt?'

'Of course not.'

'Why don't you take Mom in the other room, Dora? Sit down and tell her about it?'

'Yes, yes, you must.' Trixie gripped Dora's hand. Dora glared at Lea before she was yanked into the fray.

The Bradshaw family room was in chaos. Toys were strewn everywhere. There were shouts and yips as a remote-controlled police cruiser, operated by Michael, terrorised the family dog, Mutsy. Will Conroy, looking very New York in a dark silk shirt, entertained Missy on the piano. Richie and his father were glassy-eyed over a Nintendo game, and Quentin was well plied with eggnog.

'Quentin.' Trixie's stage voice froze all action. 'Our child was threatened.'

'I wasn't, Mom.' Dora eased her mother into a chair. 'The shop was broken into. They didn't get anything. Jed scared them off.'

'I'd've shot him dead.' Richie fired an imaginary weapon.

'Dora, you called the police?' John asked.

'Yes.' She scooped up Richie. 'And the investigating officer is the father of your good friend, frogface. Jody Chapman.'

'Jody Chapman!' Richie made gagging noises.

'She sends her love.' Dora smacked her lips. The resulting din of groans and shrieks had her convinced that the crisis had passed.

'Willowby!' Trixie cut through the noise. 'You'll stay at Isadora's tonight. I won't feel safe if your sister's alone.'

'No problem,' Will said.

'Mother knows best.' Quentin rose to kiss his wife's hand.

Will grimaced. 'What is that stench?'

'Dinner,' Lea announced, swinging through the kitchen door. 'Sorry, Mom, I seem to have burned your meatballs.'

A BLOCK AWAY, Jed was trying to ease himself out of the door. He'd enjoyed Christmas dinner at the Chapmans' more than he'd anticipated. It was hard not to get a kick out of the kids, who were still enthusiastic over their Christmas loot. Impossible not to relax with the scents of pine and turkey and apple pie sweetening the air.

But there was no way to avoid comparing the homy family scene with his own miserable childhood memories of the holiday. The shouting matches. Or worse, the frigid, smothering silences.

Mary Pat was heaping turkey leftovers into a plastic container. 'Tell me about this landlord of yours, Jed. Brent said she's gorgeous. Why don't you bring her over some time?'

'I pay her rent; I don't socialise with her.'

'You chased a bad guy for her,' Mary Pat pointed out.

'That was reflex. I gotta go.' He picked up the food container she'd just sealed. 'Thanks for dinner.'

Her arm round Brent's waist, Mary Pat waved goodbye to Jed's retreating figure. 'You know, he needs someone in his life.'

'He needs to come back to work.'

WHEN JED KNOCKED on Dora's door a little after nine on the day after Christmas, the last thing he expected was to hear a man's voice saying, 'Wait a minute.' There was a thud, a curse.

Will, a flowered sheet wrapped around his thin frame like a toga, and favouring the toe he'd just smashed, opened the door with a sneer. 'If you're selling anything,' he said, 'I hope it's coffee.'

She sure could pick them, Jed thought nastily. First an accountant with overactive glands, now a skinny kid barely out of college.

'Isadora,' Jed said, and showed his teeth.

'Sure.' Mindful of the trailing sheet, Will moved back so that Jed could step inside. 'Where the heck is she?' he muttered. 'Dora!'

Jed noticed, intrigued, the tangle of blankets on the sofa.

'You're not getting in here until I dry my hair.' Dora stepped out of the bathroom, dressed in a towelling robe and armed with a hair dryer. 'You can just—Oh.' She spotted Jed. 'Good morning.'

'I need to talk to you for a minute.'

'All right. You met my brother?'

Brother, Jed thought, annoyed with his sense of relief. 'No.'

'The guy in the sheet is Will. Will, the guy who needs a shave is Jed, from across the hall.'

'The ex-cop who chased off the burglar.' Will's sleep-glazed eyes cleared. 'Nice to meet you.'

'Here.' Dora passed Will the hair dryer. 'You can use the shower.' He headed off, trailing the sheet.

314

'My mother thought I needed a man in the house after the break-in,' Dora explained. 'We can talk in the kitchen.'

She put a kettle on to boil and scooped coffee beans into the grinder before she spoke again.

'So how was your Christmas?'

'Fine. I've got a guy coming by around noon to hook up a new security system. He's a friend of mine. He knows what he's doing.'

'A friend. Incredible. You might have discussed it with me.'

'You weren't around. You need real locks on the doors.'

Her lips pursed, Dora measured coffee into a filter cone. 'I'm debating whether to be amused, annoyed or impressed.'

'I can pick up the locks at the hardware store. I'll bill you.'

That decided her. Her smile turned into a quick laugh. 'OK, Skimmerhorn. Go make our little world safe. Anything else?'

'I figured I might measure for those shelves you want.'

'As it happens, we're not opening until noon today. Why don't you set the table for breakfast? Will makes terrific crepes.' Before he could answer, the kettle shrilled. Dora poured boiling water over the coffee. The smell was all it took.

'Where do you keep your plates?' he asked.

'First cupboard.'

'One thing,' he said, opening the cabinet. 'You might want to put some clothes on.' He sent her a slow smile. 'The sight of your damp, half-naked body might send me into a frenzy.' Dora poured her coffee and walked towards the bathroom.

'Smells good.' Will strolled in, now wearing jeans and a sweater. His hair, lighter than Dora's, had been blow-dried into artful disarray. 'Hey, would you mind switching on the tube? CNN, maybe. I haven't heard what's been happening for a couple of days.' Will poured both himself and Jed a cup before rolling up his sleeves.

He measured ingredients and stirred with careless finesse. 'So this burglary thing. Do you think it's anything to worry about?'

'I always worry when somebody shoots at me.'

'Shoot? What do you mean "shoot"?'

'A gun. Bullets.' Jed sipped his coffee. 'Bang.'

'She didn't say anything about shooting.' He dashed into the living room and down the hall and opened the bathroom door.

Dora nearly poked her eye out with her eye pencil. 'Will!'

'You didn't say anything about shooting, Dory.'

She sighed, giving Jed a hard stare over Will's shoulder. 'Thanks loads, Skimmerhorn.'

'Don't blame him.' Incensed, Will took Dora by the shoulders and shook. 'I want to know exactly what happened. Now.'

'Then ask the big-nosed cop.' She gave Will a shove. 'I'm busy,' she said, and shut the bathroom door, deliberately locking it.

Will turned towards Jed. 'Fill me in while I make breakfast.'

'There's not much to tell.' There was a sick feeling in Jed's gut. It didn't come from running over events while Will whipped up apple crepes. It came from watching the brother and sister together, in seeing Will's concern and anger—emotions that came from a deeply rooted love, not simply from family loyalty.

'So that's it?' Will demanded. 'Some joker breaks in, messes with the files, takes a couple of pot shots and runs away. Why?'

'That's what the police are paid to find out. Look, she'll be safe.'

'What kind of a cop were you?' Will asked.

'That's irrelevant, isn't it? I'm not a cop now.'

'Yeah, but . . .' Will trailed off, frowning down at the crepes he was scooping onto a platter. 'Skimmerhorn. Name sticks in the mind. I remember something from a few months ago. I'm a news junkie. Captain, right? Captain Skimmerhorn. You blew away Donny Speck. "Millionaire cop in shoot-out with drug baron." ' Will remembered the headline. He would have pressed, but there was more. The assassination of Skimmerhorn's sister with a car bomb. 'I guess anyone who could take out Speck ought to be able to look out for my sister.'

Dora came in to answer the ringing kitchen phone. 'Hello . . . Yes, Will's here. One minute.' Dora fluttered her lashes. 'Marlene.'

'Oh. I might be a while.' Will took the phone from his sister.

'Why didn't you tell him the whole story?' Jed asked Dora.

Dora kept her voice low. 'I didn't see any need to worry my family. They tend to be dramatic under the best of circumstances. My mother would have called the CIA and hired bodyguards. As it was, she stuck me with Will.'

'He's all right,' Jed said just as Will made kissy noises into the phone. Jed savoured the crepes and grinned into his coffee.

Dora rose. 'Since he's busy, I'm turning off the television.' She had nearly tapped the off button when a bulletin stopped her.

'There are still no leads in the Christmas tragedy in Society Hill,' the reporter announced. 'Prominent socialite Alice Lyle remains in a coma this morning as a result of an attack during an apparent burglary in her home on December 24th. Mrs Lyle was found unconscious. Muriel Doyle, the housekeeper, was dead at the scene. The two were discovered by Mrs Lyle's niece. A police spokesperson has stated that a full investigation is under way.'

'Oh, Lord. I know her. She was in the shop before Christmas, buying a gift for her niece. She bought a couple of doorstops. Her niece was expecting a baby.' Dora shuddered. 'How awful.'

'You can't take it to heart.' Jed got up to turn off the television.

'Is that what they teach in cop school?' she snapped, then immediately shook her head. 'Sorry. That's why I never listen to the news.' She struggled to shake off the mood. 'I think I'll open early.'

'It's tough when they're not strangers.'

'It's tough when they are. Is that why you quit?' Dora asked.

'No. I'll head out to the hardware store. Thanks for breakfast.'

Dora merely sighed when the door closed behind him. 'Will, when you finish your call, do the dishes. I'm going to the shop.'

'I'm finished.' He popped out of the kitchen. 'You're full of secrets, aren't you, Dory? How come you didn't tell me that your tenant was the big bad cop who took down Donny Speck?'

'Who's Donny Speck?'

'Jeez, what world do you live in? Speck ran one of the biggest drug cartels on the East Coast—probably the biggest. He was crazy, too. Liked to blow people up if they messed with him. Always used a pipe bomb triggered by the ignition. Jed whacked him in a real old-fashioned gunfight.'

'Killed him?' Dora asked through dry lips.

'I think he got a medal for it. It was all over the news last summer. The fact that he's the grandson of L.T. Bester Incorporated got him a lot of press, too.'

'Bester Inc? As in large quantities of money?'

'None other. Real estate, Dora. Shopping malls. Philadelphia doesn't have too many loaded cops.'

'Then why would he be renting a one-bedroom apartment?'

Will began to clear the table. 'The way I see it, the wealthy police captain is taking some time off. Last summer was pretty hairy. The Speck investigation kept him in the news for months. Then when his sister died in the car explosion—'

'Wait.' She gripped Will's arm. 'His sister?'

'They figured it was Speck, but I don't think they ever proved it.'

'Oh, that's horrible.' Paling, she pressed a hand to her stomach.

'Worse—he saw it happen. Pretty tough. The tabloids got a lot of play out of it, too. The sister'd been divorced three or four times. The parents used to have public brawls. There was stuff about Jed getting in scrapes as a juvenile. You know how people like to read about wealthy families suffering.'

'No wonder he wants to be left alone,' Dora murmured. 'But that's not the answer.' What she didn't know about Jed Skimmerhorn could apparently fill a football stadium. She leaned over and kissed Will's cheek. 'Lock up when you leave. See you New Year's?'

'Wouldn't miss it.'

THE CONROY WOMAN was asking for trouble, Jed thought grimly as he sent the power saw ripping through a board. He wasn't scared of her. Damned if he was. But she sure made him nervous.

He'd be stupid not to admit he liked the way she looked. She wasn't any wilting pushover, either. He admired the way she'd taken on the accountant, her fists raised and fire in her eye. Jed grinned.

He wasn't going to let her get to him. After all, he mused, he'd been raised to be suspicious and aloof, in the best Skimmerhorn tradition. His years on the force had only heightened the tendency.

Jed gathered up the timber and headed back inside. She was in the storeroom, sitting at her desk. Before he could come up with an appropriately sarcastic comment, he saw her face. Her cheeks were dead white, her eyes dark and gleaming.

'Bad news?' he said. When she didn't answer, he set the timber aside. 'Dora?' He stepped in front of the desk.

She lifted her face. One of the tears swimming in her eyes spilled over and slipped down her cheek. She blinked, spilling another.

'What is it?'

Battling fiercely for control, she shook her head.

'Do you want me to get your sister?' he asked.

'No.' Dora pressed her lips together. After a moment she sniffled and said, 'I met this other dealer on a buying trip right before Christmas. I just called down there to see if he had this piece my last customer wanted.' She took a long breath. 'He's dead. He was killed during a burglary last week.'

'I'm sorry.'

'I only met him once. I outbid him for a couple of lots. Lea and I went by his shop after the auction.' Her voice broke. 'He was killed the next night. That was his grandson on the phone.'

'Did they catch the guy?'

'No. I don't know the details. I didn't want to ask. How do you handle it?' she demanded, gripping Jed's hand with an urgency that surprised them both. 'How do you handle being close to the horrible, day in and day out?'

'You don't look at things the same way as a civilian. You can't.'

'Did you leave because you stopped looking at things like a cop?'

'That's part of it.' He pulled his hand away, distanced himself.

'I don't think that's a good reason.'

'I did.'

'Interesting choice of tense, Skimmerhorn.' She rose, wishing her stomach wasn't still so shaky. 'You should have said "I do"—unless you've changed your mind. I've got to go talk to Lea now.'

318

6

Dora loved a party. It didn't matter if she didn't know a single soul, as long as there was music, interesting food and plenty of people.

As it happened, she knew a great many people attending the Winter Ball. Some were friends; some were customers; some were patrons of her family's theatre. She mingled, moving from group to group to exchange pecks on the cheek and fresh gossip. Though she'd taken a chance wearing a strapless white gown, the press of bodies comfortably heated the room.

'Darling, you look fabulous.' Ashley Draper, a social climber of the first order, swooped down on Dora in a cloud of Opium.

Dora was amused. 'You look radiant, Ashley.'

'You're a dear to say so, even though I know I'm a bit washed-out. The holidays are so fatiguing, aren't they? We missed you the other night at the Bergermans' Christmas Eve.'

'I was . . . unexpectedly detained.'

'I hope he was worth it,' Ashley purred, then grabbed Dora's hand in a crushing grip. 'Look. The *grande dame* herself. Honoria Skimmerhorn Rodgers. She rarely puts in an appearance here.'

'Who?' Dora craned her neck but lost the rest of Ashley's explanation the minute she saw Jed. 'Surprise, surprise,' she murmured. 'Excuse me, Ashley, I have to go see a man about a tux.'

And he did look fabulous in it, she mused as she circled the ballroom to come up behind him. 'I know,' she said at his shoulder. 'You're undercover for the force.' She caught his soft oath as he turned. 'What is it—a ring of insidious cat burglars?'

'Conroy. Do you have to be everywhere? It's bad enough I have to be here at all without—'

'Jedidiah!' Honoria's authoritative voice halted any complaints. 'Have you lost whatever slight degree of manners I managed to teach you? Introduce your friend to your grandmother.'

'Grandmother?' Dora said.

Honoria's snowy hair was softly coiffed around her face, and her gown of royal blue set off her eyes and stately figure. Diamonds glittered at her throat, at her ears.

Dora took her narrow-boned hand. 'I'm delighted to meet you, Mrs Skimmerhorn. It destroys my theory that Jed was hatched from a very hard-shelled, very stale egg.'

'His social graces are lacking.' Honoria studied Dora with growing interest. 'And it's Mrs Rodgers, my dear. I was briefly married to Walter Skimmerhorn but rectified that as soon as possible.'

'I'm Dora Conroy, Jed's landlord.'

'Ah.' There was a world of expression in the single syllable.

'Grandmother.' Very deliberately Jed took her arm. 'Let me get you some hors d'oeuvres.'

'I'm capable of getting my own.' Just as deliberately she shook him off. 'Dance with the girl, Jedidiah.'

'Yeah, Jedidiah,' Dora said as Honoria swept off. 'Dance with the girl. Your grandma's watching.' She tugged on the sleeve of his tux.

Jed took her arm. 'Don't you have a date around here?'

'No,' Dora said as they took the floor. 'I don't usually like to bring a date to a party. Then I'd have to worry if he was having a good time. I prefer having one myself.' The orchestra was playing a silky version of 'Twilight Time'. 'You're a nice dancer, Skimmerhorn. Better than Andrew.'

'Thanks a lot. Andrew's clean, by the way. He was at his office Christmas party.'

'Of course he's clean. He washes behind his ears.'

'Why did you ever go out with him in the first place?'

'He was talking about the new tax law. I was terrified not to.' She tilted her head and smiled. 'So are you having a good time?'

'I hate these things.' It was a shame, he thought, that Dora felt so incredibly good in his arms. 'You probably love them.'

'Oh, I do.'

He slid a hand up her back, encountered bare skin. 'Do you ever go out at night in anything that doesn't glitter?'

'Not if I can help it. Don't you like the dress?'

'What there is of it.' The song ended and another began, but he'd forgotten he didn't want to dance with her. Honoria glided by in the arms of a distinguished-looking man. 'You look OK, Conroy.'

'My! Are you exuding charm for your grandmother's sake?'

He looked down at her again. Something in her smile encouraged one of his own. 'She liked you.'

'I'm a likeable person.'

'No you're not. You're a pain in the ass.' He stroked his hand up and down her bare back. 'A very sexy pain in the ass.'

'I'm getting to you, Jed.'

'Maybe.' He dipped his head and brushed her mouth with his.

She ignored the curious heads turning their way and kept her mouth an inch away from his. 'We could go home tonight and tear each other's clothes off . . . '

'An interesting image, Conroy, but it sounds like there's an "or" coming.'

'Or,' she said and tried to smile. 'We could be friends first.'

'Who said I wanted to be your friend?'

'You won't be able to help yourself because everyone needs a friend. Because it's hard to be alone in a room full of people, but you are.'

He rested his brow against hers. 'I don't want to care about you, Dora. I don't want to care about—'

'Anything?' she finished for him. When she looked up into his eyes, her heart broke. 'You're not dead,' she murmured.

'Close enough.' He pulled himself back. 'I want a drink.'

She went with him to the bar, ordered champagne while he chose Scotch. 'Tell you what.' Her voice was light again. 'We'll try something new. I won't give you a hard time—and vice versa.'

He studied her. 'What's left?'

'We'll be agreeable, have a good time. Let's check out the buffet.'

They went over together. She heaped food on the plate, then generously held it out to share. He plucked a cube of cheese from her plate while she sampled a thumb-sized spinach pastry.

'Try one of these, Skimmerhorn,' she said with her mouth full, and picked up another pastry. Before he could accept or refuse, she had it up to his mouth and in. 'Great, huh?'

'Jed.' A hand clamped on his shoulder. Jed braced, turned.

'Commissioner,' Jed said, both his face and voice neutral.

'Good to see you.' Police Commissioner James Riker gave Jed a quick but thorough study. What he saw obviously pleased him, as his thin, dark face creased in a smile. 'You're keeping fit, I see. How was your Christmas?'

'Fine.' Because he couldn't ignore Riker's pointed look towards Dora, Jed did his duty. 'Commissioner Riker, Dora Conroy.'

'Hello.' As both her hands were full with a plate and a champagne glass, Dora just beamed him a smile.

'I hope you'll forgive me, Miss Conroy,' Riker said, 'but I need to steal Jed for a minute. The mayor would like a word with him.'

Dora gave way. 'Nice to have met you, Commissioner Riker.'

'My pleasure. I'll only keep Jed a moment.'

Oh, he really hates this, she mused as she watched Jed walk away. A man would face a firing squad with more enthusiasm.

Feeling for him, Dora wondered if she could find some way to distract him when he returned, to turn whatever emotions the commissioner and the mayor managed to stir up into a different channel. She wandered away to get a refill of champagne.

Five minutes later Jed strode over to the sitting area with comfortable chairs and potted plants, where Dora had seated herself. She grinned at him. 'Give me a kiss, will you?'

'Why?'

322

'Because I'd like one. Just a friendly one.'

He touched his lips to hers. 'Friendly enough?'

'Yeah, thanks.'

She started to smile, but he shifted his hand, cupped it round her throat. He lowered his mouth to hers again. She felt a rush that left her limp. His kiss was slow, cool, devastatingly controlled. When he drew back, she kept her eyes closed, absorbing the flood of sensation. Her heart was still pounding in her ears when she opened her eyes. 'Jeez' was all she managed to say.

'Problem?' Jed asked her.

'I think so.' She pressed her lips together. 'I think . . . I'll go.' Her knees wobbled when she stood. It was very difficult, she thought, to be in charge of a situation when your knees wobbled.

7

The new security system on Dora's building brought DiCarlo a great deal of irritation. He'd hoped to get in and out of the storeroom by midnight. For surely if the Conroy woman had bought the painting, it was inside, regardless of what the idiot redheaded salesgirl had told him on Christmas Eve. Now, with the sturdier locks, he'd be lucky to be inside by midnight. And worse, a cold and nasty sleet was beginning to fall. At least there were no vehicles in the drive, he thought as he worked and shivered—which meant no one was home. He could still be in New York by morning. He'd sleep the entire day, then catch a late flight to the West Coast. Once he'd handed over Finley's toys, he'd fly back to New York for a rollicking New Year's Eve.

When the final tumbler fell, he gave a little grunt of satisfaction.

In less than fifteen minutes he was certain that the painting was not in the storeroom. Using self-control, he curbed the urge to wreck the place. He did another thorough tour of the shop, automatically picking up a few small trinkets as he went, including the jade Fo dog that the redhead had tried to sell him.

Resigned, DiCarlo went upstairs. The lock on the door at the top of the steps was basically for looks. He was through it quickly.

He listened, heard nothing. No radio, television, conversation. Still, he moved silently down the hall. Three minutes later he was inside Jed's apartment. That search was over almost before it began. There were no paintings on the wall, none tucked into the closets. He found nothing under the bed but a dogeared paperback and a balled-up sock. He did find the .38 in the bedside cupboard of some interest but, after a brief examination, replaced it.

DiCarlo was in Dora's apartment in a matter of seconds. She hadn't bothered to lock it. The search here was a different matter because of the clutter. There were several paintings, but no abstract on the wall. He moved into the bedroom. He barely had time to react when he heard the front door open. By the time it slammed, DiCarlo was hidden deep in the closet behind a colourful assortment of outfits.

I have to be crazy, Dora said to herself. She peeled off her coat and yawned. How did she let her parents talk her into it? Still muttering, she walked straight to the bedroom. Her plan had been to spend a quiet, relaxing evening at home. But oh, no, she thought, switching on the Tiffany lamp beside the bed, she had to fall into that old family trap of 'the show must go on'. Was it her fault that three stagehands had come down with the flu? Absolutely not, she decided as she undressed. I didn't give them the flu. And I didn't have to jump in just because I have a union card.

Dora sighed. She had spent hours handling props and scenery. She'd even reluctantly enjoyed it. Standing backstage and listening to the voices echo, feeling a vicarious pride when the cast took their curtain calls. After all, Dora thought, what's bred in the bone . . .

Through the crack in the closet door DiCarlo had an excellent view. The more he saw, the more his annoyance at being interrupted faded. The woman who was now stretching at the foot of the bed was wearing only a couple of lacy black patches. Very nice, DiCarlo thought, and smiled in the dark. Very nice, indeed.

She'd changed his plans, but DiCarlo prided himself on creative thinking. Once she'd got into bed, DiCarlo figured, it would be a simple matter—using his .22 automatic—to convince her to tell him where the painting was. And after business, pleasure. He might not even have to kill her afterwards.

Dora shook back her hair, rolled her shoulders. It was as if she were posing, DiCarlo thought. His blood surged.

The pounding on her door made Dora jump. In the closet DiCarlo's breath hissed out in a combination of rage and frustration.

'Hold on!' Dora shouted. She struggled into her white towelling robe. Switching on lights as she went, she hurried out to the living room. She hesitated with her hand on the knob. 'Jed?'

'Open up, Conroy.'

'You gave me a start,' she said as she opened the door. 'I was just—' The fury on his face stopped her. She stepped back.

'What did you think you were doing?'

'Uh . . . going to bed,' she said carefully.

'Cut the nonsense.' Jed yanked her into the hall. 'I know when my place has been turned over.' Enraged, he shoved her up against the opposite wall. Her muffled cry of surprised pain only added to his fury. 'What were you looking for?' he demanded.

'Let go of me.' She twisted, too terrified for denials.

'You figure because you've got me churned up inside, you can paw through my things any time you want?' He dragged her stumbling after him. 'Fine.' He slammed his door open, shoved her inside. 'Take a look now. Take a good one.'

Her breath shuddered in and out. 'You're out of your mind.'

Neither heard DiCarlo slip away. They stood apart, Dora tugging with a shaking hand at the robe that had fallen off her shoulder.

'Did you think I wouldn't notice?' He moved quickly, grabbing her robe by the lapels. 'I was a cop for fourteen years.'

'Stop it!' She pushed herself away from him. The sound of her robe ripping at the shoulder was like a scream. Tears of terror and rage sprang to her eyes. 'I haven't been in here.'

'Don't lie.' But a seed of doubt now squeezed through his fury.

'Let me go.' She tore free. Slowly, waiting for the tiger to spring again, she backed away. 'I just got home. Go feel the bonnet of my car. It's probably still warm.' Her voice sputtered in time with her heart. 'I've been at the theatre all night. You can call, check.'

He said nothing, only watched her edge for the door. She was crying now—fast, choking sobs—as she fumbled with the doorknob.

'Stay away from me,' she whispered. 'Stay away from me.' She fled, leaving his door swinging open and slamming her own.

He stood where he was, waiting for his heartbeat to slow. He hadn't been wrong. Someone had been inside. He knew it. His books had been moved, his gun examined. But it hadn't been Dora.

Sickened, he pressed his hands to his eyes. He'd snapped. He'd been waiting to snap for months. Wasn't that why he'd turned in his badge? He'd come home after a miserable day of dealing with lawyers, accountants and bankers, and he'd snapped like a twig. And if that wasn't bad enough, he'd terrorised a woman. Why her? Because she'd got to him. He took a long breath and walked over to Dora's.

At the knock she stopped rocking on the arm of the chair. Her head jerked up. She scrambled to her feet.

'Dora, I'm sorry.' On the other side of the door Jed shut his eyes and knocked again. 'Let me come in, will you?' The silence dragged on, tightening his chest. 'I swear I won't touch you. I want to see if you're OK, that's all.' In frustration, he turned the knob.

Her eyes widened as she watched it rotate. Oh, Lord, she thought in panic. She hadn't locked it. A little sound caught in her throat. She lunged for the door just as Jed opened it.

She froze, and he saw wild fear on her face. Slowly he lifted his hands, palms out. 'I won't touch you, Dora. I want to apologise.'

'Just leave me alone.' Her eyes were dry now, but terrified.

He couldn't walk away until he'd eased that fear. 'I hurt you.'

'Why?' Her hand clenched and unclenched on the neck of her robe. 'You owe me why.'

There was a hot ball in his throat. But she was right. 'Speck raided my house a week after he killed my sister. He left a snapshot of her and a news clipping about the explosion on my dresser. He just wanted me to know he could get to me, any time. He wanted to make sure I knew who was responsible for Elaine. When I came home tonight and I thought you'd been in, it brought it back.'

She had a beautifully expressive face. He could read every emotion. The fear, and the anger to combat it, faded away. In their stead were flickers of sorrow, understanding and sympathy.

She lowered her eyes. 'When you kissed me last night, I thought something was happening with us.' She lifted her gaze again, and her eyes were cool. 'But it can't be, or this wouldn't have happened. Because you'd have trusted me. And that's my mistake.'

'I can move out if you want,' he said stiffly.

'It isn't necessary, but you do what you want.'

Nodding, he stepped back into the hall. 'Will you be all right?'

For an answer she closed the door gently and turned the lock.

SHE FOUND THE FLOWERS on her desk in the morning. Daisies, wilted but smelling of spring, stuffed into a vase. Sternly Dora ignored them.

He hadn't moved out. That much had been clear from the monotonous thud of weights bumping the floor. As far as she was concerned now, Jed Skimmerhorn was a paying tenant. Nothing more. No one was going to terrify her, threaten her and break her heart, then lure her back with a straggling bunch of daisies.

Since Terri and Lea were handling the shop, she took out her accounts book and prepared to work. She sneaked a peek at the daisies and smiled. Then the sound of boots coming down the stairs had her firming her lips and staring at her electricity bill.

Jed hesitated at the base of the stairs. 'If you're going to be working in here, I can finish up those shelves later.'

'I'll be here for a couple of hours,' she said, not glancing up.

'I've got some stuff to do downtown.' He waited for a response, got nothing. 'Do you need anything while I'm out?'

'No.'

'Fine. Great. Then I'll finish the shelves this afternoon. After I go out and buy myself a hair shirt.'

Dora lifted a brow, listened to the door slam. 'Probably thought

I'd throw myself in his arms because of the flowers. Jerk.' She looked over as Terri stood in the doorway wringing her hands.

'Dora, did you take the jade dog? The little Chinese piece?'

'The Fo? No. I haven't circulated any stock since Christmas. Why?'

Terri gave a breathless laugh, a sickly smile. 'I can't find it.'

'It probably just got moved. Lea might have—'

'I've already asked her,' Terri interrupted.

Dora pushed away from her desk. 'Let me take a look around.'

Lea was busy showing tobacco jars to a customer when Dora and Terri entered the shop.

'It was in this cabinet,' Terri said quietly. 'I showed it Christmas Eve, right before closing. I'm positive I saw it here yesterday.'

'All right.' Dora patted Terri's shoulder. 'Let's look around.'

Even the first glance was alarming. Dora made sure to keep her voice calm and low. 'Terri, have you sold anything this morning?'

'A tea set—the Meissen—and a couple of cigarette cards. Lea sold the mahogany cradle and a pair of brass candlesticks.' Terri's already pale cheeks went whiter. 'Is something else gone?'

'The vinaigrette, the enamel one that was on the bonheur.' Dora controlled a curse. 'And the inkwell that was beside it.'

'The pewter?' Terri turned to the delicate desk and groaned. 'Oh, no.'

Dora shook her head and did a swift tour of the entire shop.

'The Chelton paperweight,' she said a few moments later. 'The Baccarat perfume bottle and the Fabergé desk seal.' That one, priced at fifty-two hundred dollars, was tough to swallow.

'Oh, Dora, I should have watched more carefully—' Terri began.

'It's not your fault.' Though she felt sick with anger, Dora slipped an arm round Terri's waist. 'We can't treat everyone who walks in like a shoplifter. We'd end up shoving all our stock behind glass.'

'Dora, the Fabergé.'

'I know. I'll report it to the insurance company. That's what they're for. Terri, go take your lunch break now. Clear your head.'

'OK.' Terri blew her nose. 'Aren't you mad?'

Dora's eyes blazed. 'I'm furious.'

8

Jed wondered if going back to his old precinct for the first time since his resignation was just another way to punish himself. He could have met Brent elsewhere and avoided the wrenching reminder. But Jed walked into the place where he'd spent eight of his fourteen years on the force, because he knew he had to face it. After the way he'd spun out of control the night before, he admitted there were plenty of things he was going to have to face.

Everything was the same. The air still smelt of spilt coffee and stale smoke—all with an undertone of disinfectant. The sounds—all familiar. Ringing phones, raised voices. Walking in without his weapon strapped to his side made him feel naked. He nearly walked out again, but the only way through it was ahead, he decided.

Jed stopped at the desk, waited until the sergeant turned. 'Ryan.' The man had shoulders like a bull, but he had the face of a teddy bear. When he spotted Jed, that face creased into a smile so big his eyes seemed to disappear into the soft folds of ruddy Irish skin.

'Captain.' He grasped Jed's hand. 'Really good to see you.'

'How's it going?'

'Oh, you know. Same old same old.' He leaned companionably on the desk. 'We miss you around here, Captain,' he said. 'Goldman's OK as an acting captain. I mean, he pushes paper with the best of them, but let's face it. The man's a fool.'

'You'll break him in.'

'No, sir.' Ryan shook his head. 'Some you do, some you don't. The men knew they could talk to you, straight. With Goldman you gotta tippytoe through regulations and procedure.'

Whatever Jed felt about Ryan's easy flow of information he kept to himself. 'Is Lieutenant Chapman in?'

'Sure. I think he's in his office. You can track him down.'

To get to Brent, Jed had to walk through the bull pen. His stomach clenched each time his name was called, each time he was forced to stop and exchange a word. Each time he forced himself to ignore the speculation, the unasked questions, the tension.

Brent was sitting at his overburdened desk, the phone at his ear. 'Tell me something I don't know,' he was saying. He glanced up and the irritation in his eyes cleared. 'Yeah, I'll get back to you.' He hung up. 'You were in the neighbourhood, thought you'd drop by, right?'

'No.' Jed sat down. He didn't want to ask, to get involved. But he had to. 'Is Goldman being as big a jerk as Ryan claims?'

Grimacing, Brent rose to pour two cups of coffee from the pot on his hot plate. 'Well, he's not exactly Mr Popularity.' He gave Jed a cup, then leaned against his desk. 'Come back, Jed.'

Jed lowered his eyes, slowly lifted them again. 'I can't, Brent. I'm a mess. Give me a badge right now and I don't know what I'd do.' He had to stop. 'Somebody'd been in my place last night.'

'You had another break-in over there?'

Jed shook his head. 'This was slick. A couple of things out of place, a drawer shut when I'd left it partway open—that kind of thing. I'd been out most of the day settling Elaine's estate. After that, I went to a movie. I came home, took one look around and went after Dora.' He sipped his coffee. 'I mean I went after her, Brent. Saw the crime, made the collar. I pushed her around.'

Stunned, Brent stared at Jed. 'You didn't—hit her?'

'No. I scared the heck out of her, though. Scared myself. I just snapped. Dora didn't go into my apartment. So who did?'

'Might have been a return visit from whoever broke in the other night. Looking for something to lift. What about the security?'

'I looked it over. Couldn't find anything. This guy's a pro, Brent. Could be a connection to Speck, somebody who wants revenge.'

'Speck wasn't the kind to inspire loyalty after death.' But, like Jed, Brent wasn't willing to dismiss the possibility. 'I'm going to do some checking. Why don't I put a couple of eyes on the building?'

Jed nodded. 'I'd appreciate it. If somebody wants me, I wouldn't like to have Dora caught in the middle.'

JED WAS SURPRISED to find Dora still huddled over her desk when he returned. It didn't surprise him that she ignored him as she had that morning, but this time he thought he was prepared.

'I got you something.'

Jed set a large box on the desk in front of her. When she glanced at it, he had the small satisfaction of spotting curiosity in her eyes.

'It's, uh, a robe. To replace the one that got torn last night.'

'I see.' When she looked up at him, the curiosity had been replaced by glittering anger. 'Skimmerhorn, you think that a bunch of pathetic flowers and a robe are going to clear the path?'

She rose and slapped her palms down on the box. She paused.

'Keep going,' Jed said quietly. 'Get the rest of it out.'

'All right, fine. You muscle your way into my apartment, flinging accusations. You didn't even consider that you might be wrong—you just attacked. You scared me. And worse, you humiliated me because I just took it.' Wearily she lifted a hand to push back her hair. 'Look, I've had a rough day—'

She broke off when he took her hand. She stiffened, but he persisted. 'I can keep saying I'm sorry. That doesn't mean a lot. I hurt you. And I don't know how to make it up to you.'

He tucked his hands away in his pockets and started for the steps.

'Jed.' There was a sigh in her voice. 'Wait a minute.' Sucker, she admitted, and flipped open the top of the box. The robe was nearly identical to hers but for the colour. She smoothed a finger down the deep green towelling lapel.

'They didn't have a white one. You wear bright colours, so . . .'

'It's nice. I didn't say I was forgiving you. I'm just not comfortable feuding with the neighbours.'

'You've got a right to set the rules.'

She smiled a little. 'You must really be suffering to hand over that kind of power.'

'You've never been a man buying women's lingerie. You don't know about suffering. I am sorry, Dora.'

'I know. Really, I do. I was nearly as mad at myself as I was at you this morning. Before I could cool off we had some trouble in the shop. So when you came back, I was ready for blood.'

'What kind of trouble?'

'Shoplifting.' Her eyes hardened again.

'Are you sure it was all there last night when you closed up?'

'I know my stock, Skimmerhorn.'.

'You said you'd got in just before I did last night. And you were upset when I left you. You were still upset this morning. I don't suppose you'd have noticed if anything was missing from upstairs.'

'What are you talking about?'

'Somebody was in my place last night.'

He saw the doubt on her face.

'I'm not saying that to excuse my behaviour,' he went on. 'Somebody was in my place. Cops see things civilians don't. I had an idea that some of Speck's men might have dropped around to hassle me, but it could have been somebody looking for some trinkets.'

'What about the alarm system, those locks you put in?'

'Nothing's burglarproof.'

'Oh.' She closed her eyes briefly as he took her hand and pulled her up the stairs. 'Well, that certainly makes me feel better.'

'Let's just check it out. Got your keys?'

'It's not locked.' His look made her bristle. 'Look, ace, the outside door's locked, and I was right downstairs.'

He bent down to examine the lock, saw no obvious signs of tampering. He opened the door and scanned the room. 'What happened to the painting? The new one you hung over the couch?'

'The abstract? I took it over to my mother.'

'Jewellery?'

She crossed to the bedroom. She opened a camphorwood and ebony chest that sat on a lowboy. 'It looks like it's all here.' She took out a velvet pouch and shook out a pair of emerald earrings. 'If anybody was going to rifle through here, they'd go for these.'

'Nice,' he said after a glance. It didn't surprise him that her bedroom was as crowded and homy as her living room. 'Some bed.'

'I like it. It's a Louis XV reproduction. I bought it from a hotel in San Francisco. I couldn't resist that headboard.'

It was high, covered with deep blue brocade and gently curved at the top. She'd added a quilted satin spread and fussy pillows.

'I like to sit up late and read with a fire going.' She closed the jewellery box. 'Sorry, Captain. I don't have a crime to report.'

He should have been relieved, but he wasn't. 'Why don't you give me a list of the stolen goods? We—Brent—can have some men check out the pawnshops.'

'I've already reported it.'

'Let me help.' He ran a hand down her arm. She didn't back away. So he was forgiven, he thought.

'All right. It wouldn't be smart to turn down the services of a police captain over a simple shoplifting. Let me—' She started forward, but he didn't move. Her heart stuttered in her chest with an emotion that had nothing to do with fear. 'The list's downstairs.'

'I think you should know, you were right,' he said.

'That's good to know. What was I right about this time?'

'I was tangled up about what was happening between us.'

'Oh.' It came out shaky. 'What *was* happening between us?'

His eyes darkened. 'I was wanting you. It was making me a little crazy. If you want to pay me back solid for last night, all you have to do is tell me you're not interested.'

'I think . . .' On a weak laugh she pushed both hands through her hair. 'I'm going to consider your offer and get back to you.'

He hadn't expected to fluster her, but he was enjoying it. 'You want to have dinner? We could discuss the terms.'

'I can't. I have a date—with my nephew. Richie's at that stage where he detests girls, so every now and again I take him out to the movies. A kind of guys' night out. Sitting through *Zombie Mercenaries from Hell*—that makes me one of the guys.'

'If you say so.' He grinned. 'Maybe we'll try a guys' night out tomorrow, then. Why don't we go get that list?'

When they'd passed safely out of the bedroom, Dora let out a small relieved breath. She was definitely going to think this over—as soon as some of the blood returned to her head.

DiCarlo MIGHT HAVE enjoyed his luxurious suite at the Ritz-Carlton with its soft king-size bed and fully stocked bar—if he'd had the painting in his possession. Instead, he fumed. Without the ill-timed arrival of the man in that other apartment, DiCarlo figured he would have had the painting—or known its whereabouts.

He hesitated to call Finley. There was nothing to report but failure, though he still had until the second of January.

He chewed on a nut and washed it down with the Beaujolais left over from his lunch. It baffled him that the man knew his apartment had been searched. Since the man suspected the woman next door had been in his apartment, DiCarlo's plans didn't change.

He'd do exactly what he had planned to do the night before. Only this time he knew he'd kill the woman when he was finished.

THE TEMPERATURE HAD DIPPED to a brisk 14°F under a night sky splattered with icy stars and sliced by a thin, frosty moon. The shops along South Street were locked up tightly, and traffic was light.

DiCarlo spotted the police cruiser on his first circle of the block. His hands tightened on the wheel. He hadn't counted on outside interference. He drove around aimlessly for ten minutes. By the time he'd circled around to South again, DiCarlo had his plan formulated. He pulled to the kerb in front of the police car. Taking out a Philadelphia street map, he climbed out of the car.

'Got a problem there?' The cop rolled down his window.

'I sure do.' Playing his part, DiCarlo grinned sheepishly. 'I don't know where I made the wrong turn, Officer, but I feel like I've been driving round in circles.'

'Thought I saw you drive by before. Where you trying to get to?'

'Fifteenth and Walnut.' DiCarlo pushed the map into the window.

'No problem. Make a left on Fifth. You'll run right into Walnut at Independence Square. Make another left.'

'I appreciate it, Officer.' Smiling, DiCarlo pressed his silenced pistol against the uniformed breast. Their eyes met for less than a heartbeat. There were two muffled pops. The cop's body jerked, slumped. DiCarlo checked the pulse. When he found none, he quietly opened the driver's door with his gloved hands and straightened the body into a sitting position. He rolled up the window, locked the door, then strolled back to his own car.

DORA WAS DISAPPOINTED that Richie hadn't taken her up on her invitation to sleep over. It seemed her nephew had had a better offer, so she'd dropped him off at a friend's after the movies.

The simple fact was, she didn't want to be alone.

No, she corrected, she didn't want to be alone and a few easy steps away from Jed Skimmerhorn. No matter how attractive and charming he'd been that afternoon, he was a crate of dynamite set with a very short fuse. She didn't want to be in harm's way when and if he exploded again. She turned into the gravel drive behind the shop.

His Thunderbird was gone. Dora frowned a moment, then shook her head. For the best, she thought. If he wasn't around, she couldn't think about knocking on his door and inviting trouble. Her boots crunched over the gravel, clattered up the back stairs. After entering the code into the alarm system, she unlocked the door, then secured it.

She decided to make an early night of it. A pot of tea, a fire and a book—the perfect remedies for a troubled mind.

She let herself into her apartment and turned on the Christmas tree. The cosy coloured lights never failed to cheer her. She took off her boots and coat and put everything into her hall closet.

She padded into the kitchen to heat the kettle. Her hand on the tap jerked as a board creaked in the other room. She stood frozen—water splashing into the sink—listening to her own racing heart.

'Get a grip, Conroy,' she whispered. Imagine, letting a silly film give her the willies. The building was settling, that was all.

Amused with herself, she put the kettle on to boil. She walked back into the living room and stopped dead. It was pitch-dark, with only the thin backwash of light from the kitchen illuminating the silhouettes of furniture. Which, of course, made the dark worse.

But she'd turned the tree on, hadn't she? Of course she had. A fuse? Maybe the tree lights had shorted. Shaking her head at her overactive imagination, she started across the room.

And the kitchen light went out behind her.

Her breath sucked in on a gasp. Slippery little fingers of fear slid over her skin. She didn't move, listening to every sound. There was nothing but her own drumming heartbeat and shallow breathing. Lifting a hand to her head, she laughed. A bulb blew, that was—

A hand clamped over her mouth. Before she could think to struggle, she was yanked back against a hard body.

'Now you stay real quiet.' DiCarlo kept his voice at a whisper. 'You know what this is?' He loosened his grip enough to slip his gun against her. 'You don't want me to have to use it, do you?'

She shook her head, squeezing her eyes tight.

'Good girl. Now I'm going to take my hand away. If you scream, I'll have to kill you.' When he removed the hand from her mouth, Dora pressed her lips together to stop them from trembling.

'I watched you the other night, in the bedroom, when you took off your clothes.' His breath quickened. 'You're going to do that little striptease for me again, after we take care of business.'

She groaned, repelled. Tears burned in her eyes. She thought she'd been scared the night before with Jed. But that was nothing compared with the ice-edged horror that clawed through her now.

'You cooperate, and we'll get on fine.' He slipped the barrel of the gun under her sweater. 'Now you tell me where the picture is, and I'll take the gun away.'

'The picture?' Her frantic mind whirled. She'd cooperate. But she wouldn't be powerless. 'I'll give you any picture you want. Please move the gun. I can't think when I'm so scared.'

DiCarlo lowered the gun. 'Just tell me where it is.'

'All right.' She cupped her left fist with her right hand. 'I'll tell you.' Using the force of both arms, she rammed her elbow into his stomach. He grunted with pain as he stumbled back. Dora heard a clatter behind her as she raced out of the door.

Her legs felt numb with fear. She fell into the hall, nearly lost her footing. She'd reached the rear door and was dragging at the lock when he caught her. She screamed and turned to claw at his face.

Swearing, DiCarlo hooked an arm round her throat. 'We're not going to be able to be so nice now, are we?' He cut off her air supply and began to pull her backwards towards the dark apartment.

They both heard footsteps pounding up the stairs. With a desperate swipe DiCarlo smashed the fluted hall light and waited in the shadows.

Jed came in low, weapon drawn.

'Toss it down,' DiCarlo hissed, jerking on his arm to make Dora choke. 'I've got a gun at the lady's back.'

Jed could see the outline of Dora's face and hear her struggle for air. With his eyes on DiCarlo he crouched, set his gun on the floor. 'She won't be much of a shield if you strangle her.'

'Stand up. Hands behind your head. Kick the gun over here.'

Jed straightened, linked his fingers behind his head. He nudged the gun halfway between himself and Dora, knowing the man would have to come closer if he wanted it.

'Back against the wall, damn it.' DiCarlo was beginning to sweat now. Things weren't going the way they were supposed to.

He began to sidestep down the hall towards the open door, with Dora between him and Jed. When he reached for Jed's gun, he pulled her down with him to retrieve it, loosening his hold.

Even as Jed prepared his move, she sucked in her breath. 'He doesn't have a gun,' she gasped out, and threw her body back.

Her foot hit the .38, sent it out the door. Jed dragged her aside and braced for DiCarlo's attack. But DiCarlo ran. Jed tackled him at the door. They went through together in a tangle of limbs. The banister cracked in two jagged pieces under the weight. By the time they'd hit the ground, Dora was down the steps in search of the gun.

A blow glanced off Jed's kidneys. Another caught him low in the gut. He ploughed his fist into the other man's face and saw blood.

Dora let out an outraged howl when DiCarlo grabbed part of the broken banister and took a vicious swing that missed Jed's face by inches. She took three running steps and leapt on DiCarlo's back.

She bit down enthusiastically on his neck and drew blood before he flung her aside.

Pain exploded as her head hit the edge of a step. Her vision doubled, then she blacked out completely as she crumpled to the ground.

WHEN SHE OPENED HER EYES again, everything swam in and out of focus. And it hurt. Dora tried to slip back into the void.

'No you don't. Come on, open up.' Jed tapped Dora's cheeks until he had her moaning and opening her eyes again.

The room revolved like a carousel. 'My head.' She touched a tentative hand to the back of her head and hissed in reaction.

'How many fingers?' Jed held a hand in front of her face.

'Two. Are we playing doctor?'

At least her vision and speech were clear. 'I think you're OK.' The flood of relief was instantly dammed by temper. 'Not that you deserve to be, after that idiotic piggyback move. What were you doing, Conroy?'

'I was trying to help.' It all came rushing back. Her fingers gripped his. 'Where is he? Did he get away?'

'Yeah, he got away. I'd have had him if you . . .'

Her eyes narrowed, dared him. 'If I what?'

'You went down like a tree. I thought you'd been wrong about the gun. It turned out all you'd done was crack that hard head of yours.'

'Well, why didn't you go after him?' She tried to shift, noticed she was wrapped in a crocheted shawl.

'I guess I could have left you unconscious, freezing, bleeding.'

'Oh.' She glanced round the apartment. 'He did have a gun before. I don't know what happened to it.'

'It was under the table. I've got it.'

Her smile was weak and didn't last. 'You've been busy.'

'You took your sweet time coming round.' He took her hand again, too gently for her to refuse. 'Tell me what happened. Exactly.'

'I guess you were right about somebody breaking in yesterday. It seems he was in here, too. I didn't notice anything moved or taken, but he said he'd seen me undressing.' She hesitated.

He recognised the signs—humiliation rushing through the fear, shame jockeying with anger. 'Dora, Brent's on his way. I can have him call in a woman officer if it would be easier for you.'

'No.' She took a deep breath. 'He must have been hiding in here. I went right into the kitchen to make tea—I left the water boiling.'

'I took care of it.'

'Oh, good. I'm fond of that kettle. Anyway, when I came back in here, the tree was off. I'd just turned it on, so I figured it had shorted or something. I started to go fix it, and the kitchen light went off. He grabbed me from behind.' Her voice started to shake.

He gathered her close, easing her throbbing head onto his shoulder, stroking her hair. 'It's all right now.'

'He was going to rape me.' She closed her eyes. 'I took this self-defence course last year, but I couldn't remember a thing. He kept saying I just had to cooperate. I got so mad because he thought I wasn't going to do anything to protect myself. I rammed my elbow into his stomach and I ran. Then you came in.'

'OK.' He didn't want to think of what might have happened if he hadn't come in. 'Did you know him?'

'I don't think so. I got a good look at him outside, but he wasn't familiar.' She let out a breath. 'Your new banister's busted.'

'I guess I'll have to fix it again. Got some aspirin?'

'Bathroom medicine chest.' She smiled when she felt his lips brush against her temple. 'Bring me a couple of dozen, will you?'

He brought the aspirin and some water, and she downed the pills. She winced at the knock on her door. 'Is that the cavalry?'

'I imagine. Stay here.'

She watched him, her eyes widening as she saw him reach for the gun hooked to his jeans. He stood at the side of the door. 'Yeah?'

'It's Brent.'

'It's about time.' He yanked open the door, furious all of a sudden. 'What kind of cops are you putting on these days when an armed rapist can stroll right by them and break into a building?'

'Trainor was a good man.' Brent's mouth was tight and grim. He saw Dora on the couch. 'Is she all right?'

'No thanks to Philadelphia's finest. If—' Jed broke off. '*Was?*'

'Dead. Twice in the chest, close range.'

Dora saw the look they exchanged. 'What is it? What?'

'I asked Brent to put a man on the building in case whoever broke in came back. He came back. And the cop's dead.'

'Dead?' The colour in her cheeks washed away. 'He was shot, wasn't he? Was he married?'

'That's not—' Jed began.

'A man was outside trying to protect me. Now he's dead.' She started up off the couch. 'I want to know if he had a family.'

'He had a wife,' Brent said quietly. 'Two kids in high school.'

Hugging her arms, she turned away.

'Dora.' Jed started to reach out to touch her, but he let his hand fall back to his side again. 'When a man or woman joins the force, they know what the risks are.'

'Shut up, Skimmerhorn. Just shut up.'

She pushed back her tousled hair. 'I'm going to make coffee.'

Later they sat at Dora's dining-room table going over her statement point by point.

'Funny he'd come back—we've got to figure three times.' Brent checked his notes. 'And taking out a cop to get inside. Not the pattern of your usual rapist.'

'He kept talking. He said . . . he said something about a picture.'

'He wanted pictures?' Brent asked.

'I—no. He wanted a specific picture, wanted me to tell him where it was,' Dora said. 'I wasn't really listening then.'

'What kind of pictures do you have?'

'All sorts. Family pictures, snapshots. Nothing interesting.'

'It doesn't fit,' Jed said. 'A guy doesn't kill a cop, then walk across the street to rape a woman and raid her photo album.'

'Did you get a good look at him?' Brent asked.

'Six foot, a hundred and seventy,' Jed replied. 'Dark hair, dark eyes, slim build. He had on a cashmere coat, grey, and a navy or black suit with a red tie. Funny, a guy wearing a suit and tie for a rape.'

'It's a funny world.' Brent rose. 'Tomorrow I'd like you two to come down to the station and work with the Identi-Kit. It's a little toy we have to help put together a composite. You need some rest, Dora. If you think of anything else, you call—any time.'

'I will. Thanks.'

When they were alone, Dora stacked the dishes. It was still difficult to look Jed in the eye. 'I haven't got around to thanking you.'

'You're welcome.' He put his hands over hers. 'Leave them.' He then tipped her head back to examine her eyes. What he saw was simple exhaustion. 'Go to bed.'

'I'm not tired. The coffee will probably keep me awake . . .'

Gently he laid his hands on her shoulders. 'Do you want me to call your sister? Your father or your mother?'

'No.' Dora plugged the sink, flipped on the water. 'I guess I'll have to tell them something tomorrow, and that'll be bad enough.'

She wasn't fooling with dishes out of a sense of neatness, he knew, but because she was postponing that moment of being alone again. At least that was something he could take care of.

'Tell you what. Why don't I bunk out on the couch for tonight?'

With one indulgent sigh she shut off the tap and turned to bury her face in his chest. 'Thanks.'

He put his arms round her. 'Don't thank me. I might snore.'

'I'll risk it. I'd tell you that you could share the bed, but—'

'Bad timing,' he finished.

'Yeah.' She eased away. 'I'll get you a pillow.'

9

Dora slept sprawled on her stomach. Her hair, tousled from the night, was swept back from her cheek. Her skin was like smooth white silk. She looked enormously appealing.

Jed walked over, set a mug of coffee on the bedside table, then sat on the edge of the bed. 'Isadora.' He shook her shoulder lightly.

She made a sound of annoyance and turned over on her back. The movement slithered the thick quilt down past her shoulders. Her flannel gown was an eye-popping blue. Jed made out two little pink appliqués that looked like pig's ears. Curious, he lifted the quilt. Sure enough, a fat pink pig face grinned back at him. He dropped the quilt and shook her shoulder again.

'Isadora,' he whispered close to her ear. 'Wake up.'

'Go away.'

Grinning, he leaned closer and captured her mouth. That had her eyes springing open. Dazed, she lifted a hand to his shoulder.

Jed murmured, 'You awake now?'

'Oh, yeah. Wide.' She cleared her throat.

'Who am I?'

'Kevin Costner.' She smiled and stretched her shoulders. 'Just a little harmless fantasy of mine, Skimmerhorn.'

'Isn't he married?'

'Not in my fantasies.'

Jed leaned back. Her eyes were heavy. 'How's the head?'

She lay still, taking stock. 'It hurts. My shoulder's sore, too.'

'Try these.' Jed held two aspirin in his hand.

Dora took the pills, then the mug of coffee he offered.

She sipped then sighed. 'I can't remember the last time anyone brought me coffee in bed.' Smiling, she tilted her head and studied him. With his hair damp from a shower and his chin shadowed with stubble, he made a very attractive picture. 'You're a tough one to figure, Skimmerhorn.'

He took the hand she pressed to his cheek. 'Listen to me.' He spoke carefully. 'You don't know me. You don't know what I'm capable of or what I'm not capable of. The only thing you can be sure of is that I want you, and when I'm certain you're a hundred per cent, I'm going to have you. I won't ask.'

'There's no need for that, since I've already answered yes. I also know you're not warning me. You're warning yourself.'

He let her hand go and rose. 'We've got other things to deal with today. What are you doing about the shop?'

'We're closed today.'

'Good. We've got to get down to the station house. Get yourself together and I'll make some breakfast.'

'Can you?'

'I can pour cold milk on cereal.'

'Yummy.' She tossed the quilt aside as he started out.

'Oh, Conroy,' he said over his shoulder, 'I like your pig.'

DICARLO PACED his New York apartment. He hadn't slept.

He couldn't go back to Philadelphia. The dead cop was one thing, but the two witnesses had seen his face well enough for an ID. And they'd tie him to the dead patrolman. He'd need to go underground. A couple of months, six at the most. He had plenty of contacts, plenty of liquid cash. He could spend the winter in Mexico, swilling margaritas. Once the cops finished chasing their tails, he'd return.

The only hitch was Edmund J. Finley.

DiCarlo studied the merchandise he'd stacked against the wall. They looked like sad, neglected presents. The parrot, the eagle, Lady Liberty, the china dog. Counting the figurine he'd already delivered, that made five out of six. Anyone but Finley would consider that a success. It was only one lousy painting, he thought. He'd given it his best shot. He had a black eye, a split lip and sore kidneys. His cashmere coat was ruined. As soon as he had time, he was going to make that shipping clerk, Opal Johnson, pay for her mistake.

In the meantime he figured he would approach Finley businessman to businessman. After all, Finley knew one had to take losses along with profit. First put him in a cheery mood by personally presenting him with the four newly recovered items; then elicit sympathy and admiration by detailing the specifics. He'd explain about the cop, too. Surely Finley would understand the great personal risk he'd taken.

Not enough, DiCarlo admitted, and picked up his ice pack to press it against his bruised cheekbone. It was just as well he was too busy to celebrate New Year's Eve.

He would use good faith. He would offer to put another man on the job, at his own expense. Surely that was an offer that would appeal to Finley's business sense. And his greed.

Satisfied, DiCarlo went to the phone.

'I THINK HIS FACE was just a little longer.' Dora watched the computer-generated image change on the monitor to the quick rattle of the operator's fingers on the keyboard. 'Yeah, that's it. And thinner, too. Maybe his eyes were heavier—more lid.'

Jed moved behind her chair. 'Thin out the lips and nose,' he ordered. 'The eyes were deeper set. Square off the chin some.'

'How do you do that?' Dora whispered.

'I got a better look at him than you, that's all.'

No, that wasn't all, she thought. He'd seen what she'd seen, but he'd absorbed and filed and retained. Now she was watching the image of her attacker taking shape on the monitor.

'Now deepen the complexion,' Jed suggested, narrowing his eyes, focusing in. 'Bingo.'

'That's him.' Shaken, Dora reached over to hold Jed's hand. She smiled weakly. 'That *is* him. That's incredible.'

'Give us a print-out,' Brent told the operator. 'We'll see if we can come up with a match.'

'I'd like a copy for Lea and Terri, too.' Dora got to her feet. 'In case they notice him hanging around near the shop.'

'We'll get you one.' Brent nodded to the operator. 'Why don't you come back to my office for a few minutes?' He took Dora's arm, guiding her out of the conference room and down the hall. Jed followed.

Brent opened his office door and ushered Dora inside. 'Oh, I got a call from your mother. An invitation to your parents' New Year's Eve bash tomorrow at the theatre.'

She'd all but put it out of her mind. 'I hope you can make it.'

'We're looking forward to it.' Brent cleared his throat, pushed up his glasses. 'Well, until we run this guy down,' he said, watching from the corner of his eye as Jed paced, 'we'll put a couple of guards on your building.'

'I don't want anyone else put at risk,' she said.

'Dora, there isn't a man in this precinct who wouldn't volunteer for the duty. Not after Trainor. This guy's a cop-killer. Which is why it was easy for me to put a rush on ballistics. The bullets they took out of Trainor matched the ones we dug out of your wall.'

'Surprise, surprise,' Jed muttered.

'I've got a case to build.' Brent polished his glasses on his wrinkled shirt. 'I'm sending out the ballistic report to other precincts throughout the city and the state. Something might match.'

It was a good move, Jed thought. 'Where's Goldman?'

'In Vail,' Brent said under his breath. 'Skiing. A vacation.'

'Son of a gun. He's got a dead cop at his feet—one of his own.'

Brent snatched up his shrilling phone. 'Call back,' he barked into it, and slammed it down. 'Look, I hope Goldman breaks his butt. Maybe then you'll get off yours and come back where you belong. The morale level around here's about knee-high.' He stabbed a finger at Jed. 'What are you going to do about it?'

Jed didn't speak, didn't dare. Instead, he turned and walked out.

Brent looked at Dora, grimaced. 'Sorry.'

'Don't worry about it.' Actually, she'd found the entire incident illuminating. 'I'd better go after him.'

'I wouldn't.'

She only smiled. 'See you tomorrow night.'

SHE CAUGHT UP with him half a block away. She trotted up beside him, matched her stride to his.

'Nice day,' she said. 'The temperature's up a bit, I think.'

'You'd be smart to stay away from me right now.'

'Yeah, I know.' She tucked her hand through his arm. 'You're not really mad at him, you know.'

'Don't tell me what I am.' He tried to shake her off, but she hung on like a silk-covered burr. 'Get lost, Conroy.'

'Impossible. I know my way around this neighbourhood too well.'

Jed stopped, turned. 'You're not going to quit, are you?'

'Nope. I can keep this up indefinitely.' Reaching down, she tugged up the zipper of his jacket. 'Brent's frustrated because he cares about you. It's tough being cared about, because it loads all this responsibility on you. You've had a potful of responsibility there, I imagine. It must be a relief to toss it out for a while.'

It was tough to hold on to his temper with someone who understood so perfectly. 'I had reasons for resigning. They still hold.'

'Why don't you tell me what they were?'

'They're my reasons.'

'OK. Want to hear my reasons for leaving the stage?'

'No.'

'Good. I'll tell you.' She began to walk again, leading him back around the block. 'I liked acting. I was good, too. The reviews were terrific. But it wasn't really what I wanted to do. I wanted my own shop. Then, about five years ago, I got an inheritance from my godmother. I took the money and a couple of courses in business management. When I told my family what I was going to do, they were upset. They loved me, but they wanted me to be something I couldn't. I wouldn't have been happy in the theatre. So I did what was right for me. It took a long time before I adjusted to the responsibility of being cared for, worried over and loved.'

For a moment Jed said nothing. It surprised him that he wasn't angry any longer. Some time during Dora's monologue his temper had dissipated and blown away on the wind of her persistence.

'So the moral of your story is that since I don't want to be a cop, I shouldn't get mad because a friend wants to make me feel guilty.'

Dora stepped in front of him. 'No, you missed it entirely. I made a choice that my family didn't agree with, but that I knew was right for me. You're a cop down to the bone. You just need to admit you made the right choice in the first place.'

He grabbed her arm. 'Do you know why I left?' His eyes weren't angry now, but dark and, to Dora, frighteningly empty of emotion. 'I didn't have to kill Speck. I pushed the situation to the point where I knew one of us would die. It turned out to be him. I used my badge for personal revenge. Not for the law. For myself.'

'A human frailty,' she murmured. 'I bet you've had a heck of a time adjusting to the fact that you're not perfect. Now that you have, you'll be a better cop when you put that badge back on.'

He tightened his grip on her arm. 'Why are you doing this?'

For a simple answer she grabbed him and pulled his mouth down to hers. She tasted impatience in the kiss, but there was something else twined with it. It was need—deep and human.

'There's that,' she said after a moment. 'And I guess we'd have to say that despite what I've always considered my good common sense, I care about you, too.' She watched him open his mouth, close it again. 'Take responsibility for that, Skimmerhorn.'

*I*O

Finley's home was a museum to his ambitions. High in the hills over LA, it had been built by a film director whose love of elaborate construction had outreached his means. When Finley purchased it, he had immediately installed an elaborate security system, an indoor pool for those rare rainy days, and a high stone wall around the property. Finley was a voyeur, but he objected to being watched.

As in his office, the walls in every room were white, as were the carpet, the tiles and the bleached-wood flooring. All the colour came from his treasures. Every table, every shelf, every niche held some masterpiece he had hungered for. When one began to bore him, as they always did, Finley set about acquiring more.

He was never satisfied.

Finley was waiting in the master bedroom. Paintings by Pissarro, Morisot and Manet graced the white silk walls. The furnishings here were lushly ornate, from the Louis XVI bureau to the cabriole bedside tables. Overhead, a trio of Waterford chandeliers sprinkled light. The sixteenth-century four-poster was a massive oak affair, complete with tester, headboard and footboard.

He flicked on the monitor. He watched as the cook prepared lunch in the kitchen—the pheasant salad he'd requested.

Finley switched the monitor to the drawing room. He watched DiCarlo sip at a club soda, rattle the ice, tug at his tie. That was good. The man was worried. Overconfidence bred mistakes. He supposed he should let the poor boy off the hook soon. After all, he had brought the merchandise two days ahead of deadline.

Perhaps he wouldn't have his arms broken after all.

DiCarlo TUGGED at his tie again. He couldn't shake the feeling that he was being watched. He took another swallow and laughed at himself. Anybody would feel as though they were being watched, DiCarlo decided, if they were stuck in a room with a hundred statues and paintings. All those eyes. Painted eyes, glass eyes, marble eyes.

DiCarlo rose to wander round the room. It was a good sign, he thought, that Finley had invited him to the house rather than the office. It made it friendlier. Over the phone Finley had sounded pleased. DiCarlo figured he could smooth over the missing painting.

'Mr DiCarlo, I trust I haven't kept you waiting too long.'

'No, sir. I've been admiring your home.'

'I'll have to give you the grand tour after lunch.' Finley scanned DiCarlo's bruised face. 'Dear me. Did you have an accident?'

'Yes.' DiCarlo touched the back of his neck. The memory of Dora's bite had him steaming all over again. 'Nothing serious.'

'I'm glad to hear it. I hope your plans for the holiday haven't been upset by this trip. I didn't expect you for another day or two.'

'I wanted to bring you the results as soon as possible.'

Finley smiled as the door chimes echoed down the hallway. 'Ah, that will be Mr Winesap. He'll be joining us to inspect the merchandise.

'Now, I hope you'll both forgive me, but I must see my treasures,' he said as Winesap entered. 'I believe they were taken into the library.' He gestured towards the door. 'Gentlemen?'

The library smelt of leather and lemon and roses. The roses were arranged in two tall Dresden vases set atop the mantelpiece. There were thousands of books in the room. The ubiquitous monitors were hidden behind a trompe l'oeil panel of a bookcase.

'And here we are.' With a spring in his step Finley walked to the library table and picked up the parrot. As instructed, the butler had left a small hammer, a knife and a large wastebasket. Finley took the knife and neatly disembowelled the parrot. 'Ah, here,' he said, opening a velvet pouch. The lightest of tremors passed through him when he let the sapphire brooch drop into his palm. The stone, set in an intricate gold filigree encrusted with diamonds, was a deep cornflower-blue sapphire of more than eight carats, square-cut and majestic.

'Worn by Mary, Queen of Scots,' Finley told his guests. He stroked the stone, turned it over to admire the back. 'It was part of the booty Good Queen Bess took after she'd had her pretty cousin executed. It shall have a place of honour.' He set it gently aside. Like a spoilt child on Christmas morning, he wanted more.

The engraved Gallé vase in the bowels of the Statue of Liberty thrilled him. He cooed over it. Finley's eyes had taken on a glassy sheen that had Winesap averting his own in faint embarrassment.

From within the base of the bronze eagle, Finley released a box and tore the padding aside. The box itself was rosewood. But the lid was the treasure, a miniature mosaic panel commissioned in imperial Russia for Catherine the Great. Signed by the artist, it was a wonderfully delicate reproduction of the imperial palace fused onto glass.

'Have you ever seen anything more exquisite? The pride of tsars. Now it's mine. Mine alone.'

'It's a beauty all right.' DiCarlo hated to interrupt, but it was time to make his pitch. 'I'm happy to have played a part in bringing you your merchandise. Of course, there was some difficulty—'

'I'm sure.' Finley waved him off before the mood was spoiled. 'But we must finish here.' He used the hammer on the dog, bursting its belly open. The hound gave birth to a gold cat. 'It's said to have been a gift from Caesar to Cleopatra,' Finley explained softly. 'A beautiful piece.'

His hands shook as he set it down. 'And now, the painting.'

'I, ah . . . there was a little trouble with that, Mr Finley.'

'Trouble?' Finley's smile remained fixed on DiCarlo. 'I don't believe you mentioned any trouble.'

DiCarlo's cheeks flushed. 'I wasn't able to bring it on this trip, Mr Finley. As I started to tell you, there was a problem.' He explained about the three break-ins, reminding Finley that the first had resulted in the recovery of the china hound. He highlighted his personal risk in the search for the painting. 'It would be dangerous for all of us for me to return to Philadelphia now. I do have a contact I can put on the matter—at my own expense, of course. I'm sure you'll be patient. I see no reason why the painting can't be in your hands within, say, six weeks.'

'Six weeks.' Finley nodded, tapped his forefinger to his lip. 'You say you shot a police officer.'

'It was necessary. He was watching the building.'

'Mmm. And why do you suppose he was doing that?'

'I can't be sure.' Sincerity in every pore, DiCarlo leaned forward. 'I did overhear an argument between the Conroy woman and her tenant. It might be that she asked for police protection.'

'Interesting that she simply didn't have him evicted,' Finley commented—smiling. 'Shall we dine, gentlemen?'

They enjoyed the pheasant salad along with a chilled Pouilly-Fumé in the formal dining room, with its sun-swept garden view. Finley kept the conversation away from business. He spent an hour playing jovial host, generously refilling DiCarlo's glass himself.

When the last drop of wine and the final morsel of dessert had been consumed, Finley pushed back from the table. 'I hope you'll forgive us, Abel, but Mr DiCarlo and I should conclude our business. Perhaps a walk around the grounds?' he said to DiCarlo.

DiCarlo patted his stomach. 'I could use a walk after that meal.'

Finley led DiCarlo out into a solarium, through the atrium doors and into the garden. Their shoes crunched lightly over the smooth white stones on the garden path, and they stopped to admire the view. Finley stood looking out over the Los Angeles basin, drawing deeply of the fragrances around him. Flowers—early roses, jasmine. The tang of freshly watered mulch and clipped grass.

'Your plans, Mr DiCarlo?' Finley said abruptly.

'What? Oh. I put my man on it. He'll snatch the Conroy woman, put on the pressure until she leads him to the painting.'

'And then?'

'He'll whack her, don't worry.' DiCarlo smiled a little, professional man to professional man. 'He won't leave any loose ends.'

'Ah, yes, loose ends. Most inconvenient.' Finley bent over a rose-bush, sniffed delicately at a pale pink bud. When he straightened, he held a pearl-handled revolver in his hand. And he was smiling again, charmingly. 'It's best to snip them off.'

He fired, aiming just above DiCarlo's belt buckle. The sound echoed over the hills and sent terrified birds screaming skywards.

DiCarlo's eyes glazed with pain. He pressed a hand against his belly as his knees crumpled beneath him.

'You disappoint me, Mr DiCarlo.' Finley didn't raise his voice, but bent low to let the words carry. 'Did you take me for a fool?'

He straightened and, while DiCarlo writhed in pain from the gun-shot, kicked him. 'You failed!' Finley shouted, and kicked again, and again, screaming over DiCarlo's groaning pleas for mercy. 'I want my painting. It's your fault, your fault I don't have it.'

Finley replaced the revolver in his pocket. He brushed dust from his sleeve as he walked back towards the solarium.

'Winesap!' he snapped.

'Sir.' Winesap tiptoed in, folded his nervous hands. He'd heard the shots and was very much afraid of what was coming next.

'Dispose of Mr DiCarlo.'

Winesap's shoulders slumped. He glanced through the glass wall to where DiCarlo was lying on his back. 'Of course, Mr Finley.'

346

'I realise that tomorrow's a holiday, Abel, and I wouldn't dream of interfering with whatever plans you might have,' Finley said. 'So I'll ask that you focus your attention the following day on gathering all the information you can on this Isadora Conroy in Philadelphia.' He sniffed. 'I'm afraid I'll have to take care of this matter myself.'

II

The lobby of the Liberty Theatre was fashioned in Gothic style, with yards of ornate plasterwork, pounds of curlicues and gremlins decorating the gilded moulding. Over the doors that led into the theatre itself were bronze masks of Comedy and Tragedy.

Tonight the area was packed with people who all seemed determined to be heard above the din. The space smelt of perfumes and smoke, and popcorn erupted cheerfully in a machine behind the bar. The guests' attire ranged from white tie to torn Levi's. Through the open doors Jed could hear a blistering rendition of the Rolling Stones's 'Brown Sugar'. The Winter Ball, he mused, it wasn't.

The house lights were up. He saw people crowded in the aisles, dancing or standing, talking and eating, while onstage the band pumped out rock. In the mezzanine and balcony were still more partygoers, shooting the noise level towards sonic with the help of the theatre's excellent acoustics.

Jed set about trying to find Dora. If she hadn't left for the New Year's party so early, with the excuse of being needed to help set up and keep her mother away from the caterers, he could have come with her, kept an eye on her. He didn't like the idea of her being alone when her attacker was still loose. Though he could hardly call a gathering of this size being alone.

Jed sipped Scotch and worked his way towards the stage.

Then he saw her. She was sitting on the edge of the stage, dead centre, holding an intimate conversation with two other women.

She'd done something to her hair, Jed noted. Piled it up on her head in a tangle of wild curls that looked just on the edge of control. She'd painted her eyes up so that they looked as sultry as a gypsy's. Her lips were a bold red. She wore a black and silver jumpsuit with long sleeves and sleek legs that fitted like a second skin. She might have left the stage, but she still knew how to lure the spotlight.

He wanted her. For a moment that desire blocked out everything else. Setting his glass on the armrest of an aisle seat, he pushed his way forward against the current of people.

'But he's a method actor, after all,' Dora said, grinning. 'Naturally, if he's going to pitch the product, he'd want to—' She broke off when hands hooked under her armpits and lifted her up.

She got a quick glimpse of Jed's face before he covered her mouth with his. Her heart was stuttering when he released her.

'Well, hi.' She staggered, put a hand on his arm for balance. In her spike-heeled boots she was nearly at eye level with him, and his look was intense. 'Glad you could make it. I—ah—this is . . .' She turned to her two friends and went blank.

'Excuse us.' Jed pulled her to a corner, where they didn't have to shout. 'What do you call that thing you're wearing?'

She glanced down at the catsuit. 'Sexy. Do you like it?'

'I'll tell you when my tongue rolls back into my mouth.'

'You have such a way with words, Skimmerhorn. Do you want a drink, some food?'

'I had a drink.'

She took Jed's hand and led him backstage, where another bar and a buffet were set up. He opted for club soda, while Dora chose champagne. She glanced down at his drink. 'You don't have to play designated driver, you know. We can take a cab back.'

'I'll stay with this.' He reached out, cupped a hand under her chin. 'I want a very clear head when I make love to you tonight.'

'Oh.' She lifted her own glass with an unsteady hand. 'Well.'

He grinned. 'Run out of lines, Conroy?'

'I . . . uh . . .'

'Isadora!'

Jed saw a statuesque redhead in a glitter of green that slicked down a regal body, then frothed out in stiff fans from the knees to the ankles. She looked like a ferocious mermaid.

Blessing Trixie's timing, Dora turned to her mother. 'Problem?'

'That caterer is a beast. He refused, absolutely refused, to listen to a word I said about the anchovy paste.'

It had been Will's shift to keep their mother separated from the caterer. Dora took a quick glimpse around. 'Where's Will?'

'Oh, off with that pretty girl he brought from New York,' Trixie said. She tossed up her hands and drew in a deep breath.

'Mom, you haven't met Jed.'

'Jed?' Distracted, Trixie patted her hair. Her face transformed when she took her first good look. Subtly she angled her chin and swept her mink lashes. 'I'm thrilled to meet you.'

Jed kissed her hand. 'The pleasure's mine, Mrs Conroy.'

'Oh, Trixie, please,' she crooned. 'Otherwise I'll feel old.'

'I'm sure that would be impossible. I saw you perform *Hello, Dolly!* last year. You were magnificent.'

Trixie's cheeks pinked with pleasure. 'Oh, how kind of you.'

'Mom, Jed's the tenant Dad found for me.'

'The tenant!' Instantly, maternal instincts outweighed flirtations. 'Oh, my dear, dear boy! I am so completely, so irrevocably in your debt. You saved my darling Isadora from that horrible burglar.' Trixie kissed both his cheeks. 'We'll never be able to repay you.'

Jed narrowed his eyes at Dora over her mother's shoulders.

'There you are, passionflower.' In white tie and tails, Dora's father swaggered up and gave his wife a lingering kiss. 'I've come to claim my bride for a dance.'

'Of course, dear.' Trixie slipped her arms round him. Quentin winked, dipped his wife, then tangoed her away.

'Passionflower?' Jed asked after a moment.

'It works for them.'

'Obviously.' He couldn't remember ever seeing his parents exchange even an impersonal embrace, much less a smouldering kiss.

'You never mentioned you'd been to this theatre before,' she said, drawing his attention back to her. '*Hello, Dolly!*?'

'You didn't ask.'

'Come on, I'll show you round,' Dora said. 'The building's mid-nineteenth-century. It used to be a popular music hall.' She headed away from the stage, down one of the narrow corridors.

As the evening wore on, Jed stopped questioning the fact that he was enjoying himself, and he didn't feel any impatient urges to leave early. When he ran into the Chapmans in the first balcony, he concluded that they were also enjoying themselves.

'Hey, Jed. Happy New Year.' Mary Pat kissed him, then leaned on the rail again to watch the action below. 'What a party.'

Jed checked out her view. A swarm of people, streams of colour, blasts of noise. 'The Conroys are—unique.'

'You're telling me. I met Lea's father. We jitterbugged.' Mary Pat's face flushed with laughter. 'I didn't know I *could* jitterbug.'

'Where's Dora?' Brent asked. 'I haven't seen her.'

'She moves around. Her brother Will wanted to dance with her.'

Brent looked down at his empty glass. 'Let's go get a beer.'

'Oh, no, you don't.' Mary Pat grabbed Brent's arm. 'You're going to dance with me, Lieutenant. It's almost midnight.'

'Couldn't we stay up here and neck?' Brent dragged his feet as his wife pulled him along. 'Listen, Jed'll dance with you.'

'I'm getting my own woman,' Jed said.

By the time the three had managed to elbow their way down to the orchestra level, the lead singer was shouting into the mike, holding up his hands for silence. 'Listen up, everybody. We got one minute until zero hour, so find your significant other—or a handy pair of lips—and get ready to pucker up for the New Year.'

Jed cut through the crowd. He saw her, stage right, laughing with her brother as they poured champagne into outstretched glasses.

She turned to see that the band had full glasses to toast. And she saw him. 'Will'—with her eyes on Jed's, she pushed the bottle at her brother—'you're on your own.'

'Get ready, people!' The singer's voice boomed out over the theatre. 'Count with me now. Ten, nine . . .'

She walked to the edge of the stage, her heart beating hard.

'Eight, seven . . .'

She leaned down, put her hands on Jed's shoulders.

'Six, five . . .'

The walls shook. He gripped her waist, and she stepped off into the air and hooked her legs round him.

'Four, three '

Inch by inch she slid down his body, her eyes locked on his.

'Two, one . . .'

Her mouth opened to his in a deep kiss. He continued to lower her from the stage to the ground. Even when she stood, her body remained moulded to his. He took his mouth from hers but kept her firmly against him. Her heart gave a wild leap, and she abandoned herself to the flood of sensations. She was in love with him.

'DORA, YOU LOOK terrible.'

'Lea, what would I do without you around to boost my ego?'

Unfazed, Lea studied her sister's pale face and shadowed eyes in the morning light. 'Maybe you're coming down with something.'

Dora walked round the counter as a customer came in. She put on a sunny smile. 'Good morning. May I help you?'

'Are you Dora Conroy?'

'That's right.' Dora knew she looked wan from lack of sleep, but this woman looked near collapse. 'Would you like some coffee?'

'I'd love some, but I'm not supposed to drink it.' She laid a hand on the gentle mound of her belly. 'Tea would be nice. Just black.'

'Why don't you sit down?' Taking charge, Dora guided the woman to a chair. 'We're all starting a little slow this morning. After-holiday fatigue.' When a young couple strolled in, Dora gestured for Lea to see to them. Then she poured two cups of tea.

'Thanks. I'm Sharon Rohman,' she told Dora.

'Oh.' It hit her all at once. She sat down and took Sharon's hand. 'You're Mrs Lyle's niece. I'm so sorry about what happened. The last time I called the hospital, I was told she was still in a coma.'

'She came out of it last night. But she's still critical.' Sharon lifted her cup, then rattled it back in the saucer without drinking. 'The doctors can't say if or when she'll recover.'

Dora's eyes stung in response. 'It's a dreadful time for you.'

'We've always been close.' She brushed at a tear with the back of her hand. Then she took a deep breath. 'Miss Conroy—'

'Dora.'

'Dora. I came by to thank you for the lovely flowers you sent to the hospital. The nurses told me you've called several times about my aunt. But I don't know how you're connected.'

'We only met briefly. She bought a few things here right before Christmas.' Dora didn't have the heart to tell Sharon they had been gifts for her and her baby. 'I liked her,' Dora said simply. 'And it bothered me that she'd been hurt so soon after she'd been here.'

'She was shopping for me, wasn't she?'

'She's very fond of you.' After a moment's hesitation Dora made a decision. 'Would you like to know what she bought?'

'Yes, I would, very much.'

'She said that you sewed. She bought you a Victorian doorstop so you could keep the door open and hear the baby in the nursery.'

Sharon smiled softly. 'A brass elephant—like Jumbo?'

'Exactly.'

'We found it in the corner of the living room.'

'She picked up a doorstop for the nursery, too. A china dog.'

'Oh, I didn't see that. It must have been broken. Whoever hurt my aunt also shattered the gifts she'd wrapped, and a great many of her things as well. It looked as though he'd gone crazy. I suppose he had to be, to kill one old woman and leave another for dead?' But she shook the question away. 'I'd like to take her something this morning. Could you help me pick something out?'

'I'd love to.'

'WHAT WAS THAT all about?' Lea asked as Sharon got into her car.

'That was Mrs Lyle's niece—Mrs Lyle was the woman who was attacked on Christmas Eve. She's just come out of a coma.'

Lea shook her head. 'It's awful to think that someone could break into your home that way.'

A quick shiver raced up Dora's spine as she remembered her own recent experience. 'Awful,' she agreed. 'I hope they find him.'

'In the meantime'—Lea turned Dora to face her—'back to you. Why do you look so exhausted when you had yesterday off?'

'I haven't a clue. I spent the entire day in bed,' she said, a smile playing around her mouth.

'Oh,' Lea said, drawing the word out. 'The light dawns. Just whose bed did you spend the day in?'

'My own.' Then she grinned. 'And it was incredible.'

'Really?' Lea was all ears. 'OK, spill it.'

'Well, Jed's . . . I can't,' she said, baffled. 'This is different.'

'Uh-oh,' Lea said, and grinned, ear to dainty ear.

The door rattled. 'Hi!' said Terri. 'Busy morning?'

Dora turned to her. 'You could say so. Listen, there's a new shipment in the back. Why don't you unpack it? Then I'll price it.'

Terri shrugged out of her coat on her way to the storeroom.

'We're not finished, Isadora,' Lea said.

'We are for now, Ophelia.' Dora kissed her cheek.

'Dora.' Terri poked her head out of the storeroom. The copy of the computer-generated picture of DiCarlo was in her hand. 'Why do you have a picture of the guy who came in on Christmas Eve?'

'What?' Dora struggled to keep her voice even. 'You know him?'

'He was our last customer. I sold him the Staffordshire—the mamma dog with pup.'

Dora's heart danced in her chest. 'Did he pay cash?'

'No. He charged it.'

'Would you mind digging up the receipt for me?'

'OK. He had some Italian name,' Terri added. 'Delano, Demarco, something.' Shrugging, she closed the door behind her.

'DiCarlo,' Brent said, handing Jed a sheet of paper. 'Anthony DiCarlo, New York. Small-time stuff: larceny, a couple of breaking and enterings. Did a short stretch for extortion, but he's been clean for nearly six years. NYPD faxed this to me this morning. Shouldn't be too hard to find out if our boy has an alibi for the other night.'

'If he has one, it's fantasy. This is him.' Jed tossed the file photo onto Brent's desk. 'Maybe I should take a trip to New York.'

'You look pretty relaxed for a man who wants to kick butt.'

Jed's lips twitched. 'Do I?'

'Yep.' Leaning back, Brent nodded. 'That's what I thought.' He grinned. 'Dora's quite a woman. Nice going, Captain.'

'Shut up, Chapman,' Jed said mildly on his way out.

JED WENT STRAIGHT up to his own apartment, stripped down to gym shorts before settling on the bench press. He had to decide how much to tell Dora. She had a right to know it all. But if he knew Dora, she'd want to do something about it. One of a cop's biggest headaches was civilian interference. Not that he was a cop, he reminded himself, keeping up a steady rhythm with the weights.

352

Some poking around in New York wouldn't infringe too much on the official investigation there. If he could do something tangible, he might not feel so . . . He scowled. Just how did he feel?

Useless, he realised. Unsettled. Unfinished. Nothing in his life had ever really had a closure, because nothing had ever really been open to begin with. It had been easier to keep himself shut off. But this was about protecting the woman across the hall. The woman he'd begun to feel something for.

He didn't stop lifting when he heard the knock, but his lips curved when she called his name.

'Skimmerhorn, I need to talk to you.'

'It's open.'

She walked in, looking all business in a hunter-green suit. 'Oh.' Her eyebrows lifted as she scanned his body stretched out on the bench, muscles rippling and oiled with sweat. Her heart did a fast somersault. 'Sorry to interrupt your male ritual.'

'Did you want something, Conroy?' Jed rattled the barbell back into the brace.

'You won't be so cranky after I tell you what I found out.' She paused, dramatic timing. 'Terri recognised the magic computer picture. He was in the shop on Christmas Eve. His name is—'

'DiCarlo, Anthony,' Jed interrupted, amused, as Dora's jaw dropped. 'Last known address East Eighty-third Street, New York.'

'But how did you . . . Darn. You could have at least pretended to be impressed with my skills as a detective.'

'You're a real Nancy Drew, Conroy.' He went to the kitchen, took some juice from the fridge and gulped it from the bottle. 'You did OK. The cops just work faster. Did you call and tell them?'

'No.' Her lip poked out. 'I wanted to tell you.'

'OK, spill it, Nancy.'

'Well, Terri said DiCarlo was very smooth, very polite. He said he had this aunt he wanted to buy a special gift for. Terri said she showed him the Fo dog—which I'm now sure he helped himself to when he broke in.' She scowled over that a minute. 'She said he was a snappy dresser and drove a Porsche.'

'I want to talk to her. Is she downstairs?'

'No. We're closed. You could catch her at the theatre later. Curtain's at eight. We can grab her backstage between scenes.'

'Fine.'

Dora followed him as he walked towards the bedroom. 'But what good will it do? I've already talked to her.'

'You don't know the questions to ask. He might have said something. The more we know, the easier it'll be in interrogation.'

THEY ARRIVED at the Liberty Theater in time to hear Nurse Nellie demonstrate how to wash a man out of her hair. Dora had taken Jed through the stage door and into the wings. Her father was there, mouthing the lyrics and pantomiming the moves.

'Hey.' Dora pinched his cheek. 'Where's Mom?'

'In Wardrobe. Jed, my boy. Glad you came by.' He pumped Jed's hand while keeping an eye onstage. 'Light cue,' he muttered under his breath, then beamed at the glow of a spot.

'We just dropped by to see how things were,' Dora said, and shot a warning look at Jed. 'And I need a minute with Terri during the interval. Shop business.' She slipped an arm around her father's shoulders and was soon as absorbed in the staging as he.

Jed hung back, more intrigued by Dora and Quentin than the dialogue onstage. Their heads were tilted together as they discussed the scene. Quentin's arm was wrapped round her waist.

Jed experienced a sensation that shocked him. It was envy. Had he ever felt that easy affection with his own father? he wondered. The answer was very simple and very bleak. No. Never.

The scene ended. There was applause, and then sudden chaos backstage as the cast made for the dressing rooms. Dora caught Terri's arm.

'I need to talk to you for a minute.'

'Sure,' Terri said. 'How about that dance number?'

'You were great.' With a nod to Jed, Dora steered Terri briskly past the stagehands to a corner of the dressing room.

Dora commandeered a stool. 'Sit down, Terri, get off your feet.'

'You don't know how good that feels.'

'About DiCarlo,' Dora began.

'Who? Oh, the guy from Christmas Eve.'

'What did he buy?' Jed asked her.

'Oh, a Staffordshire figure. Never even winked at the price. It was for his favourite aunt. I thought he might bite on the Fo dog, too, because he was looking for an animal.'

'An animal?' Jed's eyes sharpened, but his voice was cool.

'His aunt collects statues of dogs. He really wanted a dog like the one his aunt had had that died.' She shifted towards the mirror to freshen her lipstick. 'I remembered how we'd had that china piece that would have been perfect. You know, Dora, the one you picked up at that auction. You'd already sold it, though.'

Dora felt her blood drain. 'To Mrs Lyle.' She needed to get out. Needed air. 'Thanks, Terri.' She fumbled for the door.

Jed caught up with Dora at the stage door just as she was pushing through and drawing in deep breaths of air.

'Shake it off, Conroy.' He held her by the shoulders.

'I sold it to her.' When she tried to jerk away, he merely tightened his hold. 'And the day after he found out—'

'You sell lots of things—that's what you do. You're not responsible for what happens to the people who buy them.'

'I can't be like that!' she shouted at him, and struck out. 'I can't close myself off that way. That's your trick, Skimmerhorn.'

That twisted in his gut. 'You want to blame yourself, fine.' Gripping her arm, he pulled her towards the car. 'I'll take you home, and you can spend the night beating yourself up over it.'

'I can get myself home.'

'You wouldn't get two blocks before that bleeding heart of yours splashed on the sidewalk.'

Her temper snapped. She rounded on him, leading with her left fist. He dodged it, caught her around the waist and scooped her up over his shoulder.

She exploded with a volley of oaths, furious at the indignity of having to hammer at his back. 'Put me down, you chicken-livered bastard. You want to fight? Put me down! They'll have to pick you up with tweezers when I'm finished. They'll . . . ' The anger drained out of her. She went limp. Shut her eyes. 'I'm sorry.'

'Shut up.' He yanked out his keys and unlocked the car door.

She got in and closed her eyes, listening to him stalk round the car, open the door, slam it shut. She opened her eyes. 'I'm sorry, Jed.'

He drove out of the car park, a cool look on his face. Then he took her hand, lifted it to touch to his lips.

She mustered up a smile. 'I'm glad you're not mad at me.'

'Who said I wasn't? I just don't want to fight when I'm driving.' He lapsed into silence for a moment. 'About Mrs Lyle,' he began. 'I'm going to need to check on her condition. If she comes out of the coma, she might put some pieces together for me.'

'Us,' Dora corrected quietly. 'She's awake. Her niece, Sharon, came by the shop this morning and told me. But I won't let her be interrogated after what she's been through.'

Tyres spat out gravel when he turned into the drive. 'Do I look like the Gestapo, Conroy?'

Saying nothing, she snapped down the door handle and climbed out. He reached the steps before her and blocked the way.

'Dora.' He took her hands. 'I know what I'm doing. I'll be careful with her.' He didn't like to ask. He didn't like needing to. But he found he had no choice. 'Trust me.'

'I do.' Watching his face, she linked her fingers with his. 'Completely. This whole thing has shaken me up some, that's all.'

A bit shaken himself, he kissed her. No, he didn't like to ask. He didn't like needing to. But he did. 'Stay with me tonight.'

The worry cleared from her eyes. 'I was hoping you'd ask.'

'HE MURDERED the housekeeper for a little china dog,' Dora said. They were at the elevators. They had just come from visiting Mrs Lyle in the intensive-care unit. She was frail and weak but lucid.

'Not much doubt of it,' Brent said. 'But that's not the end of it. The bullet that killed Muriel came from the same gun that killed Officer Trainor. Matched the ones we dug out of the plaster at the shop.'

'So he came back for something else.' Calculating, Jed stepped into the elevator. 'The dog wasn't it—or wasn't all of it.'

'But the piece wasn't valuable or unique,' Dora murmured. 'It wasn't even marked. I only bid on it because it was cute.'

'You bought it at an auction.' Slowly Jed turned the possibilities over in his mind. 'Where?'

'In Virginia. Lea and I went on a buying trip. You remember. I got back the day you moved in.'

'And the next day you sold the dog.' He took her arm when they reached the hospital lobby. 'There was a break-in at the shop, Mrs Lyle was attacked, then another break-in. What else did you buy, Dora?'

'At the auction? A lot of things. I have a list at the shop.'

'What did you buy right before the dog, and right after?'

She was tired down to the bone. Her temple throbbed. 'Jeez, Skimmerhorn, how am I supposed to remember?'

'Conroy, you know everything you buy, everything you sell and the exact price. Now what did you buy before the dog?'

'A shaving mug, swan-shaped.' She snapped the words out. '*Circa* 1900. Forty-six dollars and seventy-five cents.'

'And after the dog?'

'An abstract painting in an ebony frame. Primary colours on white canvas, signed E. Billingsly. Final bid fifty-two seventy-five—' She broke off, pressed a hand to her mouth. 'Oh, my Lord.'

'Right on target,' Jed muttered.

'A picture,' she whispered, horrified. 'Not a photograph—a painting. He wanted the painting.' Dora's cheeks were the colour of paste as she groped for Jed's hand. 'I gave it to my mother.'

JED, DORA AND BRENT had dropped in on Trixie and picked up the painting. They'd chosen to work in Dora's apartment rather than the storeroom because there was both room and privacy. No one had mentioned that Brent hadn't insisted on taking the painting, or the information he'd gathered, to his superior, Goldman. It was an unspoken fact that Brent still considered Jed his captain.

Jed removed the frame from the canvas and set it carefully aside. 'Nothing in the frame. We'll let the lab boys take a look.'

'Can't be the painting itself,' Dora said. 'The artist is an unknown—I checked the day after I bought it.'

Jed turned the painting over. 'The canvas is stretched over plywood. Get me something to prise this off with, Conroy.'

'You think there might be something inside?' In the kitchen she rummaged through drawers and brought out a screwdriver. 'A cache of drugs—no, better. Diamonds. Rubies, maybe.'

'Try reality,' Jed suggested, working at the plywood backing.

'It has to be something worth killing for, and that's usually money,' she insisted.

'Nothing,' Jed muttered as he examined the backing he'd removed. 'No secret compartments.'

'That's odd. The back of that canvas has a lot of age to it,' Dora said. 'I suppose Billingsly could have painted over an old canvas.'

'Sometimes people paint over paintings to smuggle them.'

'You think there's an old master behind there?' Amused, Dora shook her head. 'Now who's dreaming?'

But he was studying the splashes of red and blue. 'We need to get this paint off, see what's under it.'

'I have some stuff in the storeroom that should work. Give me a minute.' Dora went downstairs, returning moments later with a cloth, a bottle and several rags.

Jed took the bottle. 'What's in here?'

'A solution I use when some idiot has painted over stencilling.' She knelt on the floor to roll back the rug. 'We need a careful touch. Give me a hand with this.' Brent crouched and spread the cloth, and Dora handed Jed a rag. 'I'd start on a corner if I were you.'

He knelt beside her, dampened the rag and, working in slow, delicate circles, removed the end of the signature, then the white primer. 'Something's under here.' He gently removed more of the primer.

'What is it?' Dora crouched close to the corner. 'Monet.' She whispered the name, as though in church. 'Claude Monet. Oh my God. I bought a Monet for fifty-two dollars and seventy-five cents.'

'I'm not much of an art buff,' Brent said, 'but even I know who this guy is. I don't think anybody would have painted over the real thing unless it was being smuggled. I'll see if there've been any art thefts that included our friend here.'

Jed looked at Brent. 'You'll have to take this to Goldman.'

'That's the next step.'

'I shouldn't ask you, but I'm going to.'

'How much time do you want?' Brent asked, anticipating him.

'Time enough to check out the auction house in Virginia and find the trail.' He kept his voice even.

Brent nodded, picked up his coat. 'Watch your back. See you, Dora.'

'Bye, Brent.' She stayed where she was for a moment. 'Why don't you book us a flight for Virginia? I'll be packed in ten minutes.'

'I don't want you with me,' Jed said. 'It could be dangerous.'

'Fine, I'll book my own flight.'

'You know, you're a pain in the neck.'

'So I've been told.'

12

It was raining in thin, chilly sheets when Jed drove into Front Royal after the flight into Dulles. Dora chatted away on the drive, her easy voice and casual observations relaxing him.

She used the visor mirror to freshen her lipstick. 'Make the next two rights,' she told him. 'There's a car park at the back.'

Jed pulled up into a slot beside a battered Ford pick-up. 'Remember, Conroy, you're not here on a buying jaunt.'

'I know, I know.' She rolled her eyes as they climbed out of the car. 'And you'll ask the questions,' she continued. She hooked her arm through his and started for the rear door. 'It won't be warm inside,' she told him as he pulled open the metal door. 'Mr Porter has a reputation for extreme frugality.' Her eyes kindled. 'Wow, just look at all this stuff. I think that's a Maxfield Parrish print.'

Jed grabbed Dora's arm. 'Where are the offices?'

'In the front, to the right.'

He hauled her along. The office was open but empty when they reached it. Curious, Dora poked her head inside.

'May I help you?'

Jed turned to the tidily dressed woman with glasses hanging from a gold chain. 'We'd like to speak to Mr Porter.'

Helen Owings's eyes clouded and filled alarmingly fast with hot tears. 'Oh,' she said, and dug into her pocket for a tissue.

Before Jed could react, Dora had her by the arm and was leading her into the office, into a chair. 'Can I get you some water?'

'No, no.' Helen sniffled. 'You couldn't have known, I suppose. Sherman—Mr Porter's dead. Murdered.' Her lips trembled.

'Oh, Lord.' Dora groped for a chair herself.

'Right before Christmas. I found him myself. There at the desk.'

'How was he killed?' Jed demanded.

'Shot. Through the head. Poor, poor Sherman.'

'Do the police have any suspects?' Jed asked.

'No.' Helen sighed and dropped her hands into her lap. 'There doesn't seem to have been a motive. Nothing was taken, Mr . . . ?'

'Skimmerhorn.'

'Mr Skimmerhorn. Did you know Sherman?'

'No. Miss Conroy is a Philadelphia dealer. We're here about items that were auctioned on December twenty-first. Miss Conroy bought two pieces. We're interested in where and how you acquired them.'

'Well . . .' It wasn't regular to reveal sources, but Helen couldn't find any harm in it. 'Do you remember the lot number?'

'F-15 and F-18,' Dora said dully. She'd remembered something else, something that made her stomach roll.

Helen rose and went to the filing cabinets. 'Oh, yes. The F lots were from the New York shipment. A small estate sale.' She smiled, taking the folder to the desk. 'To be frank, the quality was not what I'd expected. Conroy . . . Yes, you purchased both pieces.'

A knock on the door interrupted her. 'Miz Owings? We got a question out here about that Early American dry sink. People are in a hurry.'

'All right. I'll be right there.' Helen rose, smoothed down her hair, her skirt. 'Will you excuse me just a minute?'

Jed waited until she'd walked out before picking up the file himself. He scanned the lists, the inventories, the prices, then simply pocketed what he felt was relevant.

'What are you doing?' Dora demanded. 'You can't do that.'

'It'll save time. Come on. We'll make copies, then send the originals back.' He took her hand, but this time she didn't try to linger. Once they were outside and in the car, Jed took her chin in his hand. 'OK, spill it. You went white as a sheet in there.'

'I remembered Mr Ashworth. He was the dealer I met at the auction that day. He bought a piece from that shipment.'

'The guy who was killed during a burglary,' Jed murmured. 'You said his shop was around here.'

'Yes, just a couple of miles away, in Front Royal.'

'Then that's where we're going next. Can you handle it?'

'Yes. But I want to call my shop first. I don't want Terri or Lea anywhere near the place. I want it closed.'

'OK.' He took her hand. 'OK.'

JED HAD HOPED to make the trip to Virginia and back in one day. There was no question of doing so after visiting Ashworth's shop so they checked into a hotel near the airport. The fact that Dora had said little throughout the rainy ride from Front Royal concerned him nearly as much as the information they'd gleaned from Tom Ashworth's grandson. In addition to Ashworth's death and the damage done during the break-in, the porcelain figurine of a man and a woman had apparently been taken.

Jed unlocked the hotel-room door, set the overnight bags aside, then pointed Dora towards a chair. 'Sit down. You need to eat.'

'I'm not hungry.'

He picked up the phone and ordered two steaks, coffee and a bottle of brandy. 'Thirty minutes,' he said when he hung up.

'I . . . I think I'll have a bath,' she said numbly. She rose, picked up her bag. 'Don't you feel anything?' she asked in a voice cracking with fatigue. 'At least three people are dead. People I care about might be in danger simply because they work for me. And you order dinner. Doesn't it make you scared? Doesn't it make you anything?'

Jed met her eyes levelly. 'Yeah. It makes me mad. Go take your bath, Dora. Tune it out for a while.'

Wearily she turned away. She closed the door behind her.

He swore under his breath. She was disappointed in him—that's what had been in her eyes. And it mattered too much to him.

He heard the water running in the tub, then called Brent.

'It's Jed.'

'What have you got, Captain?'

'A couple of dead guys.' Jed automatically kept his voice low and told Brent what he knew. 'I've got the name of the guy who sent the shipment down from New York,' he concluded. 'I'm going to check him out tomorrow, in person. Franklin Flowers, Brooklyn address. Any more on the painting?'

'Still working on it.'

'Are you taking any flak on this?'

'Nothing I can't handle. Goldman decided to take an interest in Trainor's death. Did an interview in front of the courthouse.'

'We'll dump DiCarlo right in his lap.'

The disgust in Jed's voice gave Brent hope. 'If we can find him. Our boy seems to have gone underground.'

'Then we'll dig him up. I'll call you from New York.'

He hung up. The water had stopped running.

Dora was lying back in the tub while the hot water relaxed her body. It was more difficult to relax her mind. She kept seeing the way Helen Owings's eyes had filled. She kept hearing the way young Ashworth's voice had thickened when he spoke of his grandfather. She kept remembering how fragile Mrs Lyle had looked. And she could feel the memory of the cool gun barrel against her skin.

360

The water cooled. Dora dried off carefully, then reached for her robe. Her hand brushed over the vivid green towelling. Sighing a little, she slipped into the robe. She opened the door, letting out a flow of steam. Jed was standing at the window, looking out at the rain. The room-service cart was beside him, set for two. He turned to her.

'You're trying to make things easier for me.' Why hadn't she realised that before? she wondered.

'I got you some fuel, that's all.' She looked fragile and lovely. He started to pull out a chair, but she was crossing to him. Her arms went round him, her body pressed close, she buried her face against his neck. He held her like that, his hands stroking her back.

'I was scared,' she murmured.

'Nothing's going to happen to you.'

'I was scared of more than that. Scared you wouldn't be here to hold me like this when I needed you to. Or that if you were, it would be because it was a job you couldn't graciously avoid.'

'I don't worry about doing anything graciously.'

She laughed. 'I know. But I got in your way. Pushing you to feel things you can't afford to feel if you're going to do what you have to do. Wanting you to have feelings for me you don't want to have.'

'I don't know what I feel for you.'

'I know that, too.' She lifted a hand to his cheek. 'Tell me what we do next,' she said.

'We go to New York in the morning.'

DORA HAD ALWAYS LOVED New York—its unrelenting pace, its energy. The sidewalk vendors, the blatant rudeness of the cab drivers.

Jed swore as a cab cut him off with a coat of paint to spare.

Dora beamed. 'Great, isn't it?'

'Yeah. Right.'

'Oh, look!' She rolled down her window, craned her neck. 'Did you see that fabulous outfit?' She narrowed her eyes to try to make out the name and address of the shop. 'It would just take me five minutes if you could find a place to park.'

He snorted. 'I should have known better than to drive you through Manhattan. It's like offering a steak to a starving dog.'

'You should have let me drive,' she corrected. 'I wouldn't have been able to look at the shops. Besides, you're the one who wanted to check out DiCarlo's apartment.'

Jed made the turn onto Eighty-third. After a quick scan for a spot big enough to slip the rental car into, he double-parked. 'I want you to wait here while I go in and check out DiCarlo.'

'How come I can't come in?'

'Because I want the car to be here when I get back.' He kissed her and got out. 'Lock your doors, Conroy.'

Five minutes passed into ten, and ten into twenty, and Dora was beginning to consider leaving Jed a note to pick her up at the boutique when he jogged back to the car.

'The caretaker let me into DiCarlo's apartment.'

'So? What did you find?'

'Italian shoes, Armani suits, silk underwear. A chequebook with a balance of seven thousand, a porcelain Madonna and dozens of framed family photos.' He started the car and headed downtown. 'I also found some letterheads from E.F. Incorporated, based in LA, with a branch here in Manhattan, a lot of paperwork from the same, and about a dozen messages on his answering machine. No one has seen him for more than a week, and his mail hasn't been picked up.'

'Do you think he's still in Philadelphia?'

'He won't get near you, Dora. That's a promise.'

Jed fought his way from Manhattan to Brooklyn Heights. By the time he found Franklin Flowers's address, he had fitted together all the pieces he had so far, jumbled them and let them reassemble. He slipped smoothly into a parking spot.

'Looks like you're in on this one, Conroy. But don't forget—'

'I know. You'll do the talking.'

They entered the shop. It was hardly bigger than the average living room and was crammed with merchandise ranging from ratty teddy bears to standard lamps. It was deserted. As the sign on the counter instructed, Jed rang a brass bell.

'One moment, please.' A male voice came from behind a beaded curtain. Before Dora could finish her survey of a group of Avon bottles, Flowers came through the curtain with a rattle of beads. He was a big man, gone soft in the middle. Like his teddy bears, he had a round, homely face that radiated sweetness. His hair was parted nearly at his ear to allow him to comb the thin, blonde strands over a wide bald spot.

'Good morning! No, no . . .' Clucking, he glanced towards a row of ticking clocks. 'It's afternoon already. Where does the time go? I never seem to be able to keep up. Now, what may I do for you?'

Jed took the lead. 'Mr Flowers?'

'Yes, I'm Frank Flowers.' He sang the words, like a kindergarten teacher.

'Do you know Sherman Porter?'

Flowers's jolly expression disintegrated. 'Poor man. Tragic.'

'You sent a shipment to him,' Jed continued. 'It arrived in Virginia on the 21st of December.'

'Oh, yes.' Flowers smiled sadly. 'Who would have guessed it would be the last time Sherman and I would do business together?'

'There seems to be a question about the shipment. A painting.'

'Painting?' Flowers frowned. 'I didn't send a painting.'

'The abstract, signed E. Billingsly.'

'Abstract?' Tilting his head, Flowers giggled. 'Oh, my dear, no. I would *never* touch an abstract. They're so hard to sell.'

'Do you have a list of the items you shipped?'

'Naturally. I'm a stickler for organisation. I'll be back in a jiff.'

He disappeared behind the curtain and returned carrying two files—one in yellow, the other in red. 'I colour-code, you see. The yellow will be what I purchased at the estate sale.' He opened the folder and flipped through meticulously typed lists of merchandise. 'Now that would have been . . . December 12. Here we are. Woodlow estate, Catskills, December 12. There's no painting.'

Nor was there a china dog, Jed observed. Or a figurine matching the description of the one Tom Ashworth had died for.

'And this is one of my shipping files, specifically dealing with Sherman—the Lord rest him. As you can see,' he said as he opened the red folder, 'the top shipment was the last. Not a painting in sight.' He grinned. 'It must have gotten mixed up with my things after uncrating. Sherman, bless him, was a teensy bit careless.'

'Yes,' Jed said. 'I'm sure you're right.'

'HE'S WRONG,' Dora stated as she pulled open the car door. 'I saw the stock boy setting up that entire lot. It had just arrived.'

'Yeah.' Jed took out his keys, jiggling them restlessly in his hand. 'Not one item matches Flowers's list. Tell me this, Conroy. If you were smuggling a Monet and other illegal valuables—'

'I wouldn't have them shipped to auction,' she interrupted, her eyes darkening with inspiration. 'Somebody messed up. DiCarlo?'

'Might be. But the packing slips. The one in Flowers's file, and the one I lifted from Porter's. They were both from Premium Shipping.' He started the car. 'I've got some calls to make.'

They stopped at a small Brooklyn restaurant. While Jed made his calls from the payphone, Dora had coffee and a sandwich.

'Looks like the Monet's genuine.' Jed sat down and pulled Dora's plate over. 'They need to run tests, but it got a thumbs up.' He wolfed down a triangle of sandwich and signalled for coffee. 'It turns out that everybody who bought from the shipment was robbed between December 22 and New Year. In each case the piece they'd bought at the auction was taken. Sloppy jobs. And still no sign of DiCarlo. He's some sort of vice-president of the New

363

York branch of E.F. Incorporated. His staff claim not to know his whereabouts. His mother filed a missing-person report this morning.'

'I have a theory,' Dora said.

He grinned. 'Playing Nancy Drew again?'

'Well, it's obvious to me there were two shipments. The one from the estate sale and the one with the smuggled goods. Since we agree that it would have been impossibly stupid for DiCarlo to have purposely shipped off his loot to auction, the logical conclusion is that the two shipments were mixed up.'

'Go on,' he encouraged. 'You're about to earn a merit badge.'

'And since both packing slips originated from Premium, one could deduce that the mix-up happened there.'

'Nice going, Nancy. Let's go check out Premium.'

BILL TARKINGTON bounced up to his office door, beaming a smile. 'Mr Skimmerhorn?' He pumped Jed's hand. 'And Miss Conroy. I apologise for making you wait. How about some coffee?'

Before Jed could decline Dora was saying, 'I'd love some.'

Happy to serve, Tarkington turned to fill three cups and passed them out. 'Now, then.' He settled himself behind his desk. 'You had some question about a shipment, didn't you?'

'That's right.' Jed read what he'd copied from Flowers's invoice. 'December 17th from a Franklin Flowers, destination Sherman Porter, Front Royal, Virginia. Number ASB-54467.'

'We'll just call that right on up. What was the problem, exactly?'

'The merchandise shipped was not the merchandise received.'

Tarkington's face took on a pained look. 'Oh, Lordy, not again.'

'You had this happen before?' Jed demanded.

Tarkington punched keys. 'The Christmas rush this year was unusually bad. December 17th, you said.' His eyes brightened. 'That could be it! There was another complaint about a shipment that went out that day. The client was very upset.'

'DiCarlo,' Dora said involuntarily.

Before Jed could snarl at her, Tarkington was beaming again. 'Right. Do you know him?'

'We've met.' Dora kept an easy smile on her face.

'Isn't that a coincidence? I've done everything possible to locate Mr DiCarlo's merchandise, and now it seems that the two shipments were misdirected. I'll contact him immediately.'

'We'll take care of that.' Jed scanned the computer screen over Tarkington's shoulder and noted the shipping clerk's name.

'That would save me an embarrassing moment.' He slurped at his coffee and winked. 'We will, of course, reimburse both you and Mr DiCarlo for all shipping charges.'

'I was right,' Dora said under her breath as they walked away.

'Pat yourself on the back later.' Jed walked up to the nearest clerk. 'Where's Johnson?'

'Opal?' The clerk jerked his head. 'Over there. Line six.'

'What are we doing now?' Dora asked.

'Checking tedious details.'

Dora didn't find it tedious at all. They sat with Opal in the employee lunch room and listened to her story. Because Dora was obviously fascinated and sympathetic, Jed sat back and let her play good cop. He'd have said she was born for it.

'Can you believe it?' The excitement was building as they made their way across the car park. 'She mixes up invoices, and we end up with a smuggled Monet.' Dora grinned as Jed unlocked the car door. 'Maybe I like police work after all.'

'Stick with selling knick-knacks,' Jed advised.

'At least you could say I did a good job.'

'You did a good job. Don't get cocky.'

'I'm not cocky. All we have to do now is find DiCarlo.'

'Leave that one to the big boys, baby. Time to step back.'

And he had something else to check out now. Bill Tarkington's computer screen had been a fount of information: the intended recipient of DiCarlo's illicit shipment was Abel Winesap of E.F. Incorporated, Los Angeles.

THE CHILL IN THE AIR didn't keep Finley from his morning ritual. Every day, regardless of the weather, he swam fifty laps in his hour-glass-shaped pool while Vivaldi poured out of the speakers hidden in the jasmine plants. It was to him a matter of discipline.

He rose in the water, enjoyed the sensation of having it run off his skin. He strode up the wide curving steps, onto the terracotta edging and into the snowy white robe his butler held for him. 'Time?' he said, rubbing down briskly.

'Twelve minutes, eighteen seconds, sir.'

The butler always stopped the clock at precisely that time. Once, he had made the mistake of timing Finley at a bit over thirteen minutes. An ugly scene had followed.

'Excellent.' Smugly satisfied, Finley accepted his vitamin drink, a concoction of herbs and Chinese roots. Then he dismissed the butler and turned his thoughts to Isadora Conroy. He'd read the dossier on her that Winesap had prepared for him, and now he had a solution.

He chuckled. If it didn't work, well then, he would simply kill her.

13

Dora was trying not to be annoyed. It was too predictable a reaction, she told herself, much too typical. Any woman would be annoyed if she awoke alone in bed without a clue as to where her lover had gone or when he might be returning. She wasn't *any* woman, Dora reminded herself. They were both free to come and go as they pleased. She wouldn't even ask Jed where he'd been.

But when she heard the knock on the door she tugged down the hem of her oversized sweatshirt and marched into the living room. 'OK, Skimmerhorn,' she muttered. 'This better be good.'

She yanked open the door, turned and walked stiffly into the kitchen. 'I woke up alone in bed this morning.'

'Hold it. What are you talking about?'

'Nothing.' Her voice was low and furious.

'Conroy.' Caught between amusement and exasperation, he leaned against the doorjamb. 'You're miffed because I went out?'

'Why should I be? I'm used to waking up in bed alone.'

Baffled, he scrubbed his hands over his face. 'Look, I got up early. I didn't want to wake you . . . Went to the gym for an hour, caught breakfast with Brent. We had some things to go over.'

'Did I ask you for an explanation? Oh, forget it!' Disgusted with herself, she pinched the bridge of her nose.

'I really need to satisfy my curiosity,' he said. 'What does a woman wear under a baggy football jogging suit?'

'Nothing important. In fact . . .' She laughed. 'Nothing at all.'

'There's a hole in the shoulder.' He scooped her up, nuzzled her neck as he carried her to the bedroom.

'I know.' They tumbled like wrestling children onto the bed. She sighed and slid her fingers into his hair.

He kissed her, twining a lock of her hair round his finger. The sun was bright through the open curtain, spilling generously over her face, her skin. 'We could start a fire,' Jed said, 'and spend the rest of the morning in bed watching game shows.'

'That sounds incredibly tempting, Skimmerhorn. Why do I have this odd feeling that you're trying to keep me out of the way?'

'Out of whose way?'

'Yours. You and Brent are working on something, and you don't want me to know what it is.' She shrugged. 'I'll find out anyway.'

'How?'

'I'll vamp it out of you.'

'Vamp?'

She laughed, so delighted with him that she leapt into his arms. 'Skimmerhorn, I love you.'

She started to kiss him senseless and felt him stiffen. Very slowly, her heart sank to her knees. 'Whoops.' She fought for a light tone as she untangled herself from him. 'Wasn't supposed to let that one out, was I? Sorry. Chalk it up to the heat of the moment.'

He finally managed her name. 'Dora—'

'No, really.' Oh, Lord, she thought, panicked. She was going to cry if she didn't do something. 'It was just a slip of the tongue.'

His face was set, his eyes absolutely blank.

'Listen, Skimmerhorn, the L word comes real easy to me. My family boots it around like a football—you know us theatrical types.' Her voice was excessively cheerful. 'Why don't you start that fire? I'll make us something to snack on while watching game shows.'

'You meant it, didn't you?' He said it quietly, and the eyes that had fastened on her face made it impossible for her to hedge.

'Yes, I meant it. And since it obviously bothers you so much, I'll be careful not to say it again. Ever. All right?'

No, it was far from all right. He couldn't pinpoint the moment when things had changed between them any more than he could pinpoint his own feelings. But he could do something to stabilise what was becoming a dangerous situation.

'Get dressed,' he told her. 'I want to show you something.'

THE WEATHER, at least, was promising. The sun beat hard against the windscreen of Jed's Thunderbird as they drove through the city, far from the rivers with their frisky breezes, towards Chestnut Hill.

He hadn't spoken since they'd started the drive. She didn't ask where they were going. She was almost sure she knew.

Far up the hill the trees were old and stately, the homes trim and elegant. Jed pulled up in a narrow driveway beside a lovely old Colonial building. The brick had mellowed to a soft dusky rose, and the trim was a Wedgwood blue. Tall windows glinted in the strong sunlight.

It was a fine house, Dora mused. Beautifully maintained, strongly feminine, with its neat lines and dignity. She imagined it in the summer, when the roses would be sumptuously blooming. And in the autumn, when the big leafy trees would burst into golds and scarlets. The picture was completed with lace at the windows and a dog in the yard. And because she imagined so well, her heart broke a little. She doubted very much that Jed saw the house as she did.

She alighted from the car. 'This is where you grew up?'

'That's right.' He led the way to the door flanked with lovely bevelled-glass inserts. When he'd unlocked it, he stepped back and waited for Dora to go in ahead.

The foyer was two storeys, topped with a many-tiered chandelier that would graciously light the way up the grand oak staircase. The floor was tiled with large squares of black and white marble. Dora ran her hand over the gleaming newel post at the base of the banister—a banister, she thought, fashioned for a woman's trailing fingers. She was curious where Jed had fitted into the design.

'You're planning to sell it?'

He was watching her carefully as she wandered from the foyer into the front parlour. 'It's on the market.' He stayed where he was when Dora walked over to study the scrubbed and empty hearth.

A fire would take away the chill, she thought. Absently she wandered out again and down the hall. She found a library, stripped of books; another parlour, with a view of a cobbled patio that begged for flower boxes; the dining room, vast and empty; and, finally, the kitchen, with its charming hearth and brick oven. But she found no warmth there, only the cold, echoing silence of an unwanted house.

'It's a pretty view from here,' she said, to fill the void. There should be a sandpit in the yard, she thought, linking her tensed fingers together. A swing hanging from the big maple.

'You should see the rest of it.' And once she had, he thought grimly, he hoped never to walk through the door again.

She caught up with him at the base of the stairs, where he had gone to wait for her. 'Jed, this isn't necessary.'

'Let's go upstairs.' He took her arm, ignoring her hesitation. At the top he inclined his head towards a door. 'My mother's room. My father's was down the hall. As you can see, there were several rooms between.'

She sighed. 'Where was yours?'

'There.'

Dora moved down the landing and peeked into the room. It was large and airy, bright with afternoon light. The windows overlooked the rear lawn. Dora sat on the narrow window seat and looked out.

'There used to be a chestnut tree out there,' he said. 'I'd go out that way at night, hitch a ride and go down to Market Street to raise hell. One night one of the servants spotted me and reported it to my father. He had the tree cut down the next day. Then he came up here, locked the door and beat me. I was fourteen.' He said it without emotion. 'That's when I started lifting weights. He wasn't going to beat me again. If he tried, I was damn well going to be strong enough to take him. A couple of years later I did. And that's how I earned boarding school, until I got kicked out.'

368

'What about your mother?' she asked quietly.

'She preferred throwing things, expensive things. She knocked me unconscious once with a Meissen vase.'

Dora nodded, swallowed. 'Your sister?'

He shrugged. 'They vacillated between treating her like a Dresden doll and a prison inmate. Tea parties one day, locked doors the next. Sharing the misery should have made us close, but somehow it never did. I got the call to go see Elaine from one of Speck's men. They wanted me on the scene when it happened. They knew she went out every Wednesday at eleven to have her hair done. I didn't. I was minutes away from her house, and annoyed at being summoned, when the dispatch came through with the bomb threat.'

He paused for a moment. 'I was first on the scene, just as Speck planned. I could see her in the car as I ran. The roses were blooming,' he said softly, seeing it all perfectly again. 'She looked towards me. I could see the surprise on her face. Then she turned the key and the car went up. The blast knocked me back into the roses.'

'You tried to save her, Jed.'

'I didn't save her,' he said flatly. 'That's for me to live with.'

Dora sat quietly. Jed felt a jolt of surprise at how lovely she looked there with the sun pouring around her, her eyes calm and watchful, her mouth solemn. Odd, he thought, there had never been anything in this house he'd considered beautiful. Until now.

'I understand why you brought me here,' she began. 'You wanted me to see a cold, empty house, and to understand that, like the house, you have nothing to offer.'

'I don't have anything to offer.'

'You don't want to,' she corrected. 'And considering the role models in your life, it's certainly logical. The problem is, Skimmerhorn, emotions just aren't logical.' She tilted her head and the sun warmed her skin. 'I told you I love you, and you'd probably have preferred a slap in the face, but there it is. I didn't mean to say it—or maybe I did.' She smiled a little, but her eyes were dulled with sadness. 'Let me tell you how I see it. Love's a gift, and can certainly be refused. I'm not asking for a gift in return. It's not that I don't want it, but I don't expect it.'

She rose then and, crossing the room, took his face gently in her hands. There was a compassion in her eyes that humbled him. 'Take what's offered, Jed, especially when it's offered without expectations. I won't keep throwing it in your face.'

'You're leaving yourself open, Dora.'

'I know.' She kissed him, one cheek, the other, then his mouth.

'I'm not what you need.' But he gathered her close and held

on. Because she was so exactly what he needed.

'You're wrong.' She willed the threatening tears away. 'You're wrong about the house, too. You're both just waiting.'

HE KEPT LOSING his train of thought. Jed knew the details he and Brent discussed were vital, but he kept remembering the way Dora's hands had felt against his face when she'd smiled and asked him to accept love.

'Jed, what's on your mind?'

Jed blinked. 'What? Nothing.' He washed the mood away with some of the station house's atomic coffee. 'Winesap looks like he's another underling. I still think we should approach the top man, Finley.'

'What I can gather on the guy wouldn't fill a teacup,' Brent complained. 'He's the American ideal, self-made man and solid citizen.'

'Then a little digging shouldn't hurt him,' Jed pointed out. 'I want to take a trip to LA.'

'I thought that was where this was leading.' Brent shifted in his chair. 'Listen, the department wouldn't have anything on this case without you. But Goldman's asking questions.'

'I'm a civilian, Brent. There's nothing to stop me from taking a trip to the West Coast—at my own expense, in my own time.'

'Why don't you cut the crap?' Brent blurted out. 'I know you've got a meeting with the commissioner in an hour, and we both know what he's going to say. Tell me you're coming back on the job.'

'I can't tell you that. I *can* tell you I'm thinking about it.' Jed rose and paced the room. 'Lord, I miss this place. Isn't that something? I miss the tedium, the stupid reports, the snot-nosed rookies. Nine mornings out of ten I reach for my shoulder harness.'

'Hallelujah. Let me tell Goldman. Let me be the one.'

'I didn't say I was coming back.'

'Yeah, you did. What does Dora think about it?'

Jed's grin faded. 'We haven't talked about it. It doesn't concern her.' He headed for the door. 'We'll touch base tomorrow.'

IT WAS NEARLY MIDNIGHT when Dora gave up the attempt to sleep and bundled into her robe. Jed hadn't come home or called. Wandering into the kitchen, she put the kettle on to boil.

How could she have blown it like this? she wondered as she tossed a tea bag into a cup. Hadn't she known that a man would head for the hills when he heard those three fateful words? Nope. She hadn't known, because she'd never said them before. And now that she was in the real show, she'd rushed her cue.

Well, it couldn't be taken back, she decided. She was going to get on with her life—with him, she hoped. Without him, if necessary. She figured she could start now by going downstairs and putting her wide-awake brain to work. Carrying her tea, she headed out, remembering to lock the door behind her.

Once in the storeroom, she continued the tedious task of reorganising the files DiCarlo had upended. The work absorbed her.

Jed stood midway down the stairs watching her. She'd set all the lights burning, like a child left home alone at night. She was wearing the green robe and a pair of purple socks. Each time she leaned down to read a piece of paper, her hair fell softly over her cheek. Then she would push it back, the movement fluid and unstudied, before she filed the paper away and reached for another.

She turned, caught a glimpse of a figure. Papers went flying as she screamed. 'What are you doing?' she said furiously.

He came down to the base of the steps. 'What are *you* doing, Conroy? It's after midnight.'

'What does it look like I'm doing? I'm practising the minuet.'

He bent down, placed a hand over hers. 'I'm sorry I scared you. I guess you were too involved to hear me.' He tilted her face up towards the light. 'You look tired. And you're cranky, too.'

She straightened and drew a deep breath. 'If I'm out of sorts, it's because I feel useless having to keep the shop closed, and deceitful, because I'm lying to my family.'

'You don't have to be either. No reason not to open tomorrow, and you'd feel better if you came clean with your family.'

She considered it. 'I will open,' she decided, 'but I'm not telling my family. Not yet. It's for me to deal with.'

He couldn't argue. He wasn't going to tell her about his decision to pick up his badge. Not yet. 'Come upstairs. I'll give you a back rub.'

Eyes narrowed, she stepped back. 'You're being nice to me. Why, Skimmerhorn? You're planning on doing something you know I won't like.' She raced up the steps after him. 'It's something about DiCarlo, isn't it? About the painting, the whole mess.'

He wondered if it was the coward's way out to give her only one part of it. 'I'm going to LA to have a talk with DiCarlo's boss.'

'Winesap?' Her brow creased as she concentrated. 'That's who the shipment was supposed to go to, wasn't it?'

'The top man's name is Finley, Edmund G.,' Jed told her as he unlocked his door. 'I'll start with him.'

'And you think he—Finley—was expecting the shipment, that he arranged for the smuggling?'

'Yeah. And I think I know enough about him to buy a ticket for LA.' He offered her a brief run-down.

'Import-export,' she mused. 'He's probably a collector. It's possible that he was unaware of DiCarlo's sideline. But if he isn't . . .'

He caught the gleam in her eye and bit back a sigh. 'Don't think, Conroy. You can be dangerous when you think.'

'But I am thinking. And what I think is, you aren't the one who should talk to Finley. I am.'

'You're out of your mind. You're in no position to tackle something like this.'

'On the contrary.' She was warming up to the idea now and began moving round the room. 'I'm in the perfect position. I, after all, was the victim of his employee. I, the baffled innocent, will appeal to Finley's sympathies if he, in turn, is innocent and, since I too am a collector, to his imagination if he's guilty. In short, Skimmerhorn, this part is tailor-made for me.'

'It's not an audition, Conroy.'

'But it is, essentially. Now, how would I play this?'

'Dora, I don't have a handle on this guy,' Jed said. 'Walking onto his turf is risky. If Finley's involved, he's going to take one look and see through that pretty face of yours like plate glass.'

'You don't trust me. That's it, isn't it?' Her voice thickened and shook even as her eyes filled.

'It's not a matter of trust. Don't take it so personally.'

The first tear spilled over, ran a lonely trail down her cheek. 'Don't you understand that I need to do something? That I can't just sit in the background after my home and I have been violated this way? I can't bear it, Jed. I can't bear having you think of me as some helpless victim who only gets in your way.'

'Stop it.' He awkwardly lifted a hand to her hair. 'I don't think of you as helpless. You're just not trained to do this. If he suspects anything, the whole sting could fall apart before it gets started.'

She sniffled. 'Do you suspect?'

'What?'

'Do you suspect?' she demanded in a perfectly controlled voice. Leaning back, she grinned at him. 'Fell for it, didn't you?' Laughing, she patted his cheek while he stared at her. 'Don't feel too stupid, Skimmerhorn. I told you I was good. And that was just an impromptu performance.'

'You ever turn on tears again like that, I swear I'll smack you.'

'Made you feel like a heel, didn't I?' She sighed lustily. 'Sometimes I do miss the stage.' Then she shrugged. 'But not very often. Be assured, Captain, that our Mr Finley will see exactly what I want him to see.'

She could do it. He hated the fact that he was certain she could.

'I don't want you hurt.'

She softened all over—eyes, mouth, heart. 'That's one of the nicest things you've ever said to me.'

He set her down on her feet. 'Conroy, I said I didn't think you were helpless, but I never told you what I think you *are*.' She braced. 'Important,' he said simply, and melted her heart. 'Very important.'

BY NOON THE NEXT DAY Dora felt at least one part of her life was shifting back into normal gear. The shop was open for business. When Lea walked in, Dora greeted her with a fierce hug.

Laughing, Lea untangled herself. 'What's all this?'

'We're open.'

'You never explained why we were closed.'

'Too complicated,' Dora said breezily. 'I needed time off.'

'That break-in bothered you more than you let on. I knew it.'

'I guess it did. Anyway, I may have to go to LA for a couple of days. There's an import business out there I may want to cultivate. I don't want to close the shop again.' No reason to, she thought, since Brent was still pulling strings to ensure police protection.

'Don't worry about it. Terri and I can keep things going.'

The phone rang and Dora lifted the receiver. 'Hello. Dora's Parlor.'

'I'd like to speak to Miss Isadora Conroy, please.'

'Speaking.'

'Miss Conroy.' From his desk in Los Angeles, Winesap turned to his meticulously rehearsed notes. 'This is, uh, Francis Petroy.'

'Yes, Mr Petroy,' Dora said as Lea turned to greet a customer.

'I hope I'm not disturbing you, but I was given your name and number by a Mrs Helen Owings of Front Royal, Virginia.'

Dora's fingers tightened on the receiver. 'What can I do for you?'

'It concerns a painting you bought at auction in December.'

All moisture evaporated in her mouth. 'Yes, an abstract.'

'Exactly. A Billingsly. I'm a collector of abstract work. I specialise in emerging artists—in a small way, you understand. I was unable to attend that particular auction—a family emergency. It gave me some hope when Mrs Owings informed me that the painting had been sold to a dealer rather than an art collector.'

'Actually,' Dora said, playing for time, 'I'm a little of both.'

'Oh, dear.' He shuffled through his notes. 'Oh, dear.'

'But I'm always interested in a legitimate offer, Mr Petroy. Perhaps you'd like to see the painting. It would have to be some time late next week, I'm afraid.' She paused and mimed flipping through an appointments book. 'My schedule's hectic until then.'

'That would be excellent.' Relieved, Winesap mopped his sweaty neck with a handkerchief. 'What day would be good?'

'I could fit you in on Thursday. Say, at two?'

'Perfect.' Winesap scribbled down the date.

'Is there a number where I can reach you if something comes up?'

'Certainly.' As his notes instructed, Winesap gave the number for one of Finley's fronts in New Jersey. 'During business hours.'

'I understand perfectly. Next Thursday, then, Mr Petroy.' She hung up and went through to the storeroom where she found Jed calmly painting shelves.

'There you are.' He continued to paint. 'I made contact.'

'With what?' Jed laid the brush across the top of the paint can.

'With whom. I got a call from Mr Petroy—only I don't think it was Mr Petroy. It could have been DiCarlo, but—'

'Sit down, Conroy. Try sticking to the facts.'

She imagined herself filing a report, and related the phone conversation precisely. 'How's that?'

'What on earth were you thinking of, making an appointment to meet him without checking with me?'

She'd expected him to be impressed, not irritated. 'I had to say something, didn't I? Wouldn't he have been suspicious if a dealer had seemed reluctant to meet with him? And I checked on Billingsly. He doesn't even exist. There isn't any Billingsly. He wants a Monet.'

'That's brilliant, Conroy. Brilliant. But you should have put him off until I got back.' He tucked his thumbs in his pockets. 'Brent and I will work out how to handle Petroy on Thursday. We'll be back by then.'

'Back? Are you and Brent going somewhere?'

'No, you and I are.' He still wasn't happy about it, but she'd made an odd sort of sense. 'We're leaving for LA tomorrow.'

'I'm going to do it?' She pressed a hand to her heart, then tossed her arms wide and vaulted into his. 'I knew you'd see it my way.'

'I didn't. I was outvoted.' He wasn't going to admit he'd recommended her idea to Brent.

'Whatever.' She kissed him hard. 'Tomorrow?' She stopped, frowned. 'How are we going to make him want to see me?'

'Because you're going to call him. And do what you're told.'

14

In Los Angeles, Winesap entered Finley's office with a worried frown creasing his face. 'Mr Finley, sir. Miss Conroy's on line two. She's waiting to speak with you.'

'Is that so?' Finley closed Isadora Conroy's file, folded his hands on top of it. 'An interesting development.'

374

Winesap's hands twisted together like nervous cats. 'Mr Finley, when I spoke with her earlier today, she was quite cooperative. And I certainly never mentioned my connection with you.'

'Sit, Abel.' He lifted the receiver and, smiling, leaned back in his chair. 'Miss Conroy? Edmund Finley here.'

He listened, his smile growing wider and more feral. 'I'm afraid I don't follow you, Miss Conroy. You're enquiring about one of my employees—Anthony DiCarlo? . . . I see. I see. I don't know if I'll be able to help. We've told the police all we know about Mr DiCarlo's unexplained disappearance, which is, unfortunately, nothing . . . Very well,' he added after a moment. 'I'd be happy to see you. Tomorrow?' His brows rose. 'That is rather short notice. I'll see if it can be arranged. Will you hold? I'll give you to my assistant.'

Finley punched the HOLD button. 'Give her four o'clock.'

'Yes, sir.' Winesap took the receiver in his damp hand. 'Miss Conroy? This is Abel Winesap, Mr Finley's assistant. The only time that Mr Finley has open is at four . . . Yes? . . . You have the address? Excellent. We'll be expecting you.'

'Delightful.' Finley nodded approval when Winesap replaced the receiver. 'Fools rush in, Abel. I'm certainly looking forward to this. Clear my calendar for tomorrow afternoon. I want Miss Isadora Conroy to have all my attention.'

'TOMORROW FOUR O'CLOCK,' Dora said, and turned to Jed. 'He sounded puzzled but cooperative, pleasant but reserved.'

'And you sounded on the verge of hysteria but controlled.'

'There's something else.' Though she wanted to, she didn't take his hand. Hers was chilled. 'I think I just spoke with Mr Petroy.'

'Finley?'

'No.' She forced a thin smile. 'His assistant, Winesap.'

DORA WAS PLEASED when the cab pulled up in front of the pink stucco Beverly Hills Hotel. 'Skimmerhorn, you surprise me.'

'The room's booked in your name.' Jed watched Dora offer her hand to the doorman. 'You have to put it on your credit card.'

She cast a withering look at him over her shoulder. 'Thanks a bunch, big spender.'

'You want to advertise the fact that you're travelling out here with a companion?' he asked. 'A cop?'

'You left out the ex.'

'So I did.' The smart lobby of the Beverley Hills Hotel didn't seem the right setting to tell her that the ex wouldn't apply much longer.

Dora scanned the lobby—discreetly—for passing movie stars as she handed the receptionist her card for verification. 'I'm going to bill you for this, Skimmerhorn.'

'It was your idea to come.'

True enough. 'Then I'll only bill you for half.' She accepted her card back and two keys, passing one to the waiting bellman. 'Some of us are not independently wealthy.'

'Some of us,' he said as he slipped an arm round her waist, 'paid for the air fare.'

She was touched by the easy way he'd linked them together as they followed the luggage to the elevator and up to the room.

Dora quickly slipped out of her shoes and padded over to the window to check out the view. 'I haven't been in LA since I was fifteen, when my father did a part in a small, forgettable film. I guess I'm an East Coast snob, because LA doesn't do it for me. It makes me think of unnecessary eye tucks and designer yoghurt. Or maybe it's designer eye tucks and unnecessary yoghurt.' She turned back, her smile becoming puzzled when he only continued to stare at her. 'What is it?'

'You're nervous.'

'Of course I'm not nervous.' She tossed her bag onto the bed.

He laid his hands gently over hers. 'You've got a right to be nervous. I'd be more worried about you if you weren't.'

'I'll be fine. Classic opening-night jitters, that's all it is.'

TWO HOURS LATER she stepped out of the bathroom wearing a red suit that showed off every glorious curve. 'I'd forgotten how much better you feel once you're in costume,' she said. 'There's just those little ripples of nerves that keep the adrenalin up.'

'Just stick to the plan and try to remember everything you see,' he told her. 'Don't bring up the painting. You haven't got a clue about it. Try to go through Winesap. We're tracing his background. But I want your impressions.'

'I know.' She brushed her hair. 'Jed, I know exactly what to do. It's simple. Simpler, because I might have done just this if I hadn't known about the painting. It's a very logical step.'

'Just watch your back.'

'Darling, I'm counting on you to do that for me.'

DORA WAS IMPRESSED with the decor of Finley's outer office, and scoured it for helpful clues. As she'd suspected, he was a collector, and their mutual interest would give them a firm foundation.

It was difficult to hang onto her nerves, though, and character, when she really wanted to walk over and examine some of Finley's treasures first-hand. She felt favourably towards anyone who put

376

malachite vases and Chippendale furniture in his waiting area.

She hoped Finley would prove to be in the clear. She'd love to develop a business relationship. But if he wasn't . . . That thought had the nerves creeping back. She brushed at her skirt, looked at her watch. It was four ten. How long was he going to keep her waiting?

'EXCELLENT,' Finley murmured to Dora's video image. She was every bit as lovely as he'd expected from the newspaper photos Winesap had unearthed from old 'Show-' and 'Style-business' sections. Finley enjoyed the way her hands moved around restlessly. Nerves, he thought, pleased. And despite the nerves, her eyes were drawn again and again to pieces in his collection. That flattered him.

He buzzed his receptionist. It was time to begin.

'Mr Finley will see you now.'

'Thank you.' Dora rose, tucked her clutch bag under her arm and followed the woman to the double doors.

When she entered, Finley smiled and stood. 'Miss Conroy, I'm so sorry to have kept you waiting.'

'I'm just happy you could see me at all.' She crossed the rug—that pool of white—and took his extended hand. Her first impression was one of vitality and health and of well-channelled power.

'What can we offer you? Some coffee, tea, or perhaps wine?'

'Wine would be lovely.' And would give her the prop of a glass stem to twist in her hands as she told her story.

'The Pouilly-Fumé, Barbara. Please sit, Miss Conroy. Be comfortable.' In a move calculated to disarm her, he rounded the desk and took the chair beside her. 'And how was your flight?'

'Long.' Dora smiled. 'Of course, I'll go back tomorrow.'

'So soon?' His eyes glinted with a touch of curiosity. When the wine was poured, the secretary slipped soundlessly out. Finley raised his glass. 'To your health, Miss Conroy, and a safe journey home.'

'Thank you.' It was beautiful wine, silk on the tongue. 'I know it might sound foolish, coming all this way just to see you, Mr Finley. But I felt compelled.' As if overcome, she looked down.

'You're upset,' Finley said kindly. 'Take your time. You told me this had to do with Anthony DiCarlo. Are you a friend?'

'Oh, no.' There was horror in her voice, and in her eyes as she dragged them back to Finley's. She imagined DiCarlo's voice whispering in her ear to bring the revulsion into her voice. 'No. He—Mr Finley, I need to ask how much you know about him.'

'Personally?' Thinking, he pursed his lips. 'I'm afraid I don't know many of my branch employees as well as I might.'

'He's worked for you for some time?'

'Six years, I believe.' He sipped his wine. 'I have studied his file since his odd disappearance, to refresh my memory. Mr DiCarlo worked his way up the corporate ladder rather quickly. He showed initiative and ambition.' He smiled. 'The desire to better oneself—this is something I respect in an employee. I'm very much afraid of foul play. Mr DiCarlo isn't a man to neglect his responsibilities.'

'I think—I think I might know where he is.'

'Really?' There was a flash in Finley's eyes.

'I think he's in Philadelphia.' Dora took a quick sip of wine and her hand shook slightly. 'I think he's . . . watching me.'

'My dear.' Finley reached for her hand. 'Watching you?'

'I'm sorry. It's not making sense. Let me start at the beginning.'

She told the story well, with one significant pause in which she described the attack. 'And I don't understand,' she finished, with her eyes wet. 'I don't understand why.'

'How horrible for you.' Finley was all baffled sympathy while his mind performed rapid calculations. DiCarlo had left out significant details, he mused. An attempted rape and a knightly neighbour coming to the rescue. It did explain the bruises on DiCarlo's face.

As if overcome, Dora covered her face with her hand. 'I'll never forget the attack. And I identified him to the police. He killed a police officer, Mr Finley, and a woman. He left another woman for dead—one of my customers.' The thought urged the first tear down her cheek. 'I'm sorry. I've been so upset. I think he must be crazy.'

'Miss Conroy—Isadora.' He took her hand again, gently. 'This is difficult for me to take in. The idea of one of my own staff attacking women, murdering police officers. It seems I misjudged Mr DiCarlo badly. What can I do to help you?'

'I don't know. I guess if he contacted you . . .'

'My dear, I assure you, if he contacts me I will do everything to lead the authorities to him.' Finley heaved a sigh. 'I'll say, with confidence, that you won't be bothered by Mr DiCarlo again.'

'I'll try to hold onto that. You've been very kind, Mr Finley.'

'Edmund.'

'Edmund.' Her eyes were guileless and trusting. 'Just talking it out has helped. I'd like to ask, if you find anything, that you'd call me.'

'I understand. Of course. I'm going to put our security team on this. If there's a trace of DiCarlo, they'll find it.'

She closed her eyes, relaxed her shoulders. 'I knew I was right to come here. Thank you.' When she rose, he took both her hands.

'I'd consider it a favour if you'd have dinner with me tonight.'

'Dinner?' Her mind went sheet blank.

'I don't like to think of you alone and upset. I feel responsible.'

378

'That's very kind of you.'

'Then ease my conscience a bit. And, I admit, I would find it very pleasant to spend the evening with a lovely young woman who shares my interests.' Finley gestured towards a curio cabinet. 'If you run an antique shop, you'd be interested in my treasures.'

'Yes, I am. I've already admired several of your pieces. The horse's head?' She nodded towards a stone figure. 'Han dynasty?'

'Precisely.' He beamed, like a professor to a prize student.

'I love things,' she confessed. 'Owning things.'

'Ah, yes, I understand. I have a brooch I'd like you to see.' He thought of the sapphire, and the pleasure it would give him to taunt her with it. 'So it is decided. I'll have a car get you at your hotel. Say, seven thirty.'

'I . . .'

'Please, don't misunderstand. My home is fully staffed, so you'll be well chaperoned. But I don't often have the opportunity to show off my treasures to someone who recognises their intrinsic worth. I'd love your opinion on my pomander collection.'

'Pomanders?' Dora said, and sighed. If she hadn't been on a mission, she'd have agreed in any case. How could she resist a collection of pomanders? 'I'd love to.'

DORA STROLLED back into the hotel room, filled with the warmth of success. She found Jed pacing. 'What took you so long?'

'It was only an hour. I was brilliant,' she said, and wrapped her arms round his neck.

'I'll tell you if you were brilliant.' He put a hand on top of her head and pushed her into a chair. 'Tell me about Finley. Everything.'

'Is there any coffee left?' She picked up a room-service pot, poured coffee, took a sip, sat back and told him.

'He really was nice,' she concluded. 'And properly shocked by my story. I, of course, played the part of the spooked heroine to perfection. He offered his security team to track down DiCarlo.'

'What about Winesap?'

'The receptionist told me he was out of the office.'

'If he's the one who's going to keep the appointment next Thursday, he couldn't afford having you see him.'

'I thought of that. So I talked to the security guard in the lobby on the way out. I told him I'd seen Winesap's name on the board and that my father had worked with an Abel Winesap years ago. So I asked if this guy was tall and heavyset, with red hair. It turns out this Winesap is short and skinny, round-shouldered and balding.'

'Good girl, Nancy Drew.'

'Thanks.' Now came the hard part, Dora mused. She would have to work up to it carefully. 'Finley has a whole wall of monitors in his office. Kind of creepy, you know. I guess he has security cameras everywhere. But he also had a Gallé lamp that made me want to sit up and beg. And a Han horse. That barely touches on it. Anyway, I'll see his personal collection at dinner tonight.'

Jed snatched her wrist. 'Play that back, Conroy. Slow speed.'

'He asked me to have dinner with him.' She walked over to the closet and brought out a little black dress with a glittery bolero jacket in red and gold stripes. 'This is what I'm here for, isn't it? To gain his sympathy and confidence and to find out everything I can.'

'I don't like you going alone. I don't have enough on him.'

'You'll have more when I get back, won't you?'

He crossed the room to her. His face was set. 'I never had anyone to worry about before. I don't like it.'

'I can understand that. I'll be fine.'

'Sure you will.' He lowered his cheek to the back of her head. 'Dora . . .' What could he say? he wondered. Nothing that was churning inside him seemed right. 'I'll miss you tonight.'

She was wonderfully touched and nuzzled her lips to his. 'I've also got an hour before I have to get ready.'

'OK, Conroy. We'll go over the ground rules for your dinner.'

DORA STEPPED off the kerb and into a white Mercedes limo at precisely seven thirty. A single white rosebud lay across the seat.

Brushing the rose petals across her cheek, she looked up towards the window where she knew Jed would be watching. The car pulled smoothly away. Because she was looking back, she noticed a dark saloon car cruise out into the traffic behind them.

Dora closed her eyes and put all thoughts of Jed out of her mind. For the next few hours she was alone. She enjoyed the ride up into the hills and prepared for Act Two.

After her impressions of his office, she'd expected Finley's house to be lavish. She wasn't disappointed. The sweeping drive up, the quick, teasing peeks of the building through screening trees. Then the full impact of stone and brick and glass shimmering in the last fiery lights of the dying sun.

A well-set stage.

There was only a moment to appreciate the dolphin-shaped Adam knocker before the door was opened by a uniformed maid.

'Mr Finley would like you to wait in the drawing room.'

Dora didn't bother to disguise her admiration for the magnificent entrance hall. In the parlour she gave the maid a murmured assent at the offer of wine and was grateful when she had the glass in hand and was alone to worship.

When Finley joined her, she was mentally devouring a collection of Japanese netsukes. 'I see you're enjoying my toys.'

'Oh, yes.' Eyes dark, she turned from the curios. 'I feel like Alice, and I've just stumbled into the best corner of Wonderland.'

'I was certain I'd find it pleasant to share my things with you.'

'You've made my trip very worth while, Mr Finley.'

'Then I'm content.' He walked over, placed a light hand at the small of her back. It wasn't a suggestive move. She had no explanation as to why her skin crawled under the friendly pressure. 'Shall I give you the tour before dinner?'

'Yes, please.' Agreeably, she slipped a hand through his arm.

He was erudite and entertaining, Dora thought. Why she was violently uncomfortable she couldn't have said. He took a greedy delight in all he'd acquired, yet she understood greed. It took all her skill to play out her role as they moved from room to room.

'This is the pin I mentioned earlier.' Finley offered her the sapphire brooch. 'The stone is, of course, magnificent, but the workmanship of the setting and, again, the history, add intrigue.'

'It's beautiful.' It was both beautiful and tragic. Tragic, she realised, because it would be forever behind glass. Perhaps that was the difference between them. She passed her treasures on, gave them a new life. Finley locked his away.

'It was said to belong to a queen,' Finley told her, waiting, watching her face for a sign of recognition. 'Mary, Queen of Scots. I often wonder if she wore it when she was arrested for treason.'

'I'd rather think she wore it riding across the moors.'

'And this.' He now chose the smuggled étui. 'This belonged to another queen with a sad fate. Napoleon gave it to Josephine. Before he divorced her for being barren.'

'You give your treasures a sad history, Edmund.'

'I find poignancy increases their meaning. Shall we dine?'

There was lobster bisque, and Peking duck so delicate it all but melted on the tongue. The meal was served on Limoges and eaten with Georgian silver. Dom Pérignon was poured into antique Waterford. Dora fought to relax and enjoy the meal.

'Tell me about your shop,' Finley invited. 'It must be exciting for you to buy and sell every day, to handle lovely things time and again. There's something innately satisfying about making your own business out of something you love. Not everyone has the courage. I believe, Isadora, that you have a great deal of courage.'

Her stomach fluttered, but she managed to swallow a mouthful of duck. 'I hate to confess, but I frighten very easily.'

'You underestimate yourself. After all, you came here, to me.' He smiled, watching her with eyes as sharp as carved jade. 'For all you knew, Mr DiCarlo might have been acting on my orders.'

When she went pale and set down her fork with a rattle, he laughed, patted her hand. 'Now I have frightened you. I apologise. It was merely said to illustrate my point.'

She fisted and unfisted her hands in her lap. She'd never wanted to escape so badly in her life. 'You must have marvellous contacts,' she said. 'Do you do much of the travelling and acquiring?'

He signalled for dessert, and a creamy chocolate soufflé was soon served. 'Not as much as I'd like. But I take the occasional trip to the Orient or Europe. I even get to the East Coast from time to time.'

'I hope you'll let me know if you're ever in Philadelphia.'

'I wouldn't think of taking the trip without paying you a call.'

After a few moments she rose to play her final scene, the contented guest taking a reluctant leave. 'It was a wonderful meal, Edmund, a delightful evening.'

'Believe me, it was my pleasure.' He stood and kissed her hand.

She had the urge to rub her hand clean on her jacket. 'Please, call me if you—if there's any news about DiCarlo.'

'I will. I have a feeling it will all be sorted out very soon.'

WHEN SHE RETURNED to the hotel, Dora watched the limo drive away, then stood on the sidewalk and waited to calm down. She didn't want to face Jed until she had herself under control. Then she saw the dark saloon pull up across the street. She bolted into the lobby.

Jumping at shadows, Conroy, she berated herself while her heart roared in her ears. By the time she'd ridden up to her floor and slipped the key into the lock, she had herself back in line. She was even able to smile when she walked in and saw Jed scowling.

'Ah, you waited up for me.'

'You're always good for a laugh, Conroy. You really—'

He broke off after he'd turned and taken a look at her. He hadn't known anyone could appear so exhausted and still stand on both feet. She sat tiredly on the edge of the bed to pull off her dress and remove her stockings, then slipped on a nightshirt.

'The house—it's immense. I've never seen so many museum-quality pieces in one place. It's a little empire.' There were faint bruises of fatigue under her eyes. 'He spooked me, Jed. He was a perfect gentleman. And being alone with him terrified me.'

'Tell me.' He combed a hand through her hair.

'He took me all through the house,' she began. 'And there was something odd about the way he showed off his pieces. A handful of them in particular. I could feel him watching me when I looked at them. I kept telling myself I was imagining it, because he was being so charming. We had this elegant dinner in this elegant room on elegant china. But it was like being defenceless.'

'You were alone.'

She yawned. 'Not really—or not often. He has an army of servants. I wasn't really afraid that he'd hurt me. I was afraid he wanted to.' She blew out a breath, grateful that Jed didn't tell her she was being a fool. 'You might see what you can find out about a sapphire brooch—sixteenth-century. The stone looked to be about eight carats, in a horizontal setting of gold filigree, with small, round-cut diamonds. He made a real issue of showing it to me.'

'Fine. You did good.'

She gave him a sleepy smile. 'Do I get a detective's gold star?'

'That's a gold shield, Nancy. And no. You're retiring.'

She stretched out without bothering to crawl under the sheets. 'I forgot. I saw this guy in a dark saloon pull out after the limo when we left. Then he drove up a few minutes after I got back.'

'I've had you tailed all day. Local private eye.'

She smiled. 'You hired a bodyguard for me.'

'I hired him for me,' he said lightly.

After pillowing her head on her folded arms, she shut her eyes and was asleep. Quietly he turned down the covers and, lifting her, slipped her between the sheets. She never stirred. Jed turned off the lights and got into bed beside her. After a little while he gathered her close to hold her while he joined her in sleep.

THE PHONE SHRILLED beside them. Dora's heart shot to her throat.

Jed shifted to grope for the receiver. 'Skimmerhorn.'

'Jed, sorry to wake you.' There was an edge of excitement in Brent's voice. 'I've got something you might want to check out.'

'Yeah?' Jed rolled over, switched on the light and picked up the pen from the bedside table.

'I just picked up a fax from the sheriff's department out there. A couple of hikers stumbled over a body a few days ago, wedged in a shallow ravine in the hills. There was enough left for a couple of prints. We can stop looking for DiCarlo. He's real dead.'

'How long?'

'Given the exposure, some time around the first of the year. I figured you'd want to talk to the coroner, the investigating officers.'

'Give me the names.' Jed wrote down the information.

'I'll fax the guys back,' Brent continued. 'Tell them that you were on a related investigation out there. They'll be ready for you.'

'Thanks. I'll be in touch.'

Dora was sitting up in bed, her chin resting on her knees, when Jed hung up the phone. 'You've got cop all over your face.'

'DiCarlo,' he told her flatly. 'They've found him.'

15

Sheriff Curtis Dearborne harboured an innate distrust of outsiders. Since he considered any member of the LA Police Department an outsider, an East Coast cop was an entity to be watched with extra care.

He rose from his desk when Jed and Dora entered, a towering, well-muscled man. His square, handsome face was serious, his handshake firm. 'Captain Skimmerhorn, pretty handy you being out our way when we identify the stiff.'

Jed summed up his man instantly. 'I appreciate your passing on the information, Sheriff. I'm sure Lieutenant Chapman filled you in on the mess we've got back home. Your quick work will be some comfort to Officer Trainor's widow.'

It was exactly the right button. Dearborne's eyes frosted, his mouth thinned. 'Sit down, Captain, Miss Conroy.'

'Thanks.' Stemming impatience, Jed took a seat. 'I was told there was no identification on the body.'

'Not a lick.' Dearborne's chair creaked comfortably as he sat back. 'But we ruled out robbery right off. The wallet was gone, but the guy wore a diamond on his pinkie, and a gold neck chain.'

'I'd like a look at the coroner's report if that's all right,' Jed began. 'And any physical evidence you've gathered. The more I go back with, the better.'

'I think we can accommodate you there. We've got the tarp and what's left of his clothes downstairs. If you want a look at the body, we'll take a run down to the coroner's.'

'I'd appreciate that. Could Miss Conroy wait here?' Jed said.

'That's fine. You just make yourself comfortable.'

'Thank you, Sheriff. I wouldn't want to get in the way,' Dora said. 'May I use your phone to make a credit-card call?'

Dearborne gestured towards the phone. 'Use line one.'

'Thank you.' There was no use being annoyed with Jed, she mused as they trooped off. In any case, she'd let her family know she was being delayed a few hours. She smiled. She wondered if Jed realised that Dearborne had called him Captain—and that Jed hadn't even winced. He'll have his badge back by spring, she predicted.

'Good afternoon. Dora's Parlor,' Lea answered.

'You've got a great voice, honey.'

Lea chuckled. 'Hey, where are you? At thirty thousand feet?'

'No.' Dora pushed back her hair. 'Just taking care of a little business Jed wanted to handle while we were here. So we'll be taking a later plane. Everything there OK?'

'Fine. How did your meeting go with the import-export guy?'

'Oh.' Hedging, Dora thumbed a file on the desk. 'I don't think we'll be doing business after all. He's out of my league.'

'Well, call me when you get in.'

'All right. I don't imagine we'll make it before ten your time, so don't start worrying until after eleven.' Dora idly flipped open the file that the deputy had set on the desk. Her mouth went dust-dry as she stared down at the colour photo. Her head buzzed.

'Dora? Dory? Are you still there? Shoot. Did we get cut off?'

'No.' With a herculean effort Dora levelled her voice. 'Sorry, I have to go. I'll call you later.'

'OK. See you tomorrow, honey. Safe trip.'

'Thanks. Bye.' Very deliberately Dora replaced the receiver. Her hands had gone icy cold beneath a sheer layer of sweat.

It was DiCarlo. There was enough of his face left for her to be sure of that. She was also sure that he hadn't died well. With numb fingers she shifted the first police photo aside and stared at the second. She couldn't take her eyes away even when the buzzing in her head became a roar and her vision blurred.

Jed let out one concise oath when he walked in and saw her white face and the open file. Even as he strode towards her, he watched her eyes roll back. He had her sitting on a chair away from the desk and her head between her knees in two brisk moves. 'Breathe slow.' He slapped the file closed with his free hand.

'I was calling Lea,' Dora said as her stomach heaved.

'Try a little of this.' Dearborne held out a cup of water. Sympathy was in his voice. He remembered his first murder victim.

Jed kept the pressure light on Dora's head as he accepted the water. 'Would you give us a minute, Sheriff?'

'Sure. Take your time.' Dearborne closed the door behind him.

'I want you to come up real slow,' Jed told her.

'I'm OK.' But the trembling was worse than the nausea, and much more difficult to control. She let her head fall back against the chair and kept her eyes closed.

'Try some of this.' He brought the cup to her lips, urging her to swallow. 'I want you to feel better before I yell at you.'

She looked away from him. 'I wasn't playing detective.'

'You have no business being this close, Dora.'

'I have no business?' She set the cup aside and forced herself to stand. 'The man inside that file tried to rape me. He would certainly have killed me. That brings me pretty close. Even knowing all that, I can't justify what I saw in those pictures. I just can't.' She walked shakily to the door. 'I'll wait in the car.'

Jed waited until she was gone before he picked up the file and studied the photos. He swore at what Dora had seen.

'She OK?' Dearborne asked as he came back in.

'She'll do.' He handed the file over. 'I'd like to take you up on your offer of talking to the coroner.'

'No problem. You can read the autopsy report on the way. It's interesting. Our pal had a heck of a last meal.'

DORA REFUSED the snack the flight attendant offered and stuck with icy ginger ale. 'You haven't yelled at me yet.'

Jed continued to work on his crossword puzzle. He'd have preferred to read through Dearborne's reports again, but they would wait until he was alone. 'It didn't seem worth it.'

'I'd rather you did, so you'd stop being mad at me. And I think I'd handle it better if you told me what you found out. You've hardly spoken since we left LA. Speculation can be worse than reality.'

'There isn't that much to tell.' He let the newspaper fall into his lap. 'We know DiCarlo flew out to the Coast on New Year's Eve, rented a car, booked a hotel room. He didn't sleep in the room that night; he didn't return the car. That hasn't turned up yet, either. He'd also booked a flight for Cancun, but he didn't use the ticket.'

'So he didn't plan on coming back east any time soon.' She tried to think it through. 'Do you think he came out to see Finley?'

'There's no record of him going to the offices. There's no evidence to link Finley to any of it at this point. We know DiCarlo came to LA, and he died there. He was murdered some time between December thirty-first and January second—a gunshot wound to the abdomen. The bruises on the face I put there myself.'

'I see.' To keep her voice steady she continued to sip the ginger ale like medicine. 'That's like no signs of struggle, right?'

'That's right, Miss Drew.' He gave her hand an approving squeeze. She was toughing it out, he thought, and admired her for it.

'The condemned man had enjoyed a hearty last meal that included pheasant, wine, and raspberries with white chocolate. Dearborne's going to have his hands full checking restaurant menus. There were also some white stones and mulch found rolled up in the tarp he'd been wrapped in. The kind you find in flowerbeds and around ornamental shrubs. Did Finley have gardens?'

'Extensive ones.' She let out a shaky breath. 'And he's very proud of them. I admired part of them from his solarium.' Her colour had drained again when she turned to look at Jed. 'They were neat and tidy, well mulched, with narrow pathways of white stone.'

'You've got good eyes, Conroy. Now close them for a while.'

'I think I'd be better off watching the movie.' She reached unsteadily for the headphones, slipped them on and escaped.

In LA, WINESAP entered Finley's office, wringing his hands. 'You wanted to see me, Mr Finley?'

Finley gestured Winesap in. His eyes were blank as he sat back. 'How long have you worked for me, Abel?'

Winesap moistened his lips. 'Eight years now, sir.'

'Eight years.' Nodding slowly, Finley steepled his index fingers. 'I've been thinking of you, Abel, all through the morning and into the afternoon. And as I did so, it occurred to me that over these eight years I've had very little cause to criticise your work. You are prompt, you are efficient, you are—in most cases—thorough.'

'Thank you, sir. I do my best.'

'I believe you do. Which is why I find myself so disappointed today. You perhaps haven't read the morning paper?'

'Things have been a bit hectic,' Winesap said apologetically.

'One should always make time for current events.' With his eyes glittering on Winesap's face, Finley stabbed a finger at the newspaper on his desk. 'Such as this. Read it now, Abel, if you will.'

'Yes, sir.' All but shaking in terror now, Winesap approached the desk and took the paper. The article Finley referred to, circled over and over again in blood-red ink, was headlined BODY DISCOVERED BY HIKERS. Winesap felt his bowels loosen.

Finley snatched the paper away. 'I expected better from you, Abel. They will, of course, identify the body, and I will be forced to answer more questions. Naturally, I'm confident that I can handle the police. But really you should have spared me this inconvenience.'

'Yes, sir. I'm terribly sorry. I can't apologise enough.'

'No, I don't believe you can. However, I'll try to overlook this. You'll be leaving for the East Coast in a day or two. I trust you'll handle Miss Conroy with more finesse than you handled Mr DiCarlo.'

Cautious, Winesap backed out of the room. 'Thank you.'

Finley leaned back as the door closed respectfully. He would have to keep a closer eye on Abel, he thought sadly. A much closer eye. If things got too sticky over DiCarlo, he would simply throw dear devoted Abel to the wolves like so much dead meat.

IT WAS GOOD to be home in the simple routines of each day. Dora comforted herself with that and tried not to think of the meeting with Mr Petroy she still had to face. At least Jed hadn't noticed her lack of appetite. She'd covered it well. Her eyes might have been shadowed, her skin pale and drawn, but with facials and creams and powders she presented a very competent mask. She hoped it didn't slip until after Thursday.

Dora felt a need for her family. She indulged it by closing the shop an hour early and spending the evening at Lea's. The din from the family room soothed her soul.

'I think Richie's improving on the trumpet,' Dora commented.

Head cocked, Lea listened to the wet musical blasts with a mixture of pride and resignation. 'There's a band concert at school in three weeks. I'm saving you a front-row seat.'

Dora slipped onto a stool by the counter. 'I needed this.'

Lea added another touch of burgundy to the stew she had simmering. 'Something's going on.' She frowned. 'You've got that line between your eyebrows. And you're pale. You always get pale when you're worried about something.'

Passing a hand over her face, Dora took a cleansing breath. 'I guess I'm still a little jet-lagged. And my life's taken a few odd turns. I think I'll go home, take a hot bath and sleep for twelve hours.' She started to move as the knock sounded on the back door.

'Hi.' Mary Pat stuck in her head. 'I came to pick up my share of the monsters.' She listened for a moment to the blare of the trumpet. 'Ah, the patter of little feet. Wonderful, isn't it?'

'Have a seat,' Lea invited. 'Unless you're in a hurry.'

'I'd love a seat. I've been on my feet for eight straight hours.' She sighed. 'Terrific news about Jed, isn't it?'

'What news?'

'About him coming back on the job.' She missed Dora's blank look. 'Brent's really flying. He detested Goldman, of course. Who didn't? But it's more than that. The department needs Jed and Jed needs the department. Now that he's made the decision to—' One look at Dora's face made Mary Pat stumble to a halt. 'Oh, Lord. Did I jump the gun? When Brent told me, I just assumed you knew.'

'No. Jed didn't mention it.' Dora fought to work a smile onto her lips, but couldn't make it reach her eyes. 'It's great news, though. I'm sure it's just what he needs. How long have you known?'

'A couple of days. I'm sure Jed planned to tell you. Once he, uh . . .' But she couldn't think of any handy excuses. 'I'm sorry.'

'Don't be. I really am glad to hear it.' After sliding off the stool, Dora reached mechanically for her coat. 'I've got to get going.'

'Stay for dinner,' Lea said quickly. 'There's plenty.'

'No, I have things to do. Say hi to Brent,' she told Mary Pat.

'Sure.' The door closed.

IT WAS TWO O'CLOCK in the morning. Jed paced his living room, strode through the door he'd propped open and paced the corridor. As he had numerous times over the last four hours, he strode to the back door and stared out at the gravel driveway.

Where was Dora? If she wasn't home in ten minutes, he would call in all his markers and put out an all persons' broadcast. Unless she was paying him back. It was a safe, even comforting, thought, so he played with it. Was this how she'd felt when he'd come in late without leaving any word? She wasn't going to get away with it, he decided. But he was reaching for his phone when he heard her key in the lock.

He was out in the hall and at the back door before she'd opened it. 'Do you have any idea what time it is?' he demanded.

'Yes.' She closed the outer door and locked it. 'Sorry. I didn't realise I had a curfew.' She walked past him, but he caught up with her at her apartment door and spun her round.

'Just a minute, Conroy. We'll forget the personal stuff for now. The fact is, you're a prime target, and it was incredibly irresponsible of you to be out of contact for half the night.'

'I'm responsible to and for myself.' She unlocked her door and shoved it open. 'And as you can see, I'm perfectly fine.'

He followed her in. 'You had no right—'

'Don't tell me about rights,' she interrupted, very cool, very calm. 'I spent the evening as I chose to spend it.'

Anger and resentment bubbled inside him. 'And how was that?'

'Alone.' She took off her coat and hung it in the closet.

'Conroy. You knew damn well I'd be half crazy with worry. I was about to call out an all persons' broadcast.'

'Interesting, isn't it, the way those police terms slide right off your tongue? It's a good thing you're going back on, Captain. You make a lousy civilian.' Her eyes were as dull as her voice.

'It's not official until next week.' He spoke carefully, studying her. He'd never seen her eyes that cold. 'How did you find out?'

'Does it matter? It's more to the point that I didn't find out from you. Excuse me.' She brushed past him and into the living room.

He cursed himself for a fool. 'So you're angry. But that—'

'No,' she interrupted. 'I'm not angry.' Because she was unbearably tired, she sat on the arm of a chair. 'You could say I've been illuminated, devastated, but I'm not angry.'

The quiet resignation in her voice reached him. 'Dora, I didn't do it to hurt you.'

'That's why I'm illuminated. You didn't tell me because you didn't think it was any of my concern. You didn't want it to be any of my concern is probably more like. It was a major decision in your life. *Your* life,' she repeated with stinging emphasis. 'Not mine. So why should you bother to tell me?'

She was slipping away from him. He was standing two feet away from her and watching the distance grow by leaps and bounds. It terrified him. 'You make it sound as though I was keeping it from you. I needed to work it out. I didn't think you'd understand.'

'You didn't give me the chance, Jed,' she said quietly. 'Did you think I could have felt the way I did about you and not understand how important your work was to you?'

'It had nothing to do with you.' As soon as the words were out, he knew they were ill-chosen. 'I didn't mean it that way.'

'I think you did. I wish I didn't blame you for it, but I do. I know you had it rough, but you've been making your own choices for a long time. You chose not to accept my feelings for you, and you chose not to let yourself feel anything back.' Her voice didn't waver. 'I do blame you for that, Jed, and for hurting me. Since you're the first man who's ever broken my heart, I think you should know it.'

'For heaven's sake, Dora.' He started towards her, but she jumped up and stepped back.

'I don't want you to touch me now. I really don't.'

His hands fisted. 'Dora, I need you to stop this and be reasonable.'

'I am being reasonable, believe me. The day after tomorrow you should be able to tie up the loose ends about the painting. Or most of them. You shouldn't need me after that.'

'You know I need you.'

Her eyes filled then, and she fought back tears. 'You can't imagine what I would have given to hear you say that before. Just once. But I have to protect myself, Jed. When we're finished on Thursday, I intend to close the shop for a couple of weeks, take a trip someplace warm. That should give you time to find other accommodation and move out. I don't want you here when I get back.'

'Just like that?'

'Yes.'

'Fine.' He had his pride. He wouldn't beg. 'I'll go as soon as things are wrapped up.' Because it hurt—it hurt unbelievably—he covered the wounds with a professional shield. 'There'll be a team in tomorrow after closing. They'll set up the wires. We'll go over procedure when they're done.'

'All right. I'm very tired. I'd like you to go now.' She walked to the door, held it open. 'Please.'

It wasn't until he'd reached her that he realised his hands were unsteady. When he heard the door close behind him, he had the sick feeling that he'd just been shut out of the best part of his life.

'WHAT'S WITH YOU TWO?' Brent asked as Jed climbed into the surveillance van.

Jed ignored the question. 'How's the sound?'

'Loud and clear.' Though Brent offered the headphones, he was far from finished. 'Loud and clear enough to hear the two of you talking in there like polite strangers. Don't you think she could have used a morale boost instead of a lecture on procedure, Captain?'

'Drop it.' Jed checked the rear window of the van to be sure he had a clear view of the shop.

The radio crackled. 'Base, this is Unit One. A man answering subject's description just got out of a cab on the corner of South and Front Streets. He's walking west.'

'Showtime,' Brent murmured, but Jed was already reaching for the portable phone. Dora answered on the first ring.

'Good afternoon. Dora's Parlor.'

'He's half a block away,' Jed said flatly. 'I've got him in view.'

'All right. Everything's ready here.'

'Keep loose, Conroy.'

'Sure.'

'Dora—' But she'd already broken the connection. 'Damn.' He said it softly, finally, helplessly.

'She can handle it, Jed.'

'Yeah. But I don't know if I can.' He watched Winesap mince hurriedly down the sidewalk, shoulders hunched. 'I just figured out I'm in love with her.' He slipped on the headphones in time to hear the bells jingle as Winesap opened the shop door.

'Good afternoon.' Dora smiled. 'May I help you?'

'Miss Conroy? I'm Francis Petroy.'

She let her smile broaden. 'Mr Petroy, I was expecting you.' She walked to the door to flip the CLOSED sign around. Her eyes swivelled to the van, then away. 'Can I get you some coffee? Tea?'

'I'd love some tea.' It might soothe his stomach more than the Alka-Seltzer he'd downed earlier. 'Your shop is very impressive.'

'Thank you. I like to surround myself with beautiful things. But you'd understand that.'

'Excuse me?'

'Being an art collector.' She offered him a cup. 'You said you specialise in abstract, but you might find some of my nostalgia prints interesting.' She gestured to a car manufacturer's sign for a Bugatti, which hung beside a Vargas girl. Watching him, she sipped her own tea. 'But as an abstract buff, you'd be more interested in, say, a Bothby or a Klippingdale,' she said, making up names.

'Yes, of course. Exceptional talents.' The tea soured in Winesap's stomach. He'd really tried to be thorough by studying the subject, but all the names and pictures swam through his head. 'My collection isn't extensive. Which is why I concentrate on the emerging artist. I'm very anxious to see the Billingsly, Miss Conroy.'

'Then by all means.' She led the way into the side room. Jed had got an artist friend to work overtime to reproduce the painting. Now it stood in the pretty sitting room.

'Ah.' The sense of satisfaction was so great that Winesap nearly wept. 'It's everything I'd hoped for.'

'Did you have an offer in mind, Mr Petroy?' Dora asked.

'In mind, naturally,' he said, trying to be coy. 'I'd prefer it if you'd set a price—for negotiation.'

'Happy to. Why don't we start at two hundred and fifty thousand?' Winesap's prim mouth fell open. 'You can't be serious.'

'Oh, but I am. You look as though you need to sit down, Mr Petroy.' She gestured to a petit-point stool. 'Now, let's be frank,' she said. 'You don't know anything about art, do you?'

'Well, really. As I told you, I have a small collection.'

'But you lied, Mr Petroy,' she said gently. 'You haven't a clue about abstract. Wouldn't it be simpler if we admitted we're both more interested in Impressionism than Expressionism?'

For a moment he didn't follow her. Then his pasty face blanched. 'You know about the painting.'

'I bought it, didn't I?'

'Yes. But that was a mistake.' His frantic eyes widened. 'No? You knew—knew all along about the Monet? You were working with DiCarlo? You—you cheated,' he accused miserably. 'I can't imagine why I was sorry he died so badly.'

The image in the police photo flashed obscenely in Dora's mind. 'So you killed him,' she murmured. 'For this.'

But Winesap wasn't listening. 'Now I have to clean up the entire mess again. I'm not happy about the two hundred and fifty thousand, Miss Conroy.'

He rose. So did Dora. Even as he reached under his coat, two officers were bursting through the rear door.

'Freeze.'

Winesap took one look at the guns pointing at him and fainted.

16

Dora watched as two officers escorted a babbling Winesap out of the shop. She sat down, not sure her legs would support her.

'Here.' Jed shoved a cup of tea into her hands.

'Good idea.' She knocked it back like water and felt it warm her jittery stomach. 'I guess you guys got all you needed.'

'We got plenty.' He wanted to touch his fingertips to her hair, but he was afraid she'd cringe away. 'You did good, Nancy.'

'Yeah, I did.' She lifted her eyes then, made herself meet his. 'I guess on some level we didn't make such a bad team.'

Brent swept in to kiss Dora. 'You were brilliant.'

'Thanks.'

Jed felt his heart sag. 'I'm going down to interrogation with Brent. Are you going to be all right?'

'I'll be fine. Go be a cop. It looks good on you.' She softened the words with a smile. 'I'd appreciate it if you'd call me, let me know what the result of the interrogation is.'

'You'll get a full report,' Brent promised her.

'In the morning.' Steadier, she rose out of the chair. 'I'm going up to sleep.' She followed them to the door. Jed turned, closed his hand over hers on the knob. He couldn't help it. 'I'd like to talk to you tomorrow, when you're feeling up to it.'

She nearly gave in. Very nearly. There was as much hurt in his eyes as she was holding inside her. But a fast break was a clean one. 'My schedule's a little tight, Jed. I've got an early flight to Aruba.'

There was nothing in her voice, nothing in her face that offered the slightest opening.

'You move fast.'

She gave his hand a quick squeeze. 'Give 'em hell, Captain.'

She closed the door quickly and turned the lock.

ONCE SHE GOT to Aruba, Dora promised herself, she'd do nothing but sleep. She'd bake this aching depression out of her body and mind with the sunshine. She went to lock the storeroom door and engage the security alarm, and then headed up to her apartment.

She took the tea tray into her kitchen to wash up. When she turned from the sink, she was standing face to face with Finley.

'I've taken you up on your offer of hospitality, Isadora. And may I say you have a charming home. Why don't we sit down?' Finley took Dora's arm and pulled her into the living room.

'How did you get in?'

'There was such a lot of confusion today, wasn't there?' He smiled as he pushed her into a chair. 'I wasn't at all sure that Abel—Mr Winesap—could handle this matter efficiently.'

Finley took the chair beside her. He saw Dora's eyes cut towards the door, and shook his head. 'Please don't attempt to run, Isadora.'

She was certain she wouldn't get two feet. Her best bet was to play for time and wait for help. 'It was you who sent DiCarlo.'

'It's a long, sad tale. But I find you such good company.' He settled back and began to talk. He told her about the carefully planned robberies in several different countries. The network of men and finances it required to operate a successful business—legally and illegally. When he reached DiCarlo's part in it, he sighed.

'But I don't have to go into that with you, do I, dear? You're an excellent actress. I realised after your visit to my office that you and DiCarlo had been in league together.'

She was stunned. 'You think I was his partner? What I told you in your office was the truth. He broke in here and attacked me.'

'I'm quite sure you had a falling-out.' His eyes narrowed. 'Did you pit another man against Mr DiCarlo, so that he came to me with a feeble excuse for not returning my painting?'

'You stole it. And I was never involved with DiCarlo.'

'And when he didn't return,' Finley continued as if she hadn't spoken, 'you became concerned and decided to test the waters with me yourself. Oh, you were very clever. I very nearly believed you. There was just one doubt in my mind, which proved sadly true. You turned to the police, Isadora. Settling for a finder's fee.'

Terrified, she sprang to her feet. 'They have Winesap down at police headquarters. He'll be telling them all about you by now.'

Finley considered, then moved his shoulders in elegant dismissal. 'Perhaps. But Mr Winesap will very soon suffer a fatal accident. I would much rather talk about how I can retrieve my painting. Surely the police have told you where they've secured it.'

This surprised her. 'I don't know where it is.'

'Don't lie, please.' He slipped his hand into the inside pocket of his Savile Row suit and pulled out a highly polished Luger. 'Gorgeous, isn't it? Now, Isadora, where is my painting?'

She looked helplessly into his eyes. 'I don't know.'

The force of the bullet slammed her back against the wall. Even as the fire erupted in her shoulder, she didn't believe he'd shot her.

'I think you'd better tell me.' Finley stepped to where Dora lay in a heap. 'We'll give you a little time to compose yourself, shall we?'

Leaving her bleeding, he began to methodically examine her treasures, one by one.

'THE LITTLE FOOL sure did sing.' Brent felt like singing himself as they turned onto South Street. They had just left Winesap at the police station.

'I don't like cutting deals with weasels,' Jed muttered.

'Even for a big fat weasel like Finley?'

'Even for that.' He checked his watch. 'I'll feel better when I know that LAPD's picked him up.'

'The warrant's in the works, pal.'

There was some comfort in that. Some small comfort. 'You didn't have to come out of your way. I could have caught a cab.'

'Nothing's too good for the captain. Not tonight. And if I were you, I wouldn't wait until morning to give a certain gorgeous woman the good news.'

'She needs the sleep.'

'She needs some peace of mind.'

'She ought to get plenty of it in Aruba,' Jed said.

'Come again?'

'Nothing.' They turned onto South Street as light sleet began to fall.

'NOW, THEN.' Finley sat down again, pleased when Dora found the strength to sit up. The blood seeping out of her shoulder wound had slowed to an ooze. 'About the painting.'

Her teeth were chattering. She'd never been so cold. She tried to speak, but the words slurred. 'The police . . . took it. Took it away.' Her head lolled on her shoulder. The room was going grey. 'To . . . away. I don't know.'

'I can see you need an incentive.' He set the gun aside and reached for the gold buckle of his belt. He wrapped the end of the belt round his hand. 'Now, Isadora, where is the painting?'

Dully Dora saw him pick up the gun and raise the belt.

'DOOR-TO-DOOR service.' Brent pulled into the gravel driveway. 'If you had any heart, you'd ask me up for a beer.'

'I haven't got any heart.' Jed pushed the car door open and glanced back at Brent's engaging grin. 'Sure, come on in.'

'You got any of that imported stuff?' Brent asked. 'Mexican?'

They trooped to the steps. When they heard the thin cry, they each slapped a weapon into their hand and charged through the back door. Years of partnership clicked seamlessly into place. When Jed kicked open Dora's door, he went in high, Brent low.

The faintest flicker of irritation crossed Finley's face as he whirled. Two police issues fired simultaneously. Two 9mm bullets caught Finley high in the chest.

With terror singing in his head, Jed rushed to Dora. He said her name over and over like a prayer. 'Hang on, baby.'

There was so much blood, he thought frantically. When he looked at her wide dilated eyes and still, white face, he had one moment of horror, thinking she was dead. But she was shaking. He peeled off his jacket to cover her. 'You're going to be OK, Dora.'

'Use this.' Brent pushed a towel into Jed's shaking hands and folded another to place under Dora's head. 'Ambulance is on the way.' He spared a glance at the body sprawled on the rug.

'Dora, listen to me.' Jed used the towel to pad the wound. 'Hold on. Just hold on.' Then he could think of nothing else but to gather her close. 'Please. Stay with me. I need you.'

HE WOULD HAVE WEPT if it would have helped. He'd tried everything else. Swearing, pacing, praying. Now he could only wait.

The Conroys were there. Jed wondered if Dora would be surprised at how tough they were. He doubted it. There had been tears and there had been terror, but they had all drawn together in the hospital waiting room while Dora was in surgery.

He'd waited for recriminations. They had given him none. Not even when he had stood, smeared with Dora's blood, and told them that he'd left her alone, left her defenceless, had they blamed him. He wished to heaven they had.

Instead, John had got them all coffee, Lea had gone down to wait for Will to arrive from New York, and Quentin and Trixie had sat side by side on the sofa holding hands.

After the second hour had crawled by, Trixie murmured to her husband. With his nod of agreement she went to sit beside Jed.

'She'll want lots of pampering, you know,' Trixie began. 'She was never sick often, but when she was—' Trixie's voice broke, betraying her. She mopped quickly at her eyes and steadied it. 'When she was, she expected everyone's devoted attention. Dora's never been one to suffer in silence.' Gently she touched the back of his hand, then gripped it firmly. 'It's so much harder to wait alone.'

'Mrs Conroy . . .' But he didn't have the words. He simply leaned against her and let himself be held.

They all rose to their feet at the quick slap of shoes on tile. Still in her surgical gown, Mary Pat stepped through the doorway. 'She's out of surgery. It looks good. The doctor will be out soon.'

It was then that Trixie began to cry, with hard, racking sobs. Jed's arms went round her automatically as he met Mary Pat's eyes.

'When can they see her?' he asked.

'The doctor will let you know. She's a tough one.'

IT WASN'T UNTIL he was alone again that Jed started to shake. He'd gone outside and sat down on the steps. The sleet had turned to a quick, light snow. There was something hypnotic about the way it danced in the streetlights. He stared at one beam of light as he waited for the tremors to subside. Then he walked back in and rode the elevator to the floor where Dora lay sleeping.

Mary Pat smiled at him. 'Jed, you're soaked.'

'I just want to see her. I know she's sedated. I know she won't know I'm there. I just want to see her.'

'Let me get you a towel. Then I'll take you in.' When Mary Pat was satisfied he was dry enough, she led him into Dora's room.

Dora lay still and white as death. Jed's heart careered into his throat. 'Are you sure she's going to be all right?'

'She's stabilised, and there were no complications.' Mary Pat didn't want to think about the amount of blood they'd had to pump into Dora or how long it had taken to get that feeble pulse to steady. 'The bullet's out—and there's some tissue damage, but it'll heal. Why don't you just sit with her for a while. You'll feel better.'

'Thanks.'

'I go off duty in an hour. I'll check back.'

But when she did, one look had her leaving them alone.

He was still there in the morning.

SHE SLOWLY AWOKE, as if swimming towards the surface of still, dark water. He watched her break through, every flicker of the eyelid. Her hand flexed once in his, then lay still again.

'Come on, Dora.' He brushed his fingers over her pale cheek. Her lashes fluttered, then her eyes opened. 'Jed?'

'Yeah, baby. Right here.'

She shifted, sending an arrow of pain radiating through her arm. Like the pain, memory burst back. 'Finley shot me.' She moved her hand to the fire blooming in her shoulder. 'I'm in the hospital.' The panic came quickly. 'How—how bad?'

'It's all over now. You're going to be fine. You just need to rest.' None of his fourteen years on the force had prepared Jed to deal with the pain clouding her eyes. 'I'm going to get a nurse.'

'I remember.' Her fingers trembled as she groped for his. 'He was in the apartment, waiting for me. He wanted the painting back. I told him I didn't know where it was, and he shot me.'

'He won't ever hurt you again. I swear it.' He pressed his brow against their joined hands. 'I'm so sorry, baby.'

'Don't leave me alone here.'

'I won't.'

THE NEXT TIME he saw her conscious, she was surrounded by banks of flowers. She was wearing something frilly and pink, but to Jed she looked horribly frail.

'How you doing, Conroy?'

'Hi.' She smiled, held out a hand. 'How'd you break in?'

'I pulled rank.' He hesitated. Her hand felt as fragile as bird wings. Miserably awkward, he turned away to study the forest of flowers. 'Looks like you ought to go into a different business.'

'Great, isn't it? I love being fawned over.' She shifted, winced. 'So what's happening? Mary Pat tells me you kicked Goldman out early and went back to work.'

'Yeah.' He'd had to have something to fill his days, or go mad.

'Can I see your badge?'

'Sure.' He pulled out his shield.

She took it, studied it. 'Pretty cool. How does it feel?'

'Right,' he said as he slipped it back into his pocket. He kept seeing the stark white bandage beneath that frilly nightgown. 'Listen, I just stopped by to see how you were doing. I've got to go.'

'Before you give me my present?' She drummed up another smile. 'That box you're holding? Isn't it for me?'

'Yeah, it's for you.' He set it on her lap.

She reached for the fussy bow, then sat back again. 'Give me a hand, will you? I have a little trouble using my arm.'

He didn't move, but his eyes were eloquent. 'They told me there wouldn't be any permanent damage.'

'Right.' Her mouth moved into a pout. 'Like a scar isn't permanent damage. I'm never going to look the same in a bikini.'

Turning abruptly, he strode to the window and stared blindly out. 'I should have been there. You shouldn't have been alone.'

'Brent says Finley slipped right through LAPD. Nobody could have imagined he'd waltz into my apartment and shoot me.'

'It's my job to know.'

'So, it's going to your head already, supercop.' She was lifting the top off the box when he turned. 'Well, you just can't be everywhere at once.' Though her arm was beginning to throb, she dug happily into the tissue paper. 'I love presents. I don't particularly care to get shot to—Oh, Jed, it's beautiful.'

Completely stunned, she lifted out an old wood and gesso box, delicately painted and gilded with figures from mythology. When she opened the lid, it played 'Greensleeves' softly.

'I had it in storage. I figured you'd get a kick out of it.'

'It's beautiful,' she said again, and the look she sent him was so sincerely baffled he felt foolish. 'Thank you.'

'It's no big deal. I've really got to go. You, ah, need anything?'
She looked at him. 'I could use a favour.'
'Name it.'
'Can you pull some strings? I want to go home.'

IT TOOK HIM several hours, but Dora finally laid her head down on her own pillow, in her own bed. She closed her eyes, sighed deeply, then opened them again to smile at Mary Pat. 'Nothing against your workplace, M.P., but personally I hated it.'

'You weren't exactly the ideal patient, either, kiddo.' She wrapped a blood-pressure cuff round Dora's uninjured arm. 'But I'm not complaining; a few days of private duty suits me just fine.' But Dora caught the quick frown over the blood-pressure reading.

'What's wrong?'

'Nothing that quiet and rest won't fix.'

'I've been quiet. I'm tired of being in bed.'

'Live with it.' Sitting on the edge of the bed, Mary Pat took Dora's hand—and her pulse. 'I'm going to be straight with you, Dora. If Jed hadn't gotten you in when he did, you wouldn't be here to complain. It was close. You're entitled to moan and groan, but you're also going to follow orders. Or I'll report you to the captain.'

Dora smiled a little. 'You nurses have ranks?'

'I'm talking about Jed, dimwit. He's financing this operation.'

'What do you mean?'

'I mean you've got round-the-clock home care for as long as you need it, courtesy of Captain J.T. Skimmerhorn.'

'But I thought insurance was arranging it. He shouldn't feel guilty,' Dora murmured.

'He feels a lot more than guilt where you're concerned.'

Dora only shook her head.

When Mary Pat left the room, Dora reached for the music box. She opened the lid, closed her eyes and wondered what to do.

AT THE END of her shift Mary Pat marched across the hall and rapped sharply on Jed's door. When he opened it, she jabbed a finger into his chest.

'Couldn't you find the energy to walk across the hall and—' She broke off, scowling. 'What are you doing?'

'I'm packing.'

Darts of fury shot out of her eyes. 'You're not walking out on her when she's flat on her back.'

'I'm not walking out. She *asked* me to leave. It's only going to upset her if she finds out I haven't moved yet.'

400

'You're an idiot. Can you tell me you're not in love with her?'

He glared. 'No, I can't. But that's not the point. The doctor was real clear about keeping her free from stress.'

'Have you ever told her you loved her?'

'I don't see that that's any of your business.'

'I didn't think so.' Impatient, she took a quick turn round the room. 'Have you ever picked her wild flowers?'

'It's February.'

She turned on him. 'She needs to be wooed, Jed.'

He felt a flush creeping up on his neck. 'Give me a break.'

'I'd like to break your butt. You almost lost her.'

His eyes whipped round, sharp as a sword. 'Don't you think I know that? I wake up every night remembering how close it was.'

'Then do something positive. Show her what she means to you.' She kissed him. 'Find some wild flowers, Jed. My money's on you.'

THE BOX ARRIVED the following afternoon.

'More presents,' Lea announced, struggling to shove the huge box across the living room to where Dora sat on the couch.

Dora leaned down to study the box. 'No return address.'

'Ah, a secret admirer.' Lea attacked the packing tape. 'Oh,' she said, deflating when she opened the lid. 'It's just books.'

'Oh, my Lord. Carolyn Keene.' Dora leant forward. 'Nancy Drew—the complete set. And first editions. It's *The Clue of the Leaning Chimney*, *The Hidden Staircase*.' All at once she clutched at the books and began to weep.

'Oh, honey, did you hurt yourself? Let me help you to bed.'

'No.' She pressed a book against her cheek. 'They're from Jed.'

'I see,' Lea said carefully, and sat back on her heels.

'He went to all this trouble just to be sweet. Why is he being so sweet? He also sent me this bracelet. Why is he doing this?'

'Honey, don't you know when you're being romanced?'

'He's just feeling sorry for me. And guilty.' She hitched back tears, blinked them away. 'Isn't he?'

'The man I saw haunting that hospital wasn't there out of guilt.' Lea reached over to tuck her sister's hair behind her ear. 'Are you going to give him a break?'

Dora laid a book on her lap, running her hands gently over the cover. 'Before I was shot, I broke things off with him. I told him to move out. He hurt me, Lea. I don't want him to hurt me again.'

'It seems awfully unfair to make him keep suffering.' Lea rose to answer the knock on the door. 'Hi, Jed.' She smiled, took his hand and pulled him inside. 'Look who's here, Dory.'

'Hi.' Dora brushed at tears and managed a shaky smile. 'These are great.' Her eyes overflowed again. 'Really great.'

'Their value's going to plummet if they're water-damaged.'

'You're right. But I always get sentimental over first editions.'

'I was just on my way out.' Lea grabbed her coat and left.

'Listen,' Jed said to Dora. 'I've got the go-ahead to take you out for a while. You up for a drive?'

'Outside?' She scrambled to her feet. 'And not to the hospital?'

'Get your coat, Conroy.'

'I can't believe it,' she said a few minutes later as she slid luxuriously into Jed's car. 'No nurses. No thermometers.'

'How's the shoulder doing?'

'It's sore.' She opened the window just to feel the rush of air on her face. 'They make me do this physiotherapy, which is—to put it mildly—unpleasant. But it's effective.' She jockeyed her elbow to a right angle to prove it. 'Not bad, huh?'

'That's great.'

'Everything all right at work?' she asked him.

'It's fine. You were right all along. I shouldn't have left.'

'You just needed some time.' She touched his arm, then let her hand fall away. It was time, she thought, to clear the air. 'Jed, I know that—Well, before I was hurt, I know I was unkind.'

'Don't. You were right. Everything you said was right. I didn't want you to get too close, and I made certain you couldn't. You were one of the main reasons I went back on the job, but I didn't share it with you, because I would have had to admit that it mattered. That what you thought of me mattered. It was deliberate.'

She rolled up the window. 'No point in raking it up again.'

'I guess it would sound pretty convenient if I told you that I was going to ask you for another chance, before you got hurt.' He shot her a look, caught her wide-eyed stare.

'I'm not sure,' she said, 'what another chance might entail.'

He was going to try to show her. He pulled up in the driveway, set the brake, then walked round to the passenger door to help her out. Because she was staring at his house, she moved wrong and bumped her arm against the car door. Her gasp of helpless pain broke him.

'I can't stand to see you hurt.' Shielding her arm, he gathered her close. 'I just can't stand it. It rips at me, Dora. I thought you were dead. I looked at you on the floor and thought you were dead.'

'Don't.' She soothed automatically. 'I'm all right now.'

'I didn't prevent it,' he said fiercely. 'I was too late.'

'You saved my life. He'd have killed me. He wanted to, as much as he wanted the painting. You stopped him.' She lifted a hand to his cheek. He grasped at it, pressed it hard to his lips.

He stood there for a moment, with the air cool and crisp, whispering through the trees. 'You shouldn't be standing out in the cold.'

'It feels great.'

'I want you to come inside. I want to finish this inside.'

'All right.' Though she no longer felt weak, she let him support her as they went up the path. She thought he needed to.

But it was he who was unsteady as he unlocked the door, opened it, led her inside. His nerves jumped as she gasped in pleasure.

She stepped onto the Bukhara rug. 'You've put things back.'

'Some.' He watched the way she ran her fingertips over the rosewood table, the curved back of a chair, the fussy gilded mirror. 'My landlord kicked me out, so I took a few things out of storage.'

'The right things.' She walked on into the front parlour. He'd put back a curvy pinstriped settee, a lovely Tiffany lamp on a satinwood table. There was a fire burning low in the hearth. She felt a surge of pleasure and of grief. 'You're moving back in.'

'That depends.' He carefully slipped her coat off her shoulders, laid it on the settee. 'I came back here last week. It wasn't the same. I could see you sitting on my window seat, looking out of the window. You changed the house,' he said. 'You changed me. I want to move back in and make it work. If you'll come with me.'

Dora didn't think the sudden dizziness had anything to do with her healing injuries. She lowered herself to the striped cushions. 'You're going to move back here? You *want* to move back here?'

'Yeah, that's right.'

'And you want me to live with you?'

'If that's the best I can get.' He took a small box out of his pocket and pushed it into her hands. 'I'd like it better if you'd marry me.'

'Can I—' Her voice squeaked. 'Can I have some water?'

Frustrated, he bit back on his temper and nerves. 'Sure.'

She waited until he was out of the room before she worked up the courage to open the box. She was glad she had, because her mouth fell open. She was still staring dumbfounded at the ring when he came back in carrying a filled Baccarat tumbler.

'Thanks.' She took the glass, drank deeply. 'It's a whopper.'

He fumbled. 'I guess it's overstated.'

'Oh, no. There isn't a diamond in the world that's overstated.' She laid the box in her lap but kept a hand possessively round it. 'Jed, I think these past few weeks have been as hard on you as they have on me. I might not have appreciated that, but—'

'I love you, Dora.'

That stopped her cold. Before she could gather her wits, he was on the settee, his hand over hers. 'If you don't want to answer yet, Dora, I'll wait. I just want a chance to make you love me again.'

'Is that what all this has been about? The presents and all? You were trying to undermine my defences when I was down.'

He looked down at their joined hands. 'That about sizes it up.'

She nodded, then rose and took the box with her to the window. She'd want tulips out there in the spring, she thought. And daffodils.

'Good job, Skimmerhorn,' she said quietly. 'It was the Nancy Drew that really did it, though.' She opened the box again and looked down at the bold square-cut diamond. 'You exploited my weaknesses for nostalgia, romance and material gain.'

Nerves screaming, he came up behind her to touch a hand to her hair. 'I've got some flaws, sure, but I'm loaded.'

Her lips curved. 'That approach might have worked once, but I'm pretty well set myself, since I'll be awarded a fat finder's fee on the Monet. I might be greedy, but I have my standards.'

'I'm crazy about you.'

'That's better.'

'You're the only woman I've ever wanted to spend my life with.' He brushed a light kiss at the curve of her shoulder and throat and made her sigh. 'The only woman I've ever loved, or want to love.'

Tears burned her throat. 'That's excellent.'

'So does that mean you're going to fall in love with me again?'

'What makes you think I ever stopped?'

'And the marriage thing? You'll give it a shot?'

She grinned into the sunlight. It might not have been the world's most romantic proposal, but it suited her. It suited her just fine.

'I have a Chippendale bench that's waiting to sit in front of that fire, Jed.'

He turned her round, brushing her hair back so that his hands could frame her face. He only had to see her eyes. 'Kids?'

'Three.'

'Good number.' Overwhelmed, he rested his brow against hers. 'There's a bed upstairs in the master suite. A George III.'

'Four-poster?'

'Tester. Stay here with me tonight.'

She laughed her way into the kiss. 'I thought you'd never ask.'

NORA ROBERTS

Since she began writing some fifteen years ago, Nora Roberts has published more than ninety novels—with over twenty-five million copies of her books in print. As well as achieving massive sales she has also won almost every award for excellence given to romance writers in the United States. Nora Roberts started to write when her two sons were very young, aged between three and five, and the family was living in western Maryland. 'We were snowed in during the blizzard of 1979,' she recalls. 'So I really began writing to avoid being driven to murder or suicide. As soon as I started, I realised that writing was what I wanted to do.'

Athough she has made her name through writing romantic fiction, many of her novels are really romantic suspense stories. 'Relationship books are the most important to me,' she says, adding in a deadpan voice, 'but I really like to murder people. That's an awful lot of fun!'

The author grew up in Maryland, where she still lives with her second husband Bruce, a carpenter, whom she married in 1985. Like Dora in *Hidden Riches*, Nora Roberts enjoys collecting antiques and the world of the stage—her father worked in television and the theatre in Washington, DC. But the author's favourite means of relaxation is gardening. Her husband is often at her side, planting and pruning under the sun. 'He doesn't know a pansy from a petunia—he really doesn't,' she says affectionately. 'But he loves being out there.'

And what's next for this talented and astonishingly prolific writer? More romantic suspense novels with intriguing relationships, she says. She's already finished the next one. And her fans will be pleased to hear that she has no intention of slowing down.

THE MAGIC BULLET

Harry Stein

Illustrated by Ruben De Anda

Amagic bullet—a miracle cure that
will destroy cancer cells while
leaving healthy ones untouched.
That is the goal of the American
Cancer Foundation.

For their new recruit, the gifted
Dr Daniel Logan, success seems
tantalisingly close. There is only one
thing in his way: the jealousy of his
ambitious colleagues, whose attempts
at persuasion are followed by angry
confrontations—and finally sabotage.

When Daniel refuses to compromise
he realises that his life, as well as his
work, is at stake.

THE FIRST CHANGE was infinitesimal—a mutation in a single nucleotide of a single cell, deep within her right breast. It is impossible to say what caused it, or even if it was necessarily destined to have any impact. Still, from that moment on, that cell was unique among the several trillion in her body.

She was seventeen years old.

Over the next decade, the cell mutated several times. It began to behave autonomously. Its shape became slightly irregular. The structure of its nucleus changed. Its metabolism increased.

Her career was going exceedingly well.

Eight years later, the cell undergoes a sudden, dramatic change. The DNA within its unstable nucleus begins mutating hourly. Normal signals directing it to stop are ignored. Within a month, it has spawned close to a hundred daughter cells.

Between her two young children, her work and her husband, she jokes that she doesn't have time for problems.

It takes four years for the next great mutation. The malignant cells now number in the hundreds of thousands; but even if taken all together, are no larger than the head of a pin. Some, however, have already learned how to live outside the breast.

One afternoon, doing laps in the White House pool, she feels a dull pain in her lower back. She ignores it. The backache lasts twenty-four hours and disappears as suddenly as it arrived.

409

DANIEL LOGAN LAY on a trolley in a dim cubicle off the emergency room in New York's Claremont Hospital. He'd been this way for an hour—alone in the dark, seemingly forgotten by the nurses moving in the corridor just a few feet away. Heaven knows he needed the rest! He hadn't made it home from that damn party until nearly dawn, and, as senior resident in charge, he'd had to report to the Emergency Room at noon.

Logan sat up and swung his feet off the trolley. He left the cubicle and walked into the doctor's station. Through a glass partition, staff could survey newcomers and assess which cases required immediate attention, while charting the heartbeats of those already under their care on a large EKG monitor suspended from the ceiling. Logan glanced up at the monitor. Nothing going on.

He turned to Janice Richman, the shy young intern on duty. 'Janice, will you keep an eye on things? I'm gonna grab a bite to eat.'

'I'll join you,' said an attendant named Ruben Perez. 'I had a break due two hours ago.' They headed for the cafeteria.

The only food available at this hour was from vending machines. As Perez wolfed down something passing as chicken soup, Logan poked at a container of Jell-O cubes.

'How's that old guy Friedman doing?' Perez asked.

'Which one is he?' Logan had a better head for disease than for names.

'You doctors!' He shook his head. 'Fever? Abdominal pain? Low haematocrit? I brought him in around three o'clock.'

It was not unusual for orderlies to take an interest in their charges, but the depth of Ruben's concern was exceptional; as was his understanding of medicine. Born in the Dominican Republic and raised in the South Bronx, Perez was only a few years older than Logan; and the young doctor knew—and knew that Perez did too—that if he'd had the education, he'd have made a hell of a doctor himself. Over the course of dozens of conversations like this one, their mutual regard had blossomed into firm friendship.

'I sent him to intensive care,' Logan replied.

'He's a nice guy. Think he'll make it?'

'No.' Logan paused. 'You're right, after a while you almost do stop thinking of them as people. He's a nice guy, huh?'

Perez nodded. 'He was in the first wave that landed on Normandy. Great stories to tell.'

Logan smiled. 'I'll look in on him before I go. Promise.'

Perez stirred his soup. 'So . . . tell me about the party.'

'Not much to tell . . .'

'"Not much to tell"', echoed Perez sarcastically. 'The man attends

410

one of the social events of the season and makes me read about it in the *Daily News.*'

'Hey, for me it was work.' Logan smiled. 'I just went as a courtesy.'

In fact, the event, honouring Dr Sidney Karpe, one of medicine's most celebrated names, had gone well for Logan. A one-man industry, Karpe wrote books, provided medical commentary for TV news shows, and had a long roster of celebrity clients. That he was a mediocre doctor hardly seemed to matter, for his greatest skill lay in choosing associates to handle the nuts and bolts.

Which is where Dan Logan came in. The most gifted young doctor emerging that year from the city's top medical facility, he'd been wooed by the great man with a starting salary of $170,000. And last night, at Karpe's elbow, he'd been introduced to movie stars, politicians and financiers as Karpe's soon-to-be partner in the practice.

But there was no way Logan was about to report any of that to Perez, stuck at Claremont with little hope of escape.

'Fine,' said Perez, 'did you enjoy the *work*?'

Logan smiled. 'Some of the women were quite attractive. But you know how shy I am.'

'Logan, you're the kind of guy the women's magazines are always talking about.'

'"How to Meet Terrific Eligible Bachelors"?'

Perez grinned. '"Guys Who'll *Never* Commit".'

'Anyway,' said Logan, 'I felt awkward in a tuxedo. It's not me.'

'You go to that place I told you? Did it fit right?'

'Yeah, it fitted right. I wasn't about to look like a *total* jerk.'

Indeed, Logan knew he'd seldom looked better. Still boyish at twenty-nine, he was aware that his loping gait, longish hair and quick smile could lend him the air of a spirited undergraduate. Last night, he knew, he'd looked like a comer.

'So did you commit to Karpe?'

'Not yet.'

'Why not?'

Why not? The truth was, Logan wanted it several irreconcilable ways at once. Ambitious for success and status, he also clung to a brand of idealism that most of his colleagues would take as naive. He ached for plausible reasons to respect himself. There was also the matter of . . . *sport.* Medicine at its best involved the skill and gamesmanship of basketball or high-stakes poker. It could be nothing short of thrilling when a mix of intuition and hard work cracked a case that baffled other doctors. He knew full well that within Karpe's practice such opportunities would be rare.

'We both know,' he began haltingly, 'how clinical work can beat you up emotionally. That old guy Friedman—you won't believe this, but there was a time when I'd have gotten very involved with a guy like that. I mean, even the way we talk about death around here. Notice how no one ever dies in a hospital?'

Perez smiled. 'Right. They "box" or "crump".'

'Or "have their subscription cancelled",' added Logan. He paused meaningfully. 'I've been thinking about how nice it'd be to do pure research.' He reached into the pocket of his white jacket, pulled out a crumpled envelope and handed it across the table.

Perez withdrew the single page and put on his glasses to read.

Dear Dr Logan,

Thank you for your application to the American Cancer Foundation. I am pleased to inform you that you are among those selected for final consideration. As such, you are invited to visit the ACF to be interviewed by members of our staff. Please contact Dr Shein, the supervisor of the Fellowship Programme, at the number listed below, to arrange a mutually convenient date.

The signature belonged to the ACF's director, Dr Kenneth Markell, one of the world's greatest names in cancer research.

Perez let out a low whistle. 'I'm impressed.'

'That isn't why I showed it to you.'

'What, you want my advice? How the hell should I know what to tell you? Just that you should be flattered.'

'Hey, it's a form letter. They probably send out hundreds.' Logan rose. 'Aren't we supposed to do some work around here?'

BACK IN THE EMERGENCY ROOM, things had picked up. Four patients were waiting to be seen, among them a chest pain and a chronic asthmatic.

'Where's Richman?' Logan asked Nurse Clancy behind the desk.

She nodded towards the line of examining rooms. 'With a dirt-ball'—hospitalese for malingerer.

Logan peered beyond the cubicle curtain. Janice Richman was examining a woman of perhaps thirty, blonde and very attractive. 'Excuse me, Dr Richman . . .?'

Richman excused herself and joined him in the hallway.

'What's the story?'

'I don't know. Cough and fever. Vital signs are OK.'

'Well, don't take long. They're stacking up out there.'

Logan had had the chest pain and the asthmatic placed in examining rooms and turned his attention to a patient brought in by ambulance, a woman with sharp abdominal pains. He noted her yellow-grey colour and her shallow breathing and knew he had a very sick woman on his hands. He headed for the nurses' station. 'Call up to the second floor; this lady needs a surgeon in a hurry. Pour in the normal saline, cover her with triple antibiotics and give her a gram of steroid.'

As he headed back to the ER to check up on his chest pain, he was met by Janice Richman.

'Could you have a look at this woman?' She couldn't hide the panic, and was already hustling back down the hall. 'I left her alone for a few minutes and . . .' Reaching the door, she opened it.

The woman he'd seen earlier was totally transformed. Wild-eyed, her blonde hair damp with sweat, she was trying to climb over the railings of the bed. 'What's her name?' he asked.

'Betsy Morse.'

Logan rushed over to the bed. 'Betsy, calm down. We're here to help you.' He tried to ease her down by the shoulders; her skin was burning. 'Richman, I need your help.'

But the harder they tried to hold her down, the harder she fought. Her face contorted, she was kicking violently.

'Clancy,' yelled Logan, 'get in here!' Nurse Clancy appeared. 'Tie her down. Get security to sit on her. Get a rectal temperature, she's hot as a pistol. One milligram of Haldol IM stat!'

The doctors extricated themselves as security took over. 'Let's get her someplace we can hook her up to the EKG.'

The young woman's EKG tracing showed ventricular tachycardia—the chaotic fluttering of a severely injured heart. She was out cold. No blood pressure. No carotid pulse. It was what any good doctor most dreads: the utterly inexplicable. Furiously, Logan began cardiopulmonary resuscitation.

'Call a cardiac team and get a respirator up here!'

The message thundered over the loudspeakers: *'Cardiac team, emergency room. Cardiac team, emergency room.'*

Logan ordered saline pads to be applied to the woman's chest. 'Run up the paddles to three hundred watt-seconds!'

The energy of the shock literally raised her from the bed.

Logan looked at the monitor. Flat line.

'Keep pumping!' he screamed. 'Where's the respirator?'

The cardiac team rushed in. While continuing to work at the young woman's chest, they began administering drugs, desperately trying to flog the heart into action. One by one they failed.

'Well,' said Logan, pretending calm. 'Anyone have any other ideas?' Silence.

Logan snapped off the EKG. 'Thank you, everybody.'

'Another one in a box,' said one of the cardiac guys softly, trying to maintain his sanity.

Glancing across the room, Logan caught Ruben Perez's eye. He reached into his pocket and felt the envelope.

THE MOMENT HE ENTERED the grounds of the American Cancer Foundation, steering the rented Taurus onto a long, maple-lined drive, Dan Logan understood why this place was referred to as a campus. With its vast manicured lawns and elegant Federal-style buildings, it conveyed as strong a sense of dignity and purpose as any ivy-covered institution of higher learning.

There was simply no research institute in the world like the ACF. Founded in 1946, the ACF now comprised some fifteen buildings, where a small army of PhDs and MDs worked towards curing cancer. The ACF also contained its own hospital, the Eisenhower Medical Center, staffed by some of the finest oncologists in the world.

If he became a part of this place, he could *accomplish* something, Logan mused. How many times, growing up, had he heard a TV reporter soberly intone: 'Researchers at the American Cancer Foundation today announced . . .'?

He made it to his first appointment with five minutes to spare. It was with Raymond Larsen, chief of the Department of Medicine. Dan had seen his name often in the prestigious *Annals of Internal Medicine*.

Tall and ramrod straight, Larsen bore a distinct resemblance to Lee Marvin and carried himself like a marine drill sergeant, all brusque impatience and snarly command. He even wore a brush crew cut straight out of a fifties movie.

Larsen gave the younger man a quick once-over. There was no evidence to suggest he liked what he saw. How, Logan wondered fleetingly, does this guy manage to deal with patients? Larsen motioned for the younger man to be seated. As Larsen leafed through his file, Logan studied the room. The walls were bare except for diplomas from Princeton and Harvard. The broad mahogany desk bore only a telephone and a neat stack of papers. No knick-knacks. No photos of loved ones—if there were any.

'I see you have a recommendation from L.D. Greiner,' Larsen said suddenly.

'Yessir.' Logan had studied with the Nobel prize-winning chemist for a postdoctorate in molecular biology at Stanford, before opting for medicine. Greiner's glowing report on him was one of the things that made his résumé leap out from the pack.

414

'Opting out of molecular biology just six months after you got your doctorate doesn't say much for your stick-to-itiveness.'

'I loved the work,' Logan said. 'It's just that there was a . . . coldness to it. A lack of connection between what I was doing and any practical application. Whereas with medical research—'

'You get to *help people*,' Larsen finished the thought—and, with horror, Logan realised that he was mocking him.

'Something like that,' he agreed.

'You realise, of course, that we have many promising applicants for the Fellowship Programme. And only a few slots to fill.'

'Yes, I do.'

'Good. I don't like people to have any illusions.' He shut the file. 'Well, thank you for coming by. You'll be hearing from us.'

THE INTERVIEW, SCHEDULED for half an hour, had taken less than ten minutes. It was forty minutes until the next one. Shell-shocked, Logan was not even sure he wanted to go to it. Over the course of his young career he had been exposed to his share of unpleasantness: mean-spiritedness, envy, duplicity, but never before had he been the object of what he took to be outright contempt.

Taking a seat on a bench outside the administration building, he felt the beginning of a dull ache behind his eyes. Without noting the irony, he wondered if he could get an aspirin in this place.

'Hi.'

Logan looked up, startled. Before him stood a short, balding man in his early forties, his bright eyes and droopy little moustache lending him an almost comic appearance.

'Hello,' Logan returned laconically.

'I work here,' offered the other. He indicated his white lab coat, in case there was any doubt. 'I saw you just came outta Larsen's office. What an ass, right? Mind if I sit down?' He immediately did so. 'You're at Claremont, right?'

Logan's face reflected his surprise.

His companion pointed to the Claremont Hospital security pass dangling from the lapel of Dan's coat. 'I got a lot of talents but mind-reading ain't one of them. You like New York? You're not from there originally.'

'No. But I like it.' He could hardly even figure out how to talk to this guy. 'Actually, I'm from Illinois.'

'I am. From New York. You wouldn't've guessed, right? Tell me how you ended up at Claremont.'

Dan found himself running through the story of his life in medicine. The excruciating first couple of years of medical school. The joy that came in the third year with the start of hospital rounds. Internship and residency and his interest in oncology.

'Why oncology?' asked the other.

Logan glanced at his watch. 'My God!' He leapt to his feet. 'Look, I've got to go. I'm late for my interview. Nice meeting you.'

'Just hold on a sec, Logan. You ain't late for your interview. You're in the middle of it.'

Logan was speechless. 'Dr Shein?' he said at last.

'Call me Seth. Time on my hands, figured I'd come to you.'

Despite himself, Dan smiled. As head of the ACF's clinical oncology programme, Shein probably had less free time than the guy across the river in the Oval Office. 'So what now?' asked Logan.

Shein nodded towards the administration building. 'There.'

His office turned out to be immense, but Shein's personality seemed instantly to fill it.

'So,' he said, sitting in his antique swivel chair and throwing his feet up on his desk, 'tell me about your work with Greiner.'

Logan sat in the dilapidated upholstered chair at the foot of the desk. 'Well,' he began, 'we were trying to see if there were unique genes that expressed themselves in glioblastoma. We took the DNA, sliced it up with a restriction enzyme, and packaged it with a virus—'

'Then,' cut in Shein, 'you let the virus infect the bacteria and so forth. Read about it. Just wanted to hear it in your own words.'

Logan looked at him curiously.

'You'd be surprised how many people try to bullshit me.' He snorted. 'Can you believe it—*me?*'

It didn't surprise Logan that Shein, who was among the most gifted researchers in his field, should flash a huge ego. A certain arrogance was in the make-up of every successful scientist he'd ever known.

Shein paused. 'You must have some pretty good offers, no?'

He played it straight. 'A few.'

Shein nodded. 'Karpe's got a great practice, all right. You'll be in the society columns in no time.'

The younger man stared. Was there anything Shein didn't know?

'But you know what? You're not going there, you're coming here. You're gonna help us cure cancer.'

'*What?* I'm . . . accepted? But are you authorised . . .' He hesitated. 'I should tell you that Dr Larsen—'

'Look, Larsen knows you're my kinda boy and he's out to protect his turf. That's the way it works around here. Now, you'll start at fifty-one thousand.'

Logan swallowed. 'Karpe is offering three times that.'

'No negotiation. This is a non-profit foundation, remember?'

Crestfallen, Logan remained silent.

'What, you think this is a bad career move? This is the big time, Logan. Me, I got security clearance and everything. You know what a couple of years does for your résumé? The big drug companies start top researchers from the ACF at three hundred grand.'

Logan weighed this for a moment. 'Why do you need security clearance?'

'Are you kidding, where do you think the big shots'—he nodded in the direction of Washington—'come for treatment? Especially if they want to keep it under wraps?' Abruptly, Shein was on his feet. 'C'mon, I want to show you the labs. And the Medical Center.' He smiled. 'I mean, that's where you're gonna be spending most of your time, right?'

T HAT NIGHT LOGAN was unable to sleep. He went into the living room and found what he was looking for: on the top bookshelf was a 1938 edition of *Microbe Hunters*—about the pioneers of microbiology—he'd had since childhood. He flipped through to the glossy section: old-fashioned engravings and photographs of the geniuses honoured on its pages. Stiff, serious men, wearing black suits and grim expressions. All, that is, except Paul Ehrlich, the conqueror of syphilis. Slim, bearded and bespectacled, appearing to be in his mid-sixties, he stared out from the page with a quizzical, almost childlike expression. On the desk before him sat a manuscript; in one hand he held a cigar.

Studying the photograph, Logan smiled. Even now, he found the story profoundly moving: this impish little man, for more than a decade working against incredible odds to find 'the magic bullet' that would cure the ancient scourge. As a kid, he'd lionised Ehrlich the way other kids did John F. Kennedy or Reggie Jackson.

T HE BUFFET LUNCHEON at Seth Shein's home had been billed as a social occasion, but Dan Logan knew that career would be at the top of the agenda. In just two days the incoming fellows would begin working at the ACF, and this hazy June afternoon was the first time they would be meeting some key members of the hierarchy. Logan decided khaki trousers and a blue blazer were right for the occasion.

Seth Shein greeted him at the front door of his impressive mock Tudor home, a plastic cup of Scotch in his hand, wearing shorts and an extravagant Hawaiian shirt. 'Kinda overdressed, wouldn't you say, Logan? It's a damn pool party.'

Logan looked stricken. 'I guess I am.'

In fact, though the temperature hovered in the mid-eighties, most of the male junior fellows were also wearing jackets and ties, while every one of the five women had shown up in a dress-for-success suit. All but a couple of the senior fellows—those who'd been at ACF for a year—wore shorts.

Shein led Dan onto the patio, making introductions. 'Allen Atlas,' he said, moving him in the direction of a tall, hollow-cheeked young man in a tailored blue suit, 'Dan Logan.'

Dan and Atlas shook hands, eyeing one another with interest.

'Allen went to school at Vanderbilt,' noted Shein evenly. 'Now, Dan here,' he added, in apparent comparison, 'went to Princeton as an undergraduate and Stanford for his PhD.'

'Nice to meet you,' mumbled Atlas, scrutinising him coolly.

'Same here,' replied Dan. 'Looking forward to working together.'

'Oh, Seth . . .'

They wheeled to face a dowdily dressed, middle-aged woman bearing a pitcher of iced tea. Her face was incongruously pretty.

'I'm sorry to interrupt,' she said, 'but there's a telephone call.' Shein gave her a quick peck on the cheek—'Dan Logan, Allen Atlas, my wife, the endlessly patient and still beauteous Alice Shein'—and headed into the house.

There was an awkward pause. 'Well,' she said, 'I do hope you young men will be happy here at the ACF.'

They offered their thanks, and she walked away.

The newcomers seemed to be clustered by themselves in groups. Logan headed towards one of these at the far end of the pool. He already knew John Reston, the other junior associate recruited from Claremont. Though they'd never spent much time together, Logan had always liked him. 'Well,' exclaimed Reston, 'look who's here!' He made introductions: Amy, not an associate but Reston's petite blonde girlfriend; Barbara Lukas, tiny, with a staccato delivery and a degree from Duke; Paul Bernstein, quick with a smile, by the look of it a little too smooth; Sabrina Como, a striking young Italian with a mane of black hair, large green eyes and an incredible accent.

Abruptly, Seth Shein joined them from out of nowhere, 'You all making friends?'

They agreed they were.

'Good. We like to leave the back-stabbing to the *senior* staff.'

This brought an uncomfortable laugh. Dan began to suspect that the Scotch was getting to Shein.

A moment later, the thought was confirmed. Smiling at Sabrina Como, Shein announced, 'Appearances to the contrary, we recruit our foreign associates only for their *scientific* potential.'

Sabrina looked at him evenly.

'And I'm sure women are treated very well at the ACF,' offered Reston's friend Amy breezily. 'Appearances to the contrary.'

The junior associates turned to her, horrified. 'Why don't I leave you people alone to get acquainted?' Amy said, and she moved off in the direction of the buffet table. Reston offered a helpless shrug. 'Sorry.'

'Don't apologise,' interjected Shein, laughing heartily. 'Believe me, hang around here long enough, you forget what someone with guts sounds like.' And, chuckling to himself, he left them.

'You should know,' offered Sabrina, 'I really am not bothered by such things.'

'Well, you should be,' snapped Barbara Lukas. 'It was an insult. He has no business commenting on your looks one way or the other.'

'Ah,' she said. 'I must study to learn to recognise such insults.'

Logan, suppressing a smile, looked at her with interest. Lukas turned to Reston. 'She your wife?' she said, nodding after Amy.

'Girlfriend,' replied Reston. 'She's a lawyer with the Federal Communications Commission.'

'Shein's right—she's got guts. I should've said something.'

'I hate to be a realist,' said Paul Bernstein, 'but saying what you think isn't exactly the best policy around here. I had a long talk with one of the senior associates last night. There are a few people to watch out for.' With a tilt of the head, he indicated a balding young man in horn-rimmed glasses near the buffet table. 'See him? Peter Kratsas. Larsen's number two.'

'Who else?' asked Dan.

'Greg Stillman.'

There was a surprised silence. The name needed no explanation. Dr Gregory Stillman, world-renowned specialist in breast cancer, was one of those chiefly responsible for the ACF's reputation.

'C'mon,' said Logan finally, 'someone's exaggerating.'

Bernstein snorted. 'Talk to the senior associates—this is a guy who describes *himself* as "a vicious S.O.B." He thinks other people respect him for it.' He paused for effect. 'And they do.'

A few minutes later, Logan moved alongside Reston at the buffet table. 'You buy any of that?'

Reston shrugged. 'Hard to tell.'

'Well,' said Logan. 'We survived the political minefield of Claremont . . . Let's face it, all you wanted to do there was to get out of the place unscathed.'

Reston nodded. 'Damn right. No way this could be as bad as that,' he agreed. 'So? How'd you manage it?'

'I don't know.' He thought about it for a moment. 'I suppose you don't go looking for trouble. You find out early who the key players are and make a point of staying on their good side. You don't go around telling dirty jokes to senior administrators.'

'Not unless you've seen someone else get ahead doing it first. See now we're getting into my territory. It's called being obsequious.'

'Being *careful*. There's a difference.'

Reston grinned. 'All right, *strategically* obsequious.'

Logan laughed; this guy seemed to be a soul mate.

They were cut off by the roar of a motorcycle zooming up the driveway. Skidding to a stop, the driver—in black leather, his face obscured by the black-tinted Plexiglas of his helmet—dismounted and strode into the midst of the gathering.

'Who the hell is *that*?' whispered Reston.

'Stillman!' called out Seth Shein from across the patio, as if in response. 'Get that damn thing off my lawn!'

Stillman removed the helmet, revealing a beet-red face, topped by thick black hair matted with perspiration. He looked to be in his late thirties. His surprisingly unimpressive features—a doughy face and droopy eyelids—lent him a sense of sleepy disengagement.

Almost instantly half a dozen senior associates surrounded the eminent oncologist. From then on, it was Stillman's show. Purposefully, he began making the rounds of the newcomers and exchanging a few words.

Given Bernstein's earlier warning, Logan found himself surprised that Stillman seemed quite the opposite of an ogre.

'I read your recommendations,' he told the young doctor. 'We're looking for good things from you.'

'Thank you, sir,' said Logan, immensely pleased.

'Chicken, Greg?' offered Seth Shein, suddenly at their side, thrusting a plate of barbecued chicken Stillman's way. He smiled, but there was utterly no warmth in it.

Stillman speared a leg—'Why not?'—and started munching it. Suddenly he was a different man, his eyes alive, looking younger, energised.

'Why not a breast, Greg? Isn't that your speciality?'

'Not after you've been handling it, Seth. At that point the patient is usually beyond hope.'

'At least I don't run experiments that risk lives!'

'That's true. Your experiments don't do anything at all.'

Logan was aghast. It wasn't merely that Shein had had too much to drink or even that these two so clearly loathed each other. What was remarkable was how little effort either made to hide the fact.

Abruptly, Stillman turned back his way with an ingratiating smile.

'Aren't you hot in those clothes, Doctor?'

Not knowing what to do, Logan nodded tentatively.

'I know I am,' said Stillman, suddenly unzipping his leather jacket and tossing it at Shein's feet, quickly followed by his boots and leather trousers. Underneath, he wore a pair of swimming trunks.

'First rule of medical research,' he announced. 'Never shy away from the unorthodox because of what people will say.' He shot Shein a look and dived into the pool. With strong, even strokes he made his way to the other end.

'You,' hissed Shein, in Logan's direction, 'are going to have to choose sides.' And, though still dressed, dived into the pool after the other man, racing frantically to overtake him.

TWO DAYS LATER, on his first day of work, Logan reached the ACF grounds before seven, though the initiation session for incoming associates was not scheduled to begin till eight thirty. Just as he drew his newly purchased used Ford into the parking lot, the heavens opened. Using the *Washington Post* for an umbrella, he made a dash for the building, arriving soaked. He headed for the cafeteria, got a cup of tea, and took a spot at a corner table to dry out.

John Reston stopped by, with a full tray. 'Hope you don't mind me making a pig of myself,' he said. He sat down and crammed a forkful of scrambled eggs into his mouth. 'You feeling all right? You seem down.'

'Aren't you? After the other day?' The scene between the two senior scientists had thrown him badly.

'Naaah. Look, guys like this, we're hardly even in their field of vision. Anyway, they've already wrecked our personal and financial lives, what more can they do?'

Despite himself, Logan smiled. 'Who's running the orientation meeting?'

'Larsen.'

'Really?' Logan shuddered. 'The guy hates me.'

'Welcome to the club.'

LARSEN WAS PRECISELY as Logan remembered him. Sitting at the head of a large conference table, flanked by his deputy, Peter Kratsas, and a grim-faced secretary, he opened the meeting by indicating the two thick spiral-bound notebooks that had been set before each new associate. 'Your first assignment is to master the material in these books. All of it. No excuses or exceptions.'

That was it. No word of welcome. No banter.

'In your first year each of you will be responsible for charting the progress of around one hundred and twenty-five patients,' Larsen continued. 'As you know, our job here is to develop and test new cancer therapies. Every patient has agreed to take part in a carefully controlled course of treatment. You must see to it that your patients do not deviate from the instructions they have been issued. That they understand that if they fail to follow through in any way, they will be dropped from the programme.' He nodded in the direction of his deputy. 'Dr Kratsas will give you a brief overview of the trials currently in progress.'

Kratsas's sudden smile was ingratiating, a conscious effect to dispel the chill that had settled over the room.

'First,' he began, 'I want to extend a personal welcome. I'm sure I speak for the entire senior staff in saying that we are always available as colleagues and friends.'

Logan glanced at Larsen, who stared straight ahead. *Sure,* Logan thought, *that guy'll be my friend, all right—the day jellybeans cure cancer.*

'Now, then, as I'm sure you know, our experimental treatments fall into three categories. A Phase One trial is by definition a new form of treatment. Subjects' malignancies are highly advanced and we recognise going in that the chances of meaningful success are remote. Usually, what most interests us is gauging the maximum dose of a new drug the human body will tolerate. Its impact on the malignancy is often of only secondary concern.'

He cleared his throat and took a sip of water. 'Perhaps only ten per cent of the drugs that go through a Phase One test move on to a Phase Two trial, aimed at determining a compound's effectiveness against malignancy in a specific organ. In turn, no more than about ten per cent of those drugs—*one* per cent of the total—are sufficiently promising to warrant Phase Three trials, which test the new treatment against the best existing therapy.'

He picked up one of the notebooks and let it fall to the table with a bang. Several of the young associates started. 'Heavy, huh? It contains, among other things, a run-down of all current protocols—thirty-six in all. Familiarise yourself with them all by Wednesday, because that's when you assume charge of your full complement of patients.' He turned back to Larsen. 'I think that about covers it.'

Larsen nodded crisply. 'After your patient-care year, you will in turn pass on your patient roster to next year's incoming fellows. And, assuming we are pleased with you'—here he stopped for a millisecond—'you will then be attached to a lab in which to pursue your specific interest.'

A bell sounded outside the conference room, followed by a voice on the loudspeaker. 'Code blue. Twelfth floor. Room thirty-eight.'

'Never mind that,' snapped Larsen. 'Let's continue.'

'Dr Larsen . . .' The words, the first his secretary had spoken, were barely above a whisper, but Logan picked them up. 'That's Mrs Conrad.'

He hesitated an instant, frowned, then rose to his feet. 'Take over, will you, Dr Kratsas?' he said, moving briskly towards the door.

'WHO'S MRS CONRAD?' ventured Logan, several hours later.

Rich Levitt, the senior associate whose patients Dan was about to inherit, stared at him across his tidy desk. 'An ovarian patient. The wife of *Senator* Conrad . . .? North Carolina? The Senate Appropriations Committee?'

Dan nodded. Now it made perfect sense. 'Is Mrs Conrad the top VIP here at the moment?'

'Absolutely.' He paused. 'As far as I know. Sometimes—rarely— there are people who get seen only by the top guys. They might even check in under phoney names.' Levitt glanced at his watch and sighed. 'Look,' he said, rising to his feet, 'I think it's time you met some of my—soon to be your—patients.'

'At least this will be familiar,' Logan said, following suit.

'Maybe. Although the patients here may not be what you're used to. At Claremont you were treating your patients individually, improvising as circumstances changed, right?'

'Of course.'

'Well—I can't emphasise this too strongly, Logan—here you have zero treatment options. Your job is to enforce the protocol. Period. Sometimes you'll be going *against* your better judgment.'

'What happens if a patient starts questioning the protocol?'

'Happens all the time. Just make sure the patient doesn't *leave* the protocol. Because then you're messing with an entire study. When patients drop out, people start saying the work was sloppy or the treatment was too toxic.' He paused. 'Trust me, if a patient drops out on your watch, the senior guy running that study will have your tail. Some of those guys are killers.'

'I get that impression. And some of these guys . . .' Logan ventured, 'they seem to hate each other.'

Levitt nodded. 'You have any idea how fierce the competition is for funding? Every time someone wins, someone else loses.'

Levitt explained that in the case of Shein and Stillman the animosity dated to Shein's support of a young ACF researcher who had come up with a novel approach to breast cancer. Stillman vigorously resisted (and won) on the grounds that the data on which

the conclusions were based were incomplete—though soon afterwards he wrote a protocol himself based on the same idea. Quite
simply, Stillman regarded breast cancer as his turf.

'That's par for the course.' Levitt shrugged. 'The top guys all have
their own little fiefdoms and their own loyalists. The ultimate aim of
each is to defeat all the others. But sometimes, for strategic reasons,
they forge alliances against a common enemy. Get it?'

'So what you're saying is I'd better stay on *everyone*'s good side.'

'You'd better also be ready for what you'll run into from patients—'

'I've dealt with some pretty bad attitudes.'

'Our patients are a different breed. Many have moved heaven and
earth and travelled thousands of miles to undergo a treatment that
might end up doing nothing. The ACF is a roll of the dice and not
many shrinking violets take it.'

'They're fighters. Nothing wrong with that.'

Levitt nodded. 'The truth is, if you've got cancer, there's no better
place to be treated. But, basically, we and the patients have different
agendas. We're interested in finding ways to cure cancer. They want
their cancer cured.'

Rounding a corner, they came to a bank of gleaming elevators.
'Let's go see Rochelle Boudin. She's one of Larsen's.'

'Oh, right,' said Logan. He had already gone over the patient files
Levitt had prepared. 'She's in the control group for the drug combination they're testing against Hodgkin's. On ACE chemotherapy.'

The protocol in question was a Phase Three. ACE, an acronym for
the three compounds involved in the treatment, had been pioneered
almost twenty-five years before by Dr Kenneth Markell, current
head of the ACF. If it was less than completely effective, it signifi-
cantly reduced tumour mass 80 per cent of the time.

'What's the problem? The report says she's doing well.'

'This woman is the *mother* of all pains.' He paused. 'And there's
also a *father*—her husband, Roger.'

After a couple of minutes in their presence, Logan had a hard time
deciding which of them he liked less: the endlessly self-pitying
Rochelle, or the arrogant Roger. The problem today was that
Rochelle was due to start a new round of chemotherapy. 'It will have
to be postponed,' her husband put it to Levitt. 'She's not ready.'

'I'm afraid that's not possible, Mr Boudin. You know very well
that, according to the terms of the protocol—'

'Damn the protocol!' snapped Roger. 'Look at her—she's looking
great, she's feeling fine! Why put her through this now?'

'I feel like I'm losing control,' said Rochelle, her bottom lip trembling. 'Just thinking about it makes me nauseous.'

Levitt exhaled deeply, trying to maintain his composure. 'I understand, the treatment is extremely unpleasant. But we do this for a reason. We've been charting the lab values very closely and—'

'So have we,' cut in Roger, 'and we've taken the numbers elsewhere for independent evaluation.'

'You've *what?*' For a moment Logan thought his colleague might lose it. But almost instantly Levitt recovered. 'Mrs Boudin,' he said blandly, turning towards the patient, 'it is your right to take that information to anyone you see fit. It is also your right to remove yourself from the protocol.' He stared at the floor for a moment, then cleared his throat. 'If you choose to do so, kindly inform me as soon as possible so I can prepare the appropriate paperwork.'

He turned and began walking from the room. Logan followed.

'Doctor?'

They turned. It was Rochelle, her eyes moist. 'Could you come back tomorrow? Just to answer a few questions?'

He nodded crisply. 'Certainly.'

As soon as they reached the hall, Levitt clapped his hands together. 'Meaning,' he added, grinning, 'that *you'll* be back.'

THAT NIGHT, LOGAN was so immersed in the notebooks, it was nearly dawn before he was aware of the time.

Each of the thirty-six protocol proposals ran to at least twenty-five pages, but to Dan, every one was like a chapter of an epic detective story, suggesting a new approach to the age-old mystery of cancer.

Logan was not surprised by the number of compounds that had demonstrated activity against malignancy—at least in a test tube. What did take him aback was how many of the most promising drugs had been known to scientists for decades. It was just that their potential uses had never before been fathomed, let alone tested; no one, until now, having made the leaps of logic and imagination.

The next morning, Reston caught the bounce in Logan's step as soon as he saw him approaching the administration building lobby.

'Who'd *you* sleep with?'

Logan laughed. 'I have the feeling I'm not going to be sleeping with anyone for a long time—unless I find someone who gets turned on by randomised trials in Hodgkin's disease.'

'Ah, you've been going through the protocols . . .'

Logan nodded. 'Boy, some of the work that's being done here! I mean, I'm reading this stuff and thinking, *What the hell do these people need* me *for?*'

'Don't give me that false modesty rubbish. You're thinking the same thing I am: *How soon before* I *get to run a protocol of my own?*'

Logan smiled. 'Me? I'm just a humble junior associate.'

'Like hell. Logan, they know we're ambitious. Ambition is part of what they were after when they brought us here.'

'*Controlled* ambition. In the service of the greater good.'

Reston nodded. 'You're right. The first order of business is figuring out which of the senior guys to try and get as a godfather.'

'Good morning, gentlemen.'

They wheeled. There, to their intense discomfort, stood Gregory Stillman. How much had he heard? His smile gave away nothing.

'Logan and Reston, isn't it—the Claremont twins?' His eyes narrowed slightly. 'I try to get to know the junior associates personally. Tell me, do you have some time right now?'

The two young doctors exchanged a quick glance. Logan knew full well that Shein would take it as a betrayal; he also suspected that this might be precisely what Stillman had in mind.

Reston quickly made the decision for him. 'Sure, we were just going to grab a bite in the cafeteria.'

Ten minutes later they were in Stillman's office, listening to the story of his own rapid rise within the ACF hierarchy. His brilliant career, as the younger men well knew, was built on his pioneering work in the molecular origins of breast cancer.

'Would you like to hear what I'll be working on next?' he asked. 'This is going to be the next great breakthrough.'

His visitors' faces lit up. Opening a drawer, Stillman withdrew a manila folder.

'This began over a year ago,' he said. 'A patient came in with an inflammatory carcinoma. I had given up hope on her, and then, to my surprise, some of her tumours spontaneously disappeared. It turned out this woman was taking a course of drugs and enhanced vitamins for a completely unrelated condition.'

'May I ask what condition?' interjected Reston.

Stillman shot him an annoyed glance. 'Sure. After I've had our work patented.' He resumed his professorial tone—and changed the subject. 'There are a number of interesting things we've been working on in this lab.'

From the folder, he withdrew two black and white photographs. 'This is a photomicrograph of malignant breast cells growing in a culture dish. And this,' he said, displaying the second photograph, 'is the same cell growth after a six-week exposure to a chemotherapeutic agent we've been developing. It involves a new mycotoxin—one brought back last year from the Amazon.'

The change was uncanny. More than half the cells were clearly dead or dying. 'That's unbelievable!' exclaimed Reston.

Stillman nodded crisply. 'Yes. It is.' He turned to Dan. 'Bear in mind I've got more protocols going at the ACF than anyone. Almost twice as many as Shein.'

LOGAN SPENT THE REST of the day in the computer room, trying to learn the system. Every procedure at the ACF—from ordering antibiotics to tracking patients' progress—went through this machine.

When he was finally done, it was after 8:00pm. Yet Logan dragged himself back up to the twelfth floor to Rochelle Boudin's room.

'Sorry I took so long,' he said apologetically.

'Where's Dr Levitt?' replied Roger. He was clearly not a man big on pleasantries.

'He's off service.' Logan paused. 'You'll be dealing primarily with me now.'

'What do you know about my wife's case?' demanded Roger.

'I'll be working under the senior physicians, of course. But, please, I want you to feel comfortable discussing anything at all with me.'

Rochelle looked him over for the first time. 'I'm not sure any doctor can understand how we feel.'

'Try me.' With his gentle prodding, she told the story of her illness, including their stormy relationship with the doctors at the ACF. When she had finished, Logan started asking questions: What at the ACF gave them the most trouble? Was it the course of treatment or a communications problem?

'Both,' said Roger. 'This is Rochelle's life we're talking about, almost no one in this place seems to get that.'

Logan nodded. 'I heard what you said before about your sense of having no control. I understand that, and I promise you I will make a real effort to be more sensitive to it.' However, he explained, he expected that they would make an equal effort to observe the protocol. 'I've got to run now,' he said. 'I'll come by tomorrow.'

Rochelle looked at him gratefully. 'Thank you, Dr Logan.'

So, he thought, allowing himself a smile as he moved from the room, maybe *that's* how to handle these two, divide and conquer.

IT WAS NOT UNTIL the third Sunday after his arrival that Logan finally had more than a couple of hours for himself. He grabbed the *Washington Post* and headed for a small park he'd passed every morning en route to work. It was exactly what he needed on this lazy summer afternoon: high grass, lots of shady trees. He kicked off his loafers, lay down in the grass and closed his eyes. From a ballfield a hundred yards away came the sounds of a softball game: dim exhortations, the crack of ball against aluminium, an occasional cheer.

'Hey? Excuse me?'

Dan opened one eye and squinted at the silhouette looming over him. A guy with a baseball glove. 'Yes?'

'You want to play some ball?' He nodded vaguely in the direction of the field. 'A couple of our guys've left.'

Logan was a softball player from way back. 'Can I borrow a mitt?'

'You can use mine.'

For two innings Logan was exiled to the outfield. But when he finally came to bat, and lined a triple over third to drive in two runs, he was instantly transformed into a hero. As soon as he'd come around to score, Kevin—the catcher, the man in charge—sat down beside him on the rickety bench. 'You from around here?'

'I just moved here. I'm a doctor with the ACF.'

The other, impressed, gave a low whistle. 'Not bad.'

'How about you?'

'Me? I'm with the Internal Revenue Service, an attorney.' He pointed at a fellow in glasses coaching third base. 'Bruce Ryan's a doctor too. I'll introduce you.'

The next inning, Kevin was as good as his word. 'So,' said Ryan, 'you're at the ACF.'

Logan could not help but note this seemed less in the spirit of fellowship than sullen challenge. 'Right. How about you?'

'Just a radiologist, with Prince William County Hospital.'

'Ah. That's supposed to be a good facility.'

'Don't worry, I make good money.'

What kind of answer did *that* call for? 'Glad to hear it.'

'I knew another guy at the ACF. I met him at a party a few years ago. A first-year fellow. Cooper-something.'

'It doesn't ring a bell. He must be gone by now.'

'Coopersmith, I think. Real sharp guy. He was working on a protocol he'd set up.'

Logan smiled indulgently. 'No, that's not possible. First-year fellows don't run protocols. We get the scut work.'

The other shook his head. 'No, I'm sure of it. That's why it made such a big impression on me, cause he was so young.'

Just then the batter lined to centre for the third out of the inning, and Ryan headed back out to the field.

Logan walked up to Kevin behind home plate. 'Look, I've really got to get back.'

'Oh, really?' The guy looked genuinely disappointed. 'Well, look, we're out here every Sunday, you know where to find us.'

As he walked from the field, Logan made a mental note to check out a recent junior associate named Coopersmith.

BEFORE THE END of the summer Logan was entirely at home at the ACF. What was asked of him was no more than he'd always asked of himself: lots of hard work and the willingness to take on more.

The work routine was standard for junior associates: three days a week working in the hospital; the other two dealing with protocol patients in the clinic on an outpatient basis, and evaluating new candidates. Yet, almost alone among the junior associates, Logan's work had never been singled out for criticism and somehow, remarkably, he had managed to remain on good terms with everyone who mattered. Half a dozen of the senior men—even Larsen—had indicated that, in time, he would be welcome as a member of their team.

Indeed, he'd already begun viewing the day when he'd have to actually make such a choice with apprehension. The consequences for his career were incalculable: the implacable enemies it would create, the doors it would forever slam shut. Allen Atlas, the junior associate from Vanderbilt, had shown himself to be marked by ambition and seemed already to have made himself all but indispensable to Peter Kratsas, spending virtually every evening in the senior man's lab, tabulating protocol data.

'I really can't stand that guy Atlas,' said Reston to Logan one evening in his apartment. 'You notice how he's started to parrot Kratsas on every damn subject?'

'Look at it this way, he's picking up as many enemies as friends.'

'You know that from experience, right?'

'Hey, I don't need that from you.'

'I don't mean it as an insult. I'd change places with you in a second.'

Logan laughed uncomfortably. Reston was right: talented as he was, no one who counted at the ACF seemed to have noticed, and the fact was becoming a matter of some awkwardness between them. Logan wished he could say something to ease his friend's distress. 'You're just biding your time, that's all,' he said. 'And at least you've got a terrific woman.'

At that moment Reston's girlfriend, Amy, emerged from the kitchen, holding a knife and a couple of tomatoes. 'Hey, John, aren't *you* supposed to be doing dinner?'

'Yeah, yeah.'

Reston and Logan rose to follow her back towards the kitchen.

'Amy,' said Reston, 'we gotta set Logan up with someone. He's trying to use our relationship to get me to feel sorry for him.'

She stopped and smiled at Dan. 'Are you kidding, there're a thousand women on Capitol Hill who'd love a guy like you.' Amy's office was in the heart of the government district.

'I think Danny's already got someone in mind,' jibed Reston.

'Who?' asked Amy.

'Sabrina Como,' Reston said.

'Oh, the Italian bombshell.' She nodded at Logan. 'You've got good taste.'

Logan smiled uneasily. 'I really don't know where he comes up with this crap.' Actually, he knew perfectly well: Reston had been around more than once when Sabrina's very presence turned Logan into a bumbling, awkward parody of his normal self. 'Look,' he added lamely, 'I don't know a thing about the woman, except that she's a terrific doctor. For all I know she's involved with someone.'

'No, she's not,' Reston said. 'I checked it out with Sylvia'—the hospital pharmacist, also the hospital's foremost gossipmonger.

Logan shook his head. 'I tell you, Amy, if this guy put half the energy into science he does into being a wiseass, he would be *running* the ACF.'

TWO HOURS LATER, they were sitting in the living room sipping Amaretto, still savouring Reston's splendid northern Italian dinner.

'You ever hear of Ray Coopersmith?' Logan asked his friend. 'He was a first-year associate at the ACF four years ago—and he got a protocol through.'

'Like hell. That's impossible.'

'I've seen the paperwork.'

The documents were in the antique wooden filing cabinet outside Larsen's office with hundreds of other earlier protocols.

'I found the record of the proposal but not the results,' Logan went on. This was not unusual; protocol data could run to hundreds of pages and were generally filed away on computer disks. 'It was something about shooting radio-labelled antibodies straight into the bloodstream to go after prostate tumours directly instead of relying on standard chemo. Interesting idea.'

'Prostate? Who'd he get to sponsor this, Larsen?'

Logan shook his head. 'A genitourinary guy, someone named Locke. I think he's now in private practice.'

'What are you saying—you want to do something on your own? *You?*'

'*Us.* Maybe. Why not?'

'Why not? Because, frankly, I don't even register on their radar around here. But I'm perfectly willing to talk—when you've got something serious on the drawing board.'

IN FACT, LOGAN HAD BEEN toying with an idea for weeks—ever since Larry Tilley had stepped into his examining room.

A Kansas City lawyer, thirty-four and gay, Tilley was on a Phase Two AIDS protocol for a drug called Compound J, designed to interfere with viral reproduction. The protocol seemed to be totally ineffective in yielding practical results.

Tilley had come back in for tests. He'd been feeling dizzy lately, but not from overactivity. 'It usually happens when I've been resting. I get up from a chair and feel like I'm going to faint.'

'Have you been thirsty a lot lately?'—worth asking, but barely. Such changes could be symptomatic of extreme dehydration.

To his surprise, Tilley nodded. 'But that comes from taking the drug, doesn't it?'

'Well, let's see if we can clarify that. I want to run some tests.'

'How long am I gonna have to stay around?'

'Probably no more than a few days. Meantime, I'm going to give you a couple of litres of intravenous fluids and see if that helps.'

Briefly, it looked like a miracle cure. By the following day, Tilley reported he was feeling better than he had in months.

But the day after that, the dizziness was as bad as ever. As test after test came up dry, the patient's few days in Washington became almost two weeks. Logan's curiosity mounted, until finally, the tests yielded the reason for Tilley's persistent dehydration: his adrenal cortex had ceased to produce the hormones that enable the kidneys to retain salt and water. Apparently, Compound J was blocking normal kidney function.

And yet, going over the proposal, Logan found nothing to indicate that the drug might have so alarming a side effect. Nor, as far as he knew, had it so affected any other patient. What could have produced such a result? And could such a discovery have some meaningful practical application?

Logan did some of his best thinking at the ballpark, and Shein had told him that the ACF had a box at Baltimore's new Camden Yards stadium. He picked up a ticket for that evening's game.

Arriving early for batting practice, he bought himself a hot dog and beer and settled in. It wasn't until the fourth inning, with the California Angels enjoying a three-run lead, that he reached into his briefcase and withdrew Larry Tilley's case history. His plan was to review it, looking for some clue in Tilley's past.

'Dan?'

He looked up and there, to his astonishment, a cardboard food tray in her hands, stood Sabrina Como.

'I hope you do not mind to be bothered.'

432

He replaced the papers in his briefcase. 'No, of course not.'

'Most times no one else is here.' She took a seat beside him.

'Aha . . .' He stared at her wonderingly. 'You like baseball?'

She nodded. 'It is a game of numbers. I like numbers, my mother teaches statistics.' She pointed at the scoreboard. 'The Orioles, they are not doing so well. Only three hits and two errors already.'

Logan strained to think of something to say. 'So . . . what are you eating?' *Why was it that every time this woman spoke to him forty points seemed to drop from his IQ?*

She picked up the hamburger from her tray. 'Not the best.'

'Well, at least it beats the food at the ACF.' He hesitated. 'Is hospital food any better in Italy?'

'No, maybe even not so good. But there the doctors may bring their own food to eat.' She turned away to stare out at the field.

'So,' he picked up, 'are you enjoying your work at the ACF?'

'Enjoying?' She turned back to him, seeming baffled. 'It is like a medieval Italian city-state. It makes me go to read Machiavelli.'

Gratefully, Logan burst out laughing. 'That's true.'

'Some of the people there—just *horrible*! Like Larsen and Stillman. Among the greatest experts in ovarian cancer and breast cancer—no?—and they do not like women. How could such a thing happen?'

On the field, the Orioles were rallying and the crowd let out a roar as a ball shot between a pair of infielders into left field. Logan shook his head. 'I really don't know.'

'Back in Florence—where I did my training—I had a year of specialisation in endocrinology. But here'—she shrugged to indicate her frustration—'what is the use of such a specialisation?'

'I didn't know you were an endocrinologist.'

'Yes, and very good too.' She laughed. 'No good hiding it under a bush.'

Her laugh was lovely. He leaned forward. 'Listen, I've got something you might be interested in . . .'

He withdrew the pages from his briefcase and outlined Tilley's case, stressing his apparently bizarre reaction to the protocol drug. Eyes fixed on the field, Sabrina listened intently.

'You know,' she said, 'I have several patients also on the Compound J protocol. One of them, she has similar symptoms— dizziness, weakness—only not so severe.' She paused. 'You have been to the library at the Foundation? You have checked for information on Compound J?'

'I've made a start. Unfortunately,' Logan confessed, 'I'm not strong in languages. Only some German.'

Sabrina shook her head. 'This is truly a disgraceful thing about you Americans'—then, worried that she might be offending him, 'I don't mean this in a bad way.'

He couldn't keep from laughing. 'I can see that.'

'Anyway, my English is not so perfect also.'

'Just drop it, Sabrina, you're in too deep.'

'Anyway,' she added, her green eyes luminous, 'this is why I went into medicine—the fun of the hunt.'

'That's a nice way of putting it.'

'And you?'

He thought a moment. 'The same, I guess.' He glanced at his watch and reluctantly rose to his feet. 'I'm afraid I have an early flight to New York tomorrow.'

'New York? Ah, where you did your internship—no? And you maybe have a friend there?'

Incredibly—or was it his hopeful imagination?—Logan thought he detected a note of jealousy. 'Well, yeah. He's getting divorced.'

'You are a good friend,' she said, her tone betraying nothing. She rose to her feet and extended her hand—'I am pleased to know you at last. You seem to me like not such a bad guy, after all.'

Her smile was so disarming, Logan entirely missed the faintness of the praise. 'Thank you, Sabrina. That's nice of you to say.'

CATCHING A MORNING SHUTTLE out of National Airport, Logan made it into midtown Manhattan at half past twelve.

Ruben Perez was waiting in front of the Plaza Hotel. As Logan approached, Ruben held up a deli bag. 'I figured we'd eat in the park.'

'Some things never change.' Logan grinned as they shook hands. 'Why do I keep imagining you have class?'

'Hey, not all of us make doctors' dough.'

'*I* don't make doctors' dough. I'm at the ACF, remember?'

'That's why I didn't suggest a restaurant. Didn't want to embarrass you.'

Having established nothing had changed between them, they began comparing notes on their respective work environments.

'You're not gonna believe this,' said Logan, 'but a lot of people'd say the ACF's as bad as Claremont. Maybe worse.'

His friend shook his head vigorously. 'Oh, c'mon, man. You *forget* what Claremont was like.'

'I'm telling you, some of these guys at the ACF are unbelievable bullies. Cross 'em, and kiss your career goodbye.'

'So how you handling it?' They sat on a bench.

The simple question seemed to hit a raw nerve. 'You just work

434

hard and try like hell to stay out of harm's way. Problem is, you get known as a kiss-ass for the trouble.'

His friend was taken aback by Logan's intensity. 'Hey, man, sounds like they're working you too hard down there.'

'Sorry.'

'Anyway, how'd we even get started on *your* problems?'

Logan couldn't help but smile. 'Fine. Your turn. Talk to me.'

Ruben's impending divorce was far messier than Logan had realised. His estranged wife was drinking heavily. Increasingly bitter, she'd been denying him access to their young daughter. He'd begun to feel he had no alternative but a custody fight.

Having zero firsthand experience with such a nightmarish scenario, knowing nothing about the emotional needs of children beyond what he'd picked up as a medical student, Logan understood he was in no position to offer advice. He mainly listened. But this seemed to be fine with Perez.

'It's so damn hard,' Perez concluded softly, brushing a sleeve over suddenly damp eyes.

Awkwardly, Logan threw an arm over his friend's shoulder. 'You know I'll do everything I can.' He'd almost forgotten—perhaps only now fully grasped—the depth of his feelings for this man.

Half an hour later, as Perez hurried back to Claremont, Logan headed for the movies, where he spent the rest of the afternoon. Afterwards he decided to stay for dinner at his favourite Thai restaurant. After coffee he called Washington to check his messages.

The first two were routine: a hospital secretary with word of a protocol patient who'd checked back in; a college friend planning to be in town. The third caught him by surprise. Sabrina Como wanted to talk with him. She said she'd found something important.

Logan checked his watch—it was eight sixteen. Dialling Sabrina's number, he got her machine and left a message: he was hoping to make the nine o'clock shuttle. He'd try her from home.

SABRINA WAS WAITING for him at the gate at National. Her long dark hair was pulled back in a ponytail; instead of one of her stylish suits, she wore jeans and a sweatshirt.

He stood there, stunned, his heart racing.

'I hope there is no one else to meet you,' she said simply.

'No. I was going to take a cab.'

'I have brought my car.' She hesitated, seemingly embarrassed. 'I have some news.'

'What kind of news?'

'Today was my day off. I went to the library. I want to show you some references I found. They are on my computer at home. If it is not too late . . .?'

As they headed towards the garage, she began telling the story of her discovery: poring over documents well into the afternoon, she'd come upon an editorial in a vintage German chemicals periodical on what appeared to be a relative of Compound J.

'They do not give the name of the compound. But they talk about the structure. And they talk about polynaphthalene sulphonic acids, as in Compound J. And what it says in this paper is *tremendous* interesting.'

G LANCING ROUND her small apartment, Logan noted how clearly it mirrored Sabrina's personality—no-nonsense yet quietly tasteful.

She inserted a disk into her computer. 'This paper was published in 1924.'

'Nineteen twenty-four?' He tried to keep his scepticism in check. Back then almost no one had even the vaguest understanding of the nature of cancer.

The screen filled with text. 'You speak some German, no?'

Logan pulled up a chair and set about trying to decipher it. It took formidable powers of concentration not to be distracted by Sabrina sitting a few feet away, eyes alive with anticipation.

What instantly struck him about the brief article was its tone. Written in the aftermath of the German defeat in the First World War, its point was that Germany's scientists, for all their lack of financial resources, remained vastly superior to their detested counterparts in England and France. The compound—'the work of a former researcher with the great Paul Ehrlich'—was merely mentioned, its alleged cancer-fighting properties cited—without substantiation—as another example of German brilliance.

'Sabrina, there are claims made here, but there's no evidence.'

'Don't you see, Dan, they talk of cancer! This is important.'

He shook his head slowly. 'It's hard to imagine these people would even have recognised an anticancer agent.'

She flashed unexpected irritation. 'You are very arrogant, Logan, for an American living in the 1990s.'

'Sorry.' He shrugged. 'I'd like to believe, but I just don't. Anyway, Compound J has already been eliminated as an anticancer agent by cell line tests.'

'A cell line is not human,' she said heatedly. 'How human cancer cells interact with healthy cells cannot be seen in a test tube.' She was right and he knew it. 'It is a pity you do not know French,' she added sharply. She had another, longer document on the screen. 'This is from the Pasteur Institute in Paris. You have respect for them?'

He peered at the screen though he spoke scarcely a word of French. The date was 1937. 'What does it say?'

'It is observations of one of their researchers who worked in a clinic in one of the French colonies, Guinea. Two women with infections from spirochaetes—maybe syphilis, maybe yaws, it doesn't tell exactly—they had breast malignancies also. And after three injections for the infections the *tumours* began to shrink!'

'What are you saying? Some relative of Compound J was active against breast cancer?' It was so far fetched as to defy belief.

She nodded. 'Perhaps. From what it says.'

'Does it give any details of the compound's structure?'

She scrolled down. 'Consisting of fused polycyclic sulphonates.' She smiled at him. 'Sounds a little familiar, no?'

Despite himself, he was starting to share her excitement. 'Anything else? Any names attached?'

She indicated a name in a footnote: M. Nakano. 'It talks of an unpublished paper this person wrote about the compound,' she noted. 'The name is Japanese, no?'

'Nakano. Didn't Paul Ehrlich use Japanese chemists? From what I've read, he had enormous respect for their work ethic.'

Sabrina shrugged. 'That is history, not science.' Then, abruptly realising what he was getting at, 'Ah . . . the other article . . .?'

He nodded. 'Ehrlich died around the beginning of the First World War. Who's to say this Nakano character wasn't the one from his lab who continued work on this compound after the war?'

Logan could no longer hide his mounting enthusiasm. Hadn't the Tilley case already impressed on him that the compound could be enormously active? If, in certain circumstances, it inhibited the growth of healthy cells, who was to say it couldn't also block the growth of malignant ones?

They talked for the next two hours. When Sabrina yawned, Logan suddenly thought of the time. 'It's late, I should be heading home.'

She looked at him directly. 'Is this what you want to do?'

Logan was taken aback. Could this be a proposition? More likely Sabrina's English had fallen short. 'Do I want to?' he repeated.

Sabrina rose from her chair and walked over beside him. 'Do you want me to drive you home, or perhaps stay tonight with me here?' She gently stroked his cheek. 'I would like you to stay,' she added. 'It will disappoint me if you do not.'

In reaction to his startled silence, she kissed him lightly on the cheek—then began undoing his shirt buttons.

'I guess I don't want to disappoint you,' he said smiling.

U NCHECKED, THE MALIGNANCY *has begun to work at her lumbar ver-
tebrae. With every sharp twist or turn, the tension comes to bear on
the weakened bone. Though she denies it, even to herself, the condition
is starting to impact her daily routine. She is often exhausted. Usually
alert and remarkably perceptive, now she more and more lacks focus.*

*In his office, her physician won't let it rest. His training and instincts
tell him, even in the absence of hard evidence, that something is terribly wrong. He informs her that he has scheduled a series of tests at
Bethesda Naval Hospital.*

She has fourteen months to live.

L OGAN DIDN'T MEET Sabrina again until that evening, at her apartment. They'd decided to keep what had happened between them
to themselves, dealing with one another at the ACF with strict professional detachment. In that place, surely someone would find a way
to use it against them.

As soon as she closed the door behind him, she gave him a passionate kiss and pointed to a chair. 'We must talk.'

Ignoring his surprised look, she took the seat opposite and leaned
intently forward. 'I love your passion for this project, Logan,' she
said, 'it's the same as mine. But if we go ahead—'

'If?'

'—we must understand how dangerous these people can be.'

'Of course,' he said blithely. 'Let's just not get paranoid about it.'

'This is wrong, we *must* become paranoid. And you especially. You
like to trust people. And to please them. Science you know well—but
people, I think, hardly at all.'

T HEIR FIRST sharp disagreement involved John Reston. Sabrina
strongly resisted letting him in on their secret.

'Look, Sabrina, we can't do this alone. If we're to have a shot at
getting a protocol accepted, we'll have to come at them with a team
in place. Reston's a terrific doc. And I trust him.'

'I do not. There's something about him I have never liked.'

'Who, then? We have to trust someone!'

The argument exasperated Logan. Of course, he, too, would prefer to lock others out—for personal as well as professional reasons.
Already, between them, there existed the kind of respect and trust
lovers can take years trying to achieve. Why tamper with that?
Never had Logan dreamed he could find a woman like this:
someone to whom he was not just wildly attracted, but whose passion for this specialised work equalled his own. Yet he had far less
faith than she did in her intuition about human beings. Her

suspicion of others could sink them before they even got started.

It came to a head one late night when Logan reported on the unsettling conversation he'd had with Steven Locke, the former ACF genitourinary researcher who had been Coopersmith's supervisor. He'd finally tracked him down in Dallas.

'Coopersmith was bad news, that's all,' Locke had said.

'Why? I don't understand.'

The other sighed. 'He faked his data and brought other people down with him. Look, I've got patient rounds to make.'

'You don't have any idea where I can find him, do you?'

He laughed hoarsely. 'Why should I know that?' And he was off.

Now, hours later, Logan felt he had the exchange in perspective. 'It was a scandal,' he told Sabrina. 'It left some casualties. But that has zero to do with us.'

'Maybe you are right,' she replied with unexpected mildness. 'But this Coopersmith was also a first-year associate, no? This will give them another reason not to let us try a protocol.' And before long, she was using this as further reason not to include Reston.

'This Reston, you must stop looking at him as a friend.'

'I'm sorry, he *is* a friend. And he has skills we need.'

'What skills? To be a wise guy? That is mainly what I see.'

'That's not fair, Sabrina.'

'What, then? What are these special skills?'

'Look, Sabrina, we're novices. This whole thing could fall apart for lack of enough competent hands and heads. It's happened before. Who knows, *that* might've been Coopersmith's problem.'

He thought that he could sense Sabrina starting to waver. She indicated a stack of research on the table, some of the material they'd assembled to review.

'Let's get to work. In three hours I must go back to the hospital.'

'Well, I guess I should get started on the introduction to the proposal.'

'Good.' She gave him a chaste kiss on the cheek.

'Though writing has never exactly been my strong suit.'

'At least it's your own language. I'm sorry, I cannot be much of a help in this.'

'You know'—he grinned—'Reston's a *helluva* writer . . .'

'COMPOUND J?' repeated Reston, three evenings later, in the trendy Georgetown restaurant to which Logan had invited him. 'For *breast* cancer?' He snorted. 'Compound J's a dud. Everyone knows that.'

'Maybe they've just been using it the wrong way. Against the wrong disease.'

'I think we should order.' Reston flipped open the menu.

'Look, I understand your reaction. It's a lot to digest.'

'I'd say it's indigestible.'

The truth was, Logan saw his friend as a kind of test; the objections he raised were those they would face within the ACF.

Given how the discussion had started, neither man pressed it. Only with the arrival of their food did it resume.

'All right,' Reston picked up suddenly, 'let's hear some evidence.'

'Where is it written that cell lines are reliable models for what goes on in a living patient? A judgment based on cell line is like looking at an elephant's toenail and thinking you see the whole elephant.'

Reston looked up from his cassoulet. 'OK. So what?'

Logan raised the Larry Tilley case. 'If a drug seems to be that active against a healthy gland, you've got to at least wonder if it won't be active against a diseased gland.'

'That's reasonable speculation—but why does it lead to cancer?'

'Sabrina Como and I have been doing some research.' He told him about Sabrina's initial finds in the archives.

Reston was dismissive. 'You're giving me stuff from the twenties and thirties?' He shook his head.

Logan glared at him and pulled a folded sheaf of photocopied pages from his inside pocket. He handed them across the table. 'Try telling me *this* is ancient history. It's a paper presented when we were third-year residents.'

The paper's author, a Professor Engel of the University of Minnesota, was an expert on the proteins called growth factors, produced by all cells. He had shown that some tumours, especially those of the female breast, develop the ability to secrete growth factors into surrounding tissue where they interact with receptors on neighbouring cancer cells, signalling those cells to reproduce. This created an endless circle of secretion and growth.

Yet, Engel had noted a curious phenomenon: sometimes, inexplicably, drugs containing polynaphthalene sulphonic acids—like Compound J—appeared to block the binding process.

'How's that for evidence?' asked Logan. 'If we can show this stuff screws up a cancer cell just a little bit more than it does normal surrounding cells, we have ourselves an anticancer drug.'

Reston burst out laughing. 'Logan, you're crazy. Finding a drug that works among the millions of compounds out there is like hitting the lottery on your first try.'

'Come on, John, you know as well as I do that this is enough evidence for a protocol.'

Reston fell silent. 'Who else knows about this?'

'Only you, me and Sabrina.'

Reston leaned forward, and spoke softly. 'You're gonna get massacred on this, Logan. Breast cancer belongs to Stillman! You're going to have to get one of the other top guys behind it.'

'I know that.'

'And by a process of elimination . . .'

'There's only Shein.'

The implications were clear to both. For all his spirited nonconformity, indeed, largely because of it, Shein wielded far less power at the ACF than most of the others.

Logan leaned forward. 'So you with us, or what?'

Reston shook his head with resignation. 'Ah, what the hell. I guess we've gotta give it a try, right?' He paused. 'You'd better start thinking of how you're gonna suck up to Shein.'

As IT HAPPENED, Shein made things easy for him. Two days later, the senior man called Logan into his office and closed the door.

'You speak German, don't you, Logan?'

'Enough to get by.'

'Getting by doesn't impress me. I can do that with my Yiddish.'

'Actually, I've been working on it a lot lately.'

'I know. I see you've taken a lot of material out of the archives.'

Logan just stared: was there *anything* this guy didn't know?

'I'm going to the International Chemotherapy Conference next month in Frankfurt. I'm gonna need another set of eyes and ears. Yours.'

'Seriously?'

'Write it down, December 15th through the 18th. It'll give us a chance to get to know each other a little better.'

'SAY, LOGAN,' HISSED SHEIN, eyeing a tall blonde in an elegantly tailored suit, 'get a load of that.' They were standing by the baggage carousel at Frankfurt Airport. 'Trust me, Logan, we're going to enjoy ourselves here.'

Logan was already starting to have second thoughts about this venture. On the plane, while most of the other passengers dozed in the darkened cabin, Shein had downed a steady supply of Bloody Marys and recounted his exploits on other trips, such as with the research assistant at the conference in Rome, and the English physician in Tokyo.

Logan could hardly miss the desperation behind the braggadocio; the sense that this man, so widely admired, had a void in his life that could not be filled. Suddenly Logan felt himself to be less a colleague than a chaperon. A few hours before, his primary concern had been choosing the right moment for trying to enlist Shein's support for their trial. Now he had to worry about the esteemed scientist embarrassing the ACF . . . and, possibly, taking him down with him.

Half an hour later, at the Hotel International, Shein underwent another metamorphosis. Relaxed and bright-eyed, he stood in the lobby, greeting colleagues from around the world; seeming to recall effortlessly not just their names but minute details of their research.

Dead on his feet, Logan quietly excused himself and went to his room. In less than five minutes he was asleep.

When his eyes opened again, it was afternoon. He picked up the phone and asked for Shein's room. No answer. But Shein *had* left a message for him: *Papa's gone a-hunting. Don't wait up.*

Sitting alone at dinner that night in the hotel restaurant, Logan reassured himself there was no reason for concern. Shein was not due to speak to the conference until the following evening. Surely by morning . . .

But Shein was not at breakfast the next day; nor, Logan discovered, had he even picked up his credentials at the front desk.

In the end, Logan decided the best plan was to pay attention to the conference. In Shein's absence, wasn't it more vital than ever that he serve as the senior man's eyes and ears?

The work being discussed and evaluated here was of immense importance. Never before, not even at the ACF, had Logan seen so much talent in one place.

By the time the last afternoon lecture ended, it was nearly five o'clock. Shein was scheduled to speak at eight, immediately after dinner. Where could he be?

Logan made his way down to the large room off the lobby given over to 'poster sessions'. It was reminiscent of a high-school science fair. Anyone with information to display had merely to scrawl a shorthand description on a poster, pin it on an easel, paste on a bit of supporting data, and wait for interested customers. Logan slowly began to make his way past the exhibits.

'Where have *you* been?'

He would know that voice anywhere—and *never* had he been so glad to hear it. Though red-eyed, unshaven, and still wearing the same clothes in which he'd arrived, Shein appeared just fine.

'Dr Shein, I was worried about you.'

'About *me*? Didn't you get my note?' Suddenly he leaned in close. 'I gotta change for my speech. Come up with me.'

Shein was fairly bursting with news.

'Remember the woman at the airport?' he asked in the elevator.

442

'You were with *her*? How'd you find her?'

Shein smiled with pride. 'I read her luggage tag.'

As they headed down the corridor, Logan glanced at his watch. The speech was in less than twenty-five minutes. And his colleague evidently hadn't given his talk a moment's thought.

He needn't have worried. Shein was brilliant. Speaking without notes on the granulocyte colony stimulating factor—a genetically engineered protein that enables bone marrow to quickly regenerate, thus rendering tolerable extremely high doses of chemotherapy—he kept the audience in the main auditorium mesmerised, along the way getting laughs from this gathering of senior scientists that would have delighted a veteran comic.

I*T HAD BEEN EIGHTEEN YEARS since she had written on local politics for the* Sacramento Bee. *Sometimes she could see herself, hair still shoulder-length, wearing one of those ridiculous trouser suits, working away at her old Underwood typewriter, struggling to meet a deadline.*

The choice to set aside a promising career had been hers. Fourteen years ago, when Charlie was born, she had wanted to stay at home to watch her children grow up. Seven years later, by the time her second child, Allison, was old enough for school, her old life no longer seemed feasible. Now, unavoidably, John's political career came first. It wasn't easy living in his shadow, but theirs was a good marriage. She respected him. She saw herself as a partner in far more than name only. He trusted her absolutely.

Perhaps even more, she realised now, than she trusted him. For almost a week after the gnawing ache in her lower back returned, she failed to mention it to him. After all, the doctor said the biopsy was only a precaution. It was set for the day after tomorrow.

Still, she decided she'd let John know afterwards, when the results came in, when she was free and clear.

T**HE FOLLOWING MORNING,** Shein was gone again, but Logan had other things on his mind. This was the day he was to visit the building in which Paul Ehrlich had conquered syphilis, now a cancer research centre. Its directors had taken advantage of their proximity to the conference to arrange a tour. For Logan, this was a pilgrimage. He was coming to this place imagining that he might pick up some small sense of what made the great man tick.

The chartered bus deposited Logan and two dozen others before the Institute shortly before eleven. Instantly, he was disappointed. From the outside it was curiously unimpressive; a massive, ivy-covered cube of grey stone.

Entering, Logan was further disheartened to note that the reception area was filled with the kind of ultramodern furniture Logan had come to associate with eager-to-impress Park Avenue physicians like Sidney Karpe. Inwardly, Logan shuddered. This had nothing to do with the magical place that had stirred his boyhood imagination.

Midway through the conducted tour, Logan slipped down the stairs and asked the receptionist where the mens' room was.

She nodded in the general direction of the front hallway. 'Go through there and down the stairs, then straight on to the next room. Turn left, and left again. You will see it on the right.'

He was certain he'd done precisely as told—which is why he was confused suddenly to find himself in a narrow corridor that dead-ended against a wooden door. Was this it?

Tentatively, he pushed the door open—and instantly knew he should close it again. Wooden stairs led downwards into the basement. But, after a moment's hesitation, he flicked on the light.

What he saw convinced him to go the rest of the way down: vintage lab equipment, neatly arranged within old glass-fronted oak cabinets. There were oversized bronze microscopes, a polished steel balance, hand-blown glass condensers with beautiful spiral cooling coils. Over all lay a thick cover of dust.

Had these once been used by Paul Ehrlich himself?

In the corner, he noticed a stack of wooden crates. Gingerly, he lifted off the top one and set it on the floor. Within were exquisite old bottles, with raised lettering, that had once contained chemicals. Each was protectively wrapped in yellowed newspaper.

Logan's eye was drawn to a crumpled sheet of lined notebook paper, wedged in a corner of the crate. He picked up the page and smoothed it out. In pencil—difficult to read in the dim light—was the date November 25, 1916, followed by a line of tight script. But what seized his interest was the sketch beneath: twin hexagons sharing a common side and, protruding from the end of each hexagon, additional sulphonate molecules. He took a deep breath, sucking in the musty air. What he held in his hands defied all logic. A primitive version of Compound J!

Carefully, he folded the page, stuck it in his pocket and put the bottles back. His heart racing, he rejoined the group.

SABRINA GAVE JOHN RESTON no reason to suspect she'd opposed his involvement with the project. In fact, in the couple of days since Logan's departure to Europe, her ill will had dissipated. Given the handicaps under which the team would be operating, the proposal had to be flawless. And it was only now, with Reston manning the computer keyboard, that Sabrina knew that Logan had been right: Reston was a gifted editor and his involvement could be crucial.

'You are excellent with words, Reston,' she said, reading over a rough draft of the introduction to the proposal. 'Who would not wish to support such a protocol?'

'It's called piling on the bull.' He paused. 'Say, got any liquor around here? I figure it's time for a break.'

She nodded. 'But I prefer not drinking and working together.'

She turned her back on him. Suddenly, incomprehensibly, she felt his arms around her waist, his breath against her neck.

'John, what are you doing? Stop. Right now!' She twisted her upper body, trying to pull away.

'But you look so good, I can't resist.' He kissed her neck, pressing against her. 'C'mon, Sabrina, what's Logan got that I don't?'

'*Bastardo!*' With a violent lurch, she wrenched herself free.

He held up his hands like a basketball player unjustly charged with a foul. 'You're not interested, fine. It was worth a try.'

'You get out, Reston. Right now!'

'C'mon. Don't be stupid. Let's get back to work.'

'*You get out now.*'

'Look, it won't happen again.' But already he was reaching for his jacket. 'I'm sorry, Sabrina.' He stepped towards the door. 'Please, let's just keep this in perspective, all right? And to ourselves.'

TWO HOURS into the return flight, Logan was still trying to find an opening for the subject of Compound J.

'Dr Shein, I had a particularly interesting experience when I went to the place where Paul Ehrlich once worked.'

Shein appeared to be dozing. 'I know about that lab. They're not doing anything worth wasting your breath on.'

'It has nothing to do with that. I ran across some equipment in the basement. I have an idea it's from Paul Ehrlich's own lab.'

Shein sat up and looked at Logan in genuine surprise. 'What the hell were you doing in the basement? Get any *souvenirs?*'

'Well, see—' Flustered, Logan reached into his inside jacket pocket for the sheet of paper. 'I found this.'

Putting on his reading glasses, Shein looked it over, then shot him a hard look. 'Logan, when the hell you gonna come clean? You and I both know this is an early version of the chemical structure you and the Italian babe have been looking at.'

'That's right,' Logan acknowledged.

'What do the words say? Translate.'

'Well . . .' Logan hesitated. 'It basically describes the compound in the picture. But the language is stilted. I was thinking it might've been written by one of Ehrlich's Japanese researchers—'

'Deal in facts, Logan. What does this little find of yours *mean*?'

'Well'—he paused—'we'd read that this compound may have originated in Germany, way back when. It's fun to find what seems like direct confirmation.'

'Logan, you're a scientist. You want fun, go body surfing. Now, I want the whole story of what the hell you've been up to.'

So over the next couple of hours, Logan told it, starting with Larry Tilley's appearance in the examining room. Shein sometimes seemed impatient—cutting into the narrative with a sharp comment or a challenging question—but his interest never wavered.

'Compound J for breast cancer?' he said at the end. 'Well, it's a novel notion, I gotta give you that. Where do you stand now?'

'I'm hoping Sabrina and Reston will have something on paper when we get back.'

'It's just you three?' His tone was ominously noncommittal.

'So far.'

Shein settled back in his seat. 'It's a good idea. Of course, I'll wanna see your data.'

'So you're interested? You'll help us?'

'Why do you think I took you along on this trip?'

S TARING AT A PAGE of the proposal, bone-tired, Reston suddenly began to laugh. Across the room, Logan and Sabrina looked up from the pages they'd been reading.

'I don't know about you guys,' explained Reston, 'but I've read this proposal so many times, it doesn't even register any more.'

'We are all tired, Reston,' snapped Sabrina. 'That's no reason to stop working.'

'Look,' Logan said, 'we're all nervous about Shein's reaction to the draft. Why don't we try and relax until he gets here?'

'Bet I'm not as nervous as you,' offered Reston. 'Shein expects nothing of *me*.'

'Thanks a lot,' said Logan, conceding the point. 'It's great to know you're always there with a reassuring word.'

In fact, since he was the one who'd recruited Shein as their adviser, Logan had infinitely more at risk than his colleagues. So far, Shein had kept his distance, choosing to let the three junior associates work out the draft of the proposal on their own. It was a courtesy that was also a challenge: only now, having studied it, would he let them know whether he'd give them his full backing.

'Well,' said Logan, sighing, 'we'll know in'—he glanced at his watch—'any time. How do you like that, the S.O.B. is late!'

'Me, I am not worried,' reassured Sabrina. 'It is good work.'

Titled 'A Phase Two Clinical Trial of Compound J in Metastatic Breast Cancer', the proposal had, at fifty-five pages, plus reprints of six articles and other supporting data, the solid feel of a corporate annual report. That was part of the point, of course.

They'd paid unusual attention to the proposal's Informed Consent Document, listing all the possible toxicities that other researchers might have discounted. One of their toughest decisions—since Compound J could not be absorbed orally—involved the choice of which intravenous delivery system would prove more effective: a continuous drip, in hopes of wearing down cancer cells, or concentrated doses via a large slug known as a bolus, aimed at overwhelming the cancer cells with toxins—which could also place healthy cells at greater risk. They'd finally opted for the drip as the sounder choice.

'Sorry,' offered Shein, when he finally turned up at Logan's apartment, forty minutes late, 'a guy from Health and Human Services came by my office and I couldn't get rid of him.'

'That's OK. May I take your coat?' asked Logan.

'No. What I have to say won't take long.'

It felt like a blow to the solar plexus, but Logan showed nothing.

'Not a bad place,' observed Shein, glancing around the room. 'You furnish it totally through the Salvation Army?'

'Actually, Dr Shein, I went to Ikea.'

'What's wrong with you, Logan, losing your sense of humour?' From the inside pocket of his rumpled tweed jacket Shein removed a folded copy of the protocol proposal. It appeared to have been well read. 'You got something to drink in this place?'

'Please, Dr Shein. The proposal.'

Shein cast Logan a baleful glance. 'OK. It's good. Very good.' He looked from Reston to Sabrina, the relief apparent on both faces. 'Not that I don't have some criticism. I don't like the drip. You gotta go with the bolus.'

'We were trying to minimise damage,' offered Logan.

'You do a trial like this, you face that there might be fatalities. Because basically what you're doing is poisoning people within an inch of their lives. You can't make omelettes without breaking eggs.'

There was a long silence in the room.

It was Sabrina who broke it. 'Dr Shein, you are talking about the therapeutic window, no? The dose that will be toxic to cancer cells but not toxic for healthy cells.'

He nodded. 'You got it.'

'And this is a tiny, tiny margin . . . even for the best drugs.'

'The trick is finding it. That's what separates great cancer docs from the chaff—the willingness to go right to the edge and not flinch.' Shein smiled. 'Fortunately, you'll have me to help devise solutions. By the way, when you rewrite the proposal, I want you to tone down that damn Informed Consent provision. You don't have to go out of your way to imagine every possible side effect.'

'We just wanted to be candid. And responsible.'

'Listen, what you had in that list scared the hell outta *me*. The committee knows all that anyway.'

T HAT NIGHT, when Reston had gone, Logan produced a bottle of champagne. Yet, though he'd planned this moment for weeks, somehow it soon began to feel like an anticlimax.

'Is there something wrong?' he asked Sabrina as they sipped their second glass.

'This Shein,' she said, with a forced smile, 'he has the morals of a cabbage. But he is not dull.'

'No—anything but that.' He paused. 'I only wish he'd stop making nasty cracks all the time.'

She looked at him closely. At the beginning his face had struck her merely as conventionally handsome; now she was equally taken by the deepening worry lines—evidence of what she knew to be character. 'He doesn't mean it. It is a sign he likes you.'

'Much more of his friendship and I'll put a gun to my head.' He smiled. 'Look at it this way, Shein's my cross to bear. You've got Reston.'

Reston! She simply could not trust him. Logan did absolutely. As a result she now sometimes found herself hesitant to confide in Logan, even on scientific matters. She reached for the champagne. 'If I show you something,' she said suddenly, 'can we keep it just for ourselves? Nothing important—but I do not want Reston involved.'

'I guess so. If you want.'

She rose, crossed the room, and retrieved a sheet of paper from her briefcase. 'Here,' she said, handing it to him.

It was a Xerox copy of a German newspaper clipping dated August 18, 1924. Studying it, Logan quickly understood it was a sort of social announcement. Dr Mikio Nakano, associate director of the Medicinal Chemistry Division of the I. G. Farben Company, was to speak the following day at the Frankfurt League of War Wives. His subject was advances made by Farben scientists against human disease. The item identified the speaker as a native Japanese, aged thirty-four, formerly an assistant to the great Paul Ehrlich.

'Where did you get this?' asked Logan, looking up.

'I contacted all the important German chemical firms. I asked if they had any information on this man.'

'But I. G. Farben no longer exists.' As they both knew, I. G. Farben was dismantled by the Allies after the war because of its enthusiastic participation in the programme of genocide instituted by the Third Reich.

'It was in the files of Hoechst, one of the successor companies.'

'So we were right about this guy—he was with Ehrlich.' He looked at her. 'You're unbelievable, you know that?'

'No, just curious. Same as you.'

But he could see she was her old self; her intense preoccupation replaced, at least for the moment, by an openness appealing beyond description. 'You're also very beautiful,' he added, spontaneously. 'You've definitely earned some more champagne.'

'No, thank you.' She took his hand and kissed it gently. 'I think now is the time to do the rest of our celebrating.'

August 18, 1924
Leverkusen

Why did I accept work at Farben? They use me like a trained monkey! Had to waste whole afternoon giving a speech.

More proof Farben has little interest in project. Herr Direktor says too much lab time spent on compound—questions its commercial potential. Harder to get laboratory time for the work.

Compound no.157 useless. Unstable at room temperature and poorly soluble in aqueous media.

Begin tomorrow on no.158.

LOGAN WAS A BIT SHAKY when he arrived at the hospital the next morning for rounds. Splashing water on his face to wash the bleariness from his eyes, he was suddenly aware of a nurse waiting off to the side. He turned and stared at her.

'I hate to bother you with this, Doctor.'

'Boudin?'

She nodded. Over the months, Rochelle had grown ever more difficult. Almost daily—even when he was not on hospital duty—Logan received word she needed to see him. If it wasn't about her dosing schedule, it might be the quality of the hospital food, or perhaps even a TV programme on cancer research she'd seen.

The truth, of course, was that what she mainly wanted was a friend. In recent weeks Rochelle's husband, Roger, had all but disappeared. There was less and less conviction in her claim that he was just away on business. Obviously, such a scenario is always poignant, and had it been someone less manipulative, Logan might have found her circumstances more touching.

'She started asking for you as soon as she woke up this morning,' the nurse said. 'Her latest white cell count is in.'

'Oh, God.' In general, he had no problem with the ethical guideline giving patients full access to their medical records. But Boudin made a habit of abusing it. 'What is it?'

'Forty-two hundred.' She handed Logan the sheet.

'So she wants to cut down on her dosage again?'

She nodded. 'That's what she wants, all right.'

Resignedly, he started moving towards her room.

'Dr Logan?'

Logan wheeled, and was startled to see . . . Stillman!

The senior man approached him, hand extended, smiling. 'I was just wondering if you might have a couple of minutes to talk.'

'Well, I'm on my way to see a patient . . .'

'Who?'

'Rochelle Boudin.'

'Lucky you.' Another smile, one of comradely understanding. 'You'd better take care of it. Come and see me in my office afterwards.'

A moment later, stepping into Rochelle Boudin's room, it was all he could do to mask his reaction—curiosity, tinged with anxiety—to what had just occurred.

'Good morning, Rochelle,' he said with brisk efficiency.

She was propped up in bed. 'Have you seen my white cell count?'

'I have. But I assure you, we're not close to the danger zone.'

'I want to cut the dose. I *insist* on it.'

'Rochelle, you know the terms of the protocol—'

'I'm so sick,' she interrupted, 'can't you give me a break . . .?'

'Please, Rochelle, you know that I—all of us—have only your best interests at heart.'

'Do you?' she asked, suddenly girlish. 'Sometimes I can't tell.'

Logan glanced at his watch. 'Listen, Rochelle, I've got a very busy morning. I have to go.' And he turned and headed for the door.

'Will you be back to see me later?'

But he pretended not to hear, not stopping until he reached Stillman's office.

'How'd it go?' said the senior man, with unsettling pleasantness. Logan shook his head. 'The woman's a nightmare.'

Stillman laughed. 'Well, sit down, relax.' He indicated the chair facing his desk. 'Who knows, maybe we can arrange it so you don't

450

have to do that sort of thing any more.' He paused, leaning forward. 'No sense beating around the bush. I'd like you to join my team.'

'Your clinical research team?' Logan was stunned. 'Really?'

'That drug I talked about to you and what's his name?'

'John Reston.'

He nodded. 'I'm almost ready to bring it to trial, and I have to beef up on support staff. I've seen your work. You're good.' When Logan didn't respond, he pressed on. 'If things work out satisfactorily, you'll get your name on the paper.' He laughed. 'Somewhere.'

Logan knew how unusual such an offer was. He appreciated what it could mean to his career. He also knew that, because of Compound J, he had to find a reason not to accept.

'Sir, could you possibly tell me a bit more about the drug?'

Such a question from a junior researcher might have seemed presumptuous, but Stillman, utterly confident, took it in good grace. 'Well, as I told you, it's an anti-growth factor strategy. I'm not ready to go into more detail.'

Still not ready, Logan wondered, *with it almost set to go before the Review Board?* Suddenly, he was hit by a gut feeling: Stillman had zero faith in this drug. It was just another variation of the same old stuff. That's why he wouldn't come clean. Stillman was thinking only short term—the hype, and the funding it would bring in.

'Can I think about it?' Logan waffled. 'It's a huge decision.'

Stillman's eyes flickered with annoyance, but he held it in check. 'Certainly,' he said. He got to his feet and extended his hand. 'That's what I like about you, Logan. Not an impetuous bone in your body.'

BEFORE THEIR PROTOCOL could go before the Review Board, Logan and his associates had to get the man who'd be most unhappy about such a project to sign off on it. Raymond Larsen. As chief of the Department of Medicine, he ran the system into which any new protocol had to fit.

In Logan's view, there was no chance Larsen would hold up the project: he couldn't be seen to be blocking a reasonable idea. Also, Compound J had the backing of Seth Shein; and Shein enjoyed the support of Kenneth Markell, the powerful head of the ACF. If nothing else, Larsen understood the realities of institutional politics.

For Larsen, however, the Compound J protocol would be proof positive that this first-year associate, this *nothing,* had gone with his nemesis Shein. Clearly, Logan would have to make at least some attempt at damage control. Now, he walked towards Larsen's office, clutching the final draft of the protocol.

The senior man was not in.

'May I leave this?' he asked Larsen's secretary.

Looking at him dismissively, she pointedly laid the envelope to the side and went back to work.

When Logan returned at the end of the day, Larsen was back—and when he saw his face, he knew he'd read the proposal. But the man was a model of control. 'Dr Logan,' he said with a crisp nod, emerging from his office.

'Sir, I was hoping you might have a few minutes to talk.'

Larsen glanced at his watch. 'I'm afraid that's quite impossible, I'm due at the lab in five minutes. If you'll excuse me.'

The unmistakable note of anger in his voice made Logan flinch. But there was no turning back now. Logan followed him into the corridor. 'I was wondering if you've had a chance to read what I left for you.'

'I looked through it. What exactly do you want me to say?'

Logan tried not to sound unctuous. 'Sir, I'd appreciate any comments as to how it might be improved.'

'*My comments?*' Larsen smiled maliciously. 'Very nice job, Logan. My compliments to you and your little friends. And Dr Shein, of course.'

'Well . . . would you have any specific recommendations?'

He stood there a long moment, staring at him coolly. 'I'm late, Logan.' And, turning on his heel, he strode away.

ACTUALLY, THE REACTION Logan was most worried about was Stillman's. It was not long in coming. As he was about to call it a day, he saw the senior man heading his way.

'So,' said Stillman sharply, before Logan could say a word, 'I guess I've got your answer to my invitation.'

'Dr Stillman—'

'I have no interest in your explanation, Logan! Just know that I can make your life hell. You stuck a pickaxe in my back, and now you'd damn well better watch yours.'

'LOOK, LOGAN'—Sabrina's tone was less consoling than practical— 'we knew Stillman would not be so happy, right? Larsen also. And maybe others. But what can they do to us?'

Logan shrugged. 'Not much—once we get the proposal through. But they've got six weeks to try and sabotage us.'

In fact, the petty annoyances began almost immediately. Suddenly various functionaries around the labs were slower to cooperate with routine requests. Reston one day found that for no apparent reason his dial-out number—the code he needed to make long-distance calls—had been changed, and a new one was not readily available.

A week later Peter Kratsas ordered Sabrina to desist from giving her patients occasional pieces of chocolate.

'He says these diets must be strict. And, even while he tells me this,' she reported late that evening, 'he is smiling, like it is a big joke!'

'That's what it is,' concurred Logan. 'Patients' families bring them stuff to eat all the time. Ignore him. It's only temporary. Just a couple more weeks.'

For the key fact was, if their adversaries had real power to get at them, they'd never have had to resort to such pettiness.

'That's very easy for you to say, Logan,' she said, with a sudden smile. 'Me, I have four pounds of Perugina chocolates in the closet. Soon I will have the mice and roaches.'

Logan managed to smile back. 'I haven't told you the latest. Guess who just discovered he now needs clearance to get a painkiller from the hospital pharmacy?'

T HE COMPOUND J TEAM waited outside the Administration Building's third-floor conference room. Logan would represent the team before the Board members. He was already on a first-name basis with four of the seven: Dr Lauren Rostoker of Surgical Oncology; Dr Brendan Herlihy of the Department of Medicine; Dr Myra Manello of Radiation Oncology; and Marilyn Lennox of Nursing Services. The remaining three included a bioethicist based at Georgetown University; an Episcopal minister from Annandale, Virginia; and Marion Winston from Patient Services.

The Board stayed behind closed doors for fifteen minutes. Then the three junior associates were invited to join them.

'Well,' began Herlihy, chairing the meeting, 'I must say a lot of solid thinking went into this idea. However, as you know, we are able to approve only a very small number of protocols, those that meet the strictest criteria for scientific merit and ethical accountability. Dr Logan, you are speaking for the team?'

'Yessir.' Logan smiled, and began to lead them through the case for Compound J, emphasising the significance of the various reports of the drug's activity spanning decades. 'What we have already observed is clear evidence that it is capable of blocking growth factors from binding with cell-surface receptors. The thing is that, as long as this drug has been around, it has *never* undergone a rigorous clinical trial for activity against metastatic breast cancer. That is a situation that we now hope to rectify. Thank you.'

'What about your Informed Consent Document?' It was Marion Winston, the patient-care rep. 'As you've acknowledged, this is a very toxic drug. I have it on the best authority that you have not covered all likely eventualities. For example, cerebral haemorrhage. Or heart attack.'

Of all the possible calamitous effects of Compound J, the chances these were among them were infinitesimal. Still, Logan worried she might be scoring points with the others; following Shein's instructions, they *had* passed lightly over the unsettling matter of side effects. The room suddenly seemed overheated.

'Well,' Logan said evenly, 'listing every *possible* eventuality would have involved pure speculation. That's the point: we need to know more about this drug.'

'I see'—Winston again—'and you're planning to use these patients as human guinea pigs.'

'I didn't say that.' Logan collected himself. 'Isn't there a certain degree of uncertainty in a test of any new compound?' He looked hopefully at the medical personnel around the table.

No one gave a word of support.

'Dr Logan,' said Winston, her voice taking on a hard edge, 'public confidence in breast cancer trials has been badly shaken in recent years by doctors more concerned with their own reputations than with the well-being of patients. Frankly, certain aspects of your own history have been brought to our attention. Are you aware of a patient named Rochelle Boudin?'

'Yes, I've helped care for Rochelle Boudin.'

'I have interviewed Ms Boudin personally.' She held aloft a notebook in grim triumph. 'She says you are chronically indifferent to her needs, and rarely if ever tell her the full truth. I must tell you that Dr Larsen fully shares her view of the situation.'

So that was it! Larsen! 'Ms Winston, I don't know what you expect me to say. I've done my best with Rochelle Boudin, as with all—'

'Look,' he was interrupted, 'this is *absurd*. We're talking about the *wrong* things here.'

Logan jerked round to see Shein standing just inside the door.

'You want to talk about the Informed Consent Document?' he picked up. 'Fine, blame me. I'm the one who told 'em to make it short and sweet. But don't throw out the baby with the bathwater!'

Everyone knew Shein's intrusion was highly unorthodox, but no one was about to stop him. He moved to stand beside Logan.

'What are we really here for?' he continued. 'We have a problem in this country with metastatic breast cancer. Now, in my considered view, our friends here have come up with a novel and rational idea that represents hope for women who otherwise have none. If, God forbid, it were my wife, I'd sure as hell want her on this protocol—even if I don't know every one of the damned toxicities.'

I T TOOK THE REVIEW BOARD half an hour to reach its decision. The Compound J team was granted a modified protocol—a smaller and more closely monitored version of the one they'd proposed.

The note on the bottle of champagne that arrived at Seth Shein's door that evening didn't even try to be clever: *All the gratitude we can ever express will never be enough.*

According to the guidelines imposed by the Board, the Compound J team had to have a 'hit'—a demonstrably positive result—within the first fifteen patients. That placed even greater than normal importance on putting together a patient roster. 'It's easy,' as Shein pointed out, 'to kill a good drug with a bad trial.' And the easiest way to screw up a trial is to stock it with patients whose chances of doing well are already compromised going in.

Unfortunately, potential candidates for this protocol would likely fall into that category since, having proven resistant to one therapy, they would likely be resistant to others. The best the team could reasonably hope to do was locate fifteen women whose exposure to radiation or chemotherapy had been minimal.

As in every other protocol being conducted at the ACF, a summary of the Compound J test was duly recorded in the Institute's Community Outreach System. The description of the protocol was followed by a national appeal for likely candidates. Over the next few weeks, calls slowly began to come in, but three weeks into the process, only a handful of women were even being considered.

The ice was finally broken late one Friday afternoon. Sabrina got word that Rachel Meigs, a junior associate interested in the protocol, needed her in the Screening Clinic.

'I think I've got a live one for you,' said Meigs when Sabrina arrived. 'I finished the examination about half an hour ago.'

Sabrina looked into the waiting room. Except for a young woman, evidently very pregnant, it was empty. 'That one?' she asked, incredulous. A pregnant woman could not even be considered for the programme.

Meigs nodded. 'That one. I think you'll like her.'

Entering the room, Sabrina extended her hand. 'Hello, I am Dr Como.'

The woman struggled to her feet. 'Hi. I'm Judy Novick.'

Only now was it apparent: aside from her bloated midsection, the woman was emaciated, and her skin, instead of a robust pink, was sallow. She wasn't pregnant; her abdomen was full of tumour!

It took a moment to register. Of *course*, a week or so earlier Sabrina and her colleagues had studied this woman's X-rays and slides. Although tests confirmed that a breast tumour had metastasised to the liver and was laying waste her body at an awful rate, the only treatment she had undergone to date was a single course of adjuvant therapy. She'd been referred to the programme after the most active drugs available had proven useless. And she lived in Bedford, Pennsylvania, little more than two hours from the ACF.

'The first thing I will tell you,' began Sabrina, 'is that this is an out-patient trial. We might need you here in the hospital at the beginning, but afterwards you would live at home.'

'But what does it do?'

Sabrina's tone was at once straightforward and sympathetic. 'I can only tell you of our hopes. This is a very new treatment—but it is something some of us believe in very much.'

'How many patients has it been tried on?'

Sabrina hesitated. 'You will be the first—number one.' She smiled. 'This is kind of an honour, no?'

The woman looked away. 'I don't know whether to be flattered or horrified.'

Sabrina had never imagined this part of it would be so tricky. Suddenly she found herself having to sell the protocol—and to a patient she wasn't even sure she wanted. 'You are possibly a good candidate for this treatment,' she offered simply. 'And this is not a thing we can say to very many.'

For a long moment, Novick said nothing. Then, 'It's not an easy decision, but this is my only chance, isn't it? I'm not one of those people who lie to themselves.'

'Still,' Sabrina said evenly, 'before we agree, you must think about it a little. I want you to look carefully at the Informed Consent Document. And talk with your family and with your doctor. And I must talk with my colleagues.'

She nodded. 'Fine. But if we're doing this, I'd like to get started. The sooner the better.'

October 3, 1927
Frankfurt

Cannot believe my good fortune—Emma's family does not disapprove! I am proud, but must also be realistic. A Japanese son-in-law cannot be easy for any German family to accept.

Versions 284, 285, and (especially) 286 of compound continue to give hope. Melting point sharp, composition successfully determined by elemental analysis. When it works, nothing is more beautiful than chemistry. Except Emma.

Must now write my family in Japan. How will they take idea of a German-Jewish daughter-in-law?

L IKE EVERY OTHER ACF PROTOCOL, a summary of the Compound J test was available to any physician calling the Foundation hotline. As word of the protocol spread, the patient accrual phase began clicking along surprisingly smoothly.

One day in the Screening Clinic, Logan was alerted by his beeper to a call while talking with a candidate, one Sally Kober. She was missing a kidney as a result of a car accident in her teens; since she was sixty-six, this was of little consequence—but under other circumstances, it might have been used to keep her out of the programme.

Logan switched off the beeper and smiled at the patient. 'I'll get that in a few minutes.'

'Don't you have to get it now? It might be an emergency.'

'No emergency. Just a doctor calling about someone else who might be interested in this protocol. *You're* already here.'

'And immensely good company,' she observed, laughing.

Logan couldn't help but be struck by this woman. A veteran of a radical mastectomy twenty years before, she seemed to be taking the ominous appearance of the new node with amazing calm.

'Now,' she said, 'this thing I've got is pretty desperate, isn't it?'

'I wish the news were better,' he replied evenly.

Unconsciously, she passed a hand over her steel-grey hair. 'Are you a football fan?'

He nodded, confused. 'The Dallas Cowboys.'

'Oh, please, you struck me as someone with common sense!' She smiled. 'I love the Giants.'

'You're excused—you live in New Jersey.'

'I will bet you, right now, on the first game the Giants and Cowboys play next season.'

'It wouldn't be right taking your money.'

She laughed. 'It's called faith. It's a convenient way of betting on myself still to be here.'

'I've only known you fifteen minutes, but *that's* a bet I'll take.'

She waved her hand. 'Enough flattery. Go and return that call.'

A S HE DIALLED, he noted approvingly that the area code was central Virginia; little likelihood of transport problems with this one.

'Hello,' answered a male voice.

'This is Dr Daniel Logan at the American Cancer Foundation—I was given this number but no name.'

'Yes, Dr Logan. You've got the right number.'

'Did you call? Are you a doctor?'

'Yes, I'm a doctor. But I'm afraid I don't have a patient to refer to you. My name is Ray Coopersmith.'

LOGAN WALKED into the Hotel Jefferson in Richmond. It was Coopersmith's choice for their meeting. Though it was early on a Saturday evening, the lobby was nearly deserted. Logan was about to take a seat when he happened to look up. There, at a table behind a wrought-iron railing on the first floor, a man was nodding at him.

'I thought for a second you wouldn't see me,' said Coopersmith, when Logan reached the top of the stairs. He extended his hand. 'Ray Coopersmith.'

Though probably no more than a few years older than Logan, Coopersmith looked middle-aged. Tall and rail thin, with dark hollows beneath penetrating eyes and thinning hair in need of a trim, he had an edgy, unfocused quality Logan had noted in junkies.

As they took their seats at the small wicker table, Logan noticed, with a rush of sympathy, that the man's worn suit jacket didn't quite match the trousers.

Coopersmith ordered a gin and tonic, Logan a beer.

'So what are you doing these days?' Logan asked.

'I'm getting by,' he said, with sudden, unmistakable rancour. 'Don't worry about me, I'm practising medicine.'

'Where's that?'

'At a clinic. In Petersburg. Why, you gonna check me out?'

Logan chose to ignore this. 'I read your protocol. Impressive.'

The waiter brought the drinks.

Incomprehensibly, Coopersmith snickered. 'Maybe I'll read yours sometime. Breast cancer. Smart. A glamour disease. Me—genius!— I go after prostate—try to get funding for *that*.'

This was the opening Logan had been looking for. 'I heard it wasn't lack of funding that got you in trouble.'

Coopersmith's head jerked left, then right. 'Who said that?'

'Steven Locke. He said you faked your data.'

'That's bull! The data was good data,' he insisted. 'There was just too much of it. But they said it was uninterpretable.'

'Who's that?'

'Larsen. Stillman. Kratsas. That bunch. They were against me from the start. What I'd give to ream out those bastards!'

Logan stared at him. *That's* why this guy had got him down here? 'Look, Ray, I appreciate the warning, but it's not news about these guys.'

'You don't know the half of it.'

'Really, I understand what you're saying.'

'You're such an arrogant S.O.B. You fit right in at that place!' He shot him a malicious grin. 'Bet you don't like hearing that, do you?'

Logan was caught short by the savagery of the attack. 'Look, I've gotta get back. I don't think this is doing either of us any good.'

Unsettling as this meeting was, Logan found it useful. This guy was wildly unstable. Who could doubt that that had been at the heart of his problems?

Coopersmith's strangled laugh caught him by surprise. 'You're a jerk, Logan!'

LOGAN LIKED Faith Byrne the instant he met her.

'So, Doctor,' she greeted him in the examining room, 'who does a girl have to suck up to around here to get well?'

He laughed. 'I'm afraid sucking up won't do it.'

'Ah. In other words, it's you.'

The sixty-two-year-old widow came from the Boston suburb of Brookline. She was slightly overweight, with lively blue eyes beneath a halo of white hair, and was clearly going to keep him on his toes.

'I want to tell you it was my own decision to come down here and see you people,' she told him five minutes into their session. 'My doctor wanted to give me the same old stuff. But I told him no.' She looked directly at him. 'I've read up on my chances.'

The manifestation of Byrne's malignancy was unusual: hundreds of tiny pink nodules cutting an angry swath across the chest wall and around to the back. But the young doctor saw this as no impediment to her inclusion in the trial. The key fact was that she had been exposed to only minimal levels of adjuvant therapy; and that had been fifteen years ago, at the time of a mastectomy.

There was something else: Faith was an irresistible chance to stick it to Stillman. He found in her paperwork that she had recently rejected the chance to go with the senior man's protocol.

'Why's that?' he soon felt comfortable enough to ask. For a patient seeking innovative treatment to turn down a doctor with Stillman's reputation was almost unheard of.

'*Why?* You kidding? I *met* the guy. Call me weird, but I like to feel I'm gonna get more consideration than a slab of beef.'

Despite himself, Logan burst out laughing.

WHEN SHE WAS ACCEPTED five days later, Faith became the eighth woman accepted on the protocol. Half a dozen other prospects waited to be seen. The time had come to begin administering the drug.

By custom, protocol patients receive treatment in the order in which they've signed up. That meant Judith Novick led off.

Logan was aware this was not ideal. The progress of the early patients would be watched closely by their senior colleagues; and of all the patients on their growing roster, Judith was in the worst shape.

It was Reston, at a meeting one Sunday morning around Logan's dinner table, who raised the issue. 'Look,' he said, 'I say we launch with someone else. Judith Novick is too far gone.'

Sabrina stared at him murderously. 'We made a contract with Judith Novick. This cannot be changed now. Compound J can be as toxic to a person with a small tumour as a large. In fact, if Judith does well, it would look even better for us, no?'

'Sabrina . . .' Reston smiled indulgently. 'I admire your compassion. But when Judith Novick goes, she's gonna take one of our fifteen slots with her. And you know as well as I do that, because she's weak, the toxicity is likely to be heightened.'

He waited for a response, but there was none. He turned to Logan. 'Look, Dan, why can't we just drop her back a few slots?'

Logan looked towards Sabrina, then back to Reston. 'So it's up to me? Well, then, we go ahead as planned.'

Abruptly Reston was on his feet. 'Dammit, what kind of power does she have over you, anyway?'

'I'm just afraid that to change now,' Logan replied calmly, 'would be to draw the wrong kind of attention to ourselves. Either we believe in Compound J or we don't.'

But already Reston had grabbed his coat and was heading for the door. 'To hell with you both! With this whole project!'

TWO WEEKS LATER, on the morning of Judith Novick's first treatment, Reston was there with the others. This was their debut, a time, if ever there was one, to look beyond petty squabbles.

The patient, slightly propped up in bed, was pale, her midsection appearing larger than ever beneath the flimsy hospital gown. The tumour measured an astounding ten by ten centimetres.

'Don't you worry, dear,' the research nurse, Sadie McCorvey, said as she inserted the IV line into the patient's arm and taped it in place. 'It'll be over sooner than you know.'

But the items that were wheeled into the room a moment later could not have been reassuring: an EKG machine, ready to go, followed by the mobile crisis centre known as the 'crash cart'.

Novick was so focused on these that she failed to notice that McCorvey had removed the clamp on the IV sleeve. The Compound J team watched in silence. If she was to have a negative reaction, it would come within the first five minutes.

They waited eight.

'Well,' Judith Novick spoke up finally, 'when are you going to give it to me?'

Sabrina laughed and then pointed towards the liquid flowing

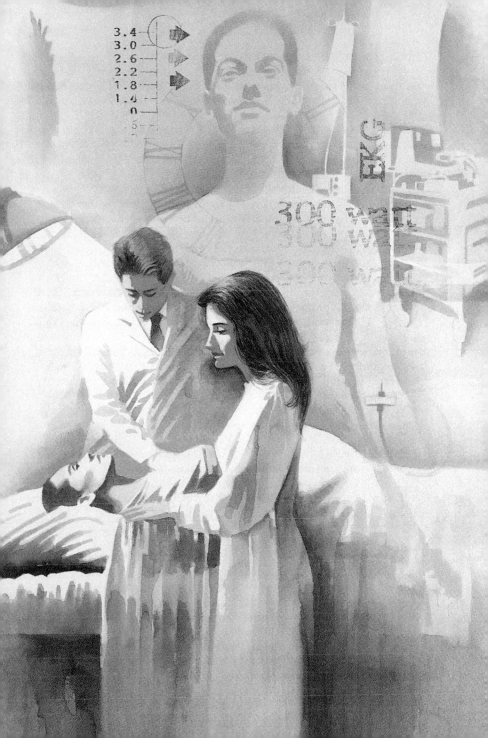

through the clear tubing. 'You see. No problems.'

If it hadn't been unprofessional, Logan might have grabbed Sabrina and kissed her. Instead, he turned from one to the other, grinning. 'Let's hear it for anticlimaxes!'

L OGAN MADE THREE VISITS to Novick's room during the next six hours. Sabrina made four. Even Reston stopped by a couple of times. Always she was resting comfortably, watching TV or reading. 'Is something wrong?' she asked Logan finally.

'Not at all,' he exclaimed. 'Just making sure you're OK.'

By the third day, she was ready to go home. Gingerly, Logan felt the tumour. By now, he knew it intimately—not only its size, but its *feel*, its distinctive contours. Could it be slightly softer than before? No, that had to be his imagination.

Abruptly, there came a knock at the door.

'What is it?'

'I'm sorry, Doctor,' said a nurse, opening the door a crack. 'Mrs Byrne is on the phone and she says it's very important.'

'OK.' He smiled at Judy Novick. 'Just keep on keeping on. We'll see you on Tuesday for your next treatment.'

He picked up the phone at the reception desk. 'Faith?' he said, with concern. 'This is Dr Logan. Is something the matter?'

'You told me I have to wait a month and a half for treatment.' There was a hardness to the voice.

'Yes.'

'So how come someone else has already got hers?'

'Who told you that?'

'Never mind who told me. That isn't the point.'

'Faith, listen to me. The drug is administered according to when patients joined the protocol.'

'I don't give a damn about that. I've got to look out for me.'

'Faith,' he said, 'we'll have to discuss this later.'

'When?'

'*Later*.'

As he headed for home a few minutes later, he felt confused, exasperated, betrayed. It wasn't hard to pinpoint Faith's most likely source: Marion Winston, the patient-care representative, who made it policy to let every patient in the protocol know that, as she put it, she 'was available to mediate misunderstandings with medical personnel'.

When Logan stopped by her office next morning, intending to raise the subject of Faith's call, Winston stopped him short with her opening words. 'I heard from Mrs Byrne. Apparently, you are not being very responsive to her needs.'

462

'Listen, our job is to be fair to everyone on the protocol.'

'Good. Well, just so we're clear: I see it as *my* job to empower these women. So that they can also help decide what's'—she made quote marks with her fingers—' "fair".'

'I see. So you suggested that Faith call?'

'She was troubled. I said it was up to her to let you know.'

'I see,' he repeated, with practised calm. 'Look, Ms Winston, I know you weren't crazy about this protocol at the start. That's all right. I'm just hoping we can work together to minimise friction.'

'Of course.' She eyed him coolly. 'That's always my intention.'

'I'm just saying that Mrs Byrne was made needlessly upset. It doesn't *matter* to her chances what order she goes in.'

'Well, then, why not move her up? We both know there are others on this protocol who truly don't care what order they go in.'

Logan's head was starting to spin. He sighed. 'I'll give it some thought.'

She smiled. 'Faith and I would appreciate that.'

WHEN JUDITH NOVICK showed up at the hospital the following Tuesday for her second treatment, the change was unmistakable. 'I'm feeling great,' she said. 'Less tired than I can remember.'

Standing beside her in the examining room, Logan and Sabrina exchanged a quick glance. Both knew that such a reaction—if indeed what they were seeing was even a reaction to the drug—could prove fleeting.

Still, there was no question the tumour was more yielding to the touch. And when they measured it, they found that it had shrunk three quarters of a centimetre—not significant, but encouraging.

In any case, Novick wasn't waiting for the doctors' authorisation to celebrate her new vigour. 'This past week has been so wonderful,' she announced. 'I've been seeing people again. My husband took me to the movies. The other day I even went out shopping.'

'That's terrific, Judy,' agreed Logan. He hesitated, not wanting to play the ogre. 'But go slow. It's still early.'

'I know. I don't have any illusions.' Suddenly she smiled, her face radiant. 'But, I'll tell you, I almost don't care. I never thought I'd ever feel this good again—even for a day.'

May 15, 1929
Frankfurt

Version 337 showing heightened activity in rats. Some tumours shrinking 25%! Must guard against over-optimism. Sixteen years on the project, and toxicity as great a problem as ever.

Was the right decision to come to Christian Thomas Company. Herr Thomas follows work closely. Very interested in progress.

Emma keeps me balanced, listens to my frustrations and complaints. If it ever comes, my success will be her success.

As SHE LAY IN BED, waiting for her treatment to begin, Faith Byrne appeared calm. 'You're not gonna feel a thing,' encouraged Nurse McCorvey, inserting the IV line into her arm.

Since Faith had assumed the fourth slot—it had previously belonged to a certain Hannah Dietz, who welcomed the delay—the procedure was starting to feel so routine that Logan was the lone Compound J team member on hand.

'That's right,' echoed Marion Winston, 'easy as pie.' She placed her hand lightly on the patient's arm. 'I wish I were as comfortable as you look in that bed.'

'Hey, feel free to change places,' said Faith. She strained to get a look at the IV bottle bearing Compound J.

'You want me to tell you when it starts?' asked McCorvey.

'Of *course*. It's my life.'

McCorvey gingerly removed the clamp. 'Now.'

The patient exhaled deeply, staring up at the ceiling.

Two minutes went by. Then a third.

'Something's not right,' spoke up Faith suddenly. 'Stop the medicine! Please!'

'What is it? Tell me.' Logan looked over at McCorvey. Her face reflected his own intense concern.

'I feel chilled all over! I'm getting nauseous!'

Logan discounted severe toxic reaction almost at once: Faith's breathing was not laboured, and her colour was good. 'What's her pressure?' he asked McCorvey.

She checked the monitor. 'One twenty-five over eighty.'

'Heart rate?'

'Seventy-five.' Both normal.

The problem, he could only conclude, was nothing more than acute anxiety. Logan nodded towards the crash cart. 'Prepare a milligram intravenous of lorazepam.' A Valium analogue.

He leaned in close to the patient and spoke soothingly. 'Faith, we're going to give you something to help you relax.'

'No! What I need is epinephrine!'

Lunacy! Epinephrine speeds up the heart rate. 'I really don't think that's necessary,' he reassured her. 'Let's just see how you do over the next few minutes.'

464

'Doctor, the woman is telling you she's in crisis! I would like you to call for back-up!' demanded Winston.

Startled, Logan looked across the bed at her. 'What Mrs Byrne is describing is not life threatening,' he replied calmly.

With a sudden wail, Faith Byrne again commanded all eyes. 'Oh, God, *please*, don't let them kill me.'

Winston took her hand. 'I promise you, that's *not* going to happen. Dr Logan, I must insist that—'

By now Logan had to make a physical effort to maintain his surface calm. 'If it'll set your mind at ease . . .' He dialled the nurses' station. 'This is Dr Logan. I'd like some back-up in room three fourteen, stat.'

As he hung up, he glanced at his watch. 'I just want to tell you, we're already past the danger point.'

Now that all concern had passed, Logan eyed the patient-care representative with cool disdain. 'Ms Winston, you are not medical personnel. I would *really* appreciate it if you would stand back now.'

'I happen to be doing my job, Doctor.'

'What is this problem?' There, in the doorway, stood Sabrina.

Logan nodded to her. 'I'm afraid we've had a bit of a misunderstanding. But everything's under control now.' He looked down at the patient. 'Feeling better, Faith?'

'I don't know. I guess so.'

'Nonetheless,' said Marion Winston, 'I believe Mrs Byrne would feel a lot more comfortable if Dr Como took over now.'

Logan stared at her. 'Is that what you want, Faith?'

Byrne didn't hesitate. 'Yes. It is.'

'Well, it's all yours, Dr Como,' he said, with a brittle smile.

And Logan strode from the room, leaving the woman he loved to supervise what had, in fact, been an entirely routine procedure.

L OGAN HOPED against hope that word of what had happened would not get around the ACF. After a week, he'd almost begun to believe it was possible.

Then, one afternoon, Allen Atlas sidled up to him in the junior associates' lounge. 'I hear you've been rejected by one of your protocol patients.' He was grinning broadly. 'Isn't it supposed to work the other way around?'

'Don't worry about me. Or our protocol.'

'Dr Stillman sends you his regrets about Mrs Byrne. He knows her, you know.'

'I heard. She turned you guys down flat.'

'Is that what she told you? Logan, you're even more gullible than I thought. The woman has a borderline personality disorder. It was in her file. Stillman took one look at it and sent her packing.'

Of course. It explained everything. When such an individual's expectations go unmet, good can turn into bad in a nanosecond. No one would ever knowingly include a borderline in a drug trial.

'I didn't see any report on that in her file,' Logan said.

'Oh, no?' Atlas smiled, even more broadly. 'Maybe that part of it didn't get sent along. These things happen.'

FORTUNATELY THERE WAS more than enough work to keep Logan from dwelling on having been duped by Stillman. Patients already on the protocol—half the eventual total—were now reporting twice weekly for administration of the drug, a thorough examination and a consultation. On top of which, Logan, Sabrina and Reston had their obligations at the hospital. Under the circumstances, their workdays often continued past midnight.

One Thursday night the phone rang in Logan's place: Sabrina needed to compare notes on a patient. While they were talking, there was a call-waiting beep on her end.

'Who could it be at this hour?' she wondered. 'Hold a second.'

A moment later she was back. 'It is Marion Winston. Something has happened to Judith Novick. I will call you back.'

The wait was less than three minutes, but it felt like a decade.

'Logan, it is terrible news. She had a bad fall. A fractured skull. She's in a coma. At the Bedford General Hospital in Pennsylvania.'

Logan was numb. 'What's Winston doing in the middle of it?'

Sabrina knew better than anyone how sensitive the topic was. 'Judith's family gave the hospital her name,' she said gently.

Logan found himself irked that Winston hadn't seen fit to notify him, the head of the team. Thirty seconds later, he had Winston on the line. He could almost see her stiffen at the sound of his voice.

'Can you tell me exactly what happened?'

'She fell. That's all we know.'

'At home?'

'No, it was at a mall. On some steps by the parking lot.'

What the hell was wrong *with her, shopping at that hour? I* warned *her to take it easy!*

'Is that all, Doctor? Obviously, keeping her on the protocol now is out of the question . . . *permanently.*'

Logan was surprised. 'Why? She seems to have had some response to the drug already.'

'Because, it could be that your drug caused her to black out. In my view, this must be regarded as a possible drug-related toxicity.'

THE ODDS WERE one in ten thousand that the drug had anything to do with Mrs Novick's fall. As for the other patients, no one, it seemed, was being made sick by Compound J, and obviously that was good. Yet none had signed up merely *not* to be made ill by the drug. The truth seemed to be that this stuff was doing nothing at all!

Early one Monday morning, busy with their respective hospital duties, Logan and Sabrina heard themselves paged over the intercom. They were to report immediately to the Outpatient Clinic.

There they found Reston, as sober as Logan had ever seen him.

'This is it,' he said. 'We can kiss our careers goodbye. We've got a toxicity problem.' He indicated the examining room to his right. 'Hannah Dietz.' Dietz, a refugee from Hitler's Germany, was the patient who'd switched places with Faith Byrne. 'She reports bleeding from the gums,' said Reston. 'Every time she brushes her teeth.'

Sabrina led the way into the examining room. 'Hello, Hannah,' she said to the heavyset woman with steel-grey hair—and then spotted the man sitting in the corner. Balding, with an unkempt moustache, he appeared in his early sixties, a few years younger than the patient. 'Hello, Phil.'

Phil, her 'companion', accompanied her on visits to the ACF.

'Well, well, the gang is all here,' said Hannah pleasantly.

'Yes,' said Logan, 'Dr Reston's told us about your problem.'

'Just some bleeding when I brush.'

'Have you noticed if you've been bruising more easily than usual?' asked Logan. The obvious thought: the drug was playing havoc with the proteins responsible for coagulation.

She shrugged. 'No. I have not noticed.'

'Well,' said Logan, 'I think we'll take a little blood. And maybe keep you here a couple of days for observation.'

Late that afternoon, the blood test showed what they'd expected: at least one of the proteins in the coagulation cascade was seriously malfunctioning. It had to be Compound J.

'Damn!' erupted Reston. He kicked a chair violently, sending it crashing to the floor. *'What now?'*

'You are a child, Reston,' said Sabrina disgustedly. 'Vitamin K should bring the prothrombin time down and with little risk.'

'That's not the point!' raged Reston. 'You realise this is going to have to be reported to the Institutional Review Board—'

'Don't overreact,' Logan cut him off. 'If we can tune up Mrs Dietz quickly, we're just about back to where we were.'

'Hold on!' Reston held up both hands. 'No *way* she stays on this protocol. The next time the bleeding could be internal—and fatal.'

'You know as well as I do, she hasn't a chance otherwise.'

'Not my problem! What are you, Logan, suicidal?'

'You can just forget it, I'm not going to cut her loose. We've already lost Judy Novick, we're down to fourteen as it is.'

'I was against keeping Novick too! That was another mistake!'

'I will arrange for the vitamin K treatment,' said Sabrina, walking briskly from the room.

WHAT ARE YOU READING?'

Startled, Logan looked up at Seth Shein. He'd deliberately chosen this spot—a bench in a quiet nook behind the Institute library—to avoid being bothered. 'Just a letter.'

'Who from?'

'A researcher, retired. An old guy. It's nothing.'

Shein sat beside him on the bench. 'Lemme see it.'

Logan handed it over and watched for a reaction.

My dear Dr Logan

Greetings and best wishes. My name is Rudolf Kistner. I live now in the city of Köln, as a pensioner.

Formerly I am an organic chemist. I write to you because I learn from my readings of the protocol you conduct at the American Cancer Foundation. Many years ago I worked also with compounds of sulphonate derivatives against cancer. In those times, we had many hopes for such drugs.

It would be a great favour if perhaps you could take a moment to tell me of your labours. I am old now, but I have much time to think and wonder. For this, one is never too old.

With very sincere regards,
Rudolf Kistner

Shein handed back the letter. 'The guy's gotta be ninety years old. Straight outta the Dark Ages.' He paused. 'Listen, Logan, I gotta tell you something. You really got Stillman going! He's scared to death he's gonna be shown up by a bunch of punk kids!'

'Us?' asked Logan, reasonably. 'Why?'

'Why?' Shein's voice dropped. 'Because Stillman's finally faced the fact that *his* protocol's gonna be a total disaster, that's why. He has the evidence in hand, and pretty soon everyone else will too.'

'That's great,' Logan said, uncertainly. 'Are congratulations in order?'

Shein clapped him on the back. 'Damn right. The bigger his failure, the bigger my success.' He stood up. 'Now what I need from you is not to let up. Wring some activity outta that stuff of yours and it'll be the stake through his heart!'

468

WHEN SABRINA REACHED Logan that night from the hospital, he could hear the exhaustion in her voice. A couple of hours earlier word had come in that Judith Novick had died.

'I have heard something today about Reston from Rachel Meigs. She says Reston makes fun of Compound J right in front of them. Even Atlas. I despise this guy.'

'You were right all along, Sabrina.'

'I don't tell you this, to be right. But we must deal with it.'

'Unless the protocol pans out. I know this guy. Believe me, if things start going better, Reston will be right back with the programme.'

SHE WAS IN HER PRIVATE OFFICE, when she was told her doctor was waiting to see her. As soon as she saw his face, she knew the news was bad.

'Mrs Rivers, I hope you'll forgive me, I've taken the liberty of—'

Abruptly, John entered the room. He was ashen-faced—not a politician now, but an ordinary husband. My God, she thought, he knows too! Wordlessly, he took a perch on the arm of her chair and kissed her cheek. 'I love you, Elizabeth,' he said.

'That bad?' she said, glaring at the doctor.

'I'm afraid that the biopsy shows a malignancy.'

There it was. The death sentence.

As he launched into the medical jargon, she scarcely even listened.

'So you're saying this is bone cancer?' asked John.

'No, sir. Based on what we see, the disease originated in the breast, and metastasised to the bone.'

'Then what are we talking about? Breast surgery?'

The doctor shook his head sympathetically. 'I'm afraid, sir, that at this point breast surgery would only eliminate a small portion of the disease. I recommend we call in Dr Markell at the ACF.'

'How dare you?' she suddenly erupted. She glared at the doctor again. 'This is my life! What gives you the right to supersede my wishes?'

'Mrs Rivers, I'm sorry, it just seemed to me that your husband had the right—'

'Well, that's not your call to make! You're worried about your own neck!'

'Elizabeth, please, you're upset.'

'Damn right I'm upset! I've got cancer! And his only thought is how he's going to look in front of the President!'

'Mrs Rivers, I assure you that's not true. I'm sorry, perhaps I did use poor judgment.'

But her fury was spent, and a moment later she was sobbing. 'I don't understand it, I've done everything I'm supposed to. Self-examinations. Mammograms.'

Her husband took her in his arms. 'It's not your fault, darling. *It's nobody's* fault. What we've got to think about now is fighting it.'

'I just want to say that there is every reason for optimism,' the doctor said. He nodded out of the window, in the direction of the ACF, across the river *in Virginia.* 'They're doing remarkable things there.'

THEIR FIRST YEAR at the American Cancer Foundation came to an end during the second week in June. With the rookies coming in to take over the hospital scut work, the second-year associates were now moving up to lab work—which, for both Logan and Sabrina, meant going to work directly under Seth Shein.

Their role was simply to clone and sequence a certain gene so that more senior people would have material to work with. Logan, with his advanced degree in organic chemistry, found it mind numbing. Day after day it was like following directions in a cookbook: *Add three lambdas of the restriction enzyme Xba to DNA; spin for fifteen minutes;* and so on. He soon began regarding the routine sessions with the protocol patients as a relief.

Increasingly, Logan was aware that the Dietz case had left Compound J ripe for ridicule. True, toxicity had been minimal and treatable. But, coming as it did within weeks of Novick's fall, there was also the psychological factor. Before, Compound J's opponents had merely been able to say it was a harebrained idea. Now they could say—with pleasure—it was a harebrained idea *that makes people even sicker.* Like it or not, the Compound J protocol was now regarded at the ACF as being in trouble.

One afternoon, when Logan and Sabrina were perusing accumulated protocol data, he started going over the numbers of a patient named Marjorie Rhome, a forty-eight-year-old dental assistant from Dover, Delaware. Reston had handled her last three visits.

Her file, like that of every other patient in the protocol, was now over a hundred pages thick. As Logan scanned the results of her blood tests from three weeks before, something caught his eye: the woman's creatinine level, a measure of kidney function, was at 1.7. Immediately, he skipped ahead to the results of last week's visit. The level had jumped to 1.8. Normal is 1.4.

'Sabrina! Look at this!'

She grasped its significance instantly. 'My God,' she said softly.

Elevation of creatinine meant the kidneys were not clearing it properly. Which could mean that they were not clearing far more dangerous substances, particularly potassium.

'Reston must've missed it,' said Logan bitterly. As far as Logan was concerned, the final straw on Reston—the definitive proof that he'd turned his back on the protocol—had been his erstwhile friend's decision to do his lab work under Larsen's associate, Kratsas.

They spent the next hour going over the files of all of the other patients on the protocol, looking for the same syndrome. They found it in one other: Faith Byrne was also at 1.8.

'This is a real problem,' said Sabrina intently. 'If the level goes to two point zero or two point one, they'll have to leave the protocol.'

'And if it continues to rise, we may be talking kidney failure.'

The fact was, Logan had been turning an idea over in his mind for a while—since Hannah Dietz's toxicity. Only now it began to seem less an intriguing possibility than an imperative.

'I think we should take this drug back to the lab,' he told Sabrina. 'Try to find some way to cut down on its toxicity.'

'But the drug we are using—*that* Compound J—by the terms of the protocol, it's the one we must stay with,' she argued.

'You're right,' he said. 'But I'm trying to think beyond that. We've got to redesign the molecule. This is the Compound J we've got, right?' He sketched an awkward rendering of two spheres, with three spikes protruding from each, connected by a long, thick tube. 'Basically, we've got three parts that more or less fit together: two naphthalene rings, each bound to three sulphonate groups—those are the spikes—and connected to one another by an organic polymer. Think of it as a modular couch, with the larger section in the middle.'

He looked up and she nodded. 'It looks more like a lobster.'

He laughed. 'Anyway, the bridge between the two outer modules might be too long. If we could shorten it . . .' He went on, explaining how, in scientific terms, what he proposed was quite elementary; how it could even be achieved in a matter of days.

WITH SHEIN'S PERMISSION, they got the lab to themselves the following weekend—by happy coincidence, the three-day Independence Day holiday. All was ready, including a dozen lab rabbits bearing tumours induced by a carcinogen.

The procedure Logan had in mind required six chemical reactions in a set sequence. If they were to succeed in concocting the slightly altered compound—Compound J-lite, as they'd begun referring to it—each step had to go flawlessly. It was intense and gruelling work—punctuated by long, frustrating breaks as they waited for one or another chemical reaction to reach completion.

That first evening, close to 1.00am, Logan noted approvingly the brown gelatinous liquid bubbling in the heating mantle. 'You want to take a nap?' He indicated a room with a bed off the lab. 'I'll do the next part.'

He worked through the night, finishing early on Saturday morning as Sabrina sauntered back into the lab. 'How is the work?'

'Terrific.' He held aloft a beaker bearing yellowish liquid. 'My turn to nap. I've written down instructions for the next step. It's simple as pie, but you know where to find me.'

Six hours later she gently jostled him awake. 'I have finished,' she said softly. 'Come and see.'

The container of liquid she held aloft seemed to be of precisely the right hue.

He beamed. 'See that? You're a natural. After we boil off the liquid and recrystallise the residue, we'll be left with a white powder. That's the material that will make up the modules.'

'What now?' she asked.

He stretched. 'Now we start on the bridge material.'

The procedure that followed took most of the next two days. Basically, as Logan told it, the various elements they were fitting together were analogous to pieces in a Tinkertoy set. 'Certain pieces fit together and others never will. You can't make an amide out of a carboxylic acid and a tertiary amine. Yet a carboxylic acid and a primary amine can fit together as neatly as a key in a lock.'

Finally, they were left with a second batch of white powder. It was seventy-five hours after they'd started. Outside, on this Monday evening—the Fourth of July—the sun was starting to set.

Logan, exhausted, allowed himself a small smile. 'Just one more step. Combining them with a condensing agent to make the Compound J-lite molecule.'

Less than two hours later, Compound J-lite was a reality. On the table before them was fully 100 grams of it.

Logan picked up the phone and called down to the animal holding facility in the basement. 'Good evening, this is Dr Daniel Logan in Dr Shein's lab . . .'

'Yessir. How may I help you?' It was Hassan, the young Bangladeshi guy, one of the crew of four or five that ran the place.

'My colleague Dr Como and I will be down shortly. I believe we have twelve rabbits with induced tumours. Could you prepare them for us?'

By the time they made it down to the basement, the animals had been moved from the holding area to an adjacent lab. The rabbits, each in its own cage, were a sorry-looking bunch: the fur of each was pocked with pink tumours—rough to the touch and rock hard. Untreated, none would live longer than three weeks.

After they'd injected each of the rabbits, Logan summoned Hassan. 'You can put these back now.'

'Yessir.' He nodded. 'Are there any special instructions?'

'Only to let us know if there is anything unusual.'

'Yes. I will.'

As A PRECAUTION, the meeting was not held at the White House but across the street in the Old Executive Office Building. One of the participants, ACF director Markell, might be recognisable; his picture had been in the newspapers. So had that of the man at his side, the renowned breast cancer specialist, Gregory Stillman.

When the two ACF doctors entered the room, Dr Paul Burke, the President's personal physician, stood up and introduced Charles Malcolm, special assistant to the President for domestic affairs. Stillman maintained a careful reserve. Markell had told him nothing in advance—a sure sign of the meeting's importance.

Dr Burke turned to Stillman. 'It's about the First Lady. She's got breast cancer—with widespread metastases to bone.'

Stillman nodded soberly. 'I see. I'm terribly sorry.' But, inside, the contradictory emotions were already stirring. This was a wide-open shot at superstar status! But it could also be a bear of a case.

Burke handed him a large manila envelope. Wordlessly, he opened it and held a CAT scan up to the light. Then he turned to the thick file of lab reports. Almost immediately he spotted two negative prognostic factors: the tumour was oestrogen-receptor negative; and the tumour cells were undergoing an extremely high rate of DNA synthesis and mitosis.

'Obviously,' said Burke, 'we hope you will take the case.'

'Of course,' concurred Stillman.

'Good,' Malcolm picked up. 'I don't know much about these things, but I assume you'll want to start immediately.'

'Yes.'

'I'll talk to Mrs Rivers today,' said Burke. 'Perhaps you could set aside Friday morning?' It was less a question than an order.

'Yes, of course.'

'Obviously, this is highly privileged information. You are to discuss it with no one. That includes family members.'

At NOON, FAITH BYRNE underwent her weekly examination at the Outpatient Clinic. So far, Logan and Sabrina had kept the creatinine problem to themselves. But they could no longer avoid facing its implications.

When Sabrina walked into the physicians' lounge after the examination, Logan could tell the news was not good.

'Her creatinine is at two point zero.'

He closed his eyes and shook his head. 'Does she know?'

'No. I wished to talk first with you.'

'We've got to be straight with her. Keeping her on the protocol will endanger her health. Shall I go in with you?'

'No,' said Sabrina. 'There could be trouble. By myself is best.'

Fifteen minutes later, Sabrina returned. 'Logan, you should come. This situation, it is impossible.'

Reluctantly, he followed her to the examining room. Byrne was perched on the edge of the examining table in a hospital gown.

'Hello, Faith,' he began pleasantly. 'Dr Como tells me you have some questions about your blood-test results.'

'Is *that* what she tells you? Well, *I'm* telling you your results are wrong. I feel fine. I have been coming here for three months and no one's said a word about this so-called problem until today. You'll have to come up with something better than this before I let you kick me out of this protocol.'

Logan was at a loss. 'Perhaps I can give you a clearer idea of what the problem is,' he said. 'You see—'

'I'm sorry, Faith, I got here as soon as I could.'

And there, stepping into the small room, was Marion Winston.

'Ms Winston,' said Logan, 'perhaps you can help Mrs Byrne understand that, for all our past differences, we're on the same side here. I know how much respect you have for the integrity of the Informed Consent Document.'

'You see,' added Sabrina, 'this is set in the terms of the protocol. If a patient's creatinine level rises above two point zero, then she *must* leave the protocol. It is too dangerous to continue.'

'No,' cut in Byrne, 'you've got it backwards. It's too dangerous for me *not* to continue. I'm going to *die* if I don't continue.'

Winston gave a decisive nod. 'Frankly I don't know anything about your experiment. And I don't really care. My concern is that you are attempting to break faith with this patient.'

'Look,' Logan said, 'we cannot in good conscience continue to administer this drug to a patient who manifests this kind of reaction. Now, Faith, as far as we're concerned this examination is over. You may get dressed.'

Winston put a hand on the patient's shoulder. 'Go ahead,' she said gently. 'You and I will talk in my office.'

As Byrne walked slowly towards the adjoining changing room, Winston lingered behind.

'Are you waiting to have the last word?' asked Logan evenly.

'I just want you both to know that we are not going to let this stand. I'm not through with you.'

ARRIVING ON CAMPUS next morning, Logan found a note in his ACF mailbox instructing him to report to Dr Raymond Larsen.

'You've done it now, Logan,' Larsen began.

'How do you mean, sir?' The senior man's obvious enjoyment of this scene only reinforced Logan's intention to play it cool.

'Do not insult my intelligence, young man. I'll come straight to the point. In the five months of this protocol, all you've established is that this drug is highly toxic.'

'I'm aware of that, sir. But it is still relatively early.'

'And,' he continued, brushing this aside, 'you do not seem to know how to get along with patients.'

Logan started to respond, then stopped. This guy wasn't interested in a dialogue. 'What do you suggest?'

'I don't *suggest* anything. You *will* do the following.' He paused. 'Inform each of the patients on this protocol, on her next visit, of the extraordinary risks we now know to be associated with this compound, and her option of leaving the protocol.'

Logan was dumbstruck. In effect, Larsen was killing the programme. *Was this the way it was going to end? Without his even making a coherent argument on its behalf?*

'That will be all, Logan. Some of us have work to do around here, you know.'

August 10, 1936
Frankfurt

The heat unbearable these last days. Still, dare not leave the apartment. Much trouble in this part of city—beatings, broken shop windows, etc.

By new laws, Emma can give piano lessons only to other Jews. Her father fears he will lose store. Some friends trying to get out.

Reduced to two days a week by Herr Thomas, so have set up alternate facility in basement. Early tests on version #531 of compound, new synthetic modification, show excellent potential. But laboratory supplies getting harder to come by, like everything else.

MORE THAN AN HOUR later, sitting on a bench in the quad on this brilliant summer morning, Logan could still scarcely believe it. He recognised the reaction: shock.

476

He would wait to call Sabrina. No need to hit her with it yet. She was stuck all morning in Shein's lab. Logan glanced at his watch. Marjorie Rhome, the other patient with a creatinine problem, was waiting for him at the Outpatient Clinic.

To date, Logan had had only a brief introductory meeting with her. Sabrina had conducted the woman's initial interview and, so far, her clinic examinations had been covered by Sabrina or Reston.

Both confirmed Logan's own first impression: that this woman was genuinely *nice*. Above all—and this was the quality often hardest to come by in such a situation—possessed of real balance. Logan recalled this by way of reassurance, for it was Logan's luck that he was going to have to conduct her examination this morning.

Even before his conversation with Larsen, that prospect had loomed as gruesome; after all, there was every reason to suppose that her creatinine level, too, had edged up to unacceptable. Even the slim possibility that her level would be encouraging offered no hope. For here he was, under orders to trash his own programme.

'Sorry I'm late,' he said, extending his hand as he entered the examining room and offered his customary reassuring smile.

'No problem, Doctor, really.' A heavyset woman with a pleasantly round face and sharp blue eyes, she seemed just as concerned with reassuring him.

'You've been feeling all right? No new special aches or pains?'

'No, actually I've been feeling pretty darn well.'

'Good. If you'll just take a seat on the examining table.'

Even as he grinned his idiot grin, he knew he'd have to work towards the subject at hand: her future with the protocol. But he'd wait for the results of her blood tests. They should be in anytime.

Logan scanned her chart. Yes, he was reminded, her problem was intraparenchymal lung nodules—a dozen or so BB-sized growths in each lung field. Her prognosis could hardly be worse.

He flipped to the page on her personal history.

'So,' he said, 'how are your kids?'

Her face lit up. 'Oh, fine, thank you.' She laughed. 'But keeping me busy. You know teens.'

'Actually, only by reputation.'

'Of course, you're hardly older than that yourself.'

He smiled; imagining the incredible degree of will this woman must possess to maintain even a semblance of a normal life.

He placed his fingertips on either side of her neck and began working down, feeling for supraclavicular nodes.

'That's good,' he concluded. 'Still clear. Mrs Rhome, would you mind getting to your feet now?'

She slipped off the examining table.

Gently, he felt her abdomen for the liver edge. He couldn't feel it. Also good—the organ wasn't yet distended.

He was interrupted by a knock on the door. 'Doctor?'

The dreaded test results. He opened the door and took them. 'Excuse me, Mrs Rhome, just a moment.'

'Take your time, Doctor.' To his surprise, she began *humming*.

There were three pages, but his eye went right for the line that mattered. 'Creatinine: 1.9.'

He didn't know whether to be pleased or despondent. On the one hand, technically, she could remain with the protocol. On the other hand, he'd just been robbed of his easy out. Now he would have to discuss the dangers of this trial.

She stopped humming. 'What's the word, Doctor? Good news?'

He laid aside the blood results. 'Status quo.'

'Well, where I come from, no news *is* good news.'

Distractedly, he slid the X-ray from its envelope. 'Mrs Rhome, there's something we've got to discuss.'

'Shoot.' He detected a trace of concern through the breeziness.

'Do you know what creatinine is?'

'Not exactly.'

He stuck the X-ray onto the view box and snapped on the light.

'Well, it's a measure of kidney function.' He turned and faced her. 'We track it through blood tests.'

'Is there a problem with mine? Because, frankly, I feel great.'

'Well, yes and no. I'm sorry to say that we've had to take one woman off the drug because her creatinine rose to dangerous levels. Yours is not quite that high yet . . .'

He paused. *That was strange.* He had turned back to look at her chest X-ray. The lungs appeared clean.

'But you're saying there's a danger of that?'

'It's something we have to watch . . .' His voice trailed off as he examined the film more closely. 'Excuse me, Mrs Rhome, you did have a chest X-ray taken this morning, right?'

'Of course. Just a little while ago.'

'And how long ago was the last one taken?'

She shrugged. 'Oh, two weeks ago.'

Taking the X-ray from the view box, he held it sideways and read the name: RHOME. Putting it back in place, he looked at it again.

No way, someone must've mislabelled this thing!

He picked up her previous X-rays—four of them, in chronological order. He stuck the most recent one up alongside the other.

No question about it. The X-rays were Rhome's. Both lacked a right breast shadow where she'd had the mastectomy. But one showed nodules. While on this new one . . .

Logan's heart began to pound. He turned to her with shining eyes, trying desperately to maintain a professional bearing. 'Mrs Rhome, I'd like to take another X-ray.' He dialled the nurses' station. 'This is Dr Logan,' he said evenly. 'I'm going to need another chest X-ray on Mrs Rhome. Stat . . .'

Hanging up, he said, 'Excuse me just a minute.'

As soon as he was out of the room, Logan dashed down the corridor to the in-house phone in the doctors' lounge. 'Sabrina, I'm at the Outpatient Clinic, can you get right over here?'

She was there in ten minutes. He handed her the two X-rays and watched as she held them up to the window.

'These are of Mrs Rhome . . .'

'Yes. And so . . .?' But now, as she looked from one to the other, he saw her expression change. She sat down on the window ledge and held the latest X-ray to the light. 'I think we must take another picture, no? To be sure.'

'Sabrina, this *is* the second X-ray.'

She nodded soberly. 'Still, we must not give false hope.'

'No. Of course not.'

Such conservatism came with the territory. Still, neither could deny what they were feeling. Complete and utter elation.

'So,' pressed Sabrina, 'what should we tell her?'

Logan erupted in a smile. 'That's the problem, isn't it? Words don't do the job.'

When they returned to the room, Sabrina put the X-rays side by side on the light box. 'Would you like to see?' she offered.

Rhome shrugged. 'I doubt it'll mean heads or tails to me.'

But as Sabrina indicated the nodules in the first picture, then indicated the same area in the second, entirely clear of tumour, Rhome turned to her with a sense of wonder that was almost childlike. 'Does that mean what I think it does?'

'It's a very hopeful sign,' agreed Logan. '*Extremely* hopeful.'

All at once there were tears in Marjorie Rhome's eyes. 'Oh, dear God!' And opening her arms, she drew them both into an embrace.

'I have to call home,' she said. 'I have to call my family.'

Logan and Sabrina left her alone to make the call. Back in the doctors' lounge, he smiled sheepishly. 'It got a little sentimental in there, didn't it?'

Sabrina's eyes were moist. 'Oh, Logan,' she said, throwing her arms wide, 'I can hardly believe this.'

He took her in his arms and held her tight. Now, she began crying in earnest. 'Shhh,' he comforted her, squeezing her even tighter. 'This is *good* news, Sabrina.' But as she continued, he fell silent, his face buried in her hair. He didn't want her to see that he was crying too.

WHEN SABRINA ANSWERED her door that evening, Logan was standing there with an armful of sunflowers. 'Just so you won't forget who's the sunshine in your life,' he announced. 'To Marjorie Rhome I sent roses.'

She laughed. 'So did I.' From behind her back she withdrew two giant packs of Chunkys. 'So you will remember who is the sweetness in yours.'

He took her in his arms. 'As usual, I got the better deal.'

She kicked the door closed behind her as they kissed.

'I tell you, Sabrina,' he said, pulling back, 'I've been flying all day. I can hardly stop myself from telling people!'

'I know. When are you seeing Reston?'

'Nine, at his place.' Something suddenly hit him. 'Oh, I've got something to show you.' From his breast pocket he withdrew a folded letter. 'It was in my box this afternoon.'

She recognised the envelope as identical to the earlier communication from the elderly German chemist. This letter was longer.

My dear Dr Logan,

Greetings and best wishes. I am pleased to hear from you in your letter of May 31. Your protocol sounds interesting indeed.

You ask me about the work we did long ago. It was under a Japanese named Mikio Nakano, who worked for the great Dr Paul Ehrlich on this problem of cancer of the human breast. I came to know Nakano in 1927, when he arrived to work in the Christian Thomas Company in Frankfurt. He was the chief chemist and I was only a young assistant. But we got on well.

Our main work at Thomas was with petrochemicals, but Herr Nakano was most interested in cancer experiments with sulphonate derivatives. He was certain he could find a cure! Herr Thomas at first believed also. But the compounds were highly toxic. Some rabbits became blind and others died. So after a time, Nakano left Thomas. But I know he did not stop working on this problem. He was determined. After all, Paul Ehrlich spent twenty years on the toxicity problem in his treatment for syphilis.

Please, sir, write me more details of your work.

With very sincere regards,
Rudolf Kistner

'You see,' Sabrina said softly, 'it does not all begin with us. This man, he had the same ideas.'

'I wish he could have seen what we saw today.'

She looked at him quizzically. 'How do we know he did not?'

A N HOUR LATER, Logan entered Reston's apartment with mixed feelings. Obviously, as a member of the team, Reston had a right to the extraordinary news; in fact, he should have been told of it hours earlier. On the other hand, he had distanced himself from the project. The thought of Reston now sharing in the glory, if, in fact, there was to be any, was almost too much to swallow.

'So, Danny boy, what's so important it couldn't wait till tomorrow?' Reston asked. 'Another damn toxicity?'

'Actually no. It's about Marjorie Rhome.' Logan held up the X-rays. 'She's clean.'

Reston sat up. '*Clean?* Really?' He got to his feet. 'Lemme see those.' He studied them momentarily. 'Amy!' he shouted. 'Get in here! Hurry!'

She came rushing in, wearing a terry-cloth robe, a towel round her hair. 'What?' Then, spotting Logan, 'Oh, Dan—'

But already Reston had her in his arms, dancing her around the room. 'We've had a hit, Amy! The drug actually works!'

'What?' She turned to Logan, what she was hearing apparently striking her as flatly impossible after months of negative talk about the drug. 'Is it really true?'

He shrugged. 'Looks good so far. Of course, it's early—'

Reston walked over and extended his hand. 'Look, buddy, I want to thank you. I guess all the rough times were worth it, right?'

'Hey, we all did our part.'

'Right.' Reston laughed. 'And don't you forget it.'

T HE NEXT MORNING, Logan was both pleased and surprised to discover that Seth Shein had not already got his hands on the information. 'Take a look at these,' he said, sliding Marjorie Rhome's X-rays across the desk.

Shein did so—but his face remained disappointingly impassive. 'This is your second creatinine patient?' he asked finally.

Logan nodded. 'That was my concern when she came in.'

'And what was her creatinine level? Or were you so swept away by this triumph that you forgot to check?'

'One point nine. Not good, but still eligible to stay on the programme.'

'We don't know if this result is going to stick, do we? Nor have you come close to licking your toxicity problem.'

'No.' *What was going on here?* Logan wondered. *Could it be that Shein resented this success?*

Shein suddenly grinned and threw out his hands. 'That said, I am bowled over! Congratulations, Logan. This is gonna kill that bastard Stillman. *Kill* him.' He actually cackled. 'And I have a pretty good idea you're going to be seeing other results.'

'Really?' Logan sat up in his seat. 'Why?'

'Paid much attention to your rabbits lately?'

'Not since yesterday, when I gave 'em their second dose.'

'Better take a look, then, don't you think?'

A moment later, in the animal-holding facility with Shein, Logan spotted the change even from across the room. At least half the animals looked healthier, their movements brisker. He went closer. On almost every one, the tumours were markedly smaller.

'My God!' exclaimed Logan. 'But it's only been four days . . .'

Shein nodded. 'I think you playing around with this molecule didn't alter the effects of Compound J, it just accelerated the process. You'll see more responses. It's just taking longer than you thought.'

'Why? What makes you so sure?'

'What seems to be happening is that this new stuff of yours isn't cleared by the body as rapidly as Compound J—which means its effects are enhanced.'

'So you think we can expect a *major* response rate?'

Shein gave him that familiar look of contempt. 'How the hell do I know? We're dealing with human beings, not rodents.' He paused. 'But it's a pretty damn good bet you're gonna get a response in more than just one.'

Logan stared at the rabbits. 'That's good enough,' he said.

IT WAS LITTLE MORE than a week before they had their second response. Reston noted it first. Back on board with a vengeance, he'd been seeing virtually every protocol patient in for her regular examination, hoping to come up with a 'hit' of his own. It was ironic that the patient turned out to be Hannah Dietz, whom Reston had tried to remove from the protocol.

Reston smiled. 'I see you've licked that bleeding gums problem, Mrs Dietz.'

'Yes, yes. No more of that, thank goodness.' She nodded. 'My Phil is such a good fellow. You know what he tells me all the time now? "We beat one, we'll beat the other." '

Dietz had a palpable, rocklike tumour of five by four centimetres, easily monitored by touch. When Reston began manipulating it, he was struck by the change. Not only had there been a significant reduction in size, but what remained was now rubbery. He made little effort to hide his excitement.

'Mrs Dietz, I swear, this tumour of yours seems almost *gone*.'

Mrs Dietz took a moment to react. 'Really?'

'What we'll need to do is a biopsy.'

The cytologist charged with performing the biopsy finished the job in less than two minutes, and the results were back before noon the next day. Not a single malignant cell had been found. Reston dashed across campus and reached Shein's lab, breathless.

'What the hell happened to you?' asked Logan.

'I got some news,' he panted. 'Come outside.' He turned to Sabrina. 'You, too, signorina.'

In the hallway, he thrust the page their way.

'Hannah Dietz is *clean*. You're holding her bill of health.'

Logan smiled broadly. 'I can hardly believe it.' He stopped. 'Wait a minute, when did you examine her?'

'Yesterday,' said Sabrina, eyeing the page.

'Why didn't you say something before this?' Logan asked.

'He wants the credit,' said Sabrina disdainfully. 'This Reston, he does not change.'

'I wanted to be *sure*,' Reston countered.

'I presume,' said Logan, betraying his irritation, 'that you told her before you came running over here.'

He hesitated. 'Not yet. I'd like to tell Shein first.'

'We can handle that.'

'I'm sure you could.' He snorted. 'I'm sure you'd love to cut me out of this thing entirely, the way you have from the beginning.'

Fixing him with a look of unapologetic contempt, Logan shook his head and sighed. 'Go ahead,' he said, gesturing towards the door to Shein's lab, 'he's all yours. We'll go and tell Hannah.'

TRUE TO FORM, Shein was publicly uncommunicative about the surprisingly positive results. But to Logan he said, 'I've been thinkin' about settin' you up at Grand Rounds.'

Logan was incredulous. Grand Rounds presentations, held every Tuesday in the main ACF auditorium, were the most prestigious forum afforded by the Foundation; speakers were generally top scientists hoping to draw attention to major research developments. 'You think I'm ready for Grand Rounds?'

'Nothin' to it,' said Shein. He paused. 'Go into detail about some of the responses you've had.'

'*Both* responses,' corrected Logan. 'There've been only two.'

'Two outta fourteen ain't bad. And I bet there'll be more.'

In fact, they had a third response only a couple of days later: sweet old Mrs Kober, whose supraclavicular node had seemingly vanished.

Sabrina, who conducted the examination, brought Logan the news—along with a note from the patient: *Dr Logan, Don't forget we have a bet on the Giants versus the Cowboys next season at the Meadowlands. Sally Kober. PS—Suddenly I am feeling much better about my chances of collecting. Thank you.*

IT WAS THE DAY after that that Logan was summoned back to Larsen's office.

The head of the Department of Medicine fixed him with a cool stare. 'I thought it was understood that I would be kept informed of the status of your protocol.'

'I'm sorry, sir,' Logan stammered, 'there must have been a misunderstanding.'

'I'm sure. How convenient for you.'

'But every patient we see is made aware of the toxicities associated with this drug, exactly as you instructed.'

'And how many patients have chosen to discontinue treatment?'

'None, sir.'

'*None?!* And you expect me to believe that you've told them the truth? You're a *liar*, young man!' he suddenly shouted. 'You should never have been accepted into this programme!'

But sitting there across from him, Logan felt a remarkable sense of well-being. Larsen was aware of the growing regard for Compound J at the ACF—and there wasn't a damn thing he could do about it.

'I'm sorry you feel that way, sir,' replied Logan.

'You'd just better pray,' Larsen spat back, 'that when all is said and done, everything you've told me holds up.'

'Yessir,' said Logan.

Abruptly, Larsen stood up. 'I really don't think,' he said scornfully, 'that you and I have anything more to say to one another.'

AS GRAND ROUNDS approached, Logan's excitement and apprehension grew. Shein was naturally keyed into his way of thinking. 'What're you worried about, Logan? You've got it made.'

'I guess I'm concerned because Markell is going to be there.'

'That's right, he is.' Shein nodded thoughtfully. 'I see what you're sayin'—you'd better be absolutely *brilliant*.'

'Thanks. I needed that.'

Logan was well aware of the extraordinary complexity of Shein's relationship with the imperious head of the ACF. They were

484

intellectual soul mates. Formerly Shein's mentor, Markell had turned into his protector; the reason, for all Shein's calculated outrageousness, his enemies couldn't touch him.

LOGAN STOOD on the stage in the vast amphitheatre, looking out over the crowd, heart pounding. Only perhaps a third of the hall was occupied, but that meant at least four hundred people. He was most conscious of the three in the centre of the second row: Raymond Larsen, Allen Atlas and Gregory Stillman.

Shein stood at the back. Sabrina, in the first row over on the left, smiled at him, then quickly averted her eyes. *She's almost as nervous as I am*, he thought. And, scanning the room: *At least Markell didn't show.*

For the first several minutes of his speech, Logan scarcely dared look at his audience. But gradually, the terror began to lift, and by the time he showed his first slide—a vintage photo of Paul Ehrlich, sitting amid mounds of journals—he'd found his rhythm, and he noticed that his audience was gratifyingly attentive.

Kenneth Markell entered the hall midway through the presentation. A short man, with a fringe of white surrounding a bald pate, he had the bearing of Caesar. He stood at the back, arms folded, listening. Shein took his place beside him.

By the time Logan reached his climax, even the occasional bout of coughing in the hall had ceased. 'I want to tell you about one of the patients on the protocol,' he said.

He nodded towards the projectionist, and the slide showing Marjorie Rhome's initial X-ray appeared on the screen. He briefly discussed her case before nodding to the projectionist again. 'This is the same patient's chest X-ray after eight cycles of treatment with Compound J.' There was a murmur in the hall. He paused a moment. 'That was only our first response. It has been followed by two others.'

For presentation purposes, these cases were less dramatic, but moments later, when he concluded the speech, it was to highly respectful applause.

Logan acknowledged this with a broad, unaffected smile. But when he glanced down at the second row, his apprehension returned with a rush. Stillman was clearly mouthing the words, 'Toxicity! What about the goddam toxicity?'

'WELL, WELL, hail the conquering Logan!' greeted Shein, half an hour after the speech, when Logan reported to work at the lab. The several other junior associates within earshot grinned. Logan noted that Sabrina was not among them. 'Thank you,' he said.

Shein led him to a quiet corner. 'I think you mighta done yourself some real good out there, boychick.'

'Really?' asked Logan. Still shaken by Stillman's taunts, he was starting to think his failure to suggest a plausible approach to the toxicity problem might outweigh all the rest.

'Listen, usually Markell walks out on these things.' Shein threw an arm over Logan's shoulder. 'I told Dr Como to take the rest of the day off. You too. You've earned it.'

'Thank you, Dr Shein . . .'

'Seth.'

'Right.' Smiling, Logan began heading for the door.

'Oh, Logan . . . That kid down in animal land wants you there.'

Logan's pretence of good humour vanished as soon as he was out of the room. *No way* this guy would call unless it was serious. When he reached the animal-holding facility, what he found exceeded his worst expectations. Every rabbit that had been dosed with Compound J-lite lay dead in its cage!

Every one.

A moment later Sabrina walked in, also summoned by Hassan. She gasped in horror. Neither had to speak the word that hovered in the air: toxicity.

Logan moved slowly down the line of cages. 'When did this happen?' he asked Hassan.

'I cannot say for certain. This is how I found them this morning.'

Logan turned to Sabrina. 'What now?'

On the one hand, to drop Compound J-lite after it had achieved such spectacular results would essentially be to write it off as a failure. But continuing to experiment with it might only kill more rabbits. And if word of *that* started getting around, it could be a disaster.

Sabrina walked to Hassan's desk and picked up the phone. A few minutes later, Dr Carrie Schneider, a friend of theirs in pathology, walked into the room and peered in at the cages, surveying the carnage. 'Whew, I see what you mean. How many you want done?'

'I don't know. At least three or four, I guess. We need to know what killed them. As soon as possible.'

THEY WERE at Sabrina's late that afternoon when Logan phoned in for the report.

'I can't be too precise here,' Schneider told him, 'but you've definitely got liver failure. That's your cause of death. I don't have any toxicology reports yet. But the three livers I've looked at so far are congested and grossly inflamed.'

486

He thanked her, and a moment later was off the line. 'Well,' he said to Sabrina, 'at least we've come up with a foolproof way of killing rabbits. That stuff is potent.'

She made no reply.

'But I keep thinking about those first results on Compound J-lite. *Something* in that molecule works.' He paused. 'Ah, well, I guess it was too much to hope for.'

THE NEXT WEEK, as reaction to the Grand Rounds talk continued to filter in, it became clear that the young doctor's star had never shone more brightly. 'You just never know the talent they've got buried away in this place,' remarked one senior staff member, with a confidential wink. 'Who'd have guessed we had one of Paul Ehrlich's heirs right here at the ACF?'

There'd been so much good news lately that the morning the phone call came in, it took a while for its gravity to register.

'Dr Logan?' said the male voice.

'Yes.'

'This is Phil Lester. I met you with Hannah Dietz?'

'Oh, yes, of course.' Abruptly, his antennae were up. Why wasn't *Hannah* on the phone?

'I think something's not right with Hannah. Last night, she started vomiting.'

'Has the vomiting been continual?' The guy's tone was so moderate, it was hard to believe anything could be seriously wrong.

'Continual? Yes, I would say so. She's just exhausted. And she's also sweating a lot. She's like a dishrag.'

This woman should be in a hospital! 'You were right to call. She should be looked at.'

The words were all it took to crack Phil's veneer of calm. 'I knew it! It's bad, isn't it? Should I take her to the hospital here?'

Where the hell were they?—somewhere in the New Jersey suburbs! Chances are no one there would even know what to look for.

'Look, if at all possible, I'd like to get her in here.' Logan's mind was racing. 'I have a thought—can I call you right back?'

A helicopter! That way she could be on site in little more than an hour. The ACF used them occasionally, but only for dire emergencies; and that required clearance by the director's office.

In seconds, he had Shein on the line. Less than a minute after that, Shein called him back with formal authorisation.

'Thank you, Dr Shein.'

'Thank me if it pans out. Otherwise, keep me the hell away from it. We're both spending a lot of capital here, Logan.'

AN HOUR AND A HALF LATER, Mrs Dietz was hustled into the hospital on a stretcher. Logan and Sabrina were waiting for her. Reston had declined an invitation to participate in the treatment.

One sight was all it took to assess the gravity of the patient's condition. She was extremely pale and completely disorientated. Most worrisome, the whites of her eyes had a distinctly yellow cast, evidence that her liver was no longer functioning properly.

Phil, alone in the waiting room, was doubled over, head in hands, when Logan touched him gently on the shoulder. 'Phil,' he said softly, 'we're going to be running a few tests, but you haven't been forgotten. If you feel you need to speak to me, tell a nurse.'

He nodded. 'I understand. Thank you, Doctor.'

Mrs Dietz was already hooked up to an IV line to counter her dehydration. The monitor over her head revealed that her heart was racing and she was hypertensive. But the greatest concern, based on her obvious sense of confusion, was the possibility that she was encephalopathic—another sign of liver failure.

Still, she appeared more alert now. Sabrina was leaning over her, talking soothingly. 'Hello, Hannah. Do you recognise me?'

The old woman smiled. 'How are you, Dr Como?'

'Good. Will you do something for me?' Sabrina asked.

'Yes?'

'Hold your arm out straight?' She demonstrated with her own.

It is the simplest test for hepatic encephalopathy. When a patient is suffering the condition, the hand will jerk back and forth spasmodically. Which is precisely what Mrs Dietz's now began to do.

Sabrina looked across to Logan. There was no need for words.

'You can put your arm down.' Sabrina managed a smile as she stroked Hannah's forehead.

'You're a very kind girl, do you know that? Very loving.'

'Thank you. From you, I consider this a great compliment.'

Hannah opened her grey eyes wider. 'I'm going to die now.'

For an instant, Sabrina thought to protest. But no, Mrs Dietz wasn't looking for reassurance. It was a declaration. Nor did the doctors doubt now that it was true.

As she drifted off to sleep, Sabrina remained watching the beautiful old face. She touched Logan's hand. 'You should get Phil.'

He was there when she fell into a hepatic coma a few minutes later; and still there early that evening when she peacefully died.

The initial autopsy report came in two days later. As he read through it, Logan physically shuddered: *A congested and grossly distended liver. Fulminent hepatic necrosis. It was almost identical to the rabbits!*

THE SPEED of the improvement startled her. Three days after she started radiation therapy, the pain in her back had begun to subside; within a week, she no longer felt it at all.

'I feel like the Tin Man in *The Wizard of Oz*,' she delightedly told her husband that night. 'Like someone took an oilcan to me and made all the stiffness disappear.'

Her husband, the President, took her in his arms. 'That's so wonderful, darling. Maybe the worst is over.'

'I hope so. They say so much of it is attitude. Well, I'm going to test that theory—because no one's going to top my attitude!'

Gregory Stillman knew not to be fooled, of course. They'd killed only a single, localised tumour—just a symptom, not the disease itself. Still, for the time being, there was no reason to disabuse the patient of her optimism—especially this patient.

'Things are looking pretty good right now,' Stillman told her at the end of ten days' course of radiation. 'I'm going to want to keep a close eye on you, of course. There's still disease there.'

'Isn't that what we should be doing now, rooting out what remains of the disease?'

'It's not that simple.' He opened his briefcase and withdrew a book—a copy of his own *Basic Principles of Breast Malignancy.* 'Read this, I'd be pleased to discuss any questions you have then.'

She looked at him, incredulous. If he hadn't just pulled off what she regarded as a minor miracle, she'd have been tempted to fire him on the spot. After their first meeting she'd been prepared to assume that his manner was a matter of shyness or discomfort due to her position. But, no, it was the real thing. Stillman might be a gifted cancer specialist, but he was hardly someone she'd choose as a friend.

'I would suggest an examination every two weeks,' he continued. 'But call me if you experience any unusual symptoms.'

The first three examinations were uneventful. But she arrived for the fourth with a dry, rasping cough. This was not necessarily cause for concern. And, in fact, when he took a chest X-ray, it was clean.

Five days later, he reached her at the White House. 'Just checking on that cough.'

Before she could respond, he heard it. 'It's no big deal,' she insisted. 'Aside from that, I'm feeling strong as a horse.'

'How you're feeling otherwise doesn't interest me. I'd like you to come in tomorrow.'

'No!' Tomorrow truly was impossible. She had meetings all day. But more than that, she resented his peremptory manner. 'It will just have to wait until next week. And frankly, Doctor, if we're going to continue, I'd appreciate a bit more courtesy.'

Like most bullies, he instantly backed off. 'I didn't mean it as it sounded, Mrs Rivers. My only concern is your health.'

'It concerns me also, Doctor. But this can wait till next week.'

'Of course.'

The following week, the new X-ray showed it clearly: a streaky density, like a cirrus cloud, in the left lung. The tumour was growing within the walls of the lymph vessels inside the lung. Radiation had taken them as far as it could. He'd have to begin chemotherapy—and soon. This was a very sick woman. He knew it—and now she knew it too. For the time being, at least, he suspected she wouldn't be giving him much trouble.

AFTER HANNAH DIETZ'S DEATH, Logan called Shein's office.

'Sorry,' Shein told Logan. 'Bad luck.' But his voice was so flat, he might have been a stranger. 'Nothing to do now but tough it out.'

Three days later, Sabrina had some more bad news as she let Logan into her apartment.

'There was a call a while ago. Mrs Rhome died today.'

He hardly reacted at all. Whether by training or instinct, they pressed on. If Compound J was killing the very women whose cancer it destroyed, there still remained one such woman unaccounted for.

When there was no answer at Mrs Kober's home, Logan suspected the worst.

'Relax, Logan,' said Sabrina, though she was thinking the same thing. 'Probably she's just not at home.'

'Where would she be at ten o'clock at night?'

'You left a message. When she gets it, she will call.'

They spent a fitful night, holding each other tight in bed. When Sabrina awoke early to call again, she spoke with diminished conviction. 'If she's in trouble, someone would call us,' she said to Logan. 'This is what happened with Mrs Dietz and Mrs Rhome.'

'Both of them had family. Mrs Kober is alone.'

November 1, 1937
Frankfurt

Today I learn Eisenstadt has been arrested in Berlin. One of our greatest chemists. For what? No reasons are needed any more!

Best results yet on version #612. Toxicity marginal—diminished energy and slight loss of appetite. Reason for hope?

Emma nearly ill with fear. Cannot blame her. Who will be next?

B ARELY A WEEK after the Grand Rounds presentation, Logan found a note from Larsen in his mailbox. He would learn it was identical to ones Sabrina and Reston found in theirs: *In light of recent developments surrounding the clinical trial of Compound J, you are requested to meet with representatives of the Department of Medicine tomorrow, October 14, at 3.00pm in the Department conference room.*

Larsen clearly intended to rake them over the coals and probably, if he could find a way to circumvent normal procedures, try to shut down the Compound J trial by executive fiat.

Beyond that, realistically, what could he do? Ten months remained on their two-year contracts. The likeliest scenario was a stern reprimand, a PR move designed to ward off potential embarrassment. Patients on this trial were dying. If the press got wind of it, the ACF had to be seen to have taken some action. Even Sabrina, the ultimate pragmatist, chose to see the positive aspects of what was obviously to be a painful encounter. They would take their shots, but at least there was to be a dialogue, a chance for them to make their case. Who could doubt, even now, that it would be a mistake to abandon this drug?

'This night will be hard, I think,' she told Logan as they pulled up before her apartment. 'Waiting is the hardest.'

'Tell me about it.'

She led him inside, then punched a button on her answering machine to check her messages.

After a brief pause, there came a familiar voice. 'What's all this fuss about?' demanded an obviously perplexed Mrs Kober. 'I get back from my sister's and there are three messages on my machine. Anyhow, if you still need me, I'll be in tonight. If not, I'll be in next week for my treatment.' She laughed. 'Hooray! The last one!'

'That's some good news, no?' said Sabrina. 'Maybe an omen.' Snatching up her book, she dialled the number.

It turned out that Mrs Kober had indeed felt ill briefly several days before. 'A little fluish, you know? A few chills, a little vomiting, and it went away. Why, what's going on?'

Sabrina shrugged. 'Some people on the protocol have got quite sick, so we are checking. But it sounds like you are fine.'

'I *am* fine, you sweet girl.'

When Sabrina got off the line, she grinned at Logan. 'For her, I really think this drug has worked.'

'Forget the omens, that's called *ammo.*'

A S SOON AS THEY WALKED into the room, it was clear the process was rigged. Larsen sat at the head of the conference table. Around him were a who's who of the protocol's enemies: Stillman, Marion

491

Winston, Peter Kratsas and, representing their peers, Allen Atlas.

Also present, of course, looking utterly miserable in his seat at the opposite end of the table, was John Reston. As Logan and Sabrina moved to their own places nearby he nodded, but edged his chair a couple of inches in the other direction.

Larsen looked solemnly around the table. 'You are all by now aware of the deaths of several patients on the Compound J trial. I am sure you share my sense of the extreme gravity of this situation.' He paused, leaning forward, his blue-grey eyes boring in on the Compound J team. 'It is my intention to rectify it.'

Only now did Logan see that there would not even be the pretence of allowing them a say. The verdict was already in.

Larsen turned to the patient-care rep. 'Ms Winston, I believe you have some preliminary observations.'

'Yes, I do,' said Winston evenly. 'There is considerable evidence that at least one member of this team, Dr Logan, has been extremely negligent in regard to patients. I would like to bring before this group two women who have had what can only be called emotionally devastating experiences under this doctor's care.'

The women, of course, were Rochelle Boudin and Faith Byrne.

Called in first, Boudin went through the litany of Logan's supposed abuses. How he'd systematically neglected her needs and failed to deliver the treatment her condition demanded. 'He just always made me feel,' she summed up softly, 'that the fact I had cancer was an inconvenience to *him*.'

Byrne, who followed, was even worse. In self-dramatising detail, she told the story of her initial treatment with Compound J, emphasising her concern—and his complete absence of same—over what turned out to be the drug's very real dangers. Never mind that she showed no danger signs; never mind that she was sitting here, right now, *alive*. Around the table, Byrne's fable was met with sympathetic nods.

'The worst of it,' chimed in Winston, 'was that, against her will, Dr Logan subsequently removed Mrs Byrne from the protocol. I personally regard this as an act of petty vindictiveness.'

At this, Logan actually came close to smiling. *Which was he? A monster for knowingly subjecting patients to a dangerous drug—or a monster for not allowing them to take it?*

But by now, logic seemed the furthest thing from anyone's mind.

'I'd like to say something,' said Atlas, when Byrne left the room. He glanced meaningfully towards Stillman and Kratsas. 'I don't know if this is the appropriate time to raise this, but Drs Logan and Como developed a second, related drug. They call it Compound J-lite.'

492

Logan was stunned. *How did Atlas even know about the variant?*

'When tested in lab rabbits,' continued Atlas, 'this compound showed a good deal of activity—followed by extreme toxicity.'

'I think what Dr Atlas is driving at,' picked up Stillman, 'is that this is the same pattern observed in the deceased patients. The possibility must be considered that these doctors substituted the second drug for the one approved for protocol use.'

Instantly, Logan was on his feet. 'That's a lie! We did *not* violate the protocol!'

'Logan is right,' said Sabrina loudly, pointing a finger Stillman's way. 'You know we did not do this thing! Why would you say so?'

It was as close to losing control as anyone had ever seen her, and momentarily Larsen seemed at a loss. 'Dr Como . . . *please.*'

'No. To say such things, *that* is wrong—not what we did!'

'All right,' said Larsen, decisive again, 'we are going to take a break now. And when we come back, I expect both of you'—he stared at Logan and Sabrina—'to control yourselves.'

Leaving the room quickly, they retreated to a quiet corner, seething. 'I'm going to bring up Mrs Kober,' said Logan quietly. 'We've gotta say something on the drug's behalf.'

'They will not let you.'

'Oh, here you are!'

And there, to their astonishment, stood Gregory Stillman.

'Sorry to interrupt,' said Stillman, ingratiatingly, 'I know it's tough in there.' He nodded back towards the meeting room.

Sabrina eyed him with undisguised loathing.

'It's not personal. We're competitors, sure, but we share the same goals. Your friend Reston understands that.' He actually managed a smile. 'I've been talking with him.'

Logan and Sabrina exchanged a glance, but made no reply.

'Look,' added Stillman, a model of sweet reason, 'no one denies you've had some interesting results. But when there are legitimate questions about methodology, we've got an obligation to raise them.'

Abruptly, Logan knew what this was about. 'You want to take over this drug, don't you?'

'Let's just say that, given the history of this protocol, it's obvious it could use an experienced guiding hand.' He looked from one to the other. 'I'd even say Compound J's finished without it.'

The bastard's intention couldn't have been clearer: Compound J was to become a Stillman project. Their dogged work would earn them nothing. For who could doubt that, once Stillman had his hands on their research, he'd cut them out entirely?

'I take it Reston's already agreed to this?' asked Logan.

'Happily. He wants only to see this drug succeed.'

Logan paused thoughtfully. 'Well, then, I hope you enjoy working with John Reston as much as we have.'

Stillman's face darkened. 'That's it?'

'Yes,' said Sabrina, taking Logan's hand, 'that is it.'

'Fine,' snapped the other, turning on his heel. 'See you inside.'

WHATEVER SATISFACTION the exchange with Stillman gave them vanished the moment they re-entered the room. At the table, where Boudin and Byrne had been, sat . . . Ray Coopersmith.

He wore the same anxious expression Logan remembered from their meeting at the Hotel Jefferson. Only, now his hair was neatly trimmed and his grey, pinstriped suit, appeared to be brand-new.

'Dr Coopersmith,' began Larsen, 'we understand you met some time ago with Dr Logan. This was at your instigation?'

'His.' He looked around the room and smiled broadly.

'That's a lie,' said Logan.

'Dr Logan, I am ready to conduct this hearing without you.' He turned to Coopersmith. 'Now, perhaps you might fill us in on your background with this institution.'

Coopersmith exhaled dramatically. 'I was a junior associate here five years ago. And I was good too. But I screwed up. I was working on a Phase Two prostate cancer trial.' He stared down at the table. 'I altered some data.'

There was a silence in the room—a sympathetic silence.

'It was stupid. I'm trying to live it down.'

'Why do you think Dr Logan wanted to see you?'

'He wanted to know how to pull the same thing. How to get away with under-reporting toxicity.'

To Logan, it was too preposterous. *What could they have offered him? Reinstatement?*

Coopersmith gave a sudden maniacal grin. 'Of course, he also wanted to talk about you, Dr Larsen. And you, Dr Stillman.' The grin grew even wider. 'He told me he hated your guts. He said you were scum.' Coopersmith, clearly improvising wildly, couldn't have been enjoying himself more. 'He said he wanted to show you up and I was the man to show him how.'

Logan felt a presence looming behind him. Instinctively, he turned—Seth Shein.

'Did he make any other remarks about senior personnel?' Larsen asked soberly.

'Yeah,' cut in Shein, 'he said everyone was scum!' He began pointing round the table. 'You, you, you, you and me, scum! That's just the

494

way we've all heard Dan Logan talk, isn't it?' He eyed Larsen with contempt. 'What the hell do you think you're doing here?'

But Larsen only smiled. 'Dr Shein, I'm so pleased you could join us. Won't you take a seat?'

'I'm comfortable here.'

'Dr Coopersmith, we thank you. You've been very helpful.'

Rising from the table, Coopersmith walked from the room, glancing blankly at Logan as he did so.

'So you found Dr Coopersmith's presentation enlightening?'

'Come on, Larsen, you really think anyone's gonna believe this?'

'The point is that these people conspired with a known fraud to fabricate data. We have just heard that—'

'We've heard lies. That's all you've got, lies!'

'Forget that,' interrupted Stillman. 'Are you ready to go on record to defend these people and their protocol? The real point, as Dr Shein knows, is that this protocol has become an embarrassment.' He cast Shein a malevolent glance. 'He gave a group of incompetent young doctors the power of life and death over a group of women, and the result has been tragic.'

'This protocol has merit, Stillman,' Shein said, but with considerably less fire.

'You are willing, then, to assume public responsibility for any further patient deaths that result?'

Shein stood there, his face showing anger and intense anxiety.

'Well, we're waiting,' piled on Larsen.

For a moment longer Shein stood silent. 'All right,' he announced finally, 'Logan got in over his head. He's got talent, but he doesn't know when to listen. He takes stupid risks.'

'Then we all agree,' said Stillman evenly. He nodded again at the chair. 'I'd appreciate your joining us. *Please.*'

Shein assumed his place at the table.

'The three of you may leave now,' said Larsen, indicating the Compound J team.

THE LETTERS Logan and Sabrina received that evening were identical: *You are hereby advised that your contract with the American Cancer Foundation has been terminated, effective immediately.*

The worst of it—which neither Logan nor Sabrina wanted to discuss—was that they'd no longer have each other. The ACF had always been, literally, their common ground. Stripped of her standing at the Foundation, Sabrina had no possibility of work at a comparable level outside Italy. They would be an ocean apart.

'At least at Regina Elena they make me feel welcome,' she said. 'Maybe they don't have the resources you have here, but what counts most is people. And they do very good work also. Serious oncology.'

He could see that already she was pulling away in self-protection. Probably he should do the same. 'When do they want you?'

'They say at the end of October. But I must go sooner, I think.' She momentarily averted her eyes. 'The faster to leave, the better.'

'You're right.'

'And you, Logan?'

He shrugged. 'Don't know yet. I'll mull things over for a while, get organised, sort out my options.' He looked at her tenderly. 'It would definitely be better if I were doing this with you beside me.'

Instantly, her reserve melted away. She gave his hand a tender squeeze. 'One day, Logan. I promise.'

'I'VE BEEN LOOKING over the latest data on Elizabeth Rivers,' said Kenneth Markell, indicating the pile of folders on his desk. 'Frankly, Greg, the bottom line is that standard chemo isn't working.'

'How aware of her progress are they at the White House?' Stillman asked.

'They're not idiots, Greg. Burke *can* read X-rays.'

The latest X-rays were what had them both so concerned. Not only was the tumour in her lung growing, it now appeared as a nodular density. 'Well, then, he also shouldn't expect magic.'

'Ah, but that's the thing of it—they do.' Markell rose. 'It's time to give it to them. I want to go experimental. Let's talk about the results of your protocol.'

'Well,' Stillman said, smiling, 'I haven't killed anybody.'

'That's not exactly the kind of endorsement I had in mind.'

'Maybe not. But in experimental breast treatments around here lately, that makes it unique.'

Markell shook his head. 'That's all the White House would have needed right now, a public stink about some kid doctor at the ACF hyping his results. Where's Logan going, anyway?'

'I have no idea. One of them's still around, though—Reston, the one who came clean. He's got promise, why not give him a break?'

Markell looked at him with sudden impatience; who was Stillman kidding with this ersatz magnanimity? 'We've already had this conversation, Greg. What I want to hear about now is your results with dyronium nitrate.'

'We've had some encouraging responses. No appreciable tumour shrinkage, but seventeen of the thirty-eight women have shown considerable periods of stabilisation.'

Markell sat back down behind his desk. 'Let's put her on this stuff of yours. Maybe she won't get better—but your job right now is to see to it she doesn't get worse.'

LOGAN SETTLED HIMSELF onto the sofa next to the phone. Glancing down at the yellow legal pad in his lap, he picked up the receiver.

His plan was simple enough. There were twenty-seven comprehensive cancer centres in the United States. Before this week was over, he intended to hit every one of them.

He knew not to be overly optimistic. Still, hadn't he been among the prize recruits in the nation just a year and a half before? And, despite the recent unpleasantness, it was reasonable to assume that his time at the ACF could only have increased his market value.

His first call, to the Washington Memorial Cancer Center in St Louis, quickly confirmed that feeling. Here, as at a dozen other institutions around the country, Logan already knew a higher-up—in this case a crackerjack oncologist named Bradley Merritt, formerly associated with Claremont Hospital.

'Dan Logan,' Merritt said. 'What a terrific surprise!'

'Well, Brad, just thought I'd say hello.'

There was some small talk about Claremont before Merritt said, 'I assume you're not calling just to reminisce.'

Logan chuckled. 'No—much as I enjoy it. Frankly, I want to find out how things are over there.'

'You're asking if there are any openings?' Logan had the impression he was trying to restrain his enthusiasm. 'Look, Dan, do me a favour. Don't call anyone else today. Let me speak to the director here and see what kind of package we can put together. Will you do that for me?'

'I guess so.' Logan couldn't believe it: the guy was *desperate* for him.

'Thanks, Dan, really. Just sit tight. I'll get back to you.'

THE CALL CAME that evening. As soon as he heard Merritt's voice he knew something had gone terribly wrong.

'Uh, listen, Dan,' he began, 'I've spoken to our top guys. It seems we're in a holding pattern right now. No new hires.'

'Oh. I see.'

'Look, I'm terribly sorry. I'm sure you'll land something terrific.'

'Oh, yeah.' But the knot in Logan's stomach meant he already suspected otherwise.

Over the next two days, he called the remaining eleven institutions in which he knew a senior staffer by a first name. At no fewer than four, the St Louis experience was repeated: strong initial enthusiasm unaccountably dissipating within twenty-four hours.

Logan knew that at every one of those institutions, someone had checked in with the ACF. There was only one office to which such calls would have been directed: that of Raymond Larsen.

On Thursday morning he set about cold-calling the second group of institutions on his list—those in which he would be known, if at all, only by reputation. The five calls he made produced not even a flicker of interest. In a couple of instances, judging from the tone on the other end, he even had the impression that his call had been *expected*. Could it be that Larsen was even seeking out potential employers and blacklisting him?

He picked up the phone and dialled the Istituto Regina Elena.

It took several minutes for the receptionist to track Sabrina down. As he waited, Logan could hear the sounds of a busy hospital, at once familiar and exotic: footfalls on a hard corridor; the chime of nearby elevators arriving and departing; a 'Dottore Ferlito' being paged; scraps of conversation, the language so melodic, it might have been poetry.

'Logan, it is you!'

'Who else?' He was determined not to show her the depth of his distress. 'I've been missing you, Sabrina. A lot.'

'I also, dear one.' She laughed, a marvellous sound. 'You see, it is so easy for me to say from far away.'

'You sound great. You doing OK?'

'Yes, I think so.' She paused and her voice fell. 'I must tell you something. Larsen, he called the *direttore* of this hospital, saying bad things about me. Untrue things.'

'How'd he respond?'

'*She*. Her name is Antonella Torrucci. She told him she doesn't want to hear this. She knows me for years, far better than him.'

He laughed, imagining Larsen's reaction. 'That's great! One small victory for humankind!' Then, despite himself, 'I envy you.'

There was an awkward silence. 'And you, Logan? What is happening?'

'I'm still looking. I'm working on it.'

There was another pause.

'You are OK?'

'Of course.'

But he suspected she'd already guessed that he wasn't, and it left him with an empty, helpless feeling.

'Listen, Logan, I must go. I am on duty.'

'I'll call you soon. As soon as I know something.'

'*Ciao*, my love.' He heard a kissing sound. '*Ti amo.*'

A moment later Logan was staring down at his yellow pad. There remained seven institutions on the list. But by now, he wasn't even sure it was worth the trouble trying them.

JOHN RESTON WAS FRUSTRATED. He hadn't expected it to be like this. What did he have to do to put his past behind him? Others at his level, a lot less sharp than he, were right at the centre of the work on Stillman's protocol, a sure road to glory. And here was he, still in Kratsas's lab, still doing scut work.

So when he got the call to report to Stillman's office, he made it over in less than five minutes. At long last, he was being ushered into the charmed circle, to hear about Stillman's wonder drug.

'Close the door,' said Stillman, 'take a seat.' He hesitated, seeming to study Reston's face. 'Tell me about Compound J.'

'Compound J?' Wouldn't they ever let him forget Compound J?

'And the other one. What'd you call it, Compound J-lite?'

Reston sat there blankly. 'The whole thing was a disaster,' he said. 'All I want to do now is forget about it.'

'Doctor,' Stillman said, with sudden impatience, 'I want you to level with me. Why was the decision made to go back to the lab? What structural problems were identified with the molecule?'

Reston hesitated and Stillman moved quickly to reassure him. 'I promise you, should we resume research on these compounds, you shall continue to play a prominent role.'

'You're thinking of doing more work on Compound J? *Why?*'

'I'm a scientist. The drug did show some activity. And as for its toxicity problem, clearly you discussed ways of mitigating it. I'd like to know what they were.'

'But aren't you focused on your own protocol?'

In the second it took Stillman to answer—'I can do both'—Reston began to suspect the truth. *Stillman's drug doesn't work!*

But simultaneously, Stillman was reaching a disturbing conclusion of his own. 'Tell me, Doctor, do you even know the chemical structure of Compound J-lite?'

There was an undercurrent of menace to the question, and Reston caught it. But there was no way he could bluff this one. 'Lab work isn't my strong suit, but I took notes. I think I still have them somewhere.'

Stillman didn't believe him for a second. Fleetingly, he wondered just how much this guy might shoot off his mouth. 'Good, I'll want to see those.' He smiled congenially. 'As I say, if we do pursue this, you'll be key.'

The meeting was clearly over. Reston rose. 'Till then, maybe you can find me something else worth doing around here.'

'Absolutely, I'll see to it.' Stillman nodded. 'In the meantime, of course, we never had this conversation.'

AMONG THE FIRST PEOPLE Logan had called after the axe fell was his friend Ruben. Perez was now working at a small start-up company in lower Manhattan, a research lab involved in AIDS drug-delivery systems. He was pretty sure the guy in charge could use someone with Logan's credentials though the pay would not be high.

Logan reached his decision. Working was better than not working, even if the job held minimal interest or prestige. He called Perez; the spot was still open.

Logan's new boss, Alex Severson, had absolute faith in his method of targeting HIV-infected cells while bypassing healthy ones. Having patented it, the young biochemist had devoted the past year to raising money for his own start-up biotech company, HIV-EX.

The problem, Logan saw immediately, was that the guy was a far better promoter than he was a scientist. Appealing as his idea might be, Logan knew that in practice it was close to an impossibility. Already in his brief career, he'd seen countless similar ideas bite the dust. Given his reservations about Severson's project, Logan just wasn't sure he could bring to the job the commitment the other had every right to expect. On the other hand, Severson was ready to give Logan unlimited use of the lab during off hours.

'I'm not really sure there's enough work here for the two of us,' Logan told him. He glanced around the converted loft that was HIV-EX world headquarters, trying to conceal his distress; the equipment looked to be reconditioned surplus.

Severson dismissed this. 'You'll be my director of basic research. My job is to get out there and round up money. Look, I know how this place must look to a guy like you. But lean and mean has its advantages, starting with the fact that you'll pretty much be your own boss. You do the work and I'm happy, period, end of story.'

No question, the pitch had its points—not the least of which was the chance to work closely with his old friend Perez, the company's only other on-site employee, a sort of all-purpose lab assistant.

As soon as they were alone, Logan threw an arm over Ruben's shoulder. 'So that's the big bonus of being here, your company?'

Perez laughed. 'Just remember, I got seniority. If it's between the Mets and the Yankees on the radio, we go with the Yanks.'

'Fine,' said Logan. 'If you're gonna play hardball—I'm gonna make *you* listen to classical music.'

'And I thought things around here couldn't get any worse.'

500

S ABRINA HAD TO MAKE the trip, if only to satisfy her curiosity. True enough, she had nothing more than an address. A call to the local directory had failed to locate even a phone number for Herr Kistner.

The first Friday in December, she flew to Cologne, arriving early in the afternoon. The address turned out to be a brick building of four storeys. The name was the first of eight listed on the directory: R. Kistner, on the ground floor.

She pushed the buzzer. No response. She rang again. Nothing.

Dispirited, she stood there a long moment. What now? She composed a note.

Having wedged it into Kistner's mailbox, she went out into the cold again and was searching for a cab, when she became aware of an old man with a shock of snow-white hair coming towards her. Though he used a cane, he moved remarkably well. She watched him enter the lobby, then proceed to the mailbox and begin reading her note.

'Herr Kistner?' she said, pushing through the front door.

He looked at her a moment; then back down at the note.

'I am from the American Cancer Foundation. I've been working on the study you enquired about. With Dr Logan? Since I happened to be in Cologne, I thought I might tell you about our progress.'

Sabrina found that even this modest lie came with great difficulty. But she'd come too far to risk being turned away now.

Wordlessly, he led her through the lobby and into his tidy apartment. She was reminded of her grandmother's place in Livorno; the same heavy turn-of-the-century furniture, Oriental rugs and leather-bound books; the same musty odour.

'May I get you some tea?' he asked.

'No, thank you.'

He took a seat in a stiff-backed chair. 'Now, please, tell me about your protocol. Your Dr Logan did not give many details.'

'We have had,' she replied, choosing her words carefully, 'very encouraging results. The drug is active, of this there is no doubt.'

He leaned forward, alert as a fan at a sporting event. 'Yes.'

'Unfortunately, toxicity remains a problem.'

'Of course. As always. Can you give me the details?'

So she began at the beginning, in broad strokes recounting the history of the protocol, except for the final, humbling chapter.

'There's something I wish to ask you,' she said. 'About Mikio Nakano—what happened to him? And to his work?'

She thought she saw him start. He shook his head. '*Nein, nein.* I do not know. After he left our laboratory, I did not see him.'

'But,' she said, 'you wrote to Dr Logan that you knew he did not stop working on this problem. How did you know?'

Again, he shook his head. 'It was very long ago, I am sorry.' Grasping the arms of his chair, he lifted himself to his feet.

Sabrina understood she was being dismissed. 'I'm sorry to keep asking, Herr Kistner, but you have no idea what became of him?'

'No, I am very sorry, miss.' Taking up his cane, he started leading the way towards the door.

As they walked, Sabrina handed him a card. 'Please,' she said, 'if you recall anything, will you let me know?'

He squinted at the card in surprise. 'The Istituto Regina Elena?'

She nodded. 'Our study had problems. You see, I am no longer welcome at the ACF. Neither is Dr Logan.'

LOGAN'S SPIRITS picked up somewhat once he got started. The work would never be challenging, but after normal working hours he was able to spread his creative wings. For at last he was free to get back to work on Compound J.

Yet the primitive conditions held him back. Animals had to be ordered from a breeding lab in Massachusetts, untreated. Logan decided on immunosuppressed rats, which at fifteen bucks were roughly one third the cost of rabbits. The human tumour cell line necessary to induce cancer had to be obtained separately.

'Damn,' exclaimed Logan, filling out the order form, 'I won't even know how to grow the tumours in the rats when everything gets here. I've never done that kind of dirty work.'

'I have,' said Perez dryly.

'Well, there you are,' said Logan, trying to make the best of it, 'you've got to help me out.'

From the outset, Perez had resisted the notion that he serve as Logan's assistant. He had quickly grasped the obvious: even if, theoretically, such a miracle drug could be concocted, the chances that it could happen here, in this miserable excuse for a lab, with him, Perez, as the entire support staff, were close to nonexistent.

'The truth is,' Ruben challenged, 'you don't even know what you're looking for. There are how many changes you could make in that molecule, ten thousand? A hundred thousand? That could take years.'

'Except we've got a head start—Compound J-lite.'

'Dan, that's a death drug. It rots livers!'

'I'm not convinced of that.' He paused meaningfully. 'Allen Atlas was in with those animals, Ruben, I'd bet my life on it.'

'You're saying he *murdered* your bunnies?'

Absolutely right, buddy! 'Well,' he said, with a stab at moderation, 'it's what I hope to find out.'

'Look, Dan, why don't you drop it,' Perez asked, 'at least for now?'

He had begun to fear for his friend's equilibrium. Hadn't Compound J inflicted enough damage already—the guy's career was a shambles, his personal life all but nonexistent.

'I know what you're saying,' said Logan. 'Really. Don't you think I know where I stand?'

'I don't. Tell me.'

Logan exhaled deeply. 'I have no standing in the scientific community. *None.* Even if we make progress with the drug, right now I'm not even in a position to get it tested. It's possible I never will be.' He managed a smile. 'Washed up by thirty.'

'I feel bad for you, man,' said Perez softly, his heart going out to his friend.

'Good. I'm not proud. Think of this as therapy for me, Ruben. Creative play. It'll keep me off the streets.'

Ruben never formally agreed. But when the rats arrived a few days later, in boxes with vents, it was he who immediately took charge of them. The breast-tumour cell line came the next day, packed in dry ice, and went immediately into a culture flask. A week later, Logan harvested the cells, mixed them in a saline solution, then watched his friend shoot half a millilitre into a tail vein of each of the six rats.

Within a week, the first tumours were visible: small bumps on the skin surface. Logan clapped his friend on the back. 'C'mon, let's mix us up a new batch of Compound J-lite.'

The procedure was identical to the one Logan had followed earlier. Soon Perez began to find himself engaged by the process—what became a crash course in advanced biochemistry. And he came to it with the one trait that can never be taught: an ability to focus on the right questions. 'What about Mrs Kober?' he asked. 'Why did she live?'

Logan had been wondering the same thing for nearly five months now. 'I don't know. I've gone over and over the charts. I've even kept in touch with her to make sure she's *still* OK.' He shrugged. 'Not even an earache.'

'It has to be something, right? These things don't happen for no reason at all.'

THEY HADN'T MADE LOVE now in nearly three months. She didn't feel like it—and, obviously, under the circumstances, John didn't press.

Although her fears about losing her hair had passed—the two cycles of standard chemotherapy had left it only slightly thinner—she'd never imagined anyone could appear so perpetually fatigued. No matter how much sleep she got, it was never enough to dispel the rings beneath her eyes, nor lend colour to her pale features.

'Does it hurt a lot?' her husband asked softly.

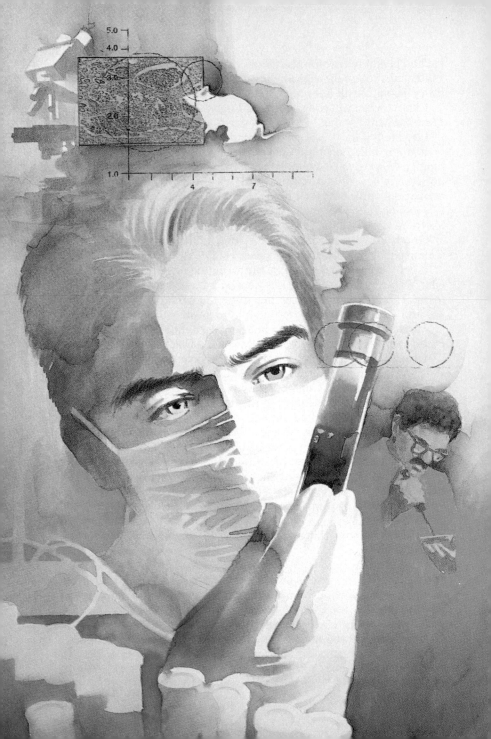

'Only when I look in the mirror.' She took his hand. 'John?' she said tentatively.

'What, my love?'

'You don't have to spend the night in here.'

'I know.' He paused. 'Are you worried about the calls waking you up?' He had a standing order that he was to be woken with any news deemed by aides to be even marginally important.

'No.' She laughed softly. 'I just wanted to make sure you really wanted to. You know how I hate pity.'

'Don't worry, you don't inspire it.'

'I worry about embarrassing you, about letting you down.'

He rolled over to face her. 'Elizabeth, I'm the one who should be embarrassed, putting you through all this pretence. I hate it.'

'I'm managing all right. Just keep me away from long flights of stairs. I'm running out of excuses for why I get winded.'

'You mean more to me than anything, you know that.'

She laughed, but the laugh quickly turned into a cough. 'No, I don't. And in the position you're in, I *shouldn't*!'

'You can't help it, can you? Always with a wisecrack.' He kissed her lightly on the cheek and took her in his arms. 'What does your doctor say about the stairs?'

'Stillman?' He couldn't see her face, but the distaste was clear in the way she spoke the name. 'Something about the tumour preventing fluid from draining from the lungs. I wish I didn't always have to drag things like that out of him.'

'Elizabeth, he's the number-one specialist at the leading cancer institute in the world.'

'Maybe. But when it comes down to it, they have no idea how to beat this. It's just trial and error. That's their big secret.'

They lay in silence for a long while, just holding hands. Suddenly he was aware that she was crying.

'Never mind. It's just me being stupid.'

He took her in his arms again. 'You're thinking about the children?'

She nodded. 'It's so trite. I so much want to be there when the children get married. I want to see my grandchildren.' Burying her face against his shoulder, she began to sob in earnest.

'It's going to be all right,' he comforted, stroking her hair.

Safe in his arms, she let the lie pass.

I T WAS PEREZ who discovered the mess: cabinets ransacked, drawers overturned, smashed beakers and test tubes everywhere.

As soon as Logan entered ten minutes later, he went ashen. 'What about the rats?'

'No problem. Better than ever.'

Logan hurried back to the storeroom. The rat cages appeared not to have been touched. Already, three days after their first dose, the animals were showing marked improvement. The tumours had begun to soften and shrink, just like the first time. Returning to the lab, he sat down heavily in a chair. 'I can't believe this.'

Perez, sweeping up, paused to face him. 'Hey, it was junkies, man. It happens—especially in a neighbourhood like this.'

'Why isn't anything missing?'

'I'm not even gonna have this conversation with you, Logan. You're paranoid!'

'We'll see.'

'YOU KNOW WHY I was most afraid of this?' demanded Perez, three mornings later, holding one of the six dead rats in his hands.

Logan stared at it. 'Because I'd say I was right.'

'Because you'd take this and misinterpret it! Face it, the drug killed the animals, just like it did before. It doesn't work!'

'Then why was Stillman so interested in it?'

'Oh, man, can't you see what a stretch that is? He's a cancer researcher, he's gonna be interested in any active drug.'

'I want to run the experiment again,' Logan suddenly decided.

Perez threw up his hands. 'Forget it. I want no part of this.'

'Please, Ruben, I need you. We can't keep them here—and I don't think my place is much safer.'

'In *my* apartment? Logan, you're way over the top, man.'

But already Perez was thinking about where to put the cages.

THE LETTER ARRIVED ten weeks after Sabrina's return from Cologne, the handwriting slightly shaky, yet still evocative of turn-of-the-century elegance. Rudolf Kistner!

My dear Doctor Como,

Greetings and best wishes. Before all else, I must offer appreciation for your kindnesses on your recent visit. Thank you so much for the many details of your protocol with Dr Logan.

Since your visit I have thought much about the question you ask me. Even now, I do not know if I can give the answers you seek.

Herr Doktor Nakano was a very great chemist, I only a young admirer. The work he did was important, but he was not treated as he should have been. I did not learn until after he was made to leave the Christian Thomas Company that Frau

Nakano was of the Jewish faith. This was in 1936. After this I
did not see him again.

You must understand that I did not support the views of the
National Socialists. Few in our laboratory did. We held
Professor Nakano in only the highest esteem. Some even
continued to correspond with him after he left for Frankfurt.
It is in this way that I learned of his continued work on the
compound.

Personally, I was not one who wrote to him. This is why I
was so surprised to receive from him a letter in November of
1938. I still have this letter, at the time he was living at
Bornheimerstrasse 138. It was quite short, only that he wished
for help in leaving Germany. Perhaps he recalled I had a friend
at the Swedish legation.

Of course, I could do nothing. At the time it was not
possible. Even now this troubles me. For Professor Nakano's
work was truly of the highest order. This is why I write you.
Perhaps it is not too late to see his work recognised at last.

Catching a three-forty flight out of Rome, she landed in Frankfurt
two hours later. By six thirty she was standing before the building
once occupied by Mikio Nakano.

Like the surrounding neighbourhood, the nineteenth-century
house had seen far better days. Several large windows had been
cracked and inexpertly repaired; the knocker and railings needed a
coat of paint.

She walked up the steps of the house and rang the bell. A middle-
aged woman with bright yellow dyed hair answered it. '*Ja, bitte?*'

'I was wondering, please, do you know where I might find the
owner of this house?' Sabrina smiled, to establish she was not bringing trouble. 'I am trying to discover what's become of an old friend
who lived here many years ago.'

The woman called over her shoulder, '*Mutter, komm bitte.*'

A moment later an elderly woman, frail but with an exceptionally
kind face, came shuffling into view wearing a tattered bathrobe.

Slowly, Sabrina explained why she was here.

The old woman shook her head. 'My late husband bought this
house in 1969. He bought it from a man called Herr Klaus. But he
also is gone, many years.'

'Well, thank you so much for your time.'

Well, thought Sabrina, back on the sidewalk, what now? She
began randomly approaching passers-by on the street; anyone who
looked to be over sixty-five. She assumed a general line of enquiry,

pretending to be a graduate student researching the recent history of the city. She heard about chronic shortages during the war; about children and grandchildren raised in these houses. It was now close to 8.00pm.

'*Entschuldigung.*' Pardon me.

Sabrina wheeled around. There stood a young girl, her pretty face framed by a tangle of dirty blonde hair.

'You wish to know about the people who have lived here?'

'Yes. This is of great interest to me.'

'Come, my grandfather will tell you. He has lived here all his life.' She extended a small hand. 'My name is Agneta.'

She shook it. '*Ich heisse Sabrina.*'

The child led her down several residential streets, emerging onto a busier thoroughfare with a number of modest commercial establishments. All but one were closed for the day: a small shop, its interior shielded by strings of beads covering the windows. When they entered, Sabrina saw it was a Middle Eastern-style coffee-house, patronised by men of the local immigrant community.

Peering through the acrid smoke, she picked up only one clearly recognisable German in the place—the individual towards whose corner table Agneta was leading her.

He greeted the child with a grin. 'Come to visit your old grand-papa or just after another pastry?'

His companion at the table, a middle-aged Turk, smiled broadly, showing several gold teeth.

'Grandpapa, this is Sabrina. She has questions about the neighbourhood.'

'Well, then'—he gestured expansively with a working man's hands—'you have come to the right person. Please, you must have some Turkish coffee.'

He ordered the coffee, and a sweet pastry for his granddaughter. 'Now, what is it you wish to know?'

He was so willing, Sabrina impulsively decided to abandon her ruse. 'I am told that many years ago, before the war, a Japanese man lived on your street. A scientist, Mikio Nakano.'

Instantly, the old man's face softened. 'Ah, yes. The professor. I was only a boy, of course. He lived with the family of his wife, Jewish people. He also had a laboratory there. We children liked him very much. He used to give us hard candy.'

Sabrina gave a convincing impression of complete calm. 'I am trying to find out what happened to him, to his work. I understand that in 1938 he was trying to leave.'

He nodded slowly. 'Yes, of course, they all were. You have heard of

Kristallnacht? The Nazis destroyed his laboratory. Everyone heard of it, even the children. It was very sad to us after all his hard work. This is when he sent away his things.'

'Pardon?' Involuntarily, Sabrina leaned slightly forward.

'Not only him, many Jews in the quarter. After *Kristallnacht*, they began sending their valuables, what was left, out of the country. I know because my brother helped carry some of their trunks to the shipping office. The professor's trunk was one of the first.'

'It went to the shipping office? Surely, they would have records there, then.'

'*Nein*. The city centre was completely destroyed.'

'Do you know if Professor Nakano got out?'

'Of course not.' He paused. 'His family was Jewish. He was not the sort of fellow who would leave them behind. Soon afterwards, many of the Jews in the quarter—and the professor too—were taken away. It was said to Dachau.'

Though none of this was surprising, Sabrina was unprepared for the force with which it registered. She knew almost nothing about Mikio Nakano, yet over the past year, working on the compound, she'd begun to feel an intimate kinship with him.

'The professor's trunk was sent to America,' the old man added, trying to be helpful. 'He had, I believe, a brother-in-law. Many had family there who had got out earlier.'

She hesitated, almost afraid to ask the obvious question. 'Do you happen to recall the family name of the professor's wife?'

'It was so long ago but, yes. I believe it was . . . Falzheim.'

'FALZHEIM,' MUSED LOGAN. 'Can you believe it, she got the name from someone who actually *remembered* Nakano?'

Ruben Perez didn't even pretend to be impressed. 'So you have the name of his in-laws—maybe. So what?'

'It's a start,' shot back Logan. 'A *good* start. The guy'd been working on this process for twenty years!'

'Right. And he wrote it all down and it's just waiting somewhere for you to find.' He picked up the telephone book. 'Manhattan. Isn't this where most of the German-Jewish refugees back then settled?'

Annoyed, Logan took it from him and flipped to the appropriate page; not at all to his surprise, there was no such name. 'I didn't say it was going to be easy,' he declared.

He started for the door.

'Where are you going?'

'Forty-second Street, the main library there. They've got phone books from all over the place there. I'll be back in a few hours.'

THE ESTIMATE PROVED way off. There were perhaps seventy directories from large and medium-sized cities throughout America at the library, and it took no more than fifteen seconds to locate in each the page where the name Falzheim might have been—but wasn't. He was back at the office in an hour and a half.

'Let's have the wisecracks now and get it over with,' Logan said, marching through the door.

To his surprise, Perez just turned from his workbench and nodded soberly towards the far end of the room.

Logan was stunned. There, atop a stool, sat Allen Atlas.

'Hello, Dan.'

'What do you want?'

'Nothing much. Just to talk.' The guy fairly oozed sincerity.

'I've got nothing to talk to you about.'

'Just ten minutes, that's all it'll take. You won't be sorry.'

To himself at least, Logan didn't deny he was intrigued. What was he after? He glanced at his watch. 'Ten minutes.'

They went to the bar two doors down from HIV-EX. 'All right,' Logan said, 'what do you want?'

'Wait a sec, will you? Won't you at least let me order us something to drink?'

He returned a minute later with two beers and placed one on the table before Logan. 'Drink up, it's on the ACF.'

'No, thanks.'

'C'mon, Logan, this is no easier for me than it is for you.'

'Hey, pal, I didn't come looking for you.' Logan took a quick swig and glanced at his watch. 'You're down to two minutes.'

'They've had second thoughts at the ACF about what happened. Dr Stillman, for one.'

Logan leaned forward, his eyes narrow. 'Which part are you talking about, Allen? What happened at the hearing, or what happened when I went looking for another job?'

'That's your imagination. We had nothing to do with that.'

'Sorry. Time's up.'

'Wait!' Atlas grabbed his arm. 'Look, Stillman's ready to bury the hatchet. You want a better job, the ACF can help you out.'

'Why, Atlas? All of a sudden they're growing consciences down there instead of tumours?'

'We're doing what we've always done, trying to cure cancer. Dr Stillman's had a chance to go over your data. He thinks your Compound J has promise. He'd like to talk it over with you.'

'Tell me something I don't know, Atlas.' He shook his arm free. 'And tell him I'm happy where I am.' He stood up and walked out.

Atlas hurried outside after him. 'Hey, Logan! Just one more thing—I'm real sorry about your friend Reston.'

'What about him?'

'Didn't you hear?' He paused meaningfully. 'They found his body in his office the other day. Barbiturates. Apparently he got tired of living.'

Logan just watched as Atlas turned and walked off in the other direction.

AMY ANSWERED on the first ring. 'Amy? It's Dan Logan.'

'Hi. How are you?'

Her flat voice made him realise she was in bad shape. 'I'm OK. How are *you*?' He paused. 'I heard about what happened.'

'I'm doing OK, better. It's been almost a week.'

'I'm so, so sorry. You know, even after everything that happened he was still my friend. It was never personal.'

'Well, thanks,' she said. 'Look, Dan, it was nice of you to call.'

Logan was caught short. He didn't want to hang up, not yet. There were too many questions demanding answers. Desperately, he plunged ahead. 'Allen Atlas told me.'

'Atlas?'

'He was in New York on business. I just couldn't believe it. It just seems so completely out of character. Do you have any explanation for it? Did he leave a note?'

'Please, Dan, I don't want to talk about it.'

'Why not?'

'Goodbye, Dan. Thank you for calling.'

Hanging up the phone, Logan turned to Perez, sweeping up the far corner of the lab. 'She wouldn't tell me a thing.'

'It's not easy being the girlfriend. She probably feels guilty about not picking up the signals.'

Logan thought for a moment. 'This isn't one of those cases. Something's off.' He paused. 'She doesn't think he killed himself.'

Perez stopped his sweeping. 'Did she say that?'

'No. But I know her. I also knew him.' He stopped. 'There's also the way Atlas told me about it. Almost like . . . a threat.'

'Oh, come *on*. Look, the guy did himself in. Period.'

Logan smiled. 'You might be right. I'm going home. What I need now's some peace and quiet.'

HEADING HOME to his studio apartment, he'd been seized by so powerful a sense of anxiety that, once inside, he ran to the medicine cabinet for a mild sedative. He was perspiring heavily. He took his pulse: 120. What was going on here? Distractedly, aware he was hungry, he was opening a can of baked beans when he was hit with sharp abdominal pains. He staggered to the next room and collapsed on the bed.

Now there came a terrific pounding in his head, so intense it all but crowded out thought. Yet he was so weak he could scarcely move. Could this be flu? But, no, it had come on too fast.

Food poisoning? What had he eaten today? His mind raced. For breakfast, only a bowl of Rice Krispies and orange juice. For lunch—what?—some chicken noodle soup, a bagel with jelly, tea.

Wait a second . . . the beer with Atlas!

The panic suddenly welling up within was even greater than the pain. He felt himself losing consciousness. He had to get to a hospital. He raised himself to his hands and knees.

But it was too much. He actually saw the blackness coming and felt it begin to wash over him.

WHEN HE AWOKE, the room was still dark. The clock read 3.23am. He was, he realised with a start, still dressed.

Tentatively, he sat up and got off the bed. So physically traumatic an experience *always* leaves after effects—at the least, wooziness and disorientation. But now there was nothing. Except for slight hunger pangs, he felt absolutely wonderful, on a natural high.

This was as frightening as anything yet. The thought was impossible to shake: this had only been a warning.

PICKING UP HIS CAR at the long-term parking lot, Logan headed into the Lincoln Tunnel as dawn was breaking. Doing seventy-five most of the way, he made it to downtown Washington in less than four and a half hours. He headed towards the National Archives.

What he needed was *The Martin Allen Directory of European SS Arrivals, 1890–1940, Port of New York*, which he'd learned at the New York Library was available only here.

Since the book provided just a record of departures and arrivals— the individual passenger lists being available only on microfilm— Logan was reduced to playing probabilities. In all likelihood, German-Jewish refugees exiting Nazi Germany would have left via Hamburg, the country's principal port, and between 1933, when Hitler was named Chancellor, and 1938. And though there were several companies that sailed between northern Germany and New York, Logan decided to concentrate on the most prominent: the Hamburg–Amerika line.

Hamburg–Amerika had three ships working the route—the

Potsdam, the *Bremen* and the *Lübeck*—each making some fifteen round trips annually. The sheer volume was staggering. Worse, when he requested the first microfilm reel bearing passenger rosters, he discovered that the lists, numbering as many as fifteen hundred names apiece, were handwritten—and not alphabetical. It was the very definition of tedium, reading down columns of names by the thousands. He'd chosen to start with the *Bremen*. Working through the morning, he did not find the single name he was after. The closest approximation, which he jotted down, was *Pfaltzstein, Ernst*.

By midafternoon, having moved on to the *Potsdam*, he was up to August 1934 when he made note of a second name that seemed close. *Forcheim, Leopold*; followed by *Forcheim, Hilda* and *Forcheim, Greta*. A whole little Forcheim clan, he realised. He pressed on.

An hour later he took a break and dialled the lab.

'You're in Washington?' exclaimed Perez. 'What the hell for?'

'Look, do me a favour. Do you have that phone book handy?'

'Oh, c'mon, man. You went down there for *that*?'

'I just want to try a couple of names on you. You got a Pfaltzstein? With a P?' He spelled it.

Logan heard the pages rustling. 'No. You know something, I oughta have you locked up.'

'How about Forcheim? With an F.'

He sighed. '. . . Hey, yeah—I got one. My neighbourhood, Washington Heights; 802 West, 190th Street.'

Logan wrote it down. 'Thanks. I'll call you when I get home.'

IT WAS PAST FOUR O'CLOCK when Logan left the National Archives building and hailed a cab. He had the driver drop him off at the Foggy Bottom Metro station and moved round a nearby corner. The spot allowed him a view of pedestrians approaching the station from the direction of the FCC Building where Amy worked.

He waited about ten minutes, and there she suddenly was; moving briskly but, as he had hoped, alone.

'Amy?' he said, feigning delight at a chance encounter.

Startled, she reflexively smiled. 'Hi.' Then she recognised him: to his surprise the smile turned genuine. 'I had a feeling you were coming.'

Taking his elbow, she led him briskly back round the corner.

'Where are we going?'

'I'm trying to figure out where we can talk.'

'I got the idea you didn't want to.'

'You caught me at a bad time—at home.' She glanced over her shoulder.

'What, you think you're being followed?'

'I don't know. Probably we should just keep walking.' She laughed uneasily. 'You can tell I'm not very good at this.'

'Amy, what happened to John?'

She turned to look behind her again. 'What'd Atlas say to you?'

'That they found him in his office. That he'd done it with pills.'

'That's what they told me too. You knew John. Did he seem the suicidal type to you?'

'No. That's what struck me.'

She said nothing for half a block. 'They were after him for information. About Compound J. They were pushing him really hard.'

Logan's blood went cold. 'Stillman?'

She nodded. 'They wanted to know things he just couldn't tell them, because—let's face it—he hadn't been that involved.'

'Right.' Logan could almost see it: the cocky, insecure Reston, desperate to play the big man, but powerless to do so.

'Obviously, they thought more of Compound J than they pretended. And John got back at them. He *taunted* them about it.'

Having walked five blocks, turning corners apparently at random, they now found themselves on busy Connecticut Avenue.

Now that she'd let it all out, Amy was more relaxed. She indicated a nearby bar-restaurant. 'I think I need a drink.'

But the conversation had had the opposite effect on Logan; his mouth was dry and he felt weightless on his feet. 'Not me, I'll take a rain check. See you, Amy. Watch yourself.'

'Funny, I was going to say the same thing to you.'

As soon as she'd disappeared into the bar, he jerked around, scanning the busy street. Nothing—but how would he know?

What, he wondered, had Atlas used on Reston? It could have been anything. Toxins from Amazonian plants, so rare and poisonous that millionths of a microgram could kill and yet leave no apparent trace. The ACF had readier access to such compounds than any intelligence branch of any government on earth.

Logan walked quickly. His car was still in the underground garage by the National Archives. When the cabbie dropped him at the entrance, he ran to it without looking back.

Seated behind the wheel, he tried to collect himself. Suddenly he knew what he had to do.

It took him no more than twenty minutes to reach Seth Shein's home in Arlington. Heading up the walk, he knew he still wasn't thinking clearly. What did he expect? An explanation? Reassurance? He was still considering when Alice Shein opened the door. He saw her shocked dismay. 'Seth,' she shouted. 'Seth, come here!'

A moment later Shein appeared at the door in baggy trousers and work shirt, hammer in hand. Seeing Logan, he recoiled—but recovered immediately. 'Logan, you look like hell. Don't think I'm gonna ask you in. No one invited you.'

Defiantly, Logan elbowed past him into the house, then wheeled on him. 'What happened to Reston? What'd they give to him?'

'Reston finally figured out what a nothing he was and did something about it. End of story.'

'Why're they killing my lab animals?'

'Killing your lab animals?' Shein laughed out loud. 'You got it wrong, Logan—*you* killed those animals. What's happened to you?'

The sight of Shein standing there with a smug smile was too much; abruptly, Logan snapped. He slammed Shein against the open front door. 'You bastard,' said Logan, breathing hard. 'You wreck people's lives and don't give it a second thought!'

Pinned tight against the door, Shein was still smiling. 'What are you gonna do, beat me up? Accept it, Logan, you just weren't good enough.'

Logan's fingers dug into Shein's arms. 'You know damn well that Compound J works! Why else was Stillman after Reston about it?'

'You're outta your head, Logan.'

Logan shook him violently. 'Tell me, damn you!'

'Let go of me,' he shouted.

Logan did so.

'Good,' said Shein, rubbing his upper arm. 'Now get the hell outta here. I got a kitchen cabinet to fix.'

'I'm not going anywhere until you tell me the truth!'

'Alice,' Shein shouted, 'call the cops, tell 'em we got a psycho threatening a guy with security clearance. And tell 'em to hurry. Also that he's driving a beat-up white Ford—a real piece of crap.'

'I swear,' Logan said softly, 'you won't get away with this.' Turning, he walked quickly out of the door.

Shein watched him drive off.

But now, staggering to his feet, he headed for his office. *Did he have the home number of the ACF pharmacist in his address book?*

Yes, there it was! Seizing the phone, Shein punched it in.

SOMEONE WAS following him—he was sure of it. For nearly fifty miles, from the start of the New Jersey Turnpike to beyond Trenton, the headlights remained at the same distance behind him, switching lanes as he did, seeming to mirror his every change of speed.

Pulling off at a rest stop, he did not leave the car—just sat staring into his rearview mirror, the exit ramp in full view behind him. Nothing—just a steady flow of cars driving up to the pumps and then off into the night. He eased back onto the turnpike.

Just outside of New Brunswick, it was back. Or maybe this was a different car. This one stayed with him for ten minutes. But when he slowed down, it zoomed past, a Volvo wagon. A family car.

Had his eyes been playing tricks on him? Or—worse—his mind?

He travelled the rest of the way to the city in the right-hand lane, at a steady fifty-five, and made it home by 1.30am.

Logan collapsed on the bed. *What time is it in Italy?* he wondered. But before he'd even done the maths, he was asleep.

AT THAT MOMENT, Seth Shein was wide awake, his every sense on full alert. His eye moved from one to another of the three files open before him on his desk at the ACF, each distinctly labelled in black marker: RHOME, KOBER, DIETZ.

Again, he picked up the Dietz autopsy report, almost identical to Rhome's: Both of these women had gone from apparent good health to total physiological decompensation and death in a matter of hours.

But what about Kober? She'd had the same initial positive reaction to the drug as the others. Why in her case had there been no comparable devastation afterwards?

Already, he'd carefully examined all the women's treatment schedules. They'd been close to identical. Kober had not missed any treatments; nor had her dosage been even marginally reduced.

For the third time, he pulled out her CAT scan. There were eight pictures, each representing a slice of the patient's body at a different level. The liver, homogeneous, took up almost one entire picture; in the next, he once again noted the upper pole of the left kidney, the kidney hilum, the indentation in it where the blood vessels enter and exit. Then . . . wait a minute, what was this? Where was the upper pole of the *right* kidney?

Quickly, he turned to the notes on her initial examination. Here was confirmation: this woman has only one kidney! Shein leaned back in his chair. On the face of it, this made no sense at all. Like many drugs, Compound J was eliminated via the kidneys. Lacking a kidney, she'd have had *more* drug in her body than the others, not less. Given the drug's established toxicity, she should've got sick and died sooner!

He cupped his hands behind his head and closed his eyes. This was always the part where it got to be *fun.*

He didn't quite have it yet, but it was coming.

LOGAN AWOKE with a jolt, the telephone jangling in his ear. The room was still semi dark. He fumbled for the receiver and answered. But there was only a click as someone hung up.

516

Instantly, the drowsiness was gone. He dialled Perez's number.

'Dan?' Ruben's voice was heavy with sleep.

'Ruben, listen to me. Something's going on.' Suddenly, he thought: what if his phone was tapped? 'Wait, stay there.' He slammed down the phone and, wild-eyed, throwing some clothes into an overnight bag, dashed out of the door.

'Ruben?' he said, ten minutes later, from a payphone.

'Logan, you're totally messin' up my life.'

'Stay there. I'm coming over!'

He caught the uptown A train at Canal Street and hid behind an open *New York Times*. It was not yet seven when he pressed the buzzer in Perez's building—and woke him again.

'Look, Ruben, I'm sorry,' he said, facing him across his tiny living room. 'I know this is tough on you.'

In the far corner, the rats scurried in their cages; the tumours, induced a week earlier, were visible even from where Logan sat. In a few days, they'd begin dosing them with the drug.

Perez, in a bathrobe, leaned forward in his chair and rubbed his eyes with both hands. 'What is it now?'

Briefly, Logan told him about his experiences in Washington.

His friend took it in soberly, aware of the sharp decline of Logan's emotional state in just two days. 'Listen, Dan,' he said softly, 'I just want you to think about what you're saying to me. I know what the girlfriend told you must've been scary. But think about where she's coming from. Her guy just killed himself.'

Logan shook his head. 'No. You don't know these people.'

'It's the ACF, Dan! They don't *do* this kind of thing.' Perez sighed. 'Look,' he said, rising. 'I gotta get ready for work. You do too.'

'I don't think so, Ruben. Not today. Would you mind if I stayed here? Just for a few days?'

Perez disappeared into the bedroom and returned with a key. He tossed it to Logan. 'What're you gonna do for clothes?'

Logan nodded at the overnight bag. 'But I was kind of rushed. I only brought a couple of things.'

'Man, don't you have any other friends?' He shook his head wearily. 'Gimme your key, I'll pick up some stuff for you after work.'

Perez had been gone a half-hour before Logan focused on it: Forcheim G; 802 W, 190th St. Not many blocks away.

Logan showered and put on the jeans and shirt he'd brought.

He walked down Broadway and up a long, curving hill. The building was perhaps twelve storeys high. The names on the panel reflected the changing face of the neighbourhood, a mix of German-Jewish and Hispanic, with a couple of Russian names as well.

Forcheim. Apt. 3C. He pushed the buzzer and waited.

'Yes?'

'Ms Forcheim?'

'Yes?'

What now? 'My name is Dr Daniel Logan. I know this might sound strange, but I'm trying to find out about a man named Nakano—'

He heard the click that signalled she'd snapped off the intercom. 'Damn,' he muttered, and pressed the buzzer again. No response. He pressed again. And again. He was about to turn away, when through the glass he saw the elevator door in the lobby open.

Coming towards him was a woman—probably in her mid-sixties, wearing a baggy housedress, but possessing one of the most beautiful faces he'd ever seen: jet-black hair, lustrous skin, dark eyes slightly crescent-shaped. He knew it even before she opened the door.

'He was my father.'

TWENTY MINUTES LATER, he sat on her faded couch, a cup of tea on the low table before him, as she told her story. She was less than a year old when she came to America with her aunt and uncle, her mother's brother. The plan was that eventually her own parents would join them. 'But my mother's parents, my grandparents, were too old to leave. Someone had to stay with them, and I suppose everyone thought because my father was not Jewish . . .'

'It would be safe.'

'I was lucky, actually. My aunt and uncle adopted me. I was never alone. My aunt just died last year.'

Logan glanced about the room, busy with colourful fabrics, plants, framed photos. His gaze fixed on the small portrait on the window ledge beside him. It showed a youngish Oriental man wearing black-rimmed glasses and a serious expression. 'This is him?'

'Yes.' She smiled. 'But I have others where he doesn't look so stern. When it became clear they weren't getting out, they sent us an album. Would you like to see it?'

'Of course.'

She reached into a shelf beside her and withdrew an album with a faded fabric cover.

Opening it, Logan was transported to another time, the Frankfurt of pre-Hitler Germany, the backdrop of many of the carefully labelled black and white pictures: elegant little shops, well-tended parks, peaceful streets. But, above all, he picked up a sense of the young family in the foreground. Mikio Nakano, usually in a business

518

suit, but occasionally showing a mischievous or even a silly side; the woman before him, as a chubby infant; her darkly pretty young mother.

'What was your mother's name?' asked Logan.

'Emma. She was a piano teacher. That's how they met. With all his work, he decided to take up the piano!' She laughed. 'I have all the details. My mother sent over her diary.'

'By any chance did your father also keep a diary?'

She shook her head. 'I don't think he had the time.'

'I mean about his work.'

'Oh.' She thought a moment. 'Actually, yes, I think there is something, a journal of some sort . . .'

She went to a closet across the room. 'Most of it I can't make head or tail of, of course.' She stood on tiptoes and gingerly pulled down a box from the top shelf. 'I think it's in here. Yes, here it is.'

She handed him a black and white marble composition book, similar to those Logan himself had used in school. He opened it. What he saw on the first page sent a shiver down his spine. A rendering of the precise compound with which Logan had been working.

'I hope it's helpful,' she was saying.

He flipped to the next page and then to the one after that, then, more rapidly, scanned perhaps ten more. It was a series of brief entries, three or four to the page, occasionally accompanied by a sketch of a chemical model. The story being told here was riveting—that of the evolution of a brilliant scientist's thinking as he struggled, over more than two decades, with a problem of almost unimaginable complexity.

Excitedly, apprehensively, Logan skipped to the back of the notebook. The final dozen pages were blank. But on the one that preceded them, there it was: the fully realised compound!

Logan deciphered the German words above it. '*Es funktioniert!*' It works! It was dated two weeks before *Kristallnacht*.

'Would you mind if I borrow this?' asked Logan, trying to maintain a veneer of calm.

She looked suddenly concerned. 'It's very important to me.'

'I understand. Of course.' *How to put this?* 'I just think you should know your father did some remarkable work here.'

'Really?' She lit up. 'That's wonderful to hear.'

'Only for a day or so. I just want to make a copy of it.' He began fumbling for his wallet. 'I'll leave you my driver's licence, my credit cards—'

With a sudden laugh, she relented. 'Never mind, of course you can. I never imagined anyone would ever be interested.'

SOMEONE ELSE might have dreaded this confrontation. Seth Shein relished it.

'Say, Stillman,' he said, strolling into his rival's office unannounced, 'haven't seen much of you lately.'

Gregory Stillman looked up from the paper he'd been working on, his lip curling in a sneer. 'Who the hell let you in here?'

'Just wonderin' if you wanna tell me what you been workin' on?' He noticed Stillman had slipped his arm over the page before him.

'I'm in no mood for your idiocy,' Stillman snapped. 'Get out!'

'Maybe that's the wrong question. What I mean to ask is—who've you been treating with Compound J?'

Stillman stopped in his tracks, bewildered. 'What?'

'Simple question. I looked at the pharmacy records. It seems you've checked out fifteen grams of the stuff. Who for?'

'For research purposes, of course,' he said. 'I've never denied Compound J seems to have some activity.'

Shein snorted. 'Don't insult my intelligence,' he said, his voice taking on a dangerous edge. 'We're talkin' fifteen grams! How many mice you planning to dose, a hundred thousand?'

'That's the most irresponsible kind of speculation!'

Shein hesitated, appearing to consider this. 'You know what Logan thinks?' he said, his tone almost conspiratorial. 'He thinks you were so desperate to discredit his research you poisoned his lab animals! So that you could take over.'

'You're throwing Logan at me? A guy who faked his data?'

Shein nodded decisively. 'You're right. J-lite's incredibly toxic. No way you killed those lab animals.' He smiled; it was impossible to tell he was operating on intuition. 'Just the women.'

'What? What the hell are you—'

'Simple enough with these new poisons, Greg. Was it chrisanthetoxin—*that* destroys the liver. All you'd have to do is get a thousandth of a microgram into the IV line.'

Stillman came back with a brittle laugh. 'Compound J killed those women, Shein. It's an established fact.'

'No, Greg, Compound J doesn't have that kind of toxicity. You know that. Why else would you take the chance of feeding it to someone else?'

The other man hesitated, his face suddenly drained of colour.

Jackpot!

Shein smiled confidentially. 'She must be pretty big stuff for you to go to so much trouble. I figure none of the conventional stuff worked, right? So what were you gonna use—*your* stuff ? Compound J had some problems, but at least it's active.'

'Where do you come up with this crap?'

'Take a look at Kober's file. She has only one kidney.'

'What the hell do I care?'

'It means she had more Compound J in her system. The stuff didn't kill her—it probably saved her. Helped her fight off the toxin.'

'You're delusional! Do you *know* what you're suggesting?'

'Well, Greg, I know this: Compound J didn't kill those ladies. Just as a matter of professional interest—did you use the same toxin on Reston? He was quite a loose cannon, wasn't he?'

'Oh God!' Stillman threw up his hands.

Shein had never imagined there'd come a time when he'd see his rival so utterly vulnerable—and he moved in for the kill. 'It's OK if you don't wanna tell me. He's only been buried—what?—a week. No problem exhuming the body and running a few tests.'

'Shein, what are you trying to do, wreck the ACF? I'm not saying there's a word of truth to this—there's not. But that's what you're going to do. It couldn't come at a worse time.'

Shein leaned forward. 'Oh, yeah? Why's that?'

Stillman closed his eyes and breathed in deeply.

'C'mon, Greg,' he urged gently, almost seductively, 'out with it. You know I'm gonna get it anyhow.'

Stillman stared at him miserably. Then he picked up the file on his desk and handed it over.

LOGAN HAD BEEN PORING over the notebook in Perez's living room for over four hours, but he was still as light-headed with excitement as at the start. What he held in his hands was close to holy—the life work of a scientist as remarkable as any he'd ever studied in the classic texts. It was a complete record of the development of the compound from theory to realisation. He could see how Nakano had built on small successes as he went; yet, too, how reluctant he'd been to discard certain key ideas that seemed virtual truisms; how slow to embrace others that appeared, at first, unlikely.

Logan understood. Nakano had also been convinced, for a dozen frustrating years, that the toxicity was linked to the length of the polymer's bridge. It was only his belated discovery that the problem lay elsewhere that enabled him to press forward; and even then, ten more years were required to reach completion.

Logan studied the final drawings. The compound Nakano discovered was, in fact, an isomer of Compound J: it had the same number of atoms, but its parts were arranged slightly differently. Logan might have gone on working for a hundred years—a thousand!—and never got it right.

He heard the click of a key in the door and looked up.

'Well,' announced Perez, a shopping bag full of Logan's clothes in each hand, 'just call me the Bag Man of Washington Heights.'

He had just closed the door and was heading towards the couch when there came the sound of heavy footfalls in the hallway, followed by a violent pounding on the door.

'What the hell?' exclaimed Perez, quickly moving for the baseball bat he kept in the corner.

In a panic, Logan slipped the notebook beneath a cushion.

Abruptly, the door crashed open, kicked in by one of the four burly men who came rushing in. Three of them had guns drawn. 'Which one of you is Logan?'

'Who the hell are you?' demanded Perez.

'Keep your mouth shut!'

Logan noticed the head man had a small photograph in his hand. It was identical to the one on his ID card at the ACF. Instantly, he knew: these guys were ACF security.

'I am,' he accepted the inevitable. 'I'm Dan Logan.'

'Who's he?' the man demanded.

'He's my friend,' Logan said. 'He didn't do anything.'

'He goes too,' came the command.

'What about these?' One of the men indicated the rats.

The leader didn't hesitate. 'Take 'em.'

Both men were jostled out of the apartment and down the stairs, where two cars waited, engines running.

'My fault, man,' called Perez, before he was pushed into one car. 'I was a stupid idiot!'

Logan couldn't manage a reply before he disappeared into the second—a Volvo. *No way*, he reflected miserably. *All mine*.

He was placed on the back floor, invisible to passers-by. 'My friend doesn't know about any of this,' he insisted. But he had no doubt that if they were ready to eliminate him to steal Compound J, Perez, caught in the crossfire, didn't have a chance.

'Don't worry about it,' said the guy in charge.

'How'd you find me?'

'No talking, Doctor. Those are our orders.'

Anyway, the answer seemed clear. Having staked out his place, he figured, they'd followed Perez uptown.

For the next thirty-five or forty minutes they drove in silence, across—he surmised, looking up from the floor—the George Washington Bridge, and into New Jersey. When they came to a halt and he was helped from the car, he was surprised to find they were at the edge of a rural airport. Now he found himself hustled aboard a

Learjet. A few moments later they were airborne. Again, he was kept from the window, an exercise that struck him as pointless.

'I know where we're going,' he said quietly.

Neither of the men flanking him replied.

They came down at a similar airfield—Virginia, he guessed, by the look of the terrain—and he was made to lie down in the back of another car, a Buick sedan.

For another half-hour there was silence—until someone tapped him on the shoulder. 'OK, you can sit up now.'

With difficulty, he struggled in the cramped space to his knees, then two pairs of hands helped lift him to the back seat.

'Why,' he said, shaking them off, 'you want me to see where—'

He stopped in midsentence, jaw literally going slack. What loomed before him was so staggering, for a moment he was actually unable to process it. They'd just driven through a gate and were heading up a drive towards the imposing structure.

'Is that the . . .'

'Yessir. The White House.'

At the East entrance Logan was helped from the car.

'I'm very sorry for the inconvenience, sir,' said the senior man. 'There was concern you might try to evade us, and our job was to bring you here as quickly as possible. Right this way, please, Doctor.' He escorted him into the building, around a corner, and then up a narrow staircase.

'Excuse me,' said Logan, 'but isn't this where—'

He nodded. 'The private quarters, yessir. Please follow me.'

He led the way down a long corridor, knocking at a door close to the end.

'Come in,' called the familiar voice.

His escort opened the door and stepped aside to let Logan pass. There, in what appeared to be a sort of sitting room, waited Kenneth Markell, Raymond Larsen and Seth Shein!

By now Logan was almost beyond surprise. He stared at them.

'Dr Logan,' nodded Markell in greeting, as if the meeting of this group, in this place, were the most natural thing in the world.

Suddenly conscious he was still dressed in his T-shirt and jeans, Logan folded his arms before him. 'What am I doing here?'

'We've got a situation,' said Markell. 'And it occurred to us that you might help.' He paused. 'Mrs Rivers has a chemotherapy refractory cancer. I'm afraid it's bad.'

The First Lady? Logan's mind raced. What Markell was telling him was that she was doomed; they'd tried all the chemo they could and nothing had worked. 'I'm sorry.'

'She's willing to try any alternative therapy we deem appropriate. The President concurs. The situation is quite desperate.'

'We understand,' added Shein, 'that you've continued to work on Compound J.'

He looked from one to the other. 'How do you know that?'

'As I expect you know, Doctor, it's our responsibility to keep tabs on such things,' replied Markell.

The break-in—it wasn't only Stillman! These monsters! Yet instead of anger, what he felt bubbling up within was something like pure joy. *They* needed *him*. *He* was in control here, *he* had the power. 'Where's my friend? They took my friend also.'

'He's fine. We had to be certain he was aware of the security implications in this.'

Logan nodded. 'Shouldn't Dr Stillman be here? Or did he object to my being called in?'

Shein fielded the question. 'He's accepted an offer to be the director of the Southwest Regional Cancer Center in Phoenix. That far away enough for you, Logan?'

'Dr Stillman was the original doctor on this case,' added Markell. 'Unfortunately, he did not agree with the course we wished to pursue.'

Throughout it all, Larsen, having taken a seat in the corner, looked as if he wanted nothing so much as to disappear into thin air. Now, Logan confidently turned his way. 'How about you, Dr Larsen? Do you agree with this course of action?'

Larsen cast a worried glance towards Markell. 'Actually, I'm new to the case myself. But, yes, it strikes me as fully appropriate.'

'It does? You're saying you've changed your mind about this compound? And me? You're offering me an apology?'

Shein spoke up. 'Why don't you let me have a few minutes alone with Dr Logan?' He smiled amiably at his colleagues.

Markell nodded. 'Absolutely.'

Shein steered Logan towards the adjacent bathroom and closed the door behind them.

'Great.' He laughed, jerking a thumb towards the room they'd just left. 'I enjoyed that as much as you did. And a lot more than the last time we got together.'

'How'd all this happen?' asked Logan coolly.

Shein shrugged. 'Hey, didn't I tell you I'm your guy?' He dropped his voice. 'You know the best part? It's a no-lose proposition. If she responds, we get the credit. If not, Stillman takes the blame. He wasted five months on useless treatment!'

'Markell's willing to back that?'

'What choice does he have? You got a desperate man in there.'

Logan smiled. 'Let's go back and talk turkey.'

'Well?' asked Markell when they emerged.

'You're right. We have to do everything we can.' Logan paused thoughtfully, then looked directly at Shein. 'I'll want to head up my own team, of course.'

Shein blanched. For the first time in Logan's experience, he appeared wholly at a loss for words.

'I understand,' agreed Markell.

'I'll pick my own people—starting with Dr Como and Ruben Perez.'

'Of course. Whoever you feel you need.'

'Good.' Logan looked from Markell, to Larsen, to Shein. 'Thank you, gentlemen. Now, where do I get some fresh clothes? I'd like to see my patient.'

O N AN EVENING ten months later, Logan felt a tap on his shoulder. 'Mrs Rivers,' he said, surprised.

'I believe you promised me a dance, Doctor.'

'It must've been one of those lies doctors tell to buck up patients.' He grinned sheepishly, aware of the eyes on them. 'I don't want to embarrass you in front of all these people.'

'That's the same thing he always says to me,' noted Sabrina. 'This is a guy who just does not know how to have fun.'

'Well, I don't embarrass easily. C'mon, here's a slow song. Don't worry, I'll lead.'

She took his hand and led him towards the crowded dance floor, other revellers at the inaugural ball clearing a path as they went.

'So . . .' he said, 'I guess congratulations are in order.'

'Thank you—but doesn't that go both ways? It looks to me like you guys are quite a success story yourselves.'

He smiled. 'Right.' The reference was to his recent appointment as Director of Basic Research at New York's prestigious Roosevelt Cancer Research Institute—with Sabrina named Director of Clinical Trials. 'They're keeping us pretty busy.'

'I just hope you'll be available, if needed.'

'Of course.'

Logan was relieved to hear her say it. She looked stupendous and—in this he took even greater pride—her CAT scans had been clean for over five months. But he knew that for some time to come, she would have to be closely monitored.

'Word is you plan to put the drug into a major clinical trial.'

'Yes, there's still a lot about this compound we need to know.'

'Have you put in for the patent?'

He grinned. 'How close are you to the Internal Revenue Service?'

'Don't worry, I can be trusted.'

'Anyway, three-quarters of the profits are going to Nakano's daughter. Believe me, money was never the point.'

Elizabeth Rivers looked at him closely. 'I know that.'

'I DON'T KNOW how to have fun?' demanded Logan, opening the hotel room door. '*Me?* You got me confused with someone else.'

Sabrina laughed. 'All right, I admit, this kind of fun you know.'

He gazed at her with a mix of tenderness and lust. She was wearing a black Versace gown, as drop-dead sexy as it was elegant.

'C'm'ere.'

'Just wait a second, please. I need to take off these fancy jewels, no? They are rented.'

He removed his dinner jacket and shoes and collapsed onto the bed. Idly, he picked up the remote and switched it on, as she took off the second earring and laid it on the bureau. 'There, ready.' She moved to the bed and fell into his arms.

They were so lost in a passionate kiss, the words in the background didn't even register.

'Authoritative sources at the renowned American Cancer Foundation announced today . . .'